M000170240

THE RUNAWAY HORSES

THE
RUNAWAY HORSES

Joyce Kotzè

JONATHAN BALL PUBLISHERS

JOHANNESBURG & CAPE TOWN

All rights reserved.
No part of this publication may be reproduced or transmitted,
in any form or by any means, without prior permission from the publisher or
copyright holder.

© Joyce Kotzè 2015

Previously published in the UK by AuthorHouse in 2012
Revised edition published in South Africa in 2015 by
JONATHAN BALL PUBLISHERS
A division of Media24 Limited
PO Box 33977
Jeppestown
2043

ISBN 978-1-86842-639-3
ebook ISBN 978-1-86842-640-9

Twitter: www.twitter.com/JonathanBallPub
Facebook: www.facebook.com/JonathanBallPublishers
Blog: http://jonathanball.bookslive.co.za/

Cover by Michiel Botha
Cover photographs by Thinkstock (upper)
and Reinhold Thiele/Thiele/Getty Images (lower)
Design and typesetting by Martine Barker
Printed and bound by Paarl Media
Set in Adobe Caslon Pro

All, everything I understand, I understand only because I love.

Leo Tolstoy,
War and Peace [1869]

CONTENTS

Background

Fact

In 1835 thousands of Cape Dutch trekked from the Cape Colony into the hinterland of southern Africa to escape British domination. They were called Boers and founded two independent republics, the Orange Free State and the Zuid-Afrikaansche Republiek, known as the Transvaal. Antagonism against the British grew among generations of Boers, and came to fever pitch following the discovery of the world's richest gold deposits, in the Transvaal in 1886.

Fiction

Sir Andrew Stewart, attached to the Cape parliament in the mid-19th century, had two daughters, Susan and Mary. They grew up in England but visited the Cape Colony regularly. Susan married a cavalry officer, Captain Stuart Henderson, and remained in England. Mary met a Transvaal Boer, Marthinus de Winter, who was at the time a student in Cape Town. She married him and settled in the Transvaal.

Thus it came about that the two sisters reared their children in very different circumstances: Charles and James Henderson as minor British gentry; their De Winter cousins, Martin, Stefanie and twin brothers Karel and Rudolf, as Boers.

In 1886, Susan Henderson brought her sons to Wintersrust, the De Winter family farm near Rustenburg, to meet their Boer cousins.

Cast of Characters

South African

Marthinus and Mary de Winter
Martin, Stefanie and twins, Karel and Rudolf – their children
Tante Koba van Wyk – sister of Marthinus
Oubaas de Winter – grandfather of Marthinus and Koba
Joep and Lettie Maree
Buks and Annecke – their children
Lena Maree – Buks's wife
Anita Verwey – nursing sister at Rustenburg
Paul Warren – lawyer for the administration of the Cape Colony
Jan Viljoen – farmer and friend of the De Winters
    His brothers – Frans, Jacob and their sister, Ester
Patrick McFee – Irish sympathiser of the Boer cause

British

General Sir Stuart Henderson and Susan, sister of Mary de Winter
Charles and James – their sons
Lord Harcourt – brother of Stuart Henderson
Beatrice, Lady Harcourt
Victoria Fairfield – only child of Lord Fairfield
Peter Radford – second son of an aristocrat
Officers of the 2nd Hussars:
    Colonel Norman Butcher: commanding officer
    Major George Hunter, Captain Murray Shaw
    Lieutenants Mark Sinclair, John Miles, William Moore, Neil Smithers
    Major Frank Crofton-Smith – surgeon

Historical Characters

Paul Kruger (Oom Paul) – President of the Transvaal
Jacobus de la Rey (Oom Koos) – Boer commander, Transvaal
Adriaan de la Rey – son of Jacobus de la Rey
Piet Cronjé – Boer commander, Transvaal
Christiaan de Wet – Boer commander, Free State
Jan Smuts – Transvaal State Attorney and Boer commander
General Kitchener – British commander-in-chief in South Africa

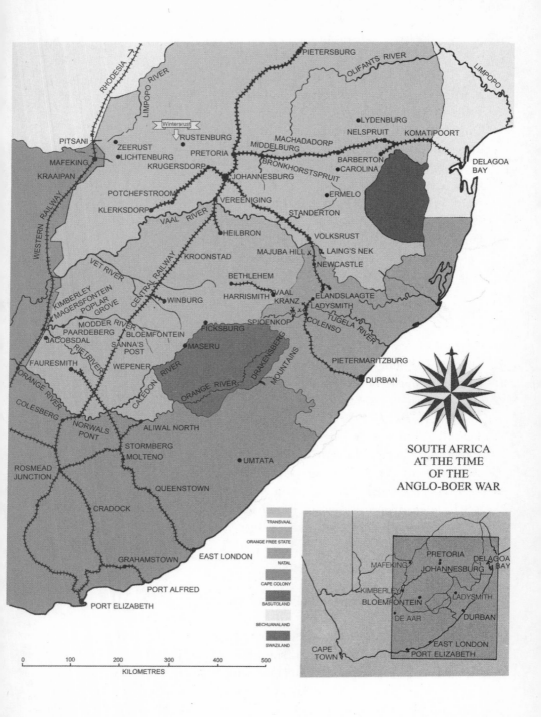

SOUTH AFRICA
AT THE TIME
OF THE
ANGLO-BOER WAR

TRANSVAAL
ORANGE FREE STATE
NATAL
CAPE COLONY
BASUTOLAND
BECHUANALAND
SWAZILAND

0   100   200   300   400   500
KILOMETRES

Prologue

Wintersrust, September 1902

THE FULL MOON sinks behind the mountain, leaving the land to dawn. At the blackened ruin of a farmstead, a man stands like a ghost, his eyes on a woman in the graveyard.

She kneels at the older tombstones. Her fingers travel over the names on the granite. At the graves of those who died recently she stands, wringing her hands. There are only wooden crosses on the mounds of earth.

The man sags to his haunches, his back against the stone wall, his hands between his knees. It started three years ago, the relentless flight of the wild horses. They followed the leader's dream, trusting implicitly, but now the dream lies shattered in the graveyard, the ravaged farmstead, the desolation of the veld. Some stayed to the end. Some broke away from the herd. Those are the runaway horses. The survivors. The wounded souls.

This day they will return to find solace in shared sorrow and forgiveness, to go to the place where guilt and blame do not exist, where only peace reigns.

The sun creeps across the farm, the light gentle, beautiful. His eyes travel over the empty cattle kraals, the unploughed fields and come to rest on the mountain in the near distance. He recalls the shrill voices of children at play in the summer of 1886 …

PART ONE

THE SUMMER OF 1886

My child, we must still think, when we
That ampler life together see,
Some true results will yet appear
Of what we are, together, here.

A.H. Clough
'What We, When Face to Face' [1849]

The Meeting of Cousins

Wintersrust, Transvaal, 1886

THE FACT THAT HE HAD BRITISH COUSINS, not ordinary English-speaking folk, but *proper* British cousins, had never troubled Martin de Winter. It belonged to his mother's distant childhood, a time that did not fit into their lives here on the farm. It was like a tale in a book or a reading from the Bible: the story was known but there was no evidence to substantiate it. Charles and James Henderson existed only in letters that his mother received from her sister in England, every month a new chapter.

But now he was about to meet head-on with the evidence; his cousins, sons of a Redcoat colonel, the enemy, were on their way to the Transvaal.

Martin balanced on a branch in the tallest milkwood tree by the drift. His father had left for Rustenburg to collect the Hendersons off the stagecoach and he was watching for the return of the horse-cart.

Waiting stretched the afternoon into eternity. The heat was unsparing. Not a breath of wind played with the leaves of the marula and wild olive trees. And in the distance the mountain fused with the scorching sky, the sun still a hand-span from the tall peak in the west. His eyes travelled to Soetvlei, the neighbouring farm. The Maree family was on a visit to Kuruman and would only return the following month. He needed Buks Maree, his friend, on this day of all days, but Buks didn't like the *Engelse* either. He would only have made matters worse.

'You're not looking properly! Dust! Over there,' came his sister's dramatic voice from under the tree. In English! Stefanie had refused to speak Afrikaans since the news of the Hendersons' visit.

Martin turned his gaze to the vlei. Plodding past the ploughed fields were the cattle, a movement of multicoloured hides, black-tipped horns, sharp as Zulu spears, catching the sun. Bleating their way to the opposite side of the vlei came the sheep. They would not drink together. Cattle, sheep, horses; each to their own kind. Like Xhosa and Zulu.

Like Boer and Brit.

'It's Old Klaas bringing the cattle to water,' he called down to Stefanie.

'Do they wear shoes, Ouboet? I won't! Never!' Karel shouted up to Martin.

'Must we speak English all the time?' Rudolf asked. 'Like Ma and Stefanie?'

Squatting under the tree, his six-year-old twin brothers gaped at him like baby barn owls.

'Of course we have to speak English,' Martin said. 'The English only speak English, stupid! They don't know a word of Afrikaans. Not a word!'

'What do they look like, I wonder?' Karel called.

Martin had no notion what his cousins looked like. He and his brothers resembled their father in all details; brownish-blond hair, deep blue eyes and square chins. Their cousins probably took after his mother: light-brown hair, slight of build.

'Well, Charles is fourteen. Short and fat?' Martin said. 'James is eleven. Thin and scrawny, like our sister?'

'I'm not scrawny! I'm small and delicate. And almost ten.' Stefanie tossed her blonde plait over her shoulder. 'Our cousins are like me. Grand and English.'

'Missy-prissy!' Karel yanked at her pinafore.

'Oh, let go, you little pest!' She aimed a kick at him.

Rudolf grabbed her foot, pulled her down and a scuffle ensued. Martin scaled down the tree and separated his siblings.

Rudolf sank back on the ground. 'We'll be called traitors. Our uncle is a Redcoat.'

'We'll be lower than baboon shit.' Karel spat to his left.

'Ma says his coat is blue, not red,' Stefanie said, 'with gold – real gold – buttons. Oh, I wish I could see it!'

'Be thankful that he's not coming.' Martin glared at her. 'Oh yes, Pa would say he's welcome. Pa welcomes all, be they British or not. But we will show the cousins that a Boer can hold his own against the British.' He turned to his brothers. 'To those who dare call us traitors, we'll say: the only way to get to know your enemy is to live with him, eat with him, speak his tongue, get to know his ways. Is this simple truth not known to them?'

'What will you tell the cousins?' Karel demanded.

'The instant the Hendersons set foot on Wintersrust, I shall tell them that the victory at Majuba made the Transvaal our country, our birthright, never to be taken ...'

'You always speak like a *predikant*.' Stefanie sniffed and strode off, but halted abruptly, pointing wildly to the dust cloud on the road. 'They're coming! They're here!'

'Run! Run!' Martin sped off, followed by the others, all calling to the house that the moment was upon them.

THEY ARRIVED breathless at the house and gathered at the steps leading onto the stone-flagged stoep. Their mother, Mary, wearing an everyday cotton dress, hair rolled into a bun at the nape of her neck, apron round her waist, stood next to the little table holding the tea things, cakes and rusks. No coffee today; the English preferred tea. Oubaas de Winter, their battle-scarred great-grandfather, nodded in his wicker chair next to the big potted fern.

The horse-cart, top-heavy with a portmanteau and suitcases, slowed down as their father reined in the horses. He alighted, opened the door and helped his sister-in-law to the ground. Stefanie sucked in her breath. The twins moved closer to each other, Rudolf twisting his pinkie around Karel's. Here, clad in a navy-blue outfit and an enormous hat with upright glossy feathers, a gauze veil covering her face, was the elegant lady who lived in their mother's stories. They had never seen the likes of her, not even in Pretoria. She stumbled delicately on the gravel, but smiled when her sister approached with open arms.

Martin did not pay attention to their tearful reunion. His eyes were riveted on the cousins emerging from the hooded cart. And there they stood, dark-haired, handsome, tall and lanky. Dressed in knee-length trousers, high socks, black boots and grey blazers, they were grand indeed.

The taller one, who wore gold-rimmed spectacles, stepped forward, hand outstretched. '*Bly te kenne. My naam is* Charles Henderson, *jou* ... hmm, *neef* ... cousin?'

Martin was struck speechless. Afrikaans! Before he could gather his wits, Charles continued: 'I've been practising Afrikaans. I want to speak it properly and hope that you will help me master it. Delighted to meet you at last. Are you Marthinus?'

Martin shook Charles's thin hand formally. 'Yes, Marthinus Johannes de Winter. I'm thirteen, the oldest and thus have my father's name, but I'm still called Martin as I'm not married yet.'

Charles's eyebrows lifted a fraction, but his smile widened.

'Say it!' Karel hissed from behind Martin.

Martin planted his bare feet apart and stood arms akimbo. 'It would serve you well to keep in mind that this is Boer country. Victory at Majuba ...' he hesitated as Charles's face lit up, his smile spreading to keen brown eyes behind the lenses.

'Majuba, 1881. Yes, the victory secured the Transvaal's independence, and rightly so. I've read all I could find on your country's history and customs. One should not rely solely on what's taught at school. It's so … well, partial, don't you think?'

Martin stared at Charles, flabbergasted. He had not imagined this from his cousins. Shame at his hostility engulfed him and all at once he was keen to make amends. 'Welcome to Wintersrust. We all hope that you will have an enjoyable stay. Welcome.' Taking Charles by the elbow, he guided him the few steps to his siblings. 'My sister, Stefanie.'

'Cousin Stefanie, delighted.' Charles pecked her on the cheek, which left her blushing, and the twins sniggering.

'My brothers, Karel, Rudolf.' Martin yanked Karel closer by the hair and twisted his neck. 'See here, this one, Karel, has this nick on the ear; that's the way to tell them apart.'

Charles inspected the scar and nodded. 'Yes, yes, I see. Karel, Rudolf. I've been looking forward to getting to know you.' He half-turned, indicating his brother.

'This is James.'

James pushed his thick brown hair from his forehead and offered his hand. Deep dimples formed in his cheeks as he produced a tentative smile.

'You are very, very pretty.' Stefanie reached for his hand.

James shot her a furious look, clasped his hands behind his back and went to the stoep.

'He doesn't like it, having such good looks,' Charles whispered.

Martin nodded, impressed that Charles was sharing secrets so soon after they had met. He led the way onto the stoep and introduced his cousins to his mother. Mary fussed over her nephews, which Charles clearly welcomed by the way he hugged her, but James bore it with a frown. Then came the turn of the De Winter children to be introduced.

Stefanie held her pinafore wide and curtsied grandly. 'I'll play the piano for you, Aunt Susan. I play well, very well indeed.'

'Braggart!' said James.

'Manners, James,' his mother chided and inclined her head towards Stefanie. 'I look forward to it, girl.' The feathers on her hat bobbed as she offered her pale cheek to the twins.

'It's our Aunt Susan. Give her a little kiss,' Martin encouraged as the two stared.

'There's a rooster on her head! She's a witch,' Karel shouted.

Martin elbowed backwards, hitting Karel on the chin. He retaliated with a kick to Martin's calf. Martin sent an apologetic smile to his aunt.

'I'm sorry, Aunt Susan.'

'Oh, it's quite all right,' she said. 'We'll get to know each other later. Won't we?'

'Susan, meet our grandfather, our dear Oubaas de Winter,' Mary intervened, taking her sister to the old man's chair. He appeared asleep, his wild grey beard resting on hands clasped around a walking stick. Mary placed her face close to his ear. 'Oubaas, my sister and her children have arrived from England.'

'Hey? Hey?' He tilted his head.

'My sister and the boys! From England!'

'Hey? *Engeland?*' He peered at the visitors and then spat into the spittoon by the side of his chair. His walking stick shot out, snaring Susan's dress at the hem.

James scowled. 'What's wrong with him?'

Martin looked to his father, who was still at the horse-cart. He was scratching his beard, hiding a smile behind his hand. 'Never mind, young James,' Marthinus said. 'He's very old and his mind is wandering.'

Charles, avoiding the walking stick, introduced himself to Oubaas.

'Zulus! *Engelse!*' Oubaas shooed him away.

'Martin, help your cousins with their luggage and then bring them for tea,' Mary ordered and led her sister to a chair.

Stefanie lifted her chin, smoothed her hair and followed her aunt. Martin eyed James and found his brown eyes sizing him up.

———

CHARLES HENDERSON HAD always been eager to meet his Boer cousins; they were his only cousins, after all. But what he found here was not what he'd imagined. Yes, the cousins were wild and sunburnt, but, although not refined in manner and speech, they were educated and spoke English without effort.

Within a few days, he became fond of them. Stefanie with her wild blonde hair and blue eyes, was assertive, fighting her brothers to establish her assumed superiority. She practised the piano with the same determination. The little ones, Karel and Rudolf, were secretive and were usually found with their father, clinging to the stirrups when Marthinus rode his daily inspection of Soetvlei, in the absence of the Marees. And Martin – a confident boy, serious-minded yet affable, making every effort to welcome them.

'Beware, this cousin is dangerously intelligent,' James had whispered to

Charles on the second night. 'Those sharp blue eyes are always searching for intent, and he never misses an opportunity to boast about the Boers and his country.'

But it was the vastness and magnificence of Wintersrust that overwhelmed Charles. The mountain to the south was imposing in its rich beauty. The foothills led to the cliffs that formed a craggy outline against the sky. Streams ran down the tree-clad gullies coming together in the vlei, an expanse of water fringed by willows. The ploughed fields sloped down to the stables and cattle and sheep enclosures. Near the house was the orchard, heavy with the summer's yield. The thatched farmstead, with its wraparound stoep, seemed to rise out of the soil.

The interior of the stone house was simple, yet gracious in its own way. The walls were plastered and whitewashed, the floors covered with animal hides. A large dining table occupied the far end of the central room. There, every night after supper, Marthinus opened the large brass-bound Bible for the nightly reading and prayers. Above the fireplace hung a lithograph depicting the Battle of Blood River. The picture seemed to fascinate James, and he pestered his uncle about every detail of the battle. The many bedrooms led off this central room. From the kitchen wafted the aromas of baking and cooking, spicing the symphony of clattering pots and pans and the chattering of Mary and her two kitchen maids. A woman's domain, his uncle had warned – bottling fruit, making jam, slapping butter, curing meat.

While Charles spent his mornings in and about the house, mostly with Stefanie at the piano or sitting with the old grandfather drinking coffee on the stoep, James roamed the farm with Martin, hunting game birds in the foothills of the mountain, riding the Boer horses at a fast gallop and even helping Martin with his chores. Yet Charles sensed that Martin's patience with James was not going to last. James was confrontational, quick to anger and reckless, never considering the repercussions of his actions. To all appearances, they were getting on well, but a silent battle was being fought for dominance.

———

JAMES BLOCKED THE furrow, allowing the water to the next row of peach trees. He leaned on his spade and looked towards the house, longing to hear the call for lunch. He saw his mother and Stefanie drinking tea on the stoep and Charles walking old Oubaas up and down.

'How old is he?'

'Oubaas? Ninety-six,' Martin said. 'He was born in 1790. It's written in our Bible, on the first page, where all our names are.'

'He's your great-grandfather, but where's your De Winter grandfather?'

'Killed by a lion, over there.' Martin pointed to the cattle kraal. 'He was a brave man.'

'If he was such a brave man, why did he let a lion get to him?'

'It was a pride, five lions. There was a terrible drought. They came for the cattle that night. The cattle trampled Uncle Servaas, my Tante Koba's husband. Grandpa de Winter tried to save him, but a lioness mauled him. They died together, Grandpa and Uncle Servaas. Pa shot the lioness. That skin in the study – that's hers.'

'A brave man indeed.' James studied the water in the furrow. Death was not something he dwelt on, but it was the way in which a man died that fascinated him. Not having a brave grandfather – their shared Stewart grandfather had died of a weak heart and Grandfather Henderson, Lord Harcourt, of cholera in India – he could not compete.

Just then a bellow from Oubaas came from the stoep as Charles settled him into his chair. 'What's he on about?'

Martin looked James squarely in the eyes. 'He is no friend of the English.'

James was astounded. 'Why ever not?'

The twins scrambled down the tree where they were searching for early fruit and came to stand behind Martin, following the words with huge eyes.

Martin dug his spade into the ground. 'Your people caused many sorrows in our lives. They hanged our people at Slagtersnek for killing Xhosas who raided the farms. They drove us out of the Cape Colony, Natal and everywhere else we tried to settle. They always try to take our country from us! That's why, James. That's why Oubaas hates the English.'

James recalled the barren land seen through the train window from Cape Town, the dusty streets of Kimberley and the potholed track on which the stagecoach had brought them to Rustenburg. 'Take your country? We don't want your uncivilised little country. You may keep it, thank you!'

Martin clenched his fists. 'Take that back. If you don't, I'm going to *bliksem* you!'

'*Bliksem* him! Hit him, Ouboet!' cried Karel, always the first of the twins to react.

James sensed his cousin's strength, saw the anger in his eyes and felt a quiver of trepidation. He searched wildly for words. 'Why did you run in the first place? You should've made a stand and fought us.'

'We fought you at Majuba. The Redcoats ran like dogs. We slaughtered them, Cousin James!'

'Take this for your petty victory!' James landed a hefty blow in Martin's face.

Martin let fly with his fist and caught James on the jaw. And then they were rolling on the ground, legs kicking and arms flying as each tried to pin the other down.

'Stop! Stop!' cried Rudolf. 'There's blood. And Pa is coming!'

Just as the two managed to get to their feet, Marthinus arrived. 'Well, now! What I see tells me that there's a dispute about a serious matter,' he said in his slow, roundabout way. 'I'll see you in my study. There are wise words only, and should they fail to come I know of a way in which to call them.'

'The *sjambok*!' Karel said as their father walked on to the house. 'You are going to get the *sjambok*.'

'It's your bloody fault!' James wiped blood from his lip and gave Martin a shove.

Marthinus looked over his shoulder. 'Come on now! Or do you prefer to have your punishment out here?'

They followed him home and into the study. James stole a look at this room that they were not allowed to enter without permission. He saw many books, racks of hunting rifles, a lion skin on the floor and, there in the corner, on a little table, a few bottles of what he took to be brandy.

Marthinus unhooked the *sjambok* from the wall and placed it on the desk. Settling in his chair, he filled his pipe. Only after he had lit it and it was drawing to his liking did he give his attention to them. 'When the battle is lost and won.' He blew smoke through his nose. 'Now then, it makes no difference to me who lost and who won, or why the *battle* was fought. What does interest me is how it was fought.'

Neither of them offered an explanation.

'James, you might not be aware of our policy in this house. Let me explain it to you; nothing good comes from violence. It only breeds more conflict. There's nought to gain if you don't take time and patience to settle your differences in a civilised manner, with wise words.'

James stared at the *sjambok* and wise words came flying to him. 'We had a difference that couldn't be settled otherwise, sir.' He had come to know his uncle as kind-hearted and open to reason. His own father's military code of discipline was absolute. Standing in his oak-panelled study awaiting punishment, the tiger's head mounted above the desk staring fixedly down, was enough to reduce him to submissiveness.

'Would you care to tell me about your unbridgeable problem?'

'I'd rather not, Uncle Marthinus. It's something that only we can resolve.' He hastily added, 'but not in the same violent manner.'

Marthinus nodded and turned to Martin. 'The reason for your behaviour can be sorted out in a more acceptable way, as James has just assured me. But son, you insulted a guest on our farm, and there's no excuse for that.'

'Uncle Marthinus,' James ignored Martin's murderous glare. 'Martin was completely in the right. We were defending the honour of our countries.'

'One should also not blindly believe in the supremacy of one's own country, refusing to acknowledge the achievements of others.' Marthinus clamped his pipe between his teeth and gestured towards the door. 'Out, both of you!'

When they closed the door, a roar of laughter followed them. James ran to the kitchen, where lunch was about to be served. He was one-up on his bold Boer cousin. He had the courage to fight him. And there in the study, he had used his superior intellect to save them both from physical pun-ishment. 'Next time it'll be your turn to save our backsides,' he said when Martin thanked him for the unexpected favour.

———◆———

IT WAS SATURDAY, the midday sun unsparing. They finished their chores for the day and sought out the shade of the milkwood by the drift. Clouds gathered to the north, only to disperse again in wispy fragments. The day stretched in endless hours of exploring and playing, but Martin rejected every suggestion offered. Stefanie wanted to have a concert, or to dress up as a queen, but the boys were not interested in her make-believe games. She stormed off.

His plan for the afternoon was of such a delicate nature that it could not include her or the twins. The previous Sunday, James had called him to the shed and shown him verses in the English Bible that Martin was convinced could not be in their Dutch Bible. His father never read from the Song of Solomon about the beauty of a bride, with breasts like clusters of grapes, skin smothered with fragrant oils and lips that tasted of wild honey. There was, however, a reference to a part that intrigued Martin. It lay between the rounded navel, filled with sweet wine, and the bronze legs that were as fleet as those of a buck. It was the strangest comparison he had heard: *the joints of thy thighs are like jewels.*

Strange images had caused unfamiliar sensations in his body all week. After much thought, he devised a plan to discover these extraordinary jewels. There was still an hour before lunch and, as he would have to set his plan in motion as soon after the meal as possible, he had to find a way of getting rid of his brothers.

He looked to where Charles sat with his back against the tree, watching the kingfishers darting across the water. James was squinting through the barrel of Martin's rifle at guinea fowl that had strayed into his view. They were just ordinary boys, he had come to accept, and posed no threat to him, the farm or the standing of the De Winter family.

'Karel! Rudi!' he called to the twins who were splashing in the water. 'Think up something to do.'

They stared at him surprised. 'Anything?' Karel asked.

'Yes, anything you want to do.' Martin squatted in front of them. 'So, what will it be?'

They looked around for inspiration. Karel's eyes lit up and he pointed to the mountain. 'We want to have a picnic on top of the mountain.'

Rudolf looked at his twin in consternation. 'Up there? God lives up there.'

'God lives up there?' James frowned.

'Yes, didn't you know, James?' Rudolf eyed him curiously.

'*He* told us so!' Karel pointed to Martin.

Charles gave Martin a searching glance. Martin turned his back to the twins and whispered, 'Just a story to keep them from wandering too far, but don't tell Pa. You see, Karel can't understand that God is invisible. He refuses to believe in anything that's not real. Well … you know what I mean.'

Charles frowned. 'Clever, I suppose, but not wise. They might get it into their heads to look Him up one day. I would advise you to let Him live in a … safer place for the time being.'

Martin saw the wisdom in this. Leopard and baboon roamed the mountain and it was easy to get lost in the gullies. He was contemplating what to say when Karel kicked him on his calf. 'What are you whispering about?'

Martin faced his brothers, scratching his head. 'Well, I've forgotten to tell you. You see, God does not live up there any more.'

'Why? What have we done wrong? Why has God moved away from here?' Rudolf's bottom lip trembled.

'God … moves around …' A bright idea struck him. 'God lives in Pretoria now!'

Rudolf nodded, but Karel stared at Martin. After a bit, Martin out-stared him and he gave up, muttering.

'Ouboet, are you going to take us up the mountain?' Rudolf asked. 'You said anything we want to do.'

Martin sighed and put his hands on Rudolf's shoulders. 'I'll tell you what. It's a grand, a very grand idea to have a picnic on the mountain. Even Charles, and you know how clever he is, couldn't have thought of that. But it'll take us all day to get there and back. Do you agree?'

The twins measured the distance to the mountain with their eyes.

'Let's go on your birthday. The Marees will be back. Little Annecke will be here! Let's wait for Annecke and Buks,' Martin said, knowing that the prospect would please them. 'We'll pack food, start out early and spend the day on the mountain. Would you like that? It will be a special birthday for you.'

Rudolf agreed, but Karel stood his ground. 'Promise! Promise on Grandpa's grave.'

Martin raised his right hand and spat on the ground. 'I promise on all the graves in the graveyard. Now, run along. Here, carry my rifle. Tell Ma we'll be there soon.'

Karel and Rudolf set off to the house. Charles was about to follow, but Martin said that they had an important matter to discuss. They squatted in a circle. Martin lowered his voice. 'Have you ever seen a naked woman?'

Charles blushed. 'No …'

James nodded casually. 'At home I saw the maid in her room. She'd taken off her dress and only had a petticoat and the … the top thing on.'

'You peeped into the servants' rooms!' Charles said, aghast.

'The door was open. I didn't peep!'

'I mean naked, no clothes at all,' Martin said. 'Right to the place where you put your stick in.' He put a stiff finger on his crotch. 'Like a stallion or a bull, you know?'

'It's not proper to look—'

James cut Charles short. 'Yes, we want to!'

'Well, Saturday the kitchen maids have the afternoon off,' Martin explained. 'After they've cleared the tables, they wash in that deep pool by the wild fig where we swam last week. Remember? We get there before they do, get up the tree and watch from there.'

James eagerly agreed, but Charles hesitated.

'Oh come on! If you want to be a doctor one day, you will have to get used to seeing naked women,' James urged.

'All right,' Charles said at last, 'but our parents must never learn of this.'

'Never!' Martin was horrified at the thought of his father finding out.

AFTER THE MEAL they set off, following the stream. They climbed into the wild fig and settled behind the foliage of the spreading crown. The chatter of the servant women announced their approach. The boys watched as they shed their dresses. James gasped at his first sight of bare breasts, but Martin silenced him with a fierce look. Boer boys had seen many a mother feeding her infant. His interest lay in the as yet unrevealed secrets.

The women stepped out of their underclothes and into the water. They splashed and washed, their breasts bobbing. One stepped out of the pool and sat on the grass, her legs apart as she rested her elbows on her knees, still taking part in the conversation. Martin craned his neck but could not get a direct view of the secret parts he wanted to see. From where the others sat, they had a perfect view. Charles blushed and closed his eyes, but James kept on staring. Martin inched forward, unwittingly obscuring James's view. James pushed him away. With a strangled cry, Martin tumbled down, arms and legs flailing in an attempt to get a grip on a branch. He landed among the women and disappeared into the water.

Martin surfaced, spluttering for breath, calling for help. The women shrieked. When they recognised Martin, they grabbed their clothes and stormed off. James scrambled to the lower branches, tearing his trousers, and jumped into the pool. Charles followed, landed on top of James and lost his glasses. Cursing, they dragged Martin out of the water. Blood flowed from his nose and from a cut down his cheek. One knee was badly bruised where he had hit a rock. Charles put his arms around his chest and squeezed hard while James slapped him on his back.

Martin coughed convulsively, water gushing from his mouth. 'You snake! You pushed me.' He made a feeble attempt to get to James.

'You were in my way!'

'By God, James, you've ruined it all,' Charles said. 'Find my glasses and keep your mouth shut.' He pulled off his shirt, ripped off the sleeve and applied pressure to Martin's nose to stop the bleeding. That achieved, he tied the bloodied sleeve around the knee where swelling had already set in.

After searching for some time, James found the glasses; one lens shattered and the frame bent. He also offered his handkerchief as a bandage for the cut on Martin's face.

'*Bliksem!* Now we are in deep shit! They will tell Old Klaas and then Pa will skin us alive. We must get away from here,' Martin said as the gravity of their position dawned. 'Back to the drift, into the milkwood. Keep a lookout and see if they come to speak to Pa. If they don't, we can always say I had a bad fall.'

Keeping to the trees, they reached the drift and helped Martin into the milkwood. Before long the tall figure of Old Klaas, the village headman, appeared in the company of the women on the footpath leading from the huts. They met Marthinus at the sheep enclosures. The women's shrill voices carried to the drift as they related their experience. Their indignation conveyed, they departed for their huts again.

'We're doomed,' James sighed.

'We did wrong,' Charles said.

'Was it like the Bible said?' Martin asked. 'A jewel? Down there between her legs?'

James thought for a bit before he came up with a description. 'Well … it's an ugly thing … looks sort of like a hairy mole rat …'

'We will burn in the Eternal Fires of Hell,' Martin said.

'No we won't. King David watched Bathsheba bathing. He went to heaven when he died.'

Charles gave his brother an irritated look. 'You know all those sort of verses in the Bible, don't you just? We might be saved from eternal damnation, but not from the *sjambok*. I suggest we get it over and done with.'

'James saved me from the *sjambok* last week,' Martin said. 'The women saw only me. Go home and pretend that you've been elsewhere and that I went off on my own.'

'It's a brave offer, but I can't accept.' Charles gestured to his dishevelled state. 'I won't get away with it, anyway; I'm going with you.'

James considered Martin's bruised face. 'I led you to those stirring verses in the Bible, and I pushed you,' he hastily added, 'accidentally. I shall not shirk from my punishment. Count me in.'

'Your backside will hurt for days,' Martin warned.

'The *sjambok* doesn't scare me. How many do you reckon we'll get?'

'Four, six perhaps. You may be last in line.' The last one suffered the least. By then his father's fury would be spent.

They left the safety of the tree. Charles, with his broken glasses askew and his torn shirt, led the way. Martin, the bloodstained handkerchief obscuring his eye, was leaning on James as they limped along. Their slow pace became a shuffle as they neared the house.

The family was on the stoep having their afternoon coffee, the mothers handing round milk tart and golden rusks. Stefanie sat on the steps, drying her hair in the sun. Karel and Rudolf were amusing Oubaas, attacking his walking stick, brandishing small wooden spears.

Marthinus was next to Oubaas, a cup of coffee in his hand, his pipe clamped between his teeth. 'Well now, what have we here?' He scratched his beard, but Martin saw the grin behind his hand. 'A tough battle, by the looks of them. Felons or victims?' He looked at Oubaas. 'How does one tell, old Grandpa?'

'The eyes! The eyes! A guilty man does not look you in the eye.'

Martin studied his dirty feet.

'There was a bit of a … mishap, sir,' said Charles, his usually confident voice wavering.

'They rescued me from certain death, Pa,' Martin said.

'And how, son, may I ask, did you get into such a position?'

James moved his foot over Martin's toes. Probably to give courage, Martin thought. His cousin had plenty to spare.

'I know what you did, so there's no need to talk your way out of the punishment you so richly deserve. Four and no supper?' Marthinus bit into a slice of milk tart. 'Or six and some of your mother's food?'

Martin caught the hungry look James cast at the table.

'Four, Pa,' he said and stole a glance at the twins. They nodded. Some rusks would not reach the kitchen and neither would some of the bobotie that their mother had prepared for supper.

Oom Paul and Tante Koba

MARTHINUS ANNOUNCED THAT the family would jour-
ney to Pretoria, the capital, for the *nagmaal* instead of joining
the district at Rustenburg for this religious occasion. James was
elated, as it entailed a two-day journey by ox-wagon. He hoped fervently
that President Kruger would be in Pretoria. He might get to see him, even if
it was just from a distance.

The women showed no interest in the trip. Susan said that she could not
bear the heat, dust and insects, which left Mary with no choice but to stay
and keep her sister company.

'The journey would be too tiresome,' Stefanie said, imitating her
aunt. 'I'll help with sewing dresses from the material Aunt Susan brought
from London.'

'Where will we stay?' James asked Martin. 'Is there a hotel in Pretoria?'

'Why, with my Tante Koba of course! She's my father's only sister. The
lion killed her husband, remember? The skin in the study? Tante Koba is
much older than Pa, but has no children. We are her brood, she says. She
clipped Karel's ear so that Ma can tell them apart.'

James looked at him askance. 'Clipped his ear? Surely not.'

'Ma is too vague, Tante Koba says. Tante Koba is a Wise Woman.
Medicines and that stuff, you know. Careful when she's around. She *feels* what
one thinks.'

The ox-wagon was being loaded with farm produce to be sold at the
market: onions, pumpkins, potatoes and dried beans. The boys forced chickens into baskets and slung them under the wagon, placed eggs in a straw-
filled wooden crate, and secured with rope the hides to be delivered to the
tannery. By late afternoon the wagon stood ready to be yoked.

Long before sunrise, Marthinus cracked the whip over the span of
sixteen oxen. The span settled into their accustomed rhythm, and the
wagon rolled on with the occasional low sigh of an ox and the creaking of
the wheels.

James did not like the unfamiliar darkness and strained his eyes for a sign of sunrise, but it was only after they had travelled for two hours that a glimmer appeared in the east. Now they could see the scattered homesteads along their route. Smoke spiralled from chimneys and farmyards bustled with activity. They waved and called out greetings. Here and there Marthinus alighted to exchange news with farmers who came to the road to meet them. The boys took turns holding the reins until he caught up with the wagon, easily outpacing the lumbering oxen.

By dusk they reached the farm of Lang Hans van Rensburg. The roads from the northwestern interior converged here, and travellers used it as a staging post on the way to Pretoria. There were stables, paddocks and drinking troughs where tired horses were exchanged. They found Lang Hans at the far end of the outspan, where he was attending to an injured ox. James stared. As thin as a rope, taller than a church tower, a greying beard down to his waist like wisps of smoke in the dusky light. *Moses. It could be Moses.*

EARLY THE NEXT MORNING they were on their way again. The road cut through the mountain at a natural pass and the oxen laboured with their load. Once through the pass the countryside was different; clumps of forest gave way to dense thickets of mimosa, their yellow puffy flowers wafting a heady perfume. The mountain range to the left looked formidable; a wall of vertical grey cliffs with barren crests overlooking the expanse of highveld bush.

With the sun setting behind them, they arrived in Pretoria, dusty and tired. Marthinus had sent word of their coming to his sister, Koba van Wyk. After the lioness had killed her husband on Wintersrust, Martin's aunt had settled in Pretoria, visiting the farm whenever she felt she was needed – a frequent occurrence. They found her waiting at the gate, waving her arms in greeting.

James stood rooted. Tante Koba was a large woman with thick arms and ample bosom, a round face, like a full moon, and blue De Winter eyes, crinkling at the corners. A real aunt, not some cross-eyed medicine woman. She gathered the twins and showered them with kisses and endearments. Martin received the same loving treatment, and Charles happily accepted a hug and a kiss. He wanted to be part of the spontaneity, but his father had always dictated that emotions should be private and kept under control. Koba beamed a welcome, but he hesitated. She placed her hands behind her back, closed her eyes and offered her cheek. He willingly, almost eagerly, placed a kiss on it.

There was just enough daylight left to see Koba's double-storey house and her two acres of land along the Apies River. Martin showed them the orchard and the beehives under the willows. They went to the stables to greet her groom and gardener, Bontes, and to see the latest additions to her stables. After a hearty supper they were ordered to bed, and the last thing James remembered was Koba's smiling face, wishing him a good night's rest.

THEY HURRIED their breakfast, eager to be off, but Marthinus ruled that they should help with the sale of the produce at the market. James sighed. Koba assured him that Church Square was a lively place, the heart of the town. Everything of importance took place there: political speeches, the gathering of the commandos before a war, as well as various sporting events.

The twins stayed with Koba, not wanting to miss her taking the honey from the hives. The other three followed Marthinus through the wide street leading to town. The gardens were pleasing, with their rose hedges, blue gums and willows. The town's water supply came from the Apies River, Marthinus explained, which had its source in a spring at the Fountains, a thickly wooded area to the southwest of the town.

'Why is Pretoria so much smaller than Kimberley, Uncle Marthinus? And why are there no trains here?' Charles asked.

'We have no diamonds, son. It's better that way, as we don't attract the unwanted elements – call them the diggers, if you like. They have no love of the land and care little about the way of life followed by our people.'

'If you had diamonds, you'd be rich,' James said. 'You could have a big army, and then you would not have to call out the farmers to fight.'

His uncle chuckled. 'No, you little hothead, the farmers *are* the army. All of us must fight to keep our country safe.'

'If we had diamonds, Pa, we could build schools,' Martin said. 'Then I wouldn't have to go all the way to Bloemfontein. It's so far away!'

'Don't you know how lucky you are to be sent away? James whispered. 'No parents to answer to.'

Marthinus ruffled Martin's hair. 'How will you get to be president if you're not prepared to study, son? You are intelligent, and,' he chuckled, 'ambitious far beyond your years. We might get you a proper education yet. In England. Our country needs educated men. God knows, there are few of them around.'

They reached Church Square as the shopkeepers were opening their stores. Low buildings with corrugated-iron roofs, some thatched, surrounded the large square, where more than fifty wagons were encamped. Smoke rose from the open fires, where women were tending black round-bellied pots. Dogs and children ran between the wagons. Bearded men stood in groups smoking their pipes. Horses were tethered to the wagon poles, munching from bales of grass. They made their way to where Marthinus had taken the wagon after their arrival, stopping frequently to greet acquaintances and friends.

Business was brisk. The eggs and chickens sold quickly, and after an hour they were left with a few pumpkins and some bags of grain.

A tall bearded man dressed in a black suit arrived at their wagon, his hand outstretched. 'Marthinus, good day, good day!' His deep-set eyes beamed down at the boys. 'Aha! The British cousins. Are you enjoying your stay in our country?'

'What brings you into town, Koos?' Marthinus asked after they had made their inquiries after the farms, wives and children.

'Volksraad business. Trouble up north again. The President has called a meeting. But I'll tell you more later. Come for coffee at my wagon when you have done here.'

Charles looked at the imposing figure walking away. 'Who's that, Martin? He looks important, and spoke English.'

'Oom Koos de la Rey. He farms a day's ride from us, near Lichten-burg. Oom Koos sits in the Volksraad. He's going to be our president when Oom Paul dies, and when he's old, I am going to be the president,' Martin declared, his blue eyes serious. 'The president is the most important man in the country. He decides when we go to war and whom we will fight, and one day I will be that man, the president!'

'Why can't your father be the president?' James said. 'He'll be old enough soon.'

'No, he can't be president.' Martin avoided James's eyes.

'But why?'

'Because he's married to an Englishwoman. Everyone knows. Even the President. I won't be so foolish. It's important to have the right wife. I'm going to marry a girl from the district – our neighbour's daughter, Annecke.'

James thought he understood; marrying into one's own class was an unwritten rule of society. 'Where's his house? The President's house?' he asked when Marthinus set them free.

On their way across the square, they passed a large white building with a thatched roof and a wide stoep. The windows had no panes and the wooden shutters were wide open. Inside was a big wooden desk, some smaller tables and old chairs scattered about. On the wall was a wooden carving of the Republic's emblem with the flag draped above it.

'This is the Raadsaal,' Martin informed them proudly.

Then he led them to a small church where many wagons were clustered around. 'The Doppers are also having *nagmaal*. What a dull lot! They don't dance or have any kind of fun. They don't even sing hymns in their church. And,' he lowered his voice, 'they're not allowed to take a *dop*. They call it the devil's brew. But Tante Koba says that in many a wagon-kist, there's a bottle of homebrew with the kick of a mule in it.'

They halted opposite a small whitewashed house with a triangular gable on each side, a stoep running its full length and a low wall separating it from the road. The Vierkleur, the four-striped banner of the Transvaal, was attached to a pole on the thatched roof. President Kruger was on the stoep, but he was partly obscured by visitors.

They sat on the pavement, feet dangling in a water-furrow, and watched the comings and goings on the stoep. Eventually there were only two men left, but they showed no sign of departing. James was impatient and badgered the others to steal a closer look at the President. They crawled behind the wall and were directly opposite where he sat.

'*Ja! Ek sien julle,*' the President roared. 'Don't hide. Stand up! Let me see you!'

They walked onto the stoep. '*Dag*, Oom Paul,' Martin said. '*Dag, Ooms,*' he greeted the other men. 'I'm the oldest son of Marthinus de Winter and these are my British cousins.'

'*Ja*, I know your father well.' The President looked at the other boys with interest. 'Did you say Englishmen?'

'It's an honour to meet you, Mr President, sir.' Charles bowed.

James stared at the President. The resemblance between the squat old man dressed in black and Queen Victoria was striking – the hooded eyes, sagging jowls and, through the scraggly beard, the double chin. 'He looks exactly like the Queen!' he exclaimed.

A very long minute ensued. The President removed his ornate meerschaum from his mouth, spat roundly in the direction of the spittoon, let out an ear-piercing bellow, slapped his knee and roared with laughter.

'*Allemagtig!* Just like old *mies* Victoria.'

James stepped backwards, slipped on the polished floor and fell to his knees. The President hoisted him by the arm. He stared into Kruger's red-veined eyes and the large mouth, split into a grin.

'I'm … I'm sorry, Your Majesty.'

'Your Majesty? *Wragtig!*' he roared again. 'What's your name, young man?'

'James … Stuart … Henderson.'

'Aha! I will write to your Queen and tell her of your compliment. Thank you, young Mr Henderson.' He made a gruff sound and released James abruptly.

James fled out of the gate and down the road, the chuckles of the men on the stoep following him. He ran past the Doppers, upsetting pots and water pails, stumbled over a dog and bumped into an old man dressed in a long frock coat. He was pushed away, but picked himself up and ran on, searching wildly for the road they had come by that morning. He arrived at Koba's front door bewildered and exhausted, and on the verge of tears.

Koba came out, took him by the arm and led him into the kitchen, where he burst into tears. 'I hate the President! I hate this country! I want to go home,' he burst out. Koba gave him a glass of lemonade, and, keeping his eyes on the table, he waited for her to ask the reason for his distress. Surprisingly, Koba just said, 'Never mind, *hartjie*; whatever it was, it's all over now.'

He watched her stirring the pots and pans, humming to herself. Her quiet presence was calming, and he found himself telling her, bit by bit, what had happened.

'No! The wily, dear old man!' She clasped her hands together. 'How could he do such a cruel thing? The President is the grandfather of a big brood. Does he not know that boys are precious?'

James saw the true emotion in her eyes, not just an affected pose for his benefit. It gave him confidence to tell her about his fears. 'Tante Koba, will the President write to the Queen? I will never be a soldier now. I know he'll write to the Queen. Even if Uncle Marthinus spares me the *sjambok*, Father will not forgive me for the shame I've brought on our name.'

'No! He'll do no such a thing. I'll see to that. Listen, *hartjie*,' she wiped her hands on her apron and sat down beside him. 'I have to buy some things for Mary: six reels of cotton, blue ribbon, spices and so on. I'll see the President and have a good talk with him.'

'Will he listen to you, Tante Koba?' She was an old widow, and the President might not grant her a minute of his time.

'But, of course, *hartjie*! Was my dear husband – God rest his poor departed soul – not the godfather of his second son, Tjaart? He will listen.' She patted his hand. 'There's nothing, not a thing, that Tante Koba cannot fix.'

After lunch, during which he had to endure the smirking faces of his brother and cousin, James hung around the kitchen until Koba left for town in her Cape cart. He collected a pile of stones and sat at the front gate to await her return. When Martin or Charles dared to put their heads around the corner of the house, taunting him with a 'your majesty', he drove them back with a well-directed stone.

The twins carefully edged their way around the opposite corner. 'Cousin James, we know that you're much older than us, but you're also younger than them,' Karel said sincerely. 'Rudi and I will help you, anytime, night or day. We know how to fight.'

'Go away! I can handle my own affairs,' he grumbled.

'You see, we are the youngest. We know,' Rudolf said, and James nodded.

A long hour later, Koba returned and James rushed to help her with her packages. She heaved her big body from the cart, untied the ribbons of her *kappie* and beckoned him closer. 'It's all settled now, *hartjie*, he will not breathe a word about it. He will never do such a thing again, the dear two-faced old Dopper. I gave him a piece of my mind!'

James offered to stay with her when the others were to return to the farm, saying that he would rather be with her. 'Thank you, *hartjie*,' she said. 'My bottling and preserving are done. It's time to see my old grandfather again. The dear old Oubaas. He needs my remedies. I'm also going to Wintersrust. I'll watch out for you.'

———

ON SUNDAY MORNING Marthinus and Koba, dressed in their Sunday black, left to attend the *nagmaal*. The boys hung about the stables for a while and then climbed into the willows to watch the bees at work around the hives.

'Where are Karel and Rudolf?' Charles asked after a while. They had been charged to keep an eye on the twins who had been acting secretively since their arrival in Pretoria.

They called and searched the house and the grounds, looked in the dark cellar, but there were only food supplies and Koba's many bottles of home remedies. They walked the nearby streets and scoured the banks of the river, but after a fruitless search they returned home. Martin contemplated whether to send for his father, but just then the Cape cart arrived and they rushed to report the disappearance of the twins.

Marthinus hung his hat on the hook behind the kitchen door and took his seat at the table where Koba was laying out lunch. 'How long ago?'

'Not even an hour, Pa,' Martin said, keeping the *sjambok* in mind.

'Well, they can't be far. Something caught their fancy and they wandered off. But let us not spoil our food.' He ate his meal unhurriedly and took his pipe and coffee onto the stoep. Eventually he saddled a horse and rode in search of the twins.

Martin and his cousins sat on the steps and waited. Before long, they spotted the twins coming down the street, hand in hand. It took Martin a while to distinguish between his brothers, as the habitual smile on Rudolf's face was absent.

Karel walked up to Martin, spat on the ground and clenched his fists. 'You lied to us! God does not live in Pretoria. We asked many people. They laughed at us! Said that God lives up there!' He pointed to the sky. At the door, Karel turned around and said with absolute finality, 'He was nailed to the cross. He died! Like Oupa did, like Uncle Servaas did.' The door slammed shut.

Martin buried his face in his hands and scratched his head. 'How on earth am I going to explain this to Pa?'

'Never mind that,' Charles said. 'How to set this right, that's the problem.'

Koba appeared a short while later. 'I fed them. They are resting in my room. I heard it all. How could you, Martin?' she asked more in sorrow than in anger. 'They need extra care. Where there should've been one, there are two, through God's strange will. What the one believes there the other must follow.'

Martin explained the problem to his aunt, knowing that she would understand. She listened with care, chewing her lip thoughtfully.

'Yes, *hartjie*, I understand now.' She sank down in a chair and wiped her brow on her apron, stared into space and started talking. Martin drew closer, for Koba's stories were spiced with intimate details, biblical quotations and meaningful silences.

'How well I remember the night they were born. Karel arrived first, a healthy but angry baby. What a noise he made! It was only after Rudolf came into the world a little while later, that Karel stopped crying. The one minute he was blue in the little face with the effort of crying, and then, when he felt his brother's body against his, he made not a sound. It was then that I understood … that I saw how it would be with them. You see, Karel is the stronger one. But, and this is what I saw that night, Karel takes his strength from his brother, the gentle spirit of Rudolf. It wells up from deep down, just here,' she placed her hand on her large bosom, 'and without that, Karel would be lost. Like an eagle in a cage, a newborn lamb bereft of his mother's milk, a hunter without his rifle, a bird without his song … Yes, that's how it would be for him. And our little Rudolf? Who'll look out for him if his brother is not there? They might not stand the separation that surely is to come.'

'Who'll separate them, Tante Koba?' Martin asked.

'Life,' Koba sighed, a meaningful sigh. 'Life doesn't always turn out the way we plan. Who knows what lies in store? Oh, yes, God does, but then, just this morning the *predikant* said: "For I the Lord thy God am a jealous God." Our God can be so gentle and kind and if we don't follow His ways, His fury and vengeance can be like lightning from angry heavens. In this hard country of ours, life doesn't always run its course. Death lurks in everything we do: hunting to keep our bellies full, fighting a war, breaking in a wild horse. And there's always disease: the dreaded fever, blood poisoning, childbirth, inflammation of the lungs …'

She tut-tutted and patted their heads. 'I'm not saying that something dreadful will happen to them. Life, I said, might separate them. What will happen when they're old enough to take wives? Will the love of a woman tear them apart? You see,' she whispered, 'there was only one afterbirth. So, before they came into this world, they'd been joined together by God, one in flesh and one in mind. Yes, always remember that.'

Koba wiped her face on her apron and heaved her body from the chair. 'You boys go rest. And don't worry your young heads any more. Tante Koba will settle this with dear Marthinus.'

As Martin followed her figure waddling through the front door, he saw the two identical faces disappear behind the windowsill in the bedroom facing the stoep. By their startled eyes, he knew that they had overheard every word through the open window.

The Home of the Fireflies

A WEEK AFTER their return to Wintersrust, a wagon approached on the road from Rustenburg. The Maree family, from the neighbouring farm, Soetvlei, had at last returned. Everyone rushed to the road to greet them.

'Uncle Joep! Uncle Joep!' Martin, followed by Karel and Rudolf, ran to meet the full-bearded man. James joined in the race, and Charles followed at a more sedate pace. He watched as Martin and the twins grabbed Joep Maree by the arms and in return received cuffs to the ears and rough tickles in the ribs with loud laughter.

Joep was a wide-shouldered, barrel-chested man, with sunburnt hairy arms and a mischievous glint in his dark eyes. His son, Buks, was a few paces behind him – a sturdy boy whose sun-freckled face and curly dark hair made him a replica of his father, all but in manner. He looked at Charles and James with suspicion, if not hostility. Annecke, his little sister, came running up, smiled at them shyly and rushed to the twins.

Marthinus assisted Lettie Maree from the wagon and helped her to the stoep, where Mary was getting coffee and rusks. Lettie was a plump woman with a jolly face. When Charles and James were introduced to her, there came a moment of unease. Lettie pinched James's cheeks and laughed shrilly. 'What a pretty young boy! Dimply cheeks and such thick lashes. You'll break many hearts, now, won't you?'

To Charles's relief, James took it in his stride. 'I'm planning on doing that, Aunt Lettie,' he said and rushed off with Martin and Buks to take the wagon to the Soetvlei farmstead.

During the following week Buks and Annecke became their daily companions. Buks soon lost his wariness and joined in the play, but he was mostly found with the livestock. Charles watched him, fascinated, as he helped his father brand the cattle and clip the sheep's ears. Annecke, being only five, could not be separated from the twins, a bond, Charles realised, that had been formed in their infancy. Stefanie spent her days with her aunt, but she joined them on Karel and Rudolf's birthday. The promise Martin had made had not been forgotten; they were going to have a picnic on the mountain.

KAREL AND RUDOLF sat on the stoep with their presents. Cloth-bags with drawstrings from Stefanie – to put their treasures in, she said. Pocket-knives from Charles and James. A sixpence each from Martin and a jar of ointment for cuts and bruises from Tante Koba. The most treasured present, however, was from Buks and Annecke: a scrawny but lively puppy.

'Dogs are hard to come by,' Buks said to Charles, 'and not easy to rear here. Ticks, snakes and baboons are their fate. We brought this one from Kuruman.'

'What's his name? He must have a name,' Annecke said.

'Hero! He looks like a brave doggy,' Karel said.

James studied the long-legged pup uncertainly. 'Let's hope it lives up to its name.'

Martin ignored James's comment and turned to Buks to discuss where to go. It was a clear summer's morning, but the tranquil air was deceptive, and a band of cloud showed to the northeast.

'We follow the kloof to a special place,' Martin told the others. 'Last summer, Buks and I discovered a pool beneath a little waterfall. We'll go there.' He checked his rifle and slung it over his shoulder.

Buks shouldered the haversack with their provisions for the day, and they set off. Martin led, followed by Buks and James. Charles was in the middle with Stefanie who, on her aunt's advice, wore a straw hat to protect her face from the sun. The twins and Annecke, the puppy trotting at their heels, brought up the rear. They skirted the cattle kraals and the ploughed fields and reached the lower slope, stopping frequently to stuff their pockets with wild raisins, sour plums and small monkey oranges.

James was in excellent spirits, Charles noticed; the next day they would be going home. He had had enough of the country, James had said to him the previous night. He wanted to go home where all was as it should be.

Charles, however, felt sad at the thought of returning to London, where his future was already mapped out. The Transvaal was not backward or hostile. The Boers were hospitable, warm and caring. And the land was fresh and unspoiled, with so much splendour in the variety of life. The birds fascinated him. Guinea fowl and francolin, twittering like startled girls, crossed their path frequently. Colourful bee-eaters and metallic sunbirds darted from bush to bush as if to show the way. Hornbills flapped ahead in their peculiar dipping movements.

It is a good thing that Tante Koba's God is a jealous God. He destroys those who come to plunder the beautiful land. Koba had learned it in the most sorrowful way. Had she not told him that her husband had been a hunter and had killed many, many elephants? And the penalty for that was death by one of His creatures. 'If the lion had not got him that fateful night at Wintersrust,' she had whispered to him, 'a buffalo or an elephant would have trampled him.'

He pondered on this tale as he searched the ground for tubers and bulbs he could take to Koba. She had showed him her jars of remedies and taught him where to look for medicinal plants. He thought about the problem facing him in the coming year. Somehow he had to convince his father that he was not cut out for Oxford and a political career. He mind was set on studying medicine, but he knew his father would disapprove.

He stopped in his tracks at the harsh call of a shrike, and searched the lower branches of the bush to his left. There it was: crimson breast flashing like a jewel with the sharp contrast of thin, perfect white lines on the pitch-black wings. 'One of God's beautiful creations,' Koba had said, 'but beneath the beauty, a savage heart.'

'Charles! You're dreaming again. Come on!' Stefanie called.

As they climbed, Charles noticed that the fleecy clouds they had observed earlier were now thickening. He also saw that little Annecke was struggling to keep up. Karel lifted her onto Rudolf's back and they carried on, alternating Annecke between them. The twins never complained or asked for assistance; they shared whatever came their way. He had watched them at play. They chatted ceaselessly, but since their return from Pretoria they were alert when Martin was around. Karel was more suspicious than before. The smile was back on Rudolf's face but there was a watchful wariness in his eyes.

They reached the promised place: a pool fed by a thin waterfall and shaded by a wild fig tree. The puppy rushed to the water and gulped thirstily. Then a lizard caught his attention and he darted off in pursuit of it.

'Get him back. That way!' Buks said to the twins, pointing to their right. 'Up those rocks and into the bushes.'

To their right was a smooth slab of rock, sloping upwards, fringed at the top by a clump of wild raisin bushes. The twins scrambled up to search. Rudolf was back within a minute, his eyes huge. 'Come! Come see!' They followed him up the rock and crawled into the thick undergrowth. They came up against a steep cliff and found themselves facing a large hole at the base. Karel was waiting there, holding the puppy.

Martin looked at the fissure in the rock and hesitated. James tried to push his way past him. Martin shoved him aside. 'You never know what's in there. Stay here!' He checked his rifle and beckoned to Buks. With great care they stepped into the opening and were gone but a few seconds before they came stumbling back, yelling wildly, enveloped in a blur of flying things. The others ducked and screamed as the dark cloud swooped away into the sky.

'What's that? Are you all right?' Charles asked.

'Bloody bats,' Martin heaved. 'We gave them a fright!'

'More like they gave you a fright,' James said.

'Come, let's try again,' Buks said. 'The bats are gone now.'

'I'm not going in there,' Stefanie said in a small voice. 'I'm a girl.'

'Wait here and a leopard will get you,' James said. 'They go for loners, your father said.'

Taking a deep breath, Martin re-entered, with the others following closely behind. For some way they tracked a narrow passage running obliquely from the entrance. Then it widened abruptly. Martin stopped and everyone bundled into him.

They gasped. An extraordinary light surrounded them. No one spoke for a full minute.

THEY WERE in a large cave, the far end barely visible. Through narrow openings in the high roof, sunbeams struck down at angles, dancing on the walls and sandy floor, giving a mysterious atmosphere to the silent interior.

Stefanie was the first to find her voice. 'So beautiful, like a palace.'

'Is this where God lived?' Rudolf whispered.

'Yes, but he died a long time ago,' Karel said.

'A fort! An entire regiment could hole up here,' James said.

'Oh yes? A commando. This is our country,' Martin reminded him.

Charles, annoyed with the constant bickering, decided that now was the moment for harmony, even if it lasted only long enough to enjoy the mystic beauty of the cave. Holding his hands above his head, he walked forward, the shadows of his hands making patterns on the floor. As he turned to face them, a shaft of light caught his face and reflected off his glasses. 'Listen! Can you hear it? Can you feel it?' His voice echoed off the walls. 'This is not a palace, nor a fort. This is a Place of Peace. It may be that God once lived here; therefore we shall not quarrel here.' He glared sternly at the silent group. 'It'll be our secret place. We shall always be safe here.'

'Safe? Safe from what, Charles?' Rudolf hooked his little finger with Karel's.

'Safe from the outside world,' he said, but still they stared at him. He searched for something dramatic to say, and struck on a passage from Isaiah that Marthinus had read a few nights ago. As he could not remember the exact words, he adjusted them to suit the occasion. 'Here shall be as a hiding place from the wind, as rivers of water in a dry place, as a shadow of a great rock in a weary land. And a shelter from the tempest of life.'

The others nodded uncertainly, stood for a while longer and then started exploring the cave. Martin found a loose flat rock, big enough for a table. Karel cleared a space where the light was at its strongest. The boys heaved and pushed and managed to get the rock there. Stefanie spread a cloth taken from the haversack on the table and laid out the food: jam sandwiches, a small cake, cold meat, fruit and a bottle of milk. They whispered, but as they grew accustomed to the overpowering silence, their voices grew stronger. They chatted about the schools they were to attend the following year: James to join Charles at Eton; Martin to Grey College in Bloemfontein; and Buks back to Rustenburg for two more years only, as farming was all that interested him.

'At least I can stay with Tante Koba over the weekends.' Stefanie had obtained a place at the Loreto Convent in Pretoria, where she would study music. 'I shall have to wear shoes and stockings all the time, but Aunt Susan says that it's about time that I do.'

Charles was impressed that his dramatic address had had the desired effect; the tranquil atmosphere at the rock table soothed even James's quarrelsome nature.

'Strange, it has been here all the time,' Buks said, 'and we passed by, just a few yards away. It's a secret.' He glared at the younger boys. 'If you breathe a word about this, there will be a curse on you!'

'It must have a name, don't you think?' James said.

'Then Karel and Rudi should have the honour of bestowing the name. It's their birthday,' Charles said before other suggestions were forthcoming.

'Let Annecke name it,' Karel said, and Rudolf nodded.

Annecke's brown eyes shone with excitement. She looked about her for a good few minutes before she said with such finality in her little voice that no one challenged her: 'The Home of the Fireflies.'

James sighed, clearly disappointed.

'That's beautiful, Annecke,' Charles smiled at her. 'Why do you want to call it that?'

She pointed to the roof, but, before she could utter a word, the light coming through the fissures faded. Within seconds they were in darkness.

'The clouds,' Martin cried. 'We must get down before the storm breaks!'

They grabbed the haversack and the puppy and rushed outside.

Blue-black clouds billowed above and around them. Wind spat dust and leaves into their faces. Then a sheet of lightning rent the air. The world trembled. The pungent smell of sulfur overwhelmed them. They stared around them and saw a wild olive cracking in half. A second later it was engulfed in flames. Then the sky opened, accompanied by ear-splitting thunder.

'Back! Get back to the cave!' Charles shouted.

They bundled into the cave and huddled together with the puppy and the three little ones in the centre. Outside, the storm raged. Inside the cave, lightning flashed through the fissures in the roof, piercing the darkness. Water poured through an opening at the far end. Then, as unexpectedly as it had started, the storm died away. Only the sound of water dripping into the puddles on the floor broke the silence.

Charles came to his feet, his hair plastered to his head, his glasses shining in the muted light. 'I told you we will always be safe here. We've just survived the most terrifying storm. Do you believe me now? The outside world cannot reach here.'

The others stretched their cramped limbs. Buks slung the haversack over his shoulder. Martin hoisted Annecke onto his back. No one showed surprise when James offered to carry the puppy. With a last look at their shelter, they filed outside. The fury of the heavens was exhausted. The clouds had moved westward, their rumblings soft and harmless now.

They gathered on the rock slab and stared at the havoc wreaked by the storm. The wild olive was broken in half, its pale bark blackened by fire. Lower down, a tamboti had snapped, taking some smaller trees with it. Water rushed down the little waterfall that had been a gentle trickle an hour ago. Far below, smoke rose from the chimneys of Wintersrust and Soetvlei, caught in a splash of sunshine. The herd boys called as they brought in the livestock. It looked peaceful, as if the storm had not touched the farms.

As they stood there, a large shadow passed swiftly over them. They looked up and saw a black eagle gliding out into the clean, fresh sky.

PART TWO

THE OUTLANDERS

Had you been
Sharer of that scene
You would not ask while it bites in keen

Why it is so
We can no more go
By the summer paths we used to know!

Thomas Hardy,
'Paths of Former Time' [1913]

The Outlanders

'A PLAGUE FROM the Almighty!' President Paul Kruger grumbled to himself.

He sat on his stoep, slurping his coffee, watching the wintry sun spread over his peaceful city. Pretoria was the pride of the *Volk* and the seat of their government. It symbolised their victory over the obstacles they had overcome to achieve their independence: the wild animals that roamed the land, the indigenous tribes, now befriended but who still plundered, murdered and stole livestock. And the British who'd followed them out here, but had been beaten, as God had ordained, at the great Battle of Majuba.

Then God had sent another burden disguised as a blessing: eight years ago, in the eventful summer of 1886, layer upon layer of gold-bearing quartz had been discovered – the richest treasure ever in the world – in the Transvaal.

He sighed and felt for his pipe. The gold had saved the country from bankruptcy, but brought Sodom and Gomorrah to his doorstep. Fifty miles to the south, a city had sprung up on the sunbaked veld at the Witwatersrand. It was named Johannesburg. Outlanders had descended like a plague of locusts to claim a share – from Germany, Russia, France, but mostly from England. Brick houses had by now replaced the sea of tents and crude dwellings, and there were gambling dens, scarlet women in houses of ill-repute, moneylenders. Philistines! All manner of offensive living in the country of his God-fearing people.

The population was over a hundred thousand and growing rapidly, causing problems with housing, food and sanitation. A Boer built his house, grew his food and dug a hole for his waste. All given freely from Nature and used wisely. But the Outlanders! Their godless ways brought moral pestilence to his *Volk*.

His people were pastoral, people of the earth. They were prepared to leave the exploitation of the gold to the foreigners as long as the newcomers, in return, were prepared to acknowledge the supremacy of the nation who had made the land safe for human settlement.

He sat sipping his coffee and puffing his meerschaum. The railway line from the two British colonies, the Cape and Natal, now reached Johannesburg and Pretoria. Soon the Boers would be outnumbered. The Englishman, Cecil Rhodes, had grabbed the country to the north and to the west. To the east there was the swampland of the Portuguese, where neither man nor beast could live. Only the republic of the Orange Free State on the southern border was a buffer between the Transvaal's gold and the avaricious Rhodes. There was nowhere to trek to this time. They would have to stay and see this through.

He placed his hand on the Bible at his side, praying for guidance through the demanding days ahead. His heart told him that the gold was the end of their independence.

———

THEY ARRIVED BARELY a minute before the train was due to leave Cape Town station. Martin de Winter, overnight bag in hand, hurried through the throng to their allotted carriage. It was midwinter, the rainy season in the Cape Colony, but the drizzle did not dampen his spirits. After three years at Cambridge, he was taking a break from his studies and heading home.

He glanced over his shoulder. Charles Henderson, loaded with luggage, was struggling to keep up. 'Where the bloody hell is he?' Charles panted, scanning the crowd frantically, but there was no sign of James.

'He'll turn up. He always does,' Martin said.

They had deposited their trunks in the baggage carriage early in the morning and had had an extended lunch at the White House Hotel. After his second bottle of wine, James had decided to find livelier entertainment. They had waited for him until the last minute, and, with no time left to hail a hansom, had run all the way from Strand Street to the station, hoping to find him there.

The first whistle sounded and there was still no sign of James. By the third whistle and the all-aboard call, they saw him – jacket crushed under the arm, waistcoat unbuttoned and two bottles in hand, running headlong through the crowd.

The train juddered into motion. James jumped onto the step of the nearest carriage, grabbed the handrail with one hand, laughing recklessly. The crowd on the platform cheered him on. He obliged with an exaggerated bow, almost losing his footing. A minute later, he burst into the compartment, face flushed, hair in disarray. He flopped down on the seat, offering them one of the open bottles.

'How do you manage? Always late, yet always making it.' Martin took the champagne. 'We searched everywhere and nearly missed the train ourselves.'

'It's obvious what you've been doing all afternoon,' Charles said. 'And that, brother, can lead to serious disease.'

'What? A few hands of cards at the docks? Disease, Dr Henderson? I, for one, refuse to live the life of celibacy that you, dear brother, manage so admirably.'

'Pretoria has no such establishments to satisfy your lusty nature.' Martin passed the champagne to Charles. 'There is, however, a splendid place in Johannesburg. Carter's. Rose Carter's. That's where I lost my fear of hairy mole rats.'

James burst into wild laughter and opened the second bottle. The cork hit Martin on his head, and champagne sprayed over the compartment amid much hooting and laughter. 'Here's to Johannesburg, then.' James took a large swig. 'The City of Gold! And Rose Carter!'

A gong sounded in the passage, announcing dinner. They hung their coats and stowed their bags. James buttoned his clothes and ran a brush through his hair. They swayed down the narrow passage to the dining saloon.

While James studied the wine list, Martin looked at their fellow diners – mainly well-dressed gentlemen, businessmen presumably, bound for Johannesburg. There were a few couples and, further down the aisle, two unescorted women who kept glancing at their table. Martin hoped that it was not going to be one of *those* nights. Since they had boarded the steamer in Southampton, James had often been the worse for drink, and his good looks had a striking effect on women.

'When faced with a choice, one has to come to a decision, even if it happens to be the mere selection of a wine,' Martin said to hurry James and beckoned the waiter to bring the first course.

They started on the soup as the train gathered speed, leaving the out-skirts of Cape Town. When the main course arrived, the conversation turned to the hunting trip Martin and James had planned. 'Come along for the fun, Charles,' James said.

Charles raised his hands. 'It will take a great deal of persuasion to get the Transvaal health authorities to allow me access to their work. And I plan to do just that.'

Charles wanted to do research on malaria, which was rife in the Transvaal in the summer. But Martin suspected that there was more to Charles's decision; over the years, he had questioned Martin about practising medicine in the Transvaal. 'I'll help where I can,' Martin said. 'You know how inflexible the elders of my *Volk* can be when it comes to progress in the medical field … well … any field, actually.'

'Spare me.' James refilled his glass. 'Has the rugby season started?'

'Yes, Pa has put in a word at Harlequins,' Martin said through mouthfuls of food. 'My place in the college XV should secure me a game.'

'Pity it's not the cricket season. Savage game, rugby.' James pushed his half-finished plate away. 'But I must say it suits your countrymen perfectly. Give me the bat, old boy. A real gentleman's game.'

Martin gave him a challenging stare, but decided to ignore the remark. Now was not the time for a drunken Boer-Brit spat. Instead he refilled their glasses and moved on to Buks Maree's forthcoming marriage, but that too was not well received.

'Ridiculous to marry so young!'

'Not ridiculous, James. In my country, wooing is overrated – choose a wife; propose by candlelight; get on with life.'

'Candlelight? Sounds hopeless!'

'Not at all,' Charles said. 'Most romantic notions seem silly in hindsight, but appear perfectly reasonable in the moment.'

'Indeed.' James yawned. 'Candlelight is fine for seducing women, but romance is for poets and lovesick fools.'

'James, there is a time to acknowledge the gentle emotions in life, and you, brother,' Charles stabbed his finger at him, 'will learn about that the hard way.'

'How dreadful.' James waved the dessert away and drained his glass. 'You've bored me to sleep.' He gave them a dimpled smile and went to find their compartment.

'Thank goodness.' Charles started on his dessert. 'Tonight we can retire early.'

———◆———

IN THE FOLLOWING two days, they steamed northeastward across the barren Karoo, arriving at Bloemfontein, the capital of the Orange Free State, late in the afternoon of the second day. Charles joined Martin, who was leaning out of the window, observing the people on the platform. A carriage arrived and deposited several trunks. A man, his black hair oiled and parted in the middle, stepped out. Under his fashionable mantle, he wore a frock coat and narrow striped trousers, a silk cravat folded over his collar, and in his gloved hands he carried a gold-tipped cane. When Charles, Martin and James arrived in the crowded dining saloon that evening, they found the man placed at their table.

'Paul Warren,' he introduced himself with a smile and invited them to share his bottle of wine before ordering another.

Polite talk about the weather, and the wind that would blow in from the frost-covered plains in the morning, soon turned personal. 'I am from Cape Town and have been spending a few days in Bloemfontein as the guest of the government,' Paul Warren said. 'I presume you're heading for Johannesburg? All roads lead to Johannesburg nowadays, they say.'

'We're bound for Pretoria, actually. Would your business be gold, Mr Warren? The business of Johannesburg, not so?' Martin asked, sipping his wine.

'No, not gold exactly, but you could say that gold is the underlying reason for the business I have to attend to.' Warren twirled the tip of his waxed moustache. 'I'm a lawyer, charged to investigate the grievances of the different nationalities in Johannesburg ...'

'Outlanders, Mr Warren. That's what they're called.'

'Are you from the Transvaal, Mr de Winter?'

'Yes I am, but I'm at Cambridge reading Law and have not been back for some years.' Martin contemplated the plate of roasted lamb that the waiter placed on the table. He was well informed on what was happening in the Transvaal, as his father regularly sent him letters, newspapers and, now that Marthinus had been elected as Volksraad member of the Rustenburg district, reports directly from the Volksraad meetings. 'What is the situation in Johannesburg? We hear very little apart from the state of the stock exchange.'

'The Transvaal needs a government that can keep up with the changing economy,' Paul Warren said. 'The concession rights are corrupt. The gold mines are taxed too heavily, and the tax laws are unjust. But the problem seems to lie in the refusal of President Kruger and most of his Raad members to accept the presence of the foreigners, the people who have rescued his country from bankruptcy.'

'So, Mr Warren, do you think these Outlanders are opposed to the President and his government?' Martin's eyes were on Warren's white hands, the manicured fingernails and the gold signet ring. Warren was sharp and intelligent, yet there was something in his dark eyes that was unsettling.

'No, they're not fundamentally opposed to the republican authorities.

It's my belief that the majority are prepared to become citizens of the Boer state, share in its responsibilities and contribute to its proper development, provided they also share the rights of its burghers.'

'How do you propose to go about the matter, Mr Warren?' Martin asked. 'How does one discover true grievances from those that are hidden in greed?'

A discussion followed on the Reform Committee, the body that brought the plight of the Outlanders to the attention of the government. They rounded off their meal with a glass of brandy, after which Paul Warren went off to his compartment.

'Good God!' burst out James, who had been strangely subdued during the evening. 'He rubbed his knee against mine. Not just once, and not by accident either!'

'Well, Warren is a little dandified, but he's certainly interesting,' said Charles. 'What nationality is he, Martin? His accent is familiar, but I couldn't place it.'

'He's an Afrikaner, an English-speaking Afrikaner from the Cape. Probably descended from British stock, as I am from Mother's side. There was something about him … something he said, or maybe the way he said it.' Martin frowned. 'But certainly interesting and extremely well informed. I thought it best to let him do the talking. From Pa's letters I formed the impression that the so-called Outlander affair is a minor matter. If Rhodes and his government take an interest in it, there must be more to it.'

DURING THE NIGHT they crossed into the Transvaal. Dawn found Martin staring out of the window at the passing landscape. Here and there, the odd homestead stood in a cluster of blue gums, with small flocks of sheep grazing on the sparse vegetation offered by the winter landscape. Miles and miles of open veld – he felt sheltered in the vastness of his homeland. A feeling of belonging took hold of him, but the feeling was badly shaken by the short stop in Johannesburg.

He had not seen the city for three years, and was overwhelmed by the size of it. The morning sun revealed vast corrugated-iron barns, smokestacks, mine headgear and huge spoil dumps, and the low hills were scarred by roads leading to fast-growing suburbs. Martin stared at the tall buildings, and breathed the smoky air. Would President Kruger be wise and consider the advantages conferred by this vast wealth? Would he listen to the engineers and financiers? It would take years, a generation possibly, before his people could take part in the mining economy. Paul Warren was right. The situation needed immediate and impartial attention.

'Listen to this!' Charles had bought a newspaper on the platform, and an item had attracted his attention. 'Paul Warren, the distinguished Capetonian lawyer and talented wing of the Villagers rugby team is due in Johannesburg today to spend the winter. The Wanderers Club expresses the hope that his work with the Reform Committee will not prevent him from playing in their team.'

'Interesting,' Martin said. 'So we are bound to meet him again.'

The journey from Johannesburg to Pretoria took less than an hour, and as the train rounded the wide bend through the thickly wooded Fountains, Martin was leaning out of the window again, restless with excitement.

'Get a grip, old boy,' James said. 'You're as excited as a hound on the hunt. Uncle Marthinus might come to the conclusion that his money was wasted on your education.'

'That's rich, coming from you!' Charles said and joined Martin at the window. The skyline of Pretoria presented a peaceful picture. The train pulled in to the station. Hope and warmth flooded back into Martin's heart when he saw the crowd on the roofless platform. There was his father, with his mother beside him, her eyes searching the carriages as the train came to a stop. The fair-haired girl in convent uniform was Stefanie, hanging on Koba's arm. And the twins, tall and lanky, looked awkward in their short trousers, their jackets too tight across the shoulders. Annecke was with them, her brown locks falling down the back of a green dress.

The need to protect them and this peaceful city, to shelter them from the ugliness and confusion he'd witnessed fifty miles to the south, took hold of his whole being.

———◆———

PAUL WARREN LEFT the Heights Hotel and strolled down Commissioner Street, swinging his cane. It was freezing, a dusty wind gusting up the dim gaslit streets. Johannesburg was cosmopolitan, noisy and ugly, a jumble of iron shacks, three-storey stone houses and gaudy wrought-iron façades. Built on greed, dressed like a whore.

He thought back to the dreadful days of his childhood; the days that had shaped his life; the foremost reason that brought him to Johannesburg. After the War of Freedom – the Boers would call it that – and the disaster at Majuba in 1881, the people of Pretoria had refused to continue to support his father's medical practice. A few months later they were bankrupt. An intense hatred of the Boers was born. When both his parents died shortly afterwards, Warren swore revenge; with the passing years this resolve grew into an obsession. He obtained a scholarship and studied Law at Oxford. On his return to the Cape he was offered a government post. The prime minister, Cecil John Rhodes, noted his brilliant academic record and his success in the courtroom. Since then he hadn't looked back. Now he was a confidant of Rhodes, and this privileged position had led to his journey to Johannesburg.

'Yes, Mr Paul Kruger, impertinent old peasant. I'll pay you back,' he muttered. 'You and your uneducated rabble! Rhodes might want you out of his way to paint the continent pink, but I want to see you stripped of all you hold dear.'

As he neared the Rand Club, his mind ran over the instructions he had received from Rhodes: take advantage of the present unrest in the city; stimulate the Outlanders, the working classes, into threatening direct action against the Boer government; persuade the big financiers to get involved in politics. An armed revolution, that's what we need. It might take time, a year or two perhaps, but it would come.

He thought about the mining magnates, the Randlords, he would be meeting in the Rand Club. Charles Leonard, a prominent lawyer, was an outspoken advocate for the Outlanders' rights. He too was a close confidant of Rhodes, and knew the real reason for Warren's visit. Robinson, rumoured to be the wealthiest man in the city, was from the Cape Colony and pro-Boer. Farrar, Bailey and Phillips were not a problem. Hays Hammond, the American engineer, was outspoken against the government, the rights of the individual being his first priority. He would be an excellent starting point.

He arrived at the club and cast a glance down the street. It was almost deserted. A couple of carriages were parked on the side and a few people hurried past, bent low against the cold wind. He walked into the spacious foyer and noted with satisfaction the plush armchairs and gilt-framed mirrors. The carpets were soft and thick, deadening the sound of his footsteps. A butler loomed out of the shadows.

'Good evening. Paul Warren, a guest for Mr Leonard. You've been informed of my visit?'

'Of course, sir. Welcome, sir.' The butler bowed, took his hat and coat. 'Mr Leonard is awaiting your arrival upstairs. Please follow me, sir.'

He was shown to a large room with a bar running the length of one wall. Comfortable leather armchairs and occasional tables stood about. A huge fireplace dominated the wall opposite the bar. Charles Leonard detached himself from the group gathered by the fire and came forward.

'Welcome, Warren, welcome! Glad to have you with us. Did you have an interesting day?' Leonard chuckled. 'Of course not. Down to real business, then? We can make a start, but don't come on too strong. Give them something to think about for the moment. We've plenty of time, my friend, plenty!'

Leonard ordered two large brandies and introduced Warren to the others. Warren found curiosity mixed with apprehension in their eyes. He smiled and acknowledged their greetings with a formal inclination of his head.

After another round of drinks, they went into an adjacent room, where dinner was served. The conversation centred around money rather than politics. It was only after the table was cleared, and cognac and cigars brought, that Leonard motioned Warren to speak.

Warren cleared his throat. 'Gentlemen, no doubt you've been informed of the official purpose of my mission, so I won't elaborate on that. You're also aware, I presume, that I act on behalf of my Prime Minster in a private capacity.'

He studied the faces around him; eyebrows lifted, expressions became guarded. Satisfied that he had their attention, he leaned forward, pressing his fingertips together. Before he could say anything further, Robinson, the Cape Afrikaner, spoke up. 'What exactly does Mr Rhodes want? More of our mines? You'd better tell us, young man, as we don't have time to waste,' he said, his moustache quivering with indignation.

'I'll tell you what he wants,' said Bailey in a noticeable German accent. 'He wants the country! We are all aware of his imperialistic greed, if you'll allow me to state a well-known characteristic of your Prime Minister.'

'Gentlemen! Allow Mr Warren to explain,' Farrar intervened.

Leonard called for order, silencing the grumbling that followed Bailey's statement.

'I'll come straight to the point, and then we can discuss your questions,' Warren said. 'First of all, I want to be in step with the feelings and needs of the city's population. I want to know if they are prepared to fight for their rights in this country, but,' he held up his hands to ward off the protest coming from Robinson, 'most importantly, I want to know how much pressure you are prepared to put on the government. You, gentlemen, *directly* control this city. That gives you control over the opinions of the masses, the workers and the smaller businessmen.'

Then he posed the question that would lead to the heart of the matter. 'Are you prepared to make more demands on the government?'

'Good heavens, Mr Warren! More demands on Kruger will border on rebellion,' Bailey warned.

'This is Boer country. It would be morally wrong to settle this dispute through force of arms,' Robinson, highly upset, flung at him.

'There are ways to put more pressure on the government: by refusing to pay the exorbitant taxes or by disobeying the ridiculous monopoly system. Import your own dynamite and mining equipment. There are many ways, gentlemen, many ways.'

'That, Mr Warren, will invite retaliation from the government.' Robinson supported himself on the arms of his chair. 'Are you familiar with the Boer way of settling disputes? Are you, Mr Warren? Corner them and they come at you with a gun in one hand and the Bible in the other. That gun, Mr Warren, will be loaded!'

'Indeed, Mr Robinson, it will be loaded,' Warren said. 'Is this city prepared for such action? Can you truly say that you can defend yourselves, your families and your mines? Do you have sufficient arms to take the fight to the Boers?'

Astonishment showed in their faces as Warren's remark struck home. 'I will not participate in treason!' said Robinson as he rose and headed for the door.

Warren turned to the others. 'May I point out that we're not talking treason? No one in this room is a citizen of the Boer republic. Shall we continue, gentlemen?'

They talked well into the night. Warren left the Club elated. Although nothing of importance had been decided, the arguments and counter-arguments showed that the seeds of rebellion had started to germinate.

He hailed a Cape cart, settled into the plush seat and chuckled to himself. 'I must keep up the pressure, gently but firmly. What you need, gentlemen, is a leader who has nothing to lose. No gold, no business concerns, no prestige. And that leader is Paul Warren. A little rebellion? No, gentlemen, a nasty little war!'

The driver put his head inside the cab. 'Where to, sir?'

'What? Oh yes, of course.' Warren consulted his notebook. 'Carter. The establishment of Madam Rose Carter. Do you know the address?'

———————

MARTIN AND HIS father sat on the stoep at Wintersrust, their eyes searching the road for Koba's new spring-wagon. The rest of the family was due to arrive from Pretoria for Buks's wedding. Charles was consulting with the health authorities and Stefanie had insisted that he and James attend her next recital. Although she was still at the Loreto Convent, she was the most sought-after pianist in Pretoria.

It was late afternoon. Martin's eyes travelled over the farms. Wintersrust and Soetvlei had prospered since the birth of Johannesburg. Joep Maree had secured contracts with businesses in the city, and the farms supplied meat, firewood, fruit, vegetables and dairy products. Wagons left weekly under the supervision of Old Klaas, bound for Pretoria, from where the produce was railed to Johannesburg.

'Pa, is the President paying sufficient attention to the problems in Johannesburg?' Martin asked in another attempt to get Marthinus to talk about the threat posed by the gold mines.

'The main issue of the Outlanders, Martin, obtaining the vote, will not add a penny to their wages. They're well aware of that,' Marthinus said firmly. 'Yes, there's a pattern they follow in presenting their demands to the government. They're playing with us; it's a game of words. Finish your studies and come back fully prepared.' He reached for his tobacco pouch, a sign that the matter was closed.

Martin suppressed a sigh of frustration; his father was shielding him from the truth. Working side by side with Buks Maree on the farm the past week, and talking to friends in Rustenburg, he had found that the President's disregard of the complaints of the Outlanders was a serious matter that could lead to unrest, or worse. But his questions concerning the Outlanders had been met with the same response from Marthinus: come back fully prepared.

Joep Maree, on his dapple-grey mare, galloped in from the veld, where the animals were grazing. He dismounted and took the bit from the horse's mouth. He settled in a chair and reported on the state of the herds while filling his pipe. 'Say, Martin,' he winked, 'has a fair English lady caught your fancy yet?'

'No, Uncle Joep. They're a different breed altogether. One has to propose before one can get as much as a kiss. What I want is a fine Boer girl.' Martin returned Joep's wink. 'Your daughter, Uncle Joep, once she's grown up.'

'Aha!' Joep laughed, his black beard shaking. 'Your brothers, it looks like, will have the final say in that. Karel, Rudolf and my little Annecke are inseparable.'

Marthinus poked his pipe at Martin. 'Son, when love grabs you by the throat—'

'And other places too!' Joep said.

'Love does not ask, are you a Boer or a Brit? Your mother turned out a good Boer wife. Her own sister is content in England. Love decides where one belongs.'

'Aunt Susan, content? Fluttering around like a nervous butterfly, especially when the General is around.'

'And the general? Come on, tell us what a British general is like,' Joep said. 'How do you call him? Uncle? Uncle General?'

'I tried "Uncle Stuart", but he didn't take to it. He's *The General* to everyone. You want to jump to attention every time you meet him. Matters outside the army simply don't interest him. By the looks of his uniform, he has had a distinguished career. Rows of medals, campaign ribbons. That's why he was knighted, I presume.'

'What's he like as a family man?'

'Not a family man at all, Pa. He rules the family with words, especially James. And those words, Pa, cut deeper than your *sjambok*. Now, this will interest you: Cousin James resembles his father to the detail. When I first set eyes on the General, I was astounded! He has dimples in his cheeks, buried under handlebar moustaches, but they're there, all right.'

Joep gathered his hat and pipe. 'My Lettie will give dimples with the sharp side of her tongue should I idle my day away. Ai, women! They find so much to do for a wedding feast.'

Martin saw him to his horse and promised to send his cousins over as soon as they arrived. Before long, Koba's spring-wagon approached with two horses tethered to the team. Marthinus had asked James to select fillies from the new arrivals at Lang Hans van Rensburg's stables on their way to the farm. They were a surprise for the twins, who had been sent on an errand to the far side of the farm.

James brought the wagon to a halt, alighted and handed Stefanie down. A vivid picture of Susan Henderson arriving on the farm years ago flashed though Martin's mind. He expected Stefanie to dab at her forehead and stumble a little, but she smiled sweetly and offered her cheek for a kiss. James caught Koba around the waist as she struggled down.

'Where's Charles?' Marthinus asked.

'We parted company at the drift, sir,' James said. 'We simply couldn't endure his incessant poetic exclamations at the beauty of the countryside. He has lost his reason completely.' He unhooked the two horses and brought them closer. 'Good fillies, Uncle Marthinus, and in excellent health. Still a bit wild, though.'

The men gathered around the horses, a chestnut and a bay, and with one glance Martin could tell that James had chosen well. The bay stood sixteen hands high, the chestnut a full hand shorter, her coat showing a deep red through the dust and lather from the journey. She was prancing, pulling at the rein. The bay stood perfectly still, only her ears flicking, her eyes steady. She was a strikingly handsome horse, a rich dark brown, almost black, not a mark on her smooth coat.

Marthinus took his time in checking them before nodding his approval.

'You chose well, James, well indeed.'

'Thank you, sir,' James said, pleasure at the compliment clear in his eyes.

Old Klaas and a stable hand arrived to see to the wagon and to water the fillies. The bay went willingly, but the chestnut neighed nervously. James led her away and arrived back as Charles came walking up the drive.

'Stretched my legs a bit. So much has changed.' Charles stepped onto the stoep, but halted by the empty chair of Oubaas de Winter. The old wicker chair was still next to the potted fern. It was as if the old man was present, shouting and groping with his stick.

'Yes, he's gone, our old grandfather. He made it to a hundred.' Marthinus explained how he had found him there one morning, peaceful in death.

James stared at the chair, mesmerised. 'And he never changed?'

Marthinus's deep laugh rang out. 'Never forgave the English, to the last.' He called into the house for the women when he saw the twins riding in from the vlei. 'James, quick, go fetch the horses before the boys reach the stables.'

'The boys will be so excited, having their own imported horses,' Mary said as she and Koba came out, drying their hands on their aprons. 'Old Lang Hans has bewitched them with tales of Arab blood.'

'Salted horses from the Lowveld are not prone to horse sickness and fever.' Koba nodded, her ample chin folding over her neck. 'It's wise to bring new blood to the farm. A good mixing of bloods, that's what I say.'

'James thought the bay for Karel and the chestnut for Rudolf,' Charles said. 'I quite agree. Rudi's calm nature should transfer to the horse, and in no time she should lose her nervousness.'

'Let the twins make the choice,' Marthinus suggested. 'The bay is an eye-catching filly, yet the chestnut shows good spirit. Yes, let them choose. Should they disagree, it will be their first argument …'

'Now, don't you upset the boys, brother!' Koba wagged her finger at him. 'Do as James says. He's wise in the way of horses.'

'Koba, the twins must differ at some time in their lives—'

'And if you drive them to that, the day will come that you will lose your sons!'

Having stabled their ponies, the twins came walking up just as James appeared from behind the house leading the fillies. Marthinus placed his hands on their shoulders. 'Now, my boys, I've promised you salted fillies, and here they are. James selected them for you.'

'The one who has the first choice of the horses,' Martin said, 'should allow the other the first choice in girls.'

'What do they know about girls?' Mary smiled at Martin. 'They are barely fourteen.'

Karel and Rudolf stood a few paces away from the horses. Despite the banter of the family, they felt all eyes on them, waiting for them to make their choice. But there was no choice to be made. Ever since they had been promised the fillies, they had discussed it. Karel dreamt of riding a black horse, and there she was, shining like polished ebony in the afternoon sun. To Rudolf, it did not matter. All he wanted was a good horse that would not succumb to horse sickness. Without so much as a glance at each other, Karel took the reins of the bay and Rudolf those of the chestnut, leaving the family astonished at their unspoken communication.

Karel placed his hand on the horse's nose, caressed her ears and spoke softly to her. The filly seemed to accept him right away and nuzzled his hand. Rudolf was not having an easy time with his chestnut; she snorted and pranced. Then her tail rose and she dropped a few pats.

'What will you name them?' Martin asked.

A flurry of suggestions came, but none appealed to the twins. 'You chose them, you name them, Cousin James,' Karel said.

'Puts me in a bit of a spot ...' said James. 'Now, let me think ... yes, I'd suggest we select names from a legend ...'

'Yes! I like that. Legend! I shall name her Legend,' Karel said.

James frowned. 'Unusual name, spirited even, but then, not an average Boer pony either. Brilliant, Karel! Yes, I approve. Legend she will be.' He gave Karel a wide smile and turned to Rudolf. 'Well now, in a legend there is, as a rule, an exceedingly courageous lady ...'

'Lady?' Rudolf said. 'Yes, she's a proper little lady, don't you think, James?'

'That she is, Rudi.'

The Wedding Feast

THE PREPARATIONS FOR Buks Maree's wedding were in full swing. The outspan at the drift was cleared for the many overnight guests. Firewood was stacked and barrels were filled with fresh water from the vlei. In the centre of the clearing, canvas was rigged over tall poles to provide shade and a communal gathering place. The aroma of baking, cooking and roasting wafted from the kitchens at Soetvlei and Wintersrust, where the women were preparing vast amounts of food.

Koba straightened her back where they were working in Mary's kitchen. She put her hands on her hips, looked sympathetically at the last suckling pig to come out of the oven and patted it on the crispy snout.

'Never mind, you dear thing,' she said, 'cool down and then I will give you your apple, right there in the mouth.'

'It's time for a cup of coffee,' Mary said, wiping her brow on her apron. 'I'm almost done with the meat. Do pour us a cup, Koba.'

'Yes, let's have our coffee on the stoep with the children,' Koba said and called to Stefanie, who was sitting in the far corner, her hands purposefully enclosed in gloves, excluding her from the hard work. 'Come, *hartjie*, surely you can cut the cake?'

They went to the stoep with the coffee tray and found Martin and Charles already there. Charles was sorting through a basket of tubers and bulbs, while Martin was engrossed in a report. James arrived from the stables, placed his hat and crop on the table and sat down next to Martin.

'Amazing how the bay took to Karel,' he said. 'It has only been a week and she follows Karel around like a lovesick hound. That boy has a way with horses.'

'And how's Lady shaping? Better hurry up with her training; Rudi wants to show her off to the *predikant*.' Martin sent him a teasing grin.

'Martin, I need a card for the wedding.' Koba winked, handing him a cup of coffee.

'A card? What kind of card, Tante Koba?'

'For James! For the dance. He wants to write his name on my card for all the waltzes. Stefanie and I showed him how to waltz the Boer way so that he could also enjoy the feast.'

Martin burst out laughing. 'My dear Tante Koba, you don't need a card. That's the way of the British at their balls.'

'Then how does one go about asking a lady for a dance at such a formal affair?'

'James, you simply take her hand and off you go,' Stefanie said. 'If someone arrives there before you, take the next one. If a girl has set her heart on dancing with you, she will ask you herself anyway.'

'Indeed! That's a bit forward. Well, I shall enjoy the dance immensely and await the pleasure of being swamped by ladies. What's the rule for smooching, then?'

'Stay out of trouble, James,' Charles said.

'Aha! Now that's where the problem usually arises,' Martin said. 'James, just a little advice; if you want to smooch, by all means do. But if a protective brother catches you at it, you'll have to run. To outsiders the girls might appear friendly and free, but they know that they are closely watched by their menfolk. As I shall have to watch my dear sister, since she's all grown-up now.'

Stefanie gave him a withering look. 'I'll spare you the trouble. I'm not planning to kiss in dark corners and I shall only dance with men of my choice.'

'Where are the boys?' Mary asked. 'I need them to get the mule-cart and bring some food over from Soetvlei. Lettie's cold room is positively overflowing, she tells me.'

'At the stables, Ma, where else? They spend all their time with the horses now,' Stefanie said. 'Men and horses!'

'It will take several trips to get all the food to the outspan.' Koba gathered the cups and turned to take the tray inside. 'We have to start early, before the service. The *predikant* always ruins a wedding.'

Charles looked up, perplexed. 'Ruins a wedding, Tante Koba?'

'Yes, *hartjie*. Such a happy-sad thing to witness two young people in love, pledging their vows in the presence of God. One never knows what He has in store for them, and that makes my old heart so sad. Four large handkerchiefs it takes to get me through the service.'

'An advantage at funerals, then?' James smiled. 'Never liked weddings myself. Lamentable spectacles, very much like funerals. Shall we skip the service, Tante Koba?'

'No, no, *hartjie*. A good cry every now and then is the best remedy for all

50

afflictions of the heart: sadness, joy, remorse …'

'Look!' Mary pointed to the road. 'The first guests are already here.'

Two wagons, flanked by riders, were making their way towards the outspan. Martin stepped off the stoep and waved his hat in greeting.

'Oom Koos de la Rey and Gert Vermaas. I'm going down to see if Buks needs help. Are you coming, Charles, James?'

BY EVENING twenty wagons had arrived at the outspan. Oxen and horses were grazing on the open veld. Fires were lit and there was a festive atmosphere as friends greeted and called to one another.

James watched spellbound from where he was helping Buks secure a piece of canvas between two wagons. The women were chattering like a flock of excited starlings and there seemed to be an endless flow of children running around. Babies cried and dogs barked and yelped. The big, bearded men were sunburnt, and most still had their hats firmly on their heads. They smoked their pipes and exchanged news in resounding voices, accompanied by much backslapping.

A crowd gathered around a man who was telling a story. Bawdy laughter accompanied his telling, but his voice rang free and boisterous above the others. '*Magtig*, Martin, it's good to see you back! Now tell us about the little island that rules the world,' barked the loud voice and James saw Martin disappear into the group.

'The *dop* is flowing freely at the Viljoens' wagon, as usual,' Buks said to James.

Two girls approached. Buks kissed the red-haired girl and introduced her to James. 'Anita Verwey, our friend from Rustenburg. She wants to be a nurse when she finishes school, so I've promised to introduce her to Charles.' When he introduced the other girl, his eyes filled with wariness, neither was she greeted with a kiss. 'And this is Ester Viljoen from Vrede, north of Rustenburg.'

Both girls had on the everyday cotton dresses, printed with flowers or stripes, worn by Boer women, the fronts buttoned up to their necks. Ester Viljoen, a pretty girl with dark brown hair and a well-rounded body, however, had two middle buttons undone, not missing, James noticed. She stared at him from cat-like green eyes in open admiration and gave him an enticing smile.

'Come to our wagon for coffee later tonight,' she said, her manner free and challenging.

She's an attractive little thing, James thought, *and well aware of it. It might be worth it.* But he was not about to clamber into one of those wagons with an irate brother lurking in the background. 'I'm rather busy now,' he said.

Ester gave him a brazen look. 'Well, tomorrow then. I will save you a dance.'

'Watch out for that girl,' Buks said as the girls walked away. 'She's only sixteen and heading for real trouble. So watch out!'

'She needs to have a few brothers, I'd say.'

'She has three brothers, big wild ones.'

———————

THE MARRIAGE ceremony was conducted the following morning at Soetvlei in the barn, which had been painted with a fresh layer of lime and decorated with streamers and bunting left over from the previous year's election campaign, lending a patriotic air. Buks was dressed in his new black suit, butterfly collar over a bow tie and a white carnation in his buttonhole. His bride, Lena, a soft girl with a ready smile, had on a pale pink dress, her light brown hair adorned with a small veil of white ribbons and lace.

It was Koba, not the *predikant*, who ruined the ceremony, James decided. She and other women kept up a steady low sobbing, Koba's just a little less subdued than that of the others. He was relieved when all was done and they filed out of the barn.

The bridal couple were lifted bodily onto Koba's spring-wagon and, with loud cheering from the guests, escorted to the outspan. Buks tucked Lena's hand through his arm and led her to the centre, where everyone was gathering to present them with their wedding gifts.

Soon the mule-cart was piled with presents; crockery, blankets, rolls of material, a cured lion skin, seedlings of fruit trees and potted plants for the stoep. Bags of seed for the coming planting season were handed over, with advice on the expected yields of the crops. There were two heifers from the Viljoens, as well as four squealing piglets, poultry in a coop and geese, which Lena was assured would give her enough down to fill all her pillows.

James handed over his gift of an Irish linen tablecloth and napkins and watched the proceedings with barely concealed amazement from where he stood with Stefanie and Charles. 'I say, Charles, how would you like one of those as a wedding gift?' He pointed to a turkey cock, legs tied together, protesting loudly as it was handed over to the twins to find a place on the cart. 'My God! I've never seen a show like this.'

Charles smiled. 'A rather unusual gift. But these are all practical gifts and, to a farmer's wife, preferable to silver candlesticks and crystal glasses.'

'One should have the finer things too,' Stefanie said.

'Tell me, cousin, when are you tying the knot?' James made a sweeping gesture over the crowd. 'Who will be the lucky one?'

She gave James a sour look. 'I've no interest in marrying a farmer.'

'Is there a problem with farmers?' Charles asked.

She folded her gloved hands together, lifting her chin. 'Yes, they live on farms. Marry a farmer, have a dozen children before I turn thirty, and then? Stagnate! Oh, certainly I don't want to be an old maid. I shall marry someday – a politician, a lawyer, someone of high standing.'

James looked askance at her. Her stylish blue dress, with tiny pearls embroidered around the neckline, her braided hair twisted around her head, gave her a regal air but also created an impression of aloofness. 'Will love be considered in this illustrious union?'

'Not necessarily. As long as the marriage provides prestige and glamour,' she said without a trace of modesty. 'I don't think much of love, James, do you? I mean, loving my family is enough for me.'

'Good heavens, Stef, you're only seventeen!'

'Are you going to be silly and fall in love, James?'

'I actually agree with you. Love is … well, an unfair business. One might not be loved in return, who knows? No, I'm not planning on getting married at all.'

'Good heavens, Jamie, you're barely twenty,' she mimicked.

'Join us in England for a spell and enjoy the social life. You never know who you might meet,' James said.

'Oh, no! I heard from Martin and Ma about the women in England. They have to be escorted everywhere and are so protected that they can't even think for themselves. Why, I do believe they have less freedom than a farmer's wife out here. I want to accomplish something, be somebody. Besides, I've already made a decision about my future.'

Before she could elaborate, Martin and Annecke, having done with their duties as best man and bridesmaid, joined them and announced that the meal would be served shortly in the barn.

'Martin, you're in serious trouble, brother.' Stefanie smiled smugly.

'Have I done something wrong?'

'Not yet. But if you don't think clearly tonight, you might!'

'Out with it!' He grabbed her arm and pulled her to him.

'Martin! No! You'll ruin my dress!' She tried to pull away, but he held her firmly. 'All right! Let go, I'll tell. I overheard some girls and their mothers speculating about you. You're a very desirable catch, brother. Careful who you ask for the first dance.'

Martin smiled. 'I have a sister who will dance with me.'

'Rotten luck, she's taken,' Charles said, placing his arm about Stefanie's waist.

'Tante Koba, then …'

'I'm afraid, cousin,' James said, 'Tante Koba promised me every waltz …'

'I'll dance the first waltz with you,' Annecke said. 'I can waltz perfectly. Pa taught me.' She looked at Martin with expectation, her hair tied up with ribbons and falling over her shoulders, large brown eyes open and honest.

'But of course, Annecke,' Martin said and smacked a kiss on her cheek. 'Promise to be at the barn before the music starts.'

'Don't put ideas into her head, Martin,' Stefanie warned as Annecke rushed off to tell the twins her news. 'She's only thirteen.'

'Well, if the old matchmakers quack-quack, let them. I might prove them right one day.' Martin led the way to where the other guests were gathering around the trestle tables laden with food.

THE WOMEN DEPARTED to the farmstead to dress for the evening's dance. The men sat in the shade, talking and smoking their pipes; some dozed after the large meal. At sunset everyone moved back to the barn. The musicians were tuning their instruments: a concertina, two guitars and a fiddle. They started hesitantly, caught the rhythm and were on their way. To loud applause, Buks waltzed Lena onto the floor to open the dancing.

James noticed many disappointed faces as Martin took Annecke in his arms. Stefanie and Charles made a handsome couple, dancing with their backs straight and taking measured steps. Joep Maree, with Lettie pressed close to him, whirled past. Marthinus and Mary danced lightly, smiling into each other's eyes. Koba arrived at his side and he led her onto the floor, now filled with laughing and singing dancers. After the long waltz, Marthinus claimed Koba.

James leaned against the wall and watched the dancers break into a lively step. A heavy hand fell on his shoulder and he turned to find a huge bearded man next to him, the man who had attracted so much attention with his boisterous laugh the previous night. '*Kom, Engelsman,* let's have a *dop*.' Outside, behind the barn.' With an arm around James's shoulders, he steered him outside. A mug containing a large measure of brandy was pushed into his hand. 'Now, I am Jan Viljoen from the farm Vrede, twenty miles north of Rustenburg,' he said in broken but understandable English. 'These are my brothers, Frans and Jacob.'

They were big men, loose-limbed and powerfully built. Black-bearded, pleasant faces, in their late twenties, James guessed. He greeted them in Afrikaans.

'*Magtig!*' Jan Viljoen said. 'This *Engelsman* can speak our *taal!*'

'I have very little Afrikaans, I'm afraid, but I do try,' James said.

'Now tell us about your Queen,' Jan Viljoen said, with an ambiguous smile. 'Will she keep her hands off our gold?'

James sighed inwardly. Jan, he surmised, wanted to provoke him into saying something about the Outlanders, but discussing politics was beyond him. He looked at the eyes watching him and chose his words carefully. 'Her Majesty has no intention of claiming your gold.'

'Shall I tell you what I think, *Engelsman*? I, Jan Viljoen, say that the old Queen wanted our diamonds at Kimberley; she took them. Now we have the Outlanders grabbing our gold. What happens next?'

James searched his mind for a suitable answer and remembered the discussion they had had with Paul Warren on the train. 'Not all the Outlanders are British. There are Germans, Australians and others. You name them, they're there.'

'Foreigners are foreigners,' Frans Viljoen said.

'Her Majesty reigns over enough territories not to need to add your republic to her list.'

'No, *Engelsman*, you're wrong. She wouldn't be such a great queen if she was satisfied without the richest gold in the world, now would she?' Jan Viljoen roared with laughter at his own wisdom and gave James an almighty slap on his back.

Further discussion on the topic ended as Martin and Charles arrived to get a drink. James made his escape while Martin fell into conversation with the Viljoens. He refilled his mug and slipped back to the barn. There he found Stefanie talking to a smartly dressed man. She seemed thrilled to see him.

'Please excuse me, I promised this waltz to my cousin,' she said to her companion, flung herself into James's arms and danced him away. 'Thank you for rescuing me. He babbled on and on about his business in Kimberley!'

James was on his third drink, leaning against the wall again, when Ester Viljoen flung her arms around his neck and steered him onto the floor. They whirled and sidestepped, James easily following her confident feet. He caught the disapproving glance of Koba as they passed her, but the brandy had taken effect and he was enjoying himself. After their second dance, a fast, long jig, they were laughing breathlessly, perspiration pouring off their faces.

She smiled into his eyes, pulling him towards the door. Once outside, she led him away from where the men were drinking. They came to a halt under a tree in the orchard and she held his hands. The next moment her hands fastened behind his neck, her body pressing into his. He looked at her upturned face and tempting mouth, her lips slightly parted. What he intended as a brief kiss turned into a wild prolonged embrace, but when she slipped her hands inside his jacket, he pulled back. He was about to close his jacket and go back to the dancing when a shout shattered the moment.

'Aha! *Engelsman!*' Jan Viljoen stood there, grinning. 'What are you doing here under the fig tree? Seducing my little sister?'

'Is this a fig tree? I hadn't noticed,' James cursed silently. *My God, does he have to be her brother?*

'If you were a decent Boer, I wouldn't have minded, but my sister will not be free with a *Rooinek*! Now clear off before I spoil that pretty face of yours!'

'We were simply taking the air ...'

Jan grabbed him by the ear, uttering a string of oaths. James was about to retaliate when Koba loomed up and kicked Jan on his shin. Jan bellowed, released James and clutched his leg.

'I was only playing with him a little bit, Tante Koba. He was seducing Ester, I caught him hot-handed, Tante Koba!'

'Seduce this lusty filly?' Koba made a threatening move towards Ester. 'It was the other way round, I'd say. Everyone in the district knows about your loose ways. You should be ashamed of yourself, Ester Viljoen!' She turned back to Jan. 'Stable your sister until she finds a husband. As for you, young man,' she glared at James and said, less harshly, 'get back to the barn where I can look out for you.'

James, still rubbing his ear, smiled apologetically to Ester and followed Koba. 'You mustn't keep company with her sort, *hartjie*,' she said when he caught up with her. 'She's not a good girl. Soft in the head, poor thing. Now, her brothers, they're good, honest men, but dear Jan Viljoen – so meddlesome, but a big-hearted man. Need I say more?'

'No, it's perfectly clear, Tante Koba.' He sank down on the nearest bench. 'I do need a drink now.'

'I've something special for you. Wait here.' She patted his shoulder and walked off.

Jan Viljoen, having seen his sister back to the barn, walked past and gave a generous laugh. 'Caught you, hey, *Engelsman*! Come, have another brandy.'

James, wary of the sudden change in the man, declined stiffly. Jan shrugged and, with another careless bellow, walked off.

Koba arrived, holding out a tumbler filled with a colourless liquid. 'Come, *hartjie*, drink this. It will help for the shock.'

'I'm not suffering from shock,' he said, but nevertheless took a sip. He spluttered as the fiery liquid caught at his throat. 'What ... what's this Tante Koba?'

'Homebrew. For medicinal purposes. I brew it from prickly pears. It'll do you good, *hartjie*; drink slowly. I must see to the soup; it must be served after the dancing.' She wagged a finger at him and planted a kiss on his forehead. 'Remember, blessed is the man who endures temptation every now and then.'

He finished the glass in one gulp and decided that the safest place would be the barn. He surveyed the noisy scene. The man with the concertina was playing a wild jig, his feet tapping out the beat, head thrown back, eyes tightly closed. Dust rose from the dancers' feet. The men had discarded their jackets and unbuttoned their waistcoats. Jan Viljoen had his wife clamped under his arm, stepping high and fast. The bridal couple whirled past, gazing into each other's eyes. Martin was dancing with a fair-haired girl who looked adoringly up at him.

Stefanie was at the far end of the floor, holding two glasses. He eased his way through the dancing couples to her. 'Hi there, Stef, shall I relieve you of those?'

'Lemonade. I fetched them for Martin and Charles, but they're enjoying themselves so much that they've forgotten their thirst. Just look at Charles and Anita Verwey. It's their third dance!'

Charles, tie undone, hair glued to his forehead, was dancing wildly but in perfect rhythm as he swung the red-haired girl around the floor.

'My brother seems to be quite an adaptable creature,' said James, tossing back the lemonade. He was about to start on the second glass when Stefanie stopped him.

'James! It's laced with brandy. You'll get drunk.'

'That's a terrible word, cousin. Shall we say intoxicated, inebriated, anything, but please, not drunk.' He sipped from the second glass, giving Stefanie a wicked smile.

Martin came walking through the dancers. 'You look distinctly bored, James.' He frowned at the empty glasses. 'Come, I need a proper *dop* to wash the dust out of my throat. Outside!' He led James to the far end of the barn, looked around briefly before extracting a bottle from behind a drum. 'Strong stuff, James, just a little at a time.'

James hesitated. 'Is this stuff concocted from prickly pear?'

'No! Only Tante Koba uses prickly pear. This is Uncle Joep's peach brandy.'

James was surprised at the delicate peach flavour and allowed himself a deep swig before handing the bottle back.

'We only use it in emergencies. Come, James! Back to the dancing.'

SITTING AROUND a fire close to a wagon, discussing the wedding with other children, were Annecke, Karel, Rudolf and Adriaan, the son of Koos de la Rey from Lichtenburg. As their fathers were both in the Volksraad, De la Rey's frequent trips to Pretoria usually necessitated a stay over at Wintersrust. Adriaan was a close friend of the twins, the only one other than Annecke allowed in their little world.

'A funny man, that *Engelsman!*' said Gert Swart, a wiry freckle-faced boy. He was not liked by the twins, as he was nurtured on hatred for the British.

'Charles? The one with the glasses?' Rudolf said.

'He's a doctor,' Annecke said importantly.

'Not him. He's nice, he spoke Afrikaans to us. The other one who walks like a bloated stork.' Gert Swart clasped his hands behind his back, pushed out his chest and strutted around. 'And he laughs like a donkey!'

The twins exchanged a look and nodded in anticipation. 'James is going to be a horse officer when he goes back to England,' Karel said smugly.

'What? And you allow him on your farm?'

'We have a British tutor,' Adriaan de la Rey said.

'Traitors!' Gert said. 'You allow the enemy on your farm?'

Karel spat on his hands and clenched his fists. 'Gert, James is our cousin and he's a good man. He chose our horses for us.'

'Your cousin is a Redcoat! Scum of the earth! And you, Karel de Winter, are a Judas!'

Karel's fist sent him sprawling. In a flash he went flying into Karel, catching him on his left eye. Karel ducked, grabbed Gert around his waist, forcing him to the ground. Gert kicked out fiercely, catching Karel on his chest and sending him backwards. With a sickening thud his head struck the wagon wheel. The children stared at the blood flowing from a cut on the back of his head. They waited, but Karel did not move.

'He's dead! He's dead!' Annecke flew into Gert, beating on his chest with her small fists. 'You killed Karel!'

Adriaan de la Rey pointed to Karel's chest. 'He's not dead! Look, he's breathing!'

'Yes! He's alive! He's alive!' cried the others.

'Adriaan, get brandy for the shock,' Rudolf said. 'Run! But don't let anyone see you.'

Adriaan ran off. Rudolf held Karel half-sitting up while Annecke tried to stop the bleeding with a cloth. Anxious minutes later, Adriaan came racing back, clutching a bottle to his chest. He fell to his knees beside Rudolf and pushed the bottle into his hands. 'I saw Martin and your cousin,' Adriaan wheezed, 'they hid this bottle under a drum. It's homebrew … stronger, it will work quicker!'

Rudolf put the bottle to Karel's mouth. He spluttered, mumbling feebly, the liquid spilling down his chin. 'It worked! Give him more!' urged the others. Rudolf forced large mouthfuls into Karel's mouth.

Adriaan pointed at Karel's blood-soaked shirt. 'Look! He'll bleed to death!'

'Annecke, go find Charles. Run, Annecke, run!' Rudolf said.

Sobbing for breath, she reached the barn, her eyes desperately searching for Charles. She spotted him in the far corner, talking to Anita Verwey. She pushed her way through the dancers and tugged at his sleeve.

Charles took in her bedraggled figure, her dress stained with blood, her hair loose and her face filled with despair. 'Excuse me,' he said to Anita, and, putting his arm around Annecke, he steered her outside. 'Dear heavens! You look awful. What's the matter, little one?'

'Oh Charles, please come quickly! Karel is dying! We can't stop the bleeding!' She grabbed his hand, forcing him to run with her.

Rudolf was still holding his twin upright when Charles arrived. He knelt beside them and lifted Karel's head, calling his name, but the only response was a feeble groan. The smell of liquor hit him full in the face. The children all tried to explain at once.

'I get the picture,' Charles held up a hand. 'He stumbled and knocked his head on the wheel. You fed him that vile stuff to bring him around.' He asked Adriaan to bring the lantern closer and examined the wound. 'Mm ... the cut is not deep. Yes, it needs a few stitches. A head wound bleeds a lot, so it looks more serious than it really is.' When he checked Karel's pupils, he saw the badly swollen eye. 'What happened to his eye?'

'He ... he fell against the wheel,' Adriaan offered lamely.

'Yes, but he hit the back of his head. If the swelling of the eye was caused by the blow to his head, then he has a cracked skull and I will have to operate tonight. Karel's life is on the line. Now, tell me.'

'We were fighting, I hit him on the eye,' Gert Swart said. 'He hit me first!'

Charles breathed a sigh of relief. He opened Karel's good eye and saw that the pupil was normal, the reflexes sluggish, but he attributed that to the drink. 'Right! Give me a hand. I must get him to the house to stitch up his wound.'

As they set off, Charles found it hard not to laugh. Karel, hanging between Rudolf and Adriaan, was hiccupping and lifting his feet as high as possible. 'Put your feet down. The ground is still where it used to be,' Rudolf implored. Karel's only response was a giggle.

A little before midnight, Charles finished attending to Karel. He hurried back to the barn to find Anita Verwey, but the dancing had ended and all were gathering to sing the *Volkslied*.

Stefanie rushed over to him. 'I've been looking for you. James is *very* drunk ... and Pa must not see him. I can't take him outside ... the Viljoens are there … James wants to fight them. Martin is nowhere to be found. Oh help, Charles. There!'

Charles followed her eyes and saw James standing by himself, looking decidedly drunk. He decided to keep an eye on him and walked over.

'I say, dear brother,' James slurred. 'Where have you been for the last hour or so? Necking young ladies under the fig tree? Or a prickly pear? I get so confused with these darn African fruits.'

'Quiet, James. We are going to sing the national anthem and can do without your contribution.'

The laughing and shuffling came to a halt. Jan Viljoen and his brothers appeared at the door, none too steady on their feet. Charles saw James's eyes fastening on them. He put out his hand to restrain him, but he was too late. James walked to where the musicians were, turned to face the Viljoens and sang: 'God save our gracious Queen, Long live our noble Queen …'

Everyone stared, while James carried on singing.

'My God, James! Now you've done it,' Charles said under his breath. He looked around quickly; his uncle was hiding a smile behind his hand and he detected an amused sparkle in Koos de la Rey's eyes. Jan Viljoen walked deliberately towards James, the people giving way to allow him through. Charles knew he had to act fast. With long strides, he arrived ahead of Jan. A hush came over the crowd as the two brothers stood a few paces apart.

'James, you're about to apologise.'

'Apologise?' James's handsome face was flushed, his eyes bright, and a smile played on his lips. 'I will most certainly not apologise. I distinctly recall you said the anthem.'

'The *Volkslied* is the anthem of this country, *Engelsman*!' There was an angry murmur from the younger men as Jan moved closer to James. 'In this country there's no place for your Queen's song!'

Charles realised that he had to prevent a brawl, and quickly. A swing from his right hand sent James sprawling as he was starting up 'God Save the Queen' again.

'I apologise to all of you on my brother's behalf,' Charles said. 'I'm ashamed to say that he's the worse for drink. He would not have acted this way had he been sober.' He pulled James up by his arm and pushed him towards the door.

'If you hadn't hit James, Jan Viljoen would've,' Stefanie said from behind him, as if reading his thoughts. 'Oh, poor Jamie!'

'Now, here is an *Engelsman* whom I respect,' Jan Viljoen roared. 'Taking on his brother for the sake of righteousness. Let me shake your hand, Dr Henderson!'

'*Allemagtig!*' Marthinus de Winter laughed thunderously from the far side of the crowd. 'I'm yet to see a Boer with more courage than James Henderson.'

'*Ja! Ja!*' agreed Koos de la Rey, joining in the laughter. 'It takes courage to sing the Queen's song when outnumbered by Transvalers.'

Joep Maree wiped tears from his eyes. Soon everyone was laughing uproariously.

'Now the *Volkslied*!' Jan Viljoen rescued Charles from the handshakes and backslapping as people sympathised and laughed with him. 'We're keeping the bridegroom from his bed. And that's a cruel thing to do!'

City of Gold

AFTER THE WEDDING, most of the De Winter family went back to Pretoria. Martin had been invited by his father to attend a meeting of the Volksraad concerning the British High Commissioner, Sir Henry Loch, who was due to discuss the matter of the Outlanders. Charles returned to his consultations with the health authorities and Stefanie was impatient to get back to her piano classes.

James took the train to Johannesburg, promising that he would be back in Pretoria for Martin's rugby match. He had not wanted to make this trip to South Africa, but it was a way out of the predicament his wild life at Oxford had created. He moved in a circle of wealthy young men fond of drinking, sport, women and gambling. With his father due back from India, he had thought it wise to disappear for a while, as there would be the devil to pay. Any whiff of scandal would stir the General into fury. And there were enough rotten odours wafting around London!

He booked into the Heights Hotel. In the bar, he met a young aristocrat who was travelling back to England from India. Peter Radford was tall and fair, with sharp features. Although his clothes were of the best quality and cut, he had a rakish, dishevelled look: his tie slack, top buttons of his shirt undone, his hair reaching his shoulders.

'You're General Sir Stuart Henderson's son? The resemblance is remarkable.' Peter squinted at James from lively brown eyes. 'Saw him in Bangalore.'

James nodded. 'Yes, perpetually absent Father.'

'Not for much longer, my dear fellow, your old man is on his way home.'

'That much I know. Home leave for a bit.'

'No, permanently, actually. Posted to the War Office.'

James cursed. 'I'm expected at Sandhurst in three months and had hoped to do it free from paternal interference and supervision.'

'So am I! Was sent down from Cambridge. Don't know what I was doing there anyway. My father spoke to yours and he vowed to turn me into a sabre-rattling, flag-waving, drum-beating soldier. I'm to join the 2nd Hussars.' Peter ordered another bottle of champagne. 'Pity we won't be in time for the scrap.'

'What scrap? Is something brewing.'

'Henderson, you're right in the middle of it.' Peter waved his hand towards the window. 'Something is about to happen here. Sir Henry Loch is on his way. The pot is about to boil over, but my guess is that old Kruger might avoid the inevitable for another year.'

'The inevitable? Surely you're not suggesting that this so-called Outlander affair will lead to military intervention.'

'The gold? Time will tell. The Empire's coffers rattle a little, the politicians say.' Peter grinned. 'So, what brings you here, Henderson? Curiosity?'

'It's quite simple. The lack of social life in the great city of Pretoria.'

'Pretoria? Hobnobbing with the Boers?'

'Visiting relatives. The De Winters. Uncle Marthinus is a member of the Volksraad, their parliament. Married to my mother's sister.' He explained briefly how it all came about.

'De Winter. Sounds familiar.' Peter frowned, pushing his hair from his eyes. 'Oh yes! Giant of a man. Met him once. Rather serious chap.'

'That's him. Cousin Martin. Serious, yes, about his studies and his future. If you care to see him play rugby, you're most welcome to join me Saturday week at the Harlequin Club in Pretoria.'

'Excellent, I'd love to see Pretoria.'

THE WEEK BECAME A ROUND OF PARTIES. There was cricket at the Wanderers Club and horse racing at Newmarket, and plenty of champagne. There were hotels and theatres, clubs and restaurants. It was said that Johannesburg had the world's largest concentration of bars and brothels.

But the city was restless, James noticed. The Zarps, the republican police force, were out in numbers whenever workmen gathered to listen to speeches. The orators egged the workers on to demand their lawful rights from the government. It was said that a Cape lawyer was the driving force behind the unrest.

On Friday night James and Peter were at the Theatre Royal. After the show, Peter suggested a visit to a brothel he had been to the previous week. 'A very discreet establishment, Henderson. Madam Carter checks her guests' credentials before admitting them. I'll vouch for you.'

They set off in a Cape cart. When they arrived, Peter announced himself to the butler, who escorted them inside. The large drawing room had fireplaces on opposite sides of the room, and the low gaslight created an intimate atmosphere. Several men were talking to expensively dressed girls.

In the far corner a girl played the piano, and a few couples danced.

James took a cigar and a glass of champagne from the silver tray held out by the waiter. An older woman in a stylish red outfit glided over and introduced herself as Rose Carter. She eyed James approvingly and inquired about his stay in Johannesburg. He explained that he was out from London, visiting relatives.

'The De Winters, from Pretoria. You might've heard about the family,' Peter said.

Rose Carter nodded thoughtfully and smiled to herself.

'You shouldn't have mentioned the name! My cousin comes here too,' James said as she walked away. 'If they get to hear about this, I'll be blamed for disgracing the family name yet again. The Boers believe this to be a sin, you know.'

'Sorry, Henderson. How indiscreet of me.'

Peter disappeared upstairs with a dark-haired girl. James settled for a buxom beauty with a French lilt to her voice. He was about to follow her upstairs when his eyes fell on two men talking intimately by the fireplace. Something compelled him to take a second look, and with a start he recognised Paul Warren. There was no mistaking the neatly parted hair and waxed moustache. He wondered what Warren was doing in a brothel. *Madam Carter must cater for all sorts*, he thought, and put it out of his mind.

When he returned to the lounge sometime later, Peter Radford, jacket draped over his shoulders, glass of cognac in hand, was sprawled on a chaise longue, flirting with Rose Carter. He hoisted himself up and came over to James. On their way out, Peter pointed to where Paul Warren was leaning against the piano. 'That fellow over there,' he said, 'is odd, Madam Rose says. All sorts of toffs come to see him. Something about Sir Henry, Kruger, Pretoria, a rally at Market Place in the morning.'

'Did he tumble about upstairs?' James asked.

'No, but he did play the piano a bit. Not a bad show, to my mind.'

JAMES COULD NOT SLEEP that night. He thought about Martin and Koba, about the farm, and his uncle. If he did not owe any loyalty to President Kruger, he did owe the De Winter family some consideration. It would do no harm to see what Warren was up to. A little intelligence could make up for his behaviour at Buks's wedding.

Early the next morning, he set off for Market Place. He had borrowed an old coat and hat from a waiter at the hotel, hoping to appear inconspicuous. A thin wind stole in from the frost-covered plains. Hugging the coat close and stepping carefully to avoid the ruts and potholes in the road, he arrived at Market Place as the sun broke through the drifting smoke. A large crowd had converged on the square, where ox-wagons and other forms of transport were outspanned.

James wrinkled his nose at the smell of fresh manure and wood smoke. He made his way through piles of bagged maize, firewood stacked next to heaps of winter vegetables and fruit, freshly slaughtered meat hanging from hooks on poles, and chickens clucking in cages, eggs piled in baskets beside them.

At the far side of the square was a large group of men, an air of anticipation about them. Half an hour later, a man wearing a cloth cap walked through the gathering to where a crate was upturned. He stepped onto it and a hush came over the crowd. James edged closer and realised it was Paul Warren.

From Warren's speech he gathered that extra trains to Pretoria had been laid on for Monday morning. He talked about the justice that would come their way should they behave in a firm but controlled manner. His speech lasted barely ten minutes. The crowd dispersed, but Warren lingered to drink coffee with a few men.

James ambled to the wagon nearest Warren, where a Boer girl was counting out potatoes for a customer. Straining his ears, James heard Warren say, 'Leave the President to me. It's important. I'll get close to him and we can take it from there.'

'The Zarps are suspicious, sir. Our spies say that they plan to get our leader before the Commissioner's train leaves for Pretoria,' said a man in a broad Scottish accent.

'Find a stooge. Anyone, just pick someone, report him to the Zarps,' Warren said. 'Any important developments, I'll be at the Corner House.' He lifted his cap and set off towards the town at a brisk pace.

James followed Warren at a distance and saw him disappear through the back door of the Rand Club. He could not follow him in there and set off for the Corner House. At a bar across the street he saw the Scot who had been with Warren earlier, talking to a few others. He sauntered over and listened for a while. They tried to draw him into the conversation. He gave a terse reply and moved on.

His curiosity was now fully aroused, and he spent the morning dashing from one place to another, but found that he was attracting curious stares, especially from the Scot, who seemed to be everywhere. By noon he returned to the Heights Hotel with two men on his tail. He looked at his watch; it was past two and the trains didn't run to Pretoria on Sundays. He had to leave that day. He scribbled a note for Peter Radford, saying that he would meet him at Pretoria station the following Saturday for the rugby match.

JAMES SAW that his bag was stowed and boarded the train. The coach was almost empty. A young woman with an infant in her arms was staring out of the window. Further down was an elderly gentleman, engrossed in his newspaper. James stretched out and soon the monotonous rhythm of the train made him drowsy. The late nights and the heavy drinking of the previous week had taken their toll.

There came a touch against his leg. A man sat opposite him and another had settled himself next to him on the narrow bench. A hard object was pushed into his ribs.

'Don't try and draw attention to us,' said the man next to him in a broad Dutch accent. 'We're going to leave this coach. Get up slowly and follow my friend. I'll be right behind you.'

James drew in his breath. 'If it's money you want, I only have a couple of pounds.'

'Get moving!'

With James between them, they walked to the last coach. When the train stopped at a siding, he was forced off. Following a narrow track through bushes for some way, they arrived at a small wooden shack. James was forced through the door. The interior was covered in black dust, and was clearly used as a coal storage room.

'Could you explain this?' he demanded furiously as they tied his hands and feet with coarse rope.

The two men said nothing. Their work finished, they walked outside and slammed the door shut, leaving James in darkness.

———————

ON MONDAY MORNING, two trains filled to capacity with Outlanders arrived at Pretoria Station.

Martin and Charles were walking to the station to witness the arrival of Sir Henry Loch. Well over a thousand people lined the streets, waving white, red and blue rosettes and Union Jacks. And through this, met with jeers and hoots, the black Presidential carriage, led by the State Artillery, moved at a dignified pace.

At the station, the carriage halted and rocked as President Kruger stepped down. He clasped his hands behind his broad back and walked through a double row of policemen to the podium, where the Union Jack and the Vierkleur fluttered in the breeze. A roar erupted as Loch stepped off the train. The crowd waved their bunting and sang enthusiastically when the Zarp band struck up 'God Save the Queen'. It came to a jubilant ending, with cheers drowning the *Volkslied* that followed.

'This could turn nasty,' Martin said to Charles, 'I'm getting closer to the President.'

He elbowed his way through the mass and managed to get to the podium. The two elderly dignitaries boarded the President's carriage just as the line of police gave way under the pressure of the crowd. A tall man jumped onto the footboard, brandishing a Union Jack. With the help of others, he pushed the carriage hood down and waved the flag over the two dignitaries. Kruger's top hat tumbled from his head.

'That's where this country belongs, old man! Under the Union Jack!' the man shouted.

Martin kicked at his legs and with a heavy thud the man hit the ground, cloth cap flying off his head. Martin saw his face clearly. It was Paul Warren. For an intense moment, their eyes met.

The carriage was forced to a standstill. Martin threw an urgent look at the President, imploring him to give a signal for his people to react, but the old man sat immovable as a rock.

A number of Outlanders unhitched the horses, grabbed the harness and set the carriage in motion. Martin looked around for support and noticed to his relief, a few mounted Boers on the edge of the crowd, their rifles at the ready. The crowd followed, keeping a wary eye on the armed Boers. The carriage was brought to a halt at the Transvaal Hotel. Sir Henry Loch attempted to make a speech but the crowd jeered. With an apologetic glance at the President, he shuffled into the hotel.

Martin looked at the President. No outward sign betrayed his humiliation. Martin grabbed the reins. Immediately some Boers joined him. They heaved the carriage into motion and set off towards the Raadsaal. He glanced back and saw Charles with the reins over his shoulder, pulling as hard as the others.

'We'll pay with our blood for the riches God has chosen to bestow on our country,' the President said as Martin helped him out of the carriage. There was the hopelessness in his voice of a man who had had a deathly premonition.

BY THE AFTERNOON most of the Outlanders had left Pretoria. Martin and Charles were eager to hear from Marthinus, who had gone to an emergency session of the Volksraad. He arrived at Koba's house long after dark. They sat down to large meal, which was Koba's way of showing sympathy with the hardships they had suffered.

'It was chaos in the Raadsaal,' Marthinus said. 'The hotheads, like Old Pieterse, shouted themselves hoarse, demanding immediate retaliation. Koos de la Rey and Joubert pleaded for restraint. A telegram from the Cape parliament arrived, apologising for "the loathsome actions of her subjects and promising to punish the rebels severely". Oom Paul says to leave the matter to the Johannesburg Council.'

'Well, at least one good thing may come out of this, Pa,' Martin said after the table was cleared and they settled down with a glass of brandy. 'Oom Paul can't ignore the Outlanders much longer. They were real today, Pa, *very real!*'

'We're sitting on a crate of dynamite, son, and the fuse is burning ever shorter.'

'Now's the time to force him to grant some concessions, Pa! You must get …'

'Slowly, young man. Your blood is young and hot, but that of the President is thin and slow. We'll give him time to digest his adventure and then take the matter from there.'

'It was disgraceful,' Charles said. 'I'm so ashamed. How can any Englishman hold up his head in this country again?'

'It was a crowd of rabble-rousers,' Marthinus said. 'Son, don't take the blame for their behaviour …'

The front gate scraped open. They waited for the knock on the door, but none came. Martin moved to the window and parting the curtains, saw a figure hanging on to the gate. He took the nearest lamp and opened the door. He recognised James. Pushing the lamp into Charles's hands, he half-carried James inside, putting him on the nearest chair. He was covered in coal dust.

'What have you been up to?' Charles asked, alarmed.

'Spent the weekend in a coal shed. Thought it might be fun.' James glared at his brother.

Martin placed his jacket around James's shoulders. 'Give him a brandy, Pa. He's shivering.'

Marthinus poured a large measure and, as James put out his hands to take the glass, they saw raw chafe-marks on his wrists. James swallowed some brandy and coughed convulsively. He attempted to tell them about the events of the preceding week, but his words were garbled. 'He was going to take the President hostage, I think … got wind that I was … to warn you … somehow set me up … the Zarps locked me … in a shed … few miles from here. Nearly froze to death … released this afternoon. Walked all the way.'

'Who are you talking about, James?' Martin asked.

'Warren ... the fellow we met on the train.' James broke into another fit of coughing. 'What happened to the President?'

'The Outlanders draped the Union Jack over his shoulders, son,' Marthinus chuckled. 'It was not to his liking.'

James broke into hysterical laughter and slipped out of the chair. Charles put a hand to his forehead. 'He's burning with fever. I thought he was drunk.'

'Koba, come see to James. Sister!' Marthinus called.

She came rushing in from the kitchen, saw James on the floor and gasped. 'Get hot water and my medicine box. Martin, help me get him to bed.'

Charles was about to follow, but was pushed aside. 'No, *hartjie*, there's no time for doctors now. He's too ill. I must see to him immediately.'

JAMES'S FEVER raged through the night and for two more days before it broke, but it took him a week to recover. Koba kept a vigil at his bedside. She treated his wounds with homemade ointments, rubbed balsam onto his chest, spooned hot broth into his mouth, talking all the time to assure him of her presence. When he opened his eyes, her round face, filled with love and concern, was always hovering above him. He felt a sense of utter contentment.

He and Charles had been brought up by nannies. His mother was a distant figure, and disillusion with his father, which had built up over the years, cut deep into James's heart and made him wary of love. The man he had hero-worshipped as a boy was merely an authority figure to rebel against.

With the De Winters, it was a different world. Aunt Mary, after twenty-three years of marriage, was still infatuated with her husband. Uncle Marthinus was still the caring, understanding man he had known as a boy, and his sister, dearest Tante Koba, was so much like her brother, only deeper; her love was a visible substance.

'I love you, Tante Koba,' James blurted out.

She placed her hand against his hot cheek and smiled down at him. 'Tante Koba loves you too. Right here,' her hand went to her large bosom and she lowered her voice, 'in the middle of my heart, there's a place big enough for only one, and it's yours.'

When he was stronger, Koba allowed the others to visit him. He told them about seeing Paul Warren and his involvement in the events of the previous Monday. Martin said that the Volksraad, at his father's insistence, had requested an official inquiry into the role Paul Warren had played in the riot. The Johannesburg Council had sent a curt reply, denying any involvement by the Capetonian lawyer. Warren had allegedly spent the day with Charles Leonard.

'I do hope Warren will be playing tomorrow,' Martin said. 'I want to tell him that I'm aware of the double role he's playing.'

'The rugby! I'd completely forgotten,' James said.

'I advise you to stay indoors,' Charles said. 'You are still ill, brother. It's entirely due to Tante Koba's care that—'

'Yes, I shall,' James cut him short, 'but I've invited Peter Radford, the fellow who's joining the 2nd Hussars. He's due on the early train tomorrow.'

'Radford? Lord Peter? The cricketer? Fast bowler, wasn't he?' Martin asked.

'Yes, a fine fellow. Always having fun. "Splendid, let's drink to that" appears to be his answer to everything.'

'Good gracious!' Charles said. 'He disappeared. Fancy him turning up here.'

'He vanished for a very good reason,' Martin said. 'A secret well kept at Cambridge at the time.'

'But word will out, it always does,' James said when Martin seemed unwilling to go on. 'So why keep us waiting?'

'Had to do with a woman, sort of. His rival was furious. Peter suggested a duel. Thought it might be fun. Unfortunately Peter's shot hit the man and nearly killed him. The family sent him away for a while.'

Charles gave a rueful smile. 'Poor Father! You and Radford. The regiment will never be the same again.'

Revenge and Honour

THE SMALL PAVILION was packed to capacity for the rugby match between the Harlequins of Pretoria and the Wanderers of Johannesburg. Around the field the spectators stood twenty deep, jostling to find a good viewpoint. Schoolboys sat squeezed on the touchline, having come early to secure their places. There were more women than usual, their parasols, *kappies* and feathered hats standing out in the sea of men.

A winter wind gusted, but did not dampen enthusiasm. With the humiliation of their beloved Oom Paul still fresh in their minds, the local supporters wanted revenge. It was to be a battle against the rude foreigners who had come into their city and shamed their president.

Paul Warren walked through the door of the changing room onto the veranda and almost collided with Martin.

'So, we meet again, De Winter,' he said pleasantly, putting out his hand.

'Yes, Warren,' Martin said, taking his hand. 'Last time we met, you were waving a Union Jack over President Kruger.'

Warren felt his hand being pressed unnecessarily hard and long. He considered Martin's powerful shoulders, and his eyes shifted to the face. The deep blue eyes were not those of an ordinary Boer. *This man is sharp, intelligent, an opponent to be reckoned with.*

'De Winter,' he said, keeping his voice neutral and pleasant, 'from our conversation on the train, I gathered that you also feel that the situation in Johannesburg needs urgent attention. Now, it appears that we are approaching the matter from different viewpoints. But still, it's a common goal, is it not?'

'Yes, Warren, but I shall not allow the honour of my country to be endangered.'

Warren read the message in Martin's eyes: a challenge, acknowledged and accepted.

STEFANIE AND HER TWO ESCORTS found a place near the centre line. Martin had fetched her from the convent and, still in her regulation navy blue with white pinafore, she'd gone with him to the station to meet James's friend, Peter Radford. They had visited James, who was still in bed. She noticed that Martin had taken to Peter straight away, judging by their ceaseless talk about London matters.

Peter was scruffy and peculiar. And discourteous. He kept calling her 'Little Sister', and burst out laughing when told about James's misfortune. If this was the sort of man James wanted her to meet in London, she wouldn't have it. And now it was left to her and Charles to entertain him.

The visiting team, accompanied by jeering from the spectators, ran onto the field. As they spread out, one player stood close to her. She drew in her breath. He was the handsomest man she'd ever set eyes on; superbly fit in black breeches and jersey, his cap set at a jaunty angle, black hair and dark eyes, his face beardless. There was an aura of a winner written in his carriage and the confident way he took the field.

'Charles,' she gestured with her eyes. 'That's the kind of man I'd like to meet. He looks so ... so right, so distinguished.'

Charles sighed and shook his head. 'My dear Stefanie! All the fuss is about that fellow. That's Paul Warren. You should not want to meet him.'

The home team burst onto the field. The spectators roared their support, but within the first minutes it was clear that the Wanderers were the better team. They scored an easy try, but failed with the conversion. Martin's experience and superior training inspired the team, and they managed a forward drive. The crowd went wild, including Radford at her side, as the wing dived over for a try. Against all expectations, the ball passed through the posts and the score stood in favour of the home team.

Charles cheered. 'Jolly good! We're ahead!'

Stefanie glared at him. 'You're supposed to be neutral.'

'One should not be neutral in anything, Little Sister,' Radford said. 'I've picked your side for the afternoon.'

'Oh really? I suppose you're right, but one could always *pretend* to be neutral.'

Warren touched down the second try for the Wanderers and undertook the conversion himself, putting his team back in the lead. Stefanie applauded.

Charles pulled a face. 'And whose side are you on?'

'It's only proper to acknowledge the achievements of the opposition,' she laughed.

With a few minutes to go, the score was still in favour of Wanderers. Then they failed to find touch with a long kick. Martin caught the ball and cut sharply infield, catching the opposition unawares. Head low on his chest, ball clamped under his arm, he charged into the loose forwards and threw off two opponents. It seemed that he had a clear field ahead and he ran at full speed.

Peter Radford roared, and even Charles gave loud voice to his excitement. But Warren came sweeping down on Martin, catching him a few yards from the goal line. Martin passed the ball into the flyhalf's outstretched hands. The crowd was jubilant when he dived over to score the try.

'Excellent! We're equal! We cannot lose!' Radford said.

'There's the chance that we might win,' Charles said, eyes bright behind his glasses.

A hush descended as the fullback set the ball for the conversion kick. A deafening roar burst over the field when it passed over the crossbar. And amid the bowlers, boaters, slouch hats and caps that filled the air, Radford took Stefanie by the waist and swung her up.

'Put me down this instant,' she hissed. 'I'm not your sister!'

MONDAY'S NEWSPAPERS carried the triumph of the Harlequin team in stirring headlines, with Martin featuring in every article. Invitations poured in, and Martin attended dinners, picnics at the Fountains and afternoon teas at the homes of many a hopeful parent with unwed daughters. Even the President sent for him, eager to hear about the victory.

'Can a jackal not outwit a lion, Oom Paul? It's their belief in their invincibility that makes them vulnerable,' Martin said, while having coffee on Kruger's stoep. 'One must study how the minds of these foreigners work and then out-think them, be one step ahead.'

The President nodded and asked Martin about England, his studies and what he planned to do on his return. As he listened, he sucked on his pipe and studied Martin through his watery eyes. 'Young man,' he said, 'your knowledge and understanding of the British can help me outwit the Outlanders.' He spat into the spittoon at his side. 'Have you found a wife?'

'I'm not married, Oom Paul.'

'*Magtig!* A man cannot do his work if there's no wife to see to his needs and comforts. I cannot take you into my government if you're ignorant in the ways of a man.'

THE SCHOOLS CLOSED for the mid-year break and everyone left for Wintersrust. Martin found that his status as a hero had reached the district. The family was gathered round the big dining table for the midday meal and Charles recounted every move of the rugby match to the twins. They listened with rapt attention and stared at him, their famous brother, with guarded admiration.

'Enough!' Martin held up his hands. 'It happened two weeks ago and you still babble on.'

'It's all there in the papers,' said Charles.

'Those who can master the written word, I suppose,' James muttered.

'Oh, James!' said Stefanie indignantly. 'There you go again! It's not proper to say things—'

'Not now, Stefanie. We do not need a lecture at the table.' Mary looked at her sternly. 'You were saying, James?'

'What I meant was, Aunt Mary, yes, it's in the papers,' James said, 'but I think the news will travel faster by word of mouth.'

Martin smiled at this ambiguous remark, pleased that James had not lost his spirit after the upheavals of the past weeks. The hunting trip would provide a much-needed outlet for his restless energy.

'Now, *hartjie*, tell me, did those clever doctors in Pretoria believe all you told them about mosquitoes?' Koba asked Charles.

'No, Tante Koba, they don't think it essential to set up a research station. They are convinced that malaria is not carried by mosquitoes but is spread by the fever tree.'

'And so it is, *hartjie*. But thank God for the quinine tree! Fusions extracted from the bark, bitter as bile, are a definite cure for fever. Any fever. Dear James was so sick, the poor thing. Just look at him now – all raring to go hunting.'

'Living proof, Dr Henderson,' James said. 'One drop of that stuff will cure one of all afflictions – for life!'

'When will you play the Wanderers again, Martin?' Stefanie asked.

'After the hunt. It's time to leave, I'm afraid.' He saw the disappointment in her eyes and winked at her. 'Why? Someone caught your fancy?'

'I saw the dear friend of James making eyes at her,' Koba said to Mary. 'Nice boy, Mary. Peter is his name – he is a lord! He is much like our James, not as handsome, but the face of an angel, so fine and delicate—'

'An angel? Good heavens, Tante Koba,' James exploded with laughter. 'He's everything *but* an angel!'

Before he could be asked to elaborate, they heard the clip-clop of horses' hooves approaching the house. Martin went to the stoep to greet the visitor. A boisterous laugh announced the arrival of Jan Viljoen. He smelled strongly of tobacco and sweat. His warm, noisy presence filled the room as he greeted all with a vigorous handshake and gave Mary a kiss on her cheek. Koba received two smacking kisses on the mouth.

'Because there's so much of you, Tante Koba,' he said.

'Mind your manners, Jan Viljoen,' she scolded playfully.

'Please join us, Jan,' Martin said. Jan took the empty chair next to James and heaped his plate with food. 'So what brings you to Wintersrust? Want to buy some cattle, perhaps?' Martin asked and joined in Jan's hearty laugh. The Viljoens were the prime cattle breeders of the district, and they were usually the sellers, not the buyers.

'I've come to invite you to my brother's wedding. Frans is taking Elsie from Groenplaas as a wife.' He asked James to pass the potatoes. 'You are also invited, *Engelsman*, that's if you promise to stay out of the orchard and learn to sing the *Volkslied* properly!' He roared with laughter and gave James a companionable slap on his back. The others joined in the laughter, but James flushed with annoyance.

'What did James do in the orchard?' Rudolf asked. Laughter rippled down the table again.

'He was *taking the air*,' Jan said, and roared again. 'So will you come to the wedding feast, *Engelsman*?'

'Thank you,' James said, 'but I'm leaving on a hunting expedition and won't be able to attend.'

'Aha! But the wedding is only next month. That brings me to the other reason for my visit. Gert Vermaas tells me that your wagon passed his farm yesterday heading northwest into the bushveld. Is that where you plan to shoot this winter? Or must I say,' he looked jokingly at James, 'have your Hunting Expedition?'

'Yes, we sent the wagon ahead with Old Klaas to find a suitable camping place. We leave in two days' time,' Martin said.

'Well, Frans and I would like to join you, if we may. You see, the farm is not big enough for all the Viljoens and their cattle. So many women in one kitchen! Ma, sister Ester, Jacob's Bettie, my lovely Hannie and now a new bride. Not to mention all the little Viljoens crawling under our feet. And I have a third son on the way.'

Jan beamed as they congratulated him. He turned to James and winked. 'You see, *Engelsman*, our talents as breeders do not stop at cattle.' He gave another thunderous laugh, with Koba and Martin joining in. 'No, we will not have a moment's peace. So we are looking for more land to buy. I've heard that there's good grazing country up there. So, what do you say, my friend? May we join you?'

'Of course, Jan,' Martin said. 'I was just thinking we would be short of hands for all the skinning and the biltong-making. Pa is still in Pretoria tied up with the Volksraad, Charles refuses to accompany us and Buks has to mind the farms. We could do with skilled hunters like you and Frans.'

Martin saw a grimace come to James's face, but Jan Viljoen was onto James again. 'So, *Engelsman*, we will hunt together. Jan Viljoen will show you how to shoot straight and—' boomed Jan, but James interrupted.

'If we are to spend two weeks in each other's company, I'd prefer that you address me by my name. My name is not *Engelsman*; it's James.'

'All right! Done!' Jan gave his loud laugh, followed by another hearty slap on James's back. 'James. We will ride and hunt together and I can teach you the ways of a real Boer.'

'James is an excellent shot and he rides very well,' Karel said. 'Even my horse, Legend, allows him on her back.'

'Pa says he was born in the saddle,' added Rudolf.

'That remains to be seen.' Jan wiped his mouth on the back of his hand and rose. 'Thank you for the nice food, Aunt Mary. It always gives me great pleasure to sit at your friendly table. I will have coffee at Soetvlei with Uncle Joep and Buks.' He made the round of handshaking and held on to James's hand a little longer. 'We'll get along. Jan Viljoen and the *Engelsman* will get along, you'll all see,' he said, searching James's face with a penetrating look.

'Don't take everything he says so seriously,' Martin said to James when Jan rode off. 'It's just his way. He's really a very agreeable chap and means no harm.'

The Hunt

A CHAOTIC SIGHT met James's eyes when the hunting party arrived at Vrede, the Viljoen farm, in the early afternoon. The rambling farmstead was bursting with life. Children, all under the age of ten, James reckoned, ran from where they were playing and came to gape at the visitors. There were cats of all colours, and a great number of dogs ran in circles around the horses, barking excitedly. The yard was littered with poultry: turkeys, geese and chickens scattered noisily at their approach.

The women of the house came out to greet the visitors. Ester was there as well, staring boldly at him. It took some time before Martin and Joep were through with the greetings and answers to questions about their health and of those at Wintersrust and Soetvlei. Only then was he introduced.

Hannie, Jan's wife, obviously pregnant, folded her arms and looked at him through narrowed eyes. 'Now, will I allow an Englishman over my threshold?' she wondered out loud and gave her husband a questioning glance.

James flushed. 'It's not my intention to inconvenience you, madam. I am on my way.' He was about to remount when Jan's strong arm grabbed him around the shoulders. There was suddenly much laughter.

Hannie took him by the arm and led him onto the stoep. 'I was only playing, Mr Henderson. You're most welcome in my house. Any friend or family of the De Winters is a friend of ours.'

After some refreshments, Jan showed them over the farm. James was astounded at the vast number of cattle and the neat layout of the camps and drinking points. He listened with interest as Jan explained his farming and export management. The Viljoens were trading with the country to the north, which had recently come under British rule.

As they were heading home, Jacob Viljoen came in from the outlying camps. Martin commented on the absence of Frans and was told that he had been sent ahead with their wagon to find Old Klaas.

During dinner, the women served the men. Hannie heaped James's plate with food and, in a comfortable mixture of English and Afrikaans, kept up a conversation as if to compensate for the discomfort she had caused him earlier. He remembered her from the wedding. A beautiful woman, her face heart-shaped, laughter always ready in her slanted eyes and a full red mouth. Jan Viljoen seemed to have the best of everything – an excellent farm, superior cattle and a bonny wife who gives him a son every year, he thought. He recalled Buks Maree's words: 'What more does a Boer want from life?'

Laughter and joking accompanied everything said and done. Ester brushed against James, and he shot her a warning glance. From the kitchen, where the children were fed, came a continuous racket. After the table was cleared and Jan had said the evening prayers, Karel and Rudolf sped back to the stables to be with their horses. The women gathered the children and saw them to bed while the men shared a bottle of homebrew on the stoep. Ester lingered in the door.

'*Gaan slaap!*' Jan said. 'We must find her a husband soon or else there'll be trouble. She's hot-blooded , like a true Viljoen. She'll make a good, willing wife.'

'No, brother, there's something wrong with her.' Jacob sucked on his pipe. 'She's hungry for men, any man. It's not normal.'

'She's young and men steer clear of her, but for how long?' Martin said.

Jan fixed his eyes on James. 'What do you think? Is she normal?'

'I beg your pardon?' James spluttered, embarrassed that they discussed domestic matters in the presence of a stranger.

'You kissed her in the orchard. Tell us if you think she's normal,' Jan said, and to his surprise James saw that he was in earnest. 'She's our only sister. She will bring shame on us.'

'Well, she's a bit … shall I say, forward, yes,' he obliged.

'You should get Koba to mix her a potion; she knows about these things,' Joep said, saving James further embarrassment.

AT SUNRISE they were on their way, travelling at a fast pace with Martin and Joep in the lead and the twins in the middle. Jan and his Boer hounds brought up the rear. He whistled to his dogs and sang lustily, love songs alternating with hymns. James forced himself to stay calm as yet another booming rendition of the *Volkslied* assaulted the morning air. He felt that it was solely for his ears.

The country became increasingly bushy and their pace slowed as they made frequent detours around thick clumps of acacia. They came across many farmsteads where they were obliged to have coffee, as it was considered impolite to pass without greetings and refreshments. James found these visits trying. The children, wives and servants all came out to gape and giggled unashamedly at his attempts to speak their language. Jan insisted on introducing him as '*my Engelsman*'. Martin took these opportunities to talk politics with the farmers.

As they moved north, the winter scenery became less harsh. Marula and white stinkwood, their branches bare now, towered over thickets of hook-thorn and the occasional mopane forest. They saw plenty of game, but Joep Maree had ruled that no shot was to be fired until they reached their camp. By afternoon they found the much-used wagon track, which they followed, skirting koppies and dongas. Martin went ahead to find the camp, but was back within minutes.

'Lion spoor on the track, Uncle Joep.' He took them a few hundred yards on. 'He walks alone, an old or perhaps injured lion, but certainly a big one.'

'Yes, the spoor is fresh. What do you reckon, Jan?' Joep said.

'Well now, it's not even an hour old. James, come, let me show you.' James squatted next to Jan and he traced the outline of the paw mark. 'See here, the earth is neat; the loose sand hasn't crumbled yet. Now, if it were this morning's spoor, there would've been insect or bird tracks crossing it. But it's clear, fresh.'

'It has smelled the oxen and will no doubt give us trouble tonight.' Joep straightened up. 'Scout ahead, Martin. Jan at the rear and you two,' he gestured to the twins, 'in the middle. Your horses are not accustomed to lion; they will bolt. Keep an open eye. We can't be far from the camp now.'

They travelled in this order for a while. Martin shouted back to them that the lion spoor was no longer on the track. The dogs whimpered and bundled around Jan's horse. 'Watch out!' he warned. 'My dogs only behave like this when there's lion near.'

James was at the rear. He desperately needed to relieve himself. Keeping a sharp lookout, he dismounted and hurriedly undid his flies. His horse whinnied and bolted down the track. Jan's dogs scattered, howling fiercely. Jan brought them back with an ear-splitting whistle and a few cuts of his whip. The twins struggled to bring their rearing horses under control. James unslung the rifle from his back, his eyes searching the undergrowth, his heart racing. There came a rustling in the dry grass. A tawny blur crashed towards him. He threw the rifle to his shoulder, pulled the trigger and stood petrified. Another shot sounded. Martin was at his side, his smoking rifle at his shoulder.

'God, James!' Martin lowered his rifle, his eyes fixed on the lion twitching in agony. 'That was close! You got him in the heart.'

Joep rushed up and flew from the saddle. The twins joined them, dragging their horses by the reins. Karel took James's rifle from his clenched hands and whispered, 'Put your hands in your pockets; they are shaking. That's what we always do.'

James did not trust his voice and, giving Karel a grateful smile, did as he had suggested.

'*Engelsman!*' Jan gave an almighty whistle, looking at James's unbuttoned flies. 'Did you piss on the lion's head? No wonder he got upset with you!'

They inspected James's first lion. The animal was in his prime, the tawny coat still handsome and the mane thick and dark. A porcupine quill protruding from his throat had made it difficult to hunt, Joep explained to James, hunger driving him to easier prey. 'Now we cover this old beast with thorn bush to keep the vultures away. Come back with a few oxen to pull it to the camp. Come on, son,' he said to James, 'this is your lion. Cut the branches.'

They reached the camp at sunset. Old Klaas had chosen the spot well, under a spreading wild fig on the bank of a slow-flowing stream. The two wagons were parallel to each other. A tarpaulin stretched between them providing shelter from the sun. The area around the camp had been cleared and enclosed with thorn scrub, the oxen and horses well protected in a similar enclosure nearby.

The fires were already lit, and the three-legged pots were emitting a delicious aroma. Frans Viljoen was there to meet them. The twins conveyed the drama of James's first lion and he offered to ride back for it. James, together with Martin and Frans, with Jan giving advice over their shoulders, wafting brandy fumes, worked well into the night skinning the lion. Finally James fell into his blanket roll, exhausted, not hearing any of the night sounds.

———

ALTHOUGH IT WAS WINTER, the temperature rose sharply in the day, only to plummet to zero at night. They hunted buck in the morning, when the air was crisp and clear. In the afternoon they prepared the meat, cutting it up, salting it and hanging it out to dry. By the end of the week the camp was festooned with strips of venison and hides pegged out in the sun. Joep kept control, ensuring that they only shot what they could handle for the day.

At night they sat around the fire, cleaned their rifles and ate from the communal pot. Joep's homebrew made the conversation easy and relaxed. Jan and Frans drank steadily, but the drink never seemed to affect them other than to make them more talkative. They told stories of previous hunts, but the talk around the fire always turned to the gold and Outlanders. The Viljoen brothers favoured taking up arms to defend their country.

Martin thought the possibility of war overrated. 'No, I don't think the presence of the gold diggers will lead to war. If there's to be a dispute, it can be settled by negotiation.'

'They went to war in '81. And they'll do so again.' Jan spat into the fire.

James slipped into his blanket roll. Although he found hunting with Jan a valuable experience, he was still wary of him and didn't want to start an argument. He knew too little about Transvaal politics and had already made the grave mistake of involving himself without first being invited.

Martin and the Viljoen brothers went north for two days and returned with a few giraffe skins that they needed to make harnesses for the draught animals. James hunted with Joep and the twins. The talk around the fire was about farming and soldiering. Although the peace was disrupted by the return of Jan, James was pleased to see Martin.

He had had enough of the hunt. The excitement of seeing lion, leopard, elephant and kudu had worn thin. He was fed up with the messy job of cutting up the hot slimy meat. He hated the unpalatable food and the smell of unwashed bodies. The twins explained to him that that made it easier to get closer to the game without being detected, but he was appalled at the sweaty smell that hung around the others.

Then there were the night sounds. The call of the jackal and nightjars he was used to, but the hysterical cackle of hyenas sneaking around the camp, attracted by the drying meat, startled him every time. Some nights there was the shattering roar of lion, followed by their deep-throated moans.

The morning before they were to break camp for the journey home, James was shaving at the stream, with Karel holding a small mirror for him. The sudden boom of Jan's voice broke the pleasant silence.

'Washing again, James? You English! You wash away all the goodness and leave nothing to protect you from the sun.' He splashed a handful of water on his face to get the sleep from his eyes. 'You shoot and ride like a proper Boer, but you must also learn to live like one.' Jan squatted in front of James and smiled broadly. 'And given time, I, Jan Viljoen, will make a real Boer out of this *Engelsman.*'

It was obvious that Jan was joking, but the nearness of his unwashed body was too much for James. 'And I, James Henderson, prefer to be an Englishman! Not a Boer!'

The smile faded from Jan's face. 'Don't get on your high horse, James. We are all people put on this earth by the Almighty, whether we are Boers or Englishmen. And I thank Him that I'm a Boer, an honest man.'

'Are you implying that the British are not honest?'

Jan looked at him for a long moment. 'Look at your history, especially in this country and answer that question yourself.' And with that, he walked back to the wagons.

'If you apologise, it will be fine again,' Karel said.

'Apologise? Whatever for?' James gathered his shaving things and got up to leave.

'He was only joking, James. Jan Viljoen is a good man, our friend. It's not right to insult him unfairly.'

Joep decided to get two more kudu. Wind-dried, the meat would last the two days of travel. James didn't relish the idea of going out in the hot sun, and that in the company of Jan, but he reluctantly collected his rifle and hat.

They followed a dry riverbed for most of the morning, but it was only at midday when they found the spoor of kudu. They dismounted and continued on foot. Martin and Frans offered to stay with the horses. James led, as it was his turn to shoot. Jan was directly behind him, and provided a constant stream of unnecessary warnings and advice. Had it been earlier in the hunt, James would have ignored it, but he was tired, hot and thirsty.

He spotted three kudu a hundred yards away and came to a halt. Jan bumped into him, spoiling his aim. The shot went wild, and the animals ran off. James bit back an angry comment. They set off again and found the kudu a few hundred yards on, as Jan had predicted. James aimed at the head of the bull and, blinking his eyes to get rid of the sweat, took a little longer than was expected.

'Now, James, pretend it's a Redcoat. Aim right in the middle of his chest, there where the heart lies,' Jan advised in a whisper.

The tension and irritation erupted inside James. He took a step forward, swung around and levelled his rifle at Jan's chest. 'I'd much rather aim at you than a Redcoat!' He held the rifle steady, the barrel almost touching Jan.

Jan didn't flinch. 'No one points a rifle at Jan Viljoen unless he has reason to kill him. That time will surely come, but not now, not yet.'

James's anger changed to shame. He lowered his rifle.

Joep stormed forward and placed his body between the two men, grabbing James's rifle and giving him a push on his chest with the butt. 'You hot-headed pup! Enough of your uncontrollable temper!' He turned to Jan and shook his head. 'Jan, *magtig*! You should've known better than to speak to *him* like that.'

'Yes, Uncle Joep,' Jan said submissively, 'it was a wrong thing to say to him.'

'You two will walk back to the camp to cool off and sort out your differences.' Joep called to the twins, who had been watching the incident from a little way off. They walked away to where Martin and Frans were waiting with the horses.

Jan looked at James, scowling. 'The camp is a long way off. I got us into this and the least I can do is get you back safely.'

They walked apart for the first few miles. Soon sweat poured off James face and his breathing became laboured. His clothes clung to his body, the speargrass penetrating his trousers and scratching against his skin. He gritted his teeth, fixing his eyes on Jan's fast-moving figure. *I will not let this Boer beat me! I will keep up!*

Jan stopped and faced him. 'James, I didn't mean to anger you. What I said was just … a manner of speaking, an old saying in this country. It was not to your liking, so I apologise. Come on, let's be friends until time gives us a reason to be enemies.'

James kept a stony silence. Jan shrugged and set off again. When they reached familiar terrain and the well-trodden path leading to the river, they spied an object in the path, placed so that it was impossible to miss.

Jan picked it up and roared joyfully. 'Frans left us some water, as I knew he would, but my kind-hearted brother chose the wrong bottle. In this one, with the scratch on the side, I carry my homebrew. For emergencies only.' He took a deep swallow and belched. 'And is this not an emergency of the greatest kind?'

James was exhausted, his thirst overwhelming. In the distance was the green vegetation that marked the stream, the spreading crown of the wild fig where they were encamped. It appeared so close, yet so far. He sank down and accepted the bottle, raised it to his lips and hesitated; it was full.

'It would be unwise to drink this on an empty stomach,' he said.

'Damn right! Just one mouthful and my head feels like a hollow pumpkin, but drink anyway. We can crawl into the camp if we need to. It's not far now and there are no women to witness our shame.'

James took a mouthful and passed the bottle back to Jan. 'Your head is a hollow pumpkin in any case.'

Jan's black eyes penetrated James's face for a tense moment. Then he slapped his thigh, bellowing with laughter. 'And your head is not empty, but stuffed with clouds of glory and fame.' Jan slugged out of the bottle and pressed it into James's hands. 'But clouds, my friend, make rain and one day you'll be just a sodden old man!'

The fiery liquid burned James's stomach. After another swig, his head felt giddy, his eyes struggling to focus. 'Will there be war, Jan?'

'Yes, James, it's coming, the war. I feel it in my bones. We can drink from the same bottle, eat from the same pot, but we cannot share the same country. The time will come for war. Yes, we'll make war, my friend.'

They drank a while in silence. 'Do you want war?' James squinted at Jan.

'Want war?' Jan looked horrified. 'No peace-loving man would wish something so terrible on his people and animals. Yes, even the animals suffer in war. I rode my black stallion to death in the last war, to save Lang Hans van Rensburg.' He lowered his voice and whispered in great earnest, 'War is not a game for the soldiers of the Queen, dressed in their fancy uniforms.'

'That war is not a game, I know perfectly well, thank you.'

Jan told stories of previous wars, the bravery of the Boers increasing as the level in the bottle dropped. They quarrelled about Boer horses and British chargers, formal warfare and hiding behind boulders, rifles and sabres.

Jan hiccupped, followed by a belch. 'Will you fight your family when the time comes?'

He looked Jan square in the eyes. 'I shall do my duty.'

'*Engelsman*, I admire your spirit. You can ride and shoot. With your courage you could be a great leader of men, a great soldier. But there's one thing you don't have. Compassion. You don't have it in your heart to feel for others. A man must first be humbled before he's truly great. How shall I put it?' He frowned, searching James's face as if to find words there. 'A proud horse; you break him first before he's truly strong. It's the same with all God's creatures. One day it'll be your turn. Until then, you carry this burden with you, this pride, this barrier that will not allow you to be truly great.'

'No, Jan Viljoen, you're wrong,' James said after a while. 'On England's coat of arms there's one of God's creatures that can't be humbled. A lion.'

Jan looked at him with regard and gave his expansive laugh. '*Allemagtig!* But you are a clever *Engelsman!*'

James brought the bottle to his lips. 'Empty.'

Jan turned the bottle upside down. One last drop fell into the sand and he looked at it sadly. 'So it is. Empty.' He rose, taking a few steps sideways to regain his balance.

James struggled up. His legs, stiff from the long walk, refused to support him and he stumbled a few paces on all fours. He grabbed Jan's offered arm, but Jan lost his balance and they sprawled in the thick sand, laughing.

Jan hoisted him to his feet, put an arm around his shoulder and they set off crookedly. 'Now, let's sing to make the journey pleasant.'

THE SUN WAS LOW when Karel and Rudolf spotted Jan and James making their way to the camp. When the two drew closer, they realised that they were drunk. Martin, Joep and Frans Viljoen came to see what it was about.

'They quarrelled at the spruit this morning,' Karel said.

'What did they quarrel about?' Martin asked.

'The usual. *Engelsman*, Boer.'

'Uncle Joep,' Frans said. 'Half a bottle of *dop*? You know that Jan can take his drink better than anyone else.'

Joep felt for his pipe in his pocket. 'Jan is not drunk at all; he's only pretending.'

'To humour James,' Martin said. 'You can see James is drunk, yet again.'

'He had nothing to eat or drink all day,' Rudolf said. 'He didn't even eat his porridge this morning.' He was ignored and exchanged a glance with Karel. They followed the conversation with wariness in their eyes.

'Why does he do it, Martin?' Joep sucked on his pipe. 'Why does it take the drink to show the human side of James? When he's sober, he's so aloof, unfeeling even. Is it like that in England as well?'

'Has he got a problem with the drink?' Frans asked. 'I mean, when drink becomes one's master—'

'No, I don't think so.' Martin looked towards the river, from where loud splashing and laughter came; Jan and James had decided to have a swim. 'When James drinks, he makes a good job of it. He drinks fast and hard. Uncle Joep, I think that there's a deep anger in him, a want of something. His father, General Henderson, has a lot to do with it.'

'You could ask him why he is angry,' Rudolf said. 'Then you could tell his father, and James won't have to drink so much.'

'No, Rudi,' Martin smiled, 'the English do not talk about these things.'

'James is young, there's time for him to come to grips with this.' Joep moved towards the wagons. 'Come, give me a hand with the loading. We leave before the sun is up.'

The men walked off, leaving the twins alone in the gathering darkness. 'Why would James be angry with his father, Karel?' Rudolf hooked his little finger around his brother's. 'What's it that he wants and can't have?'

Karel stared at Martin and then turned his eyes towards the river. 'Rudi, James has a reason to be angry. We have each other, but he … well, he has no one.'

'He has Charles.'

'Martin took Charles from James when he went to London. Martin is Charles's brother now. Martin takes what he wants. The grown-ups do that. They take everything. It's their birthright, they claim. They just don't care, Rudi.'

Home of the Fireflies

HALFWAY UP THE KLOOF on their way to the cave, Charles turned around to view the scenery below. Eight summers ago, a sea of greens, picturesque in its variety of shades, had met the eye. And now the winter's frosty nights had wrought an arresting contrast. The grassland was a carpet of burnished yellow, russet and brown, the thorny branches of the acacia stark against the showy surroundings. He could see the stream winding downwards to the vlei. The path was not as steep as it had seemed years ago. The boulders, so huge then, were just obstacles to find one's way around.

And now, looking into the distance, he finally made up his mind. He loved the Boers and wanted to be part of their future. His father's posting to England had set him free. Now he was at liberty to shape his life and career. But it would not be an easy time for James.

Charles cared deeply about his brother's wellbeing and had always smoothed things over after rows with their father. James's arrogance concealed an inner vulnerability, Koba had confided. She took extra care to love him in an unobtrusive way and James feasted on her love as a hungry child would on food. Koba had again taken James's side after the incident with Jan Viljoen on the hunting trip. 'James is a stranger to our ways, *hartjie*, and it's only human to lose your temper when you're picked on by the likes of dear old Jan Viljoen.'

Military life should channel James's adventurous spirit, Charles hoped, forcing him to think beyond the moment, to consider the repercussions of his actions, to curb his impulsiveness …

'Come on, Charles!' Stefanie's call broke into his thoughts. 'We're almost there!'

He waved and resumed climbing. Martin and Buks, some way ahead of him, were in deep conversation, but he had noticed that there was awkwardness between them and it came mostly from Buks's side. With a child on the way, Buks was content with life on Soetvlei. That was what he'd always wanted: to be a farmer, a husband and a father. He was wary of Martin's English manners, his worldly ways, he had said on occasion.

Stefanie's laugh rang out. Charles saw James helping her free her dress from a thorn bush. Where James was careless and unruly, Stefanie was annoyingly prim, yet they sought each other's company, laughing and whispering together.

At the waterfall Charles paused to catch his breath. The way to the entrance of the cave was clearer now, yet the magnificence inside the rock face would always be concealed.

The cave was as impressive as the first time they had entered it. The light danced off the walls forming patterns of light and dark. The silent interior still had the same mystical power. The wild olive that had been struck by lightning in the storm had been put to good use. Sawed into blocks, it now served as chairs around the rock table. There was a fireplace under a wide fissure, and shelves fashioned into the rock held mugs, a kettle, tins of coffee and sugar and a bag of biltong, candles and some books.

'Looks like a proper little house,' Charles said.

'Do you play here often?' Martin asked the twins.

Karel scowled. 'We don't *play* any more. We make plans for when we leave school.'

'We want to buy our own farm,' Rudolf explained.

'The eldest always inherits the farm.' Karel looked fixedly at Martin.

Martin looked taken aback, but before he could reply, Stefanie said, 'I also have *serious* plans for my future. I'm going to be a great pianist. People from all over the country will come to hear me play at concerts, in theatres.'

Charles smiled. Just like her older brother, she had her future planned to the last detail, and, just like Martin, she was determined that nothing would stand in her way.

'Are you serious?' Martin frowned. 'I know you play brilliantly, but to make a career? Pa would not like you to travel by yourself.'

'Of course I'm serious! Why, I've been offered the post as music teacher at the convent and I'm not even done with my tuition yet. And I won the first prize at the Music Hall last Christmas. I still have to tell Pa that I signed up for performances in the Royal Theatre in Johannesburg ...'

'But Uncle Marthinus will never let you go to Johannesburg,' Annecke said. 'He says the devil roams the streets there.'

'True, Annecke, he does. I saw him!' James said. 'Carries a bottle of gin and a deck of cards.' He gave an evil grin and grabbed Stefanie around her waist. 'Pretty girls like you, my dear cousin, disappear into his lair and are never heard of again.'

'James! Stop this instant!' She pried his hands away. 'The devil does not scare me.'

'I've also made a decision about my future,' Martin said, catching their attention. 'Oom Paul has offered me a position in the Attorney General's office on my return. I've decided to accept.'

'Good heavens,' Buks said. 'Only proper Dutch lawyers have been offered those posts before. You are in favour with the old man.'

'You'll be living with us? With Tante Koba?' Stefanie asked.

'Well, yes, I'll be in Pretoria mostly, I suppose. I can escort you to Johannesburg, see that you don't land in the devil's clutches. And,' he looked at the twins, 'I shall also keep an eye on you two while you are at school there.' He smiled at Annecke. 'I shall have to find a wife, as the President strongly disapproves of bachelors.'

Charles had noticed the way Martin looked at Annecke lately, and it was not a brotherly expression. The twins didn't like it either, by the look on Karel's face. 'I also have plans I'd like to share with you,' he said. He cleared his throat and polished his glasses on his handkerchief, searching for words.

All eyes turned to him. 'I've decided to settle in the Transvaal.'

A barrage of questions met him. When? Where? Why? He explained that he would first have to finish his studies in tropical diseases in London and then would be back at the same time as Martin. The twins grinned. Annecke planted a kiss on his cheek and Buks slapped him on the back.

'Permanently?' James asked.

'Yes, I rather hope so. It's not a decision I've taken lightly. I've just this morning made up my mind, actually. This is where I'm needed. I want the sunshine, I love the land and the people.'

'That'll be so marvellous,' Stefanie said. 'All of us will be home, every summer …' she looked at James. 'There are British soldiers in the Cape Colony. You can live there, come and see us often. Oh do, Jamie!'

'I'm afraid that won't be possible,' James laughed. 'I belong in England. I don't fit in here, never will.'

'I understand, James, believe me,' Martin said. 'In a way, I'm lonely in England. It's lonely being different from everybody else.'

They talked about England and how Charles's decision to move to the Transvaal would be received by his parents, about Martin's impatience to return and be part of the government.

Soon it was time to leave. Stefanie came to her feet and picked up her hat. 'Oh, the light is so beautiful in here.' She turned her face up to the roof. 'I thought it was a palace then.'

'The Home of the Fireflies, not so, Annecke?' Charles said. 'Why did you choose that name? You were little then, but can you remember?'

'Oh yes, I remember. I was five, but I do remember.' She pointed to the roof. 'Look! The light! I thought that this was where the fireflies hide during the day. You can only see them at night, so they must be somewhere in the day where their lights can still shine.'

'Yes,' Stefanie said. 'What a charming idea. Fireflies eternally dancing in the cave.'

'Like us, fireflies live for a short while only and their lights shine briefly,' James said.

Charles was startled at James's remark: was it flippant or prophetic?

PART THREE

WRITINGS ON WALLS

And yet, when all is thought and said,
The heart still overrules the head;
Still what we hope we must believe,
And what is given us receive;

A.H. Clough,
'What We, When Face to Face' [1849]

The Heart Overrules the Head

London, July 1895

MARTIN DE WINTER contemplated the sherry glass in his hand. The afternoon was hot. A cold beer was what he needed; he had barely had enough time to change into his suit after arriving from Cambridge, where a riotous party had marked his graduation. But it would not be correct to ask for a beer.

He surveyed the reception room of the Henderson residence. The usual crowd, here and there a new face, mostly people recently returned from India. He thought about the many social functions he had attended in the past five years. It was hard to get to know these people; they lived behind polite fronts. This was the class his cousins had been born into. To restrain all emotion was absurd, untruthful to one's soul. God gave man feelings, Tante Koba would say.

Now that he had almost finished his studies, the urge to go home was stronger than ever. It was time to be a Boer – to grow a beard, smoke a pipe, shed the fancy suits and ties. Find a wife. He sighed; there was still one term of postgraduate study ahead.

His eyes strayed to his uncle, who stood surrounded by other officers. General Sir Stuart Henderson, every inch the military aristocrat, with an air of authority that brooked no opposition, was preparing James's future in the army. But would he succeed in disciplining his rebellious son? James stepped out of line deliberately and persistently, and General Henderson's patience was wearing thin.

'I count on your presence, then, Mr de Winter.' A familiar singsong voice brought him out of his meditation. Beatrice, Lady Harcourt, was smiling archly at him. She was attractive, in a dangerous way, and calculating in her pursuit of status. After considerable effort, she had finally persuaded Gordon, Lord Harcourt, the General's older brother, to forsake his bachelorhood.

'The luncheon. I'll be there, Beatrice.' Martin inclined his head a little, smiling thinly. He walked over to Charles, who was at a window. Charles was still trying to placate his mother, who was upset about his decision to move to the Transvaal. She accused him of turning his back on his country and family, but Charles's resolve remained firm.

'That woman, your *aunt*, is quite demanding …' Martin said.

'Yes, another luncheon tomorrow,' Charles smiled wanly. 'Please endure, cousin. Five months and we'll be home.'

'A marriage of convenience, I tell you. A woman in her twenties marries an old dodderer like your uncle?'

'Uncle Gordon needs an heir; she needs a title.'

'Or a licence to lure whoever she desires into her bed. She and her friends are notorious at Cambridge.'

Charles shrugged. 'Well, that's how it's done.'

'Charles,' Martin tugged at his sleeve. 'Let's go to the Black Swan and get drunk.'

'You've been drunk since graduation. Father is expecting the Fairfields any minute now. I promised that you'd be present; Lord Fairfield has an interest in your country's politics.'

'Lord Fairfield? Must be an important fellow. Look at the titles hanging about.'

'He spent sixteen years in India – as an administrator. Very wealthy, has considerable investments in the gold mines. Must warn you, though: he's no admirer of President Kruger, so tread lightly.'

'All right, I'll play the dumb Boer for a while, and then I'm getting out of here.' Through the window he saw a carriage, crest emblazoned on the door, draw up. Lord Fairfield, he presumed, alighted, followed by two ladies. A few minutes later, he heard his uncle making a welcoming speech.

Then he saw her.

He stared, fascinated, at the young woman standing completely at ease next to her parents, unaffected by the attention focused on her. Her dress was a brilliant blue, in stark contrast to the pale pastels in the room. Her hair tumbled down her back, secured with a plain ribbon. The fading sunlight streaming through the high windows caught it, turning it into a halo of fire. There was an earthiness, a sensual quality, about her that was immediate and overwhelming.

There came a tap on his shoulder and he glanced around to find James, dashing in his blue and black-braided uniform.

'How is it that you're here?' Martin asked.

'Another dressing-down.' James gestured towards his father. 'I wasted only a minute of the General's precious time.'

'The verdict?' Charles gave James a sympathetic smile.

'Like being back at school, brother. Apologies all around; a drastic cut in my allowance. I can live with that. Been having a bit of luck with the cards—', he broke off when he noticed the girl, who was now being introduced to the guests. 'Who's that … apparition?'

'Don't you recognise Victoria?'

'Good heavens! Yes, so it is! They've not been home for years.'

'Poor girl,' Charles said. 'Her brother died last year – a hunting accident, they say. Now Lord Fairfield's only hope for an heir is his daughter.'

'I'll spread the word.'

'Why don't you give it some thought, James?' Charles grinned. 'Your gambling debts are scandalous.'

'No, thank you, dear brother. I'd rather face Father's wrath.'

'She's so different …' Martin interrupted.

'Yes, ladies are supposed to do up their hair when they reach a certain age to give us men an indication—'

'I wasn't referring to her hair, James. Look at her face. There's warmth there, strength.'

James rolled his eyes. 'Romantic twaddle, and from *you*, Martin.'

Martin was aware of saying the right words when introduced to the Fairfields, promising to discuss the state of affairs in his country with Lord Fairfield. Then she was standing in front of them.

'How good to see you again, Lady Victoria. Welcome home,' Charles said.

'Miss Fairfield.' James inclined his head.

'Charles. James. You used to call me Vicky. Have the years made us strangers?'

'The last time we met we were children. It's lovely to see you again, Vicky,' Charles said. 'May I introduce my cousin, Martin de Winter? Martin, Lady Victoria Fairfield.'

Martin looked into the greenest eyes he'd ever seen. They shone like jewels in her face, her skin bronzed by the Indian sun, a few freckles on her nose. 'The colour of dark honey,' he said. 'Your hair.'

'Dark honey?' Her eyes searched his face, her mouth forming a smile that broke into a delightful laugh. 'I'm glad to make your acquaintance. Your cousins told me about their visit to Africa years ago.' She turned to Charles. 'Have you been out again?'

When Charles told her about his decision to settle in the Transvaal, she seemed both sad and envious. 'That's wonderful, Charles. To be master of your own destiny, to have the freedom to choose where and how to spend your life.'

James smirked. 'Oh, to be a man!'

There was another delighted laugh before she turned to go. 'Mother is getting impatient. I do hope to see you again.' She moved off to join Lady Fairfield.

'Well done, cousin. You swept her off her feet.'

'Don't be absurd, James,' Martin mumbled, his eyes still following Victoria.

'I must placate Mother.' With a wave of his hand and a rattle of his spurs, James walked over to Susan Henderson.

'We'll see her again, won't we?' Martin said as he and Charles left through a side door.

'Yes, but remember, although Victoria was raised in India, she's as British as the rest of them.'

NEXT DAY, while driving through St John's Wood in the open carriage to lunch with Beatrice Harcourt, Charles pointed to a large house. 'The Fairfield residence. Or shall I say one of many scattered over the country.' The three-storey house was set well back from the road in wooded grounds. A cobbled driveway and wrought-iron gates formed an imposing entrance. As they passed, a couple emerged from the front door. Martin recognised Victoria and a cavalry officer, Captain George Hunter of the 5th Hussars.

'A friend of her late brother's. Same regiment,' Charles said as they moved on.

At the Harcourt residence they were ushered through the reception hall and out to the garden, where a table was set under the oak trees. The guests sprawled in deckchairs, sipping champagne. Beatrice came to meet them, but there was no sign of Lord Harcourt.

'Your uncle ... a problem on the estate, and with the grouse season only two months away ... well, come along, then!' She led them to the table and soon they each had a glass of champagne and fell into conversation with the others.

Martin's heart raced when he saw Victoria and George Hunter coming down the lawn. She was dressed in a yellow and blue dress, a scarf of vivid colours securing her long hair. The couple moved to the table and Martin turned his attention to setting out the croquet hoops as Beatrice had ordered. He looked up when a burst of laughter announced the arrival of James, with Peter Radford. As always, Peter looked somewhat dishevelled.

'Looks like they started the day with something stronger than tea,' Charles said.

'Or haven't finished last night's party yet,' Martin smiled.

Since joining the 2nd Hussars, James and Peter had lived life to the full. If James was reckless, then Peter Radford was even more so. He often engaged in dangerous pranks; the closer the shave with death, the more satisfying the risk. Peter was also pursued by women desperate to trap him into marriage. James said he gave the ladies everything they asked for – except a proposal.

As Martin hammered the last hoop into the lawn, Victoria came walking over, smiling at him. He led her to a chair and took a place on the grass beside her. 'I do admire your choice of colours,' he said. 'Your scarf, it's beautiful.'

'Oh yes, I love strong colours. Each one seems to induce a feeling of its own. Yellow makes one aware of the power of the sun.' She looked up at the cloudless sky. 'As green is for the plants. In India, before the rains, one should wear green to will the plants to endure, to wait for the rains.'

'And the lovely blue dress you wore yesterday?'

'Blue makes you feel alive. It's the colour of heaven and of the energy of the sea. Take red; you only wear red if you have a statement to make.' She leaned closer to him. 'Red puts fire in your veins. You can take on the whole world when you wear red. The Indian people love vibrant colours. It's part of their lives, their religion. Oh, I know here it's out of place, but I don't care. One should follow one's inclinations, be happy and free when one still has the chance.'

Martin searched her face, wondering what troubled her. He found himself answering her questions about Africa, but their conversation ended with Beatrice's call for lunch. 'Are you free tomorrow? For tea, perhaps?' he asked on the spur of the moment. She accepted without hesitation.

The first course was served. Martin contemplated the chilled cucumber soup and listened absent-mindedly to the conversation. His eyes kept straying to Victoria, who was seated next to George Hunter a few chairs from him.

He had seen Hunter a few times with the General, but now he looked at him with curiosity. He was in his early thirties, with dark hair, deep-set brown eyes and a waxed moustache. James had said many an unkind thing about Hunter, and Martin sensed something disturbing about him.

The next course, wafer-thin slices of smoked salmon and a variety of summer salads, was served. Martin found Victoria's green eyes watching him openly. And all at once his homesickness evaporated. He felt powerless against the anticipation that rushed through every inch of his body.

DURING THE FOLLOWING WEEKS, Martin spent a lot of time with Victoria, away from the inquisitive eyes of London society. They went out into the countryside, and took tea and sometimes lunch when the time allowed.

He had never been in love, but he had thought about falling in love. There would be a sophisticated Boer girl – Annecke, perhaps. They would be part of the elite circles in Pretoria, dance at the President's annual banquet and she would stand proudly beside him, a member of the Volksraad. And at night, in a wide feather bed, she would be warm, inviting.

But the dream, like the homesickness, had also evaporated. He had found the girl, yes, but she was the only child of an English nobleman. And falling in love was not what he thought it would be. It was powerful, physical, and it scared him. For the first time in his life, he had come up against a force that he could not manage or resist.

During his time in England he had met many women. Mostly they were aloof and class-conscious, with little conversation other than social gossip. In Victoria he found the opposite. From the first, he was acutely aware of his desire for her, yet his mind reeled with the impossibility of fulfilling that desire.

By the second week of their friendship, he admitted to himself that he was in love with her. Like him, she was trying hard not to let her spontaneous nature betray her innermost emotions. Awareness of this drove him to examine his plans for the future. He wanted to tell her that he needed to take her back to the Transvaal with him, to have her with him always. But the words stayed mere thoughts.

There was a light in her face that made it change unpredictably. She could be happy and cheerful one moment and the next her eyes would fill with a longing for something that seemed out of her reach. He uncovered the reason while they were having lunch at an inn outside London.

'I understand Charles's need to settle in your country,' she said, staring out of the window at the light rain that had set in. 'Once you have experienced the vastness of India, and I suppose Africa too, England seems so small and limited. It's not where one is born, but where one grows up that counts in the end, don't you think?'

'I know. My country, well, my country is my world, my all, if you will.' He told her about Wintersrust and his family, and about his desire to play a role in his country's politics.

She told him of her deep love of India and its people, about the heat on the dusty sunbaked plains, and about the rains that fell for weeks on end. She spoke about her desire to return to India and make a home there. 'Realising that dream is futile,' she said, a touch of forlornness in her voice. 'England has never been my home; my heart lies in India. There must be a way to get back.'

He took her hand across the table. 'Nothing is impossible if one puts one's mind to it, Vicky.'

She looked at him long and hard. 'I have a duty to my parents, and they are not planning to return there.'

He entwined his fingers with hers and returned her gaze. He hesitated before he spoke, but decided to make light of her dilemma. 'Set your sights on someone who is bound to return to India. A military man, Foreign Office, that sort.'

She withdrew her hand. The waiter brought their coffee. She stirred sugar into hers and then asked abruptly, 'Is nothing impossible in your world? Is that what you live by?'

He frowned at her questions and formulated an answer that would suit them both. 'Yes, that's how I plan my life. Five years at Grey College and four years at Cambridge proved that it works.'

CHARLES ALONE WAS AWARE of their frequent excursions, and would often accompany them. Some nights they would go to the theatre or to dine at fashionable restaurants. When James was not carousing with his friends, he would join them. At first he was wary of Victoria, but when he discovered that she had no interest in him as a future husband, he relaxed and soon enjoyed her company.

'Enchanting girl,' he declared one night after they had seen Victoria home. 'Reminds me of being with Stefanie. Wouldn't you agree, Charles?'

'Yes, I would. I find her company refreshingly ... unconventional,' Charles said. He was happy for James's sake. Vicky was not overawed by his good looks, and an easy friendship had formed between them.

But Charles was not happy for Martin.

After Martin had overcome his initial reluctance to join the social whirl, he had become quite popular. He fitted in, behaved according to the fashion, yet had not lost his identity; he was the honest and sincere Boer from the Transvaal. His effect on people was remarkable. They were attracted by his broad shoulders, serious blue eyes and golden-brown hair, yet it was his confident manner and hearty laugh that won them over. Charles remembered the General commenting to a fellow officer: 'De Winter is a born leader.'

Charles was worried about the way Martin and Victoria had taken to each other. It was obvious that she was in love with Martin. It showed in her eyes and in the small frown that worried her brow when she looked at him and thought herself unobserved. *She's British,* he thought, *and realises her duty to her parents, despite her professed indifference to the rules of society.* But Martin! He would not survive this unharmed. He appeared to be in control of the situation, but Charles was not sure if he knew where he was heading. It would be wise to talk to him, but he did not want to be thought meddlesome. Martin would probably not welcome his advice. Victoria, then? Yes, he would speak to Victoria.

A Delightfully Talented Pianist

P AUL WARREN SAT in Charles Leonard's office, a glass of port in his hand, a cigar clamped between his teeth. The time had finally come for the downfall of Kruger and his Boers – the revenge he had planned since he was a boy of fourteen.

Yes, something was in the air. He had promised the people the ideal life in exchange for their names on a petition against the corrupt government of old Kruger, the illiterate Boer who sat on his stoep, scheming about what to do with the riches he stole from the gold mines.

'Write your name on the petition, join the protest meetings and, most important of all, be ready to finish off the Boers when they ride into town with their rifles and swagger. Get rid of Kruger. A new government is needed!'

An armed rebellion was what they were planning. Hundreds of rifles and thousands of rounds of ammunition, supplied by Cecil Rhodes, had been smuggled into the city. An armed force of seven hundred under the command of a Dr Jameson was to assemble on the western border of the Transvaal, ready to invade on New Year's Eve. Nothing could go wrong. It would all be over in a day.

There was, however, an uneasiness lurking in Warren's mind. Convincing the Randlords had not been a problem; it was the ordinary workers that worried him. They demanded their lawful rights, but fighting the Boers did not appeal to them. No, the success of the mission lay with Dr Jameson and his trained men and the rapid intervention of the Cape government. British *intervention* would lead to British *occupation*: the Union Jack would replace the Vierkleur in Pretoria.

'What if the Boers get wind of this?' Charles Leonard asked, refilling Warren's glass. He was the head of the Reform Committee, which liaised with the Kruger government on improvement of the city. 'If this turns into a fiasco, we'll be arrested and thrown into Pretoria gaol.'

'Then we put it off until a later date, but the time's right now. The Boers won't fight during Christmas. The unrest in this city must start now. I've already seen to that. It has to be a long drawn-out affair so that the Boer government gets used to it, tires of it and thinks it all to be just grumbling, a nuisance that cannot come to a point. Then, just as they think it might fizzle out, we'll strike!'

Warren glanced out of the window into the street below. A lumbering ox-wagon obstructed the road. Pedestrians shouted abuse at the farmer. Soon they would be facing one another with rifles in their hands, he hoped. He looked at the portly lawyer, took in his thinning hair and florid complexion.

'If the unthinkable happens, I'll get you out, trust me, and then we'll start from the beginning. We will not stop until we succeed.'

Leonard placed his glass on the table. 'I've discovered a delightfully talented pianist. She played at the Theatre Royal last month. The audience was in raptures. I managed to book her for this evening. Exorbitant fee, but I assure you she's worth every penny, and a pleasure to behold, I might add.'

DELIGHTFULLY TALENTED? Definitely. But a pleasure to behold? Her white dress was tight at the waist, wide at the shoulders to accommodate the movement of her arms as her fingers danced over the ivory keys. Her golden-brown hair was twisted into an elegant knot, leaving her neck exposed. The fire in the blue eyes, the colour in her cheeks and her straight back – all told of dedication to her art.

She needed polishing here and there, but she was certainly the best he'd heard in years. Warren's eyes returned to her face. She would be indifferent to everything but her music, conscious only of her talent. He'd heard about the artistic type from many a disillusioned husband. They made excellent hostesses, and provided stimulating conversation, but the marriage usually ended in separate bedrooms. An adornment to a man's house; an advantage to social life and career.

And that was what he needed: a wife, that kind of wife, not to have or to hold or to share his bed, but to do away with the gossip about him, talk that threatened to ruin his standing and career. Invitations were becoming less frequent and fewer and fewer guests graced his dinner table in Cape Town. The apologies offered were wafer thin, and the servants gossiped incessantly. Warren had had his fair share of women, but now he despised them. There was no love, only greed and self-importance. For some years now, he had found truth and beauty in the attention and company of men.

He joined in the applause as the last notes of Grieg sonata died away.

Who was this woman anyway? He had not been introduced, as he had arrived late.

'EXCELLENT! BRAVO! Bravo!' Stefanie faced her small audience, inclining her head in acknowledgement. As she turned to her hostess at her side, she saw the man who had haunted her dreams for a year now. She had despaired of ever seeing him again, but there he was: tall, dark and mysterious.

'Dear Miss de Winter, a brilliant performance, I thank you for it,' Mrs Leonard said.

Stefanie smiled, trying hard not to look at Warren. 'You're very kind.'

'You're a genius, child,' said the lady on her other side and laid a hand on her forearm. 'You should be playing where you might be noticed by those who could benefit your career.'

She was about to explain her plans for the forthcoming year, but Paul Warren came walking towards them. Mrs Leonard caught sight of him and smiled an invitation. 'Ah, Mr Warren, you've not met our distinguished guest yet, Miss Stefanie de Winter.'

She extended her hand, hoping that the trembling was not noticeable. Warren touched her fingers lightly and bowed courteously. He was more charming up close, a few silver hairs on his temples, older than she had taken him to be, but that only made him more alluring.

'Miss de Winter, great opportunities await a gifted musician such as you.'

She searched her mind for something impressive to say, and instead cursed herself for being so tongue-tied.

'De Winter? Do you have a brother who plays rugby?' Warren asked.

Her heart sank. If the altercation of a year previously, when Martin had been in Pretoria, had been personal, she could wish her dreams goodbye, but if she were to get to know Paul Warren, it would be impossible to hide Martin. 'Yes, my brother, Martin. He's reading Law at Cambridge. Have you met him, Mr Warren?'

He returned her smile and her heart leapt. 'Yes, I had the pleasure of running out against him. It was quite an experience. Will he practise law in Pretoria on his return?'

'Yes … well, politics is more his line. He'll be in the Attorney General's office.'

'I dined with your brother and his friends – a doctor, if I remember correctly, and another young man, on the train from Cape Town last year.'

'My cousins, Dr Henderson and his brother.'

Warren's eyebrows shot up. 'You have British cousins?'

'My mother is English, Mr Warren.' She was about to tell him that Mary was the daughter of the late Sir John Stewart, but checked herself.

Her host came to offer his arm to escort her in to dinner. The conversation centred on the social life in the colony, horse races and trips to Europe. She thought how her stubbornness had almost prevented her from being there. She did not like playing at private parties. She preferred the acclaim of the concert stage. When Leonard had begged her to perform for his guests, she'd doubled her fee in the hope of putting him off, but he had accepted without demur. And judging by the applause, she was likely to be invited again. Performing in Johannesburg entailed a stay overnight. She took the train from Pretoria, and at the station there was always a grand hansom sent for her from the luxurious Heights Hotel.

'You have not played in Cape Town yet, Miss de Winter?' A lady from lower down the table broke into her thoughts.

'Not yet, but I will do so early in the coming year. I'm giving up my teaching post at the convent to further my studies under Herr Manfred von Hochstadt.'

'How fortunate! I would not want to miss a single performance,' Warren said.

'Do you visit Cape Town often, Mr Warren?' Stefanie prayed for an affirmative. His answer almost made her shout with excitement.

'Cape Town is my home. I live in Rondebosch.'

SHE LEFT while the men were having cigars and port and the ladies gossiping in the drawing room over cups of coffee. She reached the hotel in an exalted state. The future had never beckoned so impatiently.

She undressed, seated herself at the mirror and brushed her long hair. He was not married! A close friend of the Prime Minister! An Oxford graduate, a lawyer! She had unashamedly wheedled the information from Mrs Leonard.

'*Hartjie*, a beautiful thing God has given us,' Tante Koba had said, 'the way each of us finds our mate. The right man will come along. You will feel it in your body first and then, should he be the right man, he will creep into your heart.'

And now the right man had come along. At the dinner table, she had looked at his hands and noted the manicured fingernails, the heavy gold ring on his right hand. Hands were so much of one's character; in hands were power, feeling, power to induce feeling. She experienced that in her music. She closed her eyes and imagined his hands touching her breasts and thighs.

She *had* to see him again. He would take an interest in her, and not just in her music. She had to play her cards right, as James would have said. She would go to Mrs Heys, who lived in the beautiful Melrose House, a few blocks away from Koba, and beg her to teach her everything the perfect society wife should know.

She climbed into bed, her heart filled with dreams of glamour and love, ignoring Mrs Leonard's parting words: Mr Warren is not the marrying kind.

Glorious and Impressive Affairs

A T FIRST NO GOSSIP was forthcoming about the relationship between the well-known Boer and the only daughter of Lord Fairfield. Then, at formal occasions, it was impossible to ignore the familiar way in which they conversed and the scarcely concealed smiles exchanged across the rooms. Soon Martin and Victoria found inquisitive eyes watching their every move and listening to their every word. They took great care always to include Charles when they were in London, but the need to be alone, to laugh, to talk unrestrictedly, was uppermost in their minds. They found reasons to visit places further away from London, their meetings secretive and, although never voiced, bordering on those of lovers who had been denied their liberty.

Lovers we are not, Martin thought as he paced the platform at Cambridge waiting for the London train bringing Victoria. But they were both playing a game that could have far-reaching repercussions. He had not seen her since the previous weekend, when they had watched James and Peter Radford playing cricket at Sandhurst. She had been in the company of her parents, General Henderson and George Hunter. He had, however, managed to see her alone for a few seconds and had invited her for a picnic on the banks of the Cam.

They had never discussed the reason they met in these faraway places. Even their usual long discussions on Africa and her love for India were not mentioned any more. It was as if they had both decided that if the future was not theirs to share, it was not worth discussing.

Martin forced himself to face the truth. *She's British and I'm going home, home to the Boer girl of my dreams. This is only a passing infatuation.* But the reasoning rang false when she smiled through the window as the train steamed into the station.

The sky was cloudless, not a breath of wind stirring the willows on the banks. As he guided their punt down the slow winding river, his eyes travelled over the college spires and turrets and the Backs, where students sprawled on the grass, their books in forgotten heaps beside them. Punts drifted past, the parasols of ladies like enormous flowers floating on the water, swans following and squawking.

No parasol for Vicky – instead, a wide-brimmed straw hat with colourful ribbons.

'Take off your hat, Vicky. Let's see the sun in your hair.'

She laughed and undid the bow that held back her hair. It tumbled over her shoulders, the sun turning it into a red-gold flame.

'Like the mane of a lion in his prime. I love your hair, Vicky.'

'Dark honey and now a lion's mane?' She looked up at him, wrinkling her nose. 'Will you be at the Summer Ball tonight?'

'Yes, Lady Beatrice saw to that. So I shall have to repay her with a dance. But I won't fill in any cards until I've seen yours.'

THEY SPREAD the rug on the grass under a willow and set out the hamper. He opened the wine and handed her a glass.

'It's a beautiful spot. Do you come here often?' she asked.

His eyes went to the river flowing under the overhanging branches of the willows. It was indeed a peaceful scene, a scene he had watched changing with the seasons every year.

'Yes, this place is special to me. I come here when I need time away from my books and when the urge to go home becomes too much.'

'Is that why we're here today? Is the urge on you again?' she asked lightly, but he saw a touch of sadness in her eyes.

He took her hand in his. 'I brought you here to share this place. I knew you'd like it.'

'I simply love it, but you're evading my question, Martin.'

'I want to get home, but not yet, not today anyway. I love being with you, Vicky.'

She selected a sandwich from the spread and held out her glass for more wine. 'If the Boers are opposed to having foreigners in their country, how will Charles fit in?'

'We need trained people. Charles made his mark during his last visit and is quite popular in our district.'

'How would I be received? I mean, should I decide to pay a visit to Pretoria, what would the attitude be towards me?'

He looked up sharply, alarmed at the course their conversation was taking. 'Don't play with words, Vicky.'

'Answer my question.'

'Vicky, I … we've never spoken about this …' He looked away to escape her gaze. How to tell her that the life he had worked for all these lonely years and which was about to become a reality, could not include her? He chose his words carefully. 'As a visitor, you'd be treated with the utmost courtesy.'

'Now you're being evasive.' She stretched out on her back, resting her head on her arms.

The filtered sunlight threw shadows on her face and danced in her hair where it lay spread out around her head. He looked at the curve of her cheek, flushed from the sun and the wine, the faint freckles on her nose, the pulse beating at the base of her throat. His gaze paused on her breasts, accentuated by her uplifted arms. As always, he resisted a strong urge to reach out and touch her beautiful hair.

'Is there a girl waiting for you at home?' she asked.

'Not actually waiting. Our neighbour's daughter, Annecke. She's still at school. Why all these questions?'

'I love you, Martin.' She stretched out her hand, tracing the outline of his mouth. It was an invitation that he had to resist but, overpowered by his need for her, was unable to do. He gathered her hair into his hands and brought it to his face, and through her hair, he kissed her eyes and then found her mouth. The pent-up passion of weeks spilled over into a kiss so forceful and intense that it left them breathless.

With a supreme effort he pulled away, took her hands and held them tightly while trying to bring his emotions under control. After a while, he stood up and walked to the edge of the river, cursing. The sun, the wine and being alone: he had nearly ruined his future, and hers. And she was willing to let him do that. He made up his mind that he would not see her alone again. He cleared his throat nervously and folded his arms across his chest. 'I apologise for my behaviour, Vicky. I'd no right to force my attentions on you.'

'I gave you reason enough. I want you too.'

He wanted to tell her about the days and nights that he thought only of her. He wanted to explain that his career did not take preference over his love for her. But he said the words that needed to be said. 'I'm going back to my country. To my people.'

She sat quietly for a while. Then she smiled up at him. 'Come, we have to go. I need time to dress for the ball. You still have a few months in England. There's no reason not to enjoy them.'

THE LIGHT OF A DOZEN CHANDELIERS sparkled on exquisite ballroom dresses, gentlemen dressed in formal attire and the striking uniforms of military men. Servants moved silently between the guests offering champagne and sherry on silver trays. An orchestra was playing, the music unobtrusive and not inhibiting conversation.

Victoria arrived in the company of her parents, fully aware of her mother's disapproval. She wore a sleeveless gown of a brilliant red and in her hair had plaited thin strings of silver cord. One of the famous pieces of Fairfield jewellery adorned her throat: five fiery rubies joined by a string of diamonds, all equal in size and brilliance.

She smiled in acknowledgement of polite greetings as her eyes slowly searched the room for Martin. She spotted him in the company of Charles and a few others. Their eyes met across the crowded room and stayed riveted on each other in open admiration. She tore her gaze away when George Hunter arrived at her side, demanding her dance card.

'You may have the second number, if you like,' she smiled. 'I've promised the first and the supper dance.'

'To De Winter, I suppose,' he said frowning. 'Victoria, you're taking it too far. This will surely cause a scandal. De Winter can handle this, but he's leaving the country soon and you'll have to face the repercussions alone. You know how judgmental people can be here. This is not Bangalore.'

'I don't care, George,' she said. 'Mr de Winter is a good dancer, I want to enjoy myself. Do you like my dress?'

Hunter smiled ruefully. 'Victoria, what is the De Winter fellow to you? Do you find him amusing? Exotic perhaps?' He saw Martin and Charles approaching them. 'Dr Henderson, De Winter,' he greeted with a tight bow, his eyes boring into Martin's.

'You look splendid, Victoria. The most exquisite rubies I've ever set eyes on,' Charles said to break the charged silence that had ensued.

'Thank you, Charles. Mother laid out a pure white creation for me, but I just couldn't. These jewels, they need this dress, don't you agree?'

Martin studied her dress with interest. 'Red. Fire in your veins tonight?'

Hunter flushed at this intimate remark and turned away.

Martin took Victoria's card. 'Which number do you prefer?'

'The first is a waltz and the supper dance?'

'Are you free?'

'I was hoping you'd ask,' she laughed softly.

THEY MADE AN ELEGANT PAIR as they glided effortlessly over the floor. The lights of the chandeliers caught the rubies at her throat and threw sparks of blazing colour in her hair and on her bare shoulders. The flaming red dress gave a subtle hint of provocative sensuality. Overpowered by the soft flutter of her eyelashes and the sensuous sway of her body, his eyes could not leave her face. They danced in silence, charged with heady emotion, oblivious of the sidelong glances they attracted.

The waltz came to an end and he handed her to George Hunter. Stepping outside the French doors onto the balcony, he thought about Vicky. She might become Lady Hunter, he thought, with anguish in his heart. But then, in time to come, I might be a president. He found no comfort in the thought, only an intense yearning. He was still standing there when the supper dance was announced. Turning to go inside, he found her waiting at the door. She sensed his unhappiness and wordlessly offered her hand.

'Say you love me, Martin,' she whispered as they circled the ballroom. 'I won't hold you to it; just say it.'

'What purpose would it serve? What purpose …' his voice was unsteady, tailing off into silence, overcome by futility.

'I want to hear you say it, just once.' Her eyes were large and unnaturally bright.

'I love you, Vicky,' he said.

'Thank you,' she whispered.

He looked at the faint freckles on her nose and the hurt in her green eyes and realised that he had to put an end to this agony. He could not endure it a moment longer. 'We can't go on meeting,' he said, sadly but firmly. 'What happened at the river today … we almost … one more hour, one more meeting like that, and we'll not be friends, we'll become lovers.'

'And that's not allowed in the life you have chosen,' she asked, looking him straight in the eyes.

His feet lost the rhythm as he stared at her in bewilderment. 'Vicky! You don't know what you are suggesting,' he whispered and released her abruptly. They stood apart, their eyes not leaving each other's faces, oblivious of the couples staring at them. 'Should it come to that,' he said heatedly, 'there would be no way out. You are British; I cannot marry you. And to just take you and leave you? I was not brought up that way.'

'We love each other, Martin, we—'

'And love conquers all? Is that what you think?'

'It might! It will!'

'Not in the world in which I live,' he retorted angrily. 'And not in yours either.'

'You are a hypocrite! You only adhere to rules where they concern your precious country.'

He became aware of people staring at them. He took her arm and steered her across the floor towards a door. 'I'm going back to Cambridge. Now! My final paper is in a mess. We can meet in public, with Charles or James glued to our sides, or Hunter if you like, but I will not meet with you alone again.'

As they reached the door, Hunter appeared. 'Your mother requests your presence at supper, Victoria,' he said, his moustache bristling with rage. He took her elbow and, with a fierce glance at Martin, steered her away.

FOR TWO MONTHS he avoided London and Victoria. Two dreadful months. He was haunted by the smell of her hair, the taste of the wine on her lips and the softness of her breasts against him. He could not sleep. He would leave his room and pace the college grounds. And in the mornings he was bad-tempered, his eyes scratchy. His work suffered.

He tried to think about home. There winter was almost over. The sky would be deep blue and the grass brown. The coral trees would soon blossom, bright red flowers like splashes of blood against the winter sky. And Annecke would turn fifteen this summer. He tried to think of loving Annecke, but all he wanted, needed, was the passion, the love, of Victoria. And he knew he was wise not going to London. To resist her was no longer in his power.

However, he received an invitation he could not refuse. Charles delivered it personally. James and his fellow subalterns would receive their commissions at a ceremony to be held in London. Martin had *two weeks*, Charles warned, to get rid of his self-inflicted wretchedness and place his personal problems second to James's most important day.

'The sooner you face up to the fact that you two are not meant for each other, the sooner you'll come to terms with it,' Charles said. 'You simply can't spend the rest of your time in England avoiding Victoria and society.' He took him by the arm and hoisted him to his feet. 'Come now. We're going to have a couple of ales and find something to eat.'

They set off to The Mill, a favourite student haunt that served plain but excellent food. Charles, who was by now a familiar face to Martin's fellow students, was asked for news from various happenings in London. He obliged as he followed Martin carrying the tankards to an unoccupied table in a corner.

'I should've gone home after graduation,' Martin said as they settled down. 'Common law confounds me. It's not practised in the Transvaal.'

'It will be to your advantage when you deal with your colleagues in the Cape and Natal. That's why you chose to do it,' Charles reminded him, and turned to lighter news. 'I received a letter from Stefanie last week. She writes that she has engagements for concerts every weekend and has been to Bloemfontein twice. James had a letter from Karel—'

'A letter from Karel? He never writes to me.'

'It appears that the twins keep up a regular correspondence with James, mostly about their horses. Karel has won two first prizes in the show in Rustenburg with Legend, but Rudolf none—'

He broke off. Martin followed his gaze and found James, dressed in uniform, weaving his way through the tables crowded with drinking students.

'Thought I'd find you chained to the books!' James took a place at the table. 'I'm positively dying of thirst!'

They ordered a meal and another round of beers, but James settled for brandy. 'Big parade coming up. You'll grace us with your presence, Martin?'

'I'll be there, cousin.'

'You're supposed to be in London,' Charles said. 'I thought Father sent for you. Yet again.'

'I've been to London, dear brother.' James indicated his uniform. 'The General was fit to be tied.'

Their meal arrived – steak and kidney pie with some boiled greens. James frowned at the food and pushed his plate away. 'Have you been studying too hard, Martin? You look ill.'

'I've been busy.' Martin waved a greeting to some friends. 'You've not told us why the General was so angry.'

'Oh, nothing much. Hunter's been telling tales again.'

Martin was aware of the animosity between the two officers, but had not realised that it ran this deep. 'So what's it this time? Gambling? Drunk and disorderly? Insubordination? Womanising?'

'Three of those combined!' James laughed. 'Had a mess formal last week – commemoration of Waterloo. Radford dressed me up as Napoleon. I made a late entry with a lusty Josephine hanging on to my arm. She was a bit under the weather, I think. She tripped and her cloak slipped open …'

'And what was she wearing?'

'Not a damn thing. It had to be a realistic portrayal of history, Radford insisted. It was brilliant, simply brilliant! You should've seen Colonel Hawthorne's face. Lieutenant-Colonel Butcher, kindly fellow that he is, had to assist the poor old man to a chair.'

'James how is it that you have not been expelled yet?'

James ordered another round of drinks. 'Cousin, I am *the General's* son.'

Martin knew that it was only a half-truth. James took the army seriously, and his exploits were largely innocent fun, yet it was clear that he persisted simply to annoy his father.

'There was some talk after the Summer Ball,' James said, looking pointedly at Martin. 'It appears that Vicky has once again flouted convention. Hunter blames you. He's furious!'

Charles raised his voice over the noise of the students. 'Hunter has nothing on Martin. Vicky, as you say, follows her own rules. We missed you at the Ball.'

'Radford had an accident; took a tumble from an untrained charger. A few cracked ribs and a sprained ankle. I … well, I have to avoid London for a while.'

'I see,' Martin said, wondering whose wife had seduced James this time.

'Vicky will miss you two awfully when you leave. Hunter spends a lot of time in London these days. Lady Fairfield made a fuss over him when they visited Sandhurst last week. Looks as if he's the chosen one,' James said.

A stab of jealousy shot through Martin's heart. He felt Charles's eyes steadying him. James, he realised, was unaware of his relationship with Victoria.

The next morning, Charles and James caught the first train south. Martin, bleary-eyed and immensely tired, climbed the stairs to his room. Two weeks. London and Victoria. Hunter, the chosen one. He contemplated the mountain of notes and books and in a fit of temper swept them off the desk.

———◆———

'IMPRESSIVE, YES, but glorious?' Charles said. He and Martin were standing with officers from various regiments, generals from the War Office, politicians and members of the gentry watching the 2nd Hussars parade past. Martin scanned the officers, dressed in their regimental regalia of blue and gold, dazzling in their tight-fitting uniforms, ramrod stiff on their chargers. Peter Radford, Mark Sinclair, William Moore, Captain Murray Shaw. Men he had befriended since James had joined the army. How different their worlds were. Insulated by their wealth and privileged position, they lived carelessly, whereas he had to guard every step he took. And not for the first time he found himself envious of their carefree lives.

'Well, our presence is not required tonight,' Charles said almost gleefully. 'Mess formal for them, theatre for us.'

When the ceremony was over, Charles left, saying that he had to see a patient. Martin followed the invited guests to the hall where refreshments were laid on. He scanned the assembly, and his gaze found the Fairfields. Victoria stood a few paces behind her parents, George Hunter at her side. She wore a dress of ivory silk, her hair done up in fashionable curls, but her eyes were sad and dispirited. He guiltily averted his gaze and went to find General and Mrs Henderson.

James arrived, saluted his father and reached for a glass from a passing waiter. Martin had not seen him in full ceremonial dress before – black breeches tapering into gleaming cavalry boots, the blue fronted tunic decorated with gold and black braid, embellished sabretache, lieutenant's insignia on the shoulder straps. The plumed shako added a good few inches to his height. His half-smile made the dimples visible, accentuating his devilish charm, as Charles would have it.

Peter Radford and his family approached. Peter, for once neatly trimmed and turned out, saluted General Henderson.

Martin had met the Earl of Waltham and his family on a previous occasion and again he was struck by the Countess's exceptional beauty. It was clear from whom Peter had inherited his looks – his angel face, as Koba would say. Lord Radford came across as an affectionate man. If rumours were to be believed, he had been just as wild in his youth as his son was now. Peter's older brother, Christopher, a well-known horse breeder, was discussing hunters with James. A heavy, gloved hand on James's shoulder interrupted them.

Captain Murray Shaw, tall and heavy-set, smiled at them. He would have been better suited for the dragoons, the heavy cavalry, Martin had heard General Henderson say once.

'Welcome to the regiment, Lieutenant Henderson, Lieutenant Radford. Pleased that you've made it, notwithstanding the number of times you visited the C.O.'s office for, shall we say, outstanding achievements in the field of revelry,' Shaw said.

'And how generously you've assisted us, Captain Shaw,' Peter said.

'We have not reached the height of our abilities in that field yet, sir,' James said.

'As from today, you find yourselves in my regiment and I shall not tolerate any more irresponsible behaviour from the two of you,' General Henderson bristled.

Beatrice Harcourt, for once with her husband at her side, joined the family group. Lord Harcourt disentangled himself from his young wife's grip and joined his brother. James made his escape while his father and uncle discussed a visit to the Harcourt estate the coming weekend.

Beatrice hooked her hand through Martin's arm and pulled him aside.

'You're leaving England soon?'

'Yes, a paper due in two months and then home, after the New Year.'

'Victoria is not for you,' Beatrice said, toying with her glass. 'A pity, I think you make a magnificent pair. Rules, however, can be overstepped if done in the acceptable way.'

'Not in the world I live in, Lady Harcourt.'

'Yes, so I've been told.' Martin looked at her sharply, but she continued unperturbed, 'I'm afraid you've humiliated her, Martin.'

Martin's eyes searched for Victoria again. She was still on George Hunter's arm, her mother on her other side, talking their way through the crowd, moving towards General Henderson's group.

'Have you ever been to Italy? To Florence?' Beatrice said. 'Michelangelo's *David*?' Martin followed her gaze to where James and Peter stood. 'Was he fair- or dark-haired, I wonder? I'd like to think of him as dark-haired.'

'Beatrice, James has enough trouble as it is.'

'I was merely making a comparison.' She smiled and, lowering her voice, said, 'Your cousin's romantic exploits are not exactly a secret. He's a very desirable man, I believe, and has the rare quality of not getting emotionally involved. But he drinks far too much, Martin. He's getting careless. People talk. Please warn him. It wouldn't be proper for me to say anything.'

With that she left. He was still thinking about her remark when he saw the Fairfield party moving closer. He decided to leave. Coming face to face with Victoria, with Hunter at her side, was more than he could bear.

The Ballad of the Far-away Soldier

*T*HE *FAR-AWAY SOLDIER* was popular among London theatregoers, Charles told Martin. People from all walks of life were flocking to see the show. Most of his friends said that they went away with a feeling that they'd witnessed something that knew no class barriers: war and love.

Charles had promised to escort Beatrice to the theatre, as Lord Harcourt was spending the night at his club. 'A frequent occurrence after six months of wedded bliss,' Charles said. 'Or old habits, I suppose?'

When they arrived at their seats, they found George Hunter and Victoria seated near them. Her dress was of rose chiffon and watered silk, cut low to expose the swell of her breasts, her hair done up in curls. Martin tried to still the conflict of emotions rising in his chest: the guilt at seeing the misery in Victoria's eyes as they tried to avoid his; the passion that her nearness created; and the jealousy towards Hunter. Their eyes met for a brief but intense moment.

Confused and depressed, he turned his attention to the stage. The gaiety of the first act gave way to more sombre emotions in the second, when the soldiers bade farewell to their sweethearts and sailed for distant battlefields. The audience was swept up in scenes of battle, destruction and death. The final act brought a measure of relief when the soldiers returned home to greet their loved ones.

One girl was left standing forlornly, looking in the direction from which the soldiers had come. The lights grew dim and the audience was drawn into her lonely world of waiting for a soldier who would never return. The closing song, 'Ballad for a Far-away Soldier', told of a love that was to be carried in moonbeams and starlight to a far-off land, a love that would be kept alive in memory. The audience united in applause that was hesitant at first and then grew into thunderous intensity.

The passionate longing in the song gave Martin a glimpse of what life would be like without Victoria. He knew that he could not bear it, could not allow her to become a bittersweet memory. He thought how the future would be for her – married to George Hunter, living in England, a cold, wet country that was not her real home. And all at once nothing was important any more but to rescue her from that world, to love her and erase the sadness from her eyes.

'How enchanting,' Beatrice declared, gathering her reticule and glasses. 'I've had some supper prepared for us. Quite informal.'

Martin did not want to sit through a meal, especially not through one of Beatrice's long drawn-out affairs, where the conversation invariably revolved around society gossip, hunting, horse racing and weekends in the country.

He told Charles that he preferred to walk home. Hugging his coat close against the drizzle, he started out for the Fairfield residence. He reasoned with himself as he walked. His father had returned from his studies in Cape Town with an English wife, and *he* had made it to the Volksraad. There was nothing to stop him from doing the same. And if it were not to be, he would adjust his plans to his and Victoria's needs.

He arrived at the Fairfield residence, his breath racing. All was in darkness except for the light in the foyer. He settled under the chestnut tree opposite the house but it was long after midnight when George Hunter brought Victoria home. He did not stay long. When the carriage turned the corner, Martin hastened down the drive.

VICTORIA WAS HALFWAY up the staircase when the front door opened. Martin stood in the foyer, his damp hair glistening in the low gaslights, his eyes filled with purpose. She placed her hand on the banister and waited.

'Will you marry me, Vicky? Come home with me?' he asked.

She caught her breath sharply. Looking at him now, she realised that she would abandon everything – parents, inheritance, country – to be with him. In her dreams, she had long ago traded India for Africa, for a little town called Rustenburg and a farm nestling at the foot of a beautiful mountain. Guilt caught at her heart. *How can you destroy a future so bright, so promising?* Charles had pleaded with her after the Summer Ball. *If you truly love him, can't you find it in your heart to allow him to fulfil his destiny?*

Martin was still looking at her steadily. 'I'll be here tomorrow to speak for us, Vicky.'

There was a note of defeat in his voice and it pierced her heart. *If he can't have me forever, he shall have me for one night, the memory of one night to carry us through whatever lies ahead.* She stood for a while longer and then stretched out her hand to him. He took it wordlessly.

'Stay with me tonight,' she whispered.

As they climbed the wide staircase and walked down the passage to her bedroom, Charles's warning came back to her. *You're playing with fire, Vicky, the Boers are passionate, earthy people and Martin is no exception.*

AS HE REMOVED her clothes, all the pent-up passion, kept in control for so long, flowed from him. He whispered repeatedly that he loved her and always would. But unbidden images swam through his mind. President Kruger's disapproving face was in her hair as it tumbled over her breasts. His family's beloved faces shouted 'treason' as he moved his hands over her hips. And as he laid her on the bed and moved her legs apart, her hands on his naked back felt like blows of the *sjambok*.

And he had never before felt so vulnerable.

THE FOLLOWING afternoon, Martin stood in Lord Fairfield's study. Conflicting emotions assailed him; he felt guilt at having betrayed the trust of his people, anxiety for the future and elation at the passion still lingering in his body. But overriding all this was his love for Victoria, and he refused to think beyond that.

Lord Fairfield stood with his back to the fireplace, staring at Martin through narrowed eyes, the air pregnant with animosity and suspicion.

Martin took a deep breath. How to tell Lord Fairfield that his heirs would have Boer blood and grow up in Africa? He decided to launch straight in. 'I spent last night with your daughter, sir. I am here to ask for her hand in marriage.'

The effects of his words were profound. Lord Fairfield's mouth dropped open, his face turned puce, the anger in his eyes terrible.

'You, a Boer, seduced my daughter!'

'I did not seduce her, sir. She loves me as deeply as I love her.'

He rang for the butler and ordered him to summon Victoria. They waited in silence, Lord Fairfield pacing the length of the room. After what seemed an eternity, the door opened and Victoria stepped inside. She was ashen-faced, her eyes swollen. She had obviously been crying for hours.

'Mr de Winter is asking permission to marry you. Naturally I refuse to give—'

'I'm honoured by Mr de Winter's proposal,' Victoria interrupted, her voice so strained that she could hardly get the words out, 'but I cannot accept.'

Martin stared at her in bewilderment. Her green eyes were agonised, but in them he saw her resolution. He searched for words that would assure her, but they caught in his throat.

With great effort, he straightened his shoulders and walked out of the room, down the long passage and into the open. The late afternoon light was weak. His feet rang hollow on the cobbled drive as he walked out the gate. Chestnut leaves swirled around his feet, crunched under his boots as he walked blindly, not knowing or caring where he went. He walked desperately, his head bent against the wind that had sprung up from the west. The pain in his soul turned to anger at betrayal. But the anger turned back to pain and despair. With each step he became more confused, and he lengthened his stride until he broke into a run.

Dawn found him heading for Cambridge. His body was numb with cold and fatigue, but his mind was clear. When least expected, fate had stumbled into his life. Everything sacred, the very heart of his life, had been plunged into a whirlpool of passion. For a while he had managed to stay on the edge, but unwillingly had been dragged into the centre. Had Koba's jealous God seen a brilliant future and decided to put an end to it? Or had there been one more test, one more obstacle, to overcome? Or was it to prove that he was as fallible, as human as God had intended man to be?

No, there's only one reality; I betrayed my country and my people by wanting a British woman for my wife.

Through the early winter months, he worked for weeks on end. He sat in his room by the small fire and spent hours staring out of his window. The sky was no longer blue, the Cam murky with autumn leaves. The willows hung naked, mute in their acquiescence to nature. At night, when all was quiet except for the wind and the rain against the windows, he would abandon his books and heap more coal on the fire. In the blue flames he saw images of his home, the sun-drenched mountain, the dusty summer sunsets and the harvest ripening in the fields.

He shuddered as he thought of the madness that had taken hold of his body and soul. Like the black eagles soaring high and free on the air currents over his beloved mountain, the fire inside him had soared out of control. From the soft blue glow of the coals, Koba's face would comfort him, her eyes brimming with love. 'The eagles,' she would whisper, 'always find their way back to their nests.'

CHARLES WAS THE ONLY VISITOR Martin allowed. By silent agreement, they avoided talking about the reason for his melancholy and instead discussed their travelling arrangements and the situation in

Johannesburg. He offered to see to the gifts Martin had planned on buying for his family and to wind up his affairs in London. When the weather lifted, they went for long walks through the wintry countryside. Martin, who had always been fit and strong, tired quickly.

Charles was alarmed at his poor physical condition but he refrained from comment. Martin had enough to cope with. He was thankful that James's regiment was away on manoeuvres in Scotland. He had heard the gossip flying around London, and was relieved that the Fairfields had not mentioned Martin's marriage proposal. George Hunter, however, had heard about it from Lady Fairfield's maid.

When Martin's work was done, Charles arrived at his rooms in Cambridge in the early morning. Determined not to return to London, Martin had taken Peter Radford up on his offer of spending the Christmas season at his place, and Charles had offered to deliver Martin there. They packed a trunk with the clothes he would need for his stay and for the journey home. Books, clothes, sports equipment and framed photographs of his years at Cambridge all went into tea chests, to be sent to Southampton.

Charles checked the labels on the luggage and nodded, satisfied. 'Two weeks and we'll be on our way. The journey might be stormy, especially the first part.'

Martin looked out the window at the snow-covered fields. 'At least it's summer in Rustenburg. This has been the coldest winter I've yet experienced.'

Charles searched his mind for something cheerful to say, but the news he had was not particularly good. He cleared his throat, adjusted his spectacles and flicked at imaginary dust on his trousers. 'Lady Fairfield thought it necessary for Victoria to attend a finishing school. She left for Switzerland last week and will be away for a year.'

Martin looked up sharply. 'A year? Is she … please tell me the truth, Charles.'

'No, she's not.'

'The snow will smother her soul,' Martin said, staring out the window again. 'And Hunter? Is he the chosen one?'

'The 5th Hussars have been posted to the Sudan. General Kitchener proposes to avenge the death of General Gordon once and for all. George Hunter will be absent from London for some time. It will allow Victoria time to adjust to her future.' He had seen her off at the station when she and a chaperone had left for Switzerland, and it was clear that she was suffering in the same way as Martin. 'She asked that you forgive her, Martin,' he said and waited, but there was no answer. He placed his hand on Martin's arm. 'I have a confession to make. Some time ago, after the Summer Ball, I told her about the future awaiting you in Pretoria.

By refusing to marry you, she has given you back your future, your life. Don't judge her too harshly.'

'I know.' Martin met Charles's eyes. 'Thank you for caring so much, cousin, about me, and about my future.'

New Year's Eve, 1895

STEFANIE SAT ON the stoep at Wintersrust and fanned herself lazily. It was past noon and the heat was unbearable. It shimmered on the veld, danced on the corrugated-iron roofs of the outbuildings. A blue-green haze enveloped the mountain, and high above the cliffs the black eagles hung motionless in the air currents.

There had been little rain in the spring, none in the early summer. Still, the earth and the ploughed fields waited. The flowers in her mother's garden were wilting although they had been watered that morning. The fruit trees cast shade over the furrows between them, the water gurgling invitingly. She longed to dangle her feet in the water, as she had done as a child, but the thought of someone watching restrained her.

Nothing seemed to stir in the pressing heat except her restlessness. After meeting Paul Warren, the future had looked promising, but now there was a shadow hovering, threatening to engulf her like a summer cloud. Although Paul had been in the front row at the Theatre Royal when she performed there, he hadn't inquired after her. He had come for the music, but not for her.

Patience, patience. Tomorrow a new year begins; time to prepare for the journey to Cape Town. At least rehearsals would pass the time.

She fetched her hat and made her way to the drift, where a number of families camped for the festive season. Rifle shots cracked through the air, startling her. She shielded her eyes with the brim of her hat and looked to where the men were accustoming the horses to rifle fire. They had been doing that for days, but still the racket caught her unawares. Wild rumours were about: the Outlanders, frustrated at their inferior status, were ready to rise and take Pretoria by force. But the New Year was upon them and nothing had happened.

At the drift the tables sagged under delicacies of all kinds, while water boiled in large kettles over open fires. The smaller children splashed noisily in the stream. The men would arrive shortly and the games would start: tug-of-war, *jukskei*, races and target practice. Tonight they would dance under the stars. There would be drinking, laughing and eating, and couples would slip off into the dark.

'My pretty flower,' Koba beamed a welcome at Stefanie. 'Did you have a nice rest, *hartjie*?'

'Stefanie, there you are,' her mother said. 'Come, give us a hand; we have so much to do.'

'What? And ruin her soft white hands?' Ester Viljoen said. She had still not found a husband, and her loose ways were an embarrassment to her family. Her brothers had instructed their wives to keep a close eye on her, and now it was the turn of Hannie, Jan Viljoen's wife.

'Ester!' Hannie said, giving her a warning look.

Stefanie took a seat next to the heavily pregnant Lena Maree, who was expecting her second child. Lena had settled into married life on Soetvlei and did what Boer women did – run a home, see to the chickens and kitchen garden, and care for her child and husband. Buks surely was fortunate in having the placid Lena for his wife.

Mary and Lettie Maree were chatting continuously, making the most of the company of the women of the district. The Viljoen women and Koba changed topics in mid-sentence – ailments, cures, recipes, chicken feed, childbirth – while keeping a sharp eye on the wayward Ester.

Jan Viljoen's roar announced the arrival of the men. They smelled of horses, perspiration and the sun. 'The Outlanders can come; we are waiting for them,' he said to no one in particular and took the coffee from his wife with a playful slap on her rump.

'They will not leave their fleshpots to give us a little fight,' said his brother Jacob.

'And if they come?' Buks Maree picked up his son, who was playing at Lena's feet.

'They don't have weapons, no cannon. They make war with their mouths,' Frans Viljoen said. 'Loud mouths, that's all they seem to be.'

'And even on that score they'll not beat us. One lashing from Jan Viljoen's tongue and they will surrender unconditionally.' Joep Maree laughed and the others joined in.

'But Jan Viljoen knows what he's talking about. And that's where the difference lies. I speak from within. From here!' Jan placed his sunburnt hand on his heart. 'Their words are written by the lords who sit in the palace with the Queen.'

'What will you say to them, Jan? What words of wisdom will you use?' Marthinus asked.

'Uncle Marthinus, I will not waste my wise words on them. I won't even have to show my rifle. This is what I'll do!' He placed his hands on his knees and let out a roar, startling the dogs stretched out in the shade. His laugh, equally loud, reverberated through the air.

Stefanie sighed. Men, horses, rifles, war.

THE GAMES, FUN AND LAUGHTER carried on through the hot afternoon. Loud encouragement and wild shouting marked the progress of *stoktrek*, a game in which the challenger had to get the better of his opponent not only with sheer strength but also shrewdness. When it came down to the last game, the two strongest men were left, and everyone gathered to watch Joep Maree steal the honour from Jan Viljoen. Cries of disappointment came from the Viljoen supporters, roars of approval from the Maree camp.

'*Magtig*, Uncle Joep, you're getting stronger every year! You outwitted me with that last pull.' Jan heaved himself from the ground, spitting dust from his mouth. He shook Joep's hand and shouted to the onlookers. 'As strong as an ox and as cunning as an old lion! Joep Maree from Soetvlei is once again the winner and I, Jan Viljoen from Vrede, am humbled in the presence of such strength!'

Dusk brought a refreshing breeze from the mountain. The women fetched their evening clothes from the wagons and departed to the house to change for the evening's dancing. The young men dressed in their best shirts and waistcoats. The older ones splashed water on their faces and arms, combed their hair and got ready for the evening.

Koba busied herself setting out the food for the evening. She saw Annecke linger and called her over. 'Is something bothering you, little one?' She put her arm around Annecke's shoulders. 'What seems to be the problem? There's nothing that Tante Koba can't fix, you know.'

She nodded wistfully and moved into her arms. 'Tante Koba, no one has asked me for the first waltz and I'm almost fifteen.'

'Oh dear, now that's a problem, but not one that can't be fixed.'

'Maybe I'm not pretty.'

'No, no,' Koba tut-tutted. 'You're the prettiest girl I've ever set eyes on. Yes, dear Stefanie is also pretty, but in a different way. Now, let me think … why don't you dance with Rudi or Karel?'

'Tante Koba, which one? I can't dance with them both at the same time.'

Koba pondered Annecke's predicament. She had thought that the growing-up process would separate her from the twins the way it usually separated boys and girls, but the bond between the three was as strong as ever. To ask her to choose between the twins for a silly thing like a dance would be to hasten the day when she would have to choose for the most important reason in her life. And that the choice would be one of the twins was certain.

'I wish Martin was back. He would've asked me,' Annecke said.

'Listen, *hartjie*, put on your blue dress, the one with the tiny white flowers. Tante Koba will think a little.' She sent her on her way.

Martin was not the man for Annecke. He was not a stranger to a woman's bed. It was there in his eyes, in his hands and in the way he moved his body when he danced. She'd seen it at Buks Maree's wedding, when he and the cousins were visiting the last time. Yes, he was a man of the world and Annecke would not live up to his expectations.

'Rudolf! Karel! Come here!' She called to them where they were helping Gert Vermaas peg out the canvas on the ground for the dancing. Martin had looked the same at their age; so had her brother Marthinus. Yes, that they had the De Winter physical characteristics – the dark blue eyes and wide shoulders – was clear, but that was where it ended. The twins were secretive, not allowing anyone into their little world. Annecke and herself, yes, but they were not loving with their parents or any other adults. They would get into trouble and fight instead of talking their way out, as Marthinus had taught them.

'Yes, Tante Koba? Can we do something for you?' Rudolf kissed her on the cheek.

'No, *hartjies*, Tante Koba just wants to ask something of you, just a little thing. It's like this; no one has asked me for the first waltz, and no one has asked Annecke either. One of us might be too old and the other too young for courting, but in our hearts we also want to feel wanted. Now, here in my hand I have two sticks. Take your pick. The one who gets the shorter one will dance with me, the other with Annecke.' She held out her closed fist.

Karel smiled naughtily. 'Who do you want to go first, Tante Koba – Rudi or me? Pick!'

'Don't tempt me, young man!'

Karel stepped back when her hand shot to his ear. 'I'll dance with you, Tante Koba. Rudi must dance with Annecke.'

Koba looked at them open-mouthed. 'Did you discuss it beforehand?'

'Tante Koba.' Karel tapped his head and then Rudolf's. 'It's here!'

She waddled back to the tables, shaking her head. Surely they should've been one. God's ways were strange to grasp.

THE MUSICIANS took their places on the buck-wagon. Rudolf spotted Annecke and Stefanie coming from the house. He met them halfway.

Annecke had on her blue dress, and in her hair was a piece of sweet-smelling jasmine. Stefanie looked elegant in a dress of yellow taffeta.

'You look nice, Sis. Your dress is pretty.'

'Thank you, Rudi. Yes, a beautiful dress, but wasted on an occasion like this.'

'What's the matter with her?' Rudolf said as Stefanie strode off.

'She's been like that all day,' Annecke whispered. 'It's time to find a husband, Tante Koba says.'

'A husband? She won't find one here. She's much too grand.' He did not understand his sister's moods. It would've been so much better if she were like Annecke. No mystery there, just a soft and lovely girl. He sniffed the flowers in her hair. 'Annecke, you smell lovely. Will you dance the first waltz with me?'

Her face lit up, but doubt showed in her eyes. 'Who will Karel dance with?'

'Tante Koba complained that she'd not been asked, so we both offered. She made us draw lots, Karel won!' He touched the tip of her nose. 'I didn't mind, because I want to dance with you.' He took her hand. 'Come, they will start without us.'

The moon, nearing full, crept over the horizon, competing with the soft glow of the lanterns and fires. The air was alive with laughter and expectation. The first notes of the waltz filled the air. The men led their partners onto the floor, singing the sad words, but laughing as they did so. From where they sat, the grandmothers peered at the dancers to see whether any new choices had been made.

Rudolf placed his arm around Annecke's waist and took her small hand in his. They started slowly, caught the rhythm and soon they were dancing effortlessly. He bent his head and kissed her on the forehead. His lips lingered a while and he closed his eyes, the sweet smell of the jasmine pleasant in his nose. All at once a wild feeling rushed through him, an emotion he could not quite comprehend.

'Rudi, you are missing the steps,' she said, her large brown eyes full of trust and innocence.

He smiled at her brightly, but his mind was filled with wonder at this new intense sensation her nearness had brought. He looked around him but the world seemed to be the same. His parents danced lightly. Jan Viljoen and his pretty wife stepped high and fast, as was their manner. Lang Hans van Rensburg towered above his wife like a blue gum, his flowing white beard obscuring her face. And there was Danie Vermaas on the buck-wagon in his flashy red shirt, playing the harmonica, and his brother, Gert, with the wailing concertina. Off the floor was Buks, holding Lena's hand and Stefanie sipping sherry like a lady from a small glass. Over at the fires a few men gathered around the cask of brandy.

The feeling was so strong that his hands shook when the waltz ended. He wanted to get away from the dancing and tell Karel about it, but Koba claimed him for the next dance.

'Come, *hartjie*, let me show you the *settees*.' He followed Koba's steps, and after some concentration found the dance easy, but his eyes kept searching for Annecke. He was pleased to see that she was dancing with Karel.

Koba panted as the musicians ended the number on a drawn-out note. 'Now I must dance with old Lang Hans, the dear old man. He dances slowly, so I can get my breath back. Won't you get Tante Koba a small glass of that nice sweet wine?'

He brought her the sherry before joining his twin. 'Did you like it, Karel, the dancing?'

'Yes, same as riding Legend. I mean the rhythm. Don't tell Tante Koba I said she dances like a horse!'

'I kissed Annecke. It was so strange. I couldn't hold her without wanting to kiss her again. Did you also feel it when you danced with her?'

Karel elbowed him in the ribs. 'We're supposed to feel like that when we're with girls.'

'But not Annecke! She trusts us; she would not want us to do ... well, to do that.'

'Martin will be home soon. He'll court her and we will have to look out for her.' Karel's eyes searched her out amid the dancers. 'It's a good thing that we go to school in Pretoria. Martin will be there with the President.'

'But he's our brother!'

'Yes, yes, he's our brother, but I don't trust a man who has English ways.' Karel put his head close to Rudolf's and whispered, 'He may court her, but *you* will marry her. I'll see to that.'

THE MERRY-MAKING continued late into the night. The musicians tested their instruments and talents to the limit. Hans Ferreira twice had to replace a broken string and now the guitar was out of tune, but he played on regardless. Gert Vermaas, his eyes screwed tight shut, feet furiously tapping out the beat, tumbled off the buck-wagon with a lamenting wail of his concertina. Amid clamorous laughter and coarse comments, he was lifted back onto the wagon and took off on the same note.

Marthinus and Joep Maree doubled up with laughter. They had mounted guard over the cask of brandy to control the number of times some men paid it a visit, but now they found themselves overstepping their own limits.

'*Wragtig*, Joep, I'm glad the *predikant* is not here!' Marthinus wiped his face on the back of his hand. 'He would have us all in the eternal fires before daybreak.'

'*Ja, ja*, he would, and midnight is long past. And this old body is asking for bed and the comforting nearness of my Lettie.' Joep folded his hairy arms over his barrel chest, barring the way to the cask as Jan Viljoen walked up.

'No, Uncle Joep, it's not brandy I want. Jan Viljoen knows his limit when it comes to that stuff.' He put his hand on Joep's shoulder. 'It's a *sopie* of that excellent homebrew of yours I'm asking for, to get me through what old Lang Hans has asked.'

'What does old Lang Hans want, Jan?'

'He wants me to show the young rams the mating dance. There's no one who can do it as well as I can. And I feel that it is time to show that there is something that Jan Viljoen can do better than the great Joep Maree.' He gave his boisterous laugh and slapped Joep's back.

'Well now, Jan, why do I have the urge for a *sopie* of my brew as well?' Joep extracted the bottle from under the table, took a swig and held it out to Jan. 'And why do I have the urge to prove that I can do the mating dance just as well as you?'

'Aha! Spoken like a worthy opponent!' Jan gulped down a mouthful, gasped, recovered his breath and belched. He walked to the buck-wagon, motioning the musicians to cut the number. The dancers came to a halt, protesting loudly.

'Come! Come all of you! Come stand here around the floor! Joep Maree and Jan Viljoen will show the tip-toeing, foot-dragging, courting mules how a real Boer should dance.'

The dancers shouted approval and cleared the floor. Those who had taken a break hurried over and congregated around the canvas. Jan rolled up his sleeves and kicked off his boots. He smiled broadly at Joep.

'Quiet! Keep quiet for a moment!' The tone of Buks Maree's voice arrested their attention. 'Hear! A horse! Someone's coming!'

'Yes, someone is coming, and approaching fast,' Marthinus said.

A rider passed the homestead, hesitated briefly and then came riding into their midst. His horse, flecked with foam and flanks heaving, shied away from the fires, whinnied and rolled its eyes.

'Field Cornet Maree! Where are you?' the rider's voice was hoarse.

Joep stepped forward. 'I'm Field Cornet Maree.'

'Get your commando together! They've come! The English crossed the border in great numbers! I bring word from Pretoria! You must ride tonight!'

'Young man, get down and rest your horse,' came Marthinus's calm voice.

'Then you can explain what's happening.'

The rider dismounted wearily and Karel led the exhausted horse away. Someone placed a mug of coffee in the rider's hand. The people crowded him, overwhelming him with questions.

'Soldiers? British soldiers? Outlanders? How many? Where are they?'

'Let the man get his breath back, then we will all know his news,' Jan Viljoen hollered.

The man, his beard and face bathed in sweat and dust, drank down the coffee and explained hastily, 'The message came over the wire this afternoon. A big force of armed English crossed the border to the west two days ago, heading for Johannesburg. You must ride tonight. To the west of Krugersdorp. General Cronjé is there.' He looked around anxiously. 'Where's my horse? I have to warn the commandos north of here.'

'Your horse is done in, Oom.' Rudolf came rushing up leading a fresh horse. 'My brother is rubbing him down and we've saddled one of our horses for you.'

'Frans Viljoen, ride with the man,' Joep Maree ordered. 'Two men work better than one.'

Before long the two men thundered off. The others stood rooted, following them with their eyes. '*My Got*, Uncle Joep, the *Engelse* are upon us and there you stand like the wife of Lot!' Jan Viljoen urged. 'The rebellion has come!'

'Boys, fetch the horses!' Joep bellowed.

The rest of his commands were lost in a flurry of activity: the men ran to get their rifles and bandoliers and saddles, while the women rolled up blankets and tied food in cloths, stuffing them into saddlebags. A table was upset, the dishes and plates crashed to the ground. Children cried, dogs ran in circles, barking fiercely, searching for the cause of the excitement. Someone swore as he tripped over the pole of a wagon and plunged into some thorn bushes.

Joep dived under the table to retrieve his homebrew. A dog worried at his trousers. Lettie kicked the dog, hauling her husband to his feet. 'Joep, leave that devil's brew! It'll spoil your aim and make you the laughing stock of the district!'

He looked at her sheepishly, made as if he wanted to hand the bottle over, and then ducked round her and stuffed the bottle into his saddlebag.

The boys arrived with the horses. The saddles were thrown over the excited animals. Marthinus looked up in surprise when he saw Karel on Legend and Rudolf mounting his mare, Lady.

'No, my boys, we're riding off to war and it's no place for children,' he said, but his face shone with pride.

'We can ride and shoot as well as any of these men, Pa,' Karel said.

Marthinus removed his pipe, which had gone cold during the excitement. 'Who will protect the women and children while we are away? Who will be here to see that all goes well should things turn nasty? No, boys, we rely on you to do that.'

The twins looked at him sceptically, but Marthinus busied himself with his horse.

Most of the men were mounted, eager to be off. A few were still saying their goodbyes to wives and crying children. Someone ran back for his tobacco pouch and another for his hat. The horses neighed shrilly and pawed the ground. Lang Hans van Rensburg tumbled down as his horse reared. He scrambled back up amid much teasing and laughter.

'Their bellies are heavy with food and their minds slow with brandy,' muttered Lettie Maree.

'What a time for this to come on us,' Mary said.

'Don't fret, Mary,' Koba said. 'The ride will soon sober them.'

'Jan Viljoen!' his wife called. 'You cannot meet the *Engelse* like that! Where's your pride? *Magtig*, you will not shame me. Go dress yourself!'

Jan, who was about to mount, looked as if he was about to protest, but one glance at Hannie sent him to his wagon. He grabbed a waistcoat and his best jacket and, not finding his slouch hat, donned his Sunday hat, a felt bowler with a silk band around the rim. He mounted and the commando was ready to go.

Hannie Viljoen shouted another order but her voice was lost as the men fired into the air and, with a thundering of hooves, rode off into the warm night. The women and children stood in silence until the noise of the departing commando had faded.

Hannie was the first to speak. 'I tried to tell him ...' She was on the dance floor, holding Jan's discarded boots in her hands. 'My husband rode out to meet the enemy with bare feet.'

Lettie Maree chuckled. 'Jan Viljoen, roaring at the enemy with his fancy hat, but no shoes? How the thorns will worry him!'

The women broke into hysterical laughter, but it died abruptly. Their husbands, brothers and sons had ridden off to war again. The dance floor was deserted; the fires were dying down. The concertina Gert Vermaas had played so heartily lay forlorn on the buck-wagon. The lantern light flickered over the plates and dishes in the sand. The brandy cask was upset, the dark liquid trickling into the sand. The dogs whimpered and the children dragged at the women's skirts.

Lena Maree clung to the nearest table. Warm fluid ran down her legs.

'My time has come,' she gasped.

Koba went pale. A baby was about to be born. And it was war. *A time to give and a time to take away. God gives and God takes away that which He has given.* Her eyes searched the women gathered around Lena. Who had God singled out to carry the burden?

———

MARTIN WAS DRINKING CHAMPAGNE, surveying the riotous scene around him. Well over a hundred people were laughing, talking, drinking and dancing. Peter Radford, evening jacket, bow tie and collar discarded, whirled past with a beauty in his arms, her raven hair contrasting sharply with his blond head. Their mouths were glued together while their feet continued with the dancing. Peter lifted his face from the woman's and swigged from the bottle in his hand.

Martin had spent the past week at Peter Radford's place, a Georgian manor house set on forty acres of land. The regiment was on Christmas furlough, and the drink was flowing freely. People came and went at all hours, the many bedrooms occupied regularly by overnight visitors. Women visited often, beautiful women with notorious reputations.

He eased his way through the revellers to the dining room, hoping to find Charles, who was due to spend the night. Mark Sinclair was draped across a chair, a cigar hanging from his mouth, a glass of brandy at his elbow. He studied his cards dozily and pushed a chip to the pile in the middle of the table. Murray Shaw, stroking his huge moustache, squinted at his cards and added another. James, a thin black cheroot between his teeth, a woman leaning over his shoulders, whooped and placed his cards on the table: a straight flush.

James, with the woman following him, ambled over to Martin. Reaching for the nearest champagne bottle, he toasted Martin. '*Hail the conquering hero comes! Sound the trumpet, beat the drums!* Homebrew and necking ladies under fig trees next New Year?'

Mark Sinclair was about to join in the toast, but his expression turned sour. George Hunter had arrived. In civilian clothes he looked ordinary, Martin thought.

'Did Radford actually invite *him*?' James asked.

'Radford doesn't mind,' Mark Sinclair drawled. 'It's the most admirable thing about him; he just doesn't mind.'

True, Martin thought, unlike most of the titled individuals he had met, Peter was unpretentious and sincere, and generous to a fault.

'Evening, gentlemen. I'd urgent business to attend to and couldn't join you earlier,' George Hunter greeted them, looking in distaste at the woman at James's side.

'Business? On a night like this?' Mark Sinclair frowned.

'My business was with Lord Fairfield.' Hunter fixed Martin with a haughty stare, poured a drink and went to the table.

'London would be dismal without him to amuse us,' James said, his eyes on Hunter. 'Shall we give him a teary send-off to express our sentiments?' He lifted his girl by the hips onto the table just as Hunter picked up his cards. 'Come, Precious, let's have that song but with the words I taught you. This man is going to war in Sudan. We might not see him again.'

When she started to sing, Martin recognised her as the actress from *The Far-away Soldier*. He left for the main hall again, knowing that the noise would drown out the words and the sad melody.

Charles arrived with a stocky man, his face and hands bronzed. 'My lost friend, Dr Frank Crofton-Smith,' Charles said. 'We were students together, but his quest for adventure overcame his sense of duty. So, what did the fellow do? Joined the army medical corps!'

'No more than what you're doing now, Charles. Running off to Africa,' his friend said.

'Frank has been in Egypt with the cavalry, treating the wounded. I'd like to hear more about it,' Charles said.

'Hoping that President Kruger might call on you to accompany his commandos to war?' Frank smiled.

Cheers and hurrahs erupted, and 'Auld Lang Syne' started up. Martin joined in the singing. It was 1896 and he was on his way home. Six thousand miles away. He stopped singing. Six thousand miles away from Vicky. When the song ended, he slipped away to his room.

MARTIN WOKE to banging on his door and his name being called. Charles burst into the room, waving a newspaper, pushed it into Martin's hands, pointing at the headlines. 'The Transvaal has been invaded! It says heavily armed soldiers crossed the western border. They intend meeting up with the Outlanders. Read for yourself!'

He scanned the headlines. *Crisis in the Transvaal. Appeal from Outlanders. Dr Jameson crosses the frontier with 700 men.* 'Does it say anything about a response? Has the President called out the commandos?'

'No, it doesn't say. William Moore brought the news. They're all in the morning room.'

Martin splashed water on his face, dressed hurriedly and went downstairs. The officers were gathered around a table spread with newspapers. An uneasy hush came over them.

'I've read what *The Times* has to say. Is there more in the other papers?' Martin said, trying to hide the anger in his voice.

'Nothing,' James said. 'The reports are just speculation about the Outlanders. Will they rise, Martin? Do you think they will actually join Jameson's force and ride on to Pretoria?'

'How many in Johannesburg will support this damnable adventure?' Sinclair's expression showed clearly what he felt about the invasion.

'What will Kruger do?' Murray Shaw said.

'Who's this Jameson fellow, anyway?' Peter asked.

Frank Crofton-Smith smiled at Charles. 'A medical doctor who's forsaken his calling. The administrator of Matabeleland, a close friend of Cecil John Rhodes. Enough said. No doubt who's behind this.'

Martin knew that he had to keep calm and evaluate the circumstances objectively, but inwardly he was seething. 'I'd say that about twenty thousand Outlanders are capable of taking up arms. As to whether they will rise: no, they won't get the chance. The commandos will halt the invaders before they get halfway to Johannesburg.'

'Impossible! You don't have an army,' William Moore said.

'Not a formal army, Moore, but it takes us a day, two at the most, to assemble a commando that can deal with seven hundred men.'

Murray Shaw frowned. 'Hard to believe. My dear fellow, to mobilise a substantial force takes time. You need to be equipped – arms, uniforms and some means of transportation—'

'We ride our own horses, wear our own clothes, and use our own rifles. My people are already there.'

'Will they come through Wintersrust?' Charles asked. 'Will the Rustenburg commando be involved?'

'Yes, we're directly on their route.'

Peter went to the study and came back with a map. They spread it out on the table and pored over it. 'Johannesburg is here,' Martin pointed. 'They've crossed the border here, I presume, and must pass Krugersdorp. We should cut them off before they get there, round about here, depending on how fast they ride.'

'What if Jameson gets help from the Cape or Natal?' James asked.

An ice-cold feeling took hold of Martin. If the two British colonies supported the invasion, there would be war, not just a rising of discontented Outlanders.

'Britain is not involved, Henderson,' Sinclair said. 'It's completely unauthorised. That is stressed in *The Times*.'

Peter sent James a teasing grin. 'Well, there's only one way of finding out. Why don't you go to London and ask your father?'

'I most certainly will not,' James snapped.

'We'll know soon enough,' Martin said. 'News travels fast nowadays. After the battle of Majuba it took months—'

'De Winter, Majuba is unfinished business, fought with inadequate forces and inferior generals.' George Hunter strutted into the room, shedding his coat. 'Your countrymen are on the run.' He poured coffee and leaned against the table. 'Before this year is much older, the Union Jack will fly in Johannesburg and then, I'm afraid, De Winter, it'll be hoisted in Pretoria too. Seven hundred men and someone with courage—'

Martin felt a thumping in his temples, a prickling at the back of his neck. This man was going to marry Victoria and, if that was not enough, he was celebrating the downfall of his country. He grabbed Hunter by his arms, forcing him back over the table. Plates and cups smashed to the floor, the coffee pot overturned. Hunter struggled, but he kept him pinned to the table, their faces almost touching. 'Now listen here, *Engelsman*! Seven hundred men and one phoney doctor will be dead before this day is much older. The British flag will never fly over my country, never! We will fight you to the last man! Do you understand, *Engelsman*?' There was no reply from the ashen-faced Hunter, helpless in Martin's powerful grip. *'Answer me, Engelsman!'*

'I hear you, Boer!'

Martin released him with a shove. Hunter straightened his clothes, grabbed his coat. 'Your country has an outdated, illiterate government. British subjects are suffering the most awful inconveniences and that shall not be tolerated.' He glared at Martin, stabbing his finger at him. 'I'll be back before the day is out with news from the War Office. I shall demand an apology!' He slammed the door. They heard his horse gallop off a few moments later.

Martin stood in the middle of the room, his arms hanging by his side, his breath coming in ragged sobs. Peter handed him a glass of brandy. He accepted it wordlessly and drank it in one gulp.

'Independence is the sacred heart of a nation. Without that, no one can endure, nothing can survive,' Martin said, speaking slowly, clearly. 'I know what's happening in my country now is none of your doing, or your government's for that matter, but Majuba and all that went before it did happen. There was war; your army did invade my country.' He searched their faces, willing them to understand his reasoning. 'I bear you no ill will. You're my friends. James and Charles, my blood cousins, but you, *all of you,* are British. What I said to Hunter was no idle threat. I meant every word, *every word.* Your duty is to answer when your country calls. But friends *or family,*' he looked pointedly at James. 'I shall not spare you. As God is my witness, if the need arises to fight you, I shall do so, and fight you to the very end I shall!'

THE RUSTENBURG MEN rode hard through the night and into the hot morning trying to catch up with General Piet Cronjé and his commando. It was only near nightfall, not far from Krugersdorp, that they found him. Cronjé had harassed the invaders, who had boldly followed the road to Johannesburg, for two days. He had ordered the road to be blocked and the commando to close in.

During the night, they encircled Dr Jameson's force. Before sunrise the battle started in earnest, the Boers forcing the invaders up onto a high hill, firing from behind boulders and anthills, paying little attention to the few cannon shot that went wild and far overhead.

'We have them! Like a meerkat in his hole!' Jan Viljoen hobbled on his blistered feet to where Joep Maree was crouching behind a boulder.

'And the sun only an inch into the sky,' Joep grinned. 'Yes, the day is won despite some of us coming to battle with bare feet and bowler hats.'

'It was your peach brandy, Uncle Joep. Brave at midnight, shamefaced in the morning. How much longer? Will they *hensop?*'

'Your feet are spared, Jan.' Joep pointed to where a white rag, hanging limply from a tall stick, showed itself on the hill.

IN HIS ROOM at the Rand Club, Paul Warren's anger spilt over into destructive madness. He overturned the table, spilling books, lamps and glasses to the floor, and tore the curtains off the windows. He cursed the Boers, their land and their president.

There came a knock on the door, but still his fury raged. He banged his fists on the closed door before jerking it open. Charles Leonard entered and looked in trepidation at the destruction around him.

'Warren, you must leave at once. People are being questioned, in the streets, at the station, in the bars. Warrants for our arrest are issued in Pretoria at this very moment. The Zarps will come in the morning, perhaps tonight.'

Warren's chest was heaving, his arms at his side, his fists clenched.

'You're the only one who can get us out of jail. Please, leave tonight!' Leonard urged. 'Rhodes has resigned ... a few hours ago.'

Warren slumped down on the bed, his face in his hands. All had failed. Jameson and his force had been cornered and beaten. The Outlanders had failed to rise. Everything he had worked for had disappeared, lost on a sunburnt koppie called Doornkop, the Hill of Thorns. Rhodes, his mentor, had resigned as prime minister. His career was in ruins.

CHAMPAGNE EASED the tension at the lunch table at Peter Radford's house. James strode in, handed the first newspapers of the day to Martin, collected a champagne bottle from the dresser and took a place at the window.

Jameson surrenders at Doornkop! The headlines screamed in bold letters. *Jameson soundly beaten,* read another.

'Seventy-four wounded or killed. One Boer lost.' Martin's voice carried neither glee nor triumph. 'General Piet Cronjé and three hundred burghers. That's all it took. Three hundred.'

George Hunter, who was busy moving his luggage to a waiting carriage, came down the staircase carrying his greatcoat and helmet. Humiliation mixed with disgust was engraved on his features. He made to leave but Martin grabbed him by his sleeve, spun him around.

'The British flag in the Transvaal seems to be *white*, Hunter. First Majuba, now Doornkop.'

James popped the champagne. The cork shot close to Hunter's head.

PART FOUR

THE TIME OF THE PHARISEES

And yet the order of the acts is planned,
The way's end destinate and unconcealed.
Alone. Now is the time of Pharisees.
To live is not like walking through a field.

Boris Pasternak, 'Hamlet'
(tr. Henry Kamen)

A Living Monument

'**A** LIVING MONUMENT. The cornerstone upon which the *Volk* build their hope.'

As he crossed Church Square, his hands behind his broad back, President Paul Kruger was reminded of the *predikant*'s words spoken at the unveiling of the cornerstone on which his statue would soon be placed. For there, towering above his people, he would be, cast in bronze, complete with frock coat and tall hat. A living monument. *Ja*, spared past his allotted three score and ten to fulfil his duty to his *Volk* and land: the faithless Outlanders lay waiting like a snake, ready to strike at the heart of the nation.

Almost three years since Jameson and his riffraff had invaded the Transvaal. Jameson – a runt if ever there was one. When the judge had donned the black cap, the *Volk* had cheered: death to the invaders! But through the thick clouds of his meerschaum, the President had formulated his own verdict. It earned him international respect, just as young Martin de Winter, his legal advisor, had assured him. A wise and shrewd decision. Pack Jameson and his men off. Let England decree; let England show the world how she rules.

The President reached his house, sank down in his chair on the stoep, recovered his breath and reached for his pipe. *Ja*, Jameson had given him a dire warning and he had heeded it. Over the past eighteen months shiploads of munitions had arrived from Germany, France and Ireland through the port of Delagoa Bay: twenty-two pieces of modern artillery and thirty-seven thousand rifles. Mausers. Five bullets in a clip. Five rounds without reloading. *Wragtig, the Germans know how to make a good rifle! But, ai, a sad day when a nation arms for war.*

He lit his meerschaum and called into the house for coffee. Jameson had caused the disgrace of the *Engelsman* Rhodes. The President slapped his knee and chuckled gleefully. 'The tortoise put out his head; I cut it off!' God sent a blessing in everything.

The Outlanders were prepared to talk now that a municipality was in place, their living conditions improved. And young De Winter and his team had been making progress, until Alfred Milner was appointed British High Commissioner. A meddlesome man. Enticing the Outlanders, demanding that the franchise be lowered to ten years of residence. *Allemagtig!* The *Volk* would be outnumbered, their independence lost in the next election. Exactly what Milner wanted.

'We must talk our way clear of Milner and his demands,' General Piet Joubert had cried in the Volksraad that morning. 'We should not look at war as a solution.'

The President sighed and blew on his hot coffee. A good general, old Piet Joubert, but a true Town Boer – bow tie and fob watch draped across his stomach. He needed a little war. The President pondered a while. Chief Mpefu in the northwest had taken to gun-running again, his warriors raiding cattle that were beginning to prosper now that the rinderpest had died out. Commandos had been sent out for months and yet he had not been subdued. *Ja*, Piet Joubert would go north.

And Martin de Winter. An upright, committed young man, a formidable man. But shrewd. He had refused to consider the post of State Attorney. No, he wanted a voice, a seat in the Volksraad. The young man needed a break from his endless work – work he heaped upon himself. It was as if he needed to prove his worth. Some days there seemed to be a deep melancholy hanging about him, a sadness in his blue eyes. *Ai, ai*, if only the young man would find himself a wife!

The President knocked his pipe against his boot. He would speak to young De Winter in the morning. A little farming like a true Boer would do him good.

Father and Sons

MARTIN CRESTED THE RISE and reined in his horse. Soon this road, like the others converging on Rustenburg, would be alive with horsemen. The long-awaited day was upon them; every burgher was to receive a Mauser to fight the foreigners, to drive them out of their land.

His eyes travelled over Rustenburg against the familiar backdrop of the mountains. He saw the cypress trees in the cemetery, the church tower dominating the town, the government building, post office, general stores and Coetzee's Hotel, where he always took a drink when pressure of work allowed a visit to the district. And there was Charles's hospital on the outskirts of town. Charles had settled at Rustenburg, and had converted a large house into a hospital. The district had welcomed him and he was loved and respected. Martin smiled to himself; he wondered how much Anita Verwey contributed to Charles's obvious contentment. The red-haired girl, with whom he had been so taken at Buks Maree's wedding, was now his nursing assistant.

'The *Volk* has no respect for a man who cannot find himself a wife!' The President's parting words still rang in his ears, pricking his conscience. He needed to marry; his people demanded it. His bachelor status frustrated the President. It was also talked about in Pretoria and in the district. It baffled his father, who raised the subject often.

On his return from England, he had reluctantly courted a few interesting girls in Pretoria. Although his whole being cried out to love and to be loved, and they could give him that, he had none to give in return. Annecke was seventeen and waiting for him to propose, but she was overawed by Pretoria society and her endearing honesty did not fit there. The few times he had taken her to dinners and public events, she had rushed to the twins the moment they got home to report all that had been said and done.

And now she was back on the farm, having finished her schooling. He loved Annecke, but not in the way a man should love his wife. Not in the way he still loved Victoria. When he thought about her during his busy days, the love they'd shared seemed like a dream dreamt long, long ago. But at night, in the many strange bedrooms he slept in during his trips into the country, following the President like a faithful hound, she was real and he would feel lonely and miserable.

He flicked the reins and his horse moved on. Star, a magnificent dappled white stallion, had been a gift from the President. Martin had come to love the horse, but not in the way that Karel loved Legend. The twins had left school and were now farming. They were, in a way, strangers to him. They showed no interest in his high-profile life, his work, his court cases or his rugby career, all of which were widely reported in the newspapers. Charles, it seemed, had taken the place of an older brother, spending most of his free time at Wintersrust.

RUSTENBURG WAS COMING TO LIFE when Martin galloped in. Wagons and horse-carts were outspanned at a large tract of land that had been cleared as a shooting range to test the new Mausers. Smoke spiralled from the cooking fires, and the air was alive with children's voices, women laughing and men talking excitedly.

Martin made his way to the marquee in the centre of the hooded wagons. There he found Joep Maree checking numbers on ammunition crates against those on a paper. It was his duty as Field Cornet to hand out the rifles and cartridges. A grin broke through the concentration on Joep's face. '*Magtig*, Martin, we didn't expect you here today. Did you bring the President with you?'

'No, Uncle Joep, today I'm not Oom Paul's watchdog. Today I'm an ordinary farmer. And that I'll be for the next two weeks. Where's Pa?'

'Marthinus asked me to collect his Mauser. He's with the herds, as your brothers don't want to miss this day.' Joep placed his arm around Martin's shoulders and steered him to the Maree wagon. 'I believe that you have it in mind to prevent the war. We'll talk at Soetvlei on the stoep over a cup of coffee. No, over my homebrew! I've made an excellent batch from this year's apricots. *Magtig*, it has a kick in it! Even Jan Viljoen was cross-eyed when he tasted it.'

Lettie Maree hugged Martin, held him at arm's length and inspected his beard. 'What a fine upstanding Boer! But I'd say that you want an ostrich feather in your hat on such an important day.'

'Lettie, the man is perishing and you fret about a hat?' Joep said. 'Bring the coffee!'

Buks Maree came galloping up, his three-year-old boy on the saddle in front of him. Envy caught sharply at Martin's heart. Buks and Lena were expecting their third child and he was still a lonely bachelor.

'*Dag*, little Joep.' Martin lifted the boy from the horse and smacked a kiss on his forehead. 'How's Lena, Buks?'

Buks dismounted, a surly expression on his face. 'I've come to fetch my rifle and then I must go back. Old Klaas and his sons are coping with the crops, but the land at the far end of the vlei must be finished, the ploughing can't wait for a war to start. And the mare that foaled last week hasn't recovered. Your father sent me to find Charles to ask his advice.'

Martin handed him a mug of coffee. 'A war is not about to start, Buks. Why, I even have a week or two to help you on the farms.'

'Is this really necessary? Are we preparing for war?'

'We're preparing for the possibility. That lawyer, Paul Warren, with the Reform Committee, has made it clear that the ultimate goal is not the vote for the Outlanders but control of the goldfields—'

'Give them that, then! Why should we squabble over gold? We have our farms. Give them the city of sin before we lose our livelihood or, worse, our lives.'

Shouts announced the arrival of the State Artillery escorting a large howitzer. People surged forward to have a look. Martin caught sight of Karel and Rudolf; with them as usual was Annecke.

'*Dag*, Martin,' Karel said as the three dismounted. 'Have you seen the cannon? It takes a span of twenty to move it.'

'Yes, a howitzer. The artillery will give a demonstration so that we get used to the noise. We'll have a good *wapenskouw* today.'

Rudolf shook his hand. 'We didn't expect you. I was going to receive your Mauser on your behalf.'

'Thank you, Rudi.' He turned to Annecke, who waited patiently to be greeted. She looked radiant, her cheeks flushed from the early morning ride and her hair secured in two long plaits. 'How have you been, Annecke? I've missed you.'

She blushed and moved closer to Rudolf. 'It's good to be back on the farm, but now I miss Tante Koba so much.'

'Just as well that you're here, Martin,' Karel said as he off-saddled Legend. 'We have something important to discuss with you and Pa.' And without further explanation, he left for the marquee, followed by Rudolf, with Annecke tagging along.

Charles arrived, his bow tie slightly crooked, a straw boater on his head. He did not notice Martin until he was almost upon him. 'Good heavens!

You're here. Have you had an agreeable trip with the President?'

'Of Biblical proportions and interest!' Martin hugged him. 'This is not a good day for you. Does it bother you much?'

'No, it doesn't bother me at all, actually. I was just thinking about something else. Jan Viljoen has brought some news … well, it's rather personal. I'm going to spend a few days at Wintersrust. I have to go to the kloof to get those tubers Tante Koba has recommended. Some of my patients will not take to modern medicine. Will you be home, Martin?'

'Yes, I need a rest. And it looks like you could do with one too. What's troubling you?'

'I've had a rather upsetting morning. What with James's regiment in Sudan now, distressing news was bound to come—'

At that moment, Jan Viljoen joined them, showing off his new Mauser. 'We're allowed five shots as soon as the range has been cleared.'

'Yes, Jan, indeed a beautiful piece of workmanship. Accurate at a thousand paces, I've been told.' Martin was still looking at Charles. 'Charles, what's wrong?'

Jan also turned his attention to Charles, whose troubled expression moved him to exclaim, 'No fear, my good friend, Jan Viljoen will never point his Mauser at this *Engelsman*.' He put his arm around Charles's shoulder and gave his boisterous laugh.

'Thank you, Jan, you do set my mind at ease,' Charles smiled. 'Well, yes, the mail coach came yesterday and I went at about four to collect—'

'Charles, the mail coach comes every Friday.' Martin hurried him on. 'What's happened?'

'James was wounded last month. Father writes that he took a shot in the upper arm and a few stab wounds in his legs—'

'Do you know any more details?' Martin asked.

'Frank Crofton-Smith who treated him in Egypt, wrote that James rescued Peter Radford, who was wounded and unable to get away from the enemy. James dragged him to safety, and was wounded in the process. Peter has a chest wound and is making a good recovery. James is to receive the DSO.'

'What's this thing? This DSO? Is he in trouble again?'

'It's a medal, Jan, a medal for bravery.'

'Aha! Have I not said so often that my *Engelsman* James is a good soldier and a brave man? His chest will be covered in medals before long.'

'And what does James have to say about his medal?' Martin asked.

'Oh, well, you know James. He told the press that he only assisted Peter to run away bravely and did not need a trinket to adorn his uniform. Father is furious.'

144

'Run away bravely?' Jan slapped his thigh, bellowing with laughter. 'What a clever *Engelsman*! How does a man run away bravely? When you write to your brother again, tell him Jan Viljoen says it's all right to run away when outnumbered, but one must do so facing the enemy. Never turn your back, for if you are shot in the back, you'll be branded a coward. Then your children and your children's children will carry the burden of a coward with them and that's not fair. Will you write him that?'

CHARLES SANK DOWN in the nearest chair. What a morning! The entire district turning out to be armed and giving him apologetic glances. And then Jan Viljoen's ominous news – his sister Ester pregnant, and blaming either Karel or Rudolf. She wasn't sure which one but was adamant that it was one of them. Ester Viljoen was unstable and the Viljoen family tried to keep her out of society, but Vrede was a popular place to visit. He had examined Ester and promised Jan to settle the matter at Wintersrust with his uncle.

Little Joep climbed onto his lap and fiddled with his tie. A few mothers came to ask his advice on various ailments and to report on the progress of their infants, some of whom he had assisted into the world. The bustle around him increased as more men full of war talk came to greet Martin, who calmed them down in his most diplomatic way.

The twins arrived. The men looked enviously at the rifle Karel had selected. Charles duly inspected it. A golden flame ran through the dark wood, forming a distinctive pattern. Karel explained how he had unpacked thirty rifles before he had found this one.

Trust Karel to do that! This rifle would mean just as much to him as his horse, and Legend appeared to be the centre of his life. The mare was six years old and had only foaled once, as Karel protected her like a man protecting the woman he loves. Rudolf loved his mare, Lady, but not in the way that Karel adored, almost revered, Legend. For Rudolf was in love with Annecke. And that Annecke was unaware of this was clear, as she was still hoping that Martin would propose. In that, he could not help; it had to take its course.

He looked at Jan Viljoen, who was comparing his new Mauser to that of his brother Frans. When the rinderpest had broken out soon after his arrival in the Transvaal, Charles had rushed to Vrede to assist the Viljoens in treating their stud bulls. He would never forget those months. He still woke at night with visions of the cattle – deep, raw sores in their mouths and noses, mute and dumb and painfully thin. Exhausted by hunger and thirst, they eventually lay down and died. The vultures came in the thousands. The smell of putrefying flesh hung over the country, only to be replaced by smoke from burning carcasses. The livelihood, the very existence of the *Volk*, went up in flames.

Now he kept some cattle on Vrede. The Viljoen brothers insisted on it. These were his people now. He was beginning to understand them, especially with the help of Anita Verwey, his nurse and assistant.

The call for lunch broke into his thoughts. He took a seat at the trestle table opposite the twins and Annecke. 'I must talk to you tonight. It's rather urgent,' he said quietly.

'Why not now?' Rudolf asked. 'Tonight we're going to dance, hey, Annecke?'

Before she could reply, Martin joined them. 'Dance? Is there going to be dancing tonight?'

'Gert Vermaas has his concertina, Hans Ferreira his guitar. Uncle Lang Hans says: why waste the opportunity?' Rudolf said.

'The *predikant* wants us here tomorrow for the church service so that he can ask God's blessing on the Mausers,' Martin said.

'Not that God can do anything for or against a Mauser,' muttered Karel.

A whistle sounded from the marquee. It was time to test the rifles. Everyone rushed to the clearing, where a State Artillery sergeant explained the workings of the rifle. When everyone was satisfied, he gave them a warning. 'We want no accidents. See the barbed wire? No one goes behind there. And watch out for cattle. Down at Krugersdorp the magistrate's best milk cow was hit. We don't want a repeat of that here. Aim only at the targets.'

Remarks flew through the air. 'We don't need targets!' 'We could use Lang Hans van Rensburg!' 'No one could miss him at five hundred paces!' 'Where's Jameson? We'll use him as a target!'

'We have our own English doctor!' Jan Viljoen hoisted Charles onto the wagon. 'Does he not present a fine target with his straw hat and bow tie?'

There was an awkward silence. Charles pulled his tie straight and adjusted his glasses. 'I believe the Mauser is accurate at a thousand paces. Shall I measure it off and present myself on the spot?'

The crowd whistled and cheered.

'Jan Viljoen!' shouted Joep Maree from the back. 'Sleep with your shoes around your neck from now on. Your feet won't last another battle.'

By late afternoon every Mauser had been tested and it was time for the sergeant to fire the howitzer. Everyone strained their eyes into the distance to see where the shell would land.

Charles was now with Martin. Directly behind the wire enclosure were Annecke and the twins. An ear-splitting explosion rent the air as the gun fired. The vibration engulfed them and then silence descended. Charles saw

Karel place his arm around Rudolf's shoulders. Rudolf pulled Annecke into his arms and held her close.

Charles looked at Martin; he was staring at them.

———

PAST NOON on the following day, Karel and Rudolf left Rustenburg and took the road to Wintersrust. They halted their horses at the first stream. Karel scooped up water and bathed his head. Legend nuzzled his neck as if to convey her sympathy. For the first time in his life, Karel was suffering from the effects of having had too much to drink.

After a while they were on their way again, keeping the horses at a walk. Karel pulled his hat low over his eyes. 'Never, never will I drink with the Viljoens again! They say that I'm a man now and should be able to take my drink. Do they really think getting a rifle from the President makes one a man, Rudi? Look at old Uncle Botes – fat as a pig, can't even mount a horse or aim the rifle past his belly.'

'Jan Viljoen tried the same with me, but I spat out that stuff when he wasn't looking.'

'We are men! Not boys! Need I remind you?'

'Karel, I can't ask Annecke to choose between Martin and me. It might confuse her, and it won't be fair on Martin. And after what happened last night? Didn't you notice?'

'I could barely stand up.'

'Martin danced almost every dance with Annecke. And when he didn't, he held her hand. I'm telling you, today the district is speculating about the wedding date. This morning when I went looking for her, she'd already left with Martin.'

'Time's running out. Speak up now!' He grabbed Rudolf's arm. 'If you don't, then I shall. If a man wants something, he fights for it.'

Rudolf cast a glance at his twin. 'Karel, don't you ever think about love?'

'Love? I love Legend, I love my new Mauser, I will love our new farm and, above all, I have you. Is that not enough? A horse, a rifle, a farm and a brother?'

'A man must have a wife if he wants to farm. Especially you. We can't run off to Johannesburg every time you need a woman. And besides, I'm tired of waiting for you in the street. What is it about whores that attracts you so much?'

Karel grinned. 'Well, there's no obligation and you do it till your pound runs out. I like it, Rudi, riding a woman. I can't understand what you find so disagreeable about it.'

Rudolf thought back to the first night they had spent in Johannesburg. Karel had taken to the delights of sex straight away, but he had been glad when it was over. Karel went back several times, but he had not tried again, not even when Ester Viljoen lured them into the shed on Vrede. Karel, knowing that she was a slut, did not hesitate. Later he confessed that it had been wrong and they had steered clear of her ever since.

They rode on in silence, their knees touching now and then as the horses broke into a canter. Rudolf's eyes travelled over the mountain, fresh in the late winter air. The trees were heavy with buds. Wintersrust came into view and, a little further on, smoke rose from the Soetvlei chimney. Johannesburg and the goldfields were not far away. If there were to be a war, would the enemy come through here?

'You know what I thought when Uncle Joep wrote my name next to the number of the Mauser? I thought: could this be the rifle that kills my cousin James? That's what I thought, Karel, and it scares me.'

'Yes, I thought about James too, but there are soldiers in Natal and in the Cape. They'll be the ones to march out against us, not James's regiment.'

'Martin says that the British cavalry is a fearsome sight. He saw them on manoeuvres. Do you think he will shoot when James is in the firing line?'

Karel considered for a bit. 'Yes, I believe he will. Martin does everything that the *Volk* expects of him.'

———

MARTHINUS DE WINTER sat in his leather chair behind his desk in his study, smoking his pipe. Martin was opposite him, looking out of the window where the twilight was creeping across the farm. They were waiting for the twins, who wanted to see them both on a serious matter. Now they were still with the herd, assisting a cow that had difficulty in delivering her calf.

He looked at his eldest son. Since his arrival a few days ago, Martin had worked on the farm, helping Old Klaas with the ploughing, but now he was smartly dressed. Whipcord trousers tucked into top boots, clean white shirt, waistcoat. His golden-brown beard neatly clipped. Going courting, perhaps? Before he could raise the subject, there came a knock on the door and Karel and Rudolf entered. Their clothes were stained, exhaustion etched on their faces after the long day in the veld.

They were good farmers, strong and tall – hard workers. To a stranger they would still be identical – same curly light brown hair and clear blue eyes, the same gestures – but there was a marked difference between them.

Karel was wild, hard and uncaring, whereas Rudolf had his mother's gentle and dreamy nature.

'Well now, my boys,' he said. 'What cannot be discussed over coffee on the stoep?'

'Pa, will you hear us out before you make a decision?' Karel was as usual the spokesman.

Marthinus waved his pipe, indicating that Karel should proceed.

'Well, it's like this, Pa. Martin has Wintersrust—'

'Pa is not in the graveyard, Karel!'

Marthinus silenced Martin with a stern look. 'Carry on, Karel.'

'Sorry, Pa, I meant he will inherit Wintersrust. In the last year, you were here for a total of seven months and Martin, well, he could only manage a few weeks. His work is in Pretoria. He'll never farm like we do.' Karel looked at Martin who nodded slowly, a wary look creeping into his eyes. 'It seems to us that for the rest of our lives we will have to work Martin's farm. We have found a farm we want, Botha's farm, it's not far from here.'

'We will not neglect Wintersrust,' Rudolf said. 'Pa, you'll be here when the Volksraad is not in session and in your absence we will keep it up and look after Ma, like we do now.'

There was an uneasy silence while Marthinus thought this over. 'You will not be able to run two farms efficiently and I can't have Wintersrust neglected. I'll be resigning from the Volksraad and Martin will stand for the district in the next election. Until then you will have to wait, help us out for the next few years.'

'We found the farm we want and will not wait for an election,' Karel said.

'Steady, son, steady,' Marthinus said. 'I'd like to help you, my boys, but it's not possible to let you go now. Besides, I'm going to build a house in Pretoria. Hopefully Martin will find a wife and settle down.' He ignored Martin's irritated look. 'It's your duty to stay here for the time being.'

Rudolf turned to go, but Karel was furious. 'We shall not live like *bywoners* on our brother's farm while he prances around the country and visits his Outlander women in Johannesburg!'

There were a few uncomfortable moments and then Martin rose. 'What were you doing in Johannesburg, Karel? You have no business there!'

'Same as you! Whoring! But at the one-pound places, not at Rose Carter.'

Marthinus banged his fist on the desk. 'Enough! I will not have my sons hurling insults in my presence.' He breathed hard before regaining his calm. 'Your mother has food on the table. Let's do it justice. I want you back here after supper. All three of you!'

Mary was already at the table when they took their places. She kept up a constant flow of conversation, rewarded only with nods or grunts from her menfolk. She talked about the news from England, about James's misfortune in Sudan and about Lord Harcourt and his young wife, Beatrice, who were finally to be blessed with an heir.

THROUGHOUT THE MEAL and the Bible reading, Karel worried about the house that was to be built for Martin in the hope that he would marry soon. Annecke! And Martin was dressed for courting. He searched for his twin's hand under the table, hooked their little fingers and pressed hard. Rudolf shielded his face with his other hand and sneaked a look at him.

'Away,' he mouthed, and Rudolf nodded.

When the prayer was done, Karel rose from the table. 'We'll be back soon, Pa. There was little time today and Legend needs ... her hoof is troubling her ...'

Without waiting for permission to leave, they rushed to the stables, while Karel told Rudolf what they were about to do. They mounted bareback and sped off to Soetvlei. They found Annecke and the heavily pregnant Lena in the kitchen clearing the supper dishes.

'Lena, keep Buks and Uncle Joep away.' Karel grabbed Annecke by the arm and dragged her to the dairy room, with Rudolf following.

'What's happening?' Annecke asked, wide-eyed, drying her hands on her apron.

Karel hurriedly related the news about the house in Pretoria.

'A house in Pretoria? I don't want to live there. I want to stay here.'

'Marry Martin, you live in Pretoria.' Karel lifted her chin none too gently and forced her to look in his eyes. 'Do you want to marry him?'

Her bottom lip trembled. 'He ... he hasn't asked me yet.'

Karel sent his twin a penetrating glance. 'Rudi, don't just stand there! Say it! Pa's waiting!' He put his head out of the door, casting a quick look about. 'You have one minute.'

Rudolf put his hands on Annecke's shoulders, but she stepped back.

'Why is Karel so nasty tonight?' She wiped her nose on the back of her hand.

The childish manner spurred him to do what he had wanted to for two long years. He pressed her so close that she gasped for breath. Her breasts squashed against his chest and he knew what needed to be said could wait no longer. He took her face in his hands and kissed her hard, harder than he had meant to. Her small teeth cut into his lip. They pulled apart. 'Tomorrow ... in the afternoon ... at the vlei ...' he said and made for the door.

MARTHINUS WAS BACK IN HIS STUDY, looking at Martin sitting quietly, set for the reprimand that was to come. He felt pride competing with the anger in his heart; Martin was always prepared.

'Your brothers are taking their time.' He kept his voice stern. 'But I'll have my say. Son, visiting whorehouses is unhealthy, degrading. I thought you'd done with that in England. You're twenty-six and have accomplished what takes most men a lifetime. Don't tarnish it by careless living.'

'I'm not careless, Pa. And I do have needs ...'

'All men have needs. Find a wife and settle down.' He saw the guarded look that crossed Martin's face, the look he always had when this subject was raised. 'A man's heart is his private place. I can't ask you to bare yours, but son, is there no place for love in your life?'

Martin looked out of the window. After a while he said, 'I found love, Pa, in England. But it was not to be.'

Marthinus's heart softened at the concealed emotion in his son's voice. At last he understood Martin's attitude towards women. There were many desperate for his favours, but once he had fixed his mind, there was little that could alter the course. Now he could only hope that a girl would come along to soften the hurt in Martin's heart.

'A man conquers melancholy; he should not flounder in it.' He poured two glasses of brandy and passed Martin one. 'You will keep your visits to Johannesburg purely professional. Is that clear? I will build you a house in Pretoria, then it's up to you.'

Martin took a mouthful from his glass. 'What about Botha's farm? I have enough money put aside. I will speak to Botha about a fair price. The twins won't neglect Wintersrust or Ma. The Viljoens farm together. I think that we could do that.'

True, Marthinus thought, it would be to everyone's advantage if they farm together; Wintersrust was big and prosperous. But then, Karel was confrontational by nature, always at odds with Martin.

'What I have in mind is this; we'll buy Botha's farm and use it for grazing until I resign from the Volksraad. Then we shall have to let them go.'

There came hurried footsteps from the drive, and moments later a knock on the study door. 'You may leave, Martin, but I want you to talk to your brothers tonight, get to know them. Come!' Marthinus called and the twins stepped in. He waited until Martin had closed the door behind him before he turned his attention to his younger boys. Karel had a guilty look about him, but Rudolf, fingering his lip, seemed in a trance. He did not ask them to sit and started filling his pipe.

'Legend has trouble with her hoof? Why did you lie, Karel?' He could almost hear Karel searching his mind for an answer, but he was unprepared when it came.

'Tante Koba says that to lie a little, just a little, is sometimes necessary.'

Marthinus scratched his beard to hide his smile.

'Pa, do you want a match?' Karel indicated the unlit pipe.

Marthinus picked up the matchbox himself and said, 'Tell me about your visits to Johannesburg.' Rudolf blushed. Karel averted his eyes and moved closer to his twin. 'God forbids us to take a woman outside marriage. You're not too young to be married, neither are you too old for the *sjambok*. If you ever buy a woman for your pleasure again, Botha's farm will never be yours. Is that understood?' They nodded vigorously. He explained his decision about the farms to them. 'Is that to your liking?'

'Thank you, Pa!' they said together.

'Let's forget about the unpleasantness of today, make a new start tomorrow. Go shake hands with your brother. You see too little of him.'

'Martin lies to us, Pa,' Karel said. 'He says that war is only a distant possibility.'

'But there will be war, won't there, Pa?' Rudolf asked.

As he looked at his twin boys, it came to him, not for the first time, what a war would mean to them. Much more than it would to a man alone. They were young and vulnerable, and his heart softened again.

'Yes, my boys, there will be war. But your brother is caught up in the most important task of his life. He's already in the war, a war of words that's too complicated for us to grasp. And he believes in what he's doing; therefore he must keep the reality of war far removed from his mind. That's why he says that there won't be war.'

———

THE NEW START between father and sons lasted only for the morning. At midday Marthinus saw Charles and Jan Viljoen riding in. He waited for them on the stoep.

Jan held his hat to his chest. 'Uncle Marthinus, if God could've spared me the tidings that I bring, I would be grateful for the rest of my days.'

'Shall we go inside, Uncle Marthinus?' Charles asked.

With foreboding in his heart, Marthinus showed them to the study. For once Jan seemed at a loss for words and Charles took the lead. 'Uncle Marthinus, I've examined Jan's sister, Ester. She's with child and adamant that one of the twins is the father. Jan has come to talk it over.'

Shock and then anger rushed through Marthinus. Slowly and with care, he filled his pipe. 'Ester says it was only one?'

'For someone who doesn't know them as well as we do, it's not always easy to tell them apart,' Charles said.

The pipe lit and drawing to his satisfaction, Marthinus gazed out of the window for a long time before he spoke. 'Send for them.'

'I believe they're at the outpost …'

'Send for them, Charles. And ask your aunt for coffee.'

He did as he was told and arrived back a few minutes later carrying a tray. 'I asked Aunt Mary to send someone for them.'

'Uncle Marthinus,' Jan said, nervously stroking his beard. 'I've not come here to force one of your fine sons to marry my sister. Everyone knows about Ester. It's not a secret; she's touched.' He tapped his head. 'What I've come for is this; the child will be my nephew and your grandson. I'll take it in as my own, with your permission. Ester will be sent north to our cousin in Pietersburg. She's barren. Ester will not mend her ways. This will happen again and my cousin will be glad for the children. Up there the people are wild. They'll accept it.'

'If you've worked all this out, Jan, why have you come, then?'

'Because Jan Viljoen is not a man who carries secrets in his heart. And Ester, in her madness, has talked. Let it not be said that the Viljoens of Vrede dragged the name of the De Winters through the mud. That's why I'm here. Uncle Marthinus, it's a sad day.'

'Yes, a sad day, Jan. I didn't raise my sons to spend their seed carelessly.'

'Ester suffers from a sexual affliction. There have been others. Please allow me to ask them a few … well, intimate details …'

'Charles, I respect your medical opinion and I'm grateful for your concern for your cousins, but this will be dealt with in our fashion.'

'Is a man not a man, Uncle Marthinus?' Jan beseeched.

'A man is not a man if he can't take responsibility for his deeds. And those two need to be taught that today. I want you, both of you, to stay out of it.'

The silence grew, the tension became unbearable. Eventually the sound of approaching riders reached them. Moments later the twins entered, their faces expectant, their eyes searching their father's face.

'Has the war started, Pa? When do we ride?' Karel asked, but only a grim silence met them. Their eyes flew to Jan and Charles and then to each other.

'Ester Viljoen says that one of you is the father of her unborn child,' Marthinus said directly. 'Now, which one of you is responsible for her condition?'

Their faces went white and they moved close together. 'Both of us, Pa,' Rudolf said.

'Ester insists that it was only one. And that one is going to do his duty by her. You, Rudolf? Or you, Karel? Make up your minds or else I shall name one.'

'It was I!' said both at once.

Karel and Rudolf accused each other of lying. And then something ensued that had not happened before, that Marthinus had not expected. Karel hit Rudolf in the face. He retaliated with a blow to Karel's stomach, which winded him badly. 'Enough!' he ordered in a shaken voice.

They pulled apart and stood mutely, not meeting each other's eyes. Blood trickled from Rudolf's lips as he said, 'It was my doing, Pa, I took Ester. Karel did not.'

Karel glared at his father, then at Jan Viljoen. 'The father of the child? Take your pick: Gert Swart, Hans Buys, Danie Vermaas, any traveller who passes through your farm. They've all been there before me and since. The only difference between your sister and a whore is that she's too eager for it to ask money from the men who ride her!'

He stormed from the study, slamming the door behind him. They heard him run through the house and down the stoep. They saw through the window as he drove his heels into Legend's flanks and set off at full gallop towards the mountain.

Marthinus looked long and hard at Rudolf before turning to Charles. 'I believe you have a few questions.'

Charles cleared his throat several times, but still his voice was hoarse. 'Rudi, tell me *exactly* when you ... went with her.'

'It was just once. We went to Vrede for the breeding cows. We were washing up at the furrow by the shed. She was in there, waiting,' he said through his broken lips. 'Karel refused her because it was wrong.'

Marthinus heard the desperate lie in Rudolf's words. He had expected that Karel would be the culprit.

'Rudi, when was it?' Charles asked. 'What month?'

'It was just before winter, Charles. It was in May, the first week, after *nagmaal*.'

'Yes, that was when they came for the cows I sold you,' Jan confirmed.

Charles breathed a sigh of relief. 'Three months ago? Then the child is most definitely not yours, Rudi. Ester is six months gone.'

'As God is my witness, Ester will not be forgiven for this slander.' Jan held out his hand to Rudolf, tears filling in his eyes.

'Forgive her, Jan. She's a sick woman.' Marthinus sighed and looked at Rudolf. 'The truth, son, will stay between you, your twin and God, it seems. Go fetch your brother back.'

A DEEP ANGER surged through Rudolf. His father had set them a trap! He fled from the study to their room, rolled a few blankets, stuffed some clothing into a haversack and took all the money he could find in their kist. He could not go back to the study for the hunting rifles, so he grabbed the two new Mausers and four packets of cartridges. It was against the law to use the ammunition, but to hell with the law.

He galloped to the kloof, led Lady up to the cave and found Legend near the waterfall. He left Lady with her and rushed into the cave. When he joined Karel at the rock table, his fury subsided.

Karel touched the dried blood on his chin. 'Did it hurt?'

'Yes.' He put his hand over Karel's. 'Pa would not have forced you or me to marry Ester.'

'But Pa forced me to hit you!'

Rudolf caught the bewilderment in his voice. They sat for a while, sharing their feelings in silence. 'I've brought our things,' Rudolf said at last, 'We leave at sunrise.'

'Annecke?'

Rudolf stared into the dim light of the cave. He didn't want to leave Annecke, didn't want Martin to marry her. But the choice had been made in his father's study. The hurt in his twin's heart would turn bitter, spill over into revenge. He had to be with him above all else. Above Annecke.

'I'll go down when it's dark,' he said. 'You stay with the horses.'

Karel nodded. 'I'll bring them inside. There are leopard about.'

Rudolf waited until the moon was on the rise. He saw his way down the mountain clearly, took a short cut through the scrub, skirted the cattle kraals and entered the orchard at Soetvlei. Joep and Buks were smoking on the stoep. After a few minutes Joep rose, shook the dottle from his pipe and they both went inside. He waited a while longer before whistling softly to attract the attention of the dogs. They greeted him with wagging tails and went back to their accustomed places. Moving quietly onto the stoep, he edged his way to Annecke's bedroom window. There was light coming from within and he peered inside.

She sat in the circle of the soft lamplight, combing her long brown hair.

The light shone through the fabric of her nightdress, defining her small body, her breasts small and high, her waist narrow, her legs as delicate as those of a colt. He looked at her with deep longing in his heart, wanting to imprint her image on his mind so that he could carry her with him in the days to come. He sank down against the wall, his face in his hands, torn between his love for her and his love for his twin. By the time he had composed himself sufficiently to face her, the house was in darkness. Snoring came from Joep and Lettie's bedroom and he felt it safe to scratch on her window. Immediately she parted the curtains and peered outside, her eyes widening when she saw him. She pushed the shutter open and he quickly climbed through.

'Rudi! I waited for you at the vlei. Has something happened?' she hissed.

He placed his hand over her mouth. The moonlight caught her face and shoulders and he was acutely aware of her breasts pushing against her nightdress. He averted his eyes and concentrated on her face. 'Have you heard what happened in Pa's study today?' She shook her head and stared at him. Taking her hands in his, he made her sit on the bed. 'Annecke, we have to go away, Karel and I. Please promise that you'll try to understand.' She nodded uncertainly and bit her lower lip. He told her about Ester, the fight, and why they had to leave. She listened, her eyes fixed trustingly on his face. Once they heard the baby cry and a candle was lit in the room where Lena and Buks slept. They sat in silence until all was quiet again.

She looked down at their hands and stroked his softly. 'Where will you go? How long will you be away?'

'I don't know, Annecke. A month, or maybe two. All I know is that we have to go. Karel is very angry. I have to be with him. You understand about Karel and me, don't you?'

'Yes, you are Karel's life, Tante Koba says.'

Tears spilled down her cheeks and he wiped them away with his thumbs. 'We'll be back someday, I promise. Will it help to know … I love you, Annecke, I love you very much,' he whispered.

'I know,' she sobbed. 'And Karel loves me too, but I'll be so lonely without you.'

That was not what he had hoped, had longed to hear. Battered by emotions, he closed his eyes to hold back the tears. He pulled her into his arms and pressed her head into the hollow of his shoulder. 'It hurts me so to see you cry,' he said into her hair, 'and it hurts even more to leave you.' He placed his lips softly against hers, to kiss her goodbye.

At that moment a cat jumped through the open window and set up a loud meow in greeting. They pulled apart but paid no attention to the cat. Rudolf was breathing hard, staring at her. Her lips were parted, her breath coming in small racing sounds. But it was her eyes that held his attention. They were filled with intense wonder and, as he watched, he saw the wonder replaced by confusion. He knew that he had to get away then. With a last look at her, he jumped out of the window and scrambled to the orchard. The dogs set up a noise, but he did not care. Never in his life had he experienced emotions so intense, so desperate and so bittersweet. He ran all the way to the cave and arrived there just as the moon was reaching its zenith. Sweat poured from his body, his breath burned in his chest.

Karel was sitting by the fire, a blanket around his shoulders. Legend and Lady whinnied a welcome. It was a warm and inviting little world where his hurt would be shared and understood. He slowly walked to the fire. Nothing was said, as few words were needed when their emotions took control.

Karel placed the blanket around their shoulders. 'We stay,' he said.

'No, we go.' Rudolf's voice was raw, but final.

They did not sleep that night. Long before the first pink glow on the horizon announced the new day, they saddled their horses and left.

Stefanie's News

TWO DAYS LATER, Koba's spring-wagon was on its way to Wintersrust, bringing Stefanie and the news of her forthcoming marriage to Paul Warren.

Throughout the journey from Pretoria, Koba warned her of the difficulty she would encounter from her parents, having given her consent to a man who was to them a total stranger, but there was no doubt in Stefanie's mind that the news would be well received. She could hardly wait to see her family's pride and joy at her achievement. Like Martin, she had gone beyond the borders of her country, cultivated her God-given talent, and became someone in her own right. And now she had made a brilliant choice of husband, an influential man of high standing, a gentleman.

It was about time that they visited her. Only Charles and her mother had made the effort to attend one of her recitals in Cape Town, and then they had stayed only for a week. Martin had played rugby in Cape Town, but never at a time she had had a recital. Come to think of it, he had neglected her ever since his return from England. And the twins? Well, they had never been outside their country.

The wagon jolted and she was thrown against Koba's large body. 'Bontes! Have you no control over the horses?' she called crossly to Koba's old groom. He had changed horses at Lang Hans van Rensburg's farm, but she urged him to set a faster pace.

'Well, *mies*, at this pace,' he grumbled over his shoulder, 'the horses won't last much longer. We'll have to rest them soon.'

'There's no hurry, *hartjie*.' Koba patted her hand. 'We'll be home at sunset.'

'The dust, Tante Koba!' She pressed a handkerchief to her nose.

Before the spring rains it was always like this – dusty and oppressive. The gentle climate of the Cape suited her well, and Cape Town was such a beautiful place to live. Everybody loved her and she revelled in the attention. Then, unexpectedly, as before, Paul Warren had shown up one night when she was giving a recital at the home of Dr Jameson. For a few months he attended almost every recital she gave, and it was only then that she discovered that his absences from Cape Town were connected to his work with the Reform Committee. One evening, he told her that he regularly had contact with Martin. They were, in fact, working towards the common goal of better conditions for the Outlanders.

He courted her, not in the Boer fashion, but in an English way, taking her to dances and dinners, and even picnics. On one such picnic, on the slopes of Table Mountain, a bee sting led to his spending three days in hospital. The doctor warned him to avoid bees in the future; the poison was not something his body could tolerate. How could such a strong man be endangered by something as small as a bee?

He proposed one Saturday morning, a rainy, windy morning. She was having tea in the drawing room of the boarding house where she lived when he arrived earlier than expected. He sat down on the chair opposite her, very straight, his long legs crossed at the ankles. He said that her beauty, perfect and flawless, and her prowess as a hostess appealed to him. She would be a graceful addition to his life and would do his fine home justice.

'Miss de Winter,' he said, smiling. 'I've come to the conclusion that we complement each other. Would you do me the honour of placing a legal seal on our relationship?'

A strange proposal. No declaration of love, no taking her hand in his, just those words. Her heart raced, blood rushed to her face, the taste of victory in her mouth. She looked at him steadily, picked up her teacup, willed her hands to be calm, took a sip and replaced the cup on the little table. 'I'd like to continue with my career,' she said.

'Naturally. Your music gives me immense pleasure and is the envy of all my friends.'

'Thank you,' she smiled. 'When would you like the wedding to take place?'

'Soon, if that's to your liking. I'd prefer it to be in Cape Town, seeing that most of our friends and acquaintances are here. It would be quite an operation to get everyone to the Transvaal, don't you agree?'

'Yes, it has to be in Cape Town,' she said. No wedding on the farm, no dancing in the barn, no bearded faces and crude comments. No presents of laying hens, turkeys and rolls of cheap cotton. A grand society wedding in Cape Town. Just a faint stab of loneliness came to her heart, but it vanished when he produced a beautiful ring from his pocket: a brilliant sapphire in a nest of little diamonds. It fitted her long, thin finger perfectly. He kissed her then, his lips strangely cold and dry on her cheek, the only kiss she had thus far received from him, the closest he had come to declaring his love for her. That could wait, she decided. She was above the sentimental hogwash of lovesick girls.

Paul himself planned the wedding to the last detail, leaving her no time to inform her family. It was going to take place in the garden of Cecil Rhodes, a close friend of Paul's. There were wide lawns bordered by masses of agapanthus and sweet-smelling jasmine, and delicate potted geraniums would line the aisle down which she would walk on Paul's arm. The church? Well, it was an English church, but that her father would just have to understand. Paul was English, after all.

A LITTLE AFTER SUNSET, the spring-wagon drew to a halt in the driveway at Wintersrust. Stefanie's sudden appearance caused a stir, but, at the foreboding look on Koba's face, everyone kept their questions to themselves. Martin and Charles unloaded her suitcase and carried Koba's huge baskets inside. Mary brought tea and something for her and Koba to eat, and the family gathered in the sitting room.

'Where are the twins? Courting already?' Stefanie asked.

'Not courting ... they went ... away for a while.' Her father's face was strained, his voice tired. She noticed how the lamplight caught grey hairs down his temples and in his beard.

'Out with it, Stef. It's not proper to make us wait.' Martin winked at her.

She looked around the room. A sideboard had taken the place of her piano. On the wall above it hung a photograph of her parents, taken on their twenty-fifth wedding anniversary: her bearded father and her mother, hair rolled into a bun like all Boer women. The ebonised lithograph of the Battle of Blood River, darkened by soot now, still hung above the fireplace. Most of the zebra hides on the floor were worn thin.

Should her father refuse his permission, her name would be sullied in Cape society. A promise given was a promise kept. She didn't want to return to the Transvaal. She looked at her mother sitting close to her fine Boer husband – she always called him that – on the sofa, sewing a button onto one of his shirts. Their love was visible as she hoped her love and Paul's would also be in the future.

She picked up her cup, took a few sips, hoping that her shaking hands were not noticed. 'I've come to inform you that I'm getting married,' she blurted out, watching their faces with great care.

Marthinus handed Mary his cup and leaned back in the sofa. 'Where's this young man of yours that he hasn't come to ask me in person, as is the custom?'

'At the last minute he was informed that he was needed in court and could not make the journey, Pa.' It was a white lie, but necessary. 'Pa, he'll be in Johannesburg soon. You'll meet him then.' Martin's eyes were riveted on her. 'You work together in Johannesburg. Paul Warren. Surely he has spoken about me?'

'Paul Warren? My God, Stefanie!' Martin jumped up. 'How on earth did you get mixed up with *him*?'

'Is something the matter with him, Martin?' Mary asked.

'Ma, Paul Warren is doing all he can to bring our government down! He's an evil man!'

Stefanie was dumbfounded. She felt blood rising to her face. 'How dare you speak like that? He holds you in the highest esteem. He speaks only well of you and your work!'

'How long have you been acquainted?' Charles asked.

'I've known him for two years now. He's not what Martin thinks. He works *with* the Reform Committee to improve the plight of the Outlanders. *Exactly* what Martin is doing!'

'In all these months he hasn't once mentioned you. Not once! Explain that to me—'

'Enough, Martin.' Marthinus' voice was harsh and tired. He turned to Stefanie. 'I want to meet Paul Warren before I allow you to marry. I trust Martin's judgement.'

'Don't you trust my judgement, Pa? I want to marry him!'

'Even if it is against the wishes of your family?'

'My family's wishes? You mean Martin's wishes. Pa, you haven't even met him yet.' She stared at the cup clenched tightly in her hands. 'I've known him for *two years*. He courted me in the *proper* fashion. I *want* to marry him!'

The arguments continued. Koba watched them all through narrowed, thoughtful eyes. But at last Mary came to Stefanie's rescue.

'Only days ago you hurt our boys badly,' Mary said to her husband. 'You had not meant to. You were too harsh. And now our daughter is hurting. Stefanie has always wanted the best for herself. Two years is a long time in which to come to know a man.' She looked at Stefanie. 'Your father should know better. I went against my parents' wishes and married him. You have my blessing, child.'

The others waited for Marthinus's decision. He sighed wearily. 'I bow to your mother's good judgement. We married against her family's wishes, and what a blessed marriage it is.' He held out his arms to Stefanie. 'Come here, my kitten.'

'Now put on that beautiful ring and show it to your father, *hartjie*.' Koba reached for her handkerchief.

Stefanie brought the ring from her pocket. Her father admired it, Charles pronounced it exquisite in a strained voice, Martin refused to look at it and her mother went into raptures about the brilliance of the sapphire.

'You're wrong, Martin.' Stefanie settled on the couch opposite him when their parents had left for their bedroom. 'Paul is a good man. Do you think that I'd do something to harm my reputation? Would you harm yours by marrying unwisely?'

'I wish you the happiness that was denied me, but I refuse to acknowledge Paul Warren as my brother-in-law. I shall tell him that myself.' He rose and walked out.

Stefanie looked at Charles for an explanation. 'Charles! What happiness was denied him? Please tell me. I might understand him better then.'

'She loved him too,' Charles said simply.

'Why didn't it work out? He should've made it work.' Charles did not answer and she nodded her head. 'Of course, she's British. He couldn't bring her home.'

'I'd known all along,' Koba whispered. 'When he arrives home after a long day's work and sits down with his endless paperwork, I always sit with him for a while, knitting, darning a sock. He tells me about his day and we laugh about silly things that happened or about something Oom Paul said. But some nights, just some nights …'

Charles put his arm around her broad shoulders. 'I have to tell you about Karel and Rudi, Tante Koba.'

MARTIN WAS ON HIS WAY to Soetvlei to ask Annecke to marry him. The moon, three nights past full now, was climbing over the mountain, its light catching the bare branches of the trees, throwing mysterious shadows on the road before his feet.

Stefanie's news had cut deep into his soul. Images went through his mind of Paul Warren making love to his sister, of George Hunter making love to Vicky, of Lord Fairfield denouncing him as he would a lowly servant. The pain in Vicky's eyes, the raw pain in his heart.

A great sadness raced through him. He needed to fill the emptiness in his heart. He could not carry it for the rest of his life. He did not want to be lonely any more.

Halfway to Soetvlei he met Buks, who had come for Koba and Charles. Lena had gone into labour. He helped Buks to fetch the mule-cart and they took Charles, Koba and her huge basket to Soetvlei. Martin and Buks joined Joep in the barn, where Joep had a bottle of his homebrew to pass the time and to celebrate the birth of his third grandchild.

It was not long before the door creaked open and Charles entered. 'I'm afraid they don't want my assistance. Tante Koba threw me out of the house.' He placed his hand on Buks's shoulder. 'All's well. According to God and Nature's design, Tante Koba says.'

Joep told Martin about a letter that had come from Pretoria. 'General Joubert has asked me for forty men for the war against Chief Mpefu.'

'Uncle Joep, write my name on your list,' Martin said.

'No, son,' Joep shook his head firmly. 'Your name will not be on my list without the President's approval.'

'Uncle Joep, a new State Attorney has been appointed. Jan Smuts was three years my senior at Cambridge and is a very capable man. He will appreciate it should I disappear for a month or two so that he can settle in by himself. Write my name on your list, please.'

'But will Oom Paul let you go?'

'Let's see ...' He took a swig from the bottle. 'He'd say, "Young De Winter, the *Volk* has no respect for a man who has not proven himself in battle yet. Go, young man, but be back to quieten down the war-seeking tongues of the clever Outlanders." Yes, that's what he'd say.'

He had made the decision on impulse. It would give him time to ride the anger and hurt out of his heart. Only then could he ask Annecke to marry him. Besides, he had never been given the chance to fight in a war. With the possibility of a greater war looming, he needed to know what it was like.

'Count me in too,' Charles said.

Joep stared at him dubiously. 'You're British, son. You can't ride out with us.'

'Not to fight, Uncle Joep, but to see to the wounded. I need the experience.'

———

'WHERE HAVE THEY GONE, Annecke?' Stefanie demanded, yet again. 'If anyone should know, it would be you. Tell us, Annecke!'

It was late afternoon, and they were resting at the drift under the milkwood after the long walk back from the cave where they had gone in the hope of finding the twins.

'I don't know, Stefanie,' Annecke said.

'Leave it, Stefanie.' Martin took Annecke's hand. 'They will be back in their own time.'

Charles was leaning against the trunk, idly picking at the frayed edge of his hat. The miserable scene with the twins was still heavy in his heart. He detested scenes and now he was caught up in another. Martin and Stefanie had hardly said a word to each other all day. He was as shocked as

Martin by Stefanie's choice of husband. Martin had often confided his suspicions about Warren's private life and about his determination to bring the Transvaal government down.

Five years ago they had all been so happy and carefree. The future had been theirs. And now? Martin still hurting for Victoria. Stefanie about to marry a man Martin despised. Karel and Rudi gone to protect each other. Annecke bewildered, and James seeking solace from a private hurt in war, drink and women. *And what about yourself?* He smiled wryly. In love with Anita Verwey, and about to go to war. His decision to ride off with Joep Maree's commando to the north had not come as a surprise to himself. If there were to be a war, he would want to be prepared for it. But where would he fit in, he wondered.

'She was lying, was she not? Charles!' Stefanie dragged him out of his thoughts.

'Who lied about what?'

Stefanie sank back on the grass. 'Ester Viljoen. My little brothers could never have done that.'

'Oh, they are completely capable,' Martin said. 'They are not little brothers any more. They are grown men.'

'What will happen to Ester and her baby now?' Annecke asked.

'Jan has taken her to Pietersburg. She will not be coming back,' Martin said.

'But only the *takhaaren* live there. They don't wear shoes and they don't go to school. They are wild people! They can't leave her there, and her little baby—'

'She deserves it, Annecke. She's better off with those people,' Stefanie said primly.

'Look at all the trouble she has caused,' Martin said.

Annecke's eyes filled with anxiety. 'It's just not right. Do you think it's fair, Charles?'

'No, Annecke, it's most certainly not fair, but apparently the best way out. You can't expect an entire family to be punished for the blunder of one of its members.'

The General and His Son

England, October 1898

JAMES SQUINTED THROUGH the smoke at Peter Radford, who was sprawled in the chair opposite him. A thin scar ran from his chin, disappearing into his collar. It reminded him of Sudan, his first taste of war, the ecstasy of real danger, the closest he'd come to complete fulfilment. Rescuing Peter from encirclement by Dervishes had thrilled him.

The regiment had been part of the cavalry force charged with protecting the army of General Kitchener as it moved up the Nile to Khartoum. Five charges in ten days. And on the sixth they ran into trouble when they were cut off from the main body of the attack force. His sergeant had yelled to him to make a dash for safety, but he saw Peter struggling to free himself from under his wounded horse. He rode clear of the enemy with Peter thrown across the saddle. And only then did he realise the damage to himself and his horse.

Their friendship had developed into a close bond. Not because he had saved Peter's life, but there was a likeness of spirit, a love of danger, of not knowing or caring what the outcome would be. And now they were closer than brothers. He had discovered that he could rely on Peter in a tight situation and, although reluctant to share his feelings, had come to trust Peter.

They had come off duty and were drinking in James's bungalow at Sandhurst. Peter wanted to slip away to London, but James was in no mood for socialising. Peacetime soldiering bored him; he wanted to experience more fighting, but all seemed peaceful in the Empire now. The decisive battle of Omdurman had ended the war in Sudan, and nothing much was happening in India.

'Any hopes of a transfer?' He looked out the window at the rain falling on the parade ground.

'Perhaps.' Peter placed his glass on the table. 'We might be on our way to India in the summer. Perhaps you could ask the General for some information?'

'Radford, I'm awaiting a summons to his study. If I do get a word in edgeways, I'll try.'

When Peter left an hour later, James stretched out on his bed. The General was still furious about a comment he'd made to the press regarding his medal. But this time, he'd really done it. Bestowing sexual favours freely had caught up with him. The General was furious about his dalliance with Lady Beatrice Harcourt. It turned out that James was the father of her child. Her husband, James's doddering Uncle Gordon, had not visited her bed for months. Now Lord Harcourt had visited the General 'to arrange things', as Beatrice had put it.

THE NEXT MORNING James took the train to London. A note had been delivered to his quarters. It had an ominous ring to it. His father had, until then, only requested his presence at the soonest possible moment, not *demanded* his immediate return.

As the train steamed towards London, he stared at the passing countryside. Summer was over, the fields harvested and autumn was magnificent in the turning of the leaves. Soon the hunting season would begin. He tried to think about hunting but his mind stayed on what lay ahead in his father's study. Financial deprivation was no longer in his father's power, as James had come into a substantial inheritance on his twenty-second birthday. Perhaps a transfer? Scotland? Egypt? *Well, should it come to that, England won't be the poorer for my absence; good times were had in Cairo.*

He arrived home in St John's Wood shortly after noon. The butler took his coat and helmet with his familiar sympathetic look. 'Directly to the study, sir.'

Passing through the drawing room, he saw his mother, silent rebuke on her face. There was no sympathy from her, always siding steadfastly with the General.

'Mother,' he greeted her with a nod and clinked across the hall.

'You came by train, did you need to wear spurs?'

'Dressed for battle, Mother.' He indicated the study door.

He took his accustomed position on the rug, facing the huge oak desk. He lifted his eyes to the tiger head on the wall, winking at the yellow glass eyes. *Nothing to it, old boy, we'll get through this as well.*

His father's footsteps rang in the passage. He entered the study and stood by the window with his back to James for some time before he spoke.

'You've brought nothing but discredit to your family. I've tried to make something of you, but it has been a waste of time and energy. God knows how many times I've put my reputation on the line ...'

James concentrated on the tiger's eyes. *Does he have to be so repetitive? The same old things over and over. Getting on a bit, the old warhorse, his moustache greying to match his head, his tongue is a bit slow today, don't you think, tiger? Nothing but a disappointment ...*

'I demand an answer!' his father's voice intruded on his reverie.

'You were saying, sir?'

'You were not listening. Could you possibly be the father? Do you claim responsibility?'

'Yes, I do, sir.'

'You admit you seduced your uncle's wife?'

'No, sir. I'm always in the fortunate position of being seduced.'

The General sank down in his leather chair. James kept his eyes fixed on the tiger head. There was only the sound of crackling logs in the fireplace and his father's breathing.

'Gordon is prepared to acknowledge the child, as it happens to be a Henderson,' his father said at last, the tone of his voice clearly indicating what he thought of the arrangement. 'The regiment will embark for India this summer. It'll be stationed in the Punjab. You alone will not be allowed home leave. You will stay there for the full allotted ten years.'

Not Cairo after all, tiger! India! James almost shouted aloud, but the words that followed stunned him.

'You will marry a suitable woman to accompany you. Heaven knows if there's a woman of good standing who'd marry someone with a reputation such as yours.'

'I beg your pardon, sir? Did you suggest marriage?'

'I didn't suggest it; I ordered it. I will hear from you before the month is out. Dismissed!'

'Sir, I refuse even to consider it.'

'You have no choice!' his father barked, his moustache trembling. 'You refuse to bend to discipline. You have no sense of moral obligation. You make a mockery of everything a gentleman and an officer stands for. A wife will change all that, by God!'

'I do not intend to marry, sir.'

'Then, sir, you will be expelled from the regiment. I shall also see to it that no other regiment will accept you. Your military career will be over.'

James looked directly at his father for the first time since entering the room. General Sir Stuart Henderson, one of the most senior officers in the British Army, had the power to do that. He stood a while, staring at the forbidding face of the man who was taking his life from him.

HE ARRIVED BACK AT HIS QUARTERS late that night, found a bottle of port, poured a large measure. His eyes fell on a sepia picture of Koba, stuck behind the mirror frame. He laughed harshly. *Tante Koba! Here's something not even you can fix!* He shattered the glass against the fireplace, and then the bottle. The silver trophies he'd won over the years followed one by one. He opened a bottle of brandy and searched for a glass.

'Old man been rough on you, has he?' Peter Radford was leaning against the doorframe, surveying the disorder. 'You overlooked this one, Henderson.' He pointed at a large silver cup standing in a place of honour on a chest of drawers.

James looked at the cup, then at Peter's bemused face and his fury subsided a little. 'Not this one, Radford. I won it off Hunter.'

'Point-to-Point last winter. Shall we drink to that again?' Peter found a glass and held it out. 'Could you spare a drop?'

James handed him the bottle and sank down in a chair. 'The regiment is leaving for India in the summer. Without me.'

'Splendid! What? You won't join us? What utter rubbish!'

'I've been expelled. My deeds have caught up with me. I do give the General credit for having endured for so long …'

Peter stepped over the trophies and broken glass and revived the fire. Pouring some brandy, he settled in the chair opposite James. 'Padded up and waiting. Let rip the ball.'

'There's nothing to bowl with,' James said, but in the end it all emerged: Beatrice, the child and that marriage was the only option he had in order to stay in the regiment.

Peter burst out laughing. 'Well done, Henderson! God! How perfectly ludicrous! Don't expect me to equal you on this one.'

James looked at him in annoyance, but joined in hesitantly and soon they were laughing uproariously. Peter unbuttoned his tunic, stretched out his legs and called to his batman to bring something to eat.

'People marry all the time, haven't you noticed, Henderson? Only the motives differ: to produce heirs, secure a fortune, combine fortunes, to save the family's honour, and so on and so on. It's simple. So you have to marry to stay in the regiment. Do you have a problem with that?'

'Yes, definitely. The wife bit!'

'That need hardly hold *you* back. Infidelity is the most popular pastime in the empire.'

'And look where it landed me. Other men's wives are other men's problems, so I thought.' James pushed at a log in the fire with the toe of his boot. 'Nothing for it but to remove myself from England. Where shall I go, I wonder?'

'After the duel, I was forced out of the fold. Had to travel for a year. But you'd find life hard outside the regiment. Shall I spell it out for you? *There Be Dragons.*'

'Dragons?'

'They're fearsome, Henderson,' he said smiling, but James found sympathy in his eyes. 'They have names too: No Regiment, No Cavalry Charges, No Fellows-to-Make-Merry-With, No Cricket, and so on. The CO of this brood? No-Right-To-Society. His nickname is Outcast.'

A terrible coldness crept into James's heart as Peter's words found their mark. He didn't want to think what life would be like not being a soldier.

'You've nothing to lose,' Peter went on. 'Get it done with. At least you get to stay in the army. And it's rather good, the army, for the time being. At least we don't have to look for trouble or fun; it's given to us.'

The batman brought a plate of sandwiches and a pot of coffee. James ignored the food and reached for the bottle again. He caught Peter's secretive smile and aimed a kick at his boot. 'Why do you look so smug, sir?'

'Bet you ten you'll be at the altar soon.'

'Up the stakes, Radford.'

'And another twenty.' Peter finished his sandwich and poured some brandy into the coffee pot. 'The General could've named the bride. Still can, should you dally overlong. Some poor forgotten maid waiting in the wings. A jilted, titled soul, traded for a military favour or such. The General, sir, has been generous indeed.'

James was horrified when the truth of Peter's reasoning sank in. 'Indeed, Radford. Very generous indeed.'

Peter pulled a tin of cheroots from his pocket. 'Right! Shall we get to it? Most importantly, we need a best man to ensure that you stay sober until the ceremony is done. Seeing that Charles and Martin are absent, I'd be honoured.'

'You're welcome!' James clinked his glass against his. 'But haven't you forgotten something?'

'A bride? I was coming to that. We find a delicate little thing who won't be able to withstand the rigours of life in India. The Punjab is no place for women, they say. We'll simply send her back on the first steamer.'

'You're a genius, Radford. Let's drink to that!'

'Thank you!' He raised his glass. 'Shall we line up the batting order?

Come up with a few names and leave it to me, Henderson. Women are fickle creatures. I'll send a go-between. That's the done thing.' He hoisted James to his feet. 'Come, let's find some bubbly. Celebrate your victory over the General.'

———— • ————

FROM HER BEDROOM, Victoria Fairfield watched as a gust swept the autumn leaves into the air. She sat in the window seat, samples of materials in her lap. They were for her holiday wardrobe. Her mother and Aunt Caroline planned to *drag* her across Europe the following spring with George Hunter in tow. It was time, they said, to give George her promise of marriage, seeing that she paid no interest to other suitors whatsoever.

She did not want to go back to Switzerland, but George had never been there and insisted. She hated Switzerland, the towering mountains and the ever-present snow, the cold lonely nights and memories of Martin de Winter. As she thought back to her behaviour after her return from India, she was deeply ashamed. A deep passion had ruled her mind. Martin's earthy sensuality had inflamed her. She had led him on; she had wanted him to take her virginity. It had been a passion that had to be fulfilled, a passion only he could have fulfilled. And he had.

She had then seen herself for the first time for what she really was, the seductress of a man she loved deeply but of whom she was not worthy. But she had to refuse his offer of marriage, for the sake of his future. The deep, incalculable grief in his blue eyes had been her final abasement.

She missed the easy company of Charles Henderson and envied him his freedom in Africa. She had only seen James at a few social occasions since his return from Egypt. James was a wild one, but that made him more alluring in the eyes of many a girl frustrated by the confines of social life. She could identify with those girls. She had been like that once. And now James was in deep trouble once again. Peter Radford had paid her a visit only last week and told her about General Henderson's threat to have James expelled from the regiment. They discussed the prospects of a few women who would suit James, but Peter asked her to consider James's plight.

'The regiment will be stationed in the Punjab for ten years. *India*, Vicky!' he said. 'Life with James is fun, unpredictable!'

'I would not want to marry him,' she told him. 'Neither would he have me.' It would be unfair on both Martin and James. During Martin's time in England, she had come to know them to be competitive, but behind James's bravado was a sensitive and fragile spirit, and he would not want her should he know about Martin, his cousin whom he so admired and loved. But at the thought of returning to India, a wave of longing washing over her.

A hansom drove through the gates. That would be James coming to ask her to act as a go-between, as Peter had arranged, and wondered whom he had chosen out of the three girls Peter had suggested. She looked down at his handsome figure, the wind touching his dark brown hair when he took off his helmet. She had on previous occasions searched his face for a family trait; there was only something in his laugh and in the way he moved his hands when he spoke. That was all, nothing more to show that he and Martin were first cousins.

She tied her hair with a ribbon and descended the stairs. James was warming his hands at the fire when she entered the drawing room.

'James, you've been a stranger lately.'

'I have, and I do apologise, Victoria.' The dimples in his cheeks gave him an irresistible charm.

'Sherry?' She moved to the table holding the decanters.

'Perhaps something stronger …'

'Brandy, then?' She poured a generous measure and handed him the glass.

'We have to talk privately.'

'Yes, Peter has told me all about your dilemma,' she smiled and he grimaced.

She led him into the conservatory, settled on a wicker settee by the ferns and waited for him to speak.

He swallowed deeply and, holding the glass in both hands, stared into the amber liquid. 'I know it's ridiculous, but I have no choice. I want to go to India, Vicky. I can't stay in England. I need to get away from Father, but I'm hopeless when it comes to commitment.' He looked about the conservatory at the ferns and tropical plants. 'What are these things?'

'Most are from India. Father plucked them from the Indian soil and now they're forced to adapt. Like me, I suppose.'

'Oh, poor Vicky!' He gave her a dimpled smile. 'Fathers are beastly, aren't they?'

She watched as his fingers worried the fronds of a fern. He was impossibly attractive, and at this moment so vulnerable. True, he was impulsive and reckless, but she'd been like that once. She looked out across the garden. He need not know about Martin. It was well in the past and should surely be left there.

'There's someone who's prepared to marry you.' Her voice sounded far away to her ears. 'Someone who wouldn't be a burden to you. She'll give you back your freedom when all this has settled.'

'Who's this perfect lady? Do I know her?' He came to sit beside her.

Taking a deep breath, she faced him squarely. 'Yes, you do. Me.'

His expression turned from disbelief to disappointment. 'Don't make fun of me, Victoria!'

'I'm being perfectly serious. You could marry me.'

'Has it slipped your mind that you're promised to Hunter?'

'I've not given my promise.' She reached for his glass and took a swig. 'There will be some explaining to do, but I shall simply say that I've fallen in love with you, and that the feeling is mutual.'

'Don't be ridiculous! They won't believe you.'

'No they won't, they won't believe me. But then, I'm of age, James. If you're willing to play along, I can handle this.'

He put down his glass, shaking his head firmly. 'The scandal you're now proposing sounds splendid, but will tear your reputation to shreds.'

'To match yours? At least we know each other. Leave me in Bangalore, go off to the Punjab, or wherever you want. I won't intrude on your private life.'

'Why are you doing this, Vicky?' He searched her face with wariness in his eyes. 'Hunter will not suffer dishonour—'

'No, he will not! That's why I dare not marry him.' On seeing his perplexed look, she relented. 'I'm not an innocent woman. I loved someone once, but he couldn't have me. It was years ago.'

'Oh poor girl!' He took her hand in his. 'You're in a pickle. I too have secrets. We all do, I suppose. Whoever it was, I don't want to hear about him. But all I can offer is a name tarnished with scandal, and my everlasting gratitude.'

'Take me to India and then leave me be.'

He drained the glass, leant back and laughed. 'Radford will be bowled flat! Nicked by the go-between and Hunter's misfortune into the bargain!'

'There's one small thing. I might be able to secure my freedom, but I can't escape my obligation to my father.' He looked at her, nonplussed. 'Oh James, don't be so daft. An heir. I have to produce at least one.'

After a tense moment, he burst out laughing again. 'I could manage that!' He pulled her into an embrace, kissing her forcefully. 'This ought to give you a head-start. Your mother's maid has been spying on us.' He waved to the woman who was standing close to the glass wall, peering in.

'James, you do stir things!' But he was already halfway to the door, his laugh still ringing out.

ONCE AGAIN JAMES stood in the General's study, but this time his eyes were not fixed on the tiger head. He was past showing respect to his father. By now the resentment that had built up against him had reached breaking point.

'You ordered me to marry. Victoria Fairfield proposed to me last week. I have accepted.'

General Henderson's eyes filled with disbelief, only for an instant, and then his disparaging glare returned. 'Have you spoken to Lord Fairfield? He will naturally refuse.'

'Victoria is of age.'

'Lady Victoria is promised to Captain George Hunter. Were you aware of that?'

'She was until you made me available, sir.'

'You're turning this into a mockery, like all else in your life. Have you no sense of honour? I've searched my mind to see where I've gone wrong in raising you! I have ...'

'Don't condemn yourself for something you had no part in. You did not raise me, sir. I suppose I should thank God for that! Added together, the time I saw you before my eighteenth birthday amounts to three years and two months. Oh yes, I've kept count! The few months I spent with Uncle Marthinus in Africa taught me about life, about caring, things you have not the *faintest* concept of. As from this moment, I do not want you meddling in my life, military or personal. Mother and you! *You and Mother!*' He stabbed his finger at his father. 'If you do, I shall go out of my way to cause the biggest scandal yet, even if it destroys my future!'

A Society Wedding

PAUL WARREN, grey frock coat, top hat, grey gloves and with a white carnation in his buttonhole, made his way to the church. It was his wedding day. He was proud of his choice of bride. Stefanie de Winter was educated, refined, an excellent hostess. She was attractive, but it was her mind and her abilities that had caught his eye. With this much-admired pianist as his wife, the gossip would cease and his popularity would soar.

Her Boer family, he had come to realise, counted very much in his favour. There was the mother, daughter of Sir Andrew Stewart, and her aristocratic Henderson cousins – sons of a British general. And should he want to impress the Cape Afrikaners, what could be more striking than a father-in-law who was a Volksraad member in the Transvaal? And then, the biggest prize of them all: Martin de Winter, an enlightened man who fought for reform. Since the Jameson Raid, Warren had acted as negotiator on behalf of the Reform Committee. And Martin de Winter was on the other side of the table, the most inspired negotiator the Boer republic had ever had.

Yes, he smiled to himself; his family-in-law. The mother, soft and dreamy, very much in love with her Boer husband, forever pointing out places where he had courted her. The fat old aunt, viewing everything with suspicion. The others treated her like they would a prize milk cow, so much did they esteem her. And then there was the beautiful Boer girl who might marry De Winter, Stefanie had confided. But Martin de Winter had gone off to fight Chief Mpefu. Warren was bitterly disappointed at his absence, but not surprised. Not much was said about the twin brothers. A scandal perhaps? And the tall English doctor who spoke fluent Afrikaans. But where was the younger cousin? The handsome young man with the arrogant flashing eyes? Oh yes, wounded in Sudan.

What would a war do to this family? Was Martin de Winter aware of the conflict that was so secretly and patiently being planned against his nation, using the Outlanders as justification? It would take the British a few months to overrun the Boers. If only the War Office would comply with Sir Alfred Milner's request for more troops! He would have to work on that.

The notes from the organ broke his reverie and he took his place near the pulpit, half-facing the door. He had a good view of the congregation. Everyone of importance was there, except Martin de Winter. The bride would not be late. She was a perfectionist, like him. She appeared on her father's arm. There were no bridesmaids. She would want to be the sole object of attention today. He couldn't see her face behind the veil, but her chin was lifted in her characteristic pose, surveying the congregation as if they were an audience at one of her recitals.

———•———

STEFANIE REFUSED TO ALLOW THE MAID to help her out of her wedding gown. She wanted to be alone to savour the day and relish her beautiful house. A double-storey house in Rondebosch, the most exclusive suburb of Cape Town, on the landward side of the mountain and only a few miles from the city centre. There were fifteen rooms, and a cook, a gardener, a house-girl and a man to run errands and see to her Cape cart, which she would drive herself.

She surveyed her luxurious bedroom and the adjoining boudoir, and glanced at the connecting door that led to Paul's bedroom. He was still in his study. A man had arrived from Johannesburg and had requested an interview on a matter of great importance. She was glad. She needed time to gather her wits.

The wedding had been a success and the reception had gone off splendidly. Her parents had chatted easily with the other guests. Koba had sat quietly with an overawed Annecke, but Charles had fitted in perfectly. The officers from the Cape garrison discovered that he was the brother of Lieutenant James Henderson, recently decorated for rescuing a wounded fellow officer.

Voices drifted up from the front door. Paul's untimely visitor was leaving. She dressed in her new silk nightgown. Her hands were clammy, but she forced herself to take up the brush and gave her hair a few strokes. She stared into the mirror. Her hair rippled over her shoulders down to her waist. *No, too girlish!* She secured it with a ribbon.

The connecting door opened. Her husband entered, a red smoking jacket over his shirtsleeves, a small parcel in his hand. He gave her a disarming smile and took a seat by the window.

'I've sent for a nightcap, my dear. Cognac for me and a little champagne for you.'

There came a knock on the door and on Paul's command the maid entered. She placed a tray on the low table.

Stefanie took the chair opposite him. He indicated the packet he had placed on the table. 'My wedding gift to you, my dear.'

She found a necklace and earrings to match her engagement ring. She wondered if she ought to kiss him, but he gave no indication of his desire, so she sat with the gift on her lap.

'A splendid day! Did you enjoy it as much as I did, my dear? Tomorrow we'll take your family on a picnic to Green Point, if the weather holds.'

He talked on for a while about her father having invited him to Wintersrust when time allowed, and how he was looking forward to meeting her brothers. Putting his glass down, he leaned towards her. 'Let's see if my gift matches your eyes. Undo your hair, my dear.'

She undid the ribbon, her hands trembling slightly. He took a strand of her golden-brown hair and brushed it to his lips. She smelt cigar smoke and cognac and tried not to inhale deeply. He led her to the mirror, stood behind her, looking over her shoulder, a veiled expression in his dark eyes as he fastened the necklace around her neck. The jewels sparkled in the muted light and her eyes shone bluer and deeper. His fingers traced the outline of her chin, her throat and came to rest lightly on her breast, his eyes all the time holding hers in the mirror. She waited breathlessly, but he led her back to the chair and picked up his glass again.

'My dear, we've not talked about children.'

She sipped her champagne, puzzled by his change of manner. She had not thought about having children yet, or about how one prevented having them. Surely it was the man's responsibility?

'I have a full season ahead,' she said. 'I'd prefer to wait.'

He cocked an eyebrow. 'I thought so and I agree whole-heartedly. We both have our respective careers, and mine keeps me from home for weeks at a time.'

'Well, that's settled then,' she said with a smile she hoped looked inviting.

'Yes, that's settled.' He drained his glass, stood up and planted a light kiss on her forehead. When he reached the connecting door, he turned, his expression hooded. 'When the time comes, the key is on your side of the lock. Good night, my dear, sleep well.' He closed the door behind him.

She sat frozen, her eyes on the door, humiliation engulfing her. After a while she replaced the jewels in their box, climbed into bed and turned down the lamp. He had left the choice to her, and she would make him wait. She would never, ever allow an indication that the marriage was not perfect. But how long was she to speculate about physical love, she wondered miserably.

The President's Banquet

WHERE THE APIES RIVER cut through the Magaliesberg stood a gigantic wild fig said to be a hundred years old. The heavy branches had re-rooted themselves, creating the impression of a forest. Under this tree General Piet Joubert halted his weary commando. Word had reached Pretoria, a few miles to the south, that they were on their way, victorious yet again. The war against Mpefu was over. There had been little fighting; the artillery had seen to that. Mpefu had escaped to the north, but it had taken the commando three months to reclaim the stolen cattle.

After allowing time to refresh at the nearby stream, General Joubert ordered the commando to form up. The State Artillery led the procession, their blue-grey uniforms dirty and torn, their hats stained, the plumes hanging limp. Then came the General's tented wagon, the mobile headquarters, and behind it, the ambulance, Charles's double-axle horse-cart. Bringing up the rear was the commando, loosely bunched behind their commandant and field cornets. There were no uniforms here, except the bandoliers slung across their chests, and their slouch hats.

It was a week before Christmas, and the men were impatient to get back to their farms. 'We're not soldiers of the old Queen to ride in straight lines and parade ourselves before the *Volk*,' grumbled Jan Viljoen. 'We are men! Hungry for food and drink and for our women!'

'A victorious entry, Jan,' Charles said, 'will make us feel like heroes at least.'

'It might be your first war, Charles, my friend, but I, Jan Viljoen have fought them more times than I can count. I'm a weary, thirsty man!'

Yes, this was an annual outing, Charles thought, it was their way of life.

Charles had joined them after returning from Stefanie's wedding, but there had been little to do. The men generally treated their wounds with homebrew or even gun oil. The few wounded had already been sent home and the ambulance was filled with leaves and tubers stuffed into linen bags. Anita would help him with the infusions and extractions. She would make tea, they would settle on the back stoep and she would tell him about the births, ailments and deaths she'd seen to in his absence.

As he rode with the commando, he had been struck anew by the beauty of his adopted country. The scenery was lush after the spring rains. The trees were resplendent in fresh summer leaves. Here and there some mimosa still had a few yellow powder puffs. The thatch-grass was knee high, the afternoon sun turning the fine tufts into a sea of shiny pink. The heavy summer rains were threatening to break, the air humid with warning.

'Charles, you're dreaming again,' Martin said and slapped the horse's rump. 'Take your place at the ambulance. We are almost there.'

They reached Pretoria and paraded down Schoeman Street, lined with people waving Vierkleurs, hats and *kappies*. At Church Square, they filed past the President's house. The old man, presidential sash across his broad stomach, stood at his gate, doffing his top hat as he acknowledged the salute of the artillery. The commando, raising their hats, called greetings to Oom Paul. The artillery carried on to the barracks and the men dispersed into the crowd.

Charles saw Koba, with Annecke at her side, and rushed over. 'Is this the welcome a man gets when he returns from war? Where are the others?'

'There's too much to be done on the farms,' Annecke said. 'Tante Koba and I have bought the things for Christmas and will travel back with you when you are ready. On Thursday night there's a state banquet for General Joubert and his men. Will you go?'

'No, Annecke,' Charles smiled. 'We'll leave that to Martin. Too much work to be done on the farms? Are the twins not back yet?'

She shook her head miserably. 'It's been months now.'

Jan Viljoen and Joep Maree descended on them. Annecke flung herself into her father's arms. Jan teased Koba in his usual manner and they set off, leading their horses, stopping frequently to greet others.

'I've prepared a little dinner for you all,' Koba called as she settled into her Cape cart and took up the reins.

Charles chuckled. 'Will be enough to feed the entire commando?'

WHEN JOEP MAREE and Jan Viljoen left the following day, with promises to meet for the New Year dance, peace finally came to Koba's house. After dinner they settled in the sitting room, exchanging news about Wintersrust and the district.

Annecke went to the dresser and brought Charles a bundle of letters.

'Anita sent these. She says everything is under control, but she's not qualified to treat sick cows and horses. Martin, your letters are in your room. Shall I fetch them?'

'I'll go through them later. Come sit by me. Tell me what dress you're going to wear to the banquet.'

'Annecke, *hartjie*, wear the green one,' Koba advised, 'the one that shines like emeralds; the one that Stefanie sent.' She turned to Charles, 'Have you told Martin about Mr Rhodes?'

'No, Tante Koba, it slipped my mind.' He gave Martin a secret wink.

She launched into a description of the wonders she'd seen in Cape Town and of the splendid wedding. 'I've never seen so many gentlemen. And poor Mr Rhodes, he looked so sick. I wanted to suggest one of my remedies, but Stefanie said that it's not proper to talk about ill health at a wedding …'

There was a knock on the door. Martin found a clerk with a manila envelope containing documents for his immediate attention. Koba announced that she was ready for bed and gave them each a kiss. Annecke kissed Charles, but he saw that she only managed a hesitant kiss on Martin's forehead before following Koba to her bedroom.

Martin poured them each a glass of brandy. 'Tomorrow I'm setting the wedding date. I'm nearing thirty and running out of time, Charles. Ever since I returned from England, Pa and the President have pestered me to find a wife. I cannot let them wait much longer.'

Throughout their trip, Charles had asked from town to town, farm to farm, but no one had seen twin brothers pass by. 'Listen to yourself, Martin. Does it have to be Annecke? There are at least a hundred suitable girls, if only you take the time to get to know them …'

'But it's Annecke I want.' Martin turned his attention to the letter on his lap. He read a few lines and cursed strongly. 'I must go to Johannesburg tomorrow. A Zarp, Constable Jones, has shot an Englishman by the name of Edgar.'

'Surely it can wait?'

'No, Charles, he killed the man and the Outlanders want him to hang. They want justice, their kind of justice.' He read on and groaned. 'They've already appointed a lawyer for Edgar's widow. None other than my bloody brother-in-law! This will turn into more than a court case. Warren has a way of doing that.'

Charles flipped through his post. He opened the most recent letter from his mother, read a few lines and sighed. 'James has caused a scandal, the details too indelicate to tell, Mother writes, followed by an almighty row with Father.'

'Sounds familiar,' Martin said, still occupied with his letter.

Charles gasped when he got to the end of the page. 'Good God! James is married. *Married*, for God's sake! *Hastily arranged*, Mother writes.'

'Heavens! I thought he kept to married women. Who caught him? Do we know her?'

Charles turned the page. He couldn't bear to look at Martin, and merely said, 'James married Vicky.' Martin sat quietly, his hands on the letter on his lap. Taking a large swallow from his glass, Charles read on. The ceremony in the chapel at Sandhurst took all of ten minutes. James left directly to resume his duties and Victoria went with the Radford women to Italy to spend the winter. No reception, no wedding night, no honeymoon. A week later, George Hunter announced his engagement to a young debutante.

When he had time to collect himself, Charles said, 'The regiment is being sent to India.' Martin did not look at him. 'James was not aware of the … happenings between you and Vicky. I know it's hard, Martin, but it might help to think that love is not always considered in these matters. Don't see it as betrayal.'

THE NEXT MORNING Martin took the train to Johannesburg. He reported to the state law offices and was taken to the police station to meet the accused. At four o'clock he had the case before a magistrate and Constable Jones was released on a thousand pounds bail, scraped together by Boer businessmen. The trial was set for January, pending the arrival of Paul Warren.

An angry feeling was evident in the city. Reporters crowded around Martin, demanding to know what he made of the shooting. He answered as best as he could. Shortly before six he remembered that he needed to buy a present for Annecke and went into a shop in Commissioner Street. He indicated the music boxes on display, the first items that caught his eye.

'A fine choice, sir,' said the shop attendant. 'The large one has perforated discs with fine classical pieces. The smaller ones include a sailor turning to 'Rule Britannia', a shepherdess with 'Mary had a little lamb', and then this one with a delightful ballad taken from a London show. Very popular, sir. Shall I demonstrate?'

'No, but thank you, the one with the ballad will do.' He looked through the brooches and selected one, a basket filled with cherries, for Koba.

He checked his watch, hurried to the station and boarded the train. The heartache he had fought all day now washed over him. The image of Vicky's green eyes and honey-coloured hair enveloped him. And James, his devil-may-care cousin, was at her side. It was like a dream, a very bad nightmare. It was betrayal. Sleep, oblivion, was all he craved.

On arriving in Pretoria, he went to the office of the State Attorney, Jan Smuts, and made his report on the Edgar-Jones case. Smuts showed him a cable from Charles Leonard informing them of the rally the Outlanders planned to stage in Johannesburg the next day and about a petition that was to be sent to the Queen should Constable Jones be acquitted of murder.

'The man is innocent,' Martin said. 'He was attacked by a drunk wielding an iron bar.'

'If Jones is innocent,' Smuts retorted, 'he will be found so accordingly. We will not permit mob justice. I've just had a long meeting with Frazer, the British High Commissioner, about the treatment of British subjects in the Transvaal. He said that Britain would even go to war over such things.'

MARTIN WAS IMMENSELY TIRED when he arrived at Koba's house. There was just enough time to change into his evening clothes for the President's banquet. Charles came into his room and settled on his bed.

'How was your day in Johannesburg?' he asked.

'The case is set for next month. And Smuts says that Britain is set on war. War!'

'You're just overwrought—'

'No, Charles, there will be war!' He did up his studs and secured his collar. 'There's nothing the President or Jan Smuts or I can do about it. The only hope is that we keep them talking till something turns up. But then, I don't know if I want to fight them with words any longer. I'm sick and tired of their constant interference in our affairs.'

'For God's sake, be reasonable! Don't let James's marriage influence you.'

He pulled a brush through his hair and beard with angry strokes. 'For three years I have tried my utmost to put her out of my mind. Three years, Charles. Hoping never to come across her again. Why my very own cousin? Charles, I made her a woman.'

———

WHEN THE CAPE CART halted at the Transvaal Hotel, Annecke longed for the evening to be over. She was thankful for the gloves, her hands were sweaty. She tugged nervously at her dress. Emerald taffeta shot with blue. Stefanie had bought it in Cape Town. Stefanie was always sending her things – hats, gloves, shawls – she had no more use for. She touched her hair. Koba had tried to secure it with pins, but it would not hold.

182

Martin placed her hand on his arm and led her into the hotel. An artillery corporal greeted Martin as if he was the President himself and took them to one of the long tables. The Vierkleur was pinned to the wall above the main table, where the President and General Joubert were to take their places. White cloths on the tables, silver candelabra holding thin candles. Not the type made on the farm, but the ones in the shops. There were roses in small silver vases, crystal glasses and many knives and forks at each place.

This would be her life if she were to marry Martin. She didn't want to be a lawyer's wife. She wanted to be a *boervrou*, but Martin wanted her to be like Stefanie – at ease in the company of the cleverest people. She loved Martin, had always hoped to marry him. But now she knew about love, at least she thought she did. If only Rudi and Karel would come back. It was almost Christmas. Surely they would be home for Christmas.

Now she knew that she loved Rudi. Yes, she loved Karel, just as much as Rudi, but it was a different love, a love that had nothing to do with her body. And she knew about that now too. She'd felt it when Rudi had held and kissed her the night he had come into her room. A strange feeling had come up from her legs, her stomach and had crept into her breasts. It had been the first time she'd felt it and she knew it was love.

She looked about the tables filling up with Town Boers. The few girls present looked at her with envy. It was always like that. There was not a girl in Pretoria or the district who did not want to marry Martin, Koba said.

She stole a glance at him. He was dressed in his London clothes – black evening suit, a bow tie and a white shirt she'd pressed that morning. His face was drawn, lines down the sides of his mouth that had not been there yesterday. His eyes were red as if he had been crying. No, Martin wouldn't cry. It was the policeman who had shot the Outlander. That was what had upset him.

A trumpet sounded and everyone rose. Loud cheering saw the President, flanked by guards, to his chair at the head of the table. On his right sat General Joubert and his wife. She reminded Annecke of someone from her childhood. Aunt Susan, Charles's mother, had the same look, the look that told everyone that she was his or her better. Stefanie was like that, but only when it suited her.

A call for silence. Out of the cloud of pipe smoke the President rose, planted his huge hands on the table, cleared his throat and spat into the spittoon to his right. He spoke in his jerky voice, telling them about the Great Trek, how the Lord had led them out of the land of Egypt, out of bondage from the British, into this, the Promised Land. And now they and their sister republic of the Free State were surrounded again by the people of Egypt. He called on them not to forget their brethren's blood that had bought them this land. He banged his fist on the table and urged them to stand fast in their faith.

'The Almighty gave us victory over Mpefu, and the greater victory, Majuba. Yes, the English are threatening us again, but God will not let His people down. He gave us water when we were thirsty. Food when we were hungry. He showed us the way when we were lost. He came to our rescue in our darkest hour.'

The President always spoke like a *predikant*. Martin did that too, always quoting from the Bible to make a point. It was the way to the *Volk's* heart, he said.

The President's speech ended amid thunderous applause and everyone rose as he left. Waiters filled their glasses with wine and brought plates of food. Martin did not touch his food. 'General Joubert will make a speech and then we'll have music. Have I told you how beautiful you are tonight, Annecke?' He smiled at her, but his eyes were not smiling.

She tried to appear happy and searched for something to say, but he was already talking to a Town Boer across the table.

General Joubert came to his feet. He praised the burghers for always being ready to answer the call, and pleaded with them to set aside their differences and face the new threat hanging over them like a storm cloud. For how could they fight an enemy if they were not united? There was loud applause, and Martin shouted 'hear, hear'.

The general reminded them that war was not always the solution to a nation's problems. Some men grumbled. They wanted a war. Koba had said that men could not endure life without having a little war every now and again.

When Joubert finished his speech, the men shouted and applauded long and hard. Then the musicians started, a sign to the guests that they were free to leave their seats. Men eager to talk to Martin immediately surrounded him. It was always like that.

Annecke listened to the music. It had a sad sound to it. It was like the pieces Stefanie played when she had finished practising from her books. Then there was a dreamy look on her face and you could tell that she was thinking about love. Her husband was a good-looking man, but Koba had said that he was not a man to be underestimated. She didn't like what was hidden in his eyes.

Shortly before midnight the band struck up the *Volkslied*. The men sang loudly, the words coming from their hearts. Afterwards all filed out of the hotel, but she had to wait for Martin to finish a discussion with Jan Smuts.

Just as she wanted to return to her chair, Martin took her hand and at last they went home.

The house was quiet, but Koba had left a lamp in the sitting room and a jug of lemonade on the table. She thought that, being so tired, Martin would want to go to his room straight away, but he pulled her down next to him on the sofa and took her hands in his. His hands were large, like a Boer's, but his fingers were stained by ink. She could see the smudges where he had tried to scrub it away. He talked about the house his father was building in Pretoria and about the curtains and wallpaper she could order from Beckett's store.

'Annecke, I think that your eighteenth birthday will be a good day to get married,' he said, but there was not so much as a sweetness in his voice, as Koba would say.

She didn't know how to tell him about her love for Rudi. He was an important and respected man, his presence overpowering, everybody did what he wanted. She swallowed hard, 'Martin, you should marry one of the town girls. I cannot do what you expect of me—'

'You'll learn with time, Annecke. I know it's hard, but you must converse with people more freely.'

'I can't, Martin. I tried at Stefanie's wedding. There were many important people there. I asked her if those people will come to her house and she said that of course they would. She can do it, but I can't. I'll only embarrass you.'

'No, you won't. Once you get used to life in Pretoria—'

'I don't want to live in Pretoria.'

'Annecke! My place is in Pretoria. I can't live at Wintersrust.'

She saw that his eyes were half-closed, as if he was thinking deeply. Then he cupped her face in his hand, turned her head so that she was looking into his eyes. His eyes were the same as Rudi's, deep blue, but Rudi's eyes were always smiling and Martin's were serious, and there was so much hurt in them, pain she didn't know the cause of. He kissed her, his mouth covering hers completely, his beard soft against her chin. It was as if he was seeking for something, waiting for something.

'If it's time you need to get used to all this, I understand,' he said. 'We'll talk about marriage next year.'

She nodded. Rudi and Karel would be back long before then. She felt proud of herself. For the first time, she had had the courage to say what needed to be said. But she also felt sorry for Martin. He was so troubled and then she had to disappoint him on top of that.

He came to his feet. 'I won't be going to Wintersrust. The Outlanders are going to march through Johannesburg and the President has asked me to speak to them on his behalf.'

'Will you be home for the New Year's dance?'

'I'll try my best.' He handed her a small parcel that he took from the mantelpiece.

She removed the wrapping and found a little box covered in scarlet velvet. 'Is there something inside? Shall I open it?'

'If you want,' he said from where he was leaning against the doorframe. She unwrapped the music box, and gave a cry of surprise when a little figurine appeared and started turning. Thin silvery chords filled the room. She watched mesmerised, but the melody caught at her heart. 'It's so sad. Do you know the song, Martin?'

His face had gone pale and it was only when the song ended that he spoke again. 'It's about a girl who waits for her soldier to come back from a faraway country.'

'And does he come back?' Suddenly she had to know if the sad girl's love had returned. She had to know if Rudi would come back. The story of this song would tell her that.

'I don't know. It's not said whether he returns.' He left the room quietly.

She sat with the box on her lap, playing the song again, tears trickling down her cheeks. She closed the lid and went to Koba's room, crawled into her bed and lay against her wide comforting back, wondering if Rudolf and Karel were wandering, lost and alone in a strange land.

A Strange Land

I T WAS LONELY being a stranger in a strange land, Rudolf thought. The countryside, the animals, the clouds and wind were much the same, yet it was all so different. The smell, the feel of home, of belonging, was absent and gave a man a vulnerable feeling deep in his heart.

He shielded his eyes against the late afternoon sun, scanning for a suitable place for the night. It was wild country, very wild. Hardly a day passed that they didn't happen upon lion, sometimes several prides a day. The camp had to be in the open veld, away from high trees, for fear of an unexpected attack by a leopard at night. It was also unwise to camp too close to a water hole, as these were rare during the winter, and the game, which was followed by predators, made use of them too.

He found a flat piece of ground in the open, removed the bit from Lady's mouth to allow her to graze and set about clearing a camp site and preparing a fire. Although it was winter, it was still warm during the day, but at night the temperature dropped rapidly. He spoke softly to Lady as he worked. She was fidgety, rolling her eyes at the slightest sound or movement and pawing the ground. She whinnied shrilly and turned her head south as if to tell him that her home was there, the stable and country she was used to and longed for.

It would be dark soon and they needed something for the pot. Karel and Legend were riding in search of a buck. Rudolf collected enough firewood to see them through the night and prepared a shelter of acacia scrub. By the time he had finished, there was still no sign of Karel. He built a fire, brewed some coffee and settled down to wait.

How long since they had left the farm? It had been at the end of August and now it was winter again. Ten months! And Annecke was probably married to Martin, living in Pretoria in a new house. He should have stayed at Wintersrust, but Karel had needed him. The bond between them was so deep now that it scared him sometimes. They knew each other's thoughts before a single glance or word had been exchanged. When the scorpion had stung him on his foot, Karel had suffered the agony of the burning pain just as if he had also been stung. He knew in his heart that if he had to choose between his love for Annecke and his love for Karel, he would choose his brother. Was that not what had happened that terrible day in his father's study?

A nightjar called, greeting the approaching dusk. He stretched his legs. There was a movement in the tall grass and he spied Karel leading Legend. All was well. He pulled the coffee pot from the fire.

They had left that night under a full moon and had ridden northeast into the bushveld. After a few weeks, they had crossed into the new British territory named after the Englishman Cecil Rhodes. They made their way through country of astounding beauty. It was early summer and the grass was rich and green. There were many acacia trees, and giant sausage and leadwood trees, and strange baobabs. Herds of buffalo, elephant and giraffe walked past them, unperturbed by their presence. Beautiful sable antelope tossed their curved horns, and even Karel could not find it in his heart to shoot them.

They had come upon a few small settlements, where they bought coffee, meal and salt. When they needed money for supplies, they worked from farm to farm – breaking in horses, training draught animals and herding the cattle of the settlers. They never stayed long in one place and moved steadily northwards until they reached the administrative centre, Salisbury. There they heard about the Englishman who had been killed by a Zarp in Johannesburg.

'The Boers had their top lawyer defending the Zarp,' the barman in the small hotel told them. 'That De Winter fellow. But, you see, the judge was a Boer and the jury consisted of Boers. There's trouble to come, that's for sure!'

They had found transport work that paid well and had stayed for three months, working the route between Salisbury and the Portuguese colony on the east coast. But soon they were on the move again, southwest this time, and now they were near a place called Bulawayo. It was already July, and Karel was anxious for news, for if there was going to be a war against the English, he was not going to miss it.

'I got an impala. Good shot, right through the head,' Karel said when he walked into the enclosure. He handed Rudolf the liver and hindquarters and unsaddled Legend.

They went to the water hole to wash and to water the horses. A small family of kudu at the edge of the water looked up surprised, tossed their heads and made off into the dusty bush. Karel knelt by the water's edge and washed the blood off his hands and arms. Legend gave him a hard push from behind, which sent him sprawling into the water. She trotted away and calmly began to drink.

'Does Legend think I need a bath?' Karel said.

'We're a horrible sight.' Rudolf looked at Karel and then at himself. They were as rugged as the country they were travelling through – lean and hard, their faces tanned to a deep brown. Both had scraggly beards and Karel had tied his hair back with a leather thong. His own was wild and matted, reaching his shoulders.

They rubbed the horses down with tufts of dry grass and returned to the enclosure, where they felt secure in their own little world. The gathering dusk brought the night music. Nightjars cried as they dipped through the air, swooping on prey, a thousand crickets started their chorus, and far-off hyenas barked.

Karel built up the fire, sprinkled the last of the salt on the meat and sat close to Rudolf. 'Rudi, it's so good to be free, but I keep on thinking about the Mausers.'

'Yes, why do you think we have them?'

'We should get closer to home, Rudi. Should a war start, we will be within reach.'

He stared into the fire. 'You want to go home, don't you, Karel? I also want to, but not unless you are ready.'

'You know what I was thinking about when I was out hunting. Pa refusing us Botha's farm just for a few visits to Johannesburg and forcing you to hit me for one, just one, ride on Ester Viljoen. But now, I feel, the scores are settled. We whored away every square yard of Botha's farm.'

'Delagoa Bay! Yes, should Pa ever find out about *those* places …'

'We'd be denied the whole of the Transvaal!' Karel said and they burst out laughing.

They ate the meat from the fire and reminisced about the exotic life of the Portuguese settlers on the coast, but the talk would not leave Wintersrust. 'I've had my fill of whores. I'm going to find myself a woman with wide hips and breasts like a milk-cow, marry her and farm,' Karel said. 'I want to farm, Rudi! And Annecke is waiting for you.'

TWO DAYS LATER, they came upon the wide wagon track that led to Bulawayo, and reached the village in the late afternoon. The old Matabele capital was now just a trading station. In the centre of the village was a post office, a few houses set behind the main road, and some buildings that they took to be government offices, by virtue of the Union Jack hanging limply in the still air.

At a store, they bought coffee, sugar, a bag of meal, salt and dried beans. Karel saw the bundles of oats and paid five shillings without even haggling over the exorbitant price. They found a place that resembled an inn and asked if they could spend the night in the stables. The horses settled, they went into the bar. There were a few customers, whom they took to be farmers, prospectors or traders. Rudolf placed a pound note on the counter.

The barman shoved two glasses and a bottle towards them. 'You fellows from down south?' He gave them a closer look. 'My God! Two peas in a pod!' He made a wide sweep with his hands, calling the others. 'Come see one of the miracles of nature. For a moment there, I thought this cheap liquor had affected my vision.'

They endured the stares and comments of the others. A man with a pronounced Irish accent introduced himself as Patrick McFee and wanted to know if they were gold diggers from Johannesburg.

'Johannesburg, yes, but not gold diggers. We do a little of this and that,' Karel said.

'We've not been home since last year and wonder if you might have news of the country?' Rudolf asked.

'Then you must go home, lads. The Transvaal is preparing for war. A war against the mighty Empire,' the barman said and the men laughed to show what they thought of such a ridiculous idea.

Karel joined in the laughter. Rudolf stole a glance at his twin. He smelled trouble, but Karel hadn't had a decent brawl since that evil-looking Portuguese had tried to buy Legend off him for a hundred pounds.

'They've been preparing for war for the last three years,' Karel scoffed, pouring the brandy. He tasted it and pulled a face. 'Is this really brandy?'

'Mighty sorry, lads. Pure rotgut! Judging by your appearance, you'll not be able to afford a good brandy at two pounds the bottle.'

'You're right,' Rudolf said. 'This will do just fine. Now tell us, have there been any new developments since the Jones case?'

'But you are out of things!' McFee said. 'Just three weeks ago we heard the news about the conference.' He saw the blank look on their faces and continued, 'A conference was held at Bloemfontein. The president there, I forget his name—'

'Steyn, President Steyn,' Karel said.

'Whatever. Well, things got so bad that he invited old Kruger and the High Commissioner to come and talk things over. And they talked and talked for days, but the old President would not give in. So he gathered his men and his Bible and left.'

'Some say the old man could not read all the fancy words and left for home to save face,' someone called. More derisive comments about Kruger and the Boers followed.

'And now? What happens now?' Karel asked.

'Well, laddie, now we wait and see. Travellers coming through your country say that the Boers are just waiting for the word to mount and ride,' the Irishman said.

The men in the bar agreed that the Boers would be forced to surrender with the first shot fired. They were drinking fast and steadily now. As they poured the last drops from the bottle, Karel whispered to Rudolf to saddle the horses and bring them to the front. He left on the pretext that he was going out to relieve himself.

'Are you lads going to join up, then? It's said that the Cape Colony is raising a force,' the barman asked.

'Damned right!' Karel emptied his glass just as Rudolf appeared in the door. 'Good night, sir!' he called and thanked the men for the news.

'You're welcome, lad,' the man returned. 'Give old Kruger hell!'

Karel burst out laughing, jumped on a table and shouted in Afrikaans. 'The mighty British Empire? We will ride you and your old queen bareback. We are Boers! Come, have a taste of what's waiting for you!'

It took a moment before the men collected their wits, and then all hell broke loose. A burly prospector came for Karel. Rudolf stuck out his foot and the man fell heavily against the table. Karel jumped on his back and then the others were on them. Rudolf swung a chair and it connected with a head. He was grabbed from behind but ducked and sent the attacker rolling. A fist caught Karel squarely on the jaw and he let loose a string of curses. Rudolf went for Karel's attacker and kicked him high on the chest.

The barman shouted for order, but the Irishman and his friend had decided that they were on the side of the Boers and a free-for-all began. The noise was overpowering. Shouts, curses, wild laughing, the crunching impacts of fists, bottles crashing and furniture being overturned.

Karel caught Rudolf's arm and, amid the confusion, they made for the door. The pack followed. Karel vaulted onto Legend. 'Take them, Legend!' he shouted. The mare rose on her hindquarters and rent the air. It gave Rudolf time to calm Lady and mount. Legend hung over the men, driving them back into the bar. Karel ducked his head, urging Legend inside, sending the men fleeing to the safety of the counter. He pulled his Mauser from the blanket roll and waved it in the air.

'This is a Mauser! And I am a Boer! South of the Limpopo is my country! Come! Come fight us! We are ready for you!' And, whooping wildly, he backed Legend outside.

They rode hard for a mile, but there were no pursuers and they soon pulled the horses to a walk. Legend tossed her mane and pranced. 'You liked that, my beauty!' Karel laughed. She twitched her ears and answered with a satisfied snort.

Drunk with the exhilaration of the fight and the fiery brandy, they rode on. Blood from a gash on Rudolf's head caked his hair, and his right eye was swollen shut. His shirt was torn and the skin on the knuckles of both hands was broken. With a cut lip and blood still flowing, Karel was not in a much better state.

'How do we get to the war from here?' Karel asked.

'We follow the railway line to Mafeking, like the Irishman said. Very little water south of here. The railway has points where they take on water.'

'How long will it take us?'

'Six weeks, maybe. By the end of August, I think.'

On the Way to India

August 1899

THE TROOPSHIPS carrying the cavalry regiments to India left Southampton in the third week of August. Troops, non-commissioned officers and baggage were quartered on the lower decks. The horses were secured in the hold for the three-week journey. The officers, some with their wives, lived it up on the upper decks.

New orders were received at Gibraltar. The convoy was to sail round the Cape of Good Hope. This gave rise to much speculation among the officers gathered in the smoking room after dinner. 'Trouble in Egypt?' James suggested. 'Suez Canal unsafe to sail?'

'Nice try, Henderson,' Mark Sinclair said. 'I bet you it's trouble with Kruger and his Boers.'

William Moore frowned. 'Do you really think the Boers would be so shortsighted and make a show of it?'

'Let's not rush to conclusions, gentlemen.' Murray Shaw poured another brandy. 'I'll wager that we're being sent there as a show of force. Give them a little something to think about, cool them down a bit.'

James listened as the others discussed the situation in South Africa. He was furious about the diversion. Of course, there was the chance of seeing his family again, but the circumstances would be awkward. He was about to ask Shaw to refill his glass, when their commanding officer, Colonel Norman Butcher, entered and called for order.

James hauled Peter, who had been drinking steadily to ward off seasickness, to his feet and almost toppled over with him. They saluted the colonel hurriedly.

Butcher smiled dryly and turned to address the gathering. 'Gentlemen, a deadlock has been reached in the negotiations between Her Majesty's government and that of President Kruger. It appears that the Boers are getting ready for war. We have only ten thousand troops in the colonies, an ideal chance for the Boers should they strike now. Our orders are to strengthen the force in the Cape Colony until a settlement can be reached. General White and a large contingent are leaving England in the near future, bound for Natal. Once they reach there, we shall proceed to our original destination.'

Mark Sinclair put the question everyone wanted to ask. 'Has war been declared, sir?'

'No, war has not been declared, Lieutenant.'

'Did the War Office give an indication of the probability of war, sir?' James asked.

'The message from General Henderson is that the decision lies with the Boers. In your father's opinion, war is inevitable.'

'Then there'll be war,' Peter said to James. 'Your old man's hardly ever wrong.'

'What was that, Lieutenant Radford?' Colonel Butcher frowned.

'He said that at least the horses can disembark at Cape Town, sir,' James lied. 'The route around the Cape is very stormy.'

'Yes, provision will be made for accommodation. We dock in Cape Town in twelve days.' A flurry of questions overwhelmed Butcher. 'Later, gentlemen, inform the men first, then your wives.'

Peter prodded James in the ribs, indicating the door. 'Your wife, sir.'

MY WIFE, James thought as he made his way to Victoria's cabin. The words were still strange to his ears, but what a stroke of luck to have her come to his rescue. Married life was not as restrictive as he'd thought it would be. Indeed, it had been a wise decision not to chuck in his commission. For the time being, he could live with the fact that he was a married man. Once they reached India, Victoria would settle in the bungalow her father had provided at Bangalore and he would move on to the Punjab, a free man.

Victoria made no demands of any kind, and he enjoyed her company, as did his fellow officers. They had been stunned by the hasty marriage, but, as no explanation had been forthcoming, blamed his impulsive nature, Peter told him. George Hunter, however, predicted disaster, but James put it down to resentment.

James had not seen his parents since the day he had stormed from his father's study until he had stood at the altar, Peter Radford at his side. Lord Fairfield and General Henderson endured the service with icy composure, he noted. His mother, Victoria had told him, was over-whelmed by *this most desirable union*. And Lady Fairfield? Well, she still questioned her wilful daughter's reason for marring *this impossible young officer*. When Victoria returned from Italy, she rented a house close to the regiment's headquarters. Without consulting him, she provided him with his own quarters; bedroom, drawing room and study. The marriage had not been consummated, as there had been no wedding night, no honeymoon. Then one night she came into his bedroom.

He had been on duty the entire day and arrived home late and sober. She joined him for a late supper and they discussed their travel arrangements for India. Victoria, who had no plans to return to England, had a long list of things she wanted to be shipped over: crates of books, clothes, her bicycle and two horses. After the meal, he retired to his room and was in bed, when a soft rap came on the door. Dressed in her nightgown, her long auburn hair a thick curtain over her shoulders, hands behind her back, green eyes questioning, he immediately knew what she wanted.

'Once we get to India you might not have much time on your hands before you depart for the Punjab. Unless you don't feel like—'

'Oh, let's not put it off. I promised you a child. If that's what you want, you shall have it.'

She produced champagne and glasses from behind her back and made herself at home on his bed. Her confidence and easy laughter were infectious and they treated the coming intimacy as they had everything up to then – as a joke. But it was more than that, and the next morning she was still in his bed. An odd thought struck him then and he laughed.

'What's so funny, James?' she asked through sleepy eyes.

'I was just thinking, Vicky, waking up with my wife, not somebody else's.'

'And is that disagreeable?'

'On the contrary. I shall take advantage of it.'

Beatrice Harcourt had given birth to a girl, Sarah. His father had ordered him to pay his respects to the new addition to the family. The baby's little face evoked emotions he hadn't expected – his child, his baby girl. A sudden urge to touch her, to pick her up and feel the reality of her came to him. He left, went directly to the mess and tried to erase the disturbing emotions in drink. But the solace he'd sought in brandy, he found in Victoria's arms the following night. And since that night she had never refused him. She seemed to welcome it. And that he did not like. To sleep with her was acceptable, but to become emotionally involved was not what he wanted.

Now he rapped on her cabin door and found her sitting cross-legged on the bunk, a book on her lap.

'We've been diverted to Cape Town. Orders are awaiting us there.'

She stared at him. 'South Africa?'

'Trouble in the Transvaal, apparently. We're to hold the fort, so to speak, until General White and his lot turn up. We'll be on our way again in no time.' There was no response from her and he searched for something positive to say. 'You'll meet my cousin Stefanie. We could cable Charles to come down. Martin is caught up in all this and might not find time to meet us. Tante Koba might fancy a train ride to Cape Town, if only to meet you.'

'I thought you didn't like Stefanie's husband.'

'Warren? Insufferable fellow, only met him once,' he burst out laughing. 'The bastard had me locked up in a coal shed years ago.'

'Should there be war, it will be against your family.'

'War has not been declared, Vicky,' he said angrily.

'You leap from laughter to anger in a split second, don't you just?' She put her arms around him, pulling him to her. He stiffened and pushed her away. 'I'm bored,' she smiled. 'Would you rather drink with Peter, or spend the night with me?'

He looked into her smiling green eyes. Desire swiftly replaced the anger and a smile spread across his face. 'A wife should endure her husband's attentions, not invite or enjoy them,' he teased as he bit into the soft skin of her shoulder.

———•———

TWELVE DAYS LATER, a gale heralded the arrival of the 2nd Hussars in Cape Town harbour, making it near impossible to catch a glimpse of the famed Table Mountain. The officers braved a quick turn about the heaving deck to check the conditions, as they were anxious to land the horses safely. By midday the wind abated sufficiently to allow the steamer to come alongside the quay. Troops and baggage were offloaded first while they waited for a swing to bring the horses onto land.

Peter Radford talked his way past the officials, hailed a Cape cart and hurried to a new hotel he had heard about, the Mount Nelson. He returned an hour later with the news that the hotel was overflowing with the Johannesburg elite, but that he had managed to secure two rooms.

James left Victoria to find her way there and went to assist with the horses. Hours later, wind-blown and exhausted, he and Peter arrived at the hotel with no time to change for dinner. They were ushered to their table in the dining room, where they found Victoria waiting.

'How are the horses?' she asked when they had settled and ordered a bottle of wine.

'Done in. That roan of yours didn't travel well,' Peter said, 'and one of my chargers, Jezebel, has a swollen fetlock. The vet will have his work cut out for the next few days.'

'Well at least they'll have a rest now. Any news on the situation?'

'The regiments on their way home from India were diverted to Durban and are moving to the northern Natal border. No news from Pretoria.' James beckoned the waiter to serve the first course. 'I spoke to officers from the regiments stationed here. The government is wary of war, they say, as the Afrikaners in the colonies might join their kin in the republics.'

They started on their meal, but the conversation would not leave the possibility of war.

'What about the British in Johannesburg?' Victoria asked.

'Abandoning ship,' Peter indicated their fellow diners. 'Trainloads fleeing Johannesburg by the hour. The Boers mean business, they say. There has to be a way to find out what's really happening in Pretoria. If we could get word to Martin, surely he would tell us, don't you think?'

'Or Charles,' James said, 'but it might take days to get a cable from Rustenburg.'

'Be patient. There's nothing to do but wait,' Victoria said.

As they left the dining room, a waiter informed James that a visitor was awaiting him in the lounge. There they found Paul Warren, hat and gloves in hand, smiling at them. 'Lieutenant Henderson, welcome! I was told of the arrival of your regiment and hastened to get here.'

James reluctantly shook his hand and introduced Victoria and Peter. Warren made a slight bow. 'Lady Victoria, I wish you a pleasant stay. Delighted to meet you, Lieutenant Radford. Would you join me for a drink to celebrate your arrival?'

'Not tonight, I'm afraid,' James said. 'I would, however, like to see Stefanie tomorrow.'

'My wife is giving tuition in Wellington for the week. Education and social life must go on despite the situation. However, I've come to extend an invitation to you. My home is at your disposal. There is ample space and excellent servants. You're most welcome too,' he said to Peter.

'Thank you, but we're quite satisfied with our present situation.' James made to leave.

'Lieutenant Henderson, you'll be moving northwards soon,' Warren said, the smile still firmly in place. 'Your wife will find life in the hotel boring. I suggest that you allow her to stay with family for the duration of the war.'

'War has not been declared,' James snapped.

'But will be soon, sir, very soon.' Warren's dark eyes flashed. 'Lieutenant Radford, you'll find me in the bar should you want a cognac.'

What Peter heard from Warren over a glass of cognac was revealed the following morning over breakfast. 'Were you aware that Warren works closely with Sir Alfred Milner? I received the distinct impression that the authorities are playing for time, awaiting the arrival of General White. And there's talk of an even bigger contingent to follow. This might be it, James.'

'We haven't heard it from the Boer side yet.'

Peter started on his kippers. 'Quite frankly, Warren is not a fool. He attended a conference at Bloemfontein, the decisive one, he called it, and seated directly opposite him was his Boer counterpart, your cousin Martin de Winter. According to Warren, he is dead set against war. That other fellow from Cambridge, the State Attorney, Smuts, I think, and Martin make a formidable team, he says. If someone could have come up with a solution, it would've been them.'

'A solution to *what*, Radford? What's it all about?'

'I didn't quite get that!' Peter laughed. 'All sorts of things ... politics, I suppose.'

'We might be stuck here for some time, Radford. Not that I mind.'

'We're stuck here for some time,' Peter echoed. He buttered his toast. 'Stuck here for some time?' He pushed his plate aside and rose. 'Colonel Butcher expects us at nine. I need you to cover for me. Urgent things to attend to, amusement of the secular kind.'

———•———

VICTORIA SPENT an uneasy day sitting at the window, looking out at the rain-drenched garden. She thought about the possibility of seeing Martin de Winter again. What anguish was he suffering now, with his beloved country about to go to war? She did not want to see him, or even to be in the same country. Nor did she want to meet his family; she only wanted to get on to India. If not, James would have to find a suitable escort and send her on to India. But then, what would happen to him? He might find himself having to fight his own kin. She might be able to make this time easier for him. There was no denying that she liked him more than she had expected.

Conflicting emotions stayed with her through the day, and she was dressing for dinner when James arrived. 'You look a bit piqued, Vicky. A drink before dinner? Might cheer you a little,' he offered as he watched her struggling to do up her hair.

She sighed with frustration, ripped the pins from her hair and tied it with a ribbon at the nape of her neck. 'I thought I was done with dressing up.'

'Poor Vicky, we shall have to find you a maid.'

'Have you any news?' she asked as they walked down the stairs and into the lounge.

James waited until the waiter had served their sherry before he replied. 'Nothing new. I tried to send a cable to Charles, but there are a thousand government messages that have to be relayed first. I haven't seen Radford all day.' He pulled a face. 'God, I hate sherry.'

'I don't want to have anything to do with war, James. You might think me unpatriotic, but that's how I feel.'

'Unpatriotic? Let's say uninformed. Sounds better.' He indicated the door.

In the dining room they found Peter, his tunic dishevelled. He could barely wait for the waiter to leave after serving the soup. 'While you were fussing over the horses all day, I was swinging the bat with a number of important gentlemen. Atrocious bowlers! But I did manage to convince the *Times* reporter to give me two press passes.' He gave James an excited smile. 'You and I are leaving on the early train tomorrow.'

'Leaving? For where?'

'Pretoria, where else?' He rolled his eyes. 'To find out what's really going on. It's better than being stuck here.'

'We are about to abscond, Radford, are we?' James burst out laughing.

'Colonel Butcher is leaving tonight for Port Elizabeth,' Peter confided in a low voice. 'There he'll board a steamer to Durban for a conference. Depending on the outcome of this, the regiment might leave for Durban. He'll be gone for at least ten days. Plenty of time to get to Pretoria and back.'

Victoria sensed their anticipation at the prospect of taking a risk. 'And if word comes through to proceed to Natal during your absence?' she asked.

James smiled at her, his brown eyes twinkling. 'I'd like to think of you as a reliable wife. We'll meet up in Durban.'

'That's settled, then,' Peter grinned, beckoning the waiter. 'Six bottles of your best champagne, at once!'

It is Our Country that You Want

September 1899

AND YOU SHALL *chase your enemies, and they shall fall before you by the sword. And five of you shall chase one hundred, and a hundred of you shall put ten thousand to flight.*

As he rode on his rounds in the district, accompanied by a troop of Zarps, Martin de Winter thought about the message President Kruger had asked his trusted advisors to deliver to the *Volk*. For the past two weeks, Martin had been on the road, addressing gatherings, urging people to be ready for war. The greybeards were cautious. They knew the disruption and sorrow war brought, but the younger men were eager to fight the British. Some hotheads had already moved to the Natal border to be there when the first shots were fired.

His back ached from long hours in the saddle, and he was anxious to get back to Pretoria. He had only the Rustenburg area still to cover. He could not remember when last he'd been home, as every day, every hour, brought new developments.

He had seen the war coming on the day he walked through the jubilant crowd that greeted him at Pretoria station following his success in the Jones trial. Talk! How they had talked through endless meetings and conferences. Eventually, the relationships became so strained that they were forced to talk to Sir Alfred Milner himself. President Steyn of the Free State arranged a conference. In the cold of the winter they boarded the presidential train and left for Bloemfontein, where flags and banners proclaiming 'Blessed are the peacemakers' and 'God directs your councils' heralded their arrival. There was even a twenty-one-gun salute as President Kruger stepped from the carriage. But God sided with the British that week. Failure was obvious from the moment Milner and his advisors, Warren included, took their places at the table. Milner presented demands he knew were unacceptable and the conference ended in a deadlock four days later.

'It is our country that you want,' the President said, his voice saddened and broken.

Back in Pretoria, frantic efforts were made to avert the looming tragedy. The franchise was lowered to five years' residence, as Milner had demanded. But no reply came from Cape Town. The silence was explained when the news reached the President's office that troopships were on their way to Durban and Cape Town.

Fighting the British appeared hopeless. And now Martin could only do what he always did when faced with the possibility of failure: close his mind to it and believe in his own superiority. If he was going to fight a war, he was going to win it.

IT WAS LATE AFTERNOON when he and his escort halted at Charles's hospital in Rustenburg. Kicking his feet free from the stirrups, Martin swung to the ground. 'See to my horse and stable him at the back,' he ordered the Zarps. 'At the hotel you will find a Mr Coetzee. I'll settle the fee in the morning.'

Charles and Anita came to greet him. 'My word! You're done in! Would you like to have a wash?'

'Thank you Anita, but first a drink for a weary man.' He sank down in a chair on the stoep. 'Charles, I'm deeply sorry that it has come to this.'

'So, it's to be war.' Charles had a forlorn edge to his voice.

'British troops are on their way to Durban.' Martin passed a hand over his face. It came away thick with dust. 'Thank God James is on his way to India.'

'Oom Koos de la Rey passed through on his way to Pretoria. He is set against war but acknowledged it is inevitable. There are two ways in which we can lose our independence, he told me: give the Outlanders the vote, or fight the Empire.'

'No, Charles,' Martin said forcefully, 'we have the weapons and the men. We fight in our own country. The British will fight not only the commandos but also the land, the relentless summer sun, the cold of the winter …'

Anita brought a tray and poured two measures of brandy. 'Will you go to Wintersrust?' she asked, pouring a cup of tea for herself. 'Tante Koba has made hundreds of remedies in anticipation of war. She says she puts a tear into every jar. I can well believe it.'

'I need to sleep, but can only stay a night. There's a Volksraad meeting on Monday, and you know Pa refuses to travel on Sundays. Is Buks coping with the sowing?'

'Yes, Old Klaas and his sons are invaluable. All fields are done,' Charles said. 'Buks and Uncle Joep have the herds to care for.'

'Charles ploughed the land for the mealies last month. The lines are not that straight, but it's done.' Anita put her cup down and came to her feet. 'I've prepared a special supper. Venison stew with peach dumplings, but first I must see to Ouma Beukes. I'll join you later.' She touched Charles's shoulder as she passed. He took her hand, and planted a kiss in her palm.

Martin looked at Charles questioningly.

He nodded. 'Every evening when I walk her home … well, I want her to become my wife, but marrying an Englishman at a time like this?'

Martin sighed. The house in Pretoria was completed but stood empty. Before long he would ride off to war, and there was no son to carry on his name.

One of the Zarps arrived at the gate with a short, wiry man in tow. 'Mr de Winter, this *Engelsman* came into town and says he wants to join up. What shall I do? He might be a spy.'

'Irish! Not English! The name is Patrick McFee.' The stranger explained that he'd come from Bulawayo, hoping to reach Pretoria before the war started.

Martin invited him to take a seat. Many foreigners were offering their help – Dutchmen, Frenchmen, Russians and a great number of Irish. 'There's a group of Irish in Johannesburg eager to join. They form their own section under a Boer commandant. If you're accepted, you'll be supplied with a horse and rifle,' he informed McFee. 'Why have you decided to take our side? There will be no pay, no reward.'

'Oh yes, that much I know, sir. Thank you kindly, sir.' McFee took the drink Charles offered. 'Apart from having no love for the Crown, another thing has set me thinking. A curious thing. It happened up in Bulawayo. With your permission, sir, very few people but yourselves give the Boers a sporting chance against the Queen's soldiers. Now, I said to myself: if two Boers can fight like that and if their horses can fight like that, then I feel mighty sorry for the British, sir.'

'Boers fighting already in Rhodesia?' Charles said.

'Well, it was like this, sir; we were having a few rounds. In walked two ragged, bearded lads. The exact image of each other. My word, sir.'

Martin exchanged a glance with Charles. 'Go on!'

'Well, there was a fight. A mighty good fight, sir, spilled into the street. One flew onto his horse, drove us back into the bar. He rode the horse, black devil of a mare, sir, right into the bar room! Never have I seen a horse like that, sir. And the two men laughing at us like devils, sir. With men and horses like that, this Irishman will never be on the losing side.'

'Their names?' Charles asked, hope shining in his eyes.

McFee frowned. 'Some men don't like their names to be known, sir.'

'Apart from being alike, could you describe them?' Charles prodded.

'They're brothers, of course.' McFee frowned in concentration. 'Oh yes! Blue eyes! Yes, their eyes are dark blue, almost grey.' He looked closely at Martin. 'Like yours, sir, if you'll permit me to say so.'

'What happened to them?'

'Don't rightly know, sir. Heading south to fight, they said. More than a month ago, sir.'

Martin stood up and shook McFee's hand. 'Well, find your way to Johannesburg. And thank you for the trust you put in us.'

Martin and Charles sat in silence. A nightjar greeted the approaching dusk. The streets were deserted now; lamplight glowed through the windows of the nearby houses. A dog barked and was answered by another some distance away.

'A month? They should've been home by now,' Charles said when Anita's call for supper came.

'They might be on the Natal border already. Let's find them before we tell the others.'

'Yes, let's not raise hopes.'

———— ◆ ————

CHARLES STOOD ON THE FRINGE of the gathering around the wagon in front of the magistrate's office. There were well over two hundred men, and more arriving every minute. Their chests were crossed with full bandoliers, the new Mausers slung across their backs, the brims of their hats pinned with a cockade of the Vierkleur. Their horses were in immaculate condition.

Whistles and hoots greeted the arrival of the Viljoen brothers. Jacob and Frans were armed like the other burghers, but Jan had gone overboard. His chest was crossed with two bandoliers, his Mauser over the left shoulder and his hunting rifle over the other, his knives strapped to his legs. His hat was decorated with colourful plumes, the bridle of his big roan festooned with streamers in the colours of the flag. The men made rude comments but Jan took it in his stride, laughing heartily and showing off his arsenal.

Charles saw his uncle and Joep Maree riding in. They were unarmed and stared at the spectacle in amazement. '*Allemagtig!*' Joep said as he dismounted. 'If I were an *Engelsman*, I'd surrender at the sight of Jan Viljoen!'

Marthinus placed his arm about Charles's shoulders. 'A far cry from your country's army. God knows we've tried to avert this tragedy. Leave us to finish this business. And when it's over, we'll welcome you back. May God in His mercy protect and spare us to see that day.'

Looking at the greater part of the Rustenburg commando, the reality of war came home to Charles. As a doctor and a British citizen it was his duty to join the Medical Corps should they need his assistance, but he could not possibly serve in a war against the people who had become a binding part of his life. And to sign the oath of neutrality? Jan Viljoen had a word for it: a *draadsitter*, a fence-sitter.

The magistrate took his place on the wagon and proceeded with the election of a new commandant. Charles was not surprised when Marthinus was unanimously elected. Joep Maree was re-elected as field cornet of Ward One, and Jan Viljoen was nominated for Ward Two. Consternation ensued as Jan climbed on the wagon, holding his arms out wide.

'Commandants, friends, burghers! I'm deeply touched by the faith you have in me. But, alas, I cannot accept.' He placed his hand on his heart. 'I, Jan Viljoen, am a brave man. I have courage to take on the Redcoats all by myself.' Jeers met this but Jan carried on regardless. 'But I'm also a great coward! I cannot lead men into battle. My heart will not allow me to see my men die and then have the poor widows crying at my door. Before you, you see a man with great courage, but also of no courage at all. No, I'll fight under the man you choose as our field cornet.'

'Jan Viljoen! Where you are there's always *dop*! And does a man not need that when he finds himself away from his home comforts?' Gert Vermaas called.

'I won't ride with Jan Viljoen,' shouted Lang Hans van Rensburg. 'The enemy will hear his loud mouth five miles off!'

'Lang Hans! You will not ride next to me!' Jan threw back at him. 'The Redcoats will see us ten miles off!'

'Jan Viljoen, if your courage is as big as your mouth, we'll follow you!' Hans Ferreira said, the others shouting support. Jan had no choice but to accept.

The magistrate called for order and announced that the President had asked Martin de Winter, who was appointed to General Piet Cronjé's commando as government advisor, to deliver a special message. Martin walked through the men to loud applause, but silence fell as he mounted the wagon.

Charles was well aware that the district was in awe of Martin's superior education and his high-profile life, especially his connection with the President. He had grown up with them and had risen above them, he'd heard many a man say, but by returning to the district whenever he was needed he'd proved that he had their welfare at heart.

Martin stood easily, hands clasped behind his back, feet apart and head thrown back. 'In Psalm 83 these words are written: 'They have taken crafty counsel against thy people. They have said, come let us cut them off from being a nation. Let them be confounded and troubled forever; yes, let them be put to shame and perish.'

'Yes, burghers, friends, that's what the British government has done to us. We have talked and talked for years in our struggle to bring them to a compromise. But now we know! It was there all the time in the words of Psalm 83. *They have taken crafty council against us.* Their goal? British supremacy in southern Africa above all! We don't want war! The British want war! It's not the vote for the Outlanders they want. It's *our country* they want! Yes, they rule half the world and are greedy for more. Red! Not pink as they have on their maps. They want this land to be red, stained in blood.'

The men listened spellbound. Charles marvelled again at his cousin's gift for capturing men's imaginations, his power to influence men and move them. Martin spoke for half an hour, telling them what had happened at the conference tables over the years, using gestures to emphasise a point, dropping his voice low and then building up to a climax as he denounced the tricks of the enemy.

At the end of his address, he gave hope and courage. 'There's nevertheless one positive thing that has come from all these years of fruitless words. They've given us time! Time to prepare for war! Now we have modern equipment, cannon and a Mauser for every Boer. And we have God on our side! Yes, burghers! Fear God! Not the enemy! For our cause is just in the eyes of the world and of our God!'

For a few moments more they stood in silence, and then a roar rose. Charles joined in, as he too was swept away on a tide of trust in Martin's words and the justice of the Boer cause.

———•———

ANNECKE THOUGHT ABOUT MARTIN and his father, who had left Wintersrust with the light wagon drawn by four horses. They should arrive in Pretoria before nightfall, as they would change the team at the Van Rensburg farm and four horses didn't tire as easily as two. Martin had stabled Star at Wintersrust to fatten up before they rode off to war. He had asked her to polish his saddle. But that was not all that he'd asked her.

During the months of waiting, of scanning the road for Karel and Rudolf, she had come to the sad conclusion that she'd been forgotten. No, they were not coming home. They didn't want to come home. They had most probably found wives and settled up north, her father had said.

Then last night Martin had asked her to marry him, and she couldn't find it in her heart to disappoint him again. He'd been so kind, so expectant. The war would not interfere with their plans; they would marry at Christmas. At least she could stay on the farm. And when the war was done, she could come home as often as she wished, he'd said.

She filled the milk jug, placed it next to the rusks on the tray. It was time for the afternoon coffee. Mary was over from Wintersrust, as was her habit now. She was lonely with Marthinus away so much. Charles had come to give his opinion on her mother's trouble; Lettie was so short of breath lately.

Mary came to help carry the things to the stoep. Just then Charles appeared in the door, frowning deeply. 'I've examined Aunt Lettie. Her heart is giving her trouble. There's little we can do for her. She needs as much rest as possible and should do only light work.'

They discussed this for a while and then Joep's impatient call for coffee came from the stoep. Annecke carried the tray through and found her mother already there. Buks and her father were talking about the coming war.

'Annecke, I hope that the war will be done before your wedding,' Buks said.

'Could you not wait till the war is over?' Charles said. Annecke wondered at the solemn note in his voice, the almost pleading look in his eyes.

'People marry even if there's a war on.' Lettie fanned her face with her *kappie*. 'Leave the war to the men and let us get on with women's business.'

'I have four children and am still not a grandmother,' Mary said. 'Stefanie has been married for almost a year now.'

The women chatted on and the men talked war again. Buks was saying that everyone had crops coming in and the spring rains had only just started. There would be little for the horses to feed on in the veld.

Annecke's eyes strayed to the road to Rustenburg. It was a habit now. There were many people riding for news of the war, looking for Marthinus. She turned her attention back to the conversation. Her mother and Mary were planning the arrangements for the wedding feast. It had to be on the farm and the entire district would be welcome. Both houses would be at the disposal of the dignitaries from Pretoria. They could clear out one of the larger sheds for their own use, Mary suggested. Lettie said that Koba would help with the cooking and baking, for never had this district had such an important wedding.

She was restless and her gaze strayed to the road again. In the distance were two riders. They disappeared behind the homestead of Wintersrust. After a while, they entered the trees by the drift.

She stood up, narrowed her eyes and waited. The horses passed through the drift, emerged again. The cup dropped from her hands. A black horse and a chestnut one, the riders longhaired, tall and thin. She stepped off the stoep, stood for a few seconds. Then she started to walk, slowly at first, then gathered her dress and ran. Her hair fell free of the ribbons and flew out behind her. She stumbled once, but remained on her feet.

She called their names and wept as if her heart was breaking.

The Dusty September Sky

September 1899

THE RETURN OF the twins heightened the preparations for war at Wintersrust. Friends came riding in to greet them. Gert Swart said how it would give him the greatest of pleasure to hunt the British down like the dogs they were. Danie Vermaas was cautious, saying that the British were putting more troops on the sea.

Adriaan de la Rey spent the night on his way to Lichtenburg. 'Pa says everything hasn't been done to avert war,' he said early the next morning while walking through the wheatfields. 'He told Martin to keep on talking, but Martin says the British are not prepared to talk any more.'

'Yes, so we've heard from Buks Maree.' Karel bent down to pick a wheatear. He rubbed it between his fingers and inspected it. 'We'll bring in an excellent crop. As for the war, now is as good a time as any.'

'Yes, I'd never admit it to Pa, but I'm all for the war,' Adriaan said.

'Did Martin have anything to say about our return?' Rudolf asked.

'He said that it had come to his attention that you used your fists often in Rhodesia and that he will have you in your father's commando so that he can keep an eye on you.'

'Every man chooses his own field cornet,' Karel said. 'We ride with Jan Viljoen. We saw him in Coetzee's Hotel. He wants us to be scouts. Says that if we could ride through a strange country and not get lost, we're just the men he's looking for.'

'And did you get lost?'

Rudolf laughed. 'We weren't going anywhere, just riding with the wind.'

'Pa has been made a fighting general under General Piet Cronjé,' Adriaan said. 'He's not a popular man, General Cronjé. He doesn't take advice from others and is bull-headed. Even Martin dislikes the man.'

'Martin would probably like to take the general's place,' Karel scoffed. 'He's not satisfied with second place.'

They passed the stables and looked in on the horses. Karel leaned on the fence and Legend came trotting over. He put his arm around her neck. Her eyes were steady on him, her ears catching his every word.

Adriaan looked at her enviously. 'You have to watch her closely. A Boer will not steal another's horse, but some Outlanders will be fighting on our side, rough men from the mines.'

'No one else but Rudi can put a saddle on her back. He still has a problem, though. Lady is nervous under fire.'

'What about that dapple-white stallion?'

'Star is Martin's horse,' Rudolf said. 'I do wish I could take Lady.'

'You must take her,' Adriaan said. 'If you don't, someone else will ride her to war. Most of the Town Boers don't have mounts; the government is commandeering from the farmers.'

'That settles it,' Karel said. 'You take Lady. She'll have to get used to firing.'

Mary waved from the stoep, indicating that breakfast was about to be served. Karel and Adriaan continued talking about horses and fodder as they walked to the house. Rudolf followed behind, his eyes straying to Soetvlei.

Since her emotional outburst at seeing them again, Annecke had become withdrawn, and lately avoided them altogether. She had told them about Stefanie's wedding, her English husband, and about James having married the daughter of a wealthy lord. But it was their mother who gave them the news of Martin and Annecke's wedding, which was set for the week before Christmas. Rudolf sighed and took his place at the breakfast table. She was to marry Martin after all, but it was plain to see that she was not happy. He decided to walk over to Soetvlei as soon as the day's work was done.

While they were seeing Adriaan off, Charles arrived with his ambulance. He sat down for breakfast, and when he finished his second cup of tea he folded his napkin, cleared his throat and fidgeted with his tie and glasses.

'Aunt Mary, I'm riding to Pretoria. I shall be back in a few days. Is there anything you need me to take or bring back?'

'Sugar, Charles. With all this baking and the war coming … yes, three bags will do.'

'Why are you using your ambulance?' Karel asked.

'I thought to take it to Pretoria. The commandos might need it.'

He left shortly afterwards and they were free to carry on with their work, but Rudolf agonised the entire day about how to approach Annecke. By afternoon the decision was made for him. They were checking on the herds when Annecke rode up. She handed them a small pail of coffee. Karel put it on the ground.

'Don't you want coffee? Your mother said to bring you some.'

'We're thankful for the coffee,' Karel said. 'Get down and come sit next to me. I want to know why you are so sad.'

'I'm not sad.' She stayed in the saddle.

'You are sad. You'll tell me now or else I'll get you down and force the truth from you.'

'Why did you stay away so long?' Her voice was small and forlorn. 'I waited for you … but you came back a day too late, too late!' Her hand flew to her mouth as if to take the words back. 'You stayed away too long …' She swung her horse around and galloped away.

'She's just about said it.' Karel grabbed Rudolf by the arm. 'Go, Rudi!'

Shaken by Annecke's words, Rudolf followed her to the big willow tree by the vlei. He found her sitting on the bank, her head bent forward, her hair obscuring her face, her feet in the water as she tried to catch the leaves drifting past.

She looked up and then behind him. 'Where's Karel?'

'I'm on my own.' He sat down beside her.

She looked into the water again. 'I'm sorry for the nasty things I said.'

To hide his nervousness, he removed his boots and dangled his feet in the water as they had done when they were children. But now their carefree intimacy was gone and he had to find a way to restore it. Stealing a glance at her troubled face, he decided that she had to speak for herself and it would be her honesty that would see them through this.

'We should be on our way,' she said before he could find the right words. 'Karel's waiting for you and I must help Ma churn the butter.'

'We must talk first.' He pulled her to her feet. Her head barely reached his shoulder and she tilted her face to look up at him. Her lips were parted, her big brown eyes searching his. His hands shook as his longing for her, so long repressed, flared up.

'Annecke, why a day too late? What are you trying to say?'

'I waited for you, waited so long,' she whispered. 'I feel so … so warm inside, Rudi when I think of you. It came to me the night you kissed me.' She bit her trembling bottom lip but seemed to find courage to carry on. 'I don't … I don't want to marry Martin. I waited for you, but you stayed away.'

He steeled himself against the joy that surged through his being. 'Do you love me, not Martin?'

'I love Martin, Karel too, but not in the same way—'

He lifted her off the ground, holding her close against him. 'Karel was right! He was right! You love me.'

'Rudi, does it mean that you love me in the same way?'

'Yes, I have always loved you. As long as I can remember, I have loved you!' he laughed as he swung her round and round. 'And now I love you in the way a man loves his wife. You're going to be my wife. Not Martin's!'

———•———

FEAR AND PANIC have no master, James thought, when he and Peter arrived at the railway station in Johannesburg. People milled about, trampling one another in their frenzy to get to the ticket office. Luggage was trodden on or disappeared as the looters saw their chance in the desperate chaos. Women sat on their cases trying to restrain their screaming children.

They grabbed their bags and pushed their way through the crowd to inquire about a train to Pretoria. 'The line is blocked for the moment,' an official informed them. 'General Joubert has commandeered the open trucks to take the commandos to the Natal front. Those trucks run empty to Pretoria now. You might find a ride on one of them.'

'When will the last train to the Cape leave?' James asked.

'Don't rightly know, sir, but they'll continue running until the war starts. There are twelve leaving for Durban and Cape Town daily, but you've seen how it is at the station.'

'And when is the war to begin?' Peter asked.

'Oh, not for another week or two, sir. All the commandos are not in position yet,' he whispered smugly. 'And old Kruger is still waiting for the Free Staters to make up their minds on whether to join the war or not.'

They made their way back into the station. The train that had brought them was filled to capacity and people were fighting for places on the cattle trucks.

'Shall we turn back while there's still a chance to get out?' James said grim-faced.

'Return? Packed in like livestock?' Peter grinned, shaking his head. 'To Pretoria!'

'I knew you'd say that!' James laughed and led the way to the shunting yard.

The driver looked at their dusty clothes while he inspected their passes. 'Reporters? If it's a free ride you're looking for, jump on.' He gestured to the open trucks.

They rattled into the Boer capital early in the afternoon. The station was bustling with armed men. Soldiers of the State Artillery were manhandling a Creusot gun onto a flat truck. Rows of cattle trucks were being lined with straw to carry the horses to the front. A train laden with burghers was about to depart. It appeared that the entire populace of Pretoria, waving Vierkleurs and singing farewell songs, had come to witness their departure. It was a sea of umbrellas, *kappies* and slouch hats.

'Over there, Peter! The black carriage,' James tugged at his sleeve, pointing discreetly. 'Oom Paul has come to pay his respects.'

President Kruger emerged from his carriage amid loud cheering. They caught a glimpse of his face as he walked through the crowd to the platform. He appeared grave and tired and stood with his hands clasped behind his back. Someone started up the *Volkslied* and the crowd responded. The men removed their hats and James and Peter followed suit as not to appear conspicuous.

When the song ended, they hurriedly made their way to Koba's house, only to find it deserted. A horse whinnied in the stables and they went to investigate.

The old groom, Bontes, was milking a cow. 'You are James,' he said, rising slowly.

'Yes, you remember me, old man? This is my friend Peter.'

'I remember him too. He came here years ago when you were very sick. This is no place for you to be now. We are going to make war against your people.'

'That's why I've come. Where is Tante Koba?'

'All gone to Wintersrust. Before sunrise.'

James groaned. 'When will they be back?'

The old man shrugged his bony shoulders. 'Martin comes again to sit with the President, but Baas Marthinus, he's going to the war.'

James swore under his breath and stood undecided. Peter walked around the cow to where two horses were munching on hay.

'Rather stunted but they'll do, I suppose. Which way to Wintersrust?'

'Bles and Swartke. They pull Tante Koba's Cape cart,' James said doubtfully.

'*Ja*, they walk slow, but will get you there,' Bontes said.

'Why not?' James laughed. 'Seeing that we have come so far.'

While they prepared for their trip, Bontes told them not to stop at farmsteads or talk to anyone if the need was not urgent. 'Don't change horses at Van Rensburg farm. The district knows your face; they will not welcome you at a time like this. Rest the horses in the day, ride at night. The moon will guide you. She's almost round. You will get to Rustenburg in two nights.'

———◆———

AT SUNSET THAT EVENING Koba's spring-wagon arrived at Wintersrust, bringing the news that President Kruger had mobilised the commandos. Marthinus had come to give instructions to his field cornets and call his commando together. Martin, knowing that an ultimatum was being prepared by Jan Smuts, that war was only a week away, two at the most, had decided to help Marthinus. Stefanie had arrived in Pretoria, demanding to be taken to Wintersrust. Koba, who had heard of the return of the twins, was convinced that they needed her.

Joep Maree had just left to take the news to Jan Viljoen. Martin looked out of the window and saw his brothers and Annecke coming from the stables. Behind them the setting sun filled the dusty September sky with red and orange flames. As he watched, Rudolf leaned close to Annecke before helping her onto her horse. She galloped off to Soetvlei. He went onto the stoep, where Stefanie and Koba were waiting for the twins. Stefanie rushed over to them.

'Where have you been all this time? A year! Not a word! And you missed my wedding!' She flung her arms around them. 'Oh never mind, you're back now. How I've missed my little brothers.'

Koba gathered Karel and Rudolf to her, showering them with kisses, endearments and gentle rebukes. Just then their father emerged from the house. Koba placed her big body behind the twins and glared at her brother. 'Your sons are back to stay, Marthinus.'

Martin saw the anxiety in his brothers' eyes, unsure of how their father would greet them. Marthinus let them stand for a few uncomfortable moments, but then held out his arms and hugged them. 'Ah, my boys! You were never out of your old father's thoughts. All is forgiven, I hope.'

Martin embraced each in turn. 'I bought Botha's farm for you. I'd like to hear about your trip and what the people in Rhodesia say about the war.'

The family sat down for supper. Marthinus ruled that there would be no war talk at the table. Rudolf described the magnificent countryside they had seen on their travels. Koba and Mary discussed the rusks they would bake in the morning. Martin asked Stefanie about Cape Town and Marthinus and Karel talked about the crops and the cattle.

'Is Charles still in Pretoria? Is he coming back?' Mary asked. 'He is in such an awful position.'

'He's getting his neutrality papers signed, Ma,' Martin said. 'He doesn't qualify for resident status yet. At least he'll be able to stay in Rustenburg.'

'Charles has to come to Cape Town with me. He can't possibly stay here.' Marthinus gave Stefanie a stern look and she turned to the twins. 'How did you get that scar above your eye, Rudi?'

'An *Engelsman* beat me up.'

'An *Engelsman* like your husband,' Karel said.

'At least my husband doesn't fight like a common villain.'

'Can your illustrious husband fight at all?' Martin cut in.

She rose indignantly, but Marthinus put down his knife and fork and ordered her to bring the Bible. He took his time selecting a chapter. Martin knew that, after the prayers, he would order them to the sitting room to settle their differences while he would sit in silence, keeping note of their arguments.

Martin knew it was wrong to take out his anger on Stefanie. She was clearly distraught and had travelled in difficult circumstances to see them. He looked at his brothers; they appeared more distant than before, youthful rebelliousness still strong in their sunburnt faces. *The anger of youth*, he thought, *where has mine gone?* Karel's eyes met his, challenging him for a long moment.

'We won't have tea, my heart,' Marthinus said to Mary when the prayer was done. 'We'll celebrate a little, for have we not all our children under our roof for a change? Martin, get a bottle from the study and some sherry for the women. All of you – to the sitting room.'

Martin poured the drinks. Koba went to the kitchen to prepare for the morning's baking, but he knew that she would keep an ear close to the door. Marthinus sat quietly, evidently waiting for the confrontation. And it was instigated, as usual, by Karel.

'So, it took a war to get you back,' Martin said to the twins. 'The crops must be brought in soon. I thought you would want to do that before you join the commando.'

'We are here to fight a war, and there are other reasons also.' Karel glanced at his twin.

'We'll help until the war is over, then we go our own way,' Rudolf said. 'Thank you for Botha's farm, Martin. We'll pay you back in cattle.'

'Oh child! Do stop your nonsense,' Mary huffed. 'You cannot fend for yourself. The state you were in when you returned—'

'We've not come to stay, Ma,' Karel said. 'And we liked the state we were in.'

'Let's not argue, Karel. There's a war, but the farm can't farm itself. Old Klaas and his sons will be here, yes, but we're brothers and should stand together now,' Martin said, trying to smooth things.

'Oh, why do men always have to make war?' Stefanie cried.

'Because they're men and have to prove their courage as men,' Koba said from the kitchen door.

'One spoilt madam doesn't want war and now two nations must put aside their differences to please her,' Karel said. 'Will your husband join the British?'

'No, he won't, Karel! He did his best to prevent war.'

'Wrong, Stefanie! He tried every ploy to get this war started and he has succeeded. But now his work is done.' Martin joined in the row before he could help himself. 'We won't see Paul Warren with a rifle in his hands.'

'What kind of man did you marry?' Karel asked.

Stefanie turned to Mary. 'Ma, *please* come home with me. You can't stay here all alone!'

'Oh, do not fuss so, child. My place is here with my husband, as yours is with your husband. When is he expecting you back?'

'He doesn't know that I'm here, Ma. I've travelled for days on the train all by myself and have to leave again tomorrow.' She burst into angry tears and fled into Koba's arms.

'Pa, she can't go through Johannesburg again. The trains are swamped with Outlanders. We have to get her to Mafeking,' Martin said.

Rudolf put down his glass. 'Martin, how long will you be staying? I need to talk to you about something important.'

'What's it about this time?' he asked, but relented immediately. 'I'm sorry, Rudi, I'm sorry. I'll be here for the weekend. We need you to ride out in the district tomorrow to get the word to all the farms. Will you do that?'

'Yes, we'll ride, but I have to speak to you before you leave.'

'Can it wait till tomorrow? I'm done in—', he broke off when the crunch of hooves was heard on the driveway. They went onto the stoep and stared in amazement at Charles's ambulance, now pulled by four mules. It had a large white circle with a Red Cross in the middle painted on the side.

'What's the meaning of this, Charles?' Martin pointed to the cart.

'All in good time,' he said and asked the twins to assist him in stabling the animals.

When they returned. Charles, bow tie crooked and clothes rumpled, but eyes bright, dusted his hat against his leg, removed his glasses and replaced them. His eyes fixed on the brandy bottle. He poured himself a glass and cleared his throat. 'For many weeks now I've searched my mind for a solution to this … hmm … situation I find myself in. I'm British, as you know—'

'We *know* that; come to the point!' Stefanie said.

'That's just the point, my dear cousin. I'm no longer a British citizen. I'm now a Transvaal burgher, and here are the papers as proof.' He pulled an official envelope from the inner pocket of his jacket and handed it to his uncle. 'I was in the war against Mpefu and that left the option open to apply for citizenship. It's all in order, Uncle Marthinus, I assure you.'

———◆———

CALM DESCENDED over Wintersrust. Martin and his brothers had ridden through the district, spreading the word of mobilisation and returned late at night. Stefanie had left on the stagecoach for Mafeking to catch the train to Cape Town. After a tearful farewell, Koba had left for Pretoria convinced that she was needed there.

Charles was eager to get back to his hospital, but Martin wanted them all to visit the cave before going their separate ways. He needed to settle things with Karel, Charles suspected, and probably hoped that the tranquillity of the cave would help. He donned his hat and, walking past the cattle kraals hoping to find the twins, was told by Old Klaas told him that they had gone to the mountain.

As he neared the waterfall, he heard Annecke's tinkling laugh. He was about to call out a greeting when, through the branches, he saw Annecke and Rudolf lying on the grass, whispering, touching, kissing, totally absorbed in each other. Charles sank down against a tree and closed his eyes. There was a touch on his shoulder and he found Karel squatting at his side.

'I wanted you to see them. That's why I allowed you so close.'

'Does Martin know?'

'Not yet, but he will soon. We'll tell him. She belongs to Rudi. And Martin knows it too.'

A movement some way down caught their attention: Martin and Buks were making their way up. Karel whistled a warning to Rudolf. They gave Rudolf and Annecke a few minutes before joining them in the cave. The cool interior was welcome after the heat of the spring afternoon. Karel started a fire to brew coffee. Charles settled at the rock table with Rudolf and Annecke. They looked young and vulnerable, and Charles caught himself thinking about Koba's jealous God. Rudolf asked his advice on how to approach Martin with his news.

Charles thought about this before committing himself. 'Martin has to know, yes, but not with all he has to cope with at the moment. It's impossible to say what will happen in war.'

'But Martin has set the wedding date!'

'You simply have to tell him to wait until after the war, Annecke—', he broke off as Martin and Buks entered.

Martin sat down next to Annecke. Buks filled his pipe and offered the tobacco pouch to Martin. 'I've noticed that you no longer have a pipe.'

'I've lost my taste for tobacco,' Martin said, looking about the cave. 'It's so peaceful here. I've forgotten about it. I mean, about peace and quiet.'

They discussed how to manage the farms in wartime. Buks would stay until the harvesting was done; the twins would come back to see to the herds by the end of October; Martin would take his turn at Christmas, should the war last that long. Then there was his wedding, he said, smiling at Annecke.

There came the crunch of boots on the rock slab. The light at the entrance darkened.

JAMES WALKED IN, chest heaving, perspiration pouring off his face. In the dim light he saw his brother, gold-rimmed glasses shining; Martin, a proper bearded Boer; Buks, homely and solid, his pipe frozen in mid-air. His twin cousins were men now, tall and strong, the perfect picture of Martin when he had arrived in England. It was only Annecke who had not changed; she was as delicate as ever.

'I'd hoped that you'd keep your presence of mind,' he said. 'Aunt Mary fainted when she set eyes on me.'

'James! It's James!' Annecke gasped and rushed into his arms.

'How on earth did you get here?' Martin asked.

'Are you not on your way to India?' Charles came to his feet.

'Unfortunately not.' James greeted them all with a handshake and took the coffee Rudolf offered. Settling at the rock table, he told them briefly about the trip from Cape Town and how he and Peter had ridden at night to reach Wintersrust. 'Old Klaas said that you were all up the mountain. So, we return to the Home of the Fireflies. I left Peter with Uncle Marthinus,' he concluded and then looked at Martin. 'So it's to be war?'

'Yes, there seems to be no other way. Any news?'

'What we heard in Cape Town was that it's a wait and see situation. We're supposed to leave for India as soon as—. He turned suddenly to Charles. 'We stopped by your house in Rustenburg and found Anita Verwey. I believe congratulations are in order?'

'Yes, thank you.' Charles flushed a little. 'I've informed you by letter.'

'She prepared us a hearty breakfast and insisted that we rest for a bit. And, brother, she's pretty too. I think she suits you rather well,' James smiled. He sensed there was something his brother wasn't telling him. 'I saw several transport vehicles with the Red Cross emblem arriving at your hospital.'

'Good! So they arrived. Those are the wagons taking my medical supplies to the front.'

'Supplies? Which front?' James asked sharply.

'I'm a citizen of the Transvaal now, James. You must understand and accept it.'

'But you're *British*, for God's sake! Does that mean nothing to you?'

'This is my land now, my home, my people,' Charles said calmly.

'James, many countries have offered us their assistance. Russia, Holland

and Germany have sent hospital teams and ambulances. There's even a train fitted out specially to bring the wounded home,' Martin said.

James passed a hand over his face, struggling to take this news in. Ever since their first visit to Wintersrust as children, Charles had yearned to live in Africa. He could only admire him for his loyalty to the people and country he had made his own. And then a pleasing thought struck him and he laughed out loud. 'I'd give anything to see the General's face when the news reaches him!'

'Yes, Father will not be pleased.'

'Where is your wife?' Annecke asked.

'My wife? Yes, I have a wife now. Odd, isn't it?' He gave Charles a wan smile. 'Victoria is in Cape Town.'

'Is she also pretty?'

'Pretty, Annecke? Not pretty ... sort of ... well, striking?' The touch of longing that caught at his heart startled him. 'Red hair, green eyes. Yes, striking. Wouldn't you say, Martin?'

Martin reached for Buks's pipe. 'She's remarkable, Annecke,' Charles said when Martin broke into a fit of coughing.

'I don't want to pry, but where would your regiment be sent should you become part of the war?' Martin asked when he found his voice.

'Natal, I should think. What about you?'

'Then we'll be out of reach of your sabre,' Karel grinned. 'We're all going to the western border with General Cronjé.'

'We are riding Legend and Lady to war,' Rudolf said.

The talk turned to horses and the twins were eager to know about James's chargers. He described both in detail and explained where the names originated from: Thunder for the General's nickname and Lightning for his own quick temper, bestowed on the horse by Peter Radford. Once again James felt the deep love that bound them. He thought about his uncle, about Joep Maree and Jan Viljoen, who had given him nothing but their friendship and consideration. And he knew that he didn't want to fight them. Then he cursed himself for being sentimental.

'Why the bloody hell did you start a war? Give the gold-diggers the vote. They won't take your farms,' he burst out.

'It's not that simple, James,' Martin said after a bit.

'James, I don't want to fight over gold.' Buks reached across the rock table and put his hand on James's arm. 'But when my farm and wife and children are threatened, I take up my Mauser and fight.'

'I apologise, I'm just so bloody exhausted.' James was ashamed of his outburst and, in an attempt to lighten the mood, said, 'Radford is all by himself in enemy territory and the poor fellow can't speak the language to fend for himself.'

They filed out of the cave, lingering for a moment on the rock slab.

'James, should the war come this way, the cave is *holy* ground,' Martin said.

James weighed his words carefully. 'Do I have your word on that?'

'Yes, you have,' Martin said and the others nodded.

'Then you have my word.'

———◆———

JAN VILJOEN LOADED the bags of coffee, salt and sugar onto his wagon, secured them with rope and told his driver to go on ahead. He would catch up later. He led his horse to the hotel, hitched it to the post and entered.

He slapped his big hand on the counter. 'Mr Coetzee, this man you see in front of you has ridden all day putting the fear of God into those who have it in mind to linger at home. No one is going to say that field cornet Jan Viljoen doesn't take his position seriously. And,' he gave his thunderous laugh, 'that he cannot do justice to that fine brandy of yours!'

'That I don't doubt for a minute, Jan.' Coetzee shoved a glass over the counter and placed a bottle next to it.

Jan poured a large measure, downed it in one gulp, refilled his glass and looked around him. Gert Swart and Danie Vermaas were in the corner in deep conversation.

'Two *Engelsmanne* rode through town today. Gert Swart swears that the one is our doctor's brother. He saw them going to the hospital and talking to Nurse Anita,' Coetzee informed him in a low voice. 'He says a Redcoat has no business here. Says he's going to arrest him as a spy. Already the word has reached the Zarps to look out for him.'

'My *Engelsman* James here? It's not possible! He wrote to our doctor that he is on his way to India.'

'Jan, I saw them taking the road to Wintersrust. Boers do not sit a horse like that. It was him all right.'

Jan slapped his hand on the counter again. 'I take my hat off to that *Engelsman*, Mr Coetzee, he's a brave man. An *Engelsman*, but a brave man.'

Filling his pipe, he set his plans. He would wait until dark; he didn't want people to say that Jan Viljoen had been kind to a Redcoat on the eve of war.

A Warning from Nature

S *O THESE ARE OUR FOES*, Peter Radford thought while sitting at
the dining table at Wintersrust. He had always been curious about
James's Boer family. As a rule, ordinary farm folk did not include a
lawyer, a pianist, a British mother and a member of parliament. Wintersrust
was a farm of substance and importance, well run and prosperous. Martin's
father was a dignified and kind man, with a confidence born of authority. The warmth and affection with which he and James had greeted each
other had come as a revelation. James would never have allowed General
Henderson to embrace him.

The twin brothers fascinated him, touched something deep inside him,
but he could not define the feeling. He stole a glance at them. A small
movement attracted his attention. They had entwined their little fingers in
the space between their chairs. And then he knew. It was the possibility of
one, not both of them, getting killed. Then this bond would be no more,
destroyed in the madness of war.

After the meal, there was a long Bible reading session in guttural Dutch.
He wondered what was going through their minds. War was only a few days
away. A few days, and James would be their enemy. Charles, Peter noticed,
was not concentrating, his eyes straying from Martin to James.

Martin's father closed the huge Bible and pushed his chair back. 'Come,
boys, let's have a *sopie* on the stoep,' he said, taking Peter by the arm and
steering him outside.

As they walked onto the stoep, he wondered about the battered wicker
chair that no one had sat on all day, even though there had been a shortage
of seats. James just said, 'Old grandpa sat on it for an entire century'.

Martin was about to pour something from a bottle when a large, bearded
man came riding up. He brought his horse to a halt while greeting expansively in Afrikaans. Around his chest was a full bandolier and across his
shoulder the gleaming barrel of a Mauser. Peter watched fascinated as the
man embraced James, gave him an almighty slap on the back and exclaimed,

'Not a single shot has been fired yet and here you are!' Before someone had time to introduce him, the man approached him with an outstretched hand. 'My name is Jan Viljoen from the farm Vrede.'

'Peter Radford,' he said, his eyes fastened on this giant with the bushy black beard and intense black eyes.

A conversation in Afrikaans ensued, with much head-shaking and expressions of dismay. He saw James's face fill with apprehension. After a while the issue seemed to be resolved, and Martin explained to him that they had to avoid the Pretoria road at all cost.

Marthinus calmed them down, saying that no harm would come to them, as the war had not started yet. 'There are many people on the road in the day. A few more will not crowd it. Boys,' he said to the twins, 'ride with Jan Viljoen, take James and his friend to Mafeking in the morning. There are still trains leaving for the Cape. Stay there, we'll meet up soon.'

'Shouldn't we rather leave straight away?' James asked.

'No, son,' said his uncle, 'you might attract attention riding in the dead of night. Jan will get you through safely.'

James looked at Jan Viljoen uncertainly. 'You don't trust me, *Engelsman*?' Jan roared with laughter, placing his heavy arm about James's shoulders. 'Now, James, my friend, tell me if you believe in your heart that I, Jan Viljoen, would betray you? The war has not started yet. And I would like to give you a fair chance to fight me.'

Light banter that Peter could not understand followed, but it was clear that the relationship between Jan Viljoen and James was one of mutual respect and fondness.

'Now what about a *sopie* for a thirsty man?' Jan asked. 'In my saddlebag I just happen to have one of my finest homebrew. Do I have your permission to offer it around, Uncle Marthinus?'

'Why, yes, Jan. We'd prefer it to the brandy.'

Jan poured them each a generous drink and they settled on the steps. There were aha's and smackings of lips, followed by an approving belch from Jan. Peter's first taste of the potent brew had him gasping for breath, which caused Jan Viljoen to bellow with glee. He took another sip and waited for the conversation to start up, but nothing happened. He followed their eyes and saw what was holding their attention.

An eerie glow showed in the east, competing with the last glimmer of the sun. A deep stillness blanketed the land, a stillness charged with expectancy. Soon the moon, full and heavy, inched over the mountain, delineating the jagged outline against the velvet night sky, plunging the ravines into dark shadows. Bats squeaked and flitted frantically. A nightjar swooped past, trailing streamers from its wings. A barn owl started its ghostly cry from the outbuildings, and from the vlei came the call of a lone jackal. It appeared peaceful, yet there seemed to be a sense of foreboding, as if man, now on the brink of war, was being warned by nature of what lay ahead.

MARTHINUS DE WINTER looked at the young men sitting around him. James's handsome profile was troubled. His friend's face was filled with a curious fascination, as it had been since his arrival on Wintersrust that afternoon. Charles was pensive since they had returned from their walk. His own sons were strangely subdued.

James's sudden appearance had brought home the plight his family would be in if the war were not dealt with swiftly, but to expect a short war was foolish. He thought back to Majuba, fought when he was a young man. War changed men. Most got on with it, but some could endure it only for a short period.

'Yes, like the runaway horses,' he said aloud.

'What about the horses, Pa?' Martin asked.

'I was thinking about war, son, and about men and wild horses. Years ago, when I was studying in the Cape, I saw them, the wild horses, on the flat land near Cape Town. I watched them for hours from the cliffs. The leader, the stallion, gets it into his head to run. We don't know why, we'll never know why. Maybe he has a dream, who knows? He sniffs the air, paws the ground, mills about and circles the herd … then he starts to run, round and round in circles, ever-widening circles. The herd follows … slowly, slowly, and then they thunder off, faster and faster … the circles wider until they cover miles of veld.

'Such a magnificent sight – manes flying, nostrils flaring! And the power! Yes, the force with which they drive themselves. But then it turns into a stampede, a mad flight from an unseen, an unknown fear. They stay together for shelter against this madness that's driving them on. But some sense the futility of staying together. They sense that they'll collapse from exhaustion and die. So they break away. They run away from the herd …'

He sucked noisily at his cold pipe before returning to his story.

'Then just as inexplicably as he'd begun, the stallion comes to a halt. Maybe the dream has been fulfilled, or shattered. Who knows? But the runaway horses …'

He knocked his pipe against his boot and reached for his tobacco pouch. He was grateful that he had their attention. He lit his pipe, puffed and cleared his throat.

'War is a kind of madness, a madness to kill. It comes from a fear, a deep primeval fear of death, and yes, fear to kill. We all carry this fear within us. There are men who cannot stomach the killing for long. War, sons, wearies the soul. Strong, good men, they break down inside; they make mistakes; they die. Some men get through war with only a wounded body, as they close their minds to suffering and death. Yes, those are the fortunate ones, for the body doesn't hurt as deeply as the soul. Then there are those who fight bravely until they reach the threshold of despair. And it comes to them in their weariness – the futility of this madness. So they give up, they break away. They should have stayed, as everything has a beginning and an end, but their souls are too weary of war to reason. Those are the runaway horses. The ones with the wounded souls.'

The moon was travelling its course. A jackal called plaintively from the vlei.

'Uncle Marthinus,' James broke the silence on the stoep. 'What happens to them, sir? The runaways. When all is done, do they come back to the herd?'

Marthinus shook the dottle from his pipe. 'They are not accepted back, son.'

PART FIVE

THE WILD HORSES

Ah Christ, that it were possible,
For one short hour to see,
The souls we loved, that they might tell us
What and where they be.

Alfred, Lord Tennyson,
'Maud'

Action and Frustration

October 1899

A FAINT GLOW on the railway line reflected the brilliance of the stars. Karel de Winter lay with his ear to the rail. He had been there since darkness had fallen and now it was almost midnight. Only the occasional cough or whisper betrayed the presence of two hundred men lying on their bellies fifty yards away.

A nightjar shrilled. Karel swore. He put his head back on the track. A muffled humming became a rat-a-tat. He leapt to his feet, sped to his place next to Rudolf in the scrub.

'Jan Viljoen, it's coming. It's coming!'

The news was hissed down the line. A rumbling like a far-off thunderstorm grew into the puffing of a train. Karel's hands tightened on his Mauser, his finger curled around the trigger. The headlamp rounded the corner, piercing the darkness. Karel kept his eyes on the spot where he had strapped the dynamite to the track.

A blast shattered the night. In a cacophony of screaming steel and hissing steam, the engine flew off the track. Smoke enveloped the waiting men, obscuring their vision. Screams of agony rose from the burning wreckage.

Jan Viljoen stood up and raised his Mauser. Karel scrambled to his knees. Jan gave him an almighty push. He fell backwards, clutching his rifle.

'Jan Viljoen fires the first shot in this war,' Jan roared above the clamour.

Hardly had his shot rang out than a volley burst from the scrub into the soldiers milling around the wrecked train. Outlined against the fire, they were easy targets. A second volley drove the survivors to seek cover.

'Surrender! *Hensop!* Throw down your weapons. Come out! *Hensop!* Hands up!'

Wild shots from the train windows met Jan's call. The Boers replied instantly, but after a few more volleys Jan ordered the men to stop firing.

Karel was astounded. 'Jan Viljoen, it's war. Let's go! They'll escape to the other side.'

Jan grabbed him by the neck. 'Yes, it's war you bloodthirsty *bliksem*. Field Cornet Jan Viljoen gives the orders. Do you want your father to kill his own son on the first night of war? Have you forgotten that he's on the other side waiting for them to crawl out?'

At that moment shots rang out from the opposite side of the train as Marthinus and his men opened fire. The soldiers threw their rifles from the windows and stumbled out with raised hands. Jan signalled his men to surround the wreck.

'Let's go, my savage little friend.' He laughed thunderously, pushing Karel towards the train.

———

ELANDSLAAGTE. James Henderson rolled the unfamiliar name on his tongue. The plain of the eland. Yet now the plain was alive with British soldiers engaged in battle against a well-concealed enemy on the ridges that enclosed the plain in the form of a horseshoe. Wounded and dead littered the ground. Men crouched behind anthills and rocks while stretcher-bearers, braving the crash of artillery and rifle fire, ran between them, stooping low. Waves of soldiers advanced on the ridge where the Boer artillery fired relentlessly over them.

The 2nd Hussars, together with the 5th Dragoon Guards and the 5th Lancers, were waiting on a nearby hill. The prospect of action had shaken off James's travel-weariness. Hardly had he and Peter arrived back in Cape Town when the regiment had been ordered to Natal: three days by sea, a night in Durban, and on to Ladysmith, where General White had his headquarters. After a week for the horses to recover, the cavalry regiments had been rushed by train to Frere, near where the Boers were attempting to advance into Natal.

The horses pawed, tossed their heads, the eagerness of their riders infecting them. James dismounted and handed Thunder into a trooper's care. He walked over to where Colonel Butcher and General French, a telescope glued to his eye, were standing.

'Any chance of us joining in the outing, Colonel?'

'Not yet, Henderson, not yet.' Butcher cast a worried glance at the sky. Billowing purple clouds, the sun colouring the edges to gold, cast shadows over the battlefield. He looked to where his regiment was waiting in loose formation. 'Oh, for heaven's sake, tell Radford to get a grip on himself and his mount.'

James trudged over to Peter. Bathsheba, Peter's roan mare, pranced, pulling at the reins. James grabbed hold of the bridle when Peter pulled the horse into a rear. 'Hurry up and wait. The usual order, Radford.'

'God, what a waste of time.' Peter slid off the horse. 'We could've speared them by now.'

A crack of thunder competed with the roar of the guns, heightening the ferocity of the battle on the plain. Driving rain soon hid the carnage below.

James wiped the rain from his face and peered down the hill. The Boer guns had stopped firing. A mass of khaki swarmed towards the enemy positions. 'Radford, look,' he pointed to where a large white cloth showed through the smoke. 'The white flag!'

'A chance for us to be in the thick of it, denied,' Peter swore.

Suddenly, concentrated fire erupted from a Boer position. The advancing men fell back and took what cover they could find, but soon rallied, cheering as they drove the Boers from their positions.

At last, a single bugle sounded. Squadron advance. Within seconds, many buglers echoed the call, as did the pipers of the Gordon Highlanders. The earth shook as four hundred horsemen thundered down the hill. Reaching the plain, they extended their lines, hurtling at full gallop. The fading sunlight reflected off gleaming sabres, sending a cruel message to those fleeing before their charge. James registered the sweet smell of wet grass and earth, mixed with the acrid stench of lyddite fumes. He was aware of the battle cries of his troopers racing behind him. He glanced to his right. Peter, sabre bared, was a few lengths away.

Directly ahead of James, two Boers were running desperately. He pulled his reins to the right, swept his sabre down, catching the nearest one where the neck meets the shoulder. From the corner of his eye he saw Peter dispatching the other with a tremendous blow to the head. Now they were in the midst of the fleeing Boers, slashing and stabbing at whatever they could reach. Then they were clear of the chaos with only the open veld to their front.

Peter wheeled around and charged back. 'I beat you to it, Henderson!' Back into the melee they charged, sabres slashing, oblivious to the cries for mercy and the upraised hands of those writhing on the ground, now strewn with a bleeding mass of dead and wounded. Then it was over. James pulled a heaving Thunder into a canter. The smell of sweat, horseflesh and blood assaulted his nostrils. His ears became open to the screams of the wounded and the shrill neighs of horses.

Peter, his face streaked with dust, his tunic blood-spattered, his eyes wild, joined him. Night fell swiftly as they turned their backs on the carnage and rode back to the railway. The darkness was broken only by the lanterns of the field corpsmen collecting the many casualties.

Later that night, when they were celebrating their victory in the mess tent, James's elation faded. He recalled the faces of the enemy. Then he thought of people dancing in a barn, stealing homebrew behind their elders' backs, gathering round a table reading from the Holy Book in Dutch, praying to a God who had given the upper hand to their enemy that afternoon.

———

PRETORIA WAS DESERTED compared with the hectic, heady weeks in September. No more trains full of armed men, no more cheering crowds singing the *Volkslied* and women urging on husbands, sons and sweethearts.

Martin de Winter stared out of his office window overlooking Church Square. It was late afternoon but still women clustered around the square. The few men who hurried past were mainly those who had their neutrality papers signed or government officials, like him, whose vital work prevented them from joining the commandos.

He ran his ink-stained fingers through his hair, contemplating the mountain of paperwork on his desk. Court cases to be wrapped up. Legal action under martial law to be prepared with the State Attorney, Jan Smuts. The commandeering system to be formulated. Accounts of the gold bars confiscated from Johannesburg and brought to Pretoria.

He was impatient to be done so that he could join the commandos, but his thoughts were disturbed. He had failed his people and himself. For years he had sought to avoid war, but now, out there on his country's borders, the wild horses were running. The stallion had sniffed the air, pawed the ground and started his ever-widening circles. There was heavy fighting on the Natal front. Twenty-five thousand men and two-thirds of the artillery were concentrated there under General Joubert against the few thousand British troops. They were striking hard while they had the numerical advantage. *And James is there.*

Martin stretched across the desk and lit a lamp. He hugged his arms around his chest trying to still the shivers that plagued him lately. Since the war had begun two weeks back, he had had very little sleep and his fevered mind was now affecting his body. He lifted the lid from the pail of bean soup that Koba had sent with Bontes, but the smell of it brought on nausea and he pushed it away. He worked through the night, sleeping in snatches stretched across his desk, his hands pressed to his red-rimmed eyes. By noon the following day he finally handed his papers to Smuts and closed his office, donned his jacket and hat and set off across the square to President Kruger's house to take his leave.

The old man was dozing in his chair on the stoep, his meerschaum hanging loosely from his tobacco-stained hand. Martin stood silently, thinking how frail the President was in sleep, yet it was he, the intransigent, biblical leader of one of the smallest nations on earth, who had declared war on the acquisitiveness of the mightiest Empire. He decided against disturbing the old man's rest and made his way to Koba's house to get ready to leave.

He found her on the bench under the willows at the far end of the garden. She moved to make space for him beside her. 'My poor heart is broken,' she said as she had every day for the past two weeks. 'Fate sends him to my door—'

'Tante Koba, my work here is done,' Martin said before she could continue. Missing James by a day on his unexpected visit seemed to have affected her more than the declaration of war. 'I have to go past Wintersrust to get Star and collect my blanket roll and Mauser. Come with me ...'

'No, dear Martin, I must be here. The wounded will be brought here and I'll be needed.' She patted his hand, gasped and put a hand to his forehead. 'Martin, you have a fever. A high fever.'

'It's been another exhausting day, Tante Koba.' He stood up, but was seized by nausea and dizziness. He stood quietly, clutching at the bench for support.

Koba hustled him inside and into his room. She nursed him through a restless night, but when he left before sunrise the next morning his fever had worsened.

He hardly saw the changes the spring rain had brought to the veld. Soon he would be part of the war. The thought brought excitement but also loneliness. He was riding to war alone. A deep yearning for love came to him. Annecke's face and her child-like body filled his mind. He should have married her years ago, but the memory of Victoria had destroyed all love inside him. And she was close, her beautiful hair shining in the gentle sunshine of the Cape, her green eyes laughing into James's as they lay in each other's arms.

Overcome by sadness and the burning passion his thoughts had evoked, he slumped forward in the saddle and allowed his horse to set the pace. He did not want to think about Victoria any more. Annecke, her innocence, was all he wanted now.

IT WAS DARK and a light drizzle had set in when he reached Rustenburg, his horse exhausted and foam-flecked. He slid out of the saddle at Coetzee's Hotel. His body shook and he could hardly focus his eyes. Pulling his sodden jacket around him, he ordered brandy. Mrs Coetzee looked at him sharply, poured a glass and rushed away.

He drank a few mouthfuls, hoping to banish the chill inside him, but the urgency to get to Annecke drove him on. He picked up his hat, stumbled to the door. Anita Verwey was standing there, the reins of his horse in her hand as if waiting for him. She took his arm and led him to the hospital.

'Martin, you should take better care of yourself,' she scolded as she helped him through the front door and pushed him into the kitchen. 'Now, sit down. Do you want coffee? Something to eat perhaps?'

He sat with his head in his hands. 'No, must get to Soetvlei. Have to see Annecke.'

'She's at Wintersrust with your mother. Aunt Lettie has Lena and the children, but your mother is by herself. She took to her bed and will not be consoled. The war …' she sighed and put a hand to his forehead. 'You're terribly hot. Stay the night and let me take care of you.'

He struggled to his feet, pushing her aside. 'Just tired … very tired …' He went out into the night.

His horse broke into a gallop, sensing familiar stables. Despite the late hour a lamp glowed in the kitchen at Wintersrust. With great effort he off-saddled and made his way from the stables to the house. Outside the front door he stood for a moment, supporting himself against the frame, shaking his head.

The door opened. Vicky stood in the lamplight, but her hair was dark, and her green eyes were brown and filled with concern.

'Are you very tired? Come, I'll warm up some food.' Annecke took him by the arm, pulling him inside. He stumbled against a chair.

His mother appeared in her bedroom door. 'Heavens, Martin. What's the matter? Have you been drinking?' She felt his forehead and cheeks. 'You have a fever, child. Let's get you to bed.'

They supported him to his room. Annecke pulled off his boots and his mother arrived with a basin of water. 'Annecke, child,' he heard her say, 'get the medicine case, please. Under my bed. The key is in the small leather box on the night stand.'

While Annecke was out, his mother undressed him and sponged his body down. He was aware that she gave him something bitter to swallow. He fell into a restless sleep, visited by vivid dreams filled with desire, of women, and of lonely winter nights at Cambridge. When he opened his eyes at times, he found a worried little face bent over him. A woman's face.

ANNECKE SAT holding his hand in hers, hoping the fever would turn. She swabbed his forehead and beard often, but still he cried out words and names that she did not understand.

Following Charles's advice, Rudi had left for the war without telling Martin about their love. It would have to wait. It could wait now. Her stomach had cramped all day, a sure sign that her monthlies were about to start. Charles had said that no one knew what could happen in a war. She knew now what he meant and it scared her. Either Martin or Rudi might be killed and then they could have spared Martin the news. She did not want Martin or anyone to be killed.

She stroked his clammy hand and he opened his eyes. 'Are you feeling better?'

His arms went around her. 'Vicky, I do love you, Vicky …'

She wanted to pull away, but could not find it in her heart to do so. He was sick and would be riding to war soon. She rested her face against his beard, hoping he would fall asleep again. But he did not. He pulled her under the blankets with him. His hands went to her breasts, pulling her nightdress down over her shoulders. Struggling to free herself, her dress tore at the buttons. She wanted to cry out but was afraid that Mary would find them like this. When Martin did not move his hands to her legs and just seemed to want to get to her breasts, she stopped struggling. His mouth and hands became less insistent and his breathing easier.

She kept still for fear of waking him. Every now and then he stirred, but his face stayed between her breasts. The candle spluttered and died. She kept her eyes on the window until the first light showed through the morning mist. Her thighs were wet and sticky as she felt her flow strongly now. She had to get to her things and Mary would be awake any minute now.

Pulling free from his arms, she stole out of the bed. She risked a look at him. He was awake, his eyes on her exposed breasts. She covered herself with her hands.

'Annecke,' his voice was a mere croak. 'What have I done to you?'

She wrapped her nightdress closer around her, trying to conceal the large bloodstain. 'You were very sick last night.' She bit her trembling bottom lip. 'A bad fever and you drank too much brandy.'

He sank back on the pillows. 'I'm so sorry, Annecke. I didn't mean it to happen like this. I'm so very sorry.'

———◆———

A WEEK LATER, Martin left for Mafeking to take up his post as General Cronjé's government advisor, only to find that the reports he had seen in Pretoria had told the truth. General Cronjé had surrounded the little border town and was content to wait for the beleaguered garrison to surrender. On the Natal front General Joubert had driven the enemy into Ladysmith and gone on the defensive; the Free State commandos had encircled Kimberley. The war had come to a standstill.

Martin spent most of his days with Charles at his hospital tent, only attending General Cronjé's meetings if he was sent for. Two weeks before his arrival, the Rustenburg and the Lichtenburg commandos under General de la Rey had ridden south to carry out pre-planned missions. Reports came in affirming their successes. They had destroyed the railway on both sides of Mafeking and every village and outpost in their way had surrendered without a shot being fired.

Martin paced outside the hospital tent, scanning the flat brown horizon. The commandos were due back that night.

'Would you kindly do your tramping elsewhere,' Charles said from where he was sitting under the canvas awning. 'It's hard to keep the dust out of my instruments as it is.'

'There'll be nothing to do if it carries on like this.' Martin found a chair and sank down.

'I've enough to occupy my time, thank you. Backaches, stomach troubles and ailments brought on by boredom. Suits me fine. There's coffee brewing. Would you care for some?'

Martin nodded and Charles fetched two mugs. 'What's troubling you, Martin? You've been awfully agitated since your arrival.'

'I can't stand this inactivity.' Martin rose, but Charles pulled him back into the chair. 'The war started a month ago and look at us. We've crossed the borders and now we wait. You could say that the entire Boer army is having a picnic around three little towns. Look around you. Wagons, chickens, milk cows and even some pigs. Grazing for the horses is almost depleted. Firewood is becoming scarce.'

The encampment of Cronjé's large force was chaotic: tents and hooded wagons, cooking fires and washing strung up, children and dogs playing, men sitting idle, smoking their pipes, their women brewing coffee.

'Yes, and there will be sanitation problems soon, but I quite like having the women and children here.' Charles smiled. 'I saw the pigs. Lang Hans van Rensburg says he's fattening them up for Christmas, as we'll still be here. Doesn't want to miss his suckling pig because of a war.'

'Charles, fifty thousand British troops are due in Cape Town any day now. We have to strike before we get overwhelmed by numbers.'

'Why don't you tell General Cronjé all this?'

'I have! I have! He says that he doesn't need the immature opinion of an anglicised Boer.' Martin finished his coffee, threw the dregs on the ground.

'When Pa gets back, I'll join the commando. I'm of no use to the war if I stay with Cronjé.'

Just then shouts from the far side of the camp announced the return of the commandos. The dust-covered riders, their horses stained dark from the hard ride, entered camp and threw their hats into the air, exulting at their successes.

Martin found his father and Joep Maree with General de la Rey. They exchanged a few words before going to report to the commanding general in his tent. Cronjé did not come to greet them and Martin decided that he was in no mood for the meeting that would take only one course – following the commander's wishes.

Jan Viljoen bellowed a greeting. '*Magtig!* What a time we had. This war is almost history. The British lion sits in a cage now. Like frightened hares they were – *Hensop! Hensop!*' Jan rubbed his stiff back, while telling Martin about the capture of the armoured train on the night the war had started.

While he was talking, Martin searched the incoming riders for his brothers, but there was no sign of them, or of Jan's brothers. 'Where are Frans and Jacob?'

Jan's black eyes gleamed impishly. 'Our herds need to be seen to, Frans said, but I reckon it's their wives that need to be seen to.'

'Rudolf and Karel? How did they fare?'

Jan wiped his forehead and matted beard on the back of his hand. 'Your brothers behaved like men, true men, under fire. They were right next to me when we waited for that train and have stayed with me ever since. I sent them out to spy the land ahead; they came with correct information every time.'

'Where are they? I don't see Buks Maree either.'

'Well now, the prisoners must be escorted to Pretoria. So I put Buks Maree in charge of them. He insisted, says he wants to go home, says that the English have taken our point; we are prepared to fight for what's ours and that they'll back off now. Your brothers want to see to the herds at Wintersrust, but what help Karel will be to Rudolf I can't say. He got drunk on British firewater and fought a Colonial Boer. Good fight. A broken bone in the hand and bruised ribs.'

FOR TWO MORE WEEKS General Cronjé's army lay idle around Mafeking. Commandos sent out for reconnaissance had nothing to report.

From the telegraph office, Martin received the reports from Pretoria with growing frustration and alarm. General Sir Redvers Buller had arrived in Cape Town with fifty thousand troops and proceeded to Natal to relieve Ladysmith. Buller dispatched General Methuen to relieve Kimberley and General Gatacre to the central front where the Free Staters had entered the Cape Colony and were holding the railway.

Late one afternoon Martin sat with General Cronjé translating yet another request to the British in Mafeking to surrender. The air in the tent was thick with mutual dislike. General Koos de la Rey entered and soon a heated exchange erupted between the two generals.

General de la Rey tried to convince his commander to free at least half of his force to strike deeper into the Cape Colony. 'You don't need five thousand men to hold two hundred English. They're not even properly armed. A few outdated guns, and you bring the war to a standstill for that.' His deep-set eyes flashed, his salt and pepper beard quivered. 'You're wasting precious ammunition firing into the town every day.'

The burly Cronjé, the hero of the *Volk*, the man who had captured Jameson, resembled an irritated warthog ready to charge. 'We won the war of '81 in this way. I sat at Potchefstroom for months and in the end the *Engelse* crawled from their hiding places and begged for mercy. We've always fought in this way and we've always succeeded.'

'Potchefstroom is close to your farm. You rode home every week to see to your cattle and crops,' De la Rey said, frustration raw in his voice. 'Yes, here we are close to our farms, but we don't want to go home until we finish the war. Piet Cronjé, the day will come – and God knows I pray that I'm wrong – that the enemy will shut you away from the outside world. Do you think they'll fire a few cannon shots into your laager and wait for you to come out? Do you really think that? No, Piet Cronjé, they won't; you will beg for mercy.'

Cronjé looked as if he was going to take his *sjambok* to De la Rey, but just then salvation arrived in the form of a cable from Pretoria. Cronjé turned puce, snorted, paced the tent and said that the force of *that British Lord Methuen* was putting the fear of God into the faint-hearted Free Staters. He decided that a thousand men would hold Mafeking under siege while the greater part of the force would accompany him south.

'Koos de la Rey, take seven hundred men and ride ahead. Go to the aid of General Prinsloo. The *Engelse* are approaching the Free State border fast. That's the President's order, not mine.'

De la Rey sighed. 'They're not cowards, Piet Cronjé. They're vastly outnumbered. Seven hundred is not enough, I need cannon too.'

'Seven hundred! No cannon!' Cronjé turned to Martin, showing De la Rey that he was done with him. 'De Winter,' he pointed with the *sjambok*.

'Take the commissariat; set up supply stations along the border to Jacobsdal. I will put up my headquarters there.'

Martin stepped forward. 'I wish to be relieved of my post. I'm riding with my father and Oom Koos as from now.'

The *sjambok* slashed close to Martin's face. 'The President appointed you. You will stay until he decides otherwise. But what I want with a half-baked Boer he never said.'

Martin refrained from pushing his case. Should he desert his post, those who had been ordered to stay behind might follow suit. An hour later he left the telegraph tent, having cabled ahead, arranging for fodder and water for Cronjé's huge commando and for the railway line to be repaired to transport the mules, artillery and medical supplies. He went to the Rustenburg men, who were preparing for an early departure with General de la Rey and came across Charles handing out medicines and bandages.

'The district is riding off to a real battle, not the skirmishes that have taken place up and down the railway, but a confrontation with highly trained soldiers,' Charles said. 'It'll be the first battle most of them will experience and I, like you, have been ordered to Jacobsdal. How am I to get there in time?'

'By train. I'll get you there in no time, cousin. Have Karel and Rudolf arrived?'

'Yes, they rode in earlier with Buks. All seems to be well on the farms.' Charles carried on doling out bandages.

Martin went in search of his brothers and found them tending their horses. He cast an admiring glance at Legend. He had heard the men talking about her at night around their fires. Now, as Karel packed his saddlebag, she nuzzled his ear as if to reassure him of his presence. Rudolf's chestnut was a different horse altogether, pawing the ground nervously.

'Martin, I hear from Adriaan de la Rey that we're just in time. We're riding south.' Karel's eyes burned with excitement. 'He says there's bad trouble in the Free State.'

'Are you riding with us, Martin?' Rudolf asked.

'No, but I'll catch up soon. Do you have letters from home?'

Rudolf extracted a thick bunch from his saddlebag. 'Tante Koba sent them from Pretoria.'

'No letter from Annecke?'

'She sends her greetings.' Rudolf looked away. 'But no letter. Perhaps Buks has.'

Martin found the Marees stuffing their saddlebags with delicacies from home. 'You thought the war was over, didn't you, Buks?'

'Yes, I was wrong, though.' Buks busied himself with his horse. 'I didn't think the British would send more troops. They must want the gold badly. And since they're still outside our borders, let's keep them there. We'll be able to do that, won't we, Martin?'

'If we move now, yes, Buks, I'm confident that we shall. Do you have a letter from Annecke for me?'

'No, perhaps your brothers have.'

Martin walked a little way off, gazing into the dust-filled sunset. In the week that he had recovered from the fever, Annecke had moved back to Soetvlei and had avoided him altogether. He again tried to recall what had happened on the night he had arrived at Wintersrust, but the images were vague. He remembered her standing in the door with a lamp in her hand; he remembered holding on to a woman and he recalled the bloodstained nightdress and the tears in her brown eyes. *What did I do to her?*

———

TEN DAYS LATER, the Rustenburg commando was nearing the Modder River, on the western border of the Free State. The hot afternoon wind carried the sound of battle to them. Columns of dust and grey-black smoke directed them to a ridge where the battle was being fought. In the twilight, a pathetic scene met their eyes. Boers were breaking away, running for their horses. A team of mules hauling a Creusot gun came hurtling past, men whipping them to spur them on. Riders, holding wounded to their saddles, galloped past.

Karel de Winter stood up in his stirrups, scanning the koppies, expecting to see the enemy in pursuit, but none came. 'Why are they running, Pa?'

'They've been through what we've not experienced yet, son. The fighting is over for the day; the English won't send cavalry out at night.' Marthinus called over his shoulder to his field cornets. 'Jan Viljoen! Joep! Go to the river. Find a place for the night.'

'I won't run.' Karel turned Legend around. 'I'm going to see for myself. Come, Rudi.'

'Karel! Come back this instant. Do as I say! To the river. You will follow my or any other officer's orders or you'll find yourself in serious trouble. Is that clear, Karel?'

Karel saw that his father's grimy face was set. He reluctantly followed the others to the river. But later, when Marthinus rode off with General de la Rey to work out a strategy for the coming action, he and Rudolf slipped away to where the Free State burghers had come to a halt. They told tales of having faced overwhelming numbers of British for the past week in three consecutive battles. Karel thought they were exaggerating. By his reckoning, a small commando could easily overrun the British infantry.

The next day found the Rustenburg commando digging into the banks of the Modder River. A few men went forward to place markers at measured intervals to assist their aim. The railway bridge had been blown up during the night, and the artillery placed on higher ground. For two days they watched the veld to the south, but nothing happened. Their strength doubled on the second night with the arrival of General Cronjé's main force from Mafeking.

'Have you seen Charles, Pa?' Karel asked the next morning when they were once again waiting on the river bank. His father was brewing coffee and appeared quite at ease with the tiresome waiting.

'No, son, General Cronjé ordered the hospital to stay at Jacobsdal.'

'That's no use,' Karel said, 'but it will take General Cronjé himself or one of his family to be wounded before he allows the doctors closer to us. If he could get to the wounded straight away, he could save more lives. Charles said so himself.'

'He'll walk over to his own as soon as the opportunity presents itself,' Gert Swart muttered.

'I heard that.' Jan Viljoen rose purposefully and kicked Gert in the ribs. 'That hurt, didn't it, loudmouth? Now, if a bullet finds you, you'll be pissing your pants for the same doctor.'

Gert lunged towards his back as he turned, but a leg from Karel caught him and he fell headlong into the sand, raising a cheer from the nearby men.

'Stop this horseplay.' Marthinus pointed to the pillar of dust in the far distance. 'The enemy is on the move.'

They scrambled for the hollows in the river bank, Mausers at the ready, but it was a long hour before the enemy, marching ten deep and four abreast, became visible. Karel took his father's field glasses and gasped. 'We're fighting a bunch of women.' He passed the glasses to Jan Viljoen.

Jan's mouth fell open. 'Scots! They wear their skirts to war. *Magtig!*' They caught the sound of regimental bands marching the soldiers into battle. 'Dressed in their finery and marching to music. Do they think this is a wedding feast?'

An ear-shattering roar ripped the air as the Boer artillery opened up into the advancing soldiers. Another blast spluttered from higher up the river bank. An inferno of sound assaulted their ears as everyone fired their Mausers. The enemy crawled for what cover they could get, behind anthills, into the thorny scrub, and tried to return fire. The British artillery began firing. Shells burst overhead, showering the Boers with shrapnel. Karel fired until his rifle was hot and his shoulder bruised by the recoil.

'Steady, steady,' Marthinus repeatedly cautioned. 'Pick your target directly in your line. Don't waste ammunition. They won't come any closer.'

In the late afternoon Adriaan de la Rey and his father appeared on foot. General de la Rey looked exhausted, but in command. He squatted by the fire, helping himself to coffee. 'Marthinus, the enemy is breaking through on the left flank, the Free Staters are wavering,' De la Rey said, but his eyes were twinkling. 'I happened on a headstrong man to go to their help. Martin. He, shall we say, missed old Cronjé in this confusion and rode hard to catch up with us.'

Karel saw the satisfied smile exchanged between De la Rey and his father. De la Rey finished his coffee and called for Adriaan. They were twenty paces away when a shell exploded into the bank. Through the dust and debris raining down, Karel saw Adriaan double up and stagger on a few paces. He grabbed Rudolf by the sleeve, staring in horror. Adriaan fell to the ground, clutching his stomach, a thin trickle of blood running from his lips.

Death had passed overhead all day long, but the reality only now penetrated Karel's battle-eager mind. 'Oom Koos, we will take him to Charles,' he said, trying to quell his eagerness when De la Rey dropped to the ground by his son. 'Legend will make it, Oom Koos. She'll carry Adriaan.'

Rudolf rushed off to fetch the horses. They lifted Adriaan onto Legend, but he screamed as soon as she started moving. They lowered him down, slung him in a blanket and set out for Jacobsdal, stopping only when his groans became too pitiful. They struggled in the dark night and were thankful when they came upon a family fleeing in a mule-cart. They placed Adriaan among the children. In the early hours of the morning, they reached Jacobsdal and found the hospital tents crowded with wounded and the men who had brought them in.

Karel spotted Charles next to a stretcher, stitching up a wound. He tugged at his sleeve. 'We brought Adriaan. He's wounded … in the stomach … in a bad way. We carried him … in a blanket … Legend couldn't carry him … he's in so much pain, he cried when Legend moved. He screamed, Charles.'

Charles nodded, finished what he was doing before following Karel to where De la Rey waited with his son. Adriaan's face was grey, his eyes unfocused, his pulse fluttering feebly. Charles pulled away the blood-sodden blanket and lifted Adriaan's shirt. The wound was small, but the swollen abdomen showed that he was bleeding internally. He gently pulled the blanket to Adriaan's chin.

'Oom Koos, I'm afraid he has bled himself dry. He's out of our hands now.'

De la Rey took Adriaan's hand in both of his. He raised his eyes to where the sun was creeping across the horizon. 'A stomach wound is always fatal,' he said, his voice hoarse, tears rolling down his lined face. 'Go, Charles, there are others in need of you.'

Karel and Rudolf stood in the first light of day. The war had come home to them. Adriaan, their friend from childhood and schooldays, someone their age, had died in his father's arms. It was real and it was frightening.

Martin, battle-stained and radiating confidence, came walking towards them, carrying a mug of steaming coffee. 'Come, the English have been beaten back. But we're moving to a farm called Magersfontein. There's a range of high koppies. It might be better there.'

Magersfontein

December 1899

O UT OF THE FLAT, dust-ridden land of low scrub and thorn bush rose a cluster of hills in a triangular shape. On the right was Magersfontein Kop, a hill higher than the rest, and it was to the south of this hill that the Boer generals decided to make a stand after the retreat from the Modder River. Five miles to the south was the British force under Lord Methuen, estimated to be fifteen thousand strong.

On his way from Cronjé's tent to join the Rustenburg commando, Martin looked with satisfaction at the narrow trenches the men had dug below Magersfontein Kop in the open veld. The loose earth was piled to the back so that, while firing, heads were not visible against the skyline. And in these trenches, running a few miles in both directions, eight thousand men were now waiting.

Martin hurried over the stony ground. Although it was midsummer, the afternoon was chilly and overcast. When he had found his brothers outside the hospital at Jacobsdal, faces haggard, eyes vacant with shock, he had felt immensely sorry for them. They had experienced death, seen the agony of the wounded and tasted fear. He could tell by their eyes that they were no longer the keen boys who had set out for war two months previously.

It had also been his first battle, but he had been prepared for fear. Fear could not be ignored; he could still feel it coursing through his body, tightening his belly into a knot. But he had closed his mind to it, taken charge of the faltering men, and led them back to the firing line. It had been easy; they just needed someone to take charge. Now they did not have long to wait. That very day perhaps, or the next, the battle and the fear would be there again.

A sleety rain set in. He hunched into his jacket and broke into a run. Others were also making for the trenches, and he heard his name called. Turning around, he saw Charles struggling to catch up. Although the main hospital was still at Jacobsdal, a field hospital had been set up two miles behind the front.

'Come for a visit, have you?'

'Thought I'd bring you some food. Must be tiresome, living off rusks and biltong.'

They were fifty yards from the trench when Joep Maree shouted a greeting, but the words never reached them. An ear-splitting roar shattered the afternoon. They threw themselves flat, burying their faces in their hands. The British artillery had begun to seek out their positions, preparing the way for the infantry attack.

Jan Viljoen came racing towards them, grabbed Charles by his collar and carried him to the trench.

Martin was aware that they were shouting for him to run, but he knew the bombardment was directed at the hills. It was close and terrifying, though. He picked up his hat and made a show of dusting it before sauntering to the trench. As he lowered himself in, he saw Charles scrambling from the floor where Jan had deposited him. Charles straightened his tie, took his glasses from Karel and unfolded his bundle. There were two roast legs of lamb and four loaves of bread. They shared the unexpected luxuries while looking at the destruction the British bombardment was creating. Fragments of boulders flew high into the air, dust and tortured earth burst forth, the yellowish-green smoke from lyddite shells making colourful patterns against the red dust.

'I must get back. I left my ambulance a mile behind the hill.' Charles scrambled up. 'My colleague, Hans Vermaak, is all by himself.'

'I'll help you, if you have to go,' Jacob Viljoen said. 'There might be wounded.'

'Well now, Jacob,' Joep Maree laughed. 'How will you help our doctor? Will you catch the shells so that they don't fall on him?'

Martin thought that the laughter that followed was unnecessarily loud. The relentless shelling had an unnerving effect on the whole commando. Talk faded, and attention turned to the south, from where the attack was expected.

Rudolf, relieved from lookout duty, sank down in the narrow space next to Martin. He was shivering, Martin noticed, whether from the rain or from the waiting he couldn't tell. 'The cave,' he whispered close to his ear, 'remember how it was the day we found it? The storm, we thought it was the end of the world then. It's like that now, Rudi.'

'Yes, it's like that now, Ouboet, but this is a storm of flying death.'

Still the earth vibrated. The rain fell icy against their faces and there was no sign of the enemy, yet the thorn bush came alive at the slightest fidget of their imagination.

As darkness came, the shelling faded, but the silence was even more unsettling.

Charles went down the line, giving a pat on the back here, a few words of encouragement there. Martin went with him, taking as many water bottles as he could carry, promising to find hot coffee. They scrambled around the koppie and reached the ambulance to find Dr Vermaak waiting. He told them that only three men with slight shrapnel wounds had turned up.

Charles shook Martin's hand. 'Well, you know where to find me. Not that I expect you. Watch out for the twins, please.'

Martin made for the telegraph tent. There was news of a decisive battle fought across the Free State border in the Cape Colony. The British had been beaten back, their artillery captured and a thousand prisoners taken.

He filled the bottles with coffee and shouldered them, thankful for the warmth through his wet jacket. He ran along the trenches, spreading the news of the victory, knowing that it would help the men through the waiting. He reached the Rustenburg section and passed out the coffee, only lukewarm now, but the men were grateful.

The rain gave way to a cold wind. They talked in hushed voices, waited, and watched. Some men dozed, only to jolt awake at the slightest sound, a suppressed cough, the movement of the man next to him. The smell of waiting, the smell of men waiting, Martin thought.

Close to midnight came the rumble of a far-off thunderstorm. It grew louder and soon a streak of lightning flashed in the darkness. For a brief moment they saw the hills in stark relief around them.

Martin was acutely aware of those around him. His father had pulled his hat over his eyes and sat mutely. In a flash of light, Martin saw Rudolf, his face in his hands. Karel was staring fascinated at the heavens. The Viljoen brothers had their heads down and Buks and Joep Maree's wet faces were raised to the sky in wonder.

The storm lasted half an hour, and with a final rumbling moved on to the south. The men came to their feet, shook their bodies and rubbed their numbed hands.

'*Magtig!* The Almighty put the *Engelse* to shame. He showed them what a bombardment is,' Jan Viljoen said hoarsely.

'The Almighty,' Karel muttered, 'has been off target. He has taken us for the British.'

Silence ensued. Martin slept intermittently, gave up and joined the others, peering into the wet darkness. Looking towards the east, he discerned the faintest of light breaking through the mist. Then came a hushed but urgent warning from Jan Viljoen.

'I hear something. The bastards are out there.'

At this the men were at their posts, lying shoulder to shoulder, their cold hands clutching their Mausers. There was a single shot from the koppie at the centre of the trenches. All at once the line of trenches lit up as a solid wall of flame as thousands of Mausers fired simultaneously in the direction of the unseen enemy.

In the greying dawn the enemy became visible – Scottish soldiers, close-ly packed, milling around, some crawling, others trying to disentangle them-selves from the thorn bushes. Many were lying in tangled heaps five hundred yards from the trenches. Others returned fire, their bullets cutting the air above the slouch hats in the trenches.

As the sun broke over the battlefield, the Scots charged. The Mausers crackled in hysterical unison and flat on the ground they went once more. Orders were shouted from the back. They crawled forward, only to be pinned down again. Martin thought that there could not be even one left unwounded, but still men edged forward, and still they picked them off.

By midday there was no more movement directly in front of them. The battle continued around them, but firing was sporadic now. Calls for water and help came from the wounded enemy but they closed their minds and kept their rifles trained on the belt of thorn scrub.

Overhead the sun stood still in the now cloudless sky. To Martin it appeared as if the battle was over. But in the late afternoon, pipers skirled and a wall of Scots rose from the ground, storming headlong towards the trenches. The Mausers spat and the line seemed to dissolve as though an invisible hand had dashed the men to the ground. When the charge petered out, the ground was strewn with dead and wounded.

RUDOLF THOUGHT about Adriaan de la Rey's death – his white face, the pleading eyes, the blood, the crude coffin and Oom Koos, his face silent, deeply lined. The day became a blur: firing, reloading, firing, ripping open ammunition boxes, his father and Joep, pipes firmly in their mouths, the Viljoen brothers taking aim and commenting on their scores, Lang Hans van Rensburg falling asleep over his rifle, and Karel, always next to him, encouraging the enemy to come closer.

Rudolf ripped a piece off his sleeve, wrapped it around the red-hot barrel of his rifle. His hand was already raw. He saw Martin reaching behind him for a fresh clip, and then sprawling heavily on the mound of earth behind them, crimson spreading on his jacket. Rudolf flung himself backwards to cover Martin. Joep and Karel dragged them into the trench.

Rudolf stared at Martin, fear and guilt paralysing him. *I love Annecke, made love to her, and he's my brother and I haven't had the guts to tell him yet. It's war, don't tell him, don't tell him. One of us must die for Annecke.* He didn't want Martin to be killed. And he didn't want to die either.

'Shoot, Rudi, they keep coming on,' Karel shouted, firing into the crawling soldiers.

But instead he stared as Joep removed Martin's jacket and tore the shirt open. Blood flowed from the gaping wound, soaking Martin's trousers. Joep fumbled in his pocket for a bandage and tied his arm to his chest. Marthinus, lurching against the fighting men, came down the trench. He knelt beside Martin and took his face in his hands, saying words that Rudolf could not hear. He watched as his father and Joep supported Martin out of the trench and set off to the ambulance wagon.

Rudolf sank against the trench wall, sobbing quietly.

Dusk brought movement from the pinned-down Scots. The soldiers rose in a half-hearted rally. Only then did the Boer artillery open fire, turning back the advance. The Boers kept their rifles trained on those who had not left the battlefield, but there was no more firing from the ragged men in front of them.

The short African dusk gave way to darkness. A stunned weariness engulfed Rudolf. He looked at the others in the trench. Their eyes were red-rimmed, faces dust-streaked, hands still on the cooling barrels of their rifles. And out of the silence came the pitiful sound of the wounded.

'Never in my life have I seen such bravery,' Jan Viljoen said. The men murmured their agreement, sighing with relief as they sank down in the trench.

Rudolf sat with the Viljoens at a small fire. They brewed coffee and ate rusks and biltong while trying to ignore the pleas of the wounded enemy barely forty yards away. Soon lanterns moved haltingly over the battlefield as the British stretcher-bearers came to collect the wounded, but no one came close to their trench.

Jan Viljoen sent a message down the line that he was going out to the wounded and that the men must hold their fire. He called out, 'I am Jan Viljoen from the Rustenburg commando. You are brave men; we admire your courage. Those who can walk, leave your weapons, go back. You have the word of Jan Viljoen, with God as witness, that we will not fire on you.'

There was no response. Jan and his brothers went out with water bottles. Tears sprang to Rudolf's eyes as he watched the big bearded Viljoen brothers moving among the wounded. He saw a few rise unsteadily and stumble off.

246

CHARLES WAS SURPRISED at the few wounded who came in during the day, considering the length of the battle. By dark, a line of prisoners was escorted in, with a few wounded among them. He recognised the men of the Black Watch by their kilts. The Highland Brigade commander, Brigadier General Wauchope, had been killed in the early morning, one of the officers told him. There would be the devil to pay, as James would've said. As he worked, his thoughts went to his brother. Should he be wounded and Fate sent him into his hands, would he work as calmly as he did now? No, he smiled wanly; James would be an impossible patient.

He finished closing a chest wound and was putting drains through the man's ribs, when an orderly came to his side. 'Dr Henderson, your cousin ... he's asking for you.'

He concentrated on his task. 'Bring him in. Is it bad? The wound ... is it bad?'

'Chest and arm, Doctor. It's the older one, the clever one.'

Charles bent over the stretcher and found that Martin, though feeble with pain, was calm and coherent. He snipped away the remainder of Martin's shirt, examined the wound, and sighed with relief. 'A lucky shot. The bullet passed through and missed the bone. Your inner arm and chest wall took most of the force. It'll take only a few minutes to patch you up.'

Charles placed a wad of chloroform-saturated cotton wool to Martin's nose and smiled at his feeble protestations when the drug overwhelmed him. He stitched and bandaged the wound and told the orderly to carry Martin to the wagons, which were taking the wounded to Jacobsdal. 'Put him in my tent. I won't need my bed tonight.'

At noon the following day, a message came that the British wanted a truce to collect their wounded and they needed help. General Cronjé would allow four hours only. Charles hurried to the Rustenburg trench section to give the men news of Martin's condition. He could see the exhaustion in their eyes. The twins were sitting side by side, Rudolf's head resting on Karel's shoulder.

'It's awful,' Rudolf said. 'The wounded cried throughout the night. I wonder how many are still alive.'

'They tried to kill us, Rudi,' Karel said. 'Why feel sorry for them?'

Jan Viljoen had tears in his eyes. 'It's not right that brave men should suffer so. No one has come near those in front of our trench since they fell yesterday.'

It was indeed carnage, Charles realised, looking at the many soldiers strewn across the veld. With Jan Viljoen and Rudolf carrying his bandages and instruments, he worked as fast as he could: disinfecting lesser wounds, stitching gaping ones, probing for superficial bullets, giving morphine to those who needed it most. He knelt by a soldier who had a stomach wound. The man was still breathing and, as he looked up to see if there was a stretcher-bearer nearby, he found a familiar face smiling down at him.

'How did it go on your side?' Frank Crofton-Smith asked.

Charles straightened up and held out his bloodstained hand. 'Light in comparison.'

'We've not recovered from the battle at the river yet.' Frank shook Charles's hand. 'My tents are overflowing. How are we going to cope with this?'

'I wish I could be of assistance, but I have to get back to my people … my hospital.'

Frank nodded thoughtfully, still holding Charles's hand. 'I understand, my friend, you have made a brave decision.' He pointed to a soldier with a chest wound. 'I've found that the Mauser makes a neat hole, which results in a clean wound. The smallness of the bore, do you think?'

'The Lee-Enfield doesn't cause much internal damage either. We perform few amputations …'

Rudolf tugged at his sleeve to get him to attend the moaning man at their feet.

Frank looked at him with interest. 'I'd say that you're a De Winter.'

'Yes, Rudolf de Winter.'

'Frank Crofton-Smith. I've heard about you and your twin. How's Martin?'

'He was wounded yesterday, in the arm, but Charles says he'll be fine.'

Jan Viljoen, whose curiosity, as usual, got the better of him, came to meet Frank. 'Do you have any news of my friend James?' Jan shook Frank's hand long and hard.

'Not exactly, but as far as I know, the 2nd Hussars are in Natal.'

The Boer guns announced the end of the truce. They left the battlefield, walking steadfastly, until the cries of the men left to die faded in their ears.

AT WINTERSRUST, ANNECKE turned the lamp a little higher and frowned at the writing paper. In her hand was a thick letter to the twins that had taken all week to write. She told them about daily life on the farm – which cow had calved, the growing sugar and coffee shortages, and so on.

There was so much to write, but she was unable to pen her most pressing news. She wondered if she should wait for them to come home, but it was already the second week in December and the war showed no sign of ending. It was almost two months since Karel and Rudi had come to see to the herds. Rudi had said goodbye to her under the willow by the vlei. When she closed her eyes, she could still feel the way he had loved her that night. The way a husband loves his wife. There was a half-moon; the outline of his head and shoulders against the light falling through the branches was imprinted in her mind. An owl hooted close by, the frogs in the vlei made their music and Rudi's breath was warm in her neck and on her breasts while he whispered that he was in a place where all else except their love ceased to exist.

Now she was feeling strange in the mornings. Her breasts were tender and sore all the time. She forced herself to be calm. Lena did not show for four months. There was still time. But what if Martin should come home despite the war and marry her?

She stole a glance at Mary, who was on the other side of the table. Next to her was a pile of letters – to Martin, to the twins, to Charles, to Stefanie. There was even a letter Mary hoped would reach her sister in England.

'Come on, Annecke, it's late. These must get to Rustenburg early tomorrow.' Mary placed her hand lovingly on the sheets waiting to be put into an envelope for Marthinus.

She was thankful that Mary was unaware of the change in her. Koba would know right away. 'What shall I write to Martin, Aunt Mary? It's easy to write to Karel and Rudi about the farm, but Martin …'

Mary smiled. 'Tell him how you long for him to be back so that you can be married. And about the flowers in my garden and that you pray for his safe return. Little things like that.'

Annecke dipped the pen in the inkwell and wrote about the garden and the flowers and about Koba, who'd written that Pretoria was quiet except for the days the hospital train came in from Natal. She hesitated. Should she tell him that she could not marry him, that he did not love her that night? No, she decided, Karel would kill Martin if he found out. She finished the letter with a hope that he was safe and well.

'Well, that's done,' Mary stood up. 'I'll make us tea.'

She waited until Mary was busy in the kitchen and scribbled down one sentence on a piece of paper. *Rudi, please come home, I'll be sent to the takhaaren. I am going to have our baby.* She folded the note, wrote his name on the outside and slipped it into the twins' letter. There was no doubt in her mind that he would hurry back as soon as he read it.

General Buller's Request

JAMES SHIVERED in his greatcoat. It had rained through the night and the morning was misty and cold. But by midday the temperature would rise to over a hundred degrees, forcing man and beast to seek shelter under the sparse mimosa.

He stood with Peter Radford and Mark Sinclair watching the troops offloading the mountains of supplies that heralded the arrival of General Buller. Thousands of tents had risen in the veld and more were pitched by the minute. The dull sound of mallets forcing pegs into the ground competed with the bellowing oxen, braying mules and men shouting orders

His mind was on the humiliation they had suffered at Elandslaagte. The victory had been theirs, but no ground had been gained, no progress made. Since then the Boers had driven them back with seeming ease. Then came the humiliating day when Joubert's force had shut twelve thousand British soldiers up in Ladysmith and laid siege to the town. Luckily his regiment had been miles away at the time.

'Well, I say,' Peter prodded James, bringing him out of his thoughts. 'Look who's arrived to rescue us from the mighty General Joubert.'

George Hunter marched towards them. He had been promoted to major, and his badges, buttons and sword hilt gleamed in the sun. They saluted and looked him up and down.

'You should cover those with cow dung, sir.' James pointed to the buttons. 'Those fellows in the mountains don't like anything that resembles gold.'

Hunter gave him a contemptuous glare and Sinclair explained, 'True, sir. Excellent targets, the shiny stuff.'

'What brings you here, major?' James asked.

'Colonel Butcher has accepted me as his second-in-command, seeing that he lost Major Hughes to the Boers.'

'Welcome to the regiment, sir.' Peter cast a glance at James, who was not even trying to hide his dismay. 'How's the wife, sir?'

'I didn't deem it appropriate to bring my wife to Africa.' Hunter made to leave, but half-turned to James. 'I spoke to yours in Durban. Victoria wants to move on to India to escape the war. Could it be that she doesn't take kindly to De Winter being on the receiving end?' He touched his swagger stick to his helmet and strutted off.

The remark puzzled James for a few seconds. True, Victoria was dead set against the war, any war, and might be worried about Martin, as they had been friends once. The man was jealous, vindictive, he decided, and put it from his mind.

THE DAYS OF WAITING to go into action turned into weeks of routine camp duties: drilling the troops, training the horses and riding patrols to observe the enemy. Directly to the north of Frere was a rampart of koppies along the Tugela River. Behind those koppies, across the river, was General Joubert's force, estimated to be twenty thousand strong, and behind them, the beleaguered town of Ladysmith.

James and his fellow officers were lying stretched out on a rise outside the encampment, scanning the mountains through their field glasses.

'Have they left? Gone home to reap the mealies? I've been watching for an hour now. Not a sign of anything.' Captain Murray Shaw grumbled, lowering his field glasses.

'I'd say that they've taken fright at the sight of our force. They can tell they're outnumbered.' Hunter took the glasses from Shaw. 'We shall have to rout them out.'

'The Boers are there, right there, in the folds of that mountain,' James said. 'Major, do you see that tall mimosa to the right of that old bridge? Yes? Now follow it up to what appears to be a broken ridge, about halfway up …'

Hunter trained the glasses, following James's instructions. 'Yes, yes, I think I have it. A broken ridge.'

'Now, to the side of it is a Krupp gun. Got it, sir?'

'I can't locate it.' Hunter screwed up his eyes.

'Exactly, sir. The Boers are experts at camouflage; they don't advertise their presence as we do.'

'Don't take me for a fool, Henderson. Orders in the mess tonight.' He swung into the saddle and galloped back to camp.

'Old scores.' Shaw gave James a warning look. 'He makes a point of settling them.'

AFTER DINNER the officers settled around the tables in the mess tent with a few bottles of port, awaiting the return of Colonel Butcher, who'd been called away by General Buller. They'd been promised an attack on the Boer lines in the morning; now there was talk that Buller might have decided to postpone the attack yet again.

George Hunter sauntered in and sat down. 'I've just met Captain Saunders from the telegraph section,' he said while pouring a measure of port. 'He tells me that our fearsome General Joubert has had a mishap. Fallen off his horse.'

'How unsporting of the bloody horse,' Peter said. 'Who, then, will open the batting tomorrow, so to speak?'

'Fellow by the name of Botha, Louis Botha,' Hunter said. 'Heard of him, Henderson?'

Just then Butcher strode in, his face set as he called for order. 'General Buller has asked me to inform you of certain …' he cleared his throat, 'certain developments. On Monday, General Gatacre withdrew from the Orange River and took his force back fifty miles. He lost eight hundred men and his guns.'

Stifled exclamations rose and Butcher held up his hand. 'On Tuesday, yesterday, General Lord Methuen suffered an appalling reverse ten miles from Kimberley at a place called Magersfontein. He lost a thousand men. Sixty-seven officers wounded or killed, including General Wauchope of the Highland Brigade. He died on the battlefield.'

Silence hung in the tent as the officers struggled to take in this news.

'As for our plans,' Butcher continued, 'General Buller has decided to postpone the attack until the artillery has cleared the way. Two days at least. Inform your men accordingly, but it's advisable not to elaborate on the misfortune on the other fronts. That's all, gentlemen, thank you.' He marched out of the tent.

'Unbelievable!' John Miles, a sub-lieutenant who had arrived at the regiment a few days earlier, said. 'A handful of backward farmers defeating the Highlanders.'

'Well, that just proves it, Miles,' Murray Shaw said. 'They're not backward and neither are they just a handful. There are thousands of them, and they know exactly what they're doing, it appears.'

'But they have no military training,' John Miles said. 'Lieutenant

Henderson, you have connections, I believe. Tell me about this unconventional enemy of ours.'

James refilled his glass. 'Yes, you're right, Miles. Only their artillery is uniformed. As for the rest, well, no set rules, but they have been hunting and fighting all their lives—'

George Hunter banged his glass on the table. 'Absurd! To suggest that their experience is superior.'

'I didn't suggest that, Major, I said that the Boers are not ignorant of military matters. Kindly stop using me as a reference manual on the ability of the Boers.' James grabbed his helmet and stormed out.

James spent a night of fitful sleep. Nightmares assailed him with images of war and blood, of his father in his study. Then Victoria was in his arms, his body joined to hers as they rolled about in bed. But the dream changed and he saw a stranger in her arms. He cursed in his sleep and struggled out of the dream.

He sat up, relieved to be awake and wondered again at the man Victoria had first loved. He should have heard her out the day she had offered to marry him. But, then, that day it didn't matter. He had thought it would never matter. But now he was falling in love with his wife. He did not want to love her, he did not want to be vulnerable, but it was happening and he was powerless to stop it.

FOR TWO DAYS the artillery pounded the ridges beyond the Tugela River, dust and smoke setting the sky aflame at sunset. No reply came from the Boers. Then the troops moved into position around Colenso, a small village clinging to the banks of the Tugela. Infantry, guns, wagons and horses left a haze of dust swirling in the morning air. Eighteen thousand men. Nothing could go wrong, General Buller said. The morning was filled with the promise of victory.

The cavalry was on the left flank waiting for the infantry to advance. The heat drained their energy, and perspiration poured off their faces, staining their khaki tunics. At mid-morning a rider came with a message to stand down, as the infantry had been forced to withdraw.

Colonel Butcher swore under his breath. 'Radford! Henderson! Find out what's happening. Report back within the hour.'

Galloping past Indian stretcher-bearers and medical personnel waiting on the edge of the battlefield, James and Peter set off to where General Buller was directing the battle. There they were informed that the general's party had left for a point not far from where two batteries of field guns had been abandoned. They spurred their horses on, swerving between retreating infantry and came upon General Buller and his staff. Around them were empty gun limbers; out in the open, the deserted guns were being pounded by enemy fire.

Buller's face was mottled but he appeared calm. 'Now, my lads,' he said to the gunners. 'This is your last chance to save the guns. Will any of you volunteer to fetch them for me?'

After some hesitation, a corporal and six men came forward, holding the reins of their frightened horses. Buller turned to his staff officers, and to James and Peter. 'Some of you go and help these men.'

James's eyes flew to Peter, who was measuring the distance to the guns with his eyes. They touched their spurs and joined the men. Three more staff officers mounted. The men quickly hooked two teams of horses to the limbers and thundered off.

James felt the blood surge through his veins. He saw an officer slump in his saddle, his tunic covered in red patches. Another man gave a shrill cry and horse and rider met the ground in a cloud of dust. Something stung his elbow and his shoulder, but he ignored it.

Miraculously, they reached the guns. James noted blood on Peter's shoulder. The team hooked a gun to a limber, turned it around and sped back. They unhooked it in a frenzy and returned, back into the bullets. Something grazed James's cheek, blurring his vision. When he opened his eyes, they were halfway to the guns but there were only two men with him. He looked over his shoulder. Peter was on the ground a hundred yards back, but there was no stopping now. They hooked another gun and turned back.

'Play dead, Radford, I'm coming for you,' he shouted when they passed Peter, who had crawled a few yards to the ditch where others were seeking shelter.

When James again reached the General's party, Thunder was heaving and wild but so was James. He swung around and went to pick up Peter. But he was alone. After a hundred yards Thunder pitched forward, throwing him clear of the saddle, face down in the dirt. He saw Thunder twist as bullets smacked into his black coat. Scrambling to his feet, choking and spluttering, he doubled over and ran to where he'd last seen Peter making for the ditch. Arms pulled him into a mass of cursing men.

'We've brought your mate in, sir.' A dust-covered sergeant pointed to where they'd placed Peter.

Peter's face was ghastly white through the dust. He tried a smile, but it contorted into a grimace. James examined Peter with shaking hands – a bullet through his right shoulder, another through his lower right leg, his breeches bloodied at the groin.

The sergeant handed James bandages and he tried his best to stop the bleeding. He crouched next to Peter and willed himself to wait. There was not a breath of wind and not a patch of shade, no water to give to the groaning wounded. He used his tunic to shelter Peter, who no longer responded to his questions. All James could do was to keep the flies and insects away from Peter's wounds.

The firing stopped at midday and stretcher-bearers appeared – the most welcome sight James had seen.

THE HOSPITAL TENTS were overcrowded when the stretcher-bearers carried Peter in late that afternoon. A doctor hastily examined him and told the orderlies to take him to the operating tent, where he joined the long queue of critical cases. Darkness came, and a soft drizzle set in. James sat next to Peter's stretcher, his battle-stained tunic becoming soaked through. He stared mutely at the hundreds of wounded men weeping, cursing and praying, the orderlies scurrying back and forth, covering the wounded with tarpaulins. Their faces were dazed and weary, blistered by the scorching sun. The Indian stretcher-bearers brought in more wounded.

Two orderlies came and picked Peter's stretcher up. James helped to carry him inside. A doctor felt Peter's pulse, examined his wounds and again felt for a pulse, this time at the throat. Frowning, he called James aside.

'I'm afraid, Lieutenant, your friend is beyond help. He's lost too much blood; medically speaking he's dead.'

Desperate emotions raced through James as he stared at Peter's ashen face, his still body, refusing to believe that he was beyond help; there was still a little breath in him. In the confusion of anxious thoughts, he struck on one and clung to it. 'Then give him my blood. My brother is a doctor, he told me that it could be done.'

The doctor shook his head. 'No, I'm afraid it's hardly ever successful—'

'Give him my blood! At least give him a chance,' he shouted.

The doctor conferred with a colleague. James grabbed them by their arms. 'Give him my blood! Now!'

An orderly brought a chair and asked James to sit. He removed his tunic and the doctor forced a thin tube into his arm, the other end inserted into a vein in Peter's arm. James watched fascinated as his blood ran down the tube and disappeared into Peter's body, but soon his head felt light and he could barely focus his eyes. Minutes later, he was vaguely aware of the doctor removing the tube from his arm. The world went black and he slumped against Peter's stretcher. Mark Sinclair found him there an hour later and escorted him to his tent.

The Incident at the River

NEWS OF THE Boer victory in Natal reached General Cronjé's tent at Jacobsdal on 16 December. Following the victories at Magersfontein and on the central front, a jovial atmosphere reigned. The British press were calling it 'Black Week' – three successive defeats at the hands of an army of farmers. Three thousand casualties in one week and double that since the start of the war.

'The Almighty is on our side! Our cause is just.' Cronjé slapped his *sjambok* repeatedly on his desk, drawing curious glances from the officers gathered in the tent. 'We drove the enemy back on all three fronts. Not a single *Engelsman* is within the borders of the republics, not one British soldier. Before this day is out, that Lord Methuen will come to my tent and beg for peace.'

From where he was standing at the entrance of the tent, Martin listened in alarm. As at Mafeking, Cronjé preferred to wait for the British to seek peace. He had ordered his army to reinforce the trenches at Magersfontein. Some men had erected tents and shelters behind the koppie to be out of reach of the British artillery, which occasionally fired a few shots as a reminder that the enemy was still there. Women and children in ox-wagons, bringing milk cows, chickens and dogs, had arrived to be with their menfolk at Christmas.

The officers reminded Cronjé that the British had signalled to the besieged town of Kimberley that help was on the way. But Cronjé just called them pessimists.

'God gave us victory.' He raised his arms as if to bless his officers. 'Let's not ask more of Him.'

Martin boiled at the old man's foolishness, but it was futile to argue. He looked at General de Wet, the new commander of the Free State forces, who had arrived that morning from the Natal front, his alert eyes following the arguments. He was short and stocky, with a neat pointed beard and the bearing of a man who inspires confidence.

'What are their plans, De Winter?' Cronjé pointed his *sjambok* at Martin. 'You lived with the English. You tell us.'

Martin adjusted his shirt, covering the sling supporting his injured arm. 'General Methuen is resting his force, but if you're waiting for him to seek peace, you're mistaken, General.' He steeled himself to be polite, but failed to keep anger from his voice. 'More troops will arrive soon. We have to strike now, General, follow up our victory while the enemy is hurting, while they're down.'

'Piet Cronjé, have you hunted lion?' General de Wet stepped forward, his left hand in the pocket of his tweed jacket, his right, swishing a riding crop against his high boots. 'The wounded lion hides at a safe distance. He licks his wounds, but soon he's eager to charge again. Has a wounded lion ever charged you, Cronjé? The young man is right. I saw the cable President Kruger sent you. He urges you to attack *now* and you refuse.'

'It's not an order, but a suggestion, De Wet.' Cronjé banged his hands on the table. 'We are outnumbered five to one. It would be a senseless waste of lives. We showed *Engeland* that we are superior. My orders stand. We'll hold our position as Louis Botha does in Natal.'

'Outnumbered? Five to one now; a hundred to one in January,' Martin said before he could check himself.

General de Wet tapped his riding crop on Cronjé's desk. 'Look around you, Piet Cronjé. Your men lie idle, thinking the war to be over. It's far from over. Your army resembles the *Groot Trek*. Wagons, cattle trampling grass we need for our horses. Send them home. We can't fight like this.'

Cronjé looked as if he was going to take his *sjambok* to the man but De Wet carried on, ignoring the old man's threat. 'Piet Cronjé, when you sit in a cell as a prisoner of Her Majesty, I'll be free to fight on.' He took Martin by the elbow, steering him out into the hot morning air.

'I apologise, General, I showed no respect to my elders in there.' Martin sighed. 'At the very least, he could harass their supply lines, blow up the railway line south of the British. We can't just sit here and wait.'

'What's your name, young man?'

'Martin de Winter, General, from the Rustenburg commando.'

'The forces of the republics are combined now. We fight as one. I need men who can operate independently, think for themselves, men with the same ideas you've just expressed. Leave Cronjé to me. Is your wound bad?'

'No, General, the flesh was torn, but the bones are intact.'

'Go home, let the wound heal and then come back.'

'I leave for home in the morning. I'll be back in the New Year.'

Martin hurried to Charles's hospital tent where his father and the

Marees had already arrived for the trip to Bloemfontein. There they would catch the train to Pretoria, and then travel to Rustenburg with Koba's wagon. His wedding was a week away.

———•———

KAREL DE WINTER was disgruntled. It was his turn to do the cooking and there was no escaping it. Jan Viljoen would surely knock him flat again. He pulled the cast-iron pot onto the fire and threw the day's meat ration into it.

It was unbearably hot. Magersfontein was no place to camp in the summer; the earth was strewn with sun-blackened rocks and there was hardly a tree, just thorn bushes. And the horses had to go to central camps at night where they were provided with water and fodder. He'd protested vociferously against this, but to no avail. On the day his father, Martin, Jan's brothers and the Marees had left for home, he erected a stone wall, cut up one of the tents and made a shelter for Legend and Lady.

Karel spotted Charles on his mule-cart, making his way through the jumble of tents and crude shelters, stopping frequently to have a few words with others of the district. Charles spent much of his free time visiting Magersfontein, saying that Cronjé's Jacobsdal was too crowded for his liking. By the time Charles reached him, Karel had coffee brewing.

'On your own? Where's Rudi?'

'Gone to the river.'

The Modder River was a few miles to the south and the enemy camp five miles further on. Both sides patrolled the river, but the heat and a plague of flies drove some Boers to seek out its shade and cool water when they thought themselves unobserved by their officers and the enemy.

'Your father has forbidden you to go to the river. It's dangerous there, Karel. The British use it too, and often,' Charles said, leading his mule into the shade.

'That's why we have Mausers, Charles. And Pa is not here. Jan Viljoen turns a blind eye, and good for him. Legend and Lady can't stand the flies. We take them west, upstream, every day and there are no signs of the enemy.'

'Karel, you should really follow orders. It's best—'

'Rudi will be back soon.' He was not in the mood for one of Charles's lectures on discipline. 'It's my turn to cook, and Jan Viljoen has invited Gert and Danie Vermaas to share our pot. And the bloody meat is so tough. It takes the entire day to get it to Jan's liking.' He added salt to the pot.

'Something to cheer you a little.' Charles handed him two letters. 'The mail came in this morning. I've taken the liberty to collect yours as well as those of the Viljoens. Their women are spoiling them.' He indicated the bulky parcels on the cart. 'There might be something sweet in there. What I'd give for Anita's bottled peaches.'

'If there are peaches in those parcels,' Karel said, taking his letters, 'it's more likely to be the distilled juice.'

Karel paged through his mother's letter before opening the bulky one from Annecke. A note with Rudolf's name on it slipped out. He reached for his jacket, which was hanging on the tent pole, and tucked it into the inner pocket. Rudi would read it and share it with him.

Jan Viljoen, a sack slung over his shoulder, stomped up, dumped it next to the fire and cursed. 'Had my brothers been here, I'd have sent them to scrounge for food. *Magtig*, stumbling around these bloody rocks and all I could get my hands on was potatoes and a few onions and they're not fresh either.'

'My, my, tempers are frayed today,' Charles smiled. 'It's the heat. It's better to stay still until dusk. Come sit here in the shade, Jan, have a cup of coffee.'

AFTER RUDOLF had ridden a few miles, he was forced to slow down. Lady snorted and pawed, unwilling to carry on. Legend tossed her mane, pulling at the reins. To the south, not even a mile away, was the river. He raised the field glasses to his eyes and scanned the opposite bank – all quiet there. Standing up in the stirrups, he swept the glasses over the veld beyond the river – no sign of activity.

'All right, calm down,' he scolded the horses. 'We won't go much further. This is as good a place as any.'

He traversed a gully in the steep north bank and led the horses down to the water. Legend stepped in, but Lady stood uncertainly. The water only reached their bellies and was barely flowing, as there had been no rain since the night of the battle. When they had had their fill, he led them back up the bank to a good patch of grass under a clump of tall bush willows. He removed their bits and went back to the river for a swim.

On the opposite bank was a clear patch of sand, a perfect spot to dry off and dream of Annecke. Placing his Mauser carefully behind a rock, he stripped naked and waded into the water. He closed his eyes and float-ed face-up for a while. He thought about the last night he'd spent with Annecke under the willow at the vlei. Intense longing washed through him. That night she'd shown him a little music box Martin had given her. It played a sad melody about a soldier who had not come home.

'Hands up!' He heard through the water. He jerked his head clear and stared thunderstruck at the four men in khaki uniforms on the patch of sand, their rifles trained on his naked body. Panic and fear ate deep inside him, and he thought of Karel, not Annecke.

'Exactly what we had in mind,' said the tall one with the officer's tabs. 'It won't do to run. Come over here, slowly, slowly.'

Realising that he had no choice, he waded to the other side, shielding his nakedness with his hands.

'We mean you no harm, Boer,' the officer said kindly. 'You're on your own. We've watched you for some time. Now, sit over there. Be a good lad and I might let you go.'

Rudolf looked at them uncertainly, but did as he was told. The officer and two others stripped down and rushed into the water, leaving the fourth man to watch over him. He sat a good ten yards away, his rifle between his knees. To his left, by the water's edge, were two more rifles and, on the officer's clothes, a pistol in the holster of a Sam Browne, just out of reach. He kept his eyes on the soldiers in the water.

'Hot, sun too much,' said his guard, pointing to the sky.

'It's midsummer; it's supposed to be hot,' Rudolf said in English.

The man's eyes widened.

They eyed each other for bit. Rudolf was desperately thinking of a way to get across the river to the horses. He decided to put his trust in the officer's promise. 'Will he really let me go when you are done here?'

'He's a good sort, is Captain Patterson. What does he want with a lone Boer?' his guard said. 'Now, tell me, how's the fighting on your side?'

While they talked, the soldier told him that they were carrying dispatches to General Methuen's camp. The heat had driven them to seek out the river.

'It's safer to go that way.' Rudolf pointed over his shoulder. 'South, a little to the east. Cut through there, round that koppie. Do you see it? Our camp is a good way from there.'

'Hensop! Hensop!'

The call came from the north bank. A number of Boers stood in the undergrowth, their Mausers trained on the British. Rudolf was stunned with relief. But then his guard raised his rifle and fired rapidly into the Boers.

In the next second Rudolf saw many things: his guard clutching his throat, blood spurting through his fingers and staining the sand beside him; the naked ones in the river scurrying for their rifles amid bullets hissing into the water. He lunged for the Sam Browne and was wrenching the pistol free when the bullets found him too.

BACK IN THE CAMP Karel cocked his head, strained his ears. He thought that he had heard rifle shots. He walked a little away from the fire and looked west, an uneasy feeling knotting his stomach. Then a sharp pain stabbed through his head and he sank to the ground.

'Are you all right?' Charles asked. 'Do you have a headache?'

'I don't know. A pain. Something is wrong, Charles.'

'Karel de Winter,' Jan Viljoen said and walked over to him, 'you want out of the cooking again, not that your cooking appeals to me.' Grabbing him by the scruff of the neck, he brought Karel to the fire. 'There! Get on with it!'

'Jan, something is wrong,' Karel said. 'I need to find Rudi. Give me your horse.'

'*Magtig!* Your brother is not a pretty girl. He's as ugly as you are and can fend for himself. He's been off on his own before.'

'Something is not right … not right,' Karel muttered.

'I'll tell you what's wrong,' Jan said. 'It's almost Christmas and I have no more homebrew to comfort me. And I don't think you have it in you to bake a cake or roast a pig like my Hannie does. Not that one can find a pig here! And as for a plump chicken …'

'Oh, I clean forgot,' Charles said. 'I've brought your mail and parcels. Do forgive me. On my cart, Jan.'

Jan fetched his post, but the bickering continued while Karel stirred the pot, all the time trying to figure out how to slip away and steal Jan's horse. Jan was reading his mail, his lips forming the words as if savouring them. Charles had dozed off. Karel was about to add water to the stew when Jan's mighty swearing woke Charles.

Karel stood up. Two men, leading Legend and Lady, rode through the camp, obviously being directed to them. He waited until the riders, followed by many from the Rustenburg commando, reached them. He rushed to Legend, but found that his throat was thick with fear.

'I'm Piet Naude, from the Lichtenburg commando,' said one of the men. 'We found these horses on the river bank, to the west and were told that they belong here.'

Jan stepped forward. 'Field Cornet Viljoen. Where's the man who was with them?'

Piet Naude was clearly uneasy. 'Field Cornet, we have a riddle here …'

'Get off your horses and speak to me!'

They dismounted and squatted in the shade of the tent. Men crowded around, urging them to get on with the news. 'We patrol that stretch of river every day. We came upon these horses under a tree. There were five khakis, swimming,' Naude said through sips of coffee. 'On the bank, a leather bag, the kind they carry dispatches in. We shouted *hensop*, but their lookout fired. We had no choice; we fired back. Before we could get to the leather bag, their patrol appeared and we ran for our horses. When we went back later, we found this Mauser on our side of the river.'

The men overwhelmed Naude with questions.

'Quiet! It will not help to shout yourselves hoarse.' Jan pushed and slapped at a few men. 'Let the man speak.'

'Four horses on the other bank, but five men; three were swimming naked and one in khaki sitting next to another, also naked.' Naude's friend gestured hopelessly. 'All five spoke English. I reckon that a Boer would've *hensopped*.'

'Rudolf speaks perfect English,' Charles's voice was a croak.

'*My Got!*' Jan was on his feet, pulling Naude with him. 'Take us there. We must search.'

'Wait! Wait!' Naude freed himself from Jan's grip. 'The five men we shot have been taken away.'

'If Rudolf is wounded, they would've taken him to the British camp,' Charles said.

Naude grimaced. 'All wounded or worse. We shoot straight. I'm sorry, truly, I am.'

'It's late. We have some way to ride back. If we can be of help …' his friend offered.

Charles saw them to their horses, thanking them for their frankness and assuring them that what had happened was no fault of theirs.

Karel stood with Legend, staring south from where anxiety, frightening in its intensity, appealed to his whole being. 'Rudi is in the British camp. And I'm going there.'

'Have you lost your reason?' Jan shook him by his arm. Legend curled her lip and flattened her ears and Jan retreated a few paces.

'There must be a way to find out,' Charles removed his glasses, polishing them on his shirtsleeve. 'We have to know what has happened to him.'

'But what if he cannot speak for himself?' Gert Vermaas asked.

'Or worse – may God in his mercy let me be wrong – they won't know his name. Then how will we know?' Jan eyes were huge, beseeching.

'Let's approach this in a rational manner.' Charles replaced his glasses and stood in deep thought for a while. 'Now, let's think clearly.'

'The doctor Rudi met on the battlefield, the one who knows Martin and James,' Karel said. 'He's your friend, Charles, and he's in that camp.'

'Frank Crofton-Smith. Yes! There has to be a way to get into contact with him. Come, let's find that way. Let's go to Jacobsdal, I'll speak to General Cronjé personally.'

EARLY THE NEXT AFTERNOON, Charles and Karel, Red Cross bands around their arms, and Karel holding a white flag high, departed for the British camp. Charles had formulated a request asking for assistance with a complicated operation. He wished to consult with Frank Crofton-Smith, who had expert knowledge on the subject. Pleading with General Cronjé had only resulted in a rebuke, but General de Wet had taken pity on Charles and signed the request.

Scarcely had they crossed the river when a patrol appeared in the distance. An officer and fifteen men rode up to meet them. Charles handed the letter to the officer.

'On a mission of mercy, then. Take them in, deliver them to the hospital tents,' he ordered two of his men.

When they were escorted through the camp, Charles marvelled at the vast difference it presented to the chaos of Magersfontein. The bell-shaped tents were in lines, the mobile field kitchens parked at intervals, Lee-Enfields stacked in crowns and the horses picketed in lines, munching from nosebags.

They dismounted at the hospital tents and were shown into what he took to be a rest room for doctors by virtue of the rumpled camp cots and canvas chairs, the teacups and issues of *Punch* and *John Bull* on a table. After a lengthy wait, Frank Crofton-Smith, carrying a pot of tea, arrived, a smile on his tired face. 'What a pleasant surprise, Charles!' He extended his hand to Karel. 'Rudolf, is it?'

'No, his twin, Karel,' Charles said when Karel shook Frank's hand wordlessly.

Frank turned back to Charles. 'A complication with a spinal injury? I could come over to assist, if you want.'

'Thank you, but I'm here for another reason altogether. Frank, we need your help. Did you get any Boer wounded or … dead … in yesterday? Rudolf went missing at the river. I believe there was a shooting incident between patrols.'

By the look on Frank's face, Charles could tell that the news was not good. 'Dispatch riders from the west were shot at the river. My colleague, Major Emerton, attended them. I'll send for him.' He stuck his head through the flap and found the men who'd accompanied Charles and Karel waiting at the entrance. 'Send for Major Emerton! You'll find him in Block B.' He drew back his head. 'Let's have some tea and tell me what exactly happened.'

Charles related the incident while Karel stood quietly, refusing the tea and not taking part in the conversation.

'What a damnable business.' Frank cast a sidelong glance at Karel, who was staring outside, a concentrated frown on his face. 'Shall we give him something? He looks shocked.'

Charles shook his head. 'He hasn't eaten or drunk anything since the news reached us. Neither has he slept. I have to find his twin. They've never been apart in their lives.'

Major Emerton, a tall man with stooped shoulders, entered. Frank poured him tea and asked about the casualties of the previous day.

'One wounded, a Captain Patterson. Leg and head. Should be on his way to Cape Town with the next train. Not much hope there, but at least out of this heat he might stand a chance.' Emerton dragged a hand over his eyes. 'The rest? I signed the death certificates. Yes, there was an unknown. We took him for Boer.'

'Look at me, doctor,' Karel said. 'Does he look like me, exactly like me?'

Major Emerton frowned. 'I see so many faces, young man. Wounded, dead, sick, but yes … your face … yes, I might've seen it.'

'Where is he? I want to see him!'

The three doctors exchanged glances on hearing the raw panic in his voice.

'How … by what did you identify them?' Charles asked.

'I'll find the medics who brought them in.' Emerton gulped down his tea and left.

A medic arrived a few minutes later and Frank asked him to describe the bodies. 'We used what information was available, Doctor,' he said. 'There were four bodies. One was dressed and had his papers with him. The other three were naked, sir. Tattoos, sir, two had tattoos. The other one not. I've never come across Boer wounded or dead with tattoos, sir.'

'Show him to me,' Karel said. 'I want to see him!'

'We buried them this morning. The heat …' He fished in his pocket and held his hand out to Karel. 'We found clothes on the other side of the river. I found this in the jacket. I thought to keep it as a souvenir.'

It was Rudolf's pocketknife, the one Charles had given him on their last birthday. Karel took the knife and slipped it into the inner pocket of his jacket.

'We can only hope that the wounded man … Captain Patterson will survive and be able to tell us what really happened.' Frank patted Charles's shoulder. 'Rudolf de Winter. I'll mark the grave, draw you a map of the cemetery. I'll get it to you somehow. My condolences to you and the family.'

Charles thanked him in a voice tight with emotion. He took Karel by the arm. 'Come, we must go. We'll bring him home to Wintersrust when the war is over.'

Karel looked at the two doctors, dry-eyed. 'My brother is not dead.'

———————

KOBA LOOKED AT THE BRIDE and groom standing solemnly in the magistrate's office in Rustenburg. Annecke wore her blue dress, the one with the red flowers embroidered on the cuffs. Her face was pale, her big brown eyes overlarge, tears lying shallow in them. Martin's arm was in a sling.

Poor Martin, her golden boy. She blew her nose into the handkerchief and reached for another in her pocket. Charles had cabled the dreadful news of Rudolf's death to Rustenburg. The wedding should have been postponed out of respect for his death, as custom demanded, but Marthinus and Mary had insisted it go ahead. 'People get married in times of war, especially in times of war, son,' Marthinus had said. 'Don't deny Wintersrust and the De Winter family name an heir.'

Yes, Marthinus was right. Three sons in the war; one killed, Martin wounded. Yet, Wintersrust would have an heir. When Annecke had told her about Rudi's child and about the night Martin had tried to take her in his fevered state, she had searched her mind for a solution. They were brothers, so much alike, so very much alike. Martin need not know now about his brother's child.

'We've sinned, Rudi and I, and now he's dead and I'm being punished too,' Annecke had cried in her arms. 'I shall be a good mother and wife, Tante Koba. Perhaps God will forgive me just a little then for the lie I must tell Martin now.'

'God will forgive us. He always does in the end,' she had comforted Annecke.

As she had tended Martin's wound, Koba had reminded him of the mortality of man. 'Unlike disease and old age, a bullet does not ask whether you are young, old or weak. It reaps those who are brave and fearless, like you. Despite the killing and sorrow, women have to carry on with life as we know it, as God intended. Your father is right; don't deny little Annecke a child, and don't deny Wintersrust an heir.'

His answer had pierced her heart with guilt at the truth she had to withhold from him. And also with pride at the honourable man he was.

'Tante Koba, surely there is no need for pretence. You know that Annecke is with child. I have wronged her. I know my duty.'

A Fateful Night in Durban

January 1900

THE HOSPITAL TRAIN took most of the afternoon to make the seventy-mile journey from Frere to Durban. The patients lay under sheets, drenched in perspiration. When the train snaked through the hills and descended to the sea, the humidity became overpowering.

James put his head through the window, trying to catch what breeze the moving train created, but there was little relief. He smelled the sea and thought he saw a glimmer in the distance. A ship was waiting in the harbour to transfer those whose injuries were slow to mend to Cape Town, as the doctors believed the climate of Natal slowed the healing process.

Peter lay on an iron cot, his wounded side supported on pillows. The scar he had received in the Sudan showed red against his bronzed face. The operation on his leg had been successful and his shoulder was improving, but the wound in his groin was still suppurating. He remained on the critical list and it appeared, the doctor said, that his body found it hard to fight back. One day he was coherent, the next he relapsed into unconsciousness.

A wave of dizziness and nausea struck James, and he realised that he had reached the extreme of depletion. Since the battle, he had given blood to Peter three times. A strange lethargy had taken hold of him and he battled to perform his duties, even fainting in the presence of his troops. The doctor had insisted that he take leave, and Colonel Butcher had ordered him to Durban to spend time with his wife.

He had not been to Durban since they'd been rushed to the front three months back. He wanted to see Victoria. She would talk about India and other unmilitary things. He needed her to ease his anxiety about Peter and his despondency about the way the war was going. In her company he would forget about all that, and he would pretend that the other man, the one she'd loved, didn't matter.

He squatted next to Peter's cot. 'Almost there. Shall I give you some water?'

Peter opened his eyes. 'Champagne is what I want.'

'Happens to be the sole reason I'm doing this trip. Buller has run out of the stuff, it seems. What a mess, Peter. I never thought we'd exactly run over the Boers, but … well, Roberts and Kitchener are due in Cape Town any day now. The tide must turn.'

'I hope you're right, but somehow …'

'Am I tiring you? Are you in pain? Shall I ask the doctor for a drop of morphine?'

Peter declined with a faint gesture of his hand and closed his eyes. James wondered if he was slipping into the twilight world again. He sighed, willing himself to stay calm.

LATE THAT AFTERNOON, with Peter installed on the hospital ship, James set off towards the centre of the town. In the lingering dusk Durban looked peaceful. Only the soldiers strolling on the promenade reminded him of the war. He kept his eyes on the pavement, ignoring the salutes of troops and greetings of passers-by. As he neared the hotel, he hesitated. There had been no time to forewarn Victoria of his arrival, but he had nowhere else to go.

The clerk at reception told him that Mrs Henderson was in and directed him to the first floor. A young Indian girl answered his knock. She gazed at him in surprise.

'It happens to be a soldier, ma'am,' she called over her shoulder.

'It happens to be your husband, ma'am,' James said.

Victoria, dressed in a silk robe and tying her freshly brushed hair, appeared and smiled a welcome. He recalled the night at the Mount Nelson, the rain on the windows, and Victoria, inviting and willing, between the sheets.

She dismissed the girl, promising to send for her again in the morning.

'A bit of India. Does it please you?' James said.

'Yes, I must confess, I'm quite happy here. A bit of India, as you say.' Her eyes stayed on him, taking in his dishevelled state. 'I wouldn't mind staying here until the war is done. It won't be long, will it?'

'We're taking a beating, for the moment. I brought Peter. The hospital ship leaves for Cape Town in the morning.'

'How is he?'

'Not well, he's … not well.' He removed his helmet and stood uncertainly. 'I'll find somewhere to stay and clean up. Could we have dinner later?'

'Nonsense. You look exhausted. My suite is quite comfortable. I brought along the rest of your things from Cape Town. They're in the wardrobe.

There's a bathroom off the bedroom. Soak for as long as you like.' She pulled the bell cord. 'Champagne? Brandy?'

'Champagne will do.'

'How's your war going?'

'I lost Thunder. He was killed when I went …' he paused, unwilling to go on.

'… back for Peter,' she finished the sentence. 'It's all over town, James. Six bullet holes in your uniform, and all you suffered were a few bruises.'

He nodded. 'Yes, no damage this time, but Lightning is stuck in Ladysmith, together with Peter's chargers.'

'They probably landed in the soup pot. People are starving in Ladysmith, you know.'

He ignored the comment. She showed him the bathroom and withdrew to the sitting room. The scent of her soaps and lotions was strong, and the damp towel on the rail reminded him of her body. As he lay back in the bath, he thought again of her in someone else's arms. He cursed and climbed out of the bath, dressed and went through to the sitting room in his shirtsleeves.

The champagne had arrived and he drank thirstily. Desperate for something to talk about to keep his emotions in control, he pointed to the letters on the table at his side. 'Any news from home?'

'Those letters are for you, actually. Stefanie's arrived today. There's also one from Beatrice. I was going to send them on. Read if you like. Dinner is only at nine.' She went to stand by the window, her back to him. 'Do share any interesting news, though.'

He opened Beatrice's letter. A photograph between two sheets. A nine-month-old baby, dark curls and dimples. His daughter, Sarah. He pushed the photograph back into the envelope and sat motionless, willing the unbearable emotions away. He poured more champagne, the last of the second bottle.

Then he opened Stefanie's letter. There was only one page: *Jamie, news from Tante Koba just arrived. Rudi was shot by a patrol at Magersfontein and was buried by the English. Karel refuses to go home. Martin married Annecke despite the death in the family. He was wounded but Charles stitched him up. Oh, Jamie, what is to become of Karel? Of us all? I must find a way to get home.*

James stood up. He handed Victoria the letter, walked over to the window and stared out into the darkness. Men die in war; it was the life he'd chosen. But there was something unfair, he felt, about Rudolf's death. *Those who God has joined together, let no man put asunder.* Koba's words from so long ago came back to him.

'So bloody unfair.'

'Unfair! Is that what you think?' Victoria's voice was thick with sarcasm. 'What did you expect? Only strangers killed in war? You have cousins, an uncle, and a brother on *your enemy's* side. Do you expect none of them to be affected?'

Everything he had experienced in the past three months assailed him. He raged aloud at General Buller's folly, which had led to Peter's injury, and at the Boers for their stubborn pride in taking on the British Empire.

Victoria put her arms around his waist, slipping her hands under his shirt. 'Forgive me, James. I'm deeply sorry about your cousin's death.'

He wished he knew how to respond but was only aware of her breasts and legs through the slippery satin of her robe. He raged silently against her for tormenting him, hating her for evoking feelings that he'd never had towards any woman. The fire inside him needed to take its course.

She came into his arms and lifted her face to meet his. He pulled away, but she held lightly onto him. He could have walked out, but her nearness was overwhelming and the fury of his passion uncontrollable. He wanted to push her away, but pulled her roughly against him, his mouth on hers, forcing her head back. He tore at her robe and the silk ripped apart. *Dear God, I am raping my wife, please make her stop me, he cried silently, desperately, please make her stop me.*

She did not struggle. In his urgency he drove her across the room. The table spilled over and glasses crashed to the floor. In one swift movement he forced her onto the floor. He raised himself on one elbow, pulled up her robe, tore at her underclothes and forced himself into her. But the fire that had ravaged him died in a few seconds. He held on to her, clinging like a child, his chest heaving. He heard her sob softly before blackness descended over him.

HE RAISED HIMSELF on his elbows. Her tear-stained face was turned from him, her hair spread on the floor around her head, her left hand against her mouth, the skin broken where she had bitten into the knuckles.

He took in the rest of the room. In the muted light he saw the table, the champagne bottles, glasses and letters on the floor. He closed his eyes for a long minute. Then he gently disentangled his body from hers, fetched a blanket from the bedroom and spread it over her.

He dressed and went to the door. As he turned the knob, he heard her calling softly, 'James, please don't leave. Please don't run away.'

He hesitated but took up his helmet and left. He walked until he found the first bar, where he ordered brandy. The bartender half-filled his glass and placed the bottle next to it. With shaking hands he emptied the glass and poured another. Thoughts and images crowded his mind.

Rudi is dead. I've raped Vicky. Karel is going to die and Peter is dying. Horses. Thunder, Lady, Legend. Thunder riddled with Mauser bullets. Legend, what a mare! Black, fierce, powerful! Lady such a dainty mare, like Annecke. Fireflies dancing in the cave. Neutral ground.

His eyes focused on his hands, the hands that had violated his wife. He hung his head between his hands. Don't run away, stay, she said. *Run away? Wild horses run away. Wild horses run away in circles, round and round, on and on, faster and faster. And then? The dream! Yes, the dream shatters and they run away. Faster and faster. On and on. When do they stop? Do they ever stop? How does the bloody story end?*

They drop dead from exhaustion, it suddenly came to him. He closed his eyes, felt tears behind his eyelids. *I'm drunk and I'm crying, hopelessly drunk and so very, very tired.*

He emptied the glass and made his way into the deserted streets. He was not a wild horse, he repeatedly told himself; he was not running away. At the hotel, the night porter in the foyer did not wake up when he stumbled past. He pushed open the door of the suite. A lamp on the table, a plate of sandwiches covered with a napkin, a decanter of cognac and a glass beside it.

He poured the glass half-full, spilling on his clothes and the carpet. The bedroom door stood ajar. There was a light coming from inside. He pushed it open. She was sitting up in the bed, her hair shining copper in the lamplight, her green eyes looking steadily at him. An apology formed on his lips, but words refused to come. He crossed the room unsteadily and sat down beside her.

'Who was the man, Vicky?' His voice was thick with the brandy.

The silence filled with the crashing of the waves on the shore and the shunting of a train at the dockyard. The lamp flickered out. The train hissed in angry puffs. A horse galloped past in the street below. The sunlight crept through the window and touched Victoria's hair. He slumped forward. The glass crashed to the floor, spilling its contents onto the carpet. He was aware that she lifted his legs onto the bed and pulled off his boots. Then she lay beside him and put her arm around him.

What and Where They Be

I T TOOK THE WAR to make Stefanie realise what a disaster her marriage was. She had been blind. Martin was right; he was always right. Paul Warren was a brilliant lawyer, but he was also an enemy of her people. Paul wanted this war, and had worked ceaselessly to make it happen. He wanted the British to destroy her nation. He made no effort to hide these feelings any longer.

Night after night she hosted dinner parties, did recitals for government officials, officers and their ladies at hotels and at the homes of British sympathisers. She played her part as Mrs Warren, but only for self-preservation. Paul was dangerous when things did not go his way. He ranted and raved in his study, drinking himself wild, swearing vengeance against Oom Paul and the Boers. She could have told him this would happen. It had happened before.

She pushed the ribbons of her hat from her face. Paul had insisted they witness the arrival of Lord Roberts. Any hope that the war might end soon was crushed by the sight of thousands of soldiers pouring down the gangways.

'I want to go home. I've had enough of this,' she said to Paul.

'Patience, my dear. We take refreshments with the new arrivals at the Mount Nelson.' Paul pointed with his gold-tipped cane to the khaki-clad mass. 'They're our liberators, my dear.'

'Don't call me "my dear".'

'You're overwrought, madam. Don't hold me responsible for your brother's death. Although I do sympathise with your loss …'

'I don't want your sympathy. Take me home.'

He tucked her hand through his arm and led her to the landau, stopping frequently to welcome newly arrived officers. By the time they reached the vehicle, he had offered a ride to two staff officers. After a frustrating hour at the Mount Nelson Hotel, during which she had to make polite conversation with pale-faced, battle-eager officers and their demure wives, they arrived home. She ascended the stairs in hasty strides and slammed her bedroom door behind her.

I must get home. There must be a way. But every possibility was blocked. No trains crossed into the Free State, and along the border the fighting forces were killing each other. She had been so utterly naive, not thinking that the war would touch her family, but Rudolf's death had forced her to face reality. She wanted to see her father and Martin most of all, and to beg their forgiveness for marrying despite Martin's warning.

Martin was wounded; he could have been killed like Rudi. And now he was to become a father, her mother had written. *Annecke, sweet thing, she had loved in a way I only wonder about.* She looked at the connecting door between her bedroom and Paul's and recalled the night, many months ago, that she had plucked up the courage to open it, only to find his room empty. She had sat on his bed for hours. At sunrise she had been waiting still. Now she acknowledged the whispered innuendoes about her husband's private life. She had not thought it possible for a man to prefer the bed of another man to that of a woman.

She sank to the floor. The desperate yearning to be loved, to love some- one, was overwhelming. She was tired, tired of pretending. She needed to get home, to Tante Koba, to Wintersrust, to be with her people, to regain her place in the world.

SO IT WENT, day after day, always struggling to maintain a composed and dignified face. Only her recitals and the long hours of practice supported her through this time.

The hospital ship carrying Peter Radford had docked a week before. James had begged her in his letter to visit Peter. His friend was in a de- pressed mood and he feared for his life. She did not want to visit anyone in the military hospital. She had played for the recuperating officers a few nights back, but wild emotions had spoiled her performance.

She scraped the courage together and went the following day. Driving her Cape cart between the rows of bungalows in the hospital garden, she saw men hobbling on crutches, others with their heads and limbs swathed in bandages sunning themselves in deckchairs, visitors fussing over them. She arrived at the main building, where the officers were housed, and entered the matron's office, barely able to conceal her antipathy. When told who she had come to visit, the matron frowned and asked her name before dispatching a nurse to inform the patient.

She thought about the man that she'd come to see. She remembered Peter Radford; he had stayed over at Koba's house for the rugby, the day she'd first set eyes on her husband. How she cursed that day now! Peter was tall, fair and oh so very English. She had heard that he and James were to receive the Victoria Cross.

A nurse in her blue-striped uniform bobbed a curtsy. 'Lieutenant Radford is in a private room. He doesn't allow visitors as a rule, but is prepared to see you.'

She followed the nurse down the long corridor. When they reached the room, the nurse stood aside for her to enter and then left.

It was not a large room. There was only one bed and the man in it was not the Peter Radford she'd met years ago. His wasted body showed through the blankets, his face thin and pale, his eyes almost lifeless. She hesitated in the door, but then an appalling thought compelled her closer. The anger and fear that had built up over the past weeks exploded.

'Does life mean nothing to you? My cousin rides out to rescue you from certain death and there, you've done it again! Both of you. Oh yes, I've heard all about it. Tell me, is it death you want?' With a swish of her skirt, she swung around and left.

Halfway down the passage the absurdity and unkindness of her behaviour struck her. She burst into angry tears, headed back to Peter's room and stood at the foot of the bed. She smiled, but her eyes still smarted.

He held out his hand. She removed her gloves, walked around the bed and took it in both of hers. She raised her eyes to meet his. They were brown with gold flecks, and were filled with compassion and understanding.

'I recall a gawky girl in convent uniform,' he said, smiling into her face.

'I was not gawky.' She smiled through her tears.

———◆———

IN THE ROOM ABOVE THEM, a patient who had been unconscious for over a month opened his eyes. The light hurt. His head felt heavy. His hand began an exploratory movement but his shoulder exploded in pain. He gave a strangled cry, his hand dropping back onto his chest.

A woman's face, her head covered with a strange cloth, appeared in his vision. 'Captain Patterson, we have to keep quiet. You have a nasty head wound, sir.'

He again reached for his head. She brought his hand down, talking in a soothing voice, but he was only aware of a searing pain between his eyes before blackness claimed him again.

IT WAS FOUR WEEKS since Rudolf had been reported dead by the English doctor. Martin looked at Karel, sitting hunched over his own little fire. His heart ached to be with him, to help him carry the burden of his twin's death, but, as hard as he had tried, as everybody had tried, they had failed.

Karel had been indifferent towards those around him before, but now he had grown cold and bitter. There was a harshness in him, a deep, uncontrolled anger, replaced at times by a vacant hopelessness. He spoke to no one and ate very little. At night he slept with his head on the saddle, Legend and Lady by his side. His days were spent riding across the veld searching the banks of the river. The Boers in the trenches and camp were used to the wild-looking young man on the fierce black horse, always riding up and down, up and down, in the heat of the midsummer sun. What made the sight more pitiful was the chestnut mare, riderless and bewildered, galloping beside them.

Not a single tear, Charles had told Martin on his return from Wintersrust. Marthinus had been very gentle with him at first, but then, fearing for his son's mind, had tried to provoke him, accusing him of not being a man for not accepting the ways of war and the will of the Almighty. Jan Viljoen had walked past his sleeping place many times, lamenting noisily, in the hope that his sorrow would break down Karel's resistance. Even that had failed. The only reaction he had shown was when Martin had informed him of his marriage to Annecke. He had stared at Martin. But that had passed as well.

At least Legend was with him, Martin thought, giving fierce snorts and flattening her ears whenever anyone approached. Rudolf gone, and Annecke my wife now. No one had been surprised at the marriage, as the Rustenburg district had expected it for years. Jan had dug him in the ribs and given him a wicked wink. The war, he had said, makes a man hungry for a woman. Charles, however, had stammered his way through his congratulations.

He saw Charles on his mule-cart making his way through the camp, handing out letters and medicine. He had replaced his straw boater with a slouch hat and his clothes were showing signs of wear, the jacket patched at the cuffs and pieces of leather sewn to the elbows, but the bow tie remained.

'Good evening to you all,' Charles greeted, removed his hat dusted it against his leg.

'Have you letters for us?' Joep Maree asked. 'My Lettie was not well when we left Soetvlei.'

274

'Oh, yes, I've brought the mail and some proper tea, a gift from Frank Crofton-Smith. He sent a messenger with the details of Rudolf's grave. Here, Uncle Marthinus.' He handed him an envelope. 'I've taken the liberty of sending a copy to Wintersrust, just in case you lose this one. One never knows …'

Marthinus put the envelope in his pocket. 'Charles, is there nothing more we can do for Karel? It's been a month now.'

'I've given it a great deal of thought, actually. He *is* a bit erratic, but he won't lose his reason, Uncle Marthinus. He'll come to terms with it. We'll have to bear with him for as long as it takes. Don't argue with him, and don't tell him his twin is dead unless he specifically asks.'

'Give the man a bottle of *dop*,' Jan Viljoen said. 'It'll break him down, make him weep.'

'No, if time is what he needs, we must give him that,' Marthinus said taking the mail from Charles. He found two letters addressed to Karel, walked the little way to Karel's fire and squatted beside him. 'Here, there's a letter from your mother and one from Annecke too.' He put the letters between them, but was ignored. 'Son, come back to us. All of us are trying to fill the emptiness of Rudolf's going. He was your brother, you loved him deeply, and he was my boy, my son. As a father, I must not just be able to endure grief, I have to overcome it.'

Karel stared into the fire, his face closed. 'He is not dead, Pa,' he whispered. His father placed a hand on his shoulder and left reluctantly as it was shrugged off.

HATRED, STRONG AND INTENSE, possessed Karel. Hatred of the English, of man, of a God who only existed in Koba's world. Emptiness, his father said; Rudi's death had left an emptiness and a grief that had to be overcome.

But all he felt was agony.

Through this agony there was a voice, muted but persistent, driving him on, up and down the river bank, over the desolate countryside, searching, always searching. But some days the voice deserted him, leaving him defeated and scared.

Now, as he sat alone by his little fire, he moved his hand over the left side of his jacket. They were still there – Annecke's note and Rudi's knife. He had not touched them since Rudi disappeared. He was scared to do so. It was the evidence he did not want to acknowledge. It would drive him over the edge. He had to get to the grave and dig it up. Only then would he know. But the

English were still there. While he waited, he had to hang on to his reason, for Rudi's sake, for Annecke's sake.

He looked at Martin talking to Charles and Jan Viljoen at their fire. He stood relaxed, thumb hooked into his trouser pocket, head tilted, the firelight catching his hair and beard. His brother was a tall, strong man. Annecke was so delicate and timid. She married him, gave her body to Martin. A body that belonged to Rudi. He picked up Annecke's letter. It was only a single page. He moved closer to the fire, held it to the flickering light. *I am so scared, Karel. I married Martin. You were not here to tell me what to do. We have sinned, Rudi and I, and he paid for it and now I am paying too. Please come home. I have a secret only you and I can share. Please come home, Karel.*

He pushed the letter into the fire. Images formed in the flames, dancing, twisting. Rudi smiling, riding Lady. Rudi beside him in the trench, taking aim, shooting. Rudi telling him about loving Annecke under the willow. Then the face of the apologetic English doctor: *I see so many faces, young man, but yours ... yes ...*

Longing for his twin welled up. He stumbled into the darkness, with Legend following him. Tears blurred his vision, but he held on to Legend. He buried his face in her mane and wept in deep silent sobs. She whinnied softly. He stroked her nose, letting her nibble his fingers. There had to be a way to hang on to his sanity. One more day of riding, of searching in vain, would destroy him.

He stood for a while before he led Legend back to his fire. He looked at the Rustenburg men. Their faces beckoned to him, the smoke from their pipes, the aroma wafting from the cooking pot. He walked over and stood a little way off.

'Hey, you vagrant!' Jan Viljoen stepped up. 'What do you see there in the darkness? Nothing. What do you find out there in the day? Nothing. If you want to search, then do so, but look closer to the British camp. And while you're out there, those eyes of yours can see what we need to know.' Jan lowered his voice to a fierce whisper, 'Do you understand what I'm saying, *magtig*?'

Karel nodded. 'Yes, Jan, I want to scout.'

'Of course! At night you're as dark as a thief and in the day as cunning as a jackal. You're the best spy I've ever come across.'

'We ride alone, Legend and I.'

'Yes, you ride alone. It's not your company I want, nor the presence of that ill-bred mare of yours. You were my friend once, but now it's only your eyes I need.' Jan pushed him towards the others. 'Uncle Marthinus, tell this scarecrow son of yours where he has to go tomorrow. He'll scout for us.'

'The English are getting restless.' Marthinus glanced gratefully at Jan and handed Karel a mug of coffee. 'A big force is marching this way. Karel, tomorrow you ride with Martin to General de Wet. His scout, Captain Danie Theron, will give you work. There's to be another battle soon.'

———

JAMES STOOD AT THE FOOT OF A HILL waiting for the order to go into battle. He was not fully sober and had not eaten in days. He felt the nausea rising. Stealing a glance at his troopers, he was grateful to find that they were watching the battle that raged on the hill.

After the traumatic night in Durban, he had returned to the front, badly shaken. He tried to drown his shame in reckless living, fighting in every skirmish, riding any patrol duty, drinking himself senseless every night. He could never touch Victoria again. That night would always be a barrier between them, like the man she'd loved before.

'I say, Henderson,' Captain Murray Shaw arrived at his side. 'Buller believes that this little mountain, er, koppie, is the key to the relief of Ladysmith.'

James unscrewed his water bottle and took a gulp. 'For God's sake, can't Buller grasp that we're fighting an enemy of sharpshooters? Thousands of us down here, a few hundred of them up there firing down at us. Clear targets!'

Shaw fingered his huge moustache, frowning. 'Spioenkop. What does it mean, Henderson? Curious name.'

'Hill of the spies. The Boers can see for miles around.'

'I take exception to being grouped with the mounted infantry.' Shaw held out a tin of cheroots. 'Shortage of able bodies, Hunter says. But to get a horse up there?'

James took a cheroot from the tin. 'Take away the mounted, and we're infantry—', he broke off when he noticed a runner handing a note to Colonel Butcher.

The order came to leave the horses and scale the hill. James slid his Lee-Enfield rifle from its leather holder. Apart from his Sam Browne, he wore nothing that distinguished him from an ordinary trooper. No obvious target.

The Boer artillery now directed fire at the base of the hill. Clouds of acrid smoke and choking dust replaced the morning mist and shrouded the summit of the hill, allowing only glimpses of the soldiers further up.

'Lieutenant Henderson, get moving,' Major George Hunter, sweat running from his face, ordered from the left. 'Open formation as from the ascent.'

Halfway up the hill, they came across stretcher-bearers labouring with their bleeding loads between wounded staggering down. A few hundred yards further on, they reached a breastwork of stone and flung themselves between the bodies of the wounded and the dead. Shells burst overhead, spraying shrapnel and battering their eardrums.

James knew that they were still some distance from the front line. Stealing a glance over his shoulder, he saw Hunter come to his feet to lead the advance but fall awkwardly to the ground. Murray Shaw took his place and charged. His rifle spun from his hands as he clutched at his leg and went down.

And now I have to lead a charge. James waited for the battle lust to take over. But nothing came. There was just a rush of anxiety, bordering on … fear? His men were watching him, waiting for his order. And before the fear could settle, he stretched his arm wide, signalling the charge.

They vaulted over the stone sangar, stumbling across the rocky ground strewn with fallen bodies. They had not gone ten yards when a bullet hit James's arm and another sent his helmet flying. He lurched over and crawled for the nearest boulder.

Blood, hot and sticky, spread down to his hand. Risking a glance around the boulder, a bullet grazed his cheek. He pulled back, blood and tears streaming down his face. He ordered his men to stay put and searched the battlefield with his eyes. Mark Sinclair, stretched out on the ground, was lighting a cheroot. Someone had dragged Murray Shaw to the safety of a large rock. William Moore raised himself a little, clutched at his shoulder, and fell back. John Miles was to James's left, lying flat, his hands pressing his helmet to his head.

Suddenly there was quiet. With a sense of foreboding, James peered round the boulder again. Fifty yards ahead was a shallow trench, filled with bodies. There was movement on the other side. The Boers were advancing.

He signalled to Sinclair and Miles and hastily passed the word to fix bayonets. With the utmost willpower, he sprang from behind the rock, followed by his few remaining men. Immediately bullets ripped through the air, and men plunged forward, their rifles clattering to the ground. A bullet smacked into James's calf, and another thudded into his chest. He lay face down, gasping with shock, and then sudden pain seared through him as a trooper dragged him by the collar to the shelter of a rocky outcrop.

His body was on fire, yet he felt as though he was drowning in mud. When he drifted into consciousness, a terrible thirst raged through him and the sun blinded his eyes.

Darkness fell swiftly. The firing died down. From far behind, the bugle called the retreat. He heard his name being called. Through a haze of pain he saw

Sinclair, face streaked with dust and etched in exhaustion, crawling towards him.

'Thought you might need a bit of a chat. Shoulders up for a chest wound.' Sinclair shifted him so that his shoulders were raised, supported on one of the many dead.

Rose-lipt Maidens and Lightfoot Lads

Wynberg Hospital, Cape Town

PETER RADFORD CHECKED his watch. Almost four. Visiting hour. For the past ten days Stefanie had always left saying she might not be able to fit him in the next day. But she had always returned.

Since her first visit, she had acted with dignity, but he was aware that she was struggling to conceal her fear for her family's safety, and loneliness was always in her eyes. He was greatly saddened when she told him about Rudolf's death, and expressed the hope that Karel would find courage somehow to come to terms with this dreadful loss. She looked at him with gratitude and, in a strained voice that slowly changed to normal, told him about the Chopin recital she was preparing for a concert at the Tivoli Theatre. 'It calls for precise technique. I'm confident with the Etude and with the Grande Valse. Much too fiery for a waltz. But there's a Nocturne for which I can't find the soul. It's meant to be dreamy, but I find only longing.'

A longing for what she did not say, as, in an abrupt change of mood, she lifted her chin and looked about the room. 'I hate sitting here every afternoon.' She pointed through the window to the garden below, where patients were wheeled in chairs under the oak trees. 'Are you ever planning to get out of bed? It's been *six weeks* since you were wounded.' Now he had a surprise for her. That morning he had succeeded in walking a few paces unaided. In her eyes, in her battle not to allow fear and anxiety to get the upper hand, he had found his fighting spirit again.

He thought how unusual she was compared to the other women he knew. She didn't play games with her eyes or words, but always spoke her mind freely. Being with Stefanie was like being with James. Even tempers were not their strong points, yet there was an understanding of moods. She did all the things a visitor should do for a patient; she brought him grapes, newspapers and books, and insisted on writing his letters. The previous day he had asked her to pen a few lines to his brother. He watched her face while she wrote, and thought how attractive she was. She was unmistakably a De Winter, and yet he could see James's features in her mouth, in her slender face.

She had broken off in mid-sentence and put the pen down. 'Horses. Horses. Is that all you and your brother ever talk about? Bathsheba, Jezebel, Salome. Why do you call your horses by those names? Seductresses, all of them. Bad women.'

'Well, I only ride mares, Mrs Warren. Can't very well call a mare Queen Victoria or Joan of Arc – it wouldn't be proper.' He watched her, wondering if he had offended her. But his explanation had not offended her, something else had.

'Call me Stefanie or whatever you prefer, just not Mrs Warren.'

He thought about her husband, whom he had met at the Mount Nelson on the eve of war. There was no denying he was an impressive, influential man. If there was trouble between them, it was most probably due to the war.

He was still lost in their conversation of the previous day when she appeared in the door. She wore a blue summer dress with wide sleeves, emphasising her narrow waist, and was carrying a parcel. She was about to enter when he put out his hand. 'Stay where you are!' He lowered his legs and fastened the cord of his dressing gown. Keeping his eyes on her, he walked a few paces.

Her face lit up. She placed the parcel on the floor, stretched out her hands. 'Come, just a few steps more. Don't be such a coward. Walk all the way to me.' He reached her and held on to her arms. 'Well done! It's only a few steps, but at least it's a start. I'll get a chair and we'll go outside. It's such a beautiful day. Not a breath of wind.'

'Tomorrow, I promise.'

She sighed but nevertheless placed her arm around his waist and gently led him back to the bed. 'Your leg. It's healed; you'll play cricket again.' She pulled the blanket over him. 'And your shoulder … oh well, just practise, I suppose. Get out of bed and practise, Peter.' She opened the parcel. 'I found those black cheroots you wanted and also brought the papers and sugared fruit. You must've had your fill of grapes by now. And this!' She held up a bottle of cognac.

'Ah, thank you. Shall we have a drop?'

'Not for me. Devil's brew, Tante Koba calls it.' She handed him a glass and took the last item from her parcel, a volume of poetry. 'Fellow named Houseman. Just published.'

'Splendid. Will you read me one?' he asked, opening the cognac.

'You're perfectly capable of reading it yourself, but all right, seeing that you've achieved something today, I'll read you one poem.' She searched the pages. 'Right, here's a short one. "With rue my heart is laden ..."' Her eyes grew sad and she mumbled the words.

'Well, read on.'

'Oh, Peter, it's so sad. The last verse ...' she cleared her throat. 'By brooks too wide for leaping, the lightfoot boys are laid/The rose-lipt girls are sleeping, in fields where roses fade.'

'Yes ... touching. It says that they all died, those leaping boys and rosy girls. Sentimental twaddle, as James would say.'

'Yes, he would. He doesn't like poetry.'

'He knows but one verse.' He poured a little cognac and raised the glass in a toast. 'Drink to Fortune, drink to Chance, While we keep a little breath!/Drink to heavy Ignorance!/Hob-and-nob with Brother Death!'

She stared at him, a thoughtful expression in her eyes. 'What was it like, Peter? Doing it ... hob-nobbing with Brother Death, riding into the bullets, knowing you might not come out again.'

'You really want to know?' She nodded. 'Well, it's quite extraordinary. Fear is with you all the time, but is overridden by ... the excitement of the danger. It's exhilarating, a kind of physical thrill, intense, rewarding. One gets addicted to it.'

Her eyes, gazing steadily into his, filled with a curious fascination. She stood and leaned over him. 'Close your eyes and don't move.'

He kept still, but she seemed to be content with just keeping her mouth gently, but firmly, on his. He parted his lips a fraction and waited. She lifted her mouth and he opened his eyes to find her blue eyes inches from his.

She straightened up, bringing a finger to her lips. 'So that's what it's like.'

'I beg your pardon?'

'I was wondering ... what it would be like to kiss ... I mean, to kiss you.'

'That wasn't much of a kiss, Stefanie.'

'No, no, I suppose it wasn't. There must be more to it.'

'More to what?'

'Oh, never mind.' She sank back into the chair. 'Peter, please tell me about that night, just once more, please ...'

So again he told her about the night on the stoep of Wintersrust, about the moon over the mountains, the night sounds and about her father and the parable of war and the wild horses.

'Did Pa mention a lone mare running in the wrong direction?' she asked, guilt and dejection in her eyes. 'I must go now, Peter.' And without explanation she left.

The next day she was accompanied by an orderly with a wheelchair.

Peter obediently got into the chair and allowed her to tuck a blanket around his legs. The orderly took them as far as the path leading to the garden before Stefanie became impatient and took over, pushing him to the nearest tree. Moving a wicker chair close to him she told him in a voice filled with dread, about a bloody battle fought in Natal.

'Heard the rumours this morning. Who were the victors?'

'You are tedious. Do you really believe that the British will ever win a battle against us? You haven't even reached our borders yet and you've lost more people than we've lost in our country's history. The Boers, *my people*, once again defeated your *mighty* Empire!' She laid her hand on his arm. 'This madness has to stop.'

'It won't end until the Boers are beaten. You know that.' He looked across the garden. 'James will be in a foul mood for days now. He so hates to lose.'

'Is James there? Of course, Jamie is there. Peter, I must get the latest news.' And she hurried away.

AS STEFANIE DROVE HER CAPE CART down the oak-lined streets, her thoughts went to Peter. He was carefree, easy to talk to. It was like being with James. When he extended his hand to her that day, she felt the comfort she so desperately needed. She had set out to repay him for saving her from despair. And she had succeeded. Yesterday he had laughed out loud for the first time. He had walked. He would be well soon. Now was the time to repay another debt.

Table Mountain was already shadowing the suburbs when she arrived home. She handed the cart over to a servant and rushed inside to see the afternoon paper. The headlines told the story of the battle at Spioenkop. General Buller's force was once again retreating across the Tugela River, with thousands more wounded and dead. But a great number of Boers had also lost their lives.

She spent two hours at the piano, dined alone and went to her bedroom. Plans that had only been a possibility until then began to take shape. She had wanted to refuse an invitation to perform in Port Elizabeth, but now it seemed like a salvation. She could find a ship there to take her to Delagoa Bay in the Portuguese colony and then travel by train to Pretoria.

Hoping to find information on ships in Paul's study, she shrugged into her dressing gown and went downstairs. When she reached the study door, she heard the sound of voices inside; Paul was reading out names and addresses. Pretoria? Johannesburg?

She withdrew to the top of the landing just as Paul and another man emerged and left in a hurry. She waited until the landau clattered off before entering the study. A key dangled from the lock of the upper drawer. With a thudding heart, she willed herself to pull it open. There was a list of names and, on the last page, a paragraph stating that the abovementioned could be trusted to perform acts of sabotage – blowing up the mines, sabotaging the ammunition factory, damaging the railway to Delagoa Bay.

Grabbing a pen and paper, she copied the lists, pausing only to listen for the return of the landau. When she heard it coming through the gate, she tucked the copies inside her drawers, checked that all was in order and rushed from the study. When she was halfway up the stairs, the front door opened and Paul walked in.

'I couldn't sleep, so I came looking for you,' she said.

'Have you been visiting that officer of yours again?' His voice was low, threatening, his breath wafting brandy.

'I won't listen to you—'

He grabbed her above the elbow and twisted her hard against him.

She struggled to free herself. 'You're not my husband. I know where you spend your nights.'

His eyes clouded with anger. He forced her against the wall. 'And whose bed do you visit? Only one way to find out.'

He dragged her into the study. She fought back, but the more she struggled, the more enraged he became. She managed to free an arm and pushed her finger into his eye. He let out a howl, covering his face with his hands. She broke loose and stumbled frantically up the stairs to her bedroom. With hands that could hardly turn the key, she locked the door, her eyes searching for a hiding place for the papers. She pulled them from her underclothes, stuffed them under the mattress. Then she slumped against the wall, tears spilling down her cheeks. The sky was paling when she fell into an exhausted sleep.

A SHARP RAP ON THE DOOR woke her. 'Stefanie, my dear, I need to speak to you.' Paul's voice was controlled and normal. 'I apologise for my behaviour last night.'

'I have nothing to say to you.' She heard him curse and leave.

She looked in the mirror and gasped: her neck and throat were covered in ugly bruises. She washed and dressed in a grey travelling outfit. When she heard Paul drive off, she extracted the papers from under her mattress. For a full hour she studied the names and addresses until they were fixed in her memory. Then she selected a green felt hat with a large crown. Unpicking the thick lining, she smoothed the paper inside and sewed the lining back. With a gauze veil to cover her face, she donned the hat and secured it with a few pins.

She called for her Cape cart and left for the hospital, determined not to return home. It was an hour before visiting time, but she walked into Peter's room unannounced. A nurse was checking Peter's shoulder and looked up as she entered.

'Visiting time is not for a while yet, ma'am.'

She mumbled an excuse, her eyes on Peter's bare chest. An urge to touch him rushed through her and she moved her eyes to his face. He returned her gaze with an amused smile. She blushed, wondering if he had read her thoughts.

The nurse finished her task and left. Peter pulled himself up against the pillows. 'Why the veil today?' He peered at her and drew his breath sharply. 'What happened to you?'

'I've come to say goodbye, Peter. I'm leaving tonight.'

'Leaving? Where to?'

'Home. I want to go home, Peter. Last night … something happened …' Her hand went to her hat. He was the enemy; she could never tell him. 'I had to fight for something, something important and I almost lost,' she said, tears threatening to overwhelm her.

He took her hands in his. 'Whatever happened last night, I'd like to help you – if you'll allow me. But please, don't leave yet. I'm almost strong enough to be discharged but won't be fit for active duty for some months. We'll make a plan to get you home. I'll take you myself.'

She withdrew her hands. 'You? How will you get through the Boer lines?'

'I refuse to let *you* take such a risk.'

'I'm perfectly capable of looking after myself.'

He sank back on the pillows. 'Stefanie, please don't put yourself in danger. You've become very dear to me …'

The nurse appeared and announced another visitor.

Paul Warren entered, doffing his hat. 'Lieutenant Radford, I trust that you're getting better? I didn't have time to visit you earlier, but I believe my wife has kept you company. My dear,' he turned to Stefanie, 'a cable from Durban. I'm afraid your cousin has been wounded. He's being sent by steamer to Cape Town. His wife is accompanying him. He will be brought to the hospital straight away for surgery and Lady Victoria will stay with us.'

'James wounded?' Peter asked.

'Yes, quite severely, I believe.'

Stefanie felt utterly vanquished. She could not leave now. She nodded to Peter and walked through the door.

Into the Noose

KAREL DE WINTER licked his cracked lips, shifted his elbows and lifted the powerful field glasses to his eyes. The dusty, sun-scorched landscape distorted distances, playing havoc with a man's vision. From where he lay, in the shade of a stunted acacia on a high koppie, he could see the rail junction a mile away. Legend stood safely hidden behind a boulder, and shaded by a struggling shepherd's tree.

While scouts generally worked in pairs, he was alone, as he had demanded. No one wanted to ride with him, anyway. They feared both him and the horse, saying that they moved too close to the enemy and there was madness about them. Each time he went on a mission, they wondered whether he would return. He always did.

He blew at the flies settling on his hands. Three days now and still trains arrived without pause. Big black snakes, disgorging men, horses and equipment. White tents rose from the red soil like wheat, in lines that stretched as far as the eye could see. There were thousands of transport vehicles, the draught animals grazing on the sparse grass. The horses were picketed, feeding from nosebags. The khaki-clad soldiers were always moving, like ants scurrying about before a storm.

He wondered how many men General Roberts had brought with him. Twenty thousand? More? He moved his glasses to where the cavalry was encamped. As he watched, regiment after regiment mounted up and headed west. He moved the glasses back to the camp, watching the soldiers going about their normal tasks.

He rolled onto his back and gazed into the dust-laden sky. A dull headache throbbed behind his eyes. He pressed his fingers to his temples. He had had a vivid dream some nights back. Rudolf had called to him. He had woken with a start. Rudolf's presence was getting stronger than it had been for a long time. *Is it because I will die soon, he wondered, or is it because the grave somewhere down there with Rudi's name on it has someone else beneath the soil?*

As the sun touched the horizon, he led Legend out of their hiding place and sped back to Magersfontein.

BATTLE-STAINED AND SADDLE-WEARY, Martin and a small part of the Rustenburg commando rode into camp at sunset. They had ridden out four days previously with General de Wet and had fought for the past thirty-six hours, chasing the Highland Brigade away from the trenches on the western side. It had not been an intense battle, but a lengthy one, as they dared not leave the safety of their lines for fear of being encircled.

'Your father is with General Cronjé at Jacobsdal. Are you going there?' Buks Maree asked and handed him a mug of coffee. 'There might be more useful information to be had. Wounded?' he said on noticing the bloodstained handkerchief around Martin's hand.

'Just a scratch. I'm going to Jacobsdal to see Charles,' Martin said and moved on. Although Buks was a good fighting man, he had lost his appetite for war, refusing to ride out under General de Wet and siding with General Cronjé's belief that they should stay put and wait for the British to come with peace proposals.

'So what are the *Engelse* up to, Martin?' Frans Viljoen asked.

'We've chased the Scots back, but it's not as Cronjé thinks. The English are not making a fresh attack on the trenches.' Martin held out his mug to be refilled. 'They sent the Scots to divert our attention. General de Wet is convinced that they will head around our flank to get to Kimberley—'

'And they moved out late this afternoon, thousands of them, horsemen, no foot soldiers,' came Karel's voice from behind him. In the dark no one had seen him approach.

'You saw them moving out?' Martin asked. 'Cavalry? Which direction?'

'To the west. I watched them until they disappeared and they did not change course. Six thousand, at least.'

News like this was usually received with scepticism, but not if it came from Karel. Every bit of information he had gathered in the past month had been reliable. Martin and the men listened, asking questions only when Karel paused to drink his coffee. As usual he kept the last bit of information for Jan Viljoen. Martin thought that it was Karel's way of acknowledging Jan's part in saving him from a complete breakdown.

'I saw the lances today, Jan Viljoen,' Karel said. 'They even have little flags on the ends.'

'*Wragtig!* And here we are not in a position to run.' Jan's face lit up with awe. 'Many men are on foot now.'

'They can't be outrun, Jan. Those horses have wings.'

'Might be so, my strange friend.' Jan gave his mighty laugh. 'But Jan Viljoen knows men who grow wings when those assegais with the little flags are on their tails.'

'Six thousand cavalry!' Martin whistled through his teeth. 'Cronjé will choke on this! Karel, come with me to Jacobsdal. If he hears it from you, he might believe it. *Magtig*, it's like talking to a deaf mule.'

'I'm going to Jacobsdal to see Pa,' Karel said. 'Lady is with Charles. Old Cronjé can hear the news from you. My work is done. I don't have to listen to generals and commandants squabbling among themselves, wasting time.'

They had a hasty meal and left for the headquarters. They rode a while in silence, Martin holding his injured hand to his chest. There was a new way between them now. They never spoke of the things that had kept them apart, only about the war.

'Is the bullet still in there?' asked Karel.

'No, but it burns like hell. I want Charles to clean it up. How close did you get to the enemy this time?'

'Right under their noses. I could hear their sentries at night. Does General de Wet want me to go back tomorrow?'

'No, we must prepare for battle tonight. It might come in the morning.' Martin slumped in the saddle. 'I'm so tired, Karel. I haven't slept for three days—'

'Martin,' Karel interrupted, 'do you believe that one can feel when your time has come, I mean, to die? A kind of premonition or something?'

'Tante Koba knows about these things. But, no, I don't think so,' Martin said after some deliberation. 'God, I suppose, decides on that.'

'I had this dream. So real, so very real. Rudi was next to me. I put out my hand and touched him. He told me I will see him again, I have to be patient.'

There was a long pause and then Martin spoke with feeling. 'It doesn't mean that you are about to die, Karel. It simply means that Rudolf is still very much alive in your mind. I had a discussion with Charles about this feeling you have that he's not dead. He says only time is needed. For what, he didn't say. It would be wrong of me to support your belief that Rudi is not dead. That I cannot do. I can only hope that by some miracle you're right. I too miss him and mourn for him. Loneliness is painful, believe me, I know.'

'Here! *Just here!*' Karel pressed his fingers against his temple. 'A strange ache for days now, days. Rudi is calling me.' He moved Legend closer and put his hand on Martin's thigh. 'He is *alive*. And thank you, Ouboet, thank you for the hope in your heart.'

The endearment, not used for many years, touched Martin deeply. *Dear God, where is it to end?* Karel was painfully thin, his clothes in rags, his hair wild and matted, his eyes burning with a strange passion.

They reached Jacobsdal and dismounted outside General Cronjé's tent. There were many horses, their minders sitting on the ground, smoking their pipes. Martin, knowing that Karel stole mealies from Cronjé's stores to feed Legend, handed his reins to Karel. 'I'll see you at the hospital. Star needs a good feed and Legend always seems to find excellent, let's say, grazing, here.'

He pushed the tent flap aside and entered. Cronjé and his staff were seated at the table, others crowding around. Martin searched through the haze of pipe smoke for his father and found him with General de Wet. They nodded a greeting.

It was some time before Cronjé noticed Martin. 'What are you doing in my tent? Have you anything to say, young De Winter?'

Martin told all he had heard from Karel – the cavalry that had moved west, the trains that had arrived during the past three days.

'As I thought,' De Wet said. 'Lord Roberts is preparing to outflank us to get to Kimberley. Then he will deal with us.'

'Nonsense! It's a waterless stretch of land,' Cronjé barked. 'They'll never make it across with so many horses. Six thousand, you say?'

Martin nodded. 'Six thousand, General. They'll reach the Modder River in the morning, by my reckoning.'

'The picnic is over, Piet Cronjé,' Marthinus de Winter said. 'Send the wagons home. This is no place for them now.'

'These wagons are the private property of the burghers, Commandant de Winter. I cannot order them away.'

Pipes were refilled and the men puffed. Cronjé decided that De Wet should ride out in the morning to check the cavalry's advance. The officers were told to put their men in the trenches and to send all women and children to Jacobsdal.

Martin made his arrangements with General de Wet for the morning's ride before setting off for the hospital. He found Charles in his tent, a welcome bottle of brandy on the table.

'Haven't seen you for some time.' Charles handed Martin a drink. 'I could do with a stiff drink and Karel prefers Lady's company to mine. Ah … I see you've also brought a wound.' He took a seat opposite Martin and undid the bloody handkerchief. While he inspected the wound, he told Martin about a letter he'd received that morning. 'It travelled all the way from Delagoa Bay to Pretoria. Tante Koba sent it on post haste.'

'Bad news, Charles?'

'Very disturbing. James received multiple wounds at Spioenkop, and was taken to Cape Town. Luckily the Mauser bullet doesn't cause much damage, unless it strikes a vital spot.' He took a mouthful of brandy and sighed. 'He's out of danger, but in a devil of a mood, writes Victoria.'

'Poor James. At least he's out of the war now, Charles. Makes it easier, I mean, to know that he's safe. Wounded, but safe.'

'I suppose one should think about it like that. Vicky also wrote that James and Peter Radford are to receive the VC for their actions at Colenso. So are four others, posthumously. Peter was wounded; James rescued him. Those two are having their usual kind of war, it appears.'

Martin sipped from his glass. 'Is Vicky moving on to India? Did she say?'

'No, she didn't, and I think it's wise not to dwell on that.'

'I do dwell, Charles.'

'You're married now, soon to be a father. Now, let's sort out your hand. Hmm ... not bad, doesn't even need a stitch. Lucky shot.'

'You always say that, Charles: lucky shot.'

'I've seen worse,' he returned Martin's smile. 'It's good to see you, cousin, but you really are exhausted. Get some rest.'

Karel walked in and sat down on the floor, declining the brandy Charles offered him.

'You should have a wash, you know,' Charles said. 'Bad hygiene leads to all sorts of unpleasant diseases. There's a tub with water behind the curtain. Help yourself to the clothes in my trunk.'

Karel rummaged through the trunk and came up with whipcord trousers, a shirt and some underclothes. 'Do you have a jacket for me? Mine stinks; I don't want to be buried in it.'

'Yes, take the tweed. It's seen better days, but at least it's clean.'

WHEN THE TWO BROTHERS left for Magersfontein, Charles went behind the curtain to clean up the mess Karel had left. He picked up the discarded clothes with the intention of burning them, but felt something heavy in the jacket pocket. He found Rudolf's knife and a small folded note, dirty and crumpled. Rudolf's name was on it, in Annecke's handwriting. For a reason he could not explain to himself, he read it.

He pressed his fingers to his eyes. Rudolf's child, not Martin's. *Tante Koba's jealous God. Oh, my sweet Annecke, Rudi is dead.*

'Doctor Henderson?' an orderly called from the tent entrance. 'We're having difficulty with a patient. He has pulled the drains from his chest.'

'I'm coming, in a moment.'

BEFORE SUNRISE THE NEXT DAY, Martin and part of the Rustenburg commando rode southwest with General de Wet. As they neared the Modder River and crested a rise, an astonishing sight met their eyes. For mile upon mile the British cavalry stretched across the open veld, enveloped in red dust.

De Wet ordered a mounted attack on the flank in an attempt to slow them down. The men poured fire from their Mausers into the massed cavalry without any visible result. Overwhelmed by dust and smoke from a fire that raged through the dry grass, the commando retreated and made their way back to Magersfontein.

And into chaos. Shell craters, spent cartridges and dead animals littered the veld. At the trenches, the men were hastily saddling horses, herding oxen to the wagons, and breaking down the tents. General Cronjé had ordered his force to Bloemfontein. The Rustenburg men packed their belongings, taking only what their horses could carry. By nightfall they set off in despondent weariness to follow the long line of wagons.

The day's tempest had saturated the air with smoke and dust. The full moon rising over Cronje's fleeing burghers was not the friendly yellow orb that they knew. It was fiery red, and in the light of this strange moon, the cumbersome convoy headed east.

The morning found them by the river. They heard rifle fire and a few cannon shots as the rearguard covered their escape. By midday the convoy swung towards a drift cutting through the steep river banks at a farm called Paardeberg.

Then, as if from nowhere, the British artillery found them. Women and children screamed. Oxen stampeded and bellowed, finding strength in their fear, dragging the wagons behind them in their flight. Men shouted useless orders and watched as the wagons overturned. An ammunition wagon caught fire, spewing its contents into the air. The families fled to the riverbed and hid in the foliage and dongas.

The Rustenburg commando was soon engaged in a desperate struggle to stop the advancing enemy. The battle raged through the day, the commandos contesting fiercely and the enemy holding on to every inch they gained. As night fell, the firing stopped. Men slumped to the ground amid their dead and wounded comrades.

Marthinus rode out to find General Cronjé. He returned late that night and the news he brought was not encouraging. On the northern bank of the

Modder River, Cronjé had formed the wagons into a laager and they were almost completely surrounded. Only a narrow corridor to the southeast was still open, thanks to the determined fighting of General de Wet. He told them how the officers had urged Cronjé to break out, but that he had refused.

'Refused, Pa?' Martin said. 'We must use the cover of night, get moving while there's still time.'

'The man is adamant, son,' Marthinus said with harsh weariness. '"We will not run like buck before the hunter's gun. We will not give the *Engelse* the satisfaction. We are men. We will fight it out." That's what Cronjé said and that's what we have to do.'

'Marthinus, we have four dead and six wounded,' Joep Maree said. 'Do you have any idea where we can find Charles?'

'The doctors are overwhelmed. They are still at Jacobsdal. Get some rest now,' Marthinus said. 'Jan Viljoen, get the wounded on the ammunition cart and take them to the laager. Tomorrow will be better.'

But hardly had they struggled up at dawn, when shots ripped through the air, the ricochets showering them with splinters. Marthinus shouted orders and encouragement to those who were searching, wild-eyed, for an escape route.

In the morning, the sun grew hot and the cries of the wounded now mixed with the noise of the battle. Martin saw Buks Maree, blood streaming from his upper arm, crawling to the big boulder where their horses were hidden. His hands became raw and blistered, his shoulders bruised from the rifle's recoil and his throat parched.

In the late afternoon, events took a turn for the worse. Martin sank behind the rise of sand from which he was firing to wrap a piece of sacking around the barrel of his rifle when he heard a strangled cry from his left. Lang Hans van Rensburg came falling backwards, blood spurting from his face, covering his flowing beard. He was about to crawl to him, but a jerky movement from his father caught his attention. He was clutching his throat, his face contorted.

'Oh, dear God! Pa! Pa!' Martin crawled to where Marthinus was writhing on the ground. Joep also reached him. They dragged him behind the big boulder.

'Pa? Is it bad?' Martin pried his father's hands from the wound. 'Uncle Joep, he's going to suffocate … drown in his own blood.'

Joep grabbed Martin by the lapels of his jacket, pulling him against his chest. 'Martin, pull yourself together. Don't let the men see you like this. Go back there. Leave me to do what I have to.'

'What will you do?' Martin's voice was steadier as he fought for control.

'Cut a hole in his windpipe to help him breathe. Now go! Look out for

Karel. He's not fit to fight.' Joep shoved Martin away, and, with a last look at his father, Martin scrambled back.

His eyes searched for Karel and found him with Frans and Jan Viljoen. A British observation balloon hung in the sky in front of them. Uttering a harsh laugh, Karel jumped to his feet and emptied his rifle at the balloon. Jan Viljoen swung his rifle by the butt, hitting Karel in the small of his back. Karel's head jerked as Jan slapped him with the back of his hand. Jan turned him over on his belly and sat on him. Then he pushed his rifle over the rock and fired madly.

Martin flung himself down next to Jan. 'God Almighty! Thank you, Jan. Is he all right?'

'The madness got to him.' Jan fired another shot, tears running into his dusty beard. 'His nerve finally broke. Leave him to me, Martin.'

He looked at his brother's dirty face pressed into the sand, blood trickling from the corner of his mouth. He put out his hand to wipe the sand from his nose but a voice rising in panic reached him.

'They're coming! They're charging!'

A line of khaki figures, bayonets fixed, charged over the broken ground.

'To your left! Rise and fire! Fire!' Jan Viljoen roared above the noise and the men rose from their positions and fired frantically.

Martin saw many things. Jan Viljoen picking Karel up, shoving his rifle in his hands. Behind them was Joep, legs planted apart, taking aim. Frans Viljoen's gun jammed. He looked around him wildly, grabbed a few stones, hurled them into the advancing enemy. Martin felt hysterical laughter bubbling inside him. He remembered Karel's mad eyes and restrained himself.

Their ferocious counterattack caught the enemy by surprise. The British soldiers sought what cover they could find. The bombardment of the laager faded out, and the rifle fire died down.

Martin felt bruised and his mouth was caked with sand. His first thought was for his father. He found him where Joep had left him, behind the boulder. His beard was caked with blood, his breath whistling through the stem of Joep's pipe, forced into a cut above his breastbone. Martin laid a hand on his brow.

'Will he live? Where the bloody hell is Charles?'

Martin turned to find Karel's tormented, exhausted face. He left Karel with their father and went in search of Joep. He found him conferring with Jan Viljoen and squatted beside them. 'Uncle Joep, you have to go to Cronjé to find out what's to be done.'

Joep placed a hand on Martin's shoulder. 'No son, we talked, Jan and I.

You must take your father's place; you must lead us now. You know the ways of the English and of our generals. Lead the men we can, yes, but fight with Cronjé? Patience and the words to do that, we don't have. You're commandant now.'

'The men have faith in you, Martin.' Jan's black eyes were red-rimmed. 'Before the war they asked you for guidance, as they're doing now.'

Martin looked at the tired faces around them. Some men had lit their pipes, others stared at him with dazed eyes. Then, as his father had the night before, he picked a few men to assist him with the wounded and set out to receive Cronjé's orders.

The officers implored Cronjé to break out while there was still time. The enemy was pulling the noose ever tighter. Again he refused, ordering the commandos to dig in on the river banks. A weary Rustenburg commando limped behind Martin into the laager that night. They buried their dead in blankets, piling stones on the mounds of earth. Then they set to the task of digging trenches into the south bank of the river. To their left was a donga, deep enough to shield their horses and wounded from fire.

Martin assisted Joep in carrying Buks to the donga. There he found Karel squatting next to their father and holding Legend's reins in his hand.

'Pa's dying, and tomorrow we're all going to die. Where's Rudi?' Karel cried.

Fear and Panic

Wynberg Hospital, Cape Town

THE WORLD WAS BLANK AND BLACK. When his senses swam close to consciousness, strange faces and voices confronted him. Women in grey dresses and scarlet capes moved about the room, doing things for him, feeding him, changing his nightshirt, washing him, and all the while talking in soothing voices.

As the days went by, he became more aware of his surroundings. The women were nurses. He was in a hospital. They spoke English. Vague images pushed into his conscious moments. A river. Horses. His head ached with the effort of thinking. *Pain?*

'Charles …'

The nurse swung around. 'Are we awake this morning, Captain Patterson? Did you say you want Charles?'

Charles? His throat burned and tears squeezed from his eyelids. There came a sharp prick in his arm. And the world became a dark and lonely place again.

Day after day, he tried to fit the broken images together. Captain Patterson. *I am Captain Patterson. Who is Captain Patterson? Who am I?* Again the tears and the prick of the needle.

Then one morning, as the first rays of the sun crept through the slats of the louvres, some broken pieces fell into place. He closed his eyes, thinking quietly, not desperately. Swimming naked in the river. Wild shots. He looked about the room. There was a man in the other bed, his head swathed in bandages, his breathing rapid.

The nurse entered, carrying a dish and towels. She removed the blankets, pushed a towel under his chest and set about washing him.

'Where am I? What happened to me?'

She scrutinised his face. 'Captain Patterson, you are in the hospital in Wynberg, in Cape Town. A nasty wound to your temple.'

He touched his head; no more bandages, no more pain. 'How long have I been here?'

'Well, we're in the middle of February, so it should be eight … about nine weeks.' She buttoned his shirt before straightening the sheets.

'Nine weeks? Am I a prisoner?'

'Why, no, sir. You're not with the Boers. You're with your own people.' She turned to a doctor who had just walked in. 'Captain Patterson is quite intelligible this morning, sir.'

Then he remembered his name. 'I'm not Captain Patterson.'

The doctor moved to his bed. 'It says on your file that you are Captain John Allan Patterson from Ashford in Kent. Does that ring a bell?'

Rudolf looked at him dumbfounded.

'Is there anyone you can recall? Parents, brothers, sisters, a sweetheart perhaps?'

Karel? Where's Karel? Tears of hopelessness burned his eyes and he averted his face. *I must get to Karel!*

'Is there anything at all you can tell me?' the kind voice probed again.

'Shots … the river … had to get to the horses …'

'I see, there's at least something and that's a good sign.' The doctor lifted the sheets and flexed his knee, testing his reflexes. 'Your leg is healed. As to your memory, what you have is amnesia. It simply means that your memory was left somewhere and now it's up to you to find it again. It might take time, a few months perhaps.' He smiled reassuringly. 'You'll find letters in your night table. It might give the old memory a jolt.'

Rudolf turned his face into the pillow, trying to quell his panic and despair. He was with the enemy, as one of the enemy, too weak to walk, no horse, no way of getting home. What did his family believe? That he was captured? That he was dead?

'They go through severe emotional stress, these cases.' He heard the doctor say to the nurse. 'Give him more laudanum, let him rest.'

Rudolf watched as she measured the drops into a glass. He did not want to return to the void. He wanted to get out of there. Raising himself with difficulty, he swung his legs off the bed, but the effort left him breathless and dizzy. The nurse held out the glass.

———

IN PETER RADFORD'S PRIVATE ROOM, James struggled out of a drug-induced sleep. It was three weeks since he had been rushed to Cape Town. His fractured lower leg had been set and the bullets dug from his chest and arm. A thick scab still covered his cheek.

He looked at the door; time for the visiting hour. Victoria and Stefanie visited every day. It annoyed him, but he needed to see Victoria today. She simply had to find a way to get to India or at least back to Durban. He did not want her around any longer.

He turned his attention to Peter, who was dressed in uniform. He'd been relieved to find him almost completely recovered and in excellent spirits again.

'There was a battle at a place called Vaalkrantz.' Peter supported James's head and held a cup of tea to his lips. 'Same disastrous results, unfortunately.'

'Sinclair? Shaw?' James asked through sips.

'No, Sinclair wrote that they are still on convalescent leave in Durban. I see George Hunter in the garden sometimes, though. I keep him away from you.'

James swallowed more tea. 'Hunter! I saw him bite the dust before we were halfway—' he broke off, pushing the terror of that day from his mind.

'Yes, a chest wound. They say the Boers are sharpshooters, but I don't agree. I mean, they appear to be two inches off target every shot. Shaw would've had it through the knee, Hunter through the heart, Moore up his rear end and I ... well, I shudder to think about it.'

James pushed the cup away. 'Are you going home? You're fit to travel.'

'I'll wait for you. Besides, I prefer to see the war out. General Cronjé is surrounded on the western front. He'll be crushed any day now.'

'I've heard that before, Radford. Go home.' He looked out of the window. The Cape cart bringing Stefanie and Victoria had just turned into the gate. He was not deceived. It was obvious that Peter was besotted with Stefanie and wanted to stay in Cape Town.

'Stefanie is my cousin,' he said, 'and married at that.'

'Steady on. My attentions are completely—'

The two women arrived, their summer dresses and feathered hats brightening up the room, their subtle perfumes competing with the sharp smell of antiseptic.

Stefanie smiled at Peter and kissed James on his good cheek. 'Are you feeling better today, Jamie?' She peered into his eyes. 'You do look brighter. Tonight I'm playing for the men on the ground floor. I'll ask them to wheel you down.'

'No, Stef, I'm in no mood for music.'

'Promise at least to keep the window open. You'll be able to hear the music quite clearly.'

'I promise to put the pillow over my head.'

She tickled his toes, which were sticking out of the plaster cast.

He gasped. 'Peter, stop this meddlesome woman from torturing me.'

Peter pulled Stefanie's hand through his arm. 'Come, meddlesome woman. There's a lovely breeze outside.'

'Yes! I've not come here to be insulted.' She turned and blew James a kiss.

'How are you today?' Victoria said when they had left. 'You do look brighter.'

'I'm better, I believe.'

'Here, a letter from your father. He's concerned about you. He's asking for forgiveness …'

'I'm not in the least bit interested in what he has to say. Have you brought the paper?'

She brought it from her basket, positioned it in his uninjured hand and settled in the chair. Hardly had he read the headlines when she spoke again, a sympathetic tone to her voice. 'James, the war … your cousin's death … I might be of help, if you'd only talk to me.'

'Kindly don't meddle.' He lowered the paper. There was anger and hurt in her eyes, but now was the time to tell her, he decided. 'Victoria, I made a commitment to you. I promised to take you to India, and I will see that you get there. However, I can't be a husband to you any more. Have I not proven it in the most brutish fashion? I want you to conduct your life as you see fit.'

She cast her eyes down and sat quietly. 'You have fulfilled the other part of our arrangement, James,' she said at last. 'I'm pregnant.'

'How can you possibly be?' He groaned and turned his face to the wall. The picture of his daughter came to his mind. One child conceived in careless lust and now a child conceived in violence. He felt nauseous and swallowed hard. 'You have what you wanted. Leave now.'

When Peter returned to the room half an hour later, James was still staring at the wall.

'Is something wrong?' Peter asked. 'Shall I send for the doctor?' James shook his head. 'A little water, perhaps?' He poured water from the carafe and held the glass to James's lips. 'What's the matter, old boy?'

James kept his eyes to the wall. 'I raped Victoria.'

Peter started. 'Your mind is wandering, Henderson. You're not even fit to drop your breeches, had you any on.'

'In Durban. The night I delivered you to the ship. The war, you dying on me, Rudolf dead … I lost control …'

There was silence as Peter thought this over. 'Couldn't have been that bad? We all get a bit … well, wild at times. Vicky will forgive you; perhaps she already has. She's no stranger to your, well, volatile moods.'

'Will I ever be able to forgive myself?' He searched Peter's face. 'I lost control at Spioenkop too. That's why I'm so full of bloody holes. When

Hunter and Shaw went down, I had to lead the charge ... well, I played Boer for a while, hid behind a boulder. Fear, I think, panic. You weren't there, I suppose, to urge me on.'

'Sinclair says that you stopped the Boers from breaking through.'

'He doesn't know how I felt at that moment.'

'But I do.' Peter placed his hand on the cast on James's arm. 'I felt that too, every morning, waking up half-dead, not knowing if I'll last the day, doubting my ability to do it again, a cavalry charge, battle. Fear and panic. But at least we've experienced them now. Not exactly pleasant feelings.'

'Have we lost it, Radford? The madness?'

'Yes, I suppose, but it's somewhere out there. We'll find it again. One more charge, one more battle.'

Captain Theron

THE SUN was hardly up when the British artillery tore into the Boer laager at Paardeberg. Within minutes, the defenders were choking on dust and lyddite fumes. Horses and oxen bellowed amid the rotting carcasses of their companions. The men took up their Mausers and crawled to their positions along the river bank. Fodder and food supplies went up in flames. Ammunition wagons exploded into crackling infernos.

And then the rain started.

At first it brought a measure of relief, as the heat broke and the rising river washed away many of the carcasses, but soon the trenches in the river bank became a muddy mess. Under constant bombardment, choked by fumes and the stench of putrefaction and excrement, those within the laager were trapped in a living hell.

On the third day of the siege, General Cronjé agreed to release all wounded British prisoners, and an equal number of Boer wounded were allowed to leave for the hospital at Jacobsdal. Marthinus was one of the lucky ones. Martin realised that, by giving him over to the British, he would be a prisoner, but he was unconscious and sinking fast. In the pelting rain, Martin and Karel carried their father to the collecting point. As the British medics took him away, Martin saw a huddled group of women and children moving a few tentative paces towards the British. At once, soldiers came rushing, gathered the children and supported the women to the waiting ambulance wagons.

The rain continued for two more days. Every night Martin trudged to General Cronjé's tented hideout in the river bank for the nightly council. There was no more talk of a breakout, and many officers urged Cronjé to surrender.

Martin listened with growing dread in his heart. Surrender meant the end for him, a prisoner, unable to prove himself as a leader of his people. His mind was furiously working on a plan of escape, when, on the eighth night of the siege, the perfect opportunity presented itself. The commandants were still arguing with Cronjé when a man, his trousers ragged, his hands and knees bloodied, stumbled into the tent. It took Martin a long minute to recognise Danie Theron, captain of De Wet's scouts.

'How did you get in?' General Cronjé asked.

'Crawled, most of the way. We couldn't reach you with the heliograph, the weather.' Theron accepted a mug of coffee with trembling hands. 'General de Wet has gathered a large commando and is keeping the eastern side open ... he'll cover you, shell the British from the koppies. Tomorrow night at ten, on the koppie ...'

The despairing officers listened with a flicker of hope. Frantic suggestions followed, but Cronjé refused to leave the remaining wagons behind and ordered a bridge to be built across the flooded river. An intense argument erupted.

Martin pulled Theron aside and they left the tent. 'I want my commando out of here. We will go without that foolish old man. Explain your plan to me.'

MARTIN MADE HIS WAY back to the river bank. He woke Joep Maree and Jan Viljoen, made coffee and told them about the possibility of escape, stressing the danger from both sides.

Jan needed no urging. 'This place is a death trap. If I'm to die, let it be so, it's God's will, but Jan Viljoen and his brothers surrender to the British? Never!'

'I need to get Buks home. His wound is worrying,' Joep said.

'We take our wounded with us, those who are prepared to chance this trip,' Martin said.

'How many able horses do we have?' Jan asked.

'We'll steal horses,' Martin said. 'The enemy will get them if they remain here.'

'There'll be an outcry if men find their horses have disappeared,' Joep said.

'We steal horses just before we leave. What do you think, Uncle Joep?'

'What do I think?' Joep sipped his coffee, scratched his filthy beard and smiled at Martin. 'At this moment, I wonder if you have forgotten that you're married to my daughter.'

'No, I haven't.' He met Joep's eyes.

'Then why do you still call me Uncle and not Pa, as is the custom?'

'Of course, I'm sorry. Pa it'll be from now on.'

THE BRITISH BOMBARDMENT intensified the next day. The bridge, hastily constructed during the night, was destroyed before it had reached halfway across the river. General Cronjé refused all pleas to surrender. The following day, the twenty-seventh of February, was the anniversary of the Battle of Majuba. 'God will smite the enemy and come to our aid on the sacred day,' he said. 'He would not forsake His people in their darkest hour.'

Martin silently thanked Cronjé for not giving in to the officers and prayed for night to come. He and Jan Viljoen spied out the escape route through their field glasses during the day and checked on where horses could be had. By late afternoon, the enemy had advanced to within a few hundred yards of their positions, and he knew the end was near: they would be overrun the next day.

When the firing ceased at nightfall, Martin went in search of Karel, who had taken no part in the fighting, hiding with Legend in a donga, only emerging at night to find fodder and scrounge a few mouthfuls of food for himself. 'I have work for you.' He put his hand on Karel's shoulder. 'In the dugout behind the General's hideout, you'll find Captain Theron. Tell him that we're seventy and will be ready as arranged last night. He must get going now.'

The men prepared for the flight. They ate porridge, washing it down with weak coffee, rolled up their blankets and refilled their bandoliers. Jan told the unmounted where to find able horses, and was about to leave with them when Karel arrived back.

'Here, take Legend, Jan. Your roan won't make it.'

Jan Viljoen searched Karel's face. 'And how, my friend, will you get out?'

Karel placed Legend's reins in Jan's hand. 'Use your heels lightly, Jan, she'll obey.'

'Why, in God's name, do you want to surrender with the laager?' Martin grabbed Karel by the arms, forcing him to look into his eyes. 'Listen to me. Rudolf is dead. You will not find him with the British. *You will never find him.*'

Karel shook free of Martin's grip. 'Jan, take my Mauser. I won't need it tonight, but I could do with one of your knives.'

Jan stood undecided for a while, but Karel pushed the rifle into his hands. Jan handed him a knife. Karel spoke once more to Legend and crept away into the dark night.

'This horse is part of him, and, as God is my witness, I, Jan Viljoen, will get her through tonight,' he said with tears in his eyes.

'And God help you, Jan Viljoen, if you don't,' Joep said. 'For her master will be waiting on the outside.'

Two hours after midnight, all was in readiness. Martin would take the lead, with Joep in the middle and Jan and his brothers at the rear to help any wounded should they be fired on. They silently led the horses to the appointed place on the eastern side of the laager. The horses snorted, sensing freedom.

Martin fiddled with his bandolier, and checked his Mauser and pistol. He was grateful for the darkness; he didn't want to see his men's faces. In an hour's time they might be captured or dead. He struck a match and checked his watch – time to leave. He gave the order to mount and the word spread down the line. Leading at a slow pace, he reached the bend in the river where he knew a strong force of British infantry to be. He swung north, breaking into a gallop. The thunder of horses' hooves was overpowering, but not a single shot came from either side.

They galloped on. Star, Martin's dappled white, was an easy beacon to follow. After three miles, rifle fire crackled but the shots came nowhere near them. Martin resisted the strong urge to glance over his shoulder to check the men. Every yard felt like a mile and, bent low over Star's neck, he concentrated on the bearing Theron had given him. The air was now alive with rifle fire. De Wet's reply flashed from the koppie to their right, the howitzer and pom-pom firing on the unseen enemy to their left.

Star began to flag. Joep, leading Buks's horse, caught up with him. 'Go on! Go on! Straight ahead!' Martin shouted. 'Straight ahead!'

He was now in the midst of the commando. Star stumbled, throwing Martin headlong through the air, hitting the ground not far from the horse. Gasping for breath, he pulled himself to his knees and crawled to Star. He felt frantically for his pistol, and placed it against the horse's head. As he fired the shot, the last of the commando sped past. The Viljoen brothers, at the rear, swung around. Frans wrested Martin's saddle off the dead horse. With a powerful heave, Jacob heaved Martin onto Legend in front of Jan. Such was Legend's strength and stamina that, before they had reached the safety of De Wet's men, she caught up with the commando despite her double load.

'*Magtig!* What a horse!' Jan stroked Legend's quivering flanks. 'Never before has she allowed anyone but her master on her back and now she has carried two heavy men out. Truly, she does her name justice.'

Martin picked himself up from where Jan had deposited him. He felt his side and shoulder. Nothing broken, he noted with relief. Only his face was bloodied where he had scraped his cheek and forehead on the ground.

Joep informed Martin that not a single man had been hit or left behind. They cheered and slapped one another's backs and congratulated Martin on the success of their daring flight. Joep hastened to Buks and the other wounded. Martin and Jan Viljoen ascended the hill where they were told General de Wet was. They found him at the crest, staring at the laager through his field glasses. The breakout had created panic on both sides and the firing had not yet died down.

'I knew you'd come, but did I have to send for you?' De Wet looked grim and kept his glasses to his eyes. 'Look! You are just in time.'

In the early morning light a white flag appeared, soon followed by more in the laager. The firing stopped. After days of thunder and constant fire, the earth was strangely still.

'Four thousand Boers,' De Wet said. 'For ten days, they held thirty thousand men at bay. For them the war is over.'

At the bottom of the hill a lone figure, face blackened with mud, came towards them. With a tremendous roar Jan Viljoen ran down the hill, slipping, sliding and hollering. 'She made it! She's safe! She made it, Karel!'

'Who made it? Did you bring a woman out?' De Wet asked.

'No, General.' Martin turned his head to hide his tears. 'It has to do with a horse.'

Alias Captain Patterson

THE SAME QUESTIONS, day after day. What's your name? Where do you come from? Another letter from your mother, shall I read it to you? And all the while Rudolf was getting stronger. He ate all the food put before him, unpalatable as it was. Kippers, runny eggs, boiled vegetables, underdone meat. And he walked.

At first he did not venture from the room, just paced up and down, up and down. Then one day he scraped up the courage to walk through the door, and became familiar with the passage. The other patients tried to draw him into conversation, but he avoided talking lest his accent give him away. They soon left him alone and made sympathetic noises behind his back. When he was obliged to answer questions from the doctor or the nurses, he said the bare minimum, copying Charles's accent.

All the while a great anxiety was in his heart. Was Captain Patterson dead? What if one of Patterson's fellow officers arrived? And he thought about his twin. Karel was alive! In his heart there was a deep conviction that he would have felt differently if Karel was dead. What was his family thinking? The only conclusion he could come to was that they thought him missing.

His mind worked furiously on a plan to get home. He heard a train passing in the near distance a few times a day. He needed money to get on that train and he had to find Stefanie, but he didn't know her address and had no knowledge of Cape Town. First he needed clothes. He asked for them one day and tried them on. Captain Patterson's clothes were baggy, but he had been sick for a long time, he explained to the nurses.

'Nurse Armstrong, do I have money?' he asked the nurse who was feeding his unconscious roommate.

'Why yes, sir, there were a few pounds in your pocket. Do you need anything? Shall I get them for you?'

'Thank you, but I intend to venture out one of these days. It might refresh my memory, don't you think?'

'You really ought to get into the garden first.'

The following day, dressed in the khaki uniform, he stood at the window, looking at the visitors arriving to meet the patients. He grabbed the windowsill and stared hard. There was Stefanie coming down the garden path. There was no mistaking the way she held her head. Another woman walked beside her. A tall officer met them. Stefanie smiled up at him and when he turned, Rudolf recognised a cheerful Peter Radford. They moved to a chair under a huge oak in which another man sat, his leg in a splint. It was James.

He tried to hold back his tears, for there, after so many weeks of fear, were his sister and cousin.

The next afternoon he was at the window long before visiting time, his plans set. He would send Stefanie a note, asking her to come to an appointed place. But Stefanie didn't arrive that day and Peter Radford was also absent. Nor did she come the next day. For an entire week he waited and hoped, but there was only James, and the woman he presumed to be his wife, under the tree. James always with the newspaper, and the woman staring, just staring, at Table Mountain. When his roommate took a turn for the worse and the doctor pulled the sheet over his face, Rudolf realised he could not risk another day in the hospital. He might not be so fortunate to have another unconscious man sharing his room. If Stefanie did not come that afternoon, he would have to search for her in this strange city.

At visiting time an orderly wheeled James out to the big oak. The woman arrived, handed him the paper, but she did not stay long as it looked like rain. Few patients braved it outside, but James stayed.

Rudolf walked down the passage. At the double doors he hesitated, reluctant to leave the safety of the floor. Clutching the banister, he descended the stairs. By the time he reached the ground floor, he trembled with exertion and fear. The faces were unfamiliar, the greetings accompanied by curious stares.

He went out into the garden, searching for the big oak. James was still there, engrossed in the paper. Rudolf covered the distance and halted a few yards behind the chair. Before his nerve could fail him, he stepped round and stood in front of James.

JAMES IGNORED THE BOOTS that came into view and kept his eyes on the paper. He was in no mood for company since Peter had left, but the man did not move on and neither was he looking for conversation. Then the voice came, a very familiar voice.

'Good afternoon, James.'

306

He stared at the unexpected sight of his cousin, dressed in British uniform, his face thin and anxious, beads of perspiration on his upper lip and forehead, his hands nervously clasped at his sides. 'Karel! What are you doing here? And in that uniform?'

'I'm not Karel, I'm Rudolf.'

The paper dropped from James's hands, sliding off his lap. Rudolf bent down with difficulty, picked it up and handed it back to him.

'Rudolf is dead. He was buried, for God's sake.' The pain in his cousin's eyes brought home the truth; this was indeed Rudolf. He searched for words, but could only stare.

Rudolf raised his head. There were tears in his eyes. 'So, I'm dead. Who did they bury? Karel? Then where am I supposed to be?'

'No, they, us ... the British, for God's sake! They buried you at Magersfontein. How ... what ... how did you get here?'

'I've been unconscious for a long time. They,' he gestured to the hospital, 'they believe I'm British, a Captain Patterson. A head wound.' He turned his head showing the scar running from his temple into his hair. And then he told about the river and meeting with the patrol. 'I woke up here and everyone says I'm John Patterson, that I have amnesia. I had to play along, James.'

It took several moments more for James to absorb the news. And, with a fresh wave of shock, he realised what position he found himself in now.

'I'm sorry, James,' Rudolf said in a broken voice. 'I shouldn't have gone to the river by myself. Karel? Please tell me he's alive.' He grabbed James's arm, his eyes beseeching.

'Yes, yes, he's alive, as far as I know. That was before Cronjé surrendered. I had someone searching through the Paardeberg prisoner of war list. Not many from Rustenburg, and there's no De Winter on it, but not any information on Boer wounded or dead yet.'

Rudolf buried his face in his hands. 'Karel is alive. I must get to him, James. I have to get out of here.'

'You can't just walk out. You have to turn yourself in, or else I shall have to do it. I'll get the news to Wintersrust, but you can't simply walk away from here.'

'Turn me in? Would you really do that, James?'

'You can't expect me to turn a blind eye to this. I'm your enemy, for heaven's sake.'

'I don't expect you to help me. All I want is directions to Stefanie's house.'

James looked at the pitiful figure of his cousin, shivering in the light breeze. He forced himself to think clearly. If it were discovered that he'd helped a Boer, there would be trouble. But if he turned him in, Rudolf would be sent to a prison camp. Stefanie was the only one who could help now.

'Rudi, listen carefully. Tomorrow morning, take the train as far as Rondebosch. Go to number seventeen, Bathurst Drive. That's all I can tell you. Be careful of that brother-in-law of yours. My wife is there ...' He stiffened. From the corner of his eye, he saw George Hunter ambling towards them. 'Go now, Rudi. Someone's coming who might recognise you.'

'There's no one who would know me—'

'The man walking this way knows Martin. He might see the resemblance. For heaven's sake, go!'

Rudolf thanked James in a whisper and left.

'Ah, Henderson, anything in the paper?' Hunter said when he reached James. James kept his eyes on the newspaper. 'No, nothing, Major.'

'I say, who was the odd fellow I saw with you a moment ago?'

'Beg your pardon?'

'That fellow, the captain.' Hunter pointed towards the entrance of the building, where Rudolf had just disappeared.

'I don't know him. Patterson, I think. Amnesia, lost his memory somewhere along the line.' He turned his attention back to the paper.

AN HOUR LATER, Rudolf was making his way down Bathurst Drive. He did not want to wait for the morning and had taken the train to Rondebosch station. A hansom had delivered him a few houses from Stefanie's, as he had requested. A misty rain set in and the street was deserted. He arrived at number seventeen, a double-storey house, like the others, with thick hedges flanking the driveway.

Stepping behind the hedge, he observed the house for a while. A carriage clattered down the street, turning into the drive. A dark-haired man carrying a gold-topped cane stepped out and gave orders to the driver. Rudolf clearly heard the reply. 'Yes, Mr Warren, I'll wait.' The man was the brother-in-law whom he had never met and it was clear that he was leaving again.

He pulled deeper into the shadows. There was a dull thudding in his head and his legs buckled. He squatted, leaning his back against the rough branches. The sun was disappearing behind Table Mountain before the door opened and let through a rectangle of light. Warren emerged and, to Rudolf's relief, Stefanie was not with him. He waited until it was dark before stepping clear of the hedge, straightened his khaki uniform and replaced his helmet. At the front door, he lifted the brass knocker and tapped it. A maid, dressed in black and wearing a white apron, opened the door.

'Good evening, may I see Mrs Warren, please?' In his eagerness, he stepped inside without waiting for an answer.

The maid stared at him in a disturbing way. A woman with copper hair and a colourful robe appeared on the staircase. James's wife; the woman he'd seen visiting James.

'I'll handle this, thank you,' she said to the maid and came down the stairs. When she reached the bottom, she paused and pulled in her breath sharply.

'I'm Captain John Patterson,' he said, but still she stared.

She seemed to collect herself and approached, her eyes still on his face. She led the way to a large drawing room, showed him to a chair. 'Do forgive me. I didn't mean to be rude. It was ... for a moment, I thought ...' she faltered. 'It's nothing. Do sit down.'

He placed his helmet on a low table and took a seat on the settee.

'Mrs Warren is in Port Elizabeth. May I help? I'm Mrs Henderson. Could I get you something? A sherry, a brandy perhaps?'

He nodded and watched as she crossed the carpet to a side table. He took in the opulence of the room. His sister lived in splendour, very different from Wintersrust or Koba's homely sitting room.

She poured a glass of sherry and one of brandy and came to sit next to him. 'You've been wounded. I can tell by the way you favour your leg.'

'Yes, a long time ago.' He stared at the brandy in the glass, wondering what to do next.

There was a long pause. 'Don't be alarmed at what I'm about to say.' He looked up sharply. 'You're not a British officer; you're not British at all.' She placed her hand on his arm. 'You remind me of someone who's very dear to me. Years ago, in England, I met a Boer from the Transvaal, my husband's cousin.'

There were circles under her eyes and her face was drawn, but the green eyes above the freckled nose looked at him with love. She would not betray him, her eyes seemed to say. He decided to take the chance.

'Martin de Winter. He's my brother. My name is Rudolf.'

Her face paled. 'But Rudolf—'

'I know, I'm supposed to be dead. Only I'm not, as you can see. There was a mix-up. I was mistaken for this Patterson man.' For the second time that day, he related the circumstances of his disappearance. 'I have to get home to my brother, to my twin. When will my sister return?'

'She won't be back. Her husband thinks that she's in Port Elizabeth, but she's determined to get to Pretoria. I'm not supposed to tell anyone. She's distraught over her ... your family, and her husband. Mr Warren is not an amicable man.'

'What's happening at home? Do you know, lady ... I don't know how to address you.'

'My name is Victoria. You know that, don't you?' She smiled. 'There have been no letters since Durban, since before James was wounded. It's extremely difficult to get mail through. The last letter he had was from Stefanie about your death ...' She shook her head, smiling wanly. 'And Martin's marriage. That's all—'

'Married? Martin?'

'Yes, he married Annecke Maree after Christmas ...'

It hit him like a physical blow. Since regaining consciousness his thoughts had been bent on getting back to Karel, not Annecke. He had abandoned Annecke. The news of his death would have left her defenceless. A terrible hurt tore through him. He had to get to Karel. He turned to the window, standing with his back to Victoria.

'Will you please help me to get home, Victoria?' he asked after a while.

'Come sit by me. I'll do all in my power to help you get home. I've heard about your twin and the bond between you. I had a brother and would give anything to have him back.'

He sat down next to her. 'What happened to your brother? Was he a soldier?'

'Yes, a captain in the Lancers. He died in India.'

He noticed a deep sadness in her eyes and took her hand in his. 'A soldier who never returned home. Annecke has this little music box. Martin gave it to her. The song tells about a soldier. His sweetheart is waiting for him, but no one knows if he comes back. I'm sorry, did I upset you?' he asked as she turned her face away. 'It's only a song. I thought about it because Annecke doesn't know that I'll be back.'

She swallowed hard. 'I'm being sentimental tonight. I know the song. I saw the show in London with Martin. When I set eyes on you, I thought that it was Martin standing there. Your face, your blue eyes, the resemblance is so strong.' She smiled brightly. 'Now. We have to get you home. I can't hide you here. Warren is not to be trusted. Seeing that you are, for now, a British officer, you could get as far as the Free State without difficulty. Ask to be sent back to your unit. Insist on being sent back. Say that you might stand a better chance of regaining your memory where you lost it.'

'Would the doctor allow that?'

'Why not? And if he doesn't, come back here and I'll think of something else.' She looked at the clock on the wall. 'It's past nine. The last train leaves at ten. You should be going. Will you manage?'

'Yes, it's downhill, I'll make it.' He picked up his helmet. 'Thank you a

310

thousand times for helping me. If ever I can repay you, anything, no matter what, I'll be honoured.'

'My only reward will be to know that you'll find your twin alive.'

He kissed her softly on her mouth. 'I'll always remember you, Victoria.'

He walked down the dark street. Martin's love, the girl he could not bring home. He had seen it in her eyes, heard it in her voice. He brought his fingers to his lips. He could still feel the touch of her mouth and he prayed that there would be something he could do to replace the misery in her eyes with happiness. But then he remembered Koba saying that many things can cause misery, even the intention of bringing happiness.

PART SIX

THE WILDERNESS OF DOUBT

Weary and homesick and distressed,
They wander east, they wander west,
And are baffled and beaten and blown about
By the winds of the wilderness of doubt;
*   To stay at home is best.*

Henry W Longfellow,
'Stay, stay at home, my heart, and rest'

A New Way to Fight the War

March 1900

THE WEEKS FOLLOWING the surrender of General Piet Cronjé and his four thousand men found Commandant Martin de Winter fighting a battle of his own, a battle against despair, defeat and an overwhelming sense of hopelessness. Everything was falling apart. Ladysmith had been relieved, the Natal front was giving in, and the enemy was breaking through on the southern border of the Free State. Only Mafeking was still besieged. And around him men openly voiced their unwillingness to make a stand against General Roberts's vast force, which had crushed Cronjé and was advancing on Bloemfontein.

Martin welcomed the responsibility of being commandant. It kept him from brooding on the consequences of Cronjé's surrender and also gave him a voice at the *krygsraads*. He drew his inspiration from General de Wet, who had not lost faith in the war.

'Our burghers are demoralised,' he told Martin. They were at Poplar Grove, a small village west of Bloemfontein, watching the arrival by carriage of President Kruger, who had come to give hope to his fast-disintegrating forces. 'We need to give them back their faith and we can only do so if we stand fast. Tell them a wounded animal fights at his best; they mustn't despair.'

Kruger stepped from the carriage. The sounds of battle erupted from the surrounding hills, where the commandos were lying in wait for the enemy. De Wet bundled the old President back into the carriage, turned it around and ordered a strong force to see it to safety.

'Get to your commando. Ride north,' he told Martin, his voice raw with anger, his *sjambok* tapping his riding boots. 'I'll send for you tonight.'

Ten miles further on Martin brought the Rustenburg commando to a halt. He slid off his horse and wiped his dust-streaked face with the back of his hand. He watched as his men galloped in. They drank from their water bottles and waited in silence for his orders.

'All accounted for, except for three, but they might find us later. And again I can't find Karel,' said Jan Viljoen, taking his saddle from his horse, a sure sign of him not wanting to run any further. 'The supply wagons are a mile to the west. I saw them heading that way. Jacob, Dirk, Gert Swart,' he bellowed. 'Go get some food. Those bastards are sure to take it all to Bloemfontein and leave us with nothing.'

They prepared to wait the night out, collecting what firewood there was, taking the horses to the river to drink and ignoring the constant stream of stragglers still heading east. Soon there was order and they settled around fires waiting for the food supplies.

'Commandant, do you want me to search for Karel?' Gert Vermaas asked.

'Thank you, Gert. He will find us if he wants to. Rather see that the men boil the water. The river is badly affected by all the carcasses still drifting down,' Martin said and joined Jan and Joep at the fire. 'I must ride to find De Wet and see what he wants us to do.'

'I'll put sentries out when the men have eaten,' Jan said.

'In this commotion? That won't be necessary, Jan. Let them rest.'

'There are a good many who have the urge to flee. They might not have the courage to do so while Jan Viljoen is awake.' He handed Martin a mug of steaming coffee. 'Ride, get the orders and leave the faint-hearted to Jan Viljoen.'

MUCH LATER THAT NIGHT Martin returned from a lengthy *krygsraad*. The men had chopped up a dry acacia and there was a huge fire, with smaller ones around the periphery, to ward off the cold of night. They were lying in groups, their heads on their saddles, some already snoring, while others were talking among themselves. At his arrival most straightened up and came to the central fire to hear the new orders.

'So what's it to be, son?' Joep passed Martin a plate of food he had kept warm. 'Do we stand and fight, or do we get the English bullets in our backs?'

'We continue north, Pa. Our orders are to prevent the enemy from out-flanking General de Wet's commandos and entering Bloemfontein from the north. Captain Theron's scouts say the English are waiting for their supply wagons before they advance. Three days at least. General de la Rey will set up cannon at the line of koppies to the west,' Martin told them between mouthfuls of food. 'Any questions?'

'Will we be able to stop the advance?' someone asked.

Martin thought for a while. It would be unwise to give his men false confidence. 'Yes, we will be able to hold them – for a while, that is,' he said, carefully selecting his words. 'Let me put it this way: we will give the Free Staters enough time to put a defence line around Bloemfontein. Then we will retreat east to Brandfort and north of them—'

'Aha! Whose horse won the race today?' A voice came from the darkness, followed by a harsh laugh. 'Never in my life have I seen such an entertaining sight.'

Martin turned to face the ragged man who walked into the firelight leading his big black mare. 'Karel! Where have you been?'

Karel scratched his long dirty hair. 'It would've been unfair if I'd joined in the race. Legend would've put the riders to shame. We were so close, so close! I saw the whites of their eyes—' he broke off abruptly. 'Guess who I found today?' No one answered; everyone knew he was still looking for his twin. 'Then I won't tell, but he needs help. He's exhausted and starving.'

'Who are you talking about?' Martin asked.

'Half a mile back, that way, you'll find him,' said Karel, pointing west. 'I must water my beauty now, so you go and see. Go and see!'

Jan and his brothers went off in the direction Karel had indicated. The others kept their eyes on Karel and Legend. Karel appeared perfectly sane, and they relaxed visibly.

'Will you have something to eat, son?' Joep asked.

'I must find something for Legend first.'

'There is fodder on the wagon,' Gert Vermaas said.

Half an hour later Jan came striding back to the fire. 'Our doctor is once again with us. Come! He has travelled all week to find us.'

Charles arrived with Frans and Jacob, clearly exhausted. Martin noticed the lines of fatigue visible through the wide grin on his face. He hugged Charles and passed him on to the others.

Joep Maree folded him in his strong arms. '*Wragtig*, son, we were worried about you.'

'Uncle Joep, you were worried about getting a bullet with no doctor to see to you,' Jan said and gave an almighty laugh.

'Speak for yourself, Jan Viljoen.' Joep turned back to Charles. 'How did you get away from the English?'

Charles, still smiling widely, took a mug of coffee. 'We were released two weeks ago, actually. My colleagues left for the north, some to Bloemfontein, but I obtained permission to stay with Uncle Marthinus.'

'Pa? How is he?' Martin asked.

'He's been sent to Cape Town, but he's recovering. Where's Buks, Uncle Joep?'

'Wounded in the arm. We sent him home by train. Others weren't so lucky.'

'How did Karel find you, Charles?' Martin asked.

'I found myself in the firing line. My mules paid no heed to the roar of the guns. Then, out of the blue, or should I say out of the dust, Karel appeared and ordered me to leave my ambulance and rather save Lady and myself. I went back for my ambulance later and insisted that the British let me through and here we are.'

They talked for a while, catching up on news. Charles fell asleep with the mug still in his hands. Martin covered him with a blanket and eased his head onto a bag of meal.

FOR THE following three days the combined commandos of generals De la Rey and De Wet dug into the line of koppies between Bloemfontein and the enemy. Martin moved the Rustenburg commando to the north as ordered, but they were not idle. He sent Frans Viljoen to Bloemfontein with a request for medical supplies. Frans arrived back with more than Charles had hoped for. Dr Hans Vermaak had joined them again and also brought a few tents, two ambulance wagons and Charles's supplies.

The battle on the hills outside Bloemfontein lasted only three days. The Rustenburg commando had no part in it. On the thirteenth of March, Lord Roberts and his troops rode into the capital of the Orange Free State.

When Martin went to the *krygsraad* called for by General de Wet, the news he received was disturbing. Many men had been lost in the fighting and a great many more had decided to go home, assuming the war to be over. The last train had left the capital that evening carrying President Steyn and the state archives to Kroonstad, a hundred miles to the north.

Captain Danie Theron reported that he had had the railway blown up to the south and to the north of the city. 'I've left a few men, those who can speak English, in Bloemfontein,' Theron said to Martin when the meeting dispersed. 'Commandant, your brother was the first to offer. I've sent these scouts in on bicycles, but he took his horse. He asked that the doctor should look after his brother's horse until he returns.'

Martin wondered if he would see Karel again, but realised that things would have to run their course. Whatever the outcome, he would have to accept it.

KOBA HUMMED WHILE she helped Lena and Annecke churn the butter in the dairy room at Soetvlei. But there was a great uneasiness stirring in her soul; all was not well here on the farm. There was a restlessness, an ugliness, moving about, unspoken and unseen, in the avoiding of eyes and the wariness in choosing words.

She had been at the station waiting for the train with the large Red Cross painted on the side when Buks Maree had arrived in Pretoria. She had taken him and two other wounded Rustenburg men to her home and seen to their wounds. Although she urged Buks to stay a few days, he refused. He wanted to go home to Soetvlei, to Lena and his children, and left the following day with her spring-wagon. Last week she had found a ride with Mrs Coetzee's cart to Wintersrust to collect her wagon and visit a while. And now she found something that she could not quite place yet, could not mend, could not fix.

Buks's wound had long since healed, but still he lingered on at home. Of course, it was good to have a man on the farms, as there was so much to do. Klaas and his folk were trying their best, but Mary knew very little about farming and Lettie had a weak heart. Buks was needed. He was a good farmer and, yes, a good husband too, for now Lena was expecting their fourth child.

No, that was not where the trouble was. She turned her attention to the chattering of Lena and Annecke as they slapped the butter into blocks. Lena was advising Annecke about the coming of her baby.

Annecke, poor little lamb, Koba sighed, the sadness in her big brown eyes was not so deep now. She was carrying a strong baby, Rudi's little baby, and was totally absorbed in the changes of her body. Life was not too difficult for her, as Martin had not been home since the wedding. Men who came to Rustenburg brought the news about Martin being a fearless leader. They also said that Karel had disappeared into Bloemfontein, but that was just his way now. Buks said that Karel had often disappeared for days since Rudi's death.

Her thoughts strayed back to Buks. Would he rejoin the commando? He hardly ever spoke about the war, yet he was so generous when it came to helping out on the farms. Not just Wintersrust and Soetvlei. He spent long hours in the saddle to check that all was in order on the Swart and Vermaas farms, giving what help he could.

A few days back he had ridden off early to Vrede, the farm of the Viljoen brothers. When asked for news of the Viljoen women on his return, he had hesitated before saying that his help was not needed there. She had wondered what had occurred at Vrede, as Buks had been pensive since. It was there that the trouble brooded, her heart told her.

'Lena, *hartjie*, has Buks told you any more news from Vrede?' Koba felt it safe to ask when Annecke left the kitchen to take the coffee to the stoep.

'Oh, Tante Koba, what happened there was ugly,' Lena whispered close to Koba's ear. 'I don't know how why they treated him like that.'

'What did they do to him, *hartjie*?' Koba gathered Lena in her arms when she saw the misery in her face.

'Hannie Viljoen said that he should offer his help where it was needed, not at Vrede. She asked him where his Mauser was and … oh, Tante Koba, this is awful, it hurts so.' Lena sobbed but continued with difficulty. 'She asked him where his courage was. Their men are still fighting. Hannie also forbade him to come to Vrede as long as the war is still on.'

'Why did she say such things? Buks is not a coward,' she comforted. 'There, there, *hartjie*, don't cry. You will only upset the little ones. A woman's tongue can cause such hurt. Now, Hannie Viljoen is a strong woman, a good wife, but, like her dear husband, she is careless with her words.' She dried Lena's tears with her large handkerchief and smacked a kiss on her cheek. 'Buks is on the stoep. He should not see you cry. Come, let's have our coffee. And there is cake too. Mary is coming over and she is bringing dear Anita with her. I will speak to Buks later; he must be hurting very badly.'

The children's shrill voices and the women's chattering could not hide Buks's discomfort, Koba noticed as she cut the cake and passed the slices around. Anita Verwey made it worse by chattering about the wounded she had treated at Rustenburg in the hospital and about Charles's letters from the front.

Mary was a little more cheerful than usual. Anita had brought a letter from Rustenburg. It was from Marthinus, written from Cape Town, Mary told them. His wound had mended and he was doing fine, he wrote, a prisoner, but well looked after.

'He will be back in no time, Aunt Mary.' Buks busied himself with his pipe. 'The British will reach Johannesburg soon. That is their goal – the goldfields.'

'Will they stop there, *hartjie*?' Koba asked, thankful to draw Buks into the conversation. 'Will they be satisfied then?'

'I should think so, Tante Koba. So many of their soldiers have been killed, why would they want to lose more? They want the gold and they will have it. Martin and the State Attorney know that too. It's up to them to make a fair deal with the British. Give them Johannesburg, leave the land to us.'

The women sat in an uneasy silence, sipping their coffee. Truly, Koba thought, Buks was not a coward. He just did not want to fight for gold. The *Volk*, the land, that was his first concern.

'Should the fighting continue,' Lena cast a furtive glance at Koba, 'will you go back to the commando, Buks?'

It took Buks some time to reply. His words were sincere, yet there was a bitter edge to his voice. 'I will fight for the freedom of our *Volk*, my heart, but I shall not fight for the gold. If I do, I will be aiding in the destruction of our nation.' He picked up his hat and pipe and made his way to the cattle kraals.

'We are not fighting for the gold,' Lena said. 'We are fighting because of the gold, surely?'

'Charles says we are playing a big part in teaching a selfish empire an expensive lesson – not to destroy lesser nations,' said Anita.

'*Allemagtig*,' Lettie Maree laughed. 'Who is fighting whom now? Come Annecke, child,' she hoisted herself to her feet. 'Let's start the supper. War talk will not fill our bellies.'

Koba waited until the women had trooped into the house. She wrapped her shawl around her shoulders and set off to where Buks was leaning against the fence at the cattle kraal. How right he was, she thought; fighting for the gold would destroy the *Volk*. Oom Paul, the wily old Dopper, would have to find some other way to fight this complicated war. But for now, Buks was helpless and in need of her comfort.

PRESIDENT KRUGER SCOWLED deeply, chewing on the stem of his meerschaum. His black frock coat was crumpled and stained after the long journey to Kroonstad, the temporary capital of the Free State. He fingered the copper ring in his ear. His rheumatism warned that a cold winter was waiting.

He had called a *krygsraad* to consolidate the scattered commandos, to give hope. But, most of all, he had to find a new way to fight the war. The recent lack of success was taking its toll on the bravest of men. The *Volk* was demoralised, weary of the flight. Could they halt Lord Roberts's advance?

He squinted through the haze of pipe smoke drifting above the large mahogany table in the Railway Hotel. President Steyn of the Free State, his red beard reaching to the fourth button of his coat, the lamplight shining on his bald head, sat quietly. There was still hope and confidence in his eyes. General Piet Joubert was wrapped in a blanket. The Town Boer had not recovered from being thrown from his horse some months back. It was clear that death was near. He saw it in the pallid face, heard it in a voice devoid of authority.

Further down the table were the two State Secretaries and the members of the Executive Councils. Around the table, leaning against the wall or seated in extra chairs, were the fighting generals: De la Rey, Olivier,

Viljoen, Prinsloo, Basson and many others – Free Staters whom he had only recently met.

He tucked his pipe into his pocket. De Wet, the stocky Free Stater with the goatee might be the man to keep the demoralised Boer forces from complete disintegration. New blood, young blood. He cleared his throat noisily. 'General de Wet, will you speak? Tell us how to keep the *Engelse* at bay. Come, young man, give us your voice.'

Christiaan de Wet rose from his chair, his sharp eyes fixing the older generals with authority. 'Be done with set battles. Be done with sieges. Go from the defensive to the offensive. We split our forces into smaller units, commandos that can move swiftly, strike at the enemy and run. We harass them, blow up the railway, attack their convoys, capture their patrols, strike at different places simultaneously. We mustn't give the enemy a moment's rest. We must drive them to the point of desperation so that they give up.'

'You told your men to go to their farms to rest,' General Joubert wheezed. 'How will you get them back?'

'I cannot catch a hare, General, with unwilling dogs. The best men will return – those who are willing to fight. To get the others back, I need only one day's good work and then they'll flock back to the commandos.'

'Who will lead these smaller commandos?' General Olivier asked. 'Will they be operating at their own discretion? It will cause lawlessness.'

'We have, say, six hundred, not more than a thousand, under a general, not a commandant. These generals receive their orders directly from the fighting general in their districts. We as fighting generals hold full control over the generals and our areas. We meet only when the need arises and report to the commander-in-chief. It'll do away with these lengthy *krygsraads*.'

'Where will we find these new generals?' someone asked from the back.

De Wet flashed an impatient look. 'We choose firm men who can discipline, men who hold the respect of their commando. Men who can think clearly and quickly in battle. We don't need those who doubt their own judgement.'

'I agree,' General de la Rey spoke up. 'Smaller commandos attacking, not waiting to be attacked. The enemy is heading for the Transvaal, for the gold mines. We all know that. Should the war reach there, my men will fight as General de Wet has just outlined.'

President Kruger nodded. 'Louis Botha is being driven back from Natal. I appointed him commander-in-chief. He will approve. Koos,' he turned to De la Rey, 'where's Marthinus de Winter? Is he with you?'

'He's wounded and now a prisoner, Oom Paul. It's a great loss.'

The President sighed. 'Ai, a sad loss, but God's will. And young De Winter? He snatched his commando out of Cronjé's trap, I've heard.'

'Yes, Oom Paul, a daring young man. My first choice as a general in the Transvaal.'

The President frowned. 'A general? But has he found a wife? Men put their trust in a man with a family at home.'

De la Rey smiled. 'He married Joep Maree's daughter and is expecting a son, or so I believe.'

Bloemfontein

BLOEMFONTEIN WAS A small town, comprising a few public and government buildings, tin-roofed stores and hotels, all clustered around the single railway passing through to the goldfields of the Transvaal. Five thousand people lived in and around the town, and it provided for their needs. But their peaceful existence ended when the orange-and white-striped republican flag was replaced by the Union Jack. Thirty thousand British troops trudged into town and brought with them enteric fever caught from drinking the filthy water of the Modder River. The disease spread through the exhausted troops, and soon hundreds lay dying in the heat of the late summer months.

General Lord Roberts issued a proclamation to the Boers: those who took the oath of allegiance to the Queen would be free to return to their farms. A great number of Free Staters obliged, convinced that the war was over now that their capital had been overrun. They flocked to the town to gape at the occupying forces.

A cheerful atmosphere reigned despite the overcrowded conditions and the funeral marches to the cemetery. Soldiers and military vehicles crowded the streets. Those who found themselves free for the evening headed for the town square, where the band of the Highland Brigade entertained the townsfolk nightly.

The owners of shops and hotels made the most of the opportunity. At first they thought the British would move on quickly to the Transvaal. But when the first cold winds blew from the plains and the trees began to turn with the season they were still there.

IT WAS EARLY AFTERNOON. A light wind stirred the dust in the streets. Karel de Winter, bearded and thin, leaned against a lamppost, his eyes filled with contempt and despair. *My sister, my own sister.* Stefanie smiled at Peter Radford as he led her into a tea room. It was the second time Karel had spotted them. *Her English husband traded for a British lord.*

After the fall of Bloemfontein, Karel and five other scouts had stayed behind to spy on the enemy's movements. They slipped away at night to meet up with Captain Theron, who passed their information to the generals and the Free State government in Kroonstad. Save for Jan Viljoen's hunting knife hidden in his jacket, Karel was unarmed.

He put his arm around Legend's neck. Stefanie's betrayal upset him but there was no time to dwell on it. He needed to send an urgent message to Kroonstad. There was a purpose to the enemy's activities, an order in the bustle. The troops were spending more time in drill. Oxen were being brought in from farms and hundreds of wagons were being loaded, set to move north. Armoured trains were being readied and trucks, loaded with fodder and crates of supplies, stood waiting. Once this military machine was set in motion, he would not get past their lines easily. But first he had to get to Orange River Station to dig up Rudi's grave. The urgent need to search for his twin was driving him on again.

He looked at the sun: three hours before darkness, but there was something he needed to do. He led Legend to the Red Cross office and secured her to a post. He entered the building and inquired from a clerk about his father.

The clerk went through the names of the prisoners of war and found it among those who had surrendered with Cronjé. 'De Winter, Marthinus Johannes, Rustenburg district, Commandant. Wounded February, 1900, deported to St Helena.'

'Does it say if he has recovered from his wound?'

'I'm afraid we don't have that information. For now, you can take it that he's still with us,' the clerk said with an encouraging smile.

'His son, Rudolf. It's said that he was buried by the English in December.'

'Let me see.' The clerk took another folder from the shelves, adjusted his glasses and let his finger travel down the lists. After a while he found what he was looking for. 'Ah, here we are. De Winter, Rudolf ...'

Karel rode to the barn on the outskirts of town. He would send a message to Martin about their father's fate. At least he was alive. He changed into tattered clothes and locked Legend in the barn. Avoiding the patrols around the town, he met up with his contact man and was back before sunrise with new orders. He slept through the day, and in the afternoon changed into his city clothes and again rode into town.

A crowd was gathering in the square for the band performance. The

man he was looking for, an English-speaking Free Stater and Boer informer who allowed him into the telegraph office to tap the line, was not yet
there. He prepared to wait, but suddenly something stirred deep inside him.
Something was amiss. He carefully searched around him but there were only
khaki-clad figures and townspeople dressed in their best. He followed his
instincts and cancelled his plans for the night.

THE BLACK HORSE caught his eye, making him swing around forcefully, colliding with two privates. 'Sorry, Captain, sir!' They gave startled
salutes and edged around him.

Rudolf stared at the mare tethered outside the Red Cross office. She
was in immaculate condition, her coat shiny, her rump a little fat. He
whistled one long and three short notes. She twitched her ears, pulled
at her reins. What was Legend doing in Bloemfontein? Had the English
captured her? Now he need not look for a horse to escape from the city. He
would have to steal her. No amount of money would convince a man to sell
a horse in her condition.

His heart racing, he crossed the street and prepared to wait until her
rider came. He pretended to inspect a shop window. Glancing over his
shoulder, he recognised an officer who'd been on the train from Cape Town.
He ducked into the shop, and when it was safe to emerge Legend was gone.
He ran into the street, searching wildly, but there was no sign of her.

Late that night he was still walking the streets, searching, always hopeful
that he would find her somewhere.

He had arrived in Bloemfontein two days previously.

It had not been easy to convince the doctor in Cape Town that he
preferred to return to his unit. The doctor had agreed only on condition that
Rudolf present himself daily at the hospital in Bloemfontein. James had
pressed an envelope containing fifty pounds into his hands and urged him
to leave as soon as possible. Rudolf had not the heart to tell him that the
same officer, who had seen them on the afternoon he had come for help, was
watching from the entrance.

The train trip to Bloemfontein had taken two weeks because of the
bottlenecking of trains on the single railway. A group of red-tabbed staff
officers had tried to engage him in talk about England, the army and
cricket. He said as little as possible, watched his accent and concentrated
on his manners. His nerves were stretched to breaking point when the
train finally steamed into Bloemfontein.

At night he slept at the tented hospital; by day he disappeared into the confusion of the crowded town. He soon discovered that Boers were allowed to enter and leave the town only if in possession of a document issued by the military authorities. A horse was impossible to obtain, as the army had bought all available mounts at exorbitant prices.

After losing sight of Legend, he returned to the hospital, dejected and weary. What tremendous happiness he would bring Karel should he and Legend ride into their camp.

The next day he stood outside the Red Cross office for hours. By late afternoon, he decided that he would buy some civilian clothes, steal any horse, and take his chances at night. But something was holding him back. He started wandering, searching again, and found himself drawn to the town square. And there was Legend, with a thin, bearded man dressed in town clothes, brown hair falling to his shoulders. But no disguise could conceal the precious image of his twin, arm loosely around the neck of his beloved horse.

The suffering and loneliness of the past months vanished. He wanted to call out, but could only stare at Karel and Legend. He was still transfixed when Karel swung into the saddle and left. He raced after them and saw them veer into a side street.

He kept his eyes on Legend until she disappeared in a cloud of dust further down the street. He was out of breath, exhausted. His officer's tunic and high boots attracted attention in this poor part of town from children playing in the street, men on the stoeps and women milking cows in their back yards.

He approached a woman who was shutting her chickens in for the night. 'Did a rider on a black horse come past here in the last half hour or so?'

She looked at him through narrowed eyes. He switched to Afrikaans, repeating his question. She spat at him. '*Verraaier*. Traitor!'

He walked on and came across a man leaning on his garden gate, watching his approach. Doffing his helmet, he repeated his question. 'Oh yes,' the man said. 'That would be him, living in Venter's barn. He's not right, you know.' He made a sign indicating his head. 'Has been there for weeks. Never speaks.'

'Could you give me directions to the house?'

The man obliged and Rudolf hurried on and saw Legend in the corner of an enclosure, drinking from a trough. Karel was standing over a bucket, splashing water over his face and chest. As he watched, Legend nuzzled him and he put his arm around her neck. He wanted to call out to Karel, but found he was unable to utter a word. Through the blur of tears running down his face, he saw Karel leading Legend into the barn, casting hurried glances in his direction.

KAREL SAW THE ENGLISH SOLDIER in the middle of the road, looking directly at him. A tall man, his face obscured by the rim of his pith helmet and the setting sun behind him.

'Have we been found out, Legend?' he whispered. 'Or is it just another cavalryman who wants to buy you off me?' He waited for the soldier to approach, but the man did not move.

He picked up his shirt and led Legend into the stable. He peered through a slit in the wall. The soldier was gone. Legend gave an urgent snort, and then he heard the rusted gate creak and boots crunch on the stony ground. Pushing Legend to the back of the barn, he pulled the knife from his waistband and took up a position behind the half-closed door. The steps faltered. There came a noise, as if the man was clearing his throat. Muscles tensed, hand clenched on the knife, he waited.

The door opened. The soldier stood there, his helmet dangling in one hand. Rudolf's face was only a couple of inches from his.

Then they were in each other's arms, entangled in a desperate embrace, clinging to each other.

'You're alive, alive,' Karel wept, his voice distorted with emotion. 'I found you, Rudi, I found you. I was losing my mind, but you were with me, always calling me.'

Rudolf tried to speak, but could not control his wild sobbing. His legs gave way, and, pressing him close, Karel supported him to the straw mattress in the corner of the barn.

'I was wounded, badly, unconscious for a long time,' Rudolf managed to say as he collapsed on the straw. 'The pain was bad, unbearable.'

'Yes, I felt it too,' Karel swallowed hard at the tears constricting his throat. 'It was in your head …'

Karel lit a fire in an old paraffin tin and put some coffee on to boil. They sat close together on the straw, their arms about each other's shoulders. Legend pushed her head between their faces. A smile broke through Rudolf's tears as he stroked her nose. 'Have you run away from the commando? Why are you two hiding here?'

Karel looked at Rudolf's khaki uniform. 'I came looking for a turncoat and today I've found him,' he said, half-sobbing, half-laughing. 'I told them you were alive! Legend, see, I told you. You were the only one who believed me.'

'Lady? Is she—?'

'Fine! I left her with Charles.' He traced the scar on Rudolf's temple. 'I told him that I'd bring you back.'

'Did he believe you?'

'I don't know. He never said so.'

When emotions subsided, Rudolf told Karel what had happened at the river, about waking up in the hospital and about James and Victoria's assistance. Karel told him how he and Charles had ridden into General Methuen's camp to search for him and of the lonely months of scouting on his own. He gave him the news of their father's fate and told him about the siege at Paardeberg, how Martin had led the commando out at night.

'It was a brave thing he did,' Karel said. 'I couldn't ride with them. I thought they would be shot. I thought about you and gave Legend up to come and search for you. I crawled out. I was so near to the enemy. I killed one, Rudi, with this knife. I was wild, Rudi, I stabbed him and left him to die. It was easy ... to kill with a knife. And that scares me too.'

It was cold in the barn. Karel draped his dirty blanket around their shoulders. He brought from his jacket the pocketknife and Annecke's note, now wrapped in a piece of oilcloth. 'You left her with child, Rudi. She had to marry Martin; she had no choice. I should have gone to be with her, but I remember so little about those days. I lost my mind when I lost you, Rudi. Your child, Rudi, not Martin's ...'

RUDOLF CURLED UP on the straw, staring into the blue flames of the coal fire. Karel's arm went around him; his body was warm and comforting – the comfort without which he could not exist. Looking at the lines around Karel's mouth and his sunken eyes, he made up his mind: they had suffered enough.

'I've remembered something, Karel, something that we've forgotten. We were born the same man, just two bodies, Tante Koba said. I believe that now. Nothing, no one, not even Annecke must come between us. We can't change it. I see that now.'

IN THE AFFLUENT PART of Bloemfontein, Peter Radford sat with Stefanie in the drawing room of a boarding house. He thought what a fortunate man he was, spending his convalescent leave not carousing with his friends but travelling the country with the woman he adored.

His initial fascination had turned to infatuation. Further than that he dared not think, as what he felt for her did not tolerate closer inspection. And Stefanie's feelings were hard to read, yet, when she thought herself unobserved, he detected a yearning in her blue eyes.

It had taken five days to get from Cape Town to Port Elizabeth, but Stefanie had failed to find a ship bound for Delagoa Bay. Two weeks later, when the railway lines to the Free State had been repaired, he managed to find them places on an overcrowded train. They arrived in Bloemfontein late one evening, and found a respectable boarding house with a room for Stefanie. Peter had no difficulty in finding lodging at the officers' mess.

Stefanie was staring out of the window, frowning. 'I'm so tired of waiting. Your brave general sits here like a brooding hen on eggs instead of fixing the tracks. There must be a way to get out of here. I feel so ... so *trapped*!'

'Shall we go for a stroll?'

'It's even worse in the streets. The dust, the flies and, oh, the crowds!' She picked up the book she had left on the table.

'What are you reading?'

'Aunt Susan sent it on.' She held up the book so that he could read the title.

'*The Story of an African Farm*, hmm ... Is it worth reading?'

'Yes, except for the silly romance. Imagine falling in love with a perfect stranger. I could've warned her what would come of that.'

He looked at her closely. Another slip of the tongue. She hardly spoke about her husband, and, when his name came up, it was obvious she held him in contempt. He was about to unfold his newspaper when she asked, 'Have you ever been in love, Peter? Is there a girl waiting for you to finish this silly war?'

'If there should be ... poor thing. What a long wait! I'm off to the Punjab when all this is done with.' He saw her flush with annoyance as she opened her book again. 'And you, Stefanie? Have you ever been in love?'

'Being married doesn't necessarily mean being, or having been, in love. Take James and Victoria. He doesn't take any interest in her. Why did he marry her then? And so suddenly?'

'A private matter, I suppose.' His eyes caught the headline when he unfolded his newspaper. 'The ammunition factory in Johannesburg was destroyed by an explosion yesterday. It says here that they suspect sabotage.'

She paled visibly, snapped her book shut and got to her feet. 'I'm going out.'

'You can't venture out on your own—'

'I can take care of myself. I don't need you to watch over me.'

He heard her go into her room. A short while later the front door opened and closed. He picked up the paper and smiled. She would be back soon, imploring him to accompany her. It had happened before.

At dusk, a trap drawn by two mules stopped outside, and Stefanie alighted.

'Where have you been?' he said. 'I've searched the entire city, the country, from the Cape to Cairo—'

'Oh, stop fussing, Peter.' She hauled a few parcels from the trap. 'Take this contraption to the back of the house. Feed them. There's a bale of grass.' She swept past him.

When he arrived at her room after he had seen to the animals, he knocked on the door. 'Come!' she called. He pushed open the door. Her portmanteau was open, the room strewn with dresses, skirts and blouses. She was transferring some underclothes into a small bag.

'Those mules won't get you very far.'

'I'm going on.' She tossed a white blouse onto the pile on the floor. 'I have a pass to travel as far as Kroonstad. There I shall catch the train to Pretoria. Simple as that.'

'Absurd! You can't travel without an escort.'

'It's only a hundred miles. My forefathers travelled by ox-wagon for thousands of miles, and their women sometimes had to manage alone …'

'But now there's a war on.'

'It was even worse then. Savages and wild beasts behind every bush. There were no roads, no trains, nothing. If they could do it, so can I.'

'Please listen. I've heard that General Roberts will set out next week. It's only a few more days. You'll be on your way sooner than you imagine. I'm responsible for your safety. I will not allow you—'

'Then I relieve you of that responsibility.' She chose a pair of high boots from the pile on the floor and put them next to the bag.

He sank down in the chair by the window. 'Is there anything I can say that will persuade you not to be so foolish?'

'You leave for Cape Town next Friday and I go on to Pretoria tomorrow.' She opened her hatbox. 'I thank you for your company of the past month. I did enjoy it, but while I'm carousing from city to city, drinking gallons of champagne with British officers, things are getting worse …' She bit her bottom lip.

'Did the report in the newspaper upset you?'

She busied herself with the hats. Two went to the pile and the third, a green felt hat, went next to the bag. 'Why should it? No more ammunition, no more war. I want to get home. Is that so strange to you?'

He picked up the green hat and turned it around in his hands. 'You can't take this ridiculous hat—'

'What's so ridiculous about this hat?' She grabbed it, putting it out of his reach on top of the wardrobe.

'Well, it's a pretty little thing, but it offers no protection against the sun,' he said, but she merely shrugged her shoulders. 'Stefanie, how do you propose to travel on your own? You cannot expect me to escort you.'

She stuffed the discarded clothes into her portmanteau. 'No, I don't. A British officer riding through enemy lines? You'd find yourself in Kroonstad with no way of getting out. Unless Lord Roberts catches up with you.'

He looked at her sharply, but she avoided his eyes. She had it all worked out. Waiting for Lord Roberts to catch up! A court martial would be waiting, not Lord Roberts. He was about to protest, but checked himself. A hundred miles – four, five days? And once he had seen her safely onto the train at Kroonstad, he could lie low until the advance force reached the town, or make his way back. Ten days at the most.

On the bed were the clothes she planned to travel in. A dowdy brown dress – not like Stefanie at all. She could pass as a countrywoman in that. She would be among her people, speaking their language; she could get them through. He made up his mind. The risk alone was inviting, and to be with her would be exhilarating. He would just have to catch a later train to Cape Town. As simple as that. But he could not give in so easily. Let her fret for a while!

'Well, then, if there's nothing I can do to change your mind …' He came to his feet. 'Write to me when you get there.'

He closed the door behind him and could barely contain his laughter when he heard her cry of anger. He stood for a few minutes before entering again. 'I've arranged to meet Lord Roberts at Kroonstad, only I've no means of getting there.'

Relief flooded her face, but it was swiftly replaced by a haughty stare. 'You may share my carriage, sir.' She came up with some papers. 'Our pass: Mr and Mrs Smith, travelling to Wilgenhof, their smallholding thirty miles to the north. You'll have to be my husband for a while … I mean *pretend* to be my husband. It will just be a new game that we'll be playing.' She handed him a bulky parcel and pulled a slouch hat from under the bed. 'Once we are clear of the town, you will wear this. You will be less conspicuous.'

He looked at the rough jacket, whipcord trousers, collarless shirt and waistcoat. 'You want me to be a Boer? It won't work of course. I can't speak a word of your language.'

'Not be a Boer, but look like one. There are some English people living around here, you know. And in the Transvaal too. It's best that you leave the talking to me. Your accent … well, it's appalling.'

'A new game? You love playing games, don't you? You knew all along that I'd come along.'

She stepped up to him and placed a kiss on his cheek. 'I never doubted it for a moment. Thank you, Peter. It'll be fun. Leave the talking to me, play dumb or … or mute …' Her eyes locked on the scar running down his chin into the high collar of his tunic. 'Your scar … does it go all the way to your throat?'

'Yes, it does go some way down … but I'm terrible at pretending—'

'Show me. Please let me see.'

He undid his collar and pulled it aside. She seemed mesmerised by the scar, her fingers travelling from his chin, following it down to where it disappeared into the hair on his chest. Their eyes met, hers challenging and his searching her face closely.

'Where will we spend the nights?' he asked in a whisper.

'We … shall have to sleep under the stars.'

'Under the stars? Yes, perfect place—' he broke off, fascinated by the power she had over him. He took her chin in his hand and lightly placed his lips against hers, waiting for her to take the initiative, but she stepped back, putting her fingers to her lips.

'Peter, we ride off into the unknown. Shall we leave it at that, for now? Isn't that enough? Not knowing what lies ahead?'

'For now, yes.' He was confused. She never did anything half-heartedly and yet there was something holding her back, despite the desire he had seen in her eyes. 'Tell me, if we run into trouble, will you reveal my identity?'

'Why should I? My people would not forgive me for running around with a British officer. I would be an outcast, or worse – shot as a traitor.'

The Great Flight

THE FOLLOWING MORNING, once they were well clear of the British lines, Peter donned his Boer outfit and put on the slouch hat. Stefanie carefully stowed her green hat in the back of the cart, placed a wide-brimmed *kappie* on her head and hung a shawl over her shoulders. For a while they rode in silence.

'Don't you dare laugh at me!' she snapped out of the blue.

'I'm not!' he said, bubbling with laughter. 'But I must say, you do look … fetching.'

'Fetching? Indeed! You don't look like a Boer at all. More like a common tramp.' They burst out laughing; the tension was broken.

She glanced back at the town fading away in the distance. 'Do you think this is wise, Peter? Maybe we should turn back, maybe …'

'Yes, we could stop under the next tree, have our picnic and turn back, if that's what you want.' He smiled; that would be the last thing on her mind, turning back. 'I'm rather enjoying myself. A damsel in distress at my side, and a rather fetching one at that. Thousands of Mausers lying in wait. What more could I possibly want?'

'You have a vivid imagination.' She squared her shoulders. 'This damsel is not in distress.'

The mules pulled at a steady pace, and by sunset they had done well over twenty miles by Peter's reckoning. They watered the animals at a dam and decided to spend the night there. Darkness brought a sharp drop in temperature, and, wrapped in their blankets, they spent an uncomfortable night sitting upright against the trap. Sleep came in snatches, and long before sunrise the pre-dawn cold set their teeth chattering.

In the course of the morning, they found more traffic on the road than they had encountered closer to the city. Mounted Boers passed in the distance, skirting around koppies, disappearing into the thorny scrubland and reappearing again. Lone riders galloped past them. Wagons and carts dotted the veld heading north. Peter decided it would be wise to leave the main road and they followed a track leading northeast to avoid the town of Brandfort. Late that afternoon they came upon a deserted outpost where the mules could graze, but before dark two wagons, filled with women and children, joined them.

Peter was struck by the kindness shown to them. The women shared coffee and food, and seemed to accept his inability to understand their language. Stefanie cooked over an open fire while he made a bed of straw under the trap, following the example of the other travellers. He understood nothing that was said; Stefanie gave the answers expected of him. One old woman watched him through narrowed and thoughtful eyes. Where a simple question only required a nod or shake of the head, he could not oblige.

When Stefanie crawled in under the trap, he could tell by the scowl on her face that she was tired. 'Come, wife, the day's work is done. I kept your side of the bed warm,' he said to cheer her a little.

'How very kind.' She wrapped her blanket around herself.

'I was about to say that I hardly slept last night and neither did you. We need a decent night's sleep, and tomorrow we travel alone.'

'Good night, Peter,' he heard her whisper.

'Sleep well, my dear,' he returned.

'No, please, anything but "my dear", Peter.'

'What shall it be, then? Darling? Sweetheart?'

'Too frivolous,' she said. 'If you could come up with something more, well, romantic.'

'Will "my love" suffice?' he asked after a while.

'Yes, I quite like that,' she sighed softly.

SHE TRIED TO IGNORE the rank smell of the straw and the roughness where it met her hair and neck. If only Peter had known the truth: she had never shared her bed with anyone. She looked at his blond hair against the dark blanket. What if he should find himself stuck behind enemy lines? Would he be captured or shot? She reached for his hand. 'We'll get through, you'll see,' she whispered, more to convince herself. He squeezed her hand tightly.

When the fires around the camp died down, the cold crept into their meagre covering. She tried to control her chattering teeth and did not protest when Peter spread his blanket to cover both of them.

They travelled steadily northward over the next two days, but Peter insisted on keeping a distance from other travellers. The vegetation was sparse now, the earth dry and flat, the winter wind dusty and relentless. Only at night did they join other carts and wagons clustered around huge fires, warding off the frosty nights.

On the fourth day, Stefanie urged Peter to go faster. He played dumb, making wheezing noises and helpless gestures with his hands.

'Don't you ever stop smiling? Do you find everything in life *amusing?*' she asked, trying hard not to laugh with him. He pulled a sad face, then an angry one and then a bored one and she gave up. 'Oh, Peter! I love being with you!' she laughed.

That night, under the trap with their blankets wrapped around them, she voiced her fears to him. 'Peter, while you were watering the mules, a rider came. The English left Bloemfontein two days ago. We simply have to move on.'

'We should reach Kroonstad tomorrow afternoon, I reckon.'

'Yes, but I must have a wash somehow. I've slept in these clothes for days now.'

'You look ravishing. The straw in your hair, that smear from the kettle on your cheek, it suits you perfectly.'

'You look progressively dirtier every day. Are you planning to grow a beard? I don't like beards.'

'Oh dear, I thought I presented the perfect picture of a fearless but devoted Boer husband.'

His face was near hers as they lay whispering, the outline of his head traced against the glowing embers of the fire. 'A devoted husband? Is he not supposed to kiss his wife goodnight?'

'Oh, have I neglected my duty? Would the wife like to be kissed goodnight?'

She nodded and closed her eyes.

His mouth stayed on hers, soft and moving. She felt the touch of his tongue on her lips and reached up, placing her arms around his neck. His tongue forced her lips apart, probing into her mouth. She found the pleasure so intense she could hardly breathe.

He lifted his head, smiling at her. 'Good night, my lovely wife.'

'No,' she pulled his head back. He caressed her shoulder and his hand stayed a while in her neck. Then it slid downwards and rested on her breast, his fingers pressing lightly. Desire flared through her and she uttered a cry of surprise.

His hand shot over her mouth and he laid his cheek against hers. 'Not tonight, not here. Look over there.' He turned her face to the side. 'The children under the wagon are watching. Soon we shall have everyone gathered around.' He pulled her close into his arms. 'Come, sleep now. It's cold, and tomorrow will be a long day. You're a good liar. You'll get us through, I know.

And when we reach Kroonstad, we'll dine, dance and laugh,' he kissed her lightly on her cheek, 'and love. Now go to sleep.'

HE FELT HER SHIVERING and pulled the blankets tighter around them. Her unrestrained response had not come as a surprise. He marvelled again at the depth of his feelings for her. He would never forgive himself if anything should happen to her. *Am I in love?* he wondered and found the idea disturbing. She was another man's wife, after all. *The excitement, the danger we face, the circumstances, that is what has brought this on, he decided. It is just a passing infatuation, has to be, must be!*

<hr>

BILLOWING CLOUDS OF DUST and swarming horsemen, a vast sea of khaki-clad foot soldiers and endless lines of transport wagons and gun carriages stretched for miles on both sides of the single railway north of Bloemfontein. General Koos de la Rey and Commandant Martin de Winter trained their field glasses on the spectacle from a koppie two miles away.

'Oom Koos, they've marched seventy miles in two days,' Martin said. 'We fought them at the Sand River, at the Vet River, but still we can't halt them. They must be as exhausted as we are. Surely they will take a respite now? Give us time to regroup?'

'Yes, one more fight today, then they'll rest for a day or so. Wherever you find yourself tonight, stay put. But keep an eye out.' De la Rey lowered his glasses. His deep-set eyes were half-closed, his mouth set above his salt-and-pepper beard. 'The commandos are restless; they won't make a stand here in the open. Try to keep a rearguard together to allow President Steyn to get away from Kroonstad.'

'That's all I've done since Magersfontein, Oom Koos, fight rearguard.'

'Our commandos, Transvalers, want to fight on their own soil. We cannot hope for any confidence out here.' He put his pipe into his jacket pocket and touched his heels to his horse. 'Come, son, there's no time to watch the British at play. Move out the transport.'

Martin galloped back to where his commando was waiting. He ordered the transport on its way and the men to take up positions in the dry riverbed. The horses were fifty yards behind them, ready for a hasty retreat.

There was no joking, no cursing the enemy, just a silence heavy with anxiety. Some men were brewing coffee and smoking their pipes. Others were stretched out with their eyes closed, but whether they were asleep or unwilling to talk Martin could not tell.

When the British infantry attacked in the afternoon, there was pandemonium, and few men stayed to fight it out. Martin, together with Joep Maree, Jan Viljoen and a handful of others, fired into the advancing enemy, but the setting sun was in their eyes, and the dust and commotion made it impossible to take aim. Fearing that they might shoot their own, they joined in the frantic flight, followed by riderless, panic-stricken horses.

A few miles on, they caught up with the commando and the transport wagons. The men were tending their trembling horses, most avoiding Martin's eyes. He set about restoring order. Fires were lit, rations distributed and the wounded taken to the railway line where he had ordered the doctors to wait.

Much later, he joined Joep at the fire to discuss the next day's strategy. He was about to pour coffee when he noticed a gathering around a wagon. He walked over to find Charles operating on a wounded Gert Swart, he who had months ago predicted that Charles would go over to the British side. As if echoing his thoughts, Frans Viljoen, who was holding Gert upright while Charles worked, said to Martin, 'What did Jan tell him at the Modder River?'

'Now is not the time to remind him of that!' Martin snapped and Frans apologised profusely.

Charles finished stitching Swart's wound and asked two men to load him onto the wagon. He gave the order for the wagon to move off and went to fetch Lady.

Martin followed him into the dark. 'What are you doing here, Charles?'

'Well, it's rather obvious. I came for the wounded.'

'It was arranged that the wounded would be brought to you now that we are retreating. I explicitly ordered you to stay out of the fighting line at all times. I've sent thirty wounded to the place where I ordered you to be.'

'Dr Vermaak and three others are there—'

'Charles, I can't have you falling into enemy hands again. Don't you understand? The commando will never forgive me,' he interrupted wearily. 'Now, I want you to move the wounded to Kroonstad, get them on the train to Pretoria. There simply is no time to put up tents and treat them. Tomorrow will be the same as today. Stay close to the railway. That's where the men will be looking for you.'

'Yes, will do,' Charles said calmly and mounted Lady. 'Shall I wait for you at Kroonstad?'

'I'll find you there.'

Charles swung Lady in the direction the wagon had taken. 'Take care, Martin!' he shouted over his shoulder and disappeared into the night.

A FEW MILES to the north, Peter spent an uneasy night with Stefanie cocooned in his arms. An icy wind rustled against the trap. He could hear the sounds of battle in the distance. He toyed with the idea of waking Stefanie and of them slipping away, but gave it up immediately. Riding in the dark would be foolish.

At dawn, he was roused by the thundering of horses' hooves and wild cries urging them to move on. A large commando was heading south. He ran to get the mules, but found that one was lame and hurriedly hitched up the remaining one.

With only one mule, they travelled at a slow pace. During the night, many wagons, carts and even the odd grand carriage had caught up from the south. Frantic women and children were driving herds of livestock northward, hampering the passage of the commandos in the opposite direction. The sun disappeared behind a thick grey cloud and a cold wind beat at their faces and cut through their clothes.

Stefanie placed the fringe of her shawl over her face. 'Where are they all going, Peter?'

'They just want to get away, I'd say.' He gave her an encouraging smile. 'There's no need to panic. The British infantry can't possibly move at the speed we're travelling.'

'Go faster, Peter. Can't you hear the guns?'

The sound of artillery was distinct now. 'Boer guns, at least twenty miles off. We have time.'

It was late afternoon when they reached the outskirts of Kroonstad, dragging the exhausted mule by the reins. Tents and wagons belonging to the commandos were mixed up with civilian transport and herds of cattle and sheep. Mounted men moved to and fro. A large Creusot gun, its barrel blackened, passed them.

Peter stared but Stefanie was unsettled. 'You should never have let me do this. You are too reckless, Peter.'

'Now, it was I who talked you into this.' He squeezed her hand. 'Lower your voice. English is most definitely not spoken here.'

They managed to get the trap close to the centre of town and left it on the side of the road. There was a large gathering near the train station where a man with a flowing red beard was standing on a trestle table, talking in an imploring manner. As they made their way into the throng, Stefanie had her eyes on the speaker.

'Who is he? What's he saying?' Peter asked.

'President Steyn of the Free State. He's pleading with the burghers not to give in. So sad, so very sad …' Then something the president said caught her attention. Peter saw fear growing in her eyes. She pulled him out of the crowd, looking around her worriedly.

'You can't stay here, Peter.' She pointed to a range of hills north of the town. 'Thousands of burghers will be up there, and here, thousands more and cannon too. He asked that those not fit for fighting should leave.' She reached for his hand.

God, we've left it too late, he swore silently as the reality of their situation hit him.

'Come north with me. We'll think of something,' Stefanie pleaded anxiously. 'I'm so sorry, Peter, I've landed you in such an awful mess—'

'No, no,' he said, squeezing her hands tightly. 'I've landed us both in this mess. Getting you out of here is what's important.' He put his arm around her waist and smiled at her. 'Being in this mess with you is quite exciting. Come, let's try the train.'

They hurried through the chaos to the train station. At the roofless platform stood five ambulance wagons offloading wounded. The men still wore the clothes in which they had fought, some lying on makeshift stretchers with only a blanket around them. A grey-haired man shielded a much younger one who'd lost both legs. Next to them, a boy held the hand of a man with a bandaged face. And a little further away lay a row of bodies, sewn up in blankets.

Stefanie stopped. 'Oh, no, just look at them, Peter.'

'Yes, a ghastly sight, but that's war, I'm afraid.' He whispered, steering her on. 'To the ticket office. Ask about trains … whatever is available.'

He watched as she pushed her way to a small corrugated-iron shed. She spoke to a couple of railway officials. She stood for a few moments looking at the wounded and, as she turned to go, she froze, her eyes riveted on a man, a Red Cross band around his sleeve, bending over one of the stretchers. Then she rushed back, grabbed his hand and pulled him through the waiting crowd.

'Did you recognise someone, Stefanie?' he asked.

She nodded. 'Someone … from the district.'

'Does it mean that the Rustenburg commando might be here?'

She lifted her face and met his eyes. He saw that her eyes were bright with tears. 'The train is for wounded only.'

'Then we shall wait for the next one.'

'There won't be another, Peter.'

The daylight was fading, the rain drizzled. They were already soaked to the skin.

'How far to the next town?' he asked.

'Vereeniging, the Transvaal border. Hundred miles, nothing in between.'

The train steamed into the station and the locomotive was turned around. There were only six wagons and a few cattle trucks. Soon they were filled with wounded and government officials carrying large wooden crates. President Steyn and a small group boarded. Women and children also scrambled aboard.

In the twilight Peter pulled her to the platform. When the signal sounded, he lifted her into an overcrowded truck and jumped on. She clung to him as the train jolted into motion, but then she pulled free. '*My hat!* I have to get my hat!' She jumped off, slipped on the wet platform and stumbled back through the crowd.

The train picked up speed. He prepared to jump, but saw rolls of barbed wire, ammunition crates and supplies piled close to the line. By the time the train had passed them, it was moving fast and the ground fell away sharply from the built-up track.

———

IN CAPE TOWN, James stood at the window in his hospital room. The branches of the big oak where Rudolf had come to him for help were bare, the sky filled with a misty rain. The joy of knowing that his twin cousins might be together again was replaced by an insistent warning in his mind. If he had reported Rudolf, as he should have, it would have been the end for the twins. Tante Koba was right; the one would not make it without the other. He had seen it in Rudolf's eyes. But by letting Rudolf go, James had crossed a boundary that he had not even considered before. And George Hunter was suspicious, that much was clear. He often referred to the mysterious Captain Patterson.

Victoria's presence, the dignified way in which she handled his depressed moods, had almost helped him to succeed in blunting the edges of another guilt. But now it had returned in full force. The child had been lost through his failure to be an attentive husband. He had insisted that they meet under the oak every afternoon. The weather had changed; the days were windy and wet. He had not noticed that Victoria was ailing. She had visited him every day, yet they hardly ever spoke.

It was a simple chill at first, which turned into influenza. The illness compromised the pregnancy and the strain resulted in a miscarriage. Now he was being discharged from hospital and she had recovered sufficiently to come for him. He was nervous at seeing her again. He had to apologise for the sorrow he'd caused her and then leave it up to her to decide on their future as man and wife. The war was almost over now that Lord Roberts was on his way to Johannesburg. A few more months and they could be off to India.

An orderly came to fetch his bag and took him to the hall, where Victoria was waiting. He nodded a greeting and shrugged into the greatcoat she was holding out for him.

'Any news about Stefanie?' he asked as they settled in the covered carriage Warren had provided.

'Well, yes, she sent her husband a note from Port Elizabeth with the news that she's going to Pretoria. There was a dreadful scene when he read it. I was asked to keep it quiet but thought you should know.'

'It does sound a bit, well, drastic, running off in the middle of war. I know Warren is intolerable, but—'

'It's the war, I suppose. And Warren despises the Boers.'

James leaned back against the seat. 'What other surprises have you for me?'

She told him about a letter from his aunt Mary that had taken months to reach Cape Town and gave him the news about Marthinus's deportation to St Helena. 'Some very good news, though. Your cousin Rudolf is alive, but he's also on his way home. There was a mix-up with the wounded—'

'I saw him,' he said, avoiding her eyes. 'So did George Hunter.'

They travelled in silence, looking out at the wet, miserable day. When they turned into Bathurst Drive, he said, 'Victoria, I'm sorry about the child.' It was not enough, but it was all he could manage. 'Would you like to go back to Durban? Shall I take you there?'

'No, thank you all the same. I'm going to rent a house with Mrs Butcher, outside the city. You're welcome to join me. The choice is yours.'

He sighed inwardly with relief: she had forgiven him. Now it was up to him to make amends. When they reached the gates, he asked, 'Where's Radford? I've had no news, no letters from him since he left. It's been weeks now.'

'James, you weren't to know of this, but Peter escorted Stefanie to Port Elizabeth. No one has heard of either of them since.'

A COUPLE OF MILES outside Kroonstad the train slowed down to round a bend. Letting go of the side, Peter gathered himself into a bundle. He hit the ground and rolled into a thorn bush, gasping as a sharp pain shot through his shoulder and hip. He rose inch by inch, tested his legs and felt his shoulder. *Nothing broken, but I'll be black and bruised for days to come. A hat! A bloody hat.* He cursed wildly.

Hours later, he trudged back into the station. Huge fires lit up the night. Vehicles struggled through the muddy mess that once was the main road. A Cape cart was stuck, the horses neighing, mouths foaming. He watched as a few men lifted the cart clear and set it on its way. Wagons piled with crates of Mauser ammunition barred his way, the oxen straining under their loads. People were milling about a store that was being looted.

Riders approached at a fast gallop, holding wounded to their saddles. A white horse, blood staining its neck, the rider hanging on, passed inches from him. He watched as they swung to their right and headed for a church where the Red Cross wagons were now parked.

Weaving his way through vehicles, people and animals, he found the trap. It was deserted, the mule unharnessed, standing a few yards off. Only their blankets and his small bag were still in the back. He was about to take his bag when he saw her coming towards him, her *kappie* hanging down her back, the green hat clasped in her hands. He felt relief at having found her, anger at her foolish act, and tenderness as she fought back tears. Love surged like a powerful current through his heart and he was still searching for words when she spoke, hiding behind her flippant manner.

'What took you so long?'

'I got off at the wrong station. Had to walk a good few miles.' They stood a few moments before he spoke again. 'And now that you have your hat, how do you propose we get out of here?'

She lifted her chin, but her hands fidgeted with the hat. 'I was ... going to steal a horse ... and catch up with you and the train ...'

'So? There are plenty of horses, saddled up. Couldn't you find one with a side-saddle?' he asked, returning her flippancy.

'I'm so sorry, Peter,' she half-sobbed. 'I'm so very sorry—'

He pulled her into his arms. 'There's no need to cry.'

'I will cry if I want to. I thought you were going on without me.'

'Where to?' he asked against her cheek. 'But why the silly hat? It's just a hat.'

'The hat?' She kept her face against his shoulder. 'Not the hat, Peter. My people ... seeing them there at the station, all broken and bloodied. Oh, Peter, I've caused them ... my family, such sorrow. I want to be worthy of them. I thought about my father and my brothers fighting back there ...'

'The man you recognised, the one with the wounded, is he one of your family?'

'Yes, it was Charles.'

'Charles? Was he with the wounded?' He thought how difficult it must have been for her, getting on the train while Charles was only a few feet away. 'So you jumped off to get to him? Have you lost him, then?'

'No, he's at the church with the wounded. I went there, stood by the gate. He's frightfully busy, there are so many wounded.'

He stroked her back, trying to give her some comfort while scanning the turmoil around them. He could not stay a moment longer, but neither did he want to leave her to fend for herself. 'Stefanie, you'll be safe with the Red Cross. Come, I'll take you there ...'

'No, there's nothing I can do there. I'll only be in the way. I'm going on.'

'I have a much better chance of getting away on my own.'

'On your own?' She pulled away. 'And leave me here stranded in the middle of winter, the war coming ever closer?'

He gathered her back into his arms, kissing her long and hard. 'Come, let's get out of here.'

———

WHEN THE NEWS reached Martin that the last train had left the previous night, he called his men together and set off for Kroonstad. It was dusk when they stumbled into the town only to find it abandoned, the stores looted and huge piles of supplies aflame. The retreating commandos had taken what they could and set fire to the rest.

'*Got*,' said Jan Viljoen as he scanned the destruction around him. 'What a terrible waste.'

'Better wasted than falling into enemy hands,' Joep Maree said, stuffing a few tins of condensed milk into his saddlebag.

'We won't be able to hold them back,' Frans Viljoen said.

'Then let them drive us all the way to the Transvaal,' Gert Vermaas cried. 'I refuse to fight for these bloody Free Staters. They almost had us caught again today!'

'And while they run away and return to their farms, we have to clear their country of the *Engelse*. I've had enough; I'm going home,' Hans Ferreira grumbled.

'That Lord Roberts is driving his men just as hard as he is driving us,' Jan said. 'We have horses, but those poor foot soldiers, marching in the dust and fighting ...'

'Stop feeling sorry for the bloody *Engelse*!' Frans shouted. 'They are going to take our farms if we don't stop them now, before they reach the Vaal River!'

'Yes, they are driving us to Johannesburg and the gold mines. But then we will be on our own soil. We will make a stand there,' Martin said.

'See what food you can find. We have to move soon.'

Some men dismounted and searched through the piles for tinned food and whatever else had not been destroyed. An argument broke out over a pair of riding boots and soon developed into a fistfight.

'Leave it!' Martin ordered sharply. The men's nerves were frayed; they had been fighting from the saddle for days and the humiliation of the retreat was not easy to bear. Defeat hung heavy over them, weariness in every line of their faces, in the exhausted slump of their shoulders and in the stumbling gait of their horses. He called a few men together. 'Go to the railway. Ammunition is bound to be left there. Take all you can carry!'

His eyes travelled over the ravaged town. Broken-down and abandoned carts and wagons, a lame horse, a few exhausted mules and, here and there, stray sheep huddled together against the cold, dogs searching the rubble. There were still some civilians, darting through the destruction, disappearing into the side streets. His eyes came to rest on the church and then he saw Charles's ambulance coming towards the station. Charles was leading his mules, Lady tethered to the side. He rode up to him and dismounted.

'You told me to wait here,' Charles smiled and shook Martin's hand. 'I knew you would come, and come through safely. Any more wounded?'

'A few, not seriously. What happened here?' Martin asked despondently. 'The enemy is not even within reach ...'

'Yes, it was chaos. Hardly had President Steyn's train pulled away last night than panic ensued. The town emptied through the day; most wagons and livestock have gone east. The Red Cross wagons left in the late afternoon, also heading east. I've sent the wounded with them to nearby farms. They're safe there, I hope. I scrounged around,' he jerked his head, indicating his ambulance. 'Meal, tinned fruit and meat, blankets, some potatoes, bags of beans ... such chaos, Martin ... women and children ... I found some oranges too. The men need fresh food ...'

Martin did not interrupt Charles's monologue. That he was exhausted, on the brink of collapse was all too clear – the grey, haggard face, the stooped shoulders, the need to talk. He took Charles to where the commando was now loosely gathered, awaiting his orders. He led them out of town, rode a few miles on and found a place to off-saddle for the night. No one bothered to make a fire. They opened tins with their knives, ate the food cold and slept with their heads on their saddles.

The next day, Martin took the commando to the Renoster River, twenty miles north of Kroonstad. A week later, they were still resting, waiting. The scouts reported Lord Roberts was delayed at Kroonstad, as his troops were too exhausted to carry on and the railway line had been blown up ahead of the army.

CHARLES RODE INTO CAMP. It was late afternoon. He had just returned from visiting a nearby farm to see a few wounded he had sent there. The camp was a welcome sight – the first place they had stayed in for more than a week since the big retreat began. Fires were burning, the smell of coffee was in the air, the men sitting close to the fires to ward off the chill of the approaching night. He saw Martin and the field cornets huddled in a circle and wondered if they would be on the move soon.

He looked at the men gathered around Martin: older men, many years Martin's senior, their faces attentive and respectful. He was the youngest of them all, yet he was the one they put their trust in, the one they followed into battle. It was his belief in his own ability that made him such a remarkable leader, Charles had come to believe, but how long would he be able to stand the pressure of retreat?

It was dark when the meeting broke up and the officers dispersed. Martin, Joep Maree and the Viljoens joined Charles at the fire. Since taking command, Martin's only fireside companions were Joep and the Viljoens. Joep shielded Martin from those who needlessly bothered him with small worries. Charles was well aware of the respect and affection Martin felt for his father-in-law. Now that Marthinus was a prisoner, Joep guided him, gave him hope, was a father to him.

'The scouts have reported that the British are moving out tomorrow, Charles,' Martin said. 'We will not make a stand until we get to the Vaal River. You will have to get moving before daybreak or else you will fall behind.'

They threw more wood on the fire. The first stirring of the night wind rustled the low bush around them. They helped themselves to food from the communal pot. The waning moon rose and the men talked about the winter crops that should have been sown by now.

'Buks will cope with the sowing,' Joep said. 'His wound must be healed now. Some cattle must be taken to market ...'

A figure loomed up in the pale moonlight. Karel stood, arms akimbo. 'I told you he was alive. But you knew better, didn't you? Laughed behind my back! Said I was crazy. My brother is alive. Charles, I told you all the time that I could feel he's alive. I was right.'

'Ai, he's really gone this time,' Joep sighed.

Charles looked closely at Karel. He was clean-shaven, his hair trimmed and his eyes had lost their haunted look.

'Don't look at me like that! I haven't gone mad. Rudi was only wounded.

I found him in Bloemfontein.'

Jan Viljoen rose. '*Got*, Karel de Winter, where's your twin? Show him to us!'

Rudolf stepped into the firelight. The Viljoens backed away as though they were seeing an apparition from another world. Martin gaped, mug halfway to his mouth.

'Martin, Uncle Joep. Charles,' Rudolf called them by their names. 'Jan, Frans, Jacob.' And still they stared. 'I'm not a ghost.'

'Great merciful God!' Jan spread his arms wide. 'It's truly him.' Martin stepped forward, held Rudolf at arm's length and then embraced him, holding him long and hard.

Charles could not utter a word. Images raced through his mind – of Annecke and Rudolf kissing at the waterfall, of Martin telling the men about the son he was expecting, of Karel pleading with him to believe that Rudi was alive. Then Rudolf was standing in front of him, smiling sadly. 'I'm sorry I gave you such a fright, Charles,' he said. Charles wordlessly put out his hands and Rudolf came into his arms.

'It was so terrible, Charles,' he whispered into his neck. 'I nearly died, Charles.'

He passed Rudolf on to Joep and the Viljoen brothers, all of them holding him, slapping his back, finding their voices again. Word spread down the line and men came to see for themselves. Lady was brought and there were few dry eyes as they watched the reunion between Rudolf and his mare.

Rudolf told of the day at the river, his mistaken identity, the time in hospital and about his wounds. Karel told how Rudolf had found him after recognising Legend, and how they had slipped through the British lines.

'How did you get to us?' Frans Viljoen asked.

'Oom Koos told us where to find you.' Karel smiled at Martin. 'Fine sentries you put out.'

It took some time for the upheaval to die down. When the men drifted back to their fires, still talking about Rudolf's miraculous escape, Karel extracted a bottle from his saddlebag. 'Jan Viljoen, compliments of Lord Roberts!'

'Aha, my good friend!' Jan took the bottle in both hands. 'I knew you would not come empty-handed. It's been a long time since Jan Viljoen has had some brandy to comfort him.' He threw the dregs of his coffee on the ground, filled his mug halfway before passing the bottle on to Martin. 'We must have a *sopie*, as tomorrow we fight again. Rudolf, did you see my wounded *Engelsman* in Cape Town?'

'Yes, I saw James and his friend Peter Radford from the window. Both with new medals on their jackets. But of course I couldn't speak to James. It wouldn't have been fair on him to know that I was there as one of them. His wife helped me to get away.'

'Victoria?' Martin looked up, surprised. 'How did she help you?'

Rudolf looked into the fire. 'I went to Stefanie, but she was in Port Elizabeth. Victoria recognised me as a De Winter and offered to help me. I reminded her of you, she said.'

'So you've not come across Stefanie at all, Rudi?' Charles asked, attempting to change the subject as Martin had gone quiet, busying himself with the coffee pot. But Jan Viljoen only aggravated things. Satisfied that Rudolf had told him all about James's wounds, he wanted to know about Victoria.

'Now tell me, Rudolf, tell me about James's wife, what colour is her hair?'

'Her hair, Jan?' Rudolf frowned. 'Well, sort of gold ... not fair, more red I'd say.'

'Ah! I knew James would marry wisely.' Jan smacked his lips, swigging more brandy. 'Women with light hair need to be pampered and spoiled, make men slaves to their whims. The dark-haired ones, like my Hannie, they're the best, see to a man's comforts, breed strong children. But a red-head? She puts fire into a man's belly. A fire that never dies down. And does a man not need that in times of war?'

'He hasn't been home for months,' Joep slapped Jan's knee. 'Give him brandy and all he thinks of is his wife's bed.'

They talked for a while longer. Charles noticed that Karel was well again, but Rudolf was not the same. He stared into the fire, his eyes dispirited. When Martin suggested that the two of them should go to Wintersrust and set their mother's mind at ease, he shook his head numbly.

Karel pulled Rudolf to his feet. 'Come Rudi, we have miles to ride back. Captain Theron wants us before the English move. Jan Viljoen,' he said in parting, 'Do you want to know what the khakis are singing down there? "We are marching to Pretoria, Pretoria ..."'

'Could I have a word before you go?' Charles asked.

Rudolf held Charles's eyes for a long moment. 'If it's my scars you want to see, could it wait till tomorrow?'

Charles nodded. The twins did not want to discuss Annecke with him. He had failed them when they had needed him most. *I have to get to Annecke, have to get to her first*, he realised. *Oh dear God, what is to happen now?*

MARTIN CRAWLED into his blanket roll. The night was cold and lonely. It needed just one word, a small flame, a flicker, and the smouldering fire flared up and devoured the defences and healing that time had brought. Her hair, her beautiful hair. *Will I ever be free of her memory? Does she ever think of me? Of the night we loved so completely?*

A Fairy Tale

THE OVERCROWDED TRAIN laboured through the outskirts of Johannesburg. Peter had his arms around a sleeping Stefanie, cushioning her against the jolting and jarring. Through the dust and soot, she looked exhausted. Her clothes were dirty, the skirt torn at the hem and she had lost a heel of one of her scuffed boots.

There had been many riderless horses in the confusion in Kroonstad, but Stefanie had refused to steal from her people. They quarrelled heatedly about this and in the end she convinced a Boer to take fifty pounds for his two packhorses. They caught up with the train late the next day where it had halted at a siding. At the Transvaal border, they spent days at the station and lost their bags and blankets. Trains came in from Natal, but they were crowded with wounded. At last they managed to find space on an open truck with other refugees. And now, two weeks after they had left Bloemfontein, they were arriving far north of their destination, battered and exhausted.

He caught her hat as it slipped from her hand and wondered again why it was so important to her. There was nothing extraordinary about it, just a green felt hat, crushed and dirty now. Then he noticed where the lining had been sewn by a less expert hand. His fingers travelled inside the crown; it was not smooth. Money perhaps? No, she had a purse concealed in the folds of her skirt. He remembered snatches of conversation regarding her loyalty to her people, and a strong suspicion formed in his mind. Her husband was working with the British and she had been in a great hurry to get away from Cape Town.

He looked at the hat again. Needle and thread. The lining could easily be sewn back.

The train stuttered to a halt. Stefanie woke with difficulty, rubbed her eyes. He handed her the hat and jumped onto the platform. She struggled down into his outstretched arms. The few people who disembarked stayed close to the trucks. Some prepared to settle on the platform for the night.

Stefanie made inquiries and was told that the train would take on water and fuel and leave for Pretoria in the morning.

They stood in silence.

'There'll be other trains,' she said.

'There always will be other trains.'

He took her hand. They walked away from the station, Stefanie limping on her uneven boots. Darkness fell, and a cold wind picked up. The bright lights were gone, as if a curtain had been drawn over the city.

Peter asked a passer-by whether the Heights Hotel was open and was informed that it was the only establishment still operating. They hurried along, but as they were about to enter Stefanie stopped short.

'I'm not going in there.'

'What? I could sleep for a week if only I could find a decent bed.'

'I know exactly where to find one. It's a long walk. Come.'

'No, I've stayed at this hotel before and—'

'So have I. The management will recognise me. Oh, do come on, Peter!' She pulled him by the arm. 'I'm so very, very tired and hungry.'

'You can't be serious. Concerned about your reputation at a time like this!'

'Peter, they might let my husband know my whereabouts. He'll find a way to fetch me back. They might even lock me up until he arrives here.'

'But surely you told him that you were going home?'

'No, I did not!' She gathered her skirt and walked away with purposeful strides.

After a few wrong turns and the better part of an hour, Stefanie found the house she was looking for. 'Mr Charles Leonard's house,' she said. 'I played here a few times. He won't mind if we use it for a night. They're in Cape Town.'

They kept to the trees bordering the driveway, making their way to the house. The front door was barred with wooden beams, as were all the downstairs windows. They examined every possible way in and decided on the kitchen window. He forced the shutters open, smashed the glass and lifted the catch. Once inside, he felt through his pocket for matches and spotted a lamp. After some spluttering, the wick caught. They looked around the large kitchen. All appeared normal, as if the household had retired early for the night.

'At least we won't starve.' Peter pointed to the bottled fruit, tinned food and bottles of wine on the shelves.

They followed a passage leading to the reception rooms. There was a dining room on the one side and a drawing room on the other, the furniture covered in dustsheets.

350

He looked about the room. 'I suppose I could make a fire. Are you cold?' 'Not cold, but hungry,' she mumbled.

He went to the kitchen, taking the lamp with him. He found a sharp knife and opened a tinned ham. When he arrived back, she was curled up on the couch, fast asleep. He put a cushion under her head, covered her with the dustsheets and then made a place for himself on the floor next to the couch. Before his head touched the cushion, he was asleep.

THE FOLLOWING MORNING, Peter went into town to assess the situation. Stefanie sat at the kitchen table, her face in her hands. She had refused to go with him; it was so hostile and cold outside. She was tired of running. The madness of the retreat had led them here, to this house. Here Peter would be safe. Here he would love her. And here she would leave him. She had found love, an impossible love.

She looked at her green hat on the table. She could not, did not, want to deceive Peter for another day. All the information she'd stolen from Paul's study over the weeks of waiting to leave Cape Town was still secure in the lining of the hat. She had memorised it all while waiting in the boarding house in Bloemfontein. Tomorrow she would go to Pretoria. She did not want to be a lone mare running in the wrong direction any longer. Martin would be proud of her.

Stealing from Paul had made her feel worthy. Martin's life was constantly in danger, and the little danger while sneaking around in Paul's study was not even comparable. And, while frantically copying Paul's papers, a new feeling had caught at her senses – the challenge of danger, of the unknown. It had been intoxicating.

Being with Peter kindled the same feeling. In a few hours she would face the unknown again, but the danger would be in not disclosing her love for him. Pretending was hard, but not impossible.

She went upstairs and wandered through the rooms. She found the master bedroom at the far end of the passage. The large bed had pillows and folded blankets on it. A longing to sleep invaded her, but then she caught sight of herself in a mirror.

She turned away in disgust and hurried to where she had seen a bathroom. The taps emitted a harsh gurgle, but soon the water ran clear. It was icy, but she scrubbed herself until her skin glowed red and her hair felt straight and clean. She kicked at the dirty clothes on the floor, picked up her hat, went back to the bedroom. There were men's clothes in the first wardrobe she opened. She tried the next one and found a few dresses. A white silk dress with a low neckline caught her eye. She spread it out on the bed. Mrs Leonard was a good bit rounder than she was, but it would have to do. Her eyes went to the bed.

Perfect. She felt the now familiar desire rushing through her body.

PETER ARRIVED BACK after dark. He slipped through the kitchen window, left his parcel on the table, and felt his way down the passage to the drawing room. As he passed the dining room, he stopped in surprise. The far end of the table was set for two, and a candle in an ornate holder flickered over silverware and glasses. A bottle of wine was uncorked, slices of canned meat, preserved vegetables and fruit arranged on a platter. There was light coming from the drawing room. He was about to rush in, but pulled up at the door.

Stefanie stood next to the piano. Candlelight caught the golden lights in her hair, falling free and soft to her waist. A white veil tumbled down her back, transfiguring the plain dress into a wedding gown. The dress only reached her ankles, exposing her bare feet. She was beautiful, utterly desirable.

'A bride, or Cinderella who has lost both slippers?' He crossed the few paces that separated them, took her hand and kissed her fingers.

'Cinderella was a bride on the day the lusty prince carried her off. At least, so the story goes. Will you be my lusty prince or is it back to my wicked stepmother for me?'

His heart told him that what he felt for her was too special, too dear, to be ruined by one forbidden night of love. Yet he dared not tell her that he was hopelessly in love with her, but her unambiguous invitation left him powerless.

She brushed her hand across his clean-shaven chin and trimmed hair. 'I see you managed to find a barber at last.'

'Yes, and a hot bath at the Heights Hotel. But that's not all I found. One moment!' He hastened to the kitchen and arrived back, holding out a bottle of champagne.

She clapped her hands. 'Oh, Peter, we haven't had any since Bloemfontein. Open it immediately!'

'Such an impatient bride. First I have to transform myself into a lusty prince. I do hope there's something upstairs that I can wear to suit the occasion.'

'You'll find clothes, but the shoes won't fit.' She pointed to her bare feet.

At the stairs, he hesitated. The needle and thread he had bought felt heavy in his pocket. He half-turned and smiled at her. 'Stefanie, whatever happens tomorrow or in the future, just know that I've had a splendid time the past two months, unforgettable.'

'Yes, unforgettable.' She waved him upstairs.

In the bedroom he saw Stefanie's dirty clothes in a corner of the room, the green hat on top of the pile. With shaking hands he undid the lining and found a sheaf of pressed papers. He scanned them hastily and swore, astounded.

A while later he returned downstairs, dressed in a black evening suit. It was wide around his shoulders and waist, the trousers and sleeves a good six inches too short. She gave him an appraising look, but soon they were laughing, excited by the promise of what was to come.

He uncorked the champagne and handed her a glass. She raised it in a toast. 'We only have till midnight.'

He brought a strand of her hair to his lips. 'I've heard that Lord Roberts reached the border—'

She placed her fingers on his mouth. 'Oh, Peter, let's pretend that we are in a different country, that there's no war. Tonight we shall be merry.'

'And in love? So the story goes.'

She smiled. 'Yes! So the story goes. Oh, let's dance!'

He put the glasses on a side table and made a formal bow. 'A waltz? Shall I sing?'

'No need to sing. I've arranged musicians,' she said grandly, went to a dresser and opened the lid of a large music box. The room filled with tinkling notes. 'Come, have a look. It has these perforated discs. I found six of them. Bits of popular melodies. Mozart, Liszt and Chopin's Nocturne. Do you remember the Nocturne? I played it at the hospital.'

'The piece with ... what was it again? Oh yes! Longing. It has a certain *longing* in it, but what for, you never told me.' He found the answer in her eyes. They sparkled with love as she held out her dress and returned his invitation to dance with a curtsy.

And while they were laughing, dancing and sipping champagne, he kissed her gently, the fire of their previous encounters under control. When his lips touched the bare skin below her collarbone, she took his face in her hands and turned it towards the dining room.

Throughout the meal, they pretended they were at a wedding feast. He saw his desire reflected in her face and wanted nothing more to keep them from going upstairs.

He drained his glass. 'Come, my beautiful bride, it's almost twelve.'

'Do you believe in fairy tales, Peter?' She drank the last of her wine in a gulp.

He gave a surprised laugh. 'No, I don't think I do, never did as a child.'

'Tonight ... well, tonight you'll find one to be true.'

'Will I?' He looked at her curiously and burst out laughing. 'Right.

Cinderella was a bride. Up to midnight. And that's the game we're playing tonight?' He wound his hands into her long hair, pulling her head back, his mouth moving down her neck to her shoulders.

She pulled free and ran up the stairs. 'I refuse to be seduced on the staircase like a servant girl.'

'Seduce?' He laughed, catching up with her. 'Never was there a bride more eager to be seduced.' He swept her up in his arms. 'The bit where I carry you over the threshold?'

He shouldered the door open and then they were rolling on the bed, still laughing and kissing while he undressed her. Her naked skin was alive against him, inflaming his already overwhelmed senses. She was eager, kissing him with unrestrained passion, but her sharp cries of surprise when his hands and mouth found the secret parts of her body made it clear that the fairy tale was true. He froze and lifted his head, his breath wild as he searched her face.

'Good God, I do *not* believe this! You're married, for heaven's sake.'

'In name only, Peter.' She sought for his mouth, but he tore himself away.

'No, Stefanie, no.' He moved off her. 'I don't dare do this.'

'But you want me, don't you?' she said, hurt strong in her voice. 'You said you wanted me. More than anything in the world.'

His mind was in a tumult. Moments before, he had been prepared to spend the night loving her and to deal with his feelings later, but what she wanted him to do now would forge a bond between them that would last forever. And what he had found in the lining of her hat could not be ignored. But her eyes imprisoned him, and the ridiculous veil still fastened to her hair held him fast.

'What you want me to do can never be undone,' he said at last.

'I know. But it has to be you.'

He looked into her eyes, tearful a second ago, but now blazing with determination. He pushed her back on the pillows, but still he hesitated, fighting his conscience. 'Is this what you really want, Stefanie?'

'If you refuse me now ... I will want to die ...'

He kissed her long and tenderly, but his mind raced ahead. Brides were supposed to be meek, scared, but she was eager and passionate. Keeping his mouth crushed to hers, he drove into her. He held still, afraid that he had been too brutal. But she clung to him, her legs tightening around his waist. Astounded at the passion he had released, and swept away by the raw intensity of emotions, he moved with her until her wild cries subsided into sobs.

With returning calm, awareness of their incongruous situation came back to him. *What have you done, Radford?* he cursed himself. *War, love, an enemy informer, a married woman.*

She sat up, pushing her hair from her face. Her lips were parted, her eyes bright, her breath still racing. 'Why didn't you say it would be so wonderful, so intense, so powerful?'

'I thought you knew. You certainly gave the impression you did.'

'Do you remember the day in hospital, when I kissed you? That's when I knew it had to be you.'

He looked at her warily. *Please don't say it, don't say you love me, I don't want to hear it, there's too much at stake.*

'You told me about danger, the exhilaration, cavalry charges. You said, a physical thrill, intense and rewarding.'

'And? That's why?' he asked relieved and disappointed. 'Is that why you wanted me? Was this like that for you?'

'Oh yes! A cavalry charge, I suppose. Not knowing what's ahead.'

He broke into wild laughter and pulled her down. 'One gets addicted to cavalry charges, I've also warned you!' He placed his face in the hollow of her shoulder and refused to think beyond the moment. *Tomorrow looks after itself, it always has.*

The Seasons of War

KOBA'S EYES STRAYED out of the window towards the ridges south of Pretoria as she worked the dough at her kitchen table. It was late afternoon, the wind fresh and cold. She thought about the men having to sleep out in the open veld. There would be many coughs and fevers to see to once they arrived. Men had already come through. To arrange things, they said to those who asked them for news of the commandos. They were making their way back to their farms, she reckoned. Their courage had failed them. She'd seen it in their averted eyes.

But courage in war was like the seasons of nature. Now was deep winter, in nature and in the war. Only the brave would weather it.

A familiar voice broke into her thoughts.

'Tante Koba, I've come home.'

She stared at Stefanie open-mouthed, taking in the tattered dress, the dirty green hat and the sad face. '*Hartjie*, how on earth?' She advanced with open arms, flour up to her elbows.

'I came by train,' Stefanie smiled, but no sooner was she in her arms than she burst into heaving sobs.

'There, there, *hartjie*, cry all you want.' Koba rocked her in her arms and let her cry for a while. 'You can tell me everything when you have had a strong cup of tea. Come, *hartjie*, come sit here.'

She filled the teapot and put out the cups, the ones with the blue delft pattern on them. Stefanie picked up a cup and traced the two entwined birds in the pattern with her finger. A fresh outburst of tears poured down her cheeks.

'I've left my husband, Tante Koba. Martin is right: Paul is working against us.' She spoke about her loveless marriage, about Peter, their trip to Johannesburg and of the previous night that they had spent together.

Koba listened to every word and to the words that were not uttered. She patted Stefanie's hands, stroked her hair and poured more tea. 'How could he do this to you, *hartjie*? Then he's not your husband. You did right; you had to leave. And now we will find a way to fix everything. We'll think what to do about that nice young man, Peter. He might be a lord and an enemy, but then, love is stronger than war and war doesn't last.'

Stefanie wiped her tears, lifted her chin. 'How is everyone at Wintersrust?'

She cradled Stefanie close and gave her the news of her father's fate. She told her that Martin was commandant now, feared and fearless. They talked about Rudolf's death and of the men of the district who had died.

'I saw our people running before the enemy,' Stefanie said. 'There are thousands of English coming this way, Tante Koba. Can we get to Wintersrust while there is still time?'

'No, we won't flee. They're only men making war and will do us no harm, *hartjie*. There's much cooking and baking to be done. Martin and his men will arrive on my doorstep, hungry and worn-out. Tomorrow I'll get Bontes to slaughter two sheep and some of the hens. This morning I baked four batches of rusks. The dough for the next lot is just about done. Go have a wash. Rest a while. You'll feel so much better then.'

STEFANIE WENT UPSTAIRS to her old room and flung herself on the bed. The pattern on Koba's delft china was so familiar, but, with her body still inundated with Peter's lovemaking, it stabbed through her heart. Koba had told the story of the two doves many times. Lovers were forbidden to love, but their love was so deep, so great, that, when they died of broken hearts, God granted them eternal love. They came back to earth as doves – lovebirds, Koba called them – a symbol of hope to those who were thus bereft on earth. The war would end; Peter would go to India, their night of love a memory that would fade with time.

She needed to be worth something now, needed her people, her brothers, to be proud of her. She picked up the battered green hat and tore the lining. There was only a folded sheet of newspaper – a Johannesburg paper, the date recent.

OVER THE FOLLOWING TWO DAYS, Stefanie helped prepare pots of mutton stew and baked bread and rusks. Later that night, they settled in the sitting room with a cup of tea. Now they were spooning Koba's cough and fever remedy from a brown earthenware pot into small bottles.

Koba stilled Stefanie's hand. '*Hartjie*, when is your monthly due?'

Stefanie looked up, puzzled. 'Started this morning. You know that I'm always regular. Just like the moon, you always say.'

'That's good, *hartjie*. If you were carrying Peter's baby, there'd be no way to explain this, as your husband has never loved you.'

'Tante Koba, I never gave it a moment's thought!'

'A woman's body is much like a flower, *hartjie* – first the bud, then the bloom, and then the flower dies. That's when your monthlies start and the whole cycle is repeated. Always remember that. The seed takes in the middle week, when it's in bloom …'

There was a knock on the door. Stefanie rushed to open it, ready to throw herself into Martin's arms, but it was not Martin who stood in the door. 'Charles? Oh Charles, is it truly you? Tante Koba! It's Charles!'

Charles was taken aback at seeing her, but before he could comment he disappeared into Koba's huge embrace. She kissed him on his cheeks and held him at arm's length. 'My dear little doctor. Just look at you – so thin and tired. And the sun has turned you into a real Boer.'

'Yes, just look at him.' Stefanie took in the tweed trousers and blue collarless shirt, which made an odd contrast with the slouch hat.

Koba pulled him to the kitchen with Stefanie following. 'The poor dear is on the brink of collapse for want of food. Where are the others, *hartjie*? Will they be in tonight?' Koba set a heaped plate in front of Charles.

'They should be here in a few days. I came by train.' Charles told them about the progress of the Rustenburg commando. 'Martin has sent Uncle Joep and Gert Vermaas to the supply stores for ammunition. I was ordered to secure the medical supplies and take them to the district.'

'To the district?' Stefanie asked. 'Won't they be needed here? Especially now?'

'It was decided to hand Pretoria over intact. Oom Paul is on his way to Delagoa Bay.' Charles wiped his mouth on the napkin. 'How strange to sit at a table again, I shall have to recall my manners—'

'Charles,' Stefanie said. 'If you talk like that, there's something important you want to tell us. *Please* don't keep us waiting.'

'It's not proper? It's so good to see you, Stefanie. I've missed you.' He took the tray with the coffee cups from Koba and led the way to the sitting room. 'I have news, but before I tell it we have to be seated comfortably.'

'We've all but lost the war and you sit there with that silly grin on your face,' Stefanie said and poured the coffee.

He took their hands in his and told them about Rudolf's miraculous escape.

The women stared at him. A picture of the wounded at Kroonstad filled Stefanie's mind. An image of James, on the night they had brought him to Cape Town, came unbidden to her. His face, his beautiful face, was white.

The pain he suffered, shaking with fever and pain, muttering things. And Peter. He was barely alive when she found him there. She shivered, covered her face with her hands and fled upstairs.

KOBA SAT MOTIONLESS, her hands open in her lap. 'Annecke and Rudolf ...'

Charles put his arm around her shoulders and told her how he had found Rudolf's knife and the unopened note in Karel's pocket. 'When I handed the knife back to Karel, he asked for the note. They refuse to discuss Annecke with me. It's sad to see the two of them now, full of fear that a bullet might separate them again. Oh, Tante Koba, why has this happened?'

'One of God's cruel reminders ...' Koba tut-tutted and patted his hand. 'My three little ones, how they suffer. And Martin, my golden boy. How we have deceived him, Annecke and I. And her heart is just beginning to heal and now ...' her voice tailed off into silence.

'Martin thinks the baby is his.'

'Yes, he does. Would he have married her, knowing that she was with Rudolf's child? Martin, like dear James, will not be second choice.' She lowered her voice. 'Martin and James's wife. Yes, I know. Martin was sick. Fever and exhaustion. Annecke was watching over him. He cried for Victoria in his delirium, she tells me. My heart says that James doesn't know about that.'

'Yes, Tante Koba. He doesn't know.' He removed his glasses and rubbed his eyes. 'If Annecke wants Rudi to know about the baby, then so be it.'

'No, no, *hartjie*, this has to stay secret, for Martin's sake. And the war, *hartjie*, maybe the war will decide for Annecke, for Victoria.'

———

ANNECKE WAS PUTTING the last stitches to a rag doll she had made for her baby when Danie Vermaas came riding up with the news of Rudolf. She could not think for some time. She just stood there, joy flooding through her. Rudi was alive. Rudi was coming home.

And then reality hit her.

Not even Koba would be able to get her out of this predicament. The English, Danie said, had surrounded Pretoria. Koba could not come to her. But Martin could. She had deceived him, lied to him. He would not forgive her or Rudi. They had both deceived him. If only she could see Rudi first. He would not think her a traitor to their love.

She clutched the rag doll to her chest, and then started walking to the vlei, her eyes on the big willow. She walked slowly against the cold winter wind that had sprung up from the north, her mind empty of all thoughts except the sad song in her little music box.

'I know the end of the story now, Rudi,' she whispered. 'The soldier did come back; she didn't wait long enough.'

She reached the willow and clung to its trunk. The baby kicked sharply against her heart. Pain rose up from her chest, tore at her throat. The doll slipped from her hands, rolling down the bank into the muddy water. She raised her face to the sky, her tear-filled eyes searching despairingly.

She saw the doll sink in the water. The eyes and mouth she had worked with such care smiled up at her. She struggled down the slippery bank, her hands anxiously reaching for the doll. The water reached her knees, her dress dragged at her legs. Her feet slipped and she fell heavily into the water. Clutching the doll to her breast, she tried to get to the bank, but her feet could not get a hold on the mud.

Through the panic rising in her head, she heard the familiar voice of Old Klaas herding the cattle to the vlei. Her fingers grasped through the mud and she clutched at some reeds. She tried to call Old Klaas, but her voice was hoarse and forlorn.

———◆———

MARTIN AND THE RUSTENBURG MEN watched the British army rolling relentlessly towards Pretoria. Waves of despair engulfed him. He longed to be far away, free from the fear eating inside him, the fear of the future. He turned his eyes to his men. While many burghers had drifted back to their farm, his commando was still strong. But he knew that they could easily leave. Like actors in a play waiting for the cue to tell them that the show was over, the curtain would come down and they could go home. Following General de Wet's example, he told them to go to their farms, have a rest and to meet him in a month's time in Rustenburg. He raised his hat in greeting when they filed past.

With effort he pulled himself together and turned to get his horse. He found his brothers waiting for him, holding the horse.

'Roast leg of lamb and buttered potatoes,' Karel said.

'Steamed pudding and custard,' added Rudolf.

Martin's spirit lifted at the thought of Koba's kitchen. 'Milk tart and decent coffee.'

They started laughing, uncertainly at first, but then louder. Swinging their Mausers across their backs, they mounted and raced towards Pretoria.

They slowed down once they reached the Fountains. There were hundreds of people and all sorts of vehicles piled high as families tried to leave the city before the British forces arrived.

In the dying light of day, the city centre was an ugly sight. Shops were being looted, windows broken and doors pulled off their hinges. They wove their way through the chaos to the railway station. The government stores were wide open, and men were loading wagons, carts and wheelbarrows with provisions meant for the fighting burghers.

'You have to stop this, Martin,' Rudolf said.

'No!' Karel said. 'Why should we leave it to the English?'

'You're right. Why should we leave it to the English?' Martin said, and turned his horse to go.

'Tante Koba will get her share as well.' Karel flew off Legend and ran across the street. He grabbed two bags, heaving them onto his shoulders. Soon Rudolf joined in and they led their horses home loaded with loot.

At Koba's house, Rudolf hung back. Martin took Lady's reins and told Rudolf to go ahead. 'I asked Charles to warn Tante Koba. Go now.'

STEFANIE HEARD HER BROTHERS' VOICES in the dark as they dismounted. She waited for Martin in the front room, a lamp in her hand. But it was one of the twins who pushed the door open. She stood rooted: this was not her little brother, but a man, bandolier across his chest, a rifle gleaming dully behind his shoulder.

They were still staring at each other when Koba steamed towards Rudolf with open arms. She held him at arm's length, scrutinising his face and gently touching the scar on his temple, tears flowing down her cheeks.

'Please, Tante Koba, don't cry.' Rudolf smiled, but was as overcome as Koba.

Stefanie stood with the lamp still in her hands when Martin and Karel entered through the back door and stopped in their tracks when they saw her. If the change in Rudolf had been a shock, Martin appeared to be a stranger. He was no longer youthful, with lines on his forehead and down the sides of his mouth. Karel was as tall as Martin, his face and hair streaked with grime and soot.

'I was so wrong, Martin, I'm sorry,' she said.

'Have you come home? Home to us?'

She put down the lamp and nodded.

'Don't be too hasty, Martin,' Karel said, his eyes hostile. 'I saw her in Bloemfontein. Oh yes, I saw you with Peter Radford. Rudi saw you in Cape

Town, walking arm in arm. Tell me, sister, have you come to spy for them? Did they send you ahead?'

'Karel, Peter Radford took me to Bloemfontein. I couldn't travel unescorted.'

'And what did you give him in return?' Karel brushed past her to greet Koba.

Stefanie flushed with shame, tears pricking behind her eyes. She wanted to shout at them, explain why she had come back, but their presence overwhelmed her. She lifted her chin, went to her room and locked the door.

She pushed her face into the pillow and allowed her hurt to spill over in tears. She cried for the war, for Martin, for the hardness in his eyes and for her little brothers who'd gone to war as boys and who were now men. *I won't beg their forgiveness, they wouldn't understand, they're men fighting a war. They've no reason left save that of hate and survival.*

She dried her tears. It had been easy to steal information from her husband's study. The British would be in Pretoria soon. She could steal again. Courage was all she needed. She went to her desk and dipped the pen into the inkwell. Closing her eyes, she concentrated hard and then wrote down everything she could recall of the papers she had copied in Paul's study. The names, addresses and code numbers presented themselves on the paper without much effort.

DOWNSTAIRS, KOBA was trying to placate the brothers.

'Karel, why didn't you tell me you saw her in Bloemfontein?' Martin demanded.

'I didn't want the men to know that our sister sleeps with the enemy. That's what I saw.' Karel went into the kitchen.

While they were eating, Koba hovered around the table, refilling the plates, stroking their hair as she went past. She repeatedly kissed Rudolf to be sure he was not just a dream.

'Did Charles stay long, Tante Koba?' Martin asked through a mouthful of food.

'Only the night. He's pining for his Anita. And there's Annecke.' Three pairs of eyes flew at her.

'Is something wrong?'

'No, no, Martin, why should anything be wrong?' She babbled on to hide her concern for Rudolf. Charles was right. Martin was a great leader, like his father, her brother, would have been were he still in the war. It was unsettling to look at Martin now. One could say that it was Marthinus sitting there. She hoped that he had his father's kind-heartedness. But no, he would not forgive Annecke and Rudolf: theirs was betrayal. As he would not forgive poor Stefanie for falling in love with the young English lord.

'Did Stefanie say anything about her husband?' Martin asked.

'She has left him, she has good reason—'

'The British lord is who she wants.'

'Peter is a fine young man.' Koba wagged her finger at Karel.

'Yes, he is,' Martin said, 'but he's British. And an aristocrat. There's a war on!'

'We don't know her circumstances,' Rudolf said. 'I pretended that I was British for a while.'

'Yes, you don't know my circumstances.' Stefanie stood in the kitchen door, hurt and fire in her eyes. 'You haven't changed. A moment ago I felt sorry for you, for what the war might have done to you, but you just haven't changed. Thank you, Rudi; you're as kind as always. And you're still malicious, Karel. And my dear Ouboet. Always so concerned about his reputation.'

'No, no, *hartjie*, we won't have words.' Koba put her arm about Stefanie's waist.

'I will have my say, Tante Koba.' She shook herself free and turned back to Martin. 'The district will talk, yes, but this time you'll benefit from my dishonourable ways. I hope you can do something with this.' She held out a sheaf of papers. 'Unfortunately it took me the better part of two months to get here, so I don't know if it's still of any use.'

Martin scanned the papers. 'This is very valuable information. How on earth did you get hold of it?'

'I copied papers from my husband's study. That's why I came home.'

'And Lord Radford?' Karel asked.

'Shall we leave him out of this?' She took her place at the table and poured coffee. 'Yes, I'm on good terms with the British, seen as a sympathiser to their cause. Wrongly so. I want to be of value to you. I wanted to go to Wintersrust, to Ma, but I shall stay in Pretoria and report everything I can lay my hands on, steal information if I'm able to do so. You will just have to find a way to collect it.'

'We'll do that,' Karel offered immediately.

'If you're caught, you'll be shot. I'm sorry, I cannot, *will not*, allow it,' Martin said.

'Then I shall find a general who will allow it.'

'You will not blackmail me.'

'You will not scare me.'

'Do you realise what you're letting yourself into, Stefanie? Your life will be in danger, constantly.'

'So is yours. Do you really think I'm going to let this perfect opportunity go to waste? Or do you take me for a coward?'

Koba saw how brother and sister challenged each other, as they had since they were little. Poor Stefanie had always had a hard time keeping up with Martin. Now he stared at her long and hard, but she returned his look with determination, but also a silent plea for recognition.

'No, you're not a coward,' Martin said at last. 'There's one condition: promise me that if you find yourself in danger, you'll let me know. I'll send Karel and Rudi to get you out of here.'

She looked at him levelly. 'Done! And you'd better come for me.'

'Done! Right, Karel, let's work out a plan. Tomorrow I attend the *krygsraad* and shall convince the real cowards that the war must continue.'

———————

A FEW MILES from where Lord Roberts and his battle-weary troops were entering Pretoria, the Boer generals and commandants met in a distillery that had become a makeshift headquarters. The Commandant-General of the Transvaal, Louis Botha, followed by General Koos de la Rey, entered. Botha walked to the middle of the gathering, scowling furiously, his pipe moving up and down as he chewed the stem. He motioned to General de la Rey to open the *krygsraad*.

De la Rey angrily denounced the government for leaving them in the lurch, and he vowed to fight on. 'If you think of surrendering, then I want nothing of it. I will set up an independent republic in my districts and fight on. Was all this for nothing? Did our sons die for nothing?'

'The situation is hopeless, Koos de la Rey,' General Erasmus said. 'We've lost all our principal towns; our capital is in the hands of the English—'

'For the want of fighting! For the want of courage,' De la Rey countered. 'The British were not even within reach when the government, those who fought the war with their mouths, took all they could and scuttled to safety like frightened mice.'

'The President is fleeing the country, taking ship to Holland. He can't lead us any more. How can we organise the commandos with no one to lead us?' another officer complained.

'The commandos are scattered and the men demoralised. How will we get a commando together large enough to take on the British? The men are weary of running,' said yet another. 'We have no more supplies. The winter is here ...'

The arguments went on. Martin looked at the despondent faces around him. The fight had gone out of them. He felt the desperation and weariness that had threatened to overwhelm him in the past months knot his shoulders. Surrender meant death, the death of the republic, the death of the *Volk*.

Unbidden, he walked to the centre. The frustration that had built up in him exploded in words.

'Cowards! Spineless cowards! Yes, I call you cowards. How dare you make us run from Bloemfontein, not giving us a chance to stand firm and fight? If the men are demoralised, then it's because of the fear and despondency that you have shown in the last months. My men are willing to fight, but surrender? Never! General Piet Cronjé surrendered because of his own foolhardiness. A stubborn old man who should never have been in command. He surrendered and you fall to pieces. Shame on you! Do you call yourselves men?'

The men stared at him with shock and abhorrence. Some grumbled, took a few steps towards him, but he stood his ground.

'You say that we've lost the towns. Do we need a town to fight? You say we've lost the railways, but we have our horses. You say that all the supplies are gone, but we have our farms. Fodder, blankets, food, clothes, medicines. *It's all there on our farms.* You say the army is scattered. The army needs to be scattered. We must fight like General de Wet, small commandos in our own districts. And who will lead us, you ask? I say, be done with the government. Let them leave the country if they so wish.'

Silence ensued. As General Botha was about to speak, a burgher from the telegraph section burst in and handed him a number of dispatches. He read them through and passed them on to Koos de la Rey. 'Commandant de Winter has made his plea, and threat, at the most opportune moment, Koos,' said Botha. 'Here, read them to the men.'

The dispatches were from the Free State, proclaiming General de Wet's latest successes. This had resulted in many men taking up arms again.

'The Free Staters are willing to fight. We drew them into the war, are we to abandon them now?' De la Rey urged.

In the end, it was decided that the fight would continue until the British were exhausted and sought terms. The commandos were to disperse to their districts and wage war in General de Wet's manner. Overall authority was to be borne by General Botha. He was to lead the commandos in the east, De la Rey in the west, Ben Viljoen in the northeast and Christiaan Beyers in the northwest.

'And in the southern Transvaal,' General Botha concluded, 'Martin de Winter will be the senior general.'

———————

KOBA AND STEFANIE kissed the twins goodbye and watched as they galloped away. They ate a hurried breakfast before setting off to Church

Square to witness the arrival of the British forces.

The soldiers marched into town at mid-morning accompanied by a band. The soil clung to their clothes and faces; faces burnt red by the African sun, peeling and blistered. 'Look, *hartjie.*' Koba pointed to the feet marching past. 'Their boots are coming apart, their clothes are worn out, like our men. My heart goes out to them. Boys, they're only boys, and so far from their mothers and their homes.'

Hours later, they were still in Church Square. Stefanie looked at the khaki uniforms filing past. Excitement and fear assailed her. She could steal from them; she knew she could. She was a good liar. She swallowed hard. Peter had said that she was a brave woman and a beautiful liar.

A cheer came from the far end of Schoeman Street. The troops formed up in rows. Minutes later, a short officer rode past, his chest bedecked with medals and ribbons. Behind him was a much larger officer, sitting straight on a pitch-black horse. His eyes were blue and hard, his moustache wide and rigid.

'The little Lord and his fierce general,' someone said behind her. 'Lord Roberts and General Kitchener.'

The officers rode to the middle of the formation. The Vierkleur was lowered. The Union Jack unfolded in the afternoon breeze. A mighty cheer went up and a band struck up 'God Save the Queen'. The troops threw their helmets into the air, shouting that the war was over.

No, Stefanie thought, Martin had said that the war had just begun. And Martin was always right.

PART SEVEN

SCORCHED EARTH

*They have taken crafty counsel against
thy people.*

*They have said, come let us cut them off
from being a nation. Let them be
confounded and troubled forever; yes, let
them be put to shame and perish.*

Psalm 83

Rustenburg District

THE SUMMER OF 1900 was the most beautiful one Wintersrust had ever witnessed, Annecke de Winter thought. The rains were gentle, the thunderstorms absent. The air was balmy, the veld verdant, the mountain gentle against the azure sky. Down at the vlei, the white lilies unfolded overnight, and on the unploughed lands were carpets of wildflowers. With Christmas not a month away, the intoxicating scent of jasmine invaded the house.

She sat on the stoep nursing her baby boy. She thought about the war, and about the many hastily dug graves scattered across the district. Wooden crosses set in cairns of stones, surrounded by the beauty of the season. God looked down on these graves, Koba wrote, and called on nature to lay a wreath for these men. That's why the season was so exceptional.

But the war went on and on. Martin and his commando were fighting south and west of the mountains, always on the move. When he did come to the farm, it was always at night while his men collected ammunition from the kloof opposite the house and meal, salt and sugar from the sheds where his supplies were stored. His mother was generous, insisting that they also take sheep, vegetables and fruit.

It was easy being Martin's wife. He expected so little of her. And when he made love to her, he was gentle but quiet. It was as if his mind was always on the war, not on her. In these tender moments she would remember Rudi most. His love had been tangible, in every smile, every word and caress. But not with Martin. Afterwards he would join his guards at the drift. He did not want the English to find him in bed.

With the medical supplies stored at Wintersrust, Charles was a frequent visitor. Anita Verwey had brought Lettie to Wintersrust where she could properly care for her. Lettie busied herself with mending clothes, keeping up a constant flow of advice, chatter and jokes. With Buks back in Martin's commando, they were now a family of women and children.

She had nearly drowned in the vlei. But Old Klaas had found her in the water, still clutching the rag doll. Charles had saved her and the baby. Lena told her that Charles had cried when he was told what had happened. Charles knew the truth. That's why he'd cried – for her, for Rudi and for Martin. He had pleaded with her to keep her secret until the war was over. Martin was a general; he should not be humiliated. She had not seen Rudi yet, did not even know if he had received her note, if he knew about his son. She dared not ask. Karel had been twice at night to fetch food and clothes. Rudi, he'd said on both occasions, was in the cave with the horses. He refused to come home.

The baby stirred and she smiled down at him; her baby, little Martin. She buttoned her dress and was putting him in the crib when Lena came hurrying from the garden, carrying a basket of vegetables, clutching her large belly with her free hand.

'Annecke! Soldiers are coming!' Lena gasped, her eyes wide with alarm.

Annecke rushed Lena to the house, herding her three children to the stoep. Mary was already there with the coffee tray; Anita was helping Lettie to a chair.

'There's English at our house, Ma.' Annecke tried to act as calmly as Anita always did.

Lettie spotted the troop heading for the Soetvlei homestead. 'Go see that they leave my fowls alone. Go at once!'

Annecke hesitated; she did not have the courage to talk to the enemy. Mary came to her rescue. She stepped off the stoep, narrowing her eyes into the distance.

'No, Lettie, there's no need. They're coming here.'

The troop halted at the drift. Ten riders detached themselves from the group and came to the house. Two men, officers, Anita whispered, dismounted. The rest stayed on their horses, rifles over their knees. A florid-faced officer strutted up the steps, spurs jingling. His expression was sullen, his manner brusque.

'Major Hunter.' He touched his swagger stick to his helmet and introduced the man behind him. 'Lieutenant Sinclair.' He fixed his eyes on Mary. 'I believe you treat wounded Boers on this farm. Do you deny it?'

Mary patted her greying hair into place. 'We treat all wounded, whether they're Boer or Brit. It's not only our duty, but also our wish. There's so little else women can do in war.'

Major Hunter, obviously startled on hearing Mary's British accent, stumbled over his next words. 'Madam … it's against the law …'

'Whose law?' Anita Verwey folded her arms across her chest.

'Lord Roberts proclaimed that no farms shall supply the fighting Boers with any help whatsoever.'

'Has he really?' Anita's eyes widened with mock surprise. 'Well, we don't live under your law. We live by our country's law.'

Hunter flushed darkly and nodded to his men. They dismounted and surrounded the house while two pushed past Lettie's chair and went inside.

'Look under the beds behind the chamber pots!' she called after them. 'That's where we hide them!'

'While your men are occupied, would you join us for coffee?' Mary said, smiling. 'How rude of me! I have not introduced myself yet. I'm Mary de Winter. Mrs Lettie Maree, my neighbour—'

'De Winter?' Sinclair said. 'Family of Martin de Winter's?'

'Indeed. This is Wintersrust. I'm Martin's mother.' Mary handed him a cup of coffee and introduced the rest of the women. 'Martin's wife, Annecke; Lena Maree; and Anita Verwey, engaged to Dr Charles Henderson, my nephew. Are you also acquainted with him?'

'Indeed! An honour to meet you, ladies.' Sinclair bowed a little at the waist.

Major Hunter's manner changed instantly to that of keen interest.

'How's my old friend Martin?' Sinclair asked and added with a laugh, 'Apart from raiding our convoys.'

'My son is fine. He was wounded, but then it is war, is it not?' Mary indicated little Martin in his crib. 'His son.'

Lena's children watched in awe as Sinclair tickled the baby under the chin. 'A charming little fellow, isn't he just?' He ruffled the other children's hair. Annecke watched Hunter furtively and saw that he paid no attention to the homely scene, but was searching the homestead with his eyes.

'James informed me of your son's death, one of the twins,' Sinclair said to Mary. 'My condolences to all of you.'

'Lieutenant, we do appreciate it, but Rudolf was only wounded. He was treated in Cape Town as one of your own. I've written to the hospital authorities to thank them for the kind treatment of my son and asked them to relay our heartfelt sympathy to the family of Captain Patterson.'

'Patterson?' Hunter bolted upright. 'I saw your son, Mrs de Winter. Well, he was then Captain Patterson, claiming to suffer from amnesia. I was in the hospital at the same time and James Henderson, your nephew was also there. Imagine … How did he manage to escape? Just as a matter of interest.'

'Why, he simply took the train and left Cape Town. How is James? Has he recovered from his wounds?'

'I've seen him briefly since he was wounded, Mrs de Winter,' Sinclair said, but looking at Hunter. 'He's recovered, yes, but isn't fit for active duty. He's still in Cape Town. How's Charles?'

'With the commandos and working very hard.' Anita's tone made Annecke glance fearfully at Hunter. 'He treats more British wounded than our own, needless to say.'

The troops returned from their search and reported to Hunter that there were medical supplies in one of the rooms.

'Does Dr Henderson store his supplies here?' Hunter asked.

'I'm a nursing sister and, since you've kicked me out of my hospital at Rustenburg, I treat the women and children here.' Anita's mouth was set in a threatening line.

'Very well.' Hunter stood up. 'Perhaps you could attend to one of my men? He was stung by a scorpion and is running a fever.'

'Certainly, Major. Send him here, we'll see to him,' Mary said before Anita could snap at him again.

Hunter grabbed his helmet, clicked his heels and marched down the steps.

'It's been delightful to meet Martin's family at last,' Sinclair said in parting. 'The coffee was much appreciated, madam. My regards to Martin and Charles.'

'Oh dear! We must get the medicines out of here,' Anita said, her eyes on the officers as they rode to the drift.

'Now do stop fretting, Anita,' Mary said. 'They won't take medicines. Weapons, yes, but—'

'They searched our house, Aunt Mary,' Lena said.

'The English burned farms in the Free State because the women supplied the commandos and saw to their wounded. They took the women off to a camp as prisoners, and their poor servants too,' Annecke said.

'What rubbish, Annecke!' Mary huffed. 'British soldiers will never wage war on women and burn their houses. We shall have no more of that talk! Come, let's see to dinner while Anita treats the soldier.' She picked up the tray and went inside.

———◆———

RUDOLF SAT ON THE ROCK SLAB at the entrance of the cave as he watched the troop at Wintersrust through his field glasses. It was clear that they intended to spend the night at the drift. Two soldiers went with his mother to the kraal. She pointed out two sheep and they took them to the drift and soon had a fire going.

He thought of waking Karel, who was asleep in the cave, but decided to wait and observe them closely. The other scouts were on the other side of the mountain crest. He lowered his glasses and checked if Legend and Jessie, his new roan mare, were still near the waterfall. Lady had fallen a few weeks before, hit in the throat by a bullet after the commando had blown up the railway line between Pretoria and Johannesburg.

The scouts were an elite corps, and Karel was their undisputed leader. He was eager to take chances and refused to abide by any rules; they were for the cautious ones. Their work was to blow up trains, move close to the enemy and supply the generals with information on their movements and strength. They were a mixed bunch, forty strong, mostly men from the district, but also a few Free Staters. Patrick McFee, the Irishman who they had met in Bulawayo before the war, had served on the Natal front with the artillery, but, as that section was now non-existent, had been recommended as a scout. He was invaluable, moving freely in Johannesburg, gathering information from the Outlanders now that the mines had reopened. McFee's ability to drink hard and stay on his feet had unlocked many a secret from an unsuspecting source.

McFee was the only scout who knew that Stefanie was spying for Martin. They slipped into Pretoria on a dark moon night every month and collected the oilcloth bags with the information she had gathered. Every time Martin had received warning about the British movements, he had either avoided being caught, or had ambushed a convoy laden with supplies.

THE LIGHT WAS FADING and the British soldiers were settling down for the night. Karel emerged from the cave and Rudolf pointed to the farmsteads, handing him the glasses.

'Fifty-four. Two officers had coffee on the stoep.'

'Ma! She would have it,' Karel said. 'Have they put out pickets?'

'In all directions, but not near the house.'

'I'll go down and see what they wanted. Go tell the others to come at sunrise. We will trail them.'

Rudolf slid down the rock slab and climbed to the crest of the mountain. The scouts had a perfect place to hide out on the south-facing side of the mountain – a rock overhang with plenty of fresh water and grazing for their horses. Karel did not allow them in the cave. Neutral ground, they had promised James before the war.

He joined the men where they were stretched out around the fire with a bottle of whisky, playing cards. He related Karel's order, took a few mouthfuls of whisky and left. He climbed back over the crest and down to the cave. Karel had brought Legend and Jessie into the cave before he had left to spy on the British at the drift. The horses were now munching on the oats in their corner.

Rudolf sank down on his mattress. Even McFee's whisky could no longer dull his despair. As he sat in the cave, staring into the dim light of the lantern, he thought how his world had changed since returning from the dead. Martin might be a general, but he was as vulnerable as any of his men. Unlike other generals, he was always in the thick of battle. Annecke might again be his; he might be a father to his son. He did not want Martin to die, but neither did he want Annecke to separate him from his twin ever again.

He went out into the night to wait for Karel. The cave held too many bittersweet memories and dark thoughts. It was a long and lonely wait for Karel, who arrived back from Wintersrust after midnight.

At dawn there came the call of a nightjar. Karel gave an answering call and McFee and thirty scouts arrived. They clambered up the rock slab and studied the sleeping enemy below. When the sun showed itself, the camp came to life with the bugler's call. Five men detached themselves from the troop, loaded supplies on a mule and headed towards the mountain.

'Spies! They know the commandos come here for supplies, and who do they want?' Karel said, looking at McFee.

'Our General,' McFee said, his black eyebrows knitting together.

'Gert, do away with them,' Karel said. 'Take their places until I call you off.'

Gert Swart and two men moved off silently. Karel turned his glasses back to the enemy, who were now heading away from Wintersrust, taking the road to Pretoria. 'Right! Let's see where they're going.'

IN A HIDDEN RECESS at the foothills of the mountain range twenty miles southeast of Rustenburg, General Martin de Winter had his headquarters. Following the capture of Pretoria, Martin had had to rebuild his forces, as many men had thought the war over and gone home. It had not been difficult to persuade them to return; within the first weeks of his arrival in the western Transvaal, he had begun raiding convoys and setting the enemy to flight. Soon his commando had grown to well over a thousand men. It was a different kind of war now – a war of plundering, of hit and run, confusing the enemy, driving them to their wits' end.

Now Martin was waiting for news of a supply convoy expected at Rustenburg. As he strolled through the camp, he watched his men at work. Some were shoeing horses, some swimming in the stream running through the camp, their clothes strung out on bushes to dry. Others sat smoking their pipes, mending boots and clothes. His eyes strayed to where men were breaking in new mounts. Jan Viljoen's mighty curses and laughter rose above the din. Martin walked over and found Joep Maree watching the spectacle.

Jan was thrown clear of a bucking horse, landed at their feet, smiling sheepishly. '*Magtig!* These horses are surely from up north. Bred from wild stock.'

Martin laughed. 'Why do you need a new horse? Not happy with Lord Roberts any more?' Jan had captured an English charger and named him after the British commander.

'What a horse! Courage he has, yes, but it's his speed that worries me. When he smells his English friends, there's no stopping him! Just last week, I found myself almost through the English lines long before you'd given the order to charge.'

'Offer a bottle of your brew as a reward for the man who tames a horse for you,' Martin suggested, swatting at flies that worried at his beard. 'You'll have plenty of takers.'

'You heard the General,' Jan hollered to the men. 'My best peach brandy for a tame horse!' He picked up his hat and joined Martin and Joep.

'Let's go to Charles,' Martin said. 'The scouts should be in soon.'

They walked to the old farmstead that served as a hospital. It was on a little rise, overlooking the valley below, making it possible to observe the camp. Charles was on the stoep, sharpening his needles. Buks Maree was with him, looking through the microscope at blood samples.

'How are the men, Charles?' Martin asked.

'All out of danger. But I need operating instruments, and I'm also low on chloroform. I don't want to worry you, but Buks is looking at samples I took from two horses yesterday. I'm afraid they didn't make it through the night. Horse sickness.'

'Son, horse sickness,' Joep puffed on his pipe, 'is nearly always fatal.'

As they talked, the twins galloped into camp, dismounted and led their horses in wide circles to cool them down. They were beardless, their hair trimmed, a condition necessitated by their forays into British territory, dressed in khaki. Martin had warned them about the risks, but, as usual, Karel scorned caution.

Rudolf came rushing up, his shirt soaked and his hair matted. 'I bring bad news and Karel has good news.'

'Bad news?' Martin frowned. 'Well, let's hear it, then.'

'The *Engelse* spent the night at the drift. Anita told Karel that they're interested in General de Winter. The officers know you from London. Hunter, a major, fierce-looking man, she says, and rude.'

Martin groaned. 'What are the Hussars doing here?'

'Protecting convoys, I've heard,' Charles said. 'And the other one?'

'Anita couldn't remember his name.' Rudolf gulped down some coffee. 'They sent a heliograph team up the kloof to watch the house. Gert took care of them, so there will only be signals saying that the general hasn't arrived yet.'

Martin grunted. He did not relish being hunted. 'And the good news?' he said when Karel arrived.

'Presents for everyone,' Karel said expansively. 'Fifty wagons! Something especially for you, Martin – six guns and all the ammunition you can carry. And for you, Charles, Red Cross wagons, loaded and waiting. Uncle Joep, I saw crates of that sweetmilk you crave, and for you, Jan Viljoen, there's bound to be some brandy.'

'You won't believe this,' Rudolf cut in. 'They're encamped *right against* the mountain at Nooitgedacht.'

Martin came to his feet. 'How many men, Karel?'

'About two thousand. Six cannon, and I'll show you exactly where they are.'

'Two thousand!' Martin sighed.

'I've done your planning, General.' Karel grinned. 'I sent word to Oom Koos and to your friend General Smuts at Cypherfontein. General Beyers and his *takhaaren* are also moving here. The *Engelse* will be outnumbered, and their camp is a death trap. Their general is either very bold or bloody stupid.'

'Good work, Karel.' Martin stood in deep thought for a while. 'Pa, send word to General Kemp and Commandant Jansen to move their men to twenty miles from Nooitgedacht. Tell them to stay out of sight and wait for me there. Jan, hand out ammunition. Move out tonight. I'm riding to confer with Oom Koos.'

———

THE CRESCENT MOON disappeared behind the mountain, leaving them in the dark. Charles followed Joep's laboured breathing and muted curses as they stumbled over rocks and through acacia scrub. After they had gone about a mile, he bumped into Joep's broad back.

'Here's where the wounded will look for you,' Joep whispered, so close to his ear that he could feel his beard against his cheek. 'If things go wrong, I'll come for you. If I'm not in a position to do so, I'll send Jan.'

Joep disappeared into the night. Charles sank to his haunches, holding the reins of the mules in his hand. He longed for the comfort of a proper bed, with Anita in his arms. He simply had to find a way to marry her soon, war or no war. *War makes a man hungry for his woman, Jan Viljoen had said, if one could use such a primitive phrase!*

He made a mental note to search for decent tea in the loot that was expected. He wondered again about the Hussars in the southern Transvaal. Thankfully, James was still unfit for active duty. *My dear reckless brother. A small thing, just a little thing,* Tante Koba would say, *to be thankful for …*

An owl shrieked. He looked east. The sky was paling through the canopy of the trees. Just then a volley of shots erupted, followed by the bark of cannon and rocks rattling down the mountain. He swore and jumped to his feet. *God, will I ever get used to this racket!*

He ran to a high boulder from where he could observe the battle. No fire was returned from the British camp, but he heard shouted orders and bugles sounding. Distant cheering rose from the crest. Martin should've attacked by now. He swept his glasses to the south. In the dawn light the commando came thundering down, lying low in their saddles. Within a mile of the camp they spread out in a half-moon, and the air crackled with rifle fire.

He shifted his glasses to the British camp. Men ran back and forth, oxen bellowed, stampeding through the milling men. A wagon caught fire. He trained his glasses on it and hoorayed. It did not have a red cross on the side!

He clambered down the boulder, found a flat piece of ground under an acacia and spread out a canvas sheet. He unpacked his scant equipment and set about cutting branches from a milkwood sapling to be used as splints. As he worked, a rider galloped up with a wounded man thrown across the saddle. 'The doctor! Where's the doctor?'

Charles waved his arms. 'You've found him!'

And so his work began. By midday twenty wounded and four dead had reached him, but they told of others near the camp and of the many enemy casualties. By late afternoon, he had used the last of his lint and ran out of morphine. Fortunately no more wounded arrived.

'You'll be safe here,' he said to those he had treated. 'I must see to the others closer to the battle, but I shall send someone to bring you in.'

IT WAS DUSK when he walked into the captured camp. A scene of wilful destruction met his eyes. Boers were plundering, carrying off whatever they could lay their hands on. Some got hold of the cavalry horses, dragging them by their reins to get them away from the hands of others. Tents were pulled down, their contents searched, the ground littered with the belongings of the British. Men stripped where they stood and tried on breeches and shirts, tossing the tunics aside. Further on were the Boer horses, feasting on the English fodder.

As he walked to what he took to be the centre of the camp, he happened on cattle enclosures into which prisoners were being herded, the Boers stripping them of their boots as they entered. He saw Karel and walked over. 'You're not looting?' he asked, trying to keep disapproval from his voice.

Karel hugged him. 'No need. McFee is in charge of that.' He pointed to the prisoners. 'Oom Koos told us to get them into the kraal.'

'How did it go with your men? Any wounded?'

'We didn't fare that well, I'm afraid.' Karel pushed an unwilling soldier into the enclosure. 'Trouble with the pickets at the top. I decided to storm them. One dead, two wounded. Rudi and Gert are bringing them down.'

Jan Viljoen loomed out of the confusion, a bottle in his hand. 'My dear doctor! My good friend!' He embraced Charles forcefully.

'Did Martin manage to get the guns? I saw the enemy fleeing with two. They'd rather save their guns than their wounded.'

'Jan Viljoen saw it too. Uncle Joep and I had fun taking their toys from them.' Jan shouted to the prisoners in the enclosure, 'Hey, *Engelse*! You have a long walk to Pretoria, and no shoes!'

Charles cast his eyes over the prisoners. With a start, he saw George Hunter a few yards away. He was about to walk over, but Karel, shoving a quarrelling trooper along with the butt of his Mauser, obscured Hunter from his view. He decided it best not to complicate matters as Hunter now descended on Karel, thundering about abuse of prisoners.

'Is there anything that Jan Viljoen can do for you, my good doctor?' Jan steered Charles away from the enclosure.

'Find me a crate of tea, Jan, and help me get the wounded in.'

'I've seen to that. Brother Jacob is also there, a bullet through his knee. I've found him a good doctor, though.' Jan looked at Charles with a self-satisfied grin. 'You'll soon see him, but first, Sailor's Brandy.'

'I have to operate, but yes, maybe a restorative nip.' Charles, knowing that it was futile to argue, swallowed a mouthful of rum.

'I've taken care of your portion of the spoils. Gert Vermaas hitched the Red Cross wagons, took them west. They might catch fire in this feast.' Jan swallowed more rum. 'Our brave general says we'll stay here for the night, and so Frans and a few men are clearing the tents for your patients.'

'Why, thank you, Jan. I'm grateful.' Charles stepped aside as two men dragged a mattress past them. 'I need to find the British doctors to assist—'

'Over there. Our friend from Magersfontein, Dr Frank. The other one is full of firewater, so I tied him to the wagon wheel. He didn't feel like helping us.' Jan gave his booming laugh followed by the habitual slap on the back.

Charles, with Jan's arm around his shoulders, made his way to the hospital tents. Under a tree festooned by lanterns, the victorious generals were dining at a table, set with glasses, china and silver cutlery taken from the British mess tent. Martin's golden mane shone in the light, his eyes glowing with success. Koos de la Rey was laughing while Jan Smuts refilled his glass, raising it in a toast. Like a show in a London theatre, Charles thought, but out of place in the midst of death and plundering.

At the hospital tents, a long line of wounded waited. The British medics were putting up acetylene lamps, and Charles found Frank Crofton-Smith as Jan had promised. 'I have a friend here, Jacob Viljoen; I have to find him,' Charles said.

'That giant of a Boer who assisted me so generously,' Frank looked at Jan's departing figure, 'insisted that I see to him first. I'm afraid we'll have to amputate his leg. Come, to work!'

RUDOLF AND GERT SWART led the horses carrying the wounded down a gully. The going was slow and darkness overtook them. Rudolf lit a lantern they had looted from the pickets on the summit. When they reached the foothills, they came upon smouldering trees, craters, dead horses and oxen that had fled into the line of fire. As they neared the outer perimeter of the camp, a horse gave a warning snort. They strained their eyes into the darkness and heard an agonised groaning.

Rudolf unslung his rifle, skirting the thorn bush. 'Hands up! The battle is over!'

No reply came except the groaning. Rudolf approached cautiously and saw prone figures. Keeping his rifle on them, he called Gert. In the lantern light they examined the fallen men. There were seven, all dead except the groaning man. He was clutching his stomach, his uniform soaked in blood.

'A horse officer.' Gert pointed to the insignia on the tunic.

'Can you hold on?' Rudolf asked in English, touching the officer's arm. 'I have wounded on my horse, but I'll come back for you.'

'No ...' the man gasped. 'I'm beyond help ...'

'Leave the Englishman,' Gert said. 'Let's go!'

'Go on, it's not far,' Rudolf said.

Gert led the horses on. Rudolf wished there was something he could do to ease the officer's suffering. 'Let me take you in. I'm strong, I can carry you.'

'No, please don't move me ...'

Rudolf realised that here was nothing he could do, but he did not want to leave him dying alone in the dark. 'Here! Keep the lantern. I'll fetch the doctor.'

He raced to the camp. Men sat around fires, roasting meat, drinking, talking and singing. He dodged his way through them, searching for the hospital tents. There he pushed through the men waiting outside but an orderly shoved him away. 'The doctors are operating. You cannot go in there.'

'Charles! Charles! It's Rudolf! Charles, can you hear me?' He shouted until Charles's anxious face appeared at the tent opening, his hands and apron bloodied, his face haggard in the bright lights.

'Dear God! Rudi! Are you wounded?'

'No! Charles, there's a cavalry officer. Come help him!'

Charles disappeared into the tent and sped out a few moments later with bandages and a syringe. Rudolf grabbed his arm and they started running, swerving to avoid men, horses and fires. They reached the place where the officer lay. Charles fell to his knees beside him. Then he sank back onto his haunches, the bandages and syringe dropping to the ground at his feet.

'Sinclair?' He turned the officer's face so that he could see him. 'It's Charles. Charles Henderson. Let me have a look ...'

Sinclair stretched out a bloodied hand. Rudolf leaned closer and caught his whispered words. 'Charles? Get word to James ... Hunter ... hospital ...'

They waited but nothing more came from the man. Charles picked up the limp wrist and dropped it. He removed his glasses, pressing his thumbs to his eyes.

'Charles?' Rudolf whispered. 'He's dead, isn't he?'

'Yes. Mark Sinclair, from James's regiment.'

Hullabaloo at the Mount Nelson

Cape Town, December

CAPTAIN JAMES HENDERSON looked through his office window into the courtyard of the Castle. The sun was hot in a cloudless summer sky, the continuous rain of the winter and spring long forgotten. James hated being cooped up in an office, frustrated with the paperwork, checking the lists of wounded and dead, keeping tally of the strength of the various regiments. He picked up a file detailing a skirmish that had taken place in December at a place called Skoonspruit, west of Pretoria. Martin's commando had been involved.

'Well done, cousin!' James slammed the file shut. How on earth did Martin manage it week after week? Only yesterday the rumour had reached them of yet another battle that had taken place the previous week west of Pretoria. Another victory for Martin? General Clements and his force of fifteen hundred had been surprised thirty miles from Pretoria. Surprised? Thirty miles from thousands of British?

James was staring into the courtyard when Peter Radford sauntered in. On their return from convalescent leave, both he and Peter had been promoted to captain and assigned to temporary duty as staff officers.

'Come on, Henderson, wrap up! General Woodgate wants to see us.'

'What's up? Have we disgraced ourselves?'

A few minutes later, they were standing in front of General Woodgate's desk. They saluted and stood to attention, their eyes on Queen Victoria's portrait on the wall.

'At ease.' General Woodgate was a greying man, his voice slow and uninterested. 'A year on convalescent leave, both of you. I've come to the conclusion that you're bored here.' He stared out of the window and then turned to face them. 'Orders from General Kitchener. Empty the Mount Nelson of British staff. It's a den of iniquity. Drunk and disorderly behaviour, gambling, shooting in the bar. Not to mention the women who flock there to join in the hullabaloo. General Kitchener needs extra staff officers, I'll be glad to be rid of both of you. Never liked cavalrymen, actually. Menace when they're not on a horse.'

'And even then, sir.'

James received what could have passed for a stern look. 'You will report for duty in Pretoria before the year is out.'

Peter's face lit up, but James received the news with mixed feelings. He would rather be in the war than doing staff duties, but the Transvaal was not where he wanted to go. He was still pondering this when the general's next words hit him.

'Captain Henderson, your personal life is none of my concern, but Lord Fairfield has requested that you send his daughter home. It's rather a lengthy business, the war. You will convey this to your wife, Captain Henderson. Dismissed.'

THEY CROSSED THE BRIDGE over the moat surrounding the Castle and passed through the gate. Peter hailed a hansom, but James waved the driver on. Peter, he knew, was eager to join the war again, but there was more to it. Although Peter had told him about his journey behind the lines, he'd said little concerning Stefanie.

'Peter, Stefanie's marriage is a failure, that much is clear, but—'

Peter turned to face him. 'I owe you some consideration, I know.'

'I should bloody well think so! She's my cousin.'

'I spent only one night with her, the last. She's married in name only. I didn't believe her ... well, that was till I discovered it for myself.'

'And you went ahead? My God, Radford!'

'Demanding lady, your cousin, doesn't take no for an answer. A family trait, I suppose. When I woke up, she was gone. Taken her hat and left.'

'Her hat?'

'Yes, her bloody hat.'

James gave Peter a sidelong glance. The rim of his helmet shaded his eyes, but, by the firm set of his mouth, James could tell that Peter was unwilling to elaborate. They crossed the Grand Parade and navigated the bustling city streets.

'Carry on, Radford,' James demanded when they reached the Company's Garden and took the oak-lined avenue to the Mount Nelson. 'She took her hat and left, but that's not all.'

Peter raised his eyes to survey Table Mountain. 'The honest truth is that I'm utterly, madly in love with your cousin. A most unwelcome situation, I assure you. Like having a fatal disease. And it gets worse by the day. It takes courage to come to terms with it. Being in love, I mean, not disease.'

'Damn it, Radford!' They walked a short distance when James stopped, scowling deeply. 'Is the feeling mutual? What are you going to do about it? I should think not a damn thing.'

A troubled look crossed Peter's face. 'I don't rightly know. I've never given the future much thought. Not a habit of mine. I *must* see her again. Maybe this is just a passing obsession, who knows?'

'If it's not, Radford?'

The frown on Peter's face deepened. 'She's married. If she wants me as a lover, what more can I expect?'

'Adultery is not something Boers indulge in, Radford. It's one of Tante Koba's Big Sins. And Stefanie's head rules her heart. Always has. On the other hand, she knows exactly what she wants, when she wants it, and she always gets it.'

They passed through the hotel's wrought-iron gates, flanked by white columns, and touched their helmets to the bust of Nelson. The garden overflowed with guests seeking the refreshing afternoon breeze. The parasols of the many ladies were conspicuous among the khaki uniforms and smart attire of the well-heeled refugees from Johannesburg.

They were bored, like him, thought James. If he didn't love Victoria, why did he feel so guilty? He had spent his convalescent leave at Matjiesfontein with Peter, while she had lived outside the city until Mrs Butcher had moved to Pretoria with the regiment.

He dearly wanted to regain the undemanding relationship they had once had. It took a lot of courage to admit being in love, Peter had just said. But to say it, to actually declare yourself – why was that so hard? Fighting a war, even killing, was easier.

FROM HER WICKER CHAIR in the garden, Victoria watched as James and Peter passed through the gates. They were back to their usual ways – gambling, womanising and drinking, always together. She was restless. It was time to move on to India. Meeting Rudolf de Winter had brought back memories of Martin she had tried hard to bury. What changes would four years have brought? Every day the newspapers carried articles on the war, and Martin was often mentioned. Once there was a story of his life, about his studies, rugby and career. A general, a man fighting for what he truly believed in.

'Evening, Victoria.' James's voice brought her out of her dreams.

'Vicky!' Peter pecked her on her cheek and beckoned a nearby waiter. 'Would you like another drink before we dine? We've some rather exciting news.'

'Oh yes, thank you. News? Are we on our way to India at last?' She straightened up and placed her straw hat on the grass beside her.

'On our way, yes, but not to India.' James deposited his helmet on the table. 'Peter and I are off to Pretoria and you've been ordered home.' He related General Woodgate's order while lighting a cheroot. 'I can't escort you. If I set foot in London, my chances of getting to India will be remote. There's bound to be a remodelling of the Army after the war.'

'That's exactly what your father wants,' Victoria said. 'If you'd taken time to read his letters, you'd know that he's been trying to get you home ever since you were wounded.'

'It appears that my misfortune has touched the old fellow deeply.' James blew smoke at the flies that settled on his helmet. 'But I've been banished to India: that's where I'm going.'

'So am I, and I refuse to go back to England.'

'Life could become unpleasant if you stay. It's rumoured that Sir Alfred Milner is looking into the situation of the many ladies who hang around here.'

'I do not *hang* around, James. I'm *stuck* here!'

'Nights would've been awfully dull if the ladies didn't hang around.' Peter handed Victoria a glass of wine. 'Come to Pretoria. It's a decent-sized town. It'll be just like here.'

Victoria thought about Peter's suggestion while he and James chattered about the prospect of rejoining the regiment. All ships docking in the colonies' harbours were returning to England to load more supplies to keep the war going, making it near impossible to find passage to India. It would be wise to go back to Durban. In Pretoria she would be closer to Martin, and the dangerous longing to see him again might become a reality.

'The Boers, do they come to Pretoria?'

'Boers live in Pretoria, Vicky. It's their capital. But the commandos are in the country, in the veld.' James said. 'You could join Tante Koba and Stefanie in a trip to Wintersrust, if possible, and meet Aunt Mary. She would certainly appreciate a little company from home.'

'When do you leave?'

'Peter goes Monday, while I first have to see to the horses and my extra baggage,' he said, giving her his dimpled smile. 'About a week or so. Depends on trains—', he broke off, pointing to Lieutenant John Miles, walking briskly towards them. 'Look who's here!'

'We were about to join you in Pretoria, Miles,' Peter said when Miles reached them. 'What brings you down here?'

'I've been allowed a brief holiday. Slight wound.' Miles's thin face was troubled.

'I say, anything the matter, old boy?' Peter beckoned to the waiter again. 'Nothing that a drink can't fix, surely.'

Miles fiddled with his helmet. 'I'm afraid I have some rather disturbing news. Before I left Pretoria, Major Hunter and Shaw arrived. They were captured by the Boers, but released—'

'Excellent!' James exploded with laughter. 'Hunter caught by the Boers! They should've kept him. Tied a rope around his neck and used him as bait.'

'Captain Henderson, he brought news of Mark Sinclair—'

'Sinclair? What about him?'

'His death, Captain. The news isn't out officially, but I thought that you should know.' Miles took the offered drink and sank down in a chair. 'Happened near Rustenburg. General de Winter and others attacked General Clements. Apparently he found Major Hunter the morning after the battle and told him to keep clear of his farm. Murray Shaw heard it all.'

De Winter's brilliant success, the pro-Boer papers would label it, Victoria thought. How unfair that he should have been in command when a friend was killed. But Martin did not kill; he was a general, he gave orders to kill. James killed, not from a distance, but in cold blood with a sabre.

'By God!' James cursed. 'I can hear Jan Viljoen. *Good shot! Got him right in the middle, just there where the heart is.* Do you think Martin knows about Mark's death?'

Peter frowned. 'Does a general look at his enemy's dead?'

'He knows, Captain Radford.' Miles took a gulp from his glass. 'He told Captain Shaw that he would bury Sinclair on his farm. General de Winter did not want to leave him in the veld under a heap of stones, Shaw told me.'

Victoria gathered her things and made her way to the stone steps leading to the entrance. For James, a night's hard drinking to the memory of Sinclair would follow. But, as she reached the door, James caught up with her, took her elbow and steered her through the crowded lounge. They reached her room in silence. She held on to the door when he showed no intention of leaving.

'I thought that you'd rather be with Peter,' she said.

'I would like to be with you for a bit,' he said, closing the door and leaning against it. She felt his eyes following her as she put down her books and straw hat. She sat down at the dressing table, taking up her brush. She was going to Pretoria. Martin would be only a few miles from her. Waves of desire rushed through her. Martin had been fiery yet controlled in his lovemaking. James made love as he lived – wildly, recklessly, yet so sensually, the intensity was almost unbearable. She had not dreamt it possible. And that was what she needed to calm the turmoil into which her mind and body had been plunged.

'Where will you go tonight, James?' Anger flashed in his eyes. 'I see the way your women look at me. It doesn't bother me.'

She undid the pins and brushed her hair. He was still leaning against the door, hands in his pockets, watching her with a veiled expression.

'If it doesn't bother you,' he asked, 'why did you mention it?'

The brush stopped in her hair. Lately there was something in his attitude towards her that had changed. Tenderness perhaps, or was it love? It could have been different, she thought. She was beginning to leave Martin in the past where he belonged. His cousin. He would never forgive her. And James did not deserve betrayal.

'Oh James, it's not turning out the way we thought it would.'

'No, it isn't.' He came to stand behind her. 'I never thought that I'd … be so attracted to you.' He placed his lips against the soft skin behind her ear, moved his mouth down her throat, barely touching her skin, his breath caressing the rise of her breasts. 'I can be gentle too, Vicky.'

She sat motionless, emotions battering her. Their eyes met in the mirror, hers burning with tears. *Save me from Martin, from myself,* she beseeched silently.

General Kitchener

STEFANIE FACED HER wardrobe wondering what to wear. Vicky had kindly sent a trunk containing her evening gowns by rail from Cape Town. Stefanie was invited to Melrose House, where General Kitchener had taken up residence since Lord Roberts had declared the war over and left for England. Now she was to meet Kitchener himself. His officers spoke about him with guarded admiration – relentless in his pursuit of perfection, an enormous appetite for work, sparing little time for personal pleasures. Yet, he had invited her to perform for his staff and guests.

It was general knowledge that she was Martin de Winter's sister, but that she condemned the war was also well known. Had her husband not proclaimed that *his dear wife's* loyalty to the Crown was absolute? When asked about her famous brother, she said not a word. It was best, Koba advised.

But every month, on a dark moon night, Karel and Rudi, or sometimes the Irishman, arrived, muddy and exhausted from having crawled through the thickets along the Apies River. They brought news of the commandos and Wintersrust. Koba strapped to their chests the oilcloth bags containing newspaper cuttings and notes on troop movements, supply trains expected and new laws and proclamations. Then, just as quietly as they appeared, the dark night swallowed them again.

'Tante Koba,' she called, leaning over the balustrade. 'Shall I wear the cream satin or the lilac gauze?'

'No, *hartjie*, my mind is on the rose tulle, the one with the lace at the sleeves. It's the prettiest dress I've ever seen.' Koba held out a spray of pink rosebuds. 'I found these for your hair in Hettie Venter's garden.'

'She gave them to you, knowing they're for my hair?'

'I told her that I need them for my table tomorrow.' Koba beamed mischievously.

The contempt with which her own people treated her was obvious, and desired, but it still hurt. Getting information was not easy. The British were no fools. They treated the sister of an enemy general with utmost courtesy, but also with guarded wariness. She was in constant demand to perform at private parties and concerts, but that was where it ended. They sent an escort to collect and deliver her home. Information was hard to come by, but, with the help of a Boer clerk at the railway offices, Dolf Meyer, she'd managed to copy the secret list of train destinations, a document only seen by few. The danger was frightening, but rewarding. She would be shot if discovered, but there was no chance of that. The British were all in love with her talent – arrogant, boring snobs.

Her hands went still. They were not all like that. She had met the 2nd Hussars at a recital in the Transvaal Hotel: Shaw, Moore, Smithers and Miles. They were fun-loving, considerate men, and treated her as James's cousin and as their friend Martin's sister. She had tea with their commanding officer, Colonel Norman Butcher, and his wife. Peter and James were still drinking the champagne cellars dry, and would most probably see the war out doing staff duty in Cape Town, they said.

Six months and not a word. *What happened to those papers? Did Peter report me? Am I being watched?*

She slipped into the dress – a beautiful dress, not pink and not red either, a rich shade in between. The waist was tight, the skirt gathered in small pleats, wide sleeves and a low neckline. Paul liked the dress. She felt another rush of fear. No word from her husband either. She took up her hairbrush and pins and went downstairs.

'Now, *hartjie*, keep your sheet music with you when you go to the bathroom,' Koba said through a mouthful of pins, combing Stefanie's hair with deft strokes. 'Slip into Kitchener's office. They say that his desk looks like a mountain with all the papers on it. He'll never know if you take a few.'

'The only thing I have to accomplish tonight, dear Tante Koba, is to make sure that I'm invited there again.' She should not tell Koba about the secret telephone line that Martin had written to her about. It was connected to Johannesburg only and operated from a different exchange than the other telephone lines. She had to see which one it was and where it left the roof. Karel and the Irishman wanted to tap it. It would be simple. She knew the layout of Melrose House, as she had performed there many times before the war, when Mrs Heys still lived there.

'There!' Koba put in the last pin to secure the rosebuds to her hair and kissed her on the forehead. 'My dear little dove! You look so elegant, so much like a princess.'

Stefanie inspected herself in the mirror above the mantelpiece. Her hair was arranged into an elegant roll, the rosebuds encircling it, her skin white and flawless, her eyes bright with excitement. She collected her sheet music when she heard wheels crunching to a standstill at the gate. Major Fernfield, a fellow pianist, was her escort for the evening. Delicate Major Fernfield, so intimidated by her superior talent.

She answered the knock on the door, saw the uniform in the dark and stood aside for Fernfield to enter. Then her hand flew to her mouth.

James stepped inside. 'Stefanie, Tante Koba,' he said. 'I'm sorry to arrive here on your doorstep without so much as a warning—'

He got no further. Koba swept him into her arms. 'James! My dear James,' she cried, holding him tight. 'Let me look at you. Have they treated you well in the hospital? I don't trust those English doctors.'

'Why, I'm completely recovered, Tante Koba,' he smiled and kissed her warmly.

'James!' Stefanie recovered her voice but not her composure. '*What are you doing here?* What are you doing in Pretoria?'

'I've been posted here. The order came only last week ...'

'Are you going to stay here? In Pretoria?'

'Yes, well ... until we leave for the war again, I suppose. I've been billeted in quite a charming old house with the regiment. I'm on General Kitchener's staff. I brought Victoria with me ...'

'You've brought your little wife?' Koba asked eagerly. 'Where is she?'

'At the Hollandia Hotel, by the station. I have to find suitable—'

'That's no place for a lady who has a lord for a father!' Koba took James by the arm and steered him deftly to the door. 'Go fetch her this instant! The poor thing! Leaving her all by herself at a hotel of all places.'

'Tante Koba, I came to greet you so that you should not bump into me on the streets, not knowing I was here. I don't want to impose on your hospitality and most certainly do not want to put you in an awkward position. For all outside purposes, I'm the enemy—', he tried to explain, but Koba would have none of it.

'No, no, *hartjie*, such nonsense! You're not my enemy,' she declared and pushed him out of the door. 'Go fetch your little wife. And don't dally! Come straight back here.'

Koba watched until James had left in the hired Cape cart and closed the door, looking at Stefanie with wide eyes. 'And now, *hartjie*? What now?' she panted. 'James will be here, but it's not he that worries me. He is only a man after all. His wife, yes!'

Stefanie sank down on the sofa. Always think clearly, Martin had impressed on her before he had left. Consider both sides, all sides, think clearly! She forced herself to ignore Koba's frantic prattling. James on Kitchener's staff? He would join the regiment soon, be out in the country for most of the time. Victoria in the house? She hated the war, despised her people for it. Would their presence endanger her plans? Or might she benefit from it?

'Tante Koba! Don't you see?' she asked bursting with excitement. 'What could be better than to have Lord Fairfield's daughter living with us? No one will suspect us! We'll just have to be extra careful.'

'Ask God to set a watch before our mouths,' Koba said, wagging her finger at Stefanie. 'You do have a quick, sharp tongue, *hartjie.*'

Major Fernfield's hansom drew up at the gate. Stefanie hastily gathered her sheet music and gloves and kissed Koba on the cheek. 'Settle Victoria in, Tante Koba,' she whispered. 'We'll talk when I get back. I'll come to your bedroom.'

AS STEFANIE PASSED the bronze lions guarding the front door of Melrose House, she felt as if she was walking into the proverbial lion's den. Once inside, she glanced to her left. The large morning room now served as Kitchener's office. There were a few officers, papers in hand, coming and going.

Major Fernfield steered her out onto the lawn where the guests were gathered. She accepted a glass of sherry and mingled with officers in their fine mess dress, a few civilians in evening suits and a sprinkling of women in the latest fashion. In the far corner of the garden, red-tabbed staff officers surrounded General Kitchener.

An hour passed before the guests were invited to the drawing room, where chairs had been arranged for the entertainment. The furniture was as she remembered – ornate and elegant, thickly upholstered. Potted palms and huge flower arrangements gave the room a graceful touch. To her annoyance, she was not the only artist invited. A woman, whom she recognised as Lady Bridgeland, took her place next to the piano and nodded to the officer seated at the keyboard to commence playing.

Stefanie's eyes went to General Kitchener sitting in the front row. His long legs crossed at the ankles, his clothes immaculate, the buttons of his uniform polished to a high shine. In his left hand he held a glass, cognac she guessed, and his right hand supported his chin. His gaze was fixed on the singer, but there was no trace of emotion on his austere features.

When Lady Bridgeland finished her second song to mild applause, Stefanie still had her eyes on Kitchener. His face remained inscrutable. *You will not intimidate me. After all, you're only a man, as Tante Koba says.*

Her fame had spread, and a swell of applause followed her as she took her place at the piano. She looked at the music she had selected; a romantic Brahms sonata and the fiery Chopin Valse. Her choice was wrong, not for the occasion, but for the man. To the consternation of Major Fernfield, who was to turn the pages for her, she placed the sheets on top of the piano. Her hands hovered above the keys, her fingers chose a transcription of a Wagner overture, a piece she knew by heart, having performed it many times for British officers at the Mount Nelson. There was not a cough, a shuffle or even a whisper from her audience as she played through the piece.

PETER RADFORD HEARD THE MUSIC as he entered the front door of Melrose House. He froze, listened for a moment and walked into the drawing room. There was Stefanie, playing with complete abandon, her fingers dancing over the keys, her shoulders following the rise and fall of the melody, her cheeks flushed with pleasure. He waited until she had struck the last spirited notes, and, as the thunderous applause broke out, he left for the telegraph office.

STEFANIE WAS OVERWHELMED with praise. Major Fernfield handed her a glass of champagne, but it was a full ten minutes later that she saw General Kitchener approaching. The admirers gave way and the next instant he stood in front of her. His eyes were hard, intimidating. Somehow she managed to return his gaze without wariness.

'Magnificent. Such commitment,' he said. 'Have you considered doing a circuit in London?'

'Yes, but regrettably I had to cancel,' she lied.

'My presence is demanded elsewhere. However, I'm entertaining a few visitors next Saturday. If you're not otherwise engaged?'

'It would be my pleasure, sir.'

He thanked her for her company and turned to the other guests.

Suddenly her eyes met the gold-flecked ones that had been in her dreams for the past six months. Peter's fair hair was neatly combed, but she saw it ruffled on the pillow beside her. She looked at his mouth, felt it searching her throat, her breasts, her thighs. Her eyes travelled to his hands. She reached for them but he clasped them behind his back, leaning a little away from her. There were a thousand things to say. Unable to hide her longing for him, she lowered her eyes and fiddled with her gloves.

'My first night on duty and I find you. How lucky! Cape Town was quite dismal without you to quarrel with. I missed you. I ...' His eyes were serious as he first looked at Kitchener, standing not ten yards from them, and then back at her. 'I love you, Stefanie.' He touched her hand briefly. 'And your eyes, I'm afraid, always betray you. Now they tell me that you love me too.'

She felt trapped and could not bear his nearness for a moment longer. 'You stole my papers!' she accused in a whisper.

'Papers? What papers?'

She was still searching for an answer when Major Fernfield arrived, handing her a fresh glass of champagne.

A Pitiful Sight

A FTER THE EUPHORIA of the victory at Nooitgedacht, the summer rains set in, making observation of enemy movements near impossible. British troops drove the commandos relentlessly and harassed the women on the farms. The horse sickness Charles had seen in December spread rapidly, and many men were without mounts. Men disappeared from the commando, never to be heard from again. It was said that many had joined the British, as they feared for their farms.

Martin sent fifty men with Joep Maree to the Free State to make contact with General de Wet and obtain remounts. Karel and a few scouts accompanied them to the crossing points over the swollen Vaal River. They arrived back with fewer than sixty horses and very disturbing news.

'The English are everywhere,' Joep reported to Martin where they were having coffee in Martin's tent. 'No sooner do De Wet's forces clear a town than the English take it back again. Buks got these horses from De Wet's men. They're not much, but it was truly the best he could do.'

Joep settled on an upturned ammunition kist and took out his pipe. Karel stood behind him, fidgeting with his Mauser. Martin looked at his father-in-law's distressed face and knew there was worse to come.

'It's true that the English burn farms. The air is thick with smoke, the kraals full of carcasses. They stab them with their lances, leave them to die. The women and children roam the veld, running before the English, and when caught they are taken to camps, like prisoners. The servants and the workers too.' He shook his head and scratched his beard. 'Ai, it's a pitiful sight – not easy for a man to stand by and watch helplessly. Buks says he saw a grandfather trying to protect his few sheep. The khakis chased him, but he couldn't run, and then they shot him.'

'There's terrible sickness in these camps,' Karel said, scowling deeply. 'People die for the want of food and medicines. A girl who escaped from the Brandfort camp told us that they buried twenty-five children on one day. Measles and stomach fever, she said.'

It took a while before Martin responded. 'I would never have thought that a soldier like Kitchener would resort to these methods.'

'Rudi and I went ahead with the dispatches for General de Wet,' Karel said, still fidgeting with his rifle. 'We found him and President Steyn north of Kroonstad. It's the same all over the Free State. Only the houses of the *hensoppers* still stand.'

'Put your rifle down!' Martin said. Karel obeyed grudgingly, and Martin had to prompt him to get the rest of his report. 'Did you come across the little forts? Stefanie wrote that they were putting up little forts all along the railway line.'

'Blockhouses,' Karel said. 'McFee crossed a few of these when he blew up the line north of Kroonstad. Easy, he says, nothing to it, only a few soldiers guarding each, with rows of wire stretched in between. You simply cut the wires, split up your men, cross at different points.'

'We have to contact Jan Smuts and the others. We need to have a *krygsraad* and decide what to do,' Martin said. 'Karel, have my horse saddled.'

'There's one more thing,' Joep said when Karel left. 'General de Wet's farm was burnt down, his wife and children sent to a camp in Natal. Wintersrust is next, that's a sure thing.'

'There's no time to waste,' Martin said. 'All men within reach of their farms must go there at once. Get fodder, clothing, blankets and food; bring in all the horses. We will make smaller depots at the far end of the mountains to the west where the English fear to come. The women must take flight when the farm burning starts in their area.' He stood up, but turned back to Joep. 'What's the matter with Karel now? Was there trouble with him on the trip, Pa?'

Joep lit his pipe and called for more coffee. 'Ai, a bad thing happened, son. And I think it's eating at his insides. Well, it was like this,' he said, scratching his beard again. 'We came across two natives carrying things taken from a farm. Looters, I said, but Karel would not have it. He shot them then and there. I later heard from Rudi that Karel had found a woman's body on the stoep. She had been used.'

'What Karel did was unwise, and in the heat of the moment. I'll speak to him,' Martin said after he had thought this over. 'Pa, the war is taking a new turn now. In war, your enemy invades your country, men take up the rifle and fight. We fight for our livelihood and what has been built up through generations. Now they burn our houses, destroy our farms. But touch a hair on a woman's head, a mother, sister or wife ...'

'Hate and revenge, son.' Joep looked at Martin long and hard. 'Keep it at bay. I know it's hard, but you don't want a thousand men to turn into a murderous horde. For where you lead, not just in battle, but in mind, they will follow.'

'It won't be easy, Pa, we can't be near our farms all the time, the war will come to a standstill. Karel!' he called through the tent flap. 'Send for the officers. I want you and Rudi to leave for home at once and start clearing the barns.'

'We leave for Pretoria tonight,' Karel said, putting his head through the flap. 'Stefanie is waiting. It's dark moon.'

'Very well. Come direct from Pretoria and report to me at home. We have to get some things to the cave and I must convince Ma that this is necessary. You know how difficult she can be. Get Charles, he has to move his medicines. Where is Buks?'

'He's at Wintersrust again,' Joep said, irritation strong in his voice. 'He slipped away without my permission. What he witnessed on this trip angered him deeply. I should never have forced him to accompany me. Martin, he's my son, your brother-in-law and is taking advantage of that. Coming and going as he wishes and endangering his mother and wife ... all at Wintersrust. Son, put him in another commando away from here. Commandant Buys's or Koos de la Rey's. There's trouble to come.'

'I'll speak to him later. Come, Pa, let's find the Viljoens and get this move done.'

TWO DAYS LATER, Martin and a small group of men arrived at Wintersrust and Soetvlei with three wagons. It took an entire day to load the ammunition stored in a deep ravine opposite the house. They laboured through the cover of darkness to pick up the food supplies from the barns and get the wagons to the smaller depots far away from the farms and deeper into the mountain.

The following morning, Joep fetched the Maree women from Wintersrust and took them to Soetvlei to do their packing. Martin arrived at Wintersrust and found Charles and Anita moving the medical supplies onto the mule-cart. Mary and Annecke were on the stoep, looking at the mountain, watching out for the heliograph flashes. He had positioned men where the road could be seen in all directions, so that they would have plenty of warning should the English catch them at their work.

Martin kissed the two women, placed his rifle against the wall and picked up the baby from the crib. 'He should not play with this, Annecke.'

He tossed the rag doll aside. 'How you've grown, my boy! And you have your mother's eyes.' He looked proudly at his son. His hair was thick and curly like a De Winter, but his eyes were large and brown like Annecke's. The little hands went to the bandolier around his chest and managed to dislodge a bullet. 'No, you may not touch this, son, not yet. Pull your father's beard.' Martin pried the bullet from his fingers. 'Have you packed, Ma?' he asked over his shoulder.

'I refuse to be evicted from my house.' Mary folded her arms across her chest, a sure sign of resistance. 'I came here as a bride and will not run at the mere rumour of—'

'Ma, please, there's a war on. I simply can't be here all the time to watch over you,' Martin said. Her British tenacity, her need to act normally even though the world might be falling apart around her, irritated him. A longing for Koba's strong presence of mind and practical way of dealing with a crisis suddenly came over him.

'I had a letter from your father just last week,' Mary said. 'He has a dreadful stomach complaint he can't shake off. He wrote that the thought of this house, the farm and us waiting for him here is all that gets him through the loneliness. You can't expect me to leave.'

'Ma, I'm not asking you to leave yet. Only remove your valuable things and some furniture that would make life comfortable in the cave.'

'I will not live in a cave like a baboon.'

'Baboons don't live in caves … Oh, what's the use! Annecke, get some coffee.' Martin turned to his mother again. In her world, it was unthinkable that the British would burn houses in order to win a war. He shifted the boy to his hip and put an arm around her shoulders. 'Ma, I know that here you are closer to Pa. All that I ask is to be ready should they come to burn Wintersrust.'

'How shall I get Lettie up there?' Mary asked, taking a chair. 'She can barely manage ten paces a day.'

'I'll see to my mother, Ma,' Annecke said coming through with the coffee. 'We will have the mule-cart close by and hide in the kloof till all danger passes.'

'I leave four milk cows and fifty sheep,' Martin said. 'The rest of our herds will go with Jacob Viljoen to the bushveld. With one leg only, he can't fight any more. Jan sent him and their womenfolk far away from the farms. It's for the best.'

'Very well,' Mary said. 'Take some furniture, but I'm convinced that once I explain to the British officers that we don't keep your ammunition here, they will be reasonable.'

'Just think for one moment about those who haven't been warned, Ma,' Annecke said. 'At least we get to keep our good things.'

Martin decided to leave it at that. He handed the baby to his mother and went into the house. He selected the iron bedsteads and mattresses in the dormitory, some chairs and a table from the kitchen and the crockery Annecke had packed. He grabbed a sheet and bundled his mother's silver and odd bits he knew she treasured into it. In his father's study, he took as many books as he could, saw the *sjambok* on the wall and, with a smile, took it off the hook.

'They are flashing, Martin!' Annecke called from the stoep.

He hastened back and read the flashes. *Scouts back. Coming down.*

'Karel and Rudi. I'll meet them halfway. Come on, Annecke. Let's get the things outside. Charles will take them to the kloof when he's done with the cart.'

They carried the kitchen things and mattresses outside, while Charles and Anita lugged crates of medicines. Anita told Martin to leave the domestic arrangements to her and Charles. He hugged her thankfully and went to where his horse was tied at the stoep.

'Send your brothers here, Martin,' Mary called. 'I haven't seen them since Christmas.'

'They are frightfully busy, Ma!'

'Blowing up trains, stealing from their foe?'

'Ma, you really have no concept of war whatsoever,' Martin muttered. He rode towards the kloof and met Karel and Rudolf at the vlei. They were stumbling with exhaustion, faces haggard and grey with fatigue.

Karel handed Martin the oilcloth bags. 'Stefanie says James arrived in Pretoria last month and so has Peter Radford.'

'Oh no,' Martin said. 'Has James been to Tante Koba?'

'Yes, his wife is staying there. James spends some nights there, Tante Koba says, but Radford never comes to the house. Stefanie says that, with Lord Fairfield's daughter living with them, no one will suspect her. We'll just have to be more careful.'

An unexpected longing rushed through Martin. He had not thought about Victoria for a long time. He found his brothers watching him closely and he quickly turned his back to them. He saw Annecke still standing on the stoep, their son in her arms. Annecke, his wife, the woman with whom he had to spend the rest of his life, the woman who would bear him more children. He felt unfulfilled and miserable. How different it would have been to have the mystery of Vicky, the passion.

With an effort, he pulled himself together and placed the bags inside his shirt. 'There's a *krygsraad* at Cypherfontein in two weeks. Could you take me there?'

'No, Gert Swart reported that a convoy with many fresh horses has left Potchefstroom bound for Rustenburg,' Karel said. 'Uncle Joep needs the horses desperately and wants us to find a suitable place to ambush the convoy. And again, there are spies who have their eyes set on you. No doubt it's your Hunter friend again. I'll deal with them first. Take McFee and Danie Vermaas.'

'Tell them to meet me at my camp,' Martin said, mounted and rode to catch up with Charles, who was taking the mule-cart to the kloof. Glancing over his shoulder, he saw Karel walking towards the house, but Rudolf was making his way back to the cave.

A Dangerous Game

EVER SINCE NEW YEAR'S Eve, Stefanie had seen Peter on a few more occasions – at Melrose House recitals for Kitchener, at a dinner hosted by Colonel Butcher at the regiment's quarters on the outskirts of Pretoria and at other social gatherings in town. But she always avoided being alone with him, keeping Victoria or James at her side.

And now Victoria handed her a note from Peter, *demanding* to see her that night. Victoria and James were to take Koba to Burgers Park to hear the regimental bands. She was to wait for him at home. If not, his note said, he would search for her and drag her home.

After all these months, Peter might want the truth about the papers she had carried in her hat. She had deceived him, but now things were different. He was riding off to fight again; he might not return. She longed to be with him, to share his carefree intimacy and to be loved. There was so little time.

She looked at Victoria sitting opposite her on the sofa. Although she tried, she did not like the mysterious woman her darling cousin had married. Still, James seemed to like her. She wondered if Victoria was pleasing in bed. The thought made her blush, and she turned her mind back to her own pressing need. She would see Peter that night. She would not deny him the truth about her papers, but neither would she confess to spying. They would have to find a way to live in another world, play another game until the war ended it one way or another. There had to be a way, but she would leave it up to him.

PETER ARRIVED AT KOBA'S HOUSE long after James had come for Koba and Victoria. He led his horse to the back, hitching her to the horse-post. As he raised his hand to knock on the front door, Stefanie opened it.

She stood for a moment, taking in his taupe riding breeches, navy jacket and cravat covering most of the scar at his throat. Her eyes went briefly to his gold signet ring, which he did not wear when in uniform, on the little finger of his right hand. He stepped inside, closing the door behind him.

'Would you like tea or coffee? Brandy? James keeps a bottle.' She indicated the decanters on the dresser at his side.

'I'd like tea, please.'

While she was busy in the kitchen, he stayed by the door, his eyes taking in the room. It was a homely place – two sofas facing each other, a few comfortable chairs, a large rocker by the fireplace, vases filled with summer flowers and lamps throwing soft light about the room. *How different our worlds are,* he thought, *yet not so different.* His eye was drawn to the framed photographs above the piano: Martin and Charles on graduation day; James receiving his commission; the twin brothers, with their horses, and the dark-haired girl, Martin's wife, smiling shyly; Stefanie at the piano. He lingered on a large picture of Martin and President Kruger, taken in front of the Raadsaal.

'Martin and his predecessor.' Stefanie entered, carrying a tray. 'That's what James calls that picture.' She placed the tray on the table between the sofas and sat down, indicating the seat opposite her.

He watched her pouring the tea, her hands betraying her nervousness. She was dressed in a plain striped cotton dress, her hair rolled behind her head. Her face was pale and tense. He felt stifled, trapped.

'This is so unlike us. I don't like it a bit. We should be laughing, quarrelling …'

'I don't like it either.' She picked up her cup. Then, looking steadily at him, said, 'I shall come to the point. What happened to the papers?'

'I destroyed them.' He stirred sugar into his cup.

'You should have reported me.'

'I was rather under the impression that it's an unrepeatable incident, seeing that your husband's office is a long way from Pretoria.'

'And now you are suspicious.'

'Do I have reason to be?'

'I should think so, Peter. General de Winter's sister? Is that not reason enough?'

'On its own?' He shook his head. 'It might not be known where your sympathies truly lie, but I know, don't I? But I also know that Martin is a noble man and would not endanger his sister.' A shadow passed across her face and she lowered her eyes. 'I thought … retaliation for what happened in Cape Town was behind the papers, the bruises … your husband? I remember you saying that you had to fight for something that was very dear to you.'

She leaned back in the sofa, her eyes bright in the lamplight, but whether they were filling up with tears, he could not tell. 'Yes, what I gave to you the night in Johannesburg,' she said. 'That's what I fought for.'

He reached across the table and touched her knee. 'Thank you, my love.'

She cleared her throat, and when she spoke her voice was detached. 'I found those papers in Paul's study quite by chance and decided to give them to Martin. Tell me, Peter, should you find something again, you will report me, won't you?'

'It would be my duty.'

'Yes, your duty, but I could say you had evidence and failed to report it, that you deliberately destroyed it.'

He stared in astonishment. He dared not report her. They would both be executed. His thoughts were racing, attempting to separate truth from deception, reality from the love they so desperately needed to share. He placed his cup on the table and stood up. 'Do you realise what you've just said?'

'Yes. They'll shoot me, won't they?' Her eyes were on the Radford crest engraved on his ring.

He put his hand into his pocket. 'God, Stefanie! Facing a firing squad! Am I supposed to think you're serious?'

Her eyes, he knew, never lied. And now, through the ruthlessness she was trying to convey, they said all that she did not put into words – her fear and misery, and love. He glanced at the clock on the mantelpiece. 'I go on duty at ten. I have to change.'

When he reached the door, he turned to face her. She was sitting quietly, her hands in her lap, her eyes shining in the lamplight. 'This is a dangerous game, you have no idea how dangerous,' he warned in a whisper and left.

SHE DIDN'T SEE HIM AGAIN until the Officers' Ball at Swartkoppies Estate, a week later. As a married woman, she refused personal invitations and went with James and Victoria in Koba's Cape cart.

James brought the cart to a halt and disentangled himself from her and Victoria's billowing evening gowns. He held out his arms to receive Victoria, planting a kiss on her mouth when he delivered her to the ground.

'You look ravishing tonight, my dear. Emeralds and diamonds and yards of green stuff ...' He leaned forward, whispering something in her ear.

It's going to be one of those nights. Stefanie thought and hoped that James's cheerfulness would last the evening. His moods were so, so fragile, especially when he was not sober. She had heard his raised voice in Victoria's bedroom a few nights back.

'Come, Waterfall!' James swung Stefanie through the air. Her dress was a sparkling blue and silver, which Koba had described as a waterfall. 'You're also very … oh dear! I shall have to omit the ravishing bit.'

He released her with a kiss to her cheek. She inspected his mess dress: gold braid on the blue tunic, black trousers, his medals making a soft clinking noise as he moved. 'I've never seen you in your finery. How dashing!'

He pulled her hand through his arm. 'Thank you, cousin. But that won't get you very far. I'm your chaperone and I propose to do my duty. I shall personally check every name on your card.'

'They've dispensed with that tonight.' Victoria hooked her arm through James's. 'There are too few ladies. Stefanie, we'll be gasping on our feet by midnight.'

They joined the throng of black evening suits, imposing uniforms and rustling evening gowns. The spacious garden was lit with Chinese lanterns and flaming torches. A canvas dance floor, surrounded by tables and chairs, had been laid out on the lawn and a platform erected for the orchestra. Enormous flower arrangements and potted plants formed an aisle leading to the floor.

James led them to where he had spotted some of his regiment. Stefanie's gaze found Peter. His mess dress, the blue and gold tunic complementing his blond hair to perfection, magnetised her. Their eyes met in ill-concealed admiration and love. He was still annoyed with her, but she was going to dance in his arms and he was going to make love to her tonight; she saw it in his eyes.

'What a fortunate fellow you are, Henderson.' Murray Shaw came to meet them. 'A most charming lady on each arm.'

'And you, sir, are the fortunate man to have the first dance with my cousin.'

Stefanie caught the smug smile James sent to Peter and wondered how much James knew about the situation between them.

'I'm most honoured, Mrs Warren,' Shaw bowed. 'Champagne?'

The evening sparkled with magic and music. When the dance with Shaw ended, he brought her back to the table. James handed Victoria to Peter, took Stefanie's arm and hastily swallowed a few mouthfuls of champagne before dancing her away.

'Your next dance is with Hunter.'

'No, Jamie, I refuse to dance with that pompous fool!'

He laughed and doubled his step. 'Shall we poison him, or shall I challenge him to a duel?'

'Who? Hunter?'

'Your husband! Shall I tell you why? The most sought after, most handsome man in the empire, according to the ladies, is at your mercy.'

'And I'm dancing with him at this very moment!'

He kissed her on her cheek and pressed her close to him. 'Peter Radford loves you.' His face turned serious. 'Be careful, cousin. Peter is not in the habit of thinking beyond the day.'

She danced with Moore and Miles. The evening became a whirl of swirling dresses, gold braid and champagne. Peter's eyes met hers frequently through the dancing and laughter, increasing the desire simmering between them.

When John Miles returned her to the table, she hardly had a chance to catch her breath when Peter's hand was under her elbow. Then she was in his arms and the world ceased to exist. She kept her eyes on his Victoria Cross resting on the crimson ribbon, and only when he squeezed her hand did she raise her eyes to meet his. Yearning consumed her, and was reflected in his face. She tried to tear her gaze away, but she was mesmerised.

'You make impossible demands on my loyalty to my country,' Peter said.

'I could say the same of you.'

'Yes, I've thought about that.' After they had done another circuit, he spoke again, his voice urgent. 'Stefanie, I couldn't bear it if something should happen to you. I've never loved before. I never thought one could feel so deeply. It's frightening.'

'Yes … frightening …' She took a deep breath. 'Peter, I'd prefer to think you didn't destroy the papers.'

'Yes, let's forget about the hat,' he said after a bit. 'What you stole didn't reach Martin.'

Tears stung her eyes, but the waltz ended and she managed to conceal them from him.

'Shall we have another, or will there be talk?' He cast a glance towards James. 'Or worse?'

'There'll be talk. You have a scandalous reputation, as I've found.'

The music started up and he took her in his arms again. 'Scandalous reputation? Do you believe it?'

'Oh yes, I do. You seduced me shamelessly.'

'You wanted me too.' They danced a while in silence and then he whispered close to her ear. 'Under the willows at the far end of your garden. I'll be there when you get home.'

'Under the willows? Oh yes, no one will see us except the moon.'

'No one will hear us except the frogs, or perhaps an owl.'

IN THE EARLY HOURS of the morning, she tiptoed past Victoria's bedroom, where a lamp still burnt, and clearly heard James's laugh. She stole through the moonlit orchard, passed the stables, careful not to wake Bontes, and reached the willows. Peter sat under the middle tree, smoking, his back against the trunk. He had changed into his khaki uniform. His pistol and boots were discarded, the buttons of his tunic undone. She slipped around the tree and knelt in front of him.

His eyes travelled over her body showing through her nightdress and her hair falling free to her waist. 'Forsaken your balcony for a bed of grass?' he asked, his voice a soft caress.

She swept her hair over her shoulders. 'Juliet was just a lovelorn girl, her love a passing infatuation. But, like her, I will gladly die for you. Poison. A dagger to my breast, or whatever it was she did.'

He reached for a bottle and glasses at his side. 'Before you take such drastic measures and deprive me of your love, would you care for champagne?'

She shook her head.

'Later, then?' He crushed out the cheroot, shrugging off his tunic. Then he held out his arms to her.

The *Hensoppers*

MARTIN ARRIVED AT Cypherfontein, General Jan Smuts's headquarters, with a ten-man escort. Located seventy miles southwest of Pretoria, Cypherfontein was too remote for the enemy, which made it ideal for the meetings of the senior Boer generals. The Magalies range lay to the east, the tree-clad valleys to the north and the grassy downs of the Witwatersrand and goldfields to the southeast. And unbeknown to the British, Smuts had a constant ear on the telegraph line connecting Pretoria to Rustenburg, giving him warning of enemy movements into the area.

It was mid-March, and the heat was unsparing. As they rode through orchards towards the farmstead, a welcome coolness enveloped them. The air was filled with the smell of ripening fruit and running water. Martin noticed the tents in ordered rows under the orange trees, cooking fires laid out with stones, firewood stacked neatly within reach.

Martin raised his hat, greeting the men in the camp. He dismounted at the tents designated for his escort, and called Patrick McFee. 'See if you can get a sheep. We'll be here for a day or so. Don't spend all our money on whisky, just half of it.'

Like Karel, Martin was attached to the rough Irishman. He was dependable, and quick to point out any oversights or offer advice when he deemed it vital.

Martin found the other five generals seated around the table in the dining room.

'Trouble on your way, son?' Koos de la Rey smiled a welcome. 'We expected you yesterday.'

'No trouble, Oom Koos,' Martin shook hands with the generals in turn. 'It's my Irish scout being over-cautious again. I dare not move without his consent.'

'There's real Dutch coffee on the stove.' Jan Smuts pointed to the kitchen. 'Pour yourself a cup and come sit down. We have a long agenda.' Martin fetched a mug of coffee and took his place at the table, directly opposite Smuts as was arranged beforehand. Smuts's stern eyes met his briefly; by the set of his mouth above the goatee, Martin construed that he had already had an unproductive encounter with the older men.

'At the meeting with President Steyn and General Botha, it was decided, in order to stop this cruel policy of farm burning, to invade the Cape Colony in small commandos, attempting to gain the support of our brethren, but so far they've not been successful. Men have joined, yes, but what we want is a general uprising of Afrikaners. All it has gained for us so far is to draw some enemy out of the Free State and, in so doing, give General de Wet's commandos time to rest and refit. Fifteen thousand English are engaged in chasing Scheepers and Wessels in the Cape,' General De la Rey said. 'General Botha's attempt to invade Natal has failed. For the moment we're still relatively comfortable in comparison to the other areas, but the time will come when we will have to look towards the colonies to take the pressure off the Free State. Winter is approaching, but come spring we need to send a strong force of Transvalers south.'

They went on to discuss the plight of the women, children and servants in the concentration camps. The state of the camps was deplorable, judging by reports from the Free State. Over twelve thousand women and children had died, and their servants were suffering even more, as they were given no food or shelter.

Martin placed Stefanie's papers on the table. 'A great number of men also fled to these camps. Our source in Pretoria revealed that the British plan to organise them into a reconnaissance force. They'll be used to smell us out and will be paid handsomely.'

An outcry followed. 'Those traitors should be dealt with before the rot spreads!' General Slabbert, an old man with a full grey beard, said.

'There's a difference between a *hensopper* and a traitor,' Martin said, 'and they should be dealt with accordingly. A *hensopper* sits on his farm, unwilling to fight. But a traitor walks over to the English and offers his help.'

'What would you suggest?' Smuts exchanged a glance with Martin. They had drawn up a legal document listing penalties, which had been approved by General Louis Botha. It was drastic. The older and less educated men would find them hard to accept, but the country was under martial law. With a nod, Smuts motioned Martin to proceed.

'For the *hensoppers*: confiscate their possessions and destroy their farms. For the traitors,' Martin cleared his throat and sent a silent plea to General de la Rey for support. 'A military court will be held, and if treason is established – supplying the British with information or assisting them against the commandos and therefore against the *Volk* – the penalty is death before a firing squad.'

'Exactly the ruling of Botha and De Wet,' Smuts said emphatically. There was a disgruntled silence.

'Destroy the farm of a *hensopper*, that I can do, but shoot our own people?' General Buys shook his head.

'We make a camp in the bushveld – keep the traitors there,' General Slabbert suggested.

'And within a month the camp overflows with those who have earned their British shilling and sit out the war while we feed and protect them?' asked Martin.

'The penalty for treason against the *Volk* is death!' Smuts tapped his fingers on the table, emphasising every word.

Another long silence followed, in which Koos de la Rey sucked on his pipe noisily while the other generals muttered at the excess of the ruling.

'General Botha has already executed traitors, and so has General de Wet,' Martin said.

'Look at the situation in the Free State,' De la Rey said. 'The burghers hands-up to save their farms and families. Those who have lost everything continue to fight. What else is there for them? And now they resent those who walk over to the enemy. There will be civil war if these traitors are not dealt with severely.'

'How will these courts work, son?' General Slabbert asked, seeking out Martin's face.

'There will be a panel of five men: two generals and three commandants. Both Jan Smuts and I are lawyers. We cast the verdict when a decision cannot be reached. We'll give the accused every chance to defend himself. If guilty, he'll be shot by men not known to him. He'll be an example to others who consider treason.'

'That concludes that point. All agreed?' Smuts said and quickly turned to De la Rey. 'Oom Koos, I believe that you have news from our commander.'

De la Rey selected a document from the pile in front of him. 'Well now, the news from Botha is that the English want to talk. Kitchener asks for a conference to discuss terms of settlement.' He shook his greying head. 'There's not much hope in this, as they're bound to seek to deprive us of our independence. The Free Staters refuse the invitation, and rightly so. Louis Botha asks that I send a general to Middelburg to represent our area.'

'Won't you be going, Oom Koos? Surely they can't decide anything without your approval?'

'No, Martin, I'm not going, but you are. With your fancy words and wise ideas you'll make them see that we're not interested in empty proposals.'

'What am I to say to them?'

'Listen to what they have to say, son. See how eager they are to end the war. Your work is to convince them that we can continue this fight indefinitely.'

'Keep them talking, guessing,' Jan Smuts said. 'Buy us time to enter the Cape and start an uprising there. We need time desperately, Martin.'

'Where am I to meet General Botha? It's a dangerous trek through the bushveld to reach him. Might take weeks.'

'The English will come for you,' De la Rey said. 'You have to present yourself at a spot five miles outside Krugersdorp. They'll put you on the train and escort you to Middelburg. I'll fill you in on the details after we've had something to eat.'

The Night that Changed Everything

April 1901

SIX THOUSAND MILES AWAY, Queen Victoria had died. For a week, Church Square was draped in black, and the Union Jack flew at half-mast. Koba wiped tears from her face with her white handkerchief and joined the crowds and troopers to listen to the military bands playing sombre marches.

And it was James's twenty-sixth birthday. When the town returned to normal, she asked Bontes to carry the trestle table and wicker chairs to the willows at the far end of her garden. It was time to have James's friends over, she decided. It would allay suspicion of Stefanie, and she needed to see the young lord, Peter. She needed to look him in the eye. Twice in the past week, when the clock had struck midnight, she had seen a white nightdress stealing into the orchard. Stefanie was in love, but she was also wise and would heed Koba's warning about the unfavourable days to lie with a man. But there was the war. God had put urgency in men to replace those they had left on the battlefields, an urgency that would not be denied. Like war and nature, women also had their seasons. Victoria was given to brooding, absorbed in Martin's picture against the wall when she thought herself unobserved. It was not love. There was a want in her green eyes, an obsession. Yet, she could not perceive the love so near, the love carefully, skilfully, concealed in her husband's eyes. But, like the war, love and lust would take their course. She could only guide love.

She donned her dove-grey dress, fixed her town hat on her hair, and was helping Stefanie and Victoria carry the feast she had prepared to the willows, when James and his fellow-officers arrived with wine and champagne.

'A bottle of sweet wine especially for you, Tante Koba!' James smacked a kiss on her cheek.

'Only two small glasses a day, *hartjie*,' she reminded him.

She gave her full attention to the others when James introduced them.

Norman Butcher, his gentle colonel; Murray Shaw, a huge, friendly man; William Moore, dark-haired and stern; John Miles, short and slim and polite; Neil Smithers, a well-mannered boy; and Peter.

'I remember your face well, young man,' she said, looking into his lively brown eyes. 'The face of an angel, I told James years ago.'

James and Stefanie burst out laughing, and the other officers made ambiguous remarks, but Peter, smiling widely, accepted her scrutiny openly and sincerely.

'Coming from you, Mrs van Wyk, I take it as a compliment,' he said and kissed her hand.

'Call me Tante Koba, *hartjie*. Everyone does!'

It was a beautiful summer's day. The intoxicating scent of her flower garden wafted through the carefree voices of the young ones while they joked, laughed, ate and drank. She moved her chair a little away from them and dozed, but observed them from under half-closed eyelids. Their accents were a bit awkward on the ear, but she caught most of what was said, if not through words, then in what was written on their faces.

Stefanie found it hard to keep her eyes from Peter, who lay stretched out on the grass next to James. And Peter grinned secretly when his eyes strayed to the middle willow tree. James laughed too loudly and drank thirstily – a dark mood was gathering in him again. The big Shaw was most entertaining, plaiting the sweeping branches of the willow, saying that he had it in mind to use it as a whip on a fellow named Hunter. Something to do with cards, brandy and vindictiveness. The others found it amusing, even the dear colonel, who was unwinding now that he had had a few glasses of champagne and a good few helpings of her bobotie. The two younger ones, Miles and Smithers, were attempting to coax empty champagne bottles into an arch, but Peter ruined their efforts by aiming corks at the bottles.

Vicky was interested in the pattern on the blue china plates, telling the sad tale to the dark-haired Moore. Others joined in, giving their judgement, some downright saucy, as to why the lovers were doomed to love as two entwined white doves.

'What drivel,' laughed James. But there was hurt in his eyes. 'Kissing for all eternity! Shall we leave them to it?'

Koba caught the loving glance exchanged between Peter and Stefanie. She rose and waddled to the kitchen to get the coffee. When she had greeted Peter and had looked him in the eye, she had found no arrogance or guilt there. His was a love pure and honest and beautiful. Her little white dove had found a perfect mate.

Her hand went to her pocket, reaching for her handkerchief. Martin and Stefanie, brother and sister, zealous in pursuit of perfection, yet bestowing their passions so hopelessly. But they could not, would not be denied. It was not in their power. Their loyalties were fated to stay poised between two worlds.

It was in the mixing of the blood: Boer and Brit.

———

'LAST WEEK IT WAS THE GUNNERS. A week ago the sappers,' Stefanie said, 'now it's the cavalry's turn. He can't accommodate everyone at once.' She and James were in Koba's sitting room, dressed in formal evening attire. She was searching through a pile of sheet music, but James was pestering her to come up with a plausible reason behind the evening's invitation.

'But why a Tuesday night? If it was a Saturday night, or even a Sunday luncheon, one could oblige, but tonight? We are off in the morning.' James drained his sherry. 'And why full mess dress—'

'Oh do stop carrying on so, Jamie! General Kitchener is a busy man. I suppose it's the only night he could spare for some relaxation.'

'My dear cousin! The man is not interested in the gentler sorts of relaxation. Warring, yes, but—'

'And burning people's homes,' Victoria said as she walked into the room.

Stefanie looked up sharply. She did not want James and Victoria to argue about the war again. 'Oh yes, James, he *is* interested in music,' she said quickly.

'Yes, *hartjie*,' Koba said from the kitchen door, wiping her hands on her apron. 'He has to put his feet up once in a while. I've been telling Stefanie that she should play songs to him so that he can hum along. Not the pieces that one has to think about.'

'Brilliant! Kitchener of Khartoum putting up his feet, humming 'Greensleeves'? Play him 'The Wild Colonial Boy'. Might bring tears to the old dragon's eyes.'

'Jamie! You're impossible!' She slapped his knee. 'I'll do no such thing.'

She went back to her sheet music. Kitchener's staff had informed her only that afternoon that he was entertaining some generals from London and Cape Town at the Pretoria Club. She was nervous. Dark moon had just passed and again McFee and the twins had tapped the telephone line from Melrose House. She had given them newspaper reports from Europe concerning the concentration camps. By using the censor's stamp she had stolen from Major Fernfield's office, she was able to send and receive letters in Johannesburg when she gave recitals there.

And every time she looked into Peter's eyes, guilt threatened to engulf her. For the past two months they had met frequently under the willows. They no longer talked about the war, but found themselves far beyond the boundaries to which the war had restricted their love. The extreme position it placed them in was silently acknowledged and accepted on the surface, but not in their hearts.

'James, where will you be heading tomorrow?' Victoria asked.

'We head north and are to protect convoys, not have battles. I'm quite looking forward to it. Riding over the bushveld, chasing elephant and *takhaaren*, is preferable to guarding Kitchener's telegraph office.'

'I fail to see how you can possibly return to active duty—'

'That's enough, Victoria!' James snapped

'Please, Vicky,' Stefanie said. 'It's hard on all of us.'

'Now, now, *hartjies*,' Koba intervened. 'We won't have words about the war. Come, Vicky, let me fix your hair properly. Go fetch your brushes. There's still time.'

Victoria went to her room and came back with her brushes and a little box filled with pins. Stefanie watched Koba brushing the red hair lovingly. Victoria had completely fallen under Koba's spell. They went shopping together, driving the Cape cart to town and carrying their baskets to Church Square. Victoria had taken on the task of visiting the wounded in the hospital, as Koba did daily.

'Right, I shall play only a few short pieces tonight. But I refuse to accompany that dreadful Lady Bridgeland again. Why she insists on singing to an audience, I'll never understand.' Stefanie planted a kiss on Koba's cheek and, with a swish of her blue silk dress, ignored James's cat noises.

IT WAS AN ELABORATE AFFAIR, Stefanie noticed, when they entered the hall at the Club; mess dress only, and masses of generals and senior officers.

Peter met them at the door. 'I say! The old man really wants to treat us tonight. Could it possibly be his birthday?'

'No idea, Radford,' said James as they helped themselves to glasses of sherry. 'I say, cousin, can you punch out the old birthday tune when he appears? We should be able to judge then?'

'Oh, brilliant!' Peter dared. 'You give voice, Stefanie will tinkle along.'

'What a delightful family gathering,' George Hunter said from behind Stefanie. 'Good evening, Mrs Warren.' His eyes were haughty, with a hint of a smile under his moustache. 'Back in the saddle again, Radford, Henderson?'

'Yes, sir, tomorrow, and looking forward to it,' Peter said.

'Any news from your family, Mrs Warren?'

Stefanie saw that James was about to protest, but she knew the danger in that. 'Why, Major Hunter, I had a letter only last week,' she said. 'Our prime breeding cow threw twins last month. The summer rains are good and Mother has run out of sugar again. Shortages of war. Could you spare her a bag perhaps, Major Hunter?'

Hunter sent her a piercing glance and took his leave.

'Well done, cousin!' James burst into laughter.

'What else could I say? I don't get any letters from home.'

'James, darling,' Victoria said, taking James by the arm, 'do escort me to a seat near the piano. If I'm to stand around waiting for something to happen, then at least I'd like to be comfortable.'

Left alone, Peter and Stefanie's eyes met.

'I'm leaving tomorrow, my love,' he said, looking over her shoulder, his eyes twinkling. 'When I get back, the willows will have lost their leaves and the nights will be cold.'

'Shall we try the stables, then? We have slept on straw before.' She nodded a greeting to Colonel Butcher.

Peter lifted a gloved hand to Murray Shaw as he passed. 'I remember one night distinctly. Under a mule-cart, in midwinter. You tried to seduce me.'

'Now I know exactly how. Shall I tell you?' She smiled at Major Fernfield.

'So what's keeping us from running away? Far away, to the ends of the earth, where no one can find us.'

'We can run only as far as the willows. You know that.'

'Pity, I'd always so much wanted to elope. Let's elope to the willows, then, my love. Shall we? Midnight?'

She nodded. 'Take me to the piano. We are being stared at.'

She placed her hand on his arm and he led her through the guests. She took her place at the piano, smiling at Major Fernfield, who was already there to turn the pages for her. James and Peter went off in search of something stronger than sherry.

She looked over her shoulder and saw General Kitchener enter, followed by four red-tabbed officers. He fell into conversation with the group closest to the door. She turned back to her sheet music and did not see the door open again. She was aware only of a sudden silence, followed by an announcement.

'Ladies and gentlemen, I'm honoured to present General Kitchener's guest for the evening. General Martin de Winter, Boer commander of the southwestern Transvaal.'

Martin's hair was bleached by the sun, and his face was framed by a golden-brown clipped beard. His pressed whipcord jacket and trousers, white shirt and ordinary tie and high riding boots looked out of place amid all the uniforms, but it was his eyes that demanded attention. They were alert, the eyes of a hunter accustomed to searching the veld for the slightest movement. He was barely thirty but did not carry the arrogance of a youthful leader. And it was obvious that, here in this room, surrounded by his adversaries, he was still in command.

HE WAS ON HIS WAY to the conference at Middelburg, east of Pretoria. He had arrived by train that afternoon expecting to carry on directly, as arranged, but was escorted by ten guards in a closed carriage to Melrose House, where Kitchener awaited him. After a few carefully phrased remarks concerning the conference, Kitchener invited him to join a few generals for dinner. He refused because he had not brought suitable attire. Kitchener assured him that his circumstances would be taken into account.

And now, standing here like a prime exhibit, he knew what Kitchener was up to; he wanted to unsettle him, to put him at a disadvantage, perhaps even to provoke his anger by bringing him face to face with the people who were now destroying his country. He smiled; he was not here to duel against individuals.

He eyes fell on James and Peter standing next to a potted palm. He saw Hunter, Shaw, Moore and other familiar faces from London. Kitchener approached him and the introductions to the many generals began. The room came to life again with excited whispers. He paid attention to everyone he was introduced to, answering their questions about his time in Cambridge, moving around completely at ease. He greeted Shaw and Moore and eventually came to James and Peter.

'Cousin James.' He gave him a hug. 'Are you recovered? How good it is to see you.'

'I'm astounded! What are you doing here?'

'Let's just say I've come to pay a visit.' Martin took Peter's offered hand.

'General de Winter!' Peter shook his hand long and hard.

'Congratulations on your VCs. Jan Viljoen once said that your chest will be smothered in medals before you get to be a general, James.'

'How is Jan? And the twins? Are Legend and Lady still alive?'

'Lady was killed, nearly took Rudolf with her. What a dreadful time we had with Karel when Rudolf was missing! But he has recovered. Legend? She's living up to her name ... Oh, yes, I'm deeply sorry about Mark Sinclair.'

'How did it happen?' James asked.

'Stomach wound. Rudolf found him hours after the battle. I buried him at Wintersrust ... oh, yes ...' His voice dropped. 'Before he died, he apparently said, "Warn James, Hunter, hospital."' Are you still feuding with Hunter, cousin?'

For a moment alarm showed in James's face, but he recovered almost instantly. 'And I suppose Charles is having an interesting time?'

'Oh yes, my men refuse to go into battle unless the English doctor is within reach ...' Martin saw a woman moving towards him and he half-turned.

A hush filled the room when he faced his sister. *Oh God, Stef, this is to be a test we dare not fail.* She stood composed, but in her eyes he saw fear.

'Good evening, Martin.'

'Stefanie.' He brushed his mouth against her cheek and clasped his hands behind his back.

'How is everything at home?' she asked, perhaps a little too loudly.

'Everyone's fine. The house is still there, miraculously.' He noticed that some of the onlookers averted their eyes. 'How is Tante Koba?'

'She's ... fine. How's your son?'

'He's ... healthy. Growing fast.'

They stood in an uncomfortable silence until a captain, sent by Kitchener, invited Martin to the buffet table. While he was filling his plate, he searched the guests with his eyes. If Stefanie was here, it was just possible ...

She stood by the piano. All else faded from his mind and vision as the years of separation fell away. He walked across the crowded room. He could not touch her; he could only look, and he saw that no words or even the most passionate embrace could have conveyed the love so clear in her eyes. Outwardly he was in control, but inwardly he became unmanned, defence-less. *I have the power to command a thousand men but here I stand vulnerable to the power of one woman.*

'I so much want to see you again, Vicky,' he said, speaking from his heart before he could stop the words he dared not say.

'The war will last for a long time still. Where will I find you?'

'I don't know, but give me time ... I'll send for you. Will you come?'

She nodded. They were still staring at each other when James and Peter joined them.

'I've brought you a splendid brandy.' Peter held out a glass.

Suddenly Martin felt weary and sad. He wanted to be away from the disturbing nearness of Victoria and the fear in Stefanie's eyes. 'No, but thank you, Peter, I must keep a clear head. It was good seeing you all so unexpectedly.' He nodded to Victoria and moved to the far side of the room to join Kitchener.

JAMES WATCHED Martin walk away. Victoria's words spoken the day they had decided to marry, hit him forcefully. *I loved someone once but he couldn't have me.* Their eyes met and there was no denial in hers.

KITCHENER SMILED. His ploy had worked. He had watched as Mrs Warren had greeted her brother, and he had not been fooled.

NOR HAD Peter Radford been fooled. There could be no more nights under the willows. From now on he had to avoid Stefanie. Their lives depended on it.

The Second Winter

THE SECOND WINTER of the war was hard, the coldest in living memory, the old men said. Winds drove in from the south, and in the mornings frost covered the yellow-brown grass. The enemy had destroyed many farms to the east and the south, burning the winter crops. The livestock had been driven off or killed, their carcasses dotting the veld, and the herds of springbok had fled. Snow blanketed the highveld and the plains of the Free State, turning the world an alien white, a rare occurrence in the two republics.

Martin pulled the blanket close about his shoulders. A thin wind carried the smell of snow to his camp in the foothills of the Magaliesberg. He stared into the fire, his hands clenched around a mug of coffee, the bitterness of defeat like a weight inside him. The night sounds went by unheard: a nightjar's call, a jackal's far-off cry, the horses snorting.

His men slept at little fires, shivering under their threadbare blankets. Their women and children roamed the veld or died in the camps, their deaths far outnumbering those dying on the battlefield. Acres of white crosses next to these camps were more than most could bear. Fear for their families drove many to lay down their weapons and join them in the camps to watch over them.

That's exactly what the English want, Martin thought bitterly. Those who surrender were given a choice: be sent to the islands as prisoners of war, or join the British forces. It caused much bitterness; when caught, these men were executed. In the past three months, he had had to send twelve men to the firing squad.

But the war went on and now the commandos scavenged for themselves. There was enough meal and meat, but coffee, salt and sugar were forgotten luxuries for most. It was increasingly difficult to get to the enemy's convoys, but desperation drove them to attack, even when the odds were against them. Apart from food, they were in desperate need of ammunition.

As Jan Smuts had predicted, the conference at Middelburg had failed. In Kitchener's hostile eyes, Martin had seen the naked truth: their struggle was in vain; their refusal to give in now would result in the destruction of their nation and land.

He thought about his father, a sick prisoner on the island of St Helena. He would have seen the futility in carrying on and put an end to the devastation. *But I cannot, Pa! The wild horses are running at breakneck speed, Pa. The dream, Pa, lies shattered in blackened ruins of farms, in thousands of white crosses, and our land, trampled by our foe. And I'm running headlong, blindly now, the circles ever wider, the pace faster, faster, and now, I don't know how to end the flight! You did not tell me how to do that, Pa.*

The pain of his nation filled his chest. Tears ran warm into his beard. His soul was weary of war, but somewhere he had to find the will, the strength to see the war through to the end, whatever end.

He had walked into Kitchener's lair, invincible, a general feared by his enemy, revered by his nation. But he had drowned in Victoria's eyes, in the love that still bound them, evoking a passion to be whole again, to be fulfilled.

He reached for the coffee pot as a huddled figure approached. With great effort he collected himself, but relaxed when the fire reflected off Charles's glasses.

'I couldn't sleep for the cold.' Charles took the coffee from Martin. 'Oh, what I'd give for a cup of tea.'

They listened to the cackling of guinea fowl disturbed in their rest. Martin's eyes travelled over the sleeping men at the nearby fires and he deemed it safe to confide in Charles. 'I leave for the Cape in two weeks. Jan Smuts, being a Cape Afrikaner himself, is riding to seek support. I'm to go ahead openly, draw the enemy away from his commando, see them through the Free State. Those are my orders from General Botha.'

'The Cape?' Charles lowered his voice. 'But General de Wet's attempt failed miserably. It's clear that the Cape Afrikaners are not prepared to assist. And in this deplorable weather? Why not wait for spring?'

'Time is of the utmost importance. I'll be back, if all goes well, by November.'

'Where are we now?' Charles frowned. 'Beginning July? Five months. Well, I'll have to get my things in order, then.'

'No, cousin, it's a long and dangerous ride across the Free State plains. There are sixty thousand British. And the blockhouses. There'll be nowhere for you to hide.'

Charles refilled their mugs and pushed a log onto the fire. 'Who will you take?'

'Uncle Joep. Charles, I cannot imagine going anywhere without him. He is my father now, guiding me, caring … and a hundred men from the Rustenburg commando. Fifteen of Karel's scouts. No more. The British will know soon that I've left. Then Wintersrust will be burned. Charles, I want you to get the women to the cave. Will you do that for me?'

'It's bound to happen. Mrs De la Rey and her children are hiding in the dry west. Their house was gutted. Jan Viljoen said that Vrede was burned a few weeks ago.'

'Yes, I know, Charles. As long as I am in the vicinity, they will try to lure me in, to corner me on Wintersrust.' Martin looked into the night before he spoke again. 'Shall we go to the cave? We could slip into the house for a few hours. I want to see my boy before I go.'

'Yes, we could. It's a dark moon. Rudolf and Karel are in Pretoria. They will come to the cave to rest.'

Martin looked at the stars, bright in the moonless sky. An owl called, his mate answering from nearby. Pretoria and Vicky, a day's ride. *At night in my bed, I seek her that my soul loveth. I seek her but find her not.* He moved a little closer to Charles, hoping that his nearness would grant some comfort.

———•———

KAREL AND RUDOLF were making their way out of Pretoria. The night was dark, the air so cold it hurt to breathe, but the going was easy, as few sentries strayed outside their observation huts. They headed south through the thickly wooded Fountains. At the railway they went down on their bellies to inspect the open area on both sides of the line. Nothing was seen or heard and they slithered forward.

'Halt! Who goes there?' came the challenge from their right.

They froze for a second, and then, doubling over, crossed the line and headed for the safety of the trees. Swerving to their left, they sped down a well-used path. A burst of rifle fire split the night and flat on their bellies they went. Karel felt frantically over Rudolf's back. His hands came away sticky with blood.

Rudolf pushed himself up on his arms. 'Just … winded … knocked me over …' he wheezed, 'bullet from the side … I'm … all right.'

Karel hoisted Rudolf to his feet, and, with his arm around his waist, they stumbled off the path into the wood. They came to rest against the trunk of a wild fig. Karel hurriedly lifted Rudolf into the lower branches and pulled him into his arms, keeping his back against his chest. The blood seeped through onto his jacket, and he held Rudolf tighter in an effort to stop the bleeding.

Footsteps came down the path. 'I saw someone running this way,' a voice travelled up to them. 'Probably searching for food. We'll never catch him.' There was a half-hearted attempt to search the bush before the order came to return to the railway.

Karel and Rudolf sat motionless, their breaths misting around their faces. The heat of the chase soon left their bodies and they began to shake. Karel judged that there were only two hours before dawn, too little time to make it to the rendezvous point and get away. At sunrise the troops would start combing the area.

'Rudi, is it bad? Can you make it?'

'It hurts, but I'll make it if you can get me going.'

Karel helped Rudolf down from the tree. They set off at walking pace, stopping every hundred feet to give Rudolf a rest and to listen for patrols.

Dawn brought swirling grey mist, assuring them of another hour's invisibility. Karel looked at Rudolf in the early morning light. His face was ashen, his mouth clenched. The cave and Charles were a full night's ride away.

'Rudi, spit.' He placed his hand under Rudolf's chin. 'Come on, spit!' Rudolf worked his dry mouth and came up with some spittle.

'The bullet didn't touch your lungs. Just a flesh wound, Rudi.'

They continued at a slow run and reached the hill behind the barn belonging to the Widow Eloff, who helped them on their night raids. Karel searched the smallholding with his eyes. The cows had been milked and were grazing at the far end of the camp. Widow Eloff was scanning the hills around the house. She was waiting for them, Karel realised. He rushed into the barn, but found only the horses at the trough. McFee and seven others had gone to Johannesburg to exchange dispatches with General Botha's man and to collect information from their source in the city. They were obviously delayed.

Widow Eloff helped Karel settle Rudolf in the barn. She brought coffee and bread, and patted his forehead as Rudolf fell into an exhausted sleep. Karel kept a constant vigil from the high window, searching the veld for enemy patrols as he waited the day out. Night came, with no sign of McFee. Karel paced the barn until, two hours later, the door creaked open. He struck a match; there were only four faces.

'They didn't make it,' McFee said, breathing hard.

'Captured or dead?'

'Dead, all four. We were trapped between blockhouses. Hid in an old mineshaft. I went back, saw them lying where they fell, Danie Vermaas in the barbed wire. They were taking him down as I watched.'

'What went wrong, Irishman?'

'The patrols have doubled. We've bothered them too frequently.' McFee sank to the floor. 'Did you get the parcels? How's our dear old aunt? And our brave spy?'

'We got the parcels, all right, but we were shot at, crossing the track. Rudi is wounded.'

'Holy Mary!' McFee crossed himself and struck a match. He lit a stub of candle and held it to Rudolf's face. 'Are you all right, lad?'

Rudolf struggled upright, but McFee held him back. 'Karel, in my saddlebag, a bottle. Whisky helps for pain, my father always says. It will make the trip easier for the lad.'

Karel came up with the whisky and watched McFee force Rudolf to drink a good amount. They helped him onto Jessie and secured him to the saddle with a rope.

'I'll see you to the cave, but I'll be back here soon,' McFee said. 'I will not allow these British bastards to get the better of an Irishman.'

'What will you do?' Karel took Legend's and Jessie's reins, leading the way out of the barn.

'Find a better way to your aunt's place. The Fountains has always been too crowded for my liking. I will be one of them. What's another soldier in the streets of Pretoria to them?'

They rode through the night, changing horses often, as there were now four extra. Morning found them in the foothills of the kloof, on the southern side of the mountain. They led the horses up the hidden path to the shelter. Rudolf lay slumped in the saddle, blood dripping down his fingers. Gert Swart and two other scouts came to assist them. They looked at their battered comrades and the empty saddles and silently took over the care of the horses.

Rudolf was placed on a mattress in the rock overhang where a fire crackled. While the others flung themselves down, exhausted after two nights without sleep, Karel set about cleaning Rudolf's wound. There were bits of cloth in the wound, and Rudolf was incoherent.

'I'll fetch the doctor,' Gert offered. 'He's only ten miles from here. Martin called the Rustenburg commando together. Something big is brewing, I think.'

'Only ten miles!' Karel sighed with relief. 'I must get to Martin myself.' He tapped on the bulky oilcloth bag strapped to his chest. 'Stuff from Pretoria ...'

'Legend is exhausted and so are you. I'll take the stuff. I'll be back with Charles before sunset.'

'Martin is not going to like it, but just this once ...' Karel struggled out of his jacket and fumbled with his shirt buttons.

Gert helped him unwrap the oilcloth bag. 'The outbuildings and barns at Wintersrust and Soetvlei are burned, all the livestock driven off, but the house still stands. Your womenfolk are all there. I almost met my death when I went in last night to see if they are all right. Aunt Lettie was aiming at my stomach with a blunderbuss, Anita was behind the door with a spade. The officer who ordered this devil's work told them that, if Martin doesn't surrender, the house would be next.'

'Little chance of Martin doing that! Thank you, Gert.'

Gert took his Mauser and hat, and Karel was soon asleep, stretched out next to Rudolf.

CHARLES REACHED THE HIDEOUT after sunset. The scouts were preparing for the night's work, stuffing bandoliers and cleaning their Mausers, Karel in their midst, giving instructions. He found Rudolf lying near the fire with McFee watching over him.

Charles touched Rudolf's shoulder gently. 'Rudi, can you sit up and lean with your chest over your knees? Patrick will hold you upright.'

Rudolf struggled up. Charles held a piece of chloroform-soaked cloth over Rudolf's nose. McFee suspended a lantern from a tripod and Charles set to work, probing for the bullet and picking out the pieces of cloth from the wound.

'Is he bad?' McFee asked.

He removed his glasses, pressing his fingers to his eyes. 'No, Patrick, it's only a flesh wound. He should be fine in a week's time.'

'Why do you look so worried, then, Doctor?' McFee helped Charles to lower Rudolf back onto the mattress.

'It's not the wound that I'm concerned about, Patrick. The poor boy is worn out.' While Patrick went to get them whisky, Charles thought about what his uncle had said about men fighting until they were exhausted, not just in their bodies but in their souls too. Rudolf might have reached that point.

'He doesn't like the killing, Doctor,' McFee said when he returned with two mugs of whisky. 'Only uses his rifle when his brother is around. Strange, these two brothers; they are like one, yet so different. He's a dreamer, Karel a killer.'

'Patrick, get them both to the cave tomorrow. The General will be here in a few days. He has new orders. They must rest until then.'

'They will do just that, Doctor. Karel will not ride without his brother at his side. Brings bad luck, he says. I'm off to Pretoria tomorrow. I'm worried about our spy. There's a watch on her and she knows it, but will the lady admit it? You rest yourself. I'll go help Karel with the horses. Legend sleeps here when those two are around. They stink the place out. Oh the love he has for that horse!'

Charles dragged a mattress next to Rudolf's. He drifted off to sleep thinking of Stefanie's stubborn courage and Martin's depressed state, the enormous burden they both carried.

He awoke with a vision of Anita's auburn hair spread over his face, but what he was seeing was the first light of day burnishing Legend's coat. She stood quietly, with Karel sleeping on the ground close to her. Sleep robbed Karel's face of its harshness, leaving him vulnerable and forlorn. Suddenly Charles's eyes filled with tears; Legend nuzzled Karel's hair, her breath misting the cold morning air over his face.

'Thank you, Charles, for coming,' Rudolf whispered.

Charles felt for his glasses. Rudolf's blue eyes were sunken, his brown hair matted against his forehead. 'Your wound is slight, Rudi; it should heal in no time.' He put his face close to Rudolf's. 'It would help if you have a word with Annecke.'

Rudolf looked at him for some time before he answered. 'An inch ... I would've been dead. A reminder from Tante Koba's jealous God to stay away.'

'No, please, I implore you; men are wounded all the time. It's war, for heaven's sake! Leave God out of it.'

'Or leave it up to God?' Rudolf gave a wan smile. 'Martin is my brother. I respect and love him and will not humiliate him.'

———◆———

WHILE THE TWINS were resting in the cave and McFee was making his way into Pretoria, Stefanie was thinking about the unexpected search carried out on the house the previous day. Victoria had confided that Major Hunter had come to warn her that the house was under observation, but, being a jealous and vindictive man, he might have said so merely to scare them.

They were having their midday meal in the kitchen, still discussing this, when there was a loud knocking at the door. They looked at one another, startled. Victoria offered to go, but Stefanie who was pouring the tea, waved her back to her seat and went.

And there he was – her husband, his dark eyes triumphant and malicious. Fear twisted her stomach and left her speechless. She took a few steps back, clutching at a chair for support.

'Thought I'd never catch up with you, my dear?' Warren said with grin, dumping his cane and hat on the sofa. 'Thought you could humiliate me, make me the laughing stock of the country?'

'What … what do you want?' Stefanie croaked.

'You, my dear, I want you. You are my wife and you will continue to be my wife until I decide that I have no further use for you.'

'I'm not *your wife*! I have *never* been your wife and I have a *man* who can testify to that!' she blurted, her hand immediately going to her mouth as if to take back the words.

His head jerked sharply and he advanced a few steps. 'Whore! You've been sleeping with that cad Radford.' His voice was so low that she could hardly catch the words.

'If you dare touch me, if you come any closer—' She grabbed a large vase from the mantelpiece, flinging it at him with all the power she could muster. It missed his head by inches and shattered on the floor.

Koba came flying in, brandishing a broom. 'You black devil of a man!' she wheezed. 'Leave my Stefanie and get out of my house!'

Then came Victoria's calm voice. 'Mr Warren, I'm sure this could be settled in a more agreeable fashion. I was just about to make some tea. Would you like some?'

'I do not want tea, Lady Victoria, but settle this matter in a more civilised way, I shall.' He looked at Stefanie. 'Shortly after the fall of Pretoria, my communication lines were destroyed, my men disappeared and half a ton of dynamite with them.'

He let this hang in the air for a moment. Stefanie shook uncontrollably and clung to Koba's arm. Koba was pale and speechless, but Victoria kept her head. 'I fail to see what this has to do with us,' she said.

'Precisely, Lady Victoria,' Warren said in an icy voice. 'My work has nothing whatsoever to do with any of you. The British do not treat informers kindly.'

There was silence. *Oh, dear God,* Stefanie cried inwardly, *he is going to have me shot! I have to escape, but Karel and Rudi will not be in for another month! The Irishman! Where is McFee?*

'You will not take Stefanie away from me!' Koba spat the words at him.

'No, old woman, I won't take her from you. However, she will do as I wish.' He turned to Stefanie. 'As my spouse, you will perform your social duties as expected. You've made a good impression in the city. Even Kitchener seems to hold you in high regard. But I will not be humiliated. If you, madam, put just one foot out of line, I'll drag you down with me.'

He took his hat and cane and went to the door. 'I have taken a room in the Pretoria Club. Tonight I am hosting a dinner for General Hamilton and his staff. You will compose yourself and prepare to play a few suitable pieces. Not Chopin! I will come for you at seven.' In the doorway he turned around, his eyes raking Stefanie with contempt. 'You will not see or exchange a single word with Peter Radford again. If you should attempt to meet him in secret, I shall find out and the consequences will be extremely unpleasant for both of you.'

The Greatest of the Three

MARTIN TOLD JOEP Maree and Jan Viljoen to pick one hundred men to ride with them to the Cape Colony. Charles and the rest of his commando were to stay with General Jansen.

'I'll see the scouts tonight and work out our route,' Martin said where they were convening in a deep gorge a few miles from Wintersrust. 'Jan, tell the men they may leave for their families now but to be back here in a week's time. Pa, please take care when you go to Wintersrust. I can't have you caught now.'

'I'll take care, son, but it's Buks you must speak to,' Joep said when Jan was out of earshot. 'We had bitter words about his trips to the farm. Order him to come to the Cape with us.'

Martin busied himself with his papers. 'Pa, we're all weary of fighting, but we know what we're fighting for – our independence. Buks fights only for Soetvlei, Lena and his children. I cannot take him away from them.'

'At least speak to him, Martin.' Joep picked up his hat and slung his Mauser across his back. 'See you at Wintersrust later.'

Martin went in search of Buks, who had been avoiding his company for months. He'd heard that Buks had spoken of the futility of continuing the war. Some branded him a *hensopper*, but he was still with the commando, although he stayed at the rear when an attack was made and sometimes could not be found at all.

He came upon Buks, stretched out in the sun, whittling at a piece of wood. 'Buks, I can't allow you to visit Wintersrust any longer. You'll have to wait until our families are in the cave. And while I'm away, you may visit only with General Jansen's permission. I can't have men leaving the commando whenever they feel the need to do so.'

'If you say so, General de Winter,' he said, without looking up.

Martin stood a while longer but Buks carried on with his whittling. 'Why are you ignoring me, Buks? You are my brother-in-law and are placing me in a difficult situation ...'

Buks plunged his knife into the wood. 'You are pathetic, Martin. The war is *lost*! And the longer you go on deceiving yourself, refusing to come to terms with failure, the more women and children will be imprisoned, farms burned and men sent to their deaths before your firing squads. This country will be a graveyard.'

Martin felt his anger and remorse rise. There was truth in what Buks was saying. He gave himself time to collect his thoughts before answering. 'It's concern for Lena and your children that rules your mind. I sympathise with that. It might be tough for now, but when our people in the Cape take up arms, the English will give in. That's why I'm riding to the Colony.'

'You won't make it through the Free State. You are taking my father to his death. Martin, I've fought as well as any other man, but the war is over! We're not the first to lose a war against Britain. Greater nations, the French, the Russians, fought them and were beaten. The British won't give in.'

'Then they will destroy themselves in the process—'

'We are being destroyed! Be it on your head if my family and farm are destroyed. Stop fighting a lost cause and *think*, for God's sake!'

'Get your horse, Buks. Jan and Frans Viljoen leave for the north in an hour's time. They'll take you to Oom Koos de la Rey with a letter explaining why you will stay there until my return.'

RUDOLF LAY ON HIS STOMACH at the waterfall, his back bared to the sun. Charles had advised that a wound healed faster when exposed to air and sunlight. It was late afternoon, and he watched Karel scrubbing Legend in the pool, the horse protesting at the coldness of the water. Suddenly she tossed her head and gave her warning snort. A few seconds later came the call of a nightjar.

'McFee? But he was here last night,' Karel said. 'We must tell that Irishman that a nightjar doesn't call before dusk.'

A few minutes later, Martin and Charles appeared, bags slung over their shoulders. 'We brought whatever we could spare for the women,' Martin said, lowering his burden.

'Could I trade this for a few tea leaves?' Charles handed over a bag of coffee. 'Our last raid didn't produce any.'

'Tea? Well, come along *Engelsman*!' Karel steered Charles to the cave. 'You're so much of a Boer, yet you still drink tea like a proper Englishman.'

'Martin, the English might decide that burning the barns was not enough.'

Rudolf reached for his shirt. 'Next time it will be the house. Please speak to Ma.'

'Yes, Rudi, tonight I will insist that they move up here. I don't need to worry about their safety when we are away, but we'll talk in the cave. Do you perhaps have brandy?'

'Karel has a few bottles. But I've heard that the General doesn't drink at all.'

'The General could do with a *sopie* tonight,' Martin smiled.

Martin had not been in the cave for months and now commented on the homely look. There were animal hides on the floors, water barrels, tinned food and cooking utensils, beds with spare mattresses stowed underneath them. Karel and Rudolf's beds were next to the fire. At the far end was a straw-strewn area for Legend and Jessie.

Rudolf joined Charles where he was brewing tea on the cast-iron foot-warmer. He squatted in front of him to have his wound inspected.

Charles gave a satisfied grunt. 'Splendid! Well on the mend.' He dressed the wound, took his tea and joined the others at the rock table. 'Ah, the peace and tranquillity of this place reminds me so—'

'—much of better times,' Martin cut Charles's reminiscence short. 'Karel, I need fifteen expert scouts to ride with me to the Colony.'

'I have already picked them,' Karel said.

'How long will we be away?' Rudolf put a bottle of brandy next to Martin's hand.

'Four months at the most. Now, every man needs two horses and as many supplies as he can comfortably carry. General de Wet will provide us with ammunition on our way. Work out a route that will best get us across the Vaal and Orange rivers.'

'What about Stefanie?' Rudolf asked. 'McFee said the house was searched the day after we were shot at. It's that Major Hunter, she thinks. Luckily Stefanie kept her temper and was helpful, so was Tante Koba.'

'There's worse,' Karel said. 'Her bloody husband arrived from the Cape.'

'Warren! What does *he* want in Pretoria?'

'She found out straight away that he's come to organise *hensoppers* into scouting units. The National Scouts. McFee has arranged to meet Stefanie in town now. No one can get near the house. Warren knows about the information she brought from the Cape.'

'Warren will not be fooled. She's no match for that devil!'

'McFee told her to give up, but she snapped, said she's not a coward,' Rudolf said. 'She'll try to get us a list of the traitors and their orders, but thinks it will take some weeks.'

'Paul Warren already has evidence against her.' Martin frowned. 'But would he dare use it against his wife? No, he'll use it to create a situation she won't be able to escape from.' He poured brandy and looked up to find the others staring at him.

'Order her to stop, Martin,' said Charles. 'She's done more than can be expected of her.'

'Yes, she has,' Martin said. 'But we still need information on the traitors. Where are her papers?'

'In a box under a beehive. She told McFee that Warren landed in hospital once after just one bee had stung him.' Karel laughed scornfully. 'So he won't be looking there.'

'I want her to send them out with McFee. From now on, only he will keep contact with her. Should things turn ugly, he must smuggle her out of Pretoria. Is that possible, Karel?'

'Nothing to it, but will she come?'

'I'll send some chloroform with Patrick,' Charles said. 'He can carry her out if he has to. What about Tante Koba? Won't she also be in danger?'

'Can you imagine her being in danger?' Karel shook his head. 'No, she takes care of James's wife, keeps her out of Stefanie's way. We don't know how much Tante Koba knows about what Stefanie is doing, anyway.'

The light slanting through the fissures of the roof faded swiftly as the sun disappeared behind the mountain. Rudolf lit a lamp and a few candles, stoked up the fire and heated up a few tins of beef while Charles and Martin went to the pool to wash. Karel brought Legend and Jessie in and settled them in their corner.

After they had had their meal, Martin set out his inkwell and papers. 'Many reports to do. Rudi, take Charles to the house. Karel, go tell McFee I want to see him in the morning. And get a few men to watch the house. The English have taken to riding at night and we don't want them to catch our cousin courting in the dark.'

'I beg your pardon!'

'I saw you, Charles. Smooching in the kitchen after the midnight hour.'

'The midnight hour! Indeed!'

'Cousin Charles? In the kitchen?' Karel hung his arm around Charles's shoulders. 'Why not the bedroom?'

'May I remind you we're not married, not yet!'

'Then do so, Charles. I could marry the two of you. Perfectly legal in times of war.' Martin gave him a teasing smile, pulled the lamp closer and started writing.

Karel reached for his rifle. 'Rest assured, cousin, tonight no one will disturb your ... what was it, Martin? Smooching in the kitchen?'

WHEN RUDOLF RETURNED two hours later, Martin was still writing. There were many pages on the table and the level in the bottle had dropped substantially.

Rudolf stretched out on his mattress by the fire and watched Martin at work. He carried the world on his shoulders, but that was the life he wanted; the heavier the load, the better he worked. But now the old sadness he had brought from England was back; the same sadness as Victoria's. Their sadness. His heart went out to Martin, for he also knew the suffering of a love lost.

Martin screwed the inkwell shut, folded the papers and put them into several oilcloth bags. He leaned with his elbows on the table, staring into the flickering lamp, a concentrated frown on his face. 'McFee. How does he get into Pretoria? Same way as you?' he asked, refilling his glass.

'No, he goes through Johannesburg and dresses as a corporal, sometimes as a worker. He has all the necessary papers and renews them every month.'

'Is it possible for him to bring her ... Stefanie, to Johannesburg?'

'She plays in Johannesburg often. In the Theatre Royal. Why?'

'I so much want to see her,' Martin mumbled, staring into the lamp again.

He was planning to meet Victoria, Rudolf realised with a start. He had it all worked out. Victoria might be willing to meet him somewhere safe, in Johannesburg. McFee could arrange that.

'You can trust McFee with your life,' he said.

Martin nodded and strapped his pistol to his waist. 'It's late. I'm going down.'

Rudolf brought a note from his pocket. 'Charles made me wait at the drift. He said to give it to you before you came down.'

Martin read the few lines and gave a surprised laugh. 'Rudi, we have a wedding at Wintersrust tonight. At the midnight hour, to be precise!'

Rudolf pulled on his boots, picking up his Mauser. There was no escaping the hurt waiting down at Wintersrust. He would have to be like Karel – harsh and uncaring.

The house was in a flurry of activity when they arrived. The children were in bed, Lena was laying the table, Lettie pressing Charles's shirt, Mary dressing Anita in her bedroom and Joep searching through the Bible. Martin and Charles went to the study to prepare the papers.

Karel stoked the fire. 'Get us clothes for the trip, Rudi. An extra shirt will do me.'

In their bedroom, Rudolf found Annecke readying the room for the bridal couple. A vase of winter flowers and two candles in the ornate silver holder stood on the kist. Between him and Annecke was the bed, now adorned with the white lace cover that was normally on his parents' bed. Annecke was smoothing it into place, but, on seeing him, brought her hands to her face.

She was no longer the young girl he had known. Her breasts had filled out, her face was older, her eyes were anxious. Love surged through him, but he felt no desire, could not conjure up the mystery he had found in her body, at the depth of possessing her, the miracle he could not share with his twin.

He stood uncomfortably, fumbling for words. 'Clothes ... I need my grey jacket and a shirt.' He pointed to the kist.

She moved the flowers, opened the kist and found what he wanted. Clutching the jacket close to her, she said, 'I waited for you, Rudi.'

'I know ... I know. What happened was terrible. And now you are my brother's wife, the mother of his child.'

Her eyes welled up and she bit her bottom lip. 'The baby—'

'He's lovely, Annecke,' he said when she faltered. 'I stood by the window one night. I saw Martin holding him.' He took the clothes from her and walked out. She followed him to the sitting room where everyone was gathered facing Martin. They went to stand next to Lettie and Lena. Karel, rifle at the ready, stood by the front door. Charles and Anita held hands while Martin read their vows. Charles looked happy and serene. Anita, in Mary's wedding dress, had tears brightening her eyes.

Joep read from the Bible. *Love is patient and kind.* Charles looked into his bride's eyes. *Love does not keep a record of wrongs.* Rudolf stole a glance at Martin, who was staring at the floor, his face closed. *Love never gives up, and love's faith, hope and patience never fails.* Rudolf looked at Annecke. Misery caught at his throat; tears were running down her cheeks. *And now abideth faith, hope, love, these three; but the greatest of these is love.*

Rudolf saw Martin lift his eyes to the Bible in Joep's hands. His stern blue eyes softened to grey and the lines running into his beard transformed into a soft, soft smile.

He will go to James's wife, Rudolf knew then.

A FEW DAYS LATER, Annecke was in the vegetable garden, transferring onion seedlings into the beds, but her mind was not on the task. For long periods she stared at the mountain. She had only ever thought of it as one of nature's miracles, but now it was a salvation. So thickly wooded and deep were the gorges that it was impossible for the English to discover the many hiding places there. Three miles to the west was the tannery where old men fixed boots and saddles. There was also the miller who ground their corn and mealies. Before the English had burnt the barns, Old Klaas had taken a few cows and sheep into the kloof; now they still had meat and milk. Anita said that families from the district had also taken refuge there, just as they would soon.

If we ever get up there. The night of the wedding, when they had gathered at the table to celebrate, Mary had again refused to leave her house. Joep, Lena, everyone, had tried to reason with her, but Martin had had enough. 'Ma, you will go to the cave!' he had said in his general's voice.

Annecke sighed. Martin had said that he would be gone for months, Karel and Rudi too. She tossed a few carrots into the basket and made her way to the house. The other women were on the stoep, Lena nursing her new baby girl, Anita with her arms folded, staring at the mountain. She looked furious, her thin lips pursed. Lettie hummed to herself while patching a pair of trousers. Mary was writing yet another letter, to Marthinus, Annecke presumed, judging by the loving smile on her face. The children were playing at their feet.

'Annecke, child.' Mary looked up from her writing. 'Come, have a cup of coffee. Are you done with the garden? I shall have to see if there are eggs in the orchard. I still think it was foolish to let the hens loose. They were much safer in their coop. The wild cats caught four of them in the last week.'

'It was clever of Annecke to let them out when the English came. They would've taken them also.' Lettie bit off a thread.

'Oh nonsense, Lettie! They burnt the barns because they thought we were feeding the commandos. They won't take our chickens.'

'They took most of our sheep and cattle, Aunt Mary,' Anita said over her shoulder. 'Also our last horse. We only have the mules left.'

'They requisitioned the livestock, Anita. It happens in war,' Mary said doggedly.

'Annecke, Lena, come with me.' Anita threw Mary an unpleasant look, her face flushed and angry as she led the way inside.

'On my way back from Rustenburg yesterday morning, I saw another cloud of smoke to the north. It could be the Coetzee house. We have to move now. Aunt Mary is going to get us caught if we stay here.'

'We can't leave her by herself. Martin said to get her up there,' Lena said, handing the baby to Annecke and buttoned her dress. 'She might come when we have Ma up there.'

'Let's get Aunt Lettie there, then. Lena, get the children ready and I'll get the mule-cart. But first, we tell Aunt Mary that she has no choice!'

Anita led them back to the stoep. Lettie and Mary looked up questioningly. 'We are moving to the cave now!' Anita said, her hands on her hips, her manner final. 'Aunt Lettie, we'll put you on the cart. Aunt

Mary, you get food for a few days. We will come down here only to see to the chickens and vegetable garden.'

Mary gave her an obstinate glance and continued with her writing. Lettie put her sewing in the basket. 'Mary, I've been your friend and neighbour for thirty years now. Not once have we had a disagreement. But now I say you're acting very selfishly. I'll do all in my power to save my daughters and grandchildren from the camps, even if it means living in a cave like a savage. I'm sure you would too.'

'I was brought here as a bride.' Mary smoothed her hair into place.

Lettie rose from her chair with difficulty. Then she gave a strangled cry, clutched at her chest with both hands and collapsed. Her face contorted, her breath coming in small gasps. The children wailed at seeing their grandmother on the floor.

'It's her heart.' Anita felt Lettie's pulse. 'Oh, where's Charles now?'

Mary's eyes were wide with shock. 'Lettie! I'm so sorry; I shall go if we have to—'

'It's too late now! Lena, get a pillow, a blanket. Annecke, get the strychnine.' Anita searched in her apron pocket for her keys. 'In the box under my bed.'

'Strychnine? Poison?'

'Yes, it helps for heart failure. You give a few drops. We can't move her until her heart has settled. Hurry up, Annecke! For heaven's sake, don't stare so!'

Annecke rushed for the medicine box, stifling heartbroken sobs. They would not get to the cave now. She would never see Rudi again.

———————

THAT NIGHT, PATRICK McFEE waited outside the Heights Hotel in Johannesburg, huddled into his coat against the harsh wind. He had been horrified at the idea of taking his General anywhere near Johannesburg. The General had not given him any details, merely the request. On Saturday morning, in Church Square, he had dropped a note into Victoria's basket, and waited a little way off. She found him with her eyes and nodded. He stood with his back to her while they made the arrangements. Before Thursday night, outside Pretoria. She would spend Wednesday at the Heights Hotel, as Stefanie was to play in the Theatre Royal.

'I'll come for you at ten, after the show. Leave by the side door. The General says you can be trusted, but it won't do to trap him.'

'I'd rather die,' she said and he believed her.

Now he lit another cigarette. Extraordinary man, the young General de Winter, a man to be feared, a man with the power of a king. And now he was meeting his cousin's wife. A long-lost love? It would be a magnificent union, the lady and the Boer general. There would only be an hour, but it would be enough for the General. He would spend his fire as he was fighting the war – dauntless, demanding. He thought about the husband, the British cousin. He was nothing like his brother, the gentle doctor. No, he was an arrogant one, his chest bedecked with medals and a familiar face at the city's high-class brothels.

He glanced at his watch; the show was over. His waited until Stefanie and Victoria emerged from a closed carriage, escorted by the devil Warren and the Hunter fellow. They went into the hotel, and after a short while the men reappeared and left with the carriage. *Off to Rose Carter's, no doubt.*

He crushed his cigarette and turned the hired Cape cart into the side street. Ten minutes later Victoria appeared, a dark cloak covering her from head to toe.

VICTORIA SAT QUIETLY next to McFee as they made their way west from the town centre. Vehicles passed them, steam misting from the horses. Soldiers walked from the railway station in clusters, heading to the many bar-rooms in the alleys. Victoria pulled her cape over her face, hoping to blot out the vulgar encouragement women were calling to the soldiers.

For three months she had lived suspended between hope and despair, but now, as she was finally on her way to see Martin, something deep in her stirred. Her unease was more profound. She tried to define it, but still it eluded her.

On the outskirts of the city, they arrived at an isolated house surrounded by a stone wall. McFee drove the cart through the gates and into the stable. With the wind snatching at her cloak and beating at her face, she followed McFee down a footpath that led to a cottage in a clump of trees. He ushered her inside and closed the door. A match flared, a candle was lit. She saw a fireplace, a table and chairs, but Martin wasn't there.

'Is that wise?' she asked in a whisper when McFee kindled the fire into life.

'Don't fear, ma'am. You'll be safe. I wouldn't have brought my General here if it weren't.' He pulled a chair to the fireplace. 'Sit here next to the fire, it's cold.'

'Thank you,' she said, but remained standing.

McFee checked his watch and stood for a while. 'The signal, I'm waiting for his signal. I could wait outside if you prefer?'

'No, that won't be necessary.' She watched the flames leaping into the wood. Again the lurking fear clutched at her heart. Her eyes flew to the door. She wanted to escape, run while there still was time.

A night bird shrilled close by. McFee waited until the call was repeated twice and left. Moments later the door opened, a blast of wind blew out the candle. Martin was leaning against the door – a bearded Boer, the smell of the winter veld and wood smoke on him. His windblown hair and beard shone golden in the firelight. His face was impassive, but he looked steadily at her, as if condemning her.

'Martin? How are you?' she asked to break the silence.

'I'm well. I couldn't see my way open earlier.'

'I quite understand. The war ...'

He looked into the fire. 'Yes, the war. It's too long, exhausting. I've killed so many men, my own people. Yes, I've ordered the execution of my own people. Their crime? They're desperate.'

She saw anguish in his eyes, in the harsh lines on his face, the weariness in the way he held himself. She wanted to touch him, comfort him, but dared not. He was not talking to her. He was isolated in a world of doubt and regret, ridding his soul of the torment he could not admit to those who followed him so blindly.

'The war killed them, not you,' she said.

'Yes, the war killed them, that's what they all say. They also say I'm fearless, Vicky, but I have fear. I fear where I am leading, I fear it, for there's nowhere to lead but to the termination of all we have.'

His admission of defeat, not of losing the war, but the loss to himself as a man, touched her deeply. Tears burned her eyes. Would he die? Sacrifice his life and thereby force his men to give up? No, he would stand firm, unbroken to the end. She met his eyes. All at once she was afraid of him.

'Martin? Why did you come?'

'I came because I had to.'

He came to find solace from the devastation of his spirit, she knew then, but she was going to fail him. *As I failed James.* He had used her violently, fighting his anger and sorrow. Martin would embrace his feelings, let them take their course, but it would not be love, simply a release of an all-consuming passion.

He undid the pistol strapped to his waist, put it on the table and came to stand in front of her. 'And you, Vicky, why did you come?'

'I came because I love you.' It sounded insignificant and she swallowed hard.

He lowered her cape and spread her hair over her shoulders. 'I so much want to touch your hair once more. Many nights, I touch your hair ...' Her cloak slipped to the floor when his hands went to the nape of her neck, letting her hair fall through his fingers. 'Why did you marry him, Vicky?'

'He needed me.'

'I also needed you, years ago. I still do,' he sighed, taking her into his arms. 'Don't be afraid. I only want to hold you again.'

He was giving her the chance to deny him, but she could not bear to let him go. She lifted her face to his, her hands going under his jacket and closing over his shoulders. He looked into her eyes, his lips moving as if he wanted to speak, but instead he buried his face in her hair.

'I'm not afraid,' she whispered.

He spread a blanket by the fireplace. Brushing her hair from her face, he laid her down. She watched as he took off his jacket and shirt before coming to lie down beside her. She touched the scar on his chest, her fingers feeling the roughness of it.

His mouth came down to hers, his lips barely moving. 'My only love.'

She felt passion rising in him when he undressed her. The roughness of his beard was on her breasts, on her belly and on her thighs. She slipped into a whirlpool of emotions, the intensity unbearable. She saw James, his brown eyes clouded with desire, the dimples deep in his cheeks, James between her breasts, lying spent and content. The memory tore at her, she wanted to cry out in her anguish, but Martin was drowning her with his passion.

AS HIS PASSION SUBSIDED, he felt the chains of the past slip loose. He laid his head on her shoulder and stared into the flickering embers of the fire. His mind was at peace for the first time in months. A picture of his son, the little hands exploring Annecke's face, filled his mind and a stifled sob came to his throat. *Everything has a beginning and an end. Another dream shattered, but I saw it through to the end. I did not run away, Pa, I came to her and saw it through to the sorrowful end.*

A nightjar called. McFee. His small commando was waiting twenty miles to the west. They needed the darkness to slip away and on to the Cape. He stood up and reached for his clothes.

'Did I abuse you by coming here?'

She sat up, wrapping the cloak around her. 'No, but I failed you.'

He strapped his pistol to his waist, and shrugged into his jacket. 'No, you gave me back what you took from me that day in your father's study, the day you did fail me. How deeply I loved you then, Vicky. It will stay with me forever.'

'James is my husband, Martin. I will stay with him as long as he wants me.'

He squatted in front of her and looked into her eyes. It was as if their forlorn passion had led to this point, a point where honesty triumphs over illusion and leaves behind the wanting. Their love had been a dream, a youthful desire that had to be fulfilled. He felt it in his heart and was grateful. He saw it in her eyes, in her smile, a poignant smile that told of forgiveness.

'Take good care of him, Vicky.' He kissed her softly on her mouth and disappeared into the cold dark night.

The Invisible Enemy

August 1901

JAMES WOKE WITH the taste of wine and tobacco in his mouth and
the smell of cheap perfume in his nose. His head pounded and his body
felt leaden. He brought his hand up. It was shaking badly. He looked at
the woman lying on her back, her arms flung out, her mouth half-open.
Bile rose to his throat. He lowered his legs to the floor, hung his head
between his knees and retched.

It had been like this since Martin had appeared in Pretoria and the
truth of Victoria's past had been revealed. After the 2nd Hussars had
returned from their expedition to the north, he and Peter had booked into
the Heights Hotel, he finding solace at Rose Carter's establishment, and
Peter gambling at Newmarket.

The pattern was set. Back into the country, chasing the Boers from the
convoys that the regiment was guarding, a skirmish here and there, watching how those they were protecting burned houses, herding families to the
nearest camp. Then back to Johannesburg for a week's rest, only to start the
operation all over again.

The cold crept across his body. Winter was not over. He picked up his
clothes and dressed, making an effort to straighten the rumpled tunic and
breeches. He placed a fistful of notes on the pillow, slipped down the passage, through the empty reception room and out into the street. Halfway
down the block a Cape cart stopped. He thankfully ordered the driver to
the Heights Hotel, paid him off and climbed the stairs to his room on the
first floor. He flung his helmet on the bed and sat with his head in his hands
before reaching for the brandy on the nightstand. His stomach protested but
he forced the liquid down. When he had finished the second glass, his hands
stopped shaking and the tightness in his chest eased a little.

He ran a bath, lowering his tired body into it. The war was no longer a
war as he had known it. No more set battles, no roar of cannon, no cavalry

charges, only hit-and-run strikes by slouch-hatted riders. It was ghostly to fight an invisible enemy. Every ravine or thicket could bring bearded, ragged riders shooting from the saddle.

He took another swig of brandy. Carrying on could only end in death or a weary victory. He felt no exhilaration at the thought of victory, not even relief. They were destroying a country, steadily laying it waste.

It was a pathetic sight to witness, the burning of a farm. The dogs, the huge Boer hounds, were shot first, whimpering amid the shouts of the troops and the wailing of the children. The women scrambled to save what they could from the flames, swearing revenge with raised fists. He'd seen a boy breaking loose from his mother's dress, attacking a soldier's legs. He'd seen women crying at the death of their fowls. One grandmother had a rooster hidden under her dress. A trooper had dragged it out and wrung its neck. He remembered the bird well. It had burnished wings with trailing feathers, iridescent chest and a blood-red comb.

He wanted no part of the burning. He didn't want to take defenceless women and children to the camps. The shame was bearable when he was in the veld, but every time he thought about Koba, it was bad, very bad, and he wanted to press his face into her warm bosom and beg for forgiveness for not refusing the cruel task Fate had bestowed upon him.

He shuddered as he thought of the last house they had burnt, outside Pietersburg. It had been a large, dirty dwelling with a stream of women and children running frantically. He had been sitting on his horse, as usual, a good way from the house, taking no part in the proceedings. Just as Sergeant Adams was about to order the wagon loaded with the inhabitants of the farm on its way, a woman broke loose, her bare feet and legs visible as she lifted her dress and ran to him. 'James! James! It is Ester Viljoen,' she shouted. 'You do remember me? Please help me! I was good to you once. Don't you remember, James?'

She clung to his stirrups, pleading and wailing. He hardly recognised her; her hair was matted, her dress dirty and torn across her pregnant belly. His troops stared at him, astonished. He ordered them to take her away and they dragged her back to the wagon, but she broke free, lifted her dress and laughed shrilly, insanely. 'Come take it! It's warm and wet inside!' she shouted before they forced her onto the wagon.

JAMES FINISHED THE BRANDY and towelled himself dry. Peter, newspaper in hand, walked in and settled in a chair.

'Brandy?' James coughed as he lit a cigarette.

'No, but thank you.' Peter glanced at the bottle. 'Steady on, old chap, you've had nothing to eat for two days now.'

James started dressing. 'Where are we heading next? North again?'

'Yes, so I've heard … heavens! Listen to this: *General Martin de Winter and a commando numbering over a hundred crossed into the Free State causing havoc as they went. His daring methods can only be compared to the elusive Flying Fox.* Referring to General de Wet, as you know. It goes on to say that Martin might be heading for the Cape. Good Lord, the man has dash! I'd give anything to ride with him.'

James poured more brandy and took a seat opposite Peter. 'I'm tired of this, Radford. Fighting a war I've no objection to, but the rest? What are we? Plunderers? Raping and pillaging like Attila the Hun?'

'Yes, it is a disagreeable task, but see it from Kitchener's viewpoint. Boer women can't be classified as non-combatants. They supply food, shelter and information to their men. The farms must be destroyed to prevent exactly that. And we could not possibly burn their houses and leave them in the veld. Ergo, the need for the concentration camps.'

'Makes sense Radford, but why do they die in the camps?'

'Well, the name says it, doesn't it?' Peter kept his eyes on the paper. 'Concentration camp; a place where people concentrate in large numbers. The conditions are primitive and there's bound to be deficiencies in sanitation, therefore the diseases.'

James stared out of the window. His mind was dull with fatigue and lack of sleep. 'Do you believe all that gibberish you've just uttered, Radford?'

'I hate this business as much as you. And I have not a thing against the Boer women. Don't exactly know why we're destroying them.'

'Radford, we are the Army. We are instruments.'

'I don't want to be an instrument,' Peter grimaced. '*God slaap nie, Engelsman.* Know what that means? *God does not sleep, Englishman.* An old woman shouted it to my face repeatedly. The troops were a bit rough-handed; I went in to calm things. She grabbed hold of my arm. Well, I felt like saying that I hope God keeps a good score.'

James stretched out in the chair. Peter was fractious of late. It was as if the abrupt ending of his brief affair with Stefanie had stunned him. *It was rapturous, I love her deeply, always will, he'd said, but it's not meant to be.* But what had happened to end it, he didn't say. And there was that note from Victoria, saying that Paul Warren had arrived and that Peter should stay clear of Stefanie at all costs.

'Come, let's get to Pretoria.' James came to his feet.

'Are you going to visit Vicky? You haven't been for months—'

'Visit Victoria? No, Radford. I have discovered that, like everyone else in this country, she belongs to the great General de Winter.' James buttoned his tunic. 'She was Martin's lover, Peter. I knew that there had been someone before me, but did it have to be him? My cousin?'

'Good God! She didn't tell you beforehand?'

'She should have. She wanted to, but I thought, well, fortunate man. I didn't ever imagine that it could've been him. Would never have taken up her offer of marriage knowing that.'

'Yes, quite. One doesn't want to compete with *him*.'

'We have been competing ever since we were boys. But in this?'

'Well, then, what has changed?' Peter teased. 'He must've said the same when he heard about your marriage. Why my own cousin?'

James gave a sardonic chuckle. 'Yes! Never thought about it that way.'

———

A HUNDRED MILES to the south, Martin had led his small commando across the Vaal River into the Free State. They lost track of time and reality in the weeks of desperate exertion to stay ahead of their pursuers. At night they struggled on, as neither man nor horse would survive the cold if they did not keep moving. Some days, dust storms drove them into what shelter they could find in the war-ravaged plains: a dry watercourse, a rise high enough to shield them from the enemy's eyes. There they fell to the ground, snatched a few hours' sleep and prepared a hasty meal, but always Joep Maree's call of 'Saddle up! Saddle up!' drove them on.

The enemy was forever behind the koppie they'd just skirted or the donga they'd just left. Many days they lost ground, having to double back as they fought their way out of a seemingly hopeless situation. Fifteen hastily dug graves and the carcasses of forty horses marked the way they had come. Twelve men were left in the enemy's path, too severely wounded to carry on. Six more, including Joep Maree, were nursing wounds.

They met up with General de Wet and took refuge with him, resting their horses and replenishing their bandoliers. They tried to close their minds to the devastation of the Free State plains. Blackened ruins of farms, some still smouldering, overturned wagons, decaying carcasses of draught animals in their harnesses, unploughed lands and groups of bewildered women running before the enemy. Dismal sights that they witnessed day after day.

A few miles from Bethulie, they crested a rise and involuntarily reined in their horses. In the distance they sighted the rows of white tents of a concentration camp, enclosed by barbed wire. Through their field glasses they saw women and children carrying wood and pails of water. A little way from the camp were hundreds of white crosses.

Martin kept his glasses trained into the distance. He did not want his men to see the emotion in his eyes. They would recognise it; it lived in their hearts and in the eyes of the women in the veld: hate, raw and bitter.

The Irish Corporal

October 1901

STEFANIE TRIED TO CONCENTRATE on the conversation around the table while feigning interest in the food on her plate. She and Paul Warren were lunching with the 2nd Hussars at their head-quarters, at the invitation of George Hunter, who was commanding the regiment in Colonel Butcher's temporary absence.

Paul talked about the exaggeration of the pro-Boer newspapers about the conditions in the concentration camps. Hunter, seated opposite them, inquired about the Boer men in the camps and Paul elaborated on their eagerness to join *his* National Scouts.

Paul's arrival in Pretoria had again trapped Stefanie in her role as Mrs Warren, the perfect hostess and devoted wife. The past three months had been a battle to conform to his wishes, while hating him with a passion so strong that it frightened her. Only Koba's love kept her going. James had not visited in months, and he and Peter were hardly ever with the regiment when in Pretoria.

'Mrs Warren, I'm looking forward to the concert tonight,' John Miles said from across the table. 'I believe you will perform for the entire second half?'

She smiled. 'Yes. Thank you, Lieutenant Miles.'

The officers had discovered that Paul did not take kindly to the relaxed relationship they'd shared with her before his arrival. And now they kept their distance. She was glad of it. These men were driving families to concentration camps and destroying farms, not just fighting a war. Koba had an answer to that too. 'My heart is breaking for the suffering of our people, *hartjie*, but then I think about how, in the past, the commandos, yes, your dear father as well, put flaming torches to the huts of poor women and children.' And, wagging her finger, Koba had said; 'God keeps a record of wrongs, *hartjie*. The English will suffer in their turn. Women must love everyone with extra care in times of war, not ponder on which side God has forced them to be.'

She wanted to bow to Koba's eccentric wisdom. She could never hate Peter and James.

'Unfortunately I won't be able to escort you tonight, my dear. A meeting in Johannesburg.' Paul brought her thoughts back to the dreadful present. 'Would it be in order if Major Hunter stands in for me?'

'I'd be delighted.' Hunter inclined his head, but in his eyes she saw disdain.

'May I inquire after captains Radford and Henderson?' Paul asked. 'Have they taken themselves off to the pleasures of Johannesburg as usual?'

'Yes, they represented the regiment in the inter-regimental cricket cup,' Murray Shaw said. 'We expect them back today. We leave the day after tomorrow.'

Paul knew well enough where they were. Peter was safe as long as he stayed away; at Paul's request, Koba's house was being guarded by six soldiers camped under the willows.

Martin would be in the Cape by now. If he could undertake such a dangerous mission, she should be ashamed of her failing courage. She had to get into Paul's room at the Pretoria Club while he was in Johannesburg. She was his wife, after all; no one would question her. The formation of the National Scouts would be completed in a few weeks, she gathered from the conversation. Most of these traitors would ride with the British, but a few would be sent to the commandos to lead them into ambushes. She had to get hold of those names.

She looked at the crepes filled with cherries on her plate and toyed with her fork and spoon. It would be risky to meddle with Paul's personal papers. If caught it would be the end of her. *But if I'm to die, let me die honourably, a name remembered for courage. But dear God, I couldn't leave this world without being with my love one more time. Just once more, finally.* She searched her mind for a way to see Peter. The regiment would be riding out soon, and wouldn't be back until Christmas. *It has to be tonight. Patrick McFee will be at Beckett's store ...*

'Well, Radford! Henderson! Back so early? How did it go with the cricket?' came Murray Shaw's voice.

James and Peter were walking towards the table, Peter's smile fading when he saw her and Paul. James looked haggard, and it was obvious that he was not fully sober.

'We brought the cup home despite Henderson scoring only three runs.' Peter nodded in their direction. 'Mr Warren, Mrs Warren.'

'Ah! My dearest cousin.' James leaned over her, breathing brandy fumes into her face. 'You've survived. So have I!' He kissed her full on the mouth. 'A kiss from me, and,' he kissed her again, 'another kiss I've been asked to pass on,' he whispered in her ear, just loud enough for Paul to hear.

John Miles saved the moment. 'Hectic night, sir?'

'And suffering the consequences, sir.' James laughed.

Hunter looked distastefully at James. 'Orders at three.'

'An hour's rest can work wonders, sir.' James took his leave, but he turned at the door. 'Stef, the devil doesn't roam the streets of Johannesburg any more. He prowls around Pretoria now, in broad daylight!'

Warren flushed darkly. James gave a taunting laugh.

PETER TOOK A CHAIR next to Shaw and poured coffee. Shaw asked Stefanie about the music she had selected for the evening. Peter was shocked at the change in her. She was thin, nervous, her voice strained and tense. Impotent rage welled up in him, and he challenged Warren with his eyes.

Warren rose abruptly. 'Thank you, gentlemen. I have a meeting shortly. My driver will see you home, my dear.' He placed his hand under Stefanie's elbow.

Peter watched as they walked away and heard her say to Warren, 'I have to stop off at Beckett's store for a hat I've ordered from Cape Town and …'

Their voices faded. The officers finished their coffee and dispersed. Peter called for his horse, making straight for Church Square, arriving in time to see Stefanie going into Beckett's store. He dismounted and watched her through the window. The shop attendant brought a hatbox from under the counter and handed it to her. Then a soldier, a corporal, came to stand directly behind her.

A few minutes later she emerged, and he was about to call to her when the corporal fell in step with her, carrying her parcel. He left his horse at the store and followed them. At the post office, they came to a halt. Stefanie scribbled on a piece of paper and gave it to the corporal. Peter looked closely at the man: short with a straight moustache and unusually dark eyebrows.

Peter stood in deep thought, not knowing what to make of the incident. He checked his watch; half an hour before Hunter's briefing. He returned to the mess with enough time to order a pot of coffee and a few sandwiches for James.

James forced the food down. 'Where to this time? North again?'

'No, west actually, Rustenburg district.' Peter watched James closely. 'As Colonel Butcher is only due back in early December, Hunter saw his chance and offered our services in that area. But take heart, Henderson, Hunter's quarry is still in the Cape.'

'God, Radford.' James had a forlorn edge to his voice.

An orderly arrived with a sealed note for Peter. *After the concert, at the bandstand in Meyers Park, my love*, it said in Stefanie's handwriting.

Peter asked the orderly who had delivered the note.

'He didn't give his name, sir. A corporal, sir, Irishman, I could tell by the accent.'

'A corporal? Could you describe him?'

'Short and wiry, and a moustache, sir. He said he didn't need a reply, sir.'

Peter thought Stefanie had probably bribed the corporal he'd seen her with earlier to deliver the message. The description fitted the man. Meyers Park was not far from Koba's house and was deserted at night. He was desperate to see her, if only to beg her to leave Pretoria and get as far away from her husband as possible.

AFTER DINNER in the mess, Peter and James went to the room they shared. James slumped onto his bed. Another hectic weekend of drinking had taken its toll. Peter called his batman for a fresh uniform and started dressing.

'Going somewhere?' James asked.

'I'm going for a gallop and then there's a recital at the Transvaal Hotel. Interested?'

'Spare me!' James divested himself of his clothes and crawled between the sheets. 'Stefanie playing?' Peter nodded, reaching for his helmet. 'Oh Radford, impossible as it may seem, forget about my cousin. Do you ever think ahead? No, you don't. Neither do I. But sometimes, just sometimes it's wise to do so. Stefanie is a Boer; you are a Brit. Remember your Dragons.' He turned onto his side and was soon snoring.

Peter stared at the ceiling, his mind still on the Irish corporal. Could he be working for Martin? If so, what a way to get information out of the city! And if it were true, he could only stand in awe of Stefanie's courage. To defy Warren was a formidable challenge. But to meet with a Boer spy in the middle of the night?

He blew out the lamp and headed back to town.

At the Transvaal Hotel, the recital had already begun and he found a seat at the back. He spotted Stefanie with Hunter and Major Fernfield. When the interval came, the audience gathered in groups, taking refreshments from passing trays. He edged closer to Stefanie's group, taking care to keep out of Hunter's sight. She met his eyes. Shaking his head clearly, he mouthed 'no'. Colour rose in her cheeks but she turned back to Murray Shaw.

He went back to his quarters. James was sleeping soundly. He lay down fully clothed and stared into the dark in abject misery. *There are many Irish corporals, only a coincidence, just a suspicion, the evidence is too fragile*, his heart beseeched. *I must report this*, his reason said. He sat up, ran his hands through his hair, picked up his helmet and left quietly.

STEFANIE JUMPED from the carriage before Hunter could assist her. 'I *refuse* to invite you in for a drink, or pleasant chat. So don't even *suggest* it!' She stormed through the gate, pushed the front door open. 'Tante Koba!' she slammed the door shut.

'In my bed, *hartjie*. Come, I have a nice cup of tea ready for you.'

She sank down on the bed, close to tears. 'Tante Koba, I can't stand it for a day longer.'

'There, there *hartjie*, not so loud. You will wake dear Vicky. She's feeling poorly today. Drink your tea now and tell Tante Koba everything.'

'There's nothing to tell Tante Koba. I played, they applauded and that horrible Hunter—'

'The cruel man! But it will not do to anger him now, *hartjie*. Come, let me brush your hair. It calms you down for a good sleep. A war has a life of its own, we cannot hurry it. Martin is doing his best and you're so brave ...'

Stefanie listened to Koba's dear, familiar twittering as the brush moved skilfully through her hair. When Peter had refused her, her world had ended. But now she had to erase all else from her mind if she was to succeed in the last, most dangerous stage of her mission. *You make mistakes if you don't think with absolute clarity*, the Irishman had so often warned her. The only way to survive until she could get her hands on the papers in Paul's room was to go back to the beginning. She had first stolen papers when enraged by degradation and had had to use courage she never knew she possessed.

She planted a kiss on Koba's cheek, took the candle from the dressing table and climbed the stairs to her bedroom. She placed the candle on the night table, stepped out of her dress and undid the drawstrings of her petticoats, watching as they fell to the floor. Her stockings and underclothes followed them. She heaped her clothes over the chair and pulled her nightdress over her head. She prayed for courage but courage refused to come, only Peter's face denying her request. She bit her lip, lifted her chin, willing herself not to cry. 'Brother Death is dancing with this rose-lipt maiden,' she said aloud and swallowed hard at the tears in her throat. 'Where do they go again, those rose-lipt maidens?'

'To fields where roses fade, if my memory serves me ...'

Her hands flew to her mouth. In the deep shadow of the wardrobe stood a khaki-clad figure, a wide smile on his face. 'Peter! How did you get in?'

'Did some lightfoot leaping past the guards and Tante Koba's bedroom,' he whispered. His eyes travelled over her body, her hair and then to her discarded clothes. 'You're as beautiful as ever, my love. No … more beautiful.'

'Oh, Peter, why did you stay away so long?'

'It was the hardest thing I've ever done in my life, staying away from you.'

Then they were in each other's arms, moving across the floor, their hands urgently seeking each other's faces and bodies. They collided with the bed and fell onto it.

'*Hartjie?*' Koba's voice came from the stairs. 'I thought I heard voices!'

They froze. 'Tante Koba,' Stefanie barely managed to keep her voice normal. 'I'm talking to myself.'

'Yes, *hartjie*, it'll do you good,' Koba returned after a long pause.

They waited breathlessly until they heard her door close again. Stefanie looked deep into Peter's eyes. The passion and love shining in them was intense, overpowering. In her heart she knew that this would be their last time together, their last night of love. Her remaining courage evaporated; all she wanted, needed, was to be with him. 'Love me one last time,' she whispered, her lips barely moving. He raised himself a little and undid the clasp of his belt. His pistol clattered to the floor, but her legs were already wrapped around his waist. He opened his breeches and entered her easily. Just in time his hand shot over her mouth, smothering her cry. Their lovemaking was swift and fierce; keeping his hand on her mouth, they waited for sounds from downstairs, but all was quiet, and in the room was only their ragged breathing.

He supported himself on his elbows and took her face in his hands. 'Will you marry me, Stefanie?' He kept his eyes locked with hers. 'I will not, could not, possibly live without you.'

She searched his face closely; this was not her teasing, smiling love. There was a serious light in his eyes, not even a trace of a smile on his lips. 'Is it not the danger, our circumstances, that brought you here tonight, my love, and makes you say such impossible things?' she asked miserably.

'I didn't want to chance it here, but I came. For months now I've been caught in something that I only now fully understand. Love. I was on my way to India, but halfway across the world, this war intervened, brought me to you. It was meant to be.'

The candle spluttered, casting fleeting shadows across their faces. Through the window came the call of a night bird, the muted laughter from the soldiers under the willows.

'I love you more than anything else in the world, but I cannot make idle promises,' she whispered, pressing her fingers to her lips to prevent her sobs from coming, but soon she was crying helplessly. 'Why, oh why, does it have to be like this? Why do you have to make war on my people?'

He did not answer for a while, just kept his eyes on her face. 'We've kept the war as far away as possible ... between us, I mean. If we allow it to come between us, we will destroy each other.'

'Is the war not already between us, my love?' It was not a question, but a statement. His eyes confirmed her fears; he had his suspicions about her activities. She would expect him to do his duty and report her; that had been understood from the day he had declared himself, with Kitchener not ten yards from them. And that was where the answer to the incredible power of their love lay. Had it not been for courage and loyalty, all might have faded between them, left under the willows. All she could do for now was to pray desperately that he would not find definite proof.

'The war will come to an end and we'll be free,' he said. 'I'll come for you, my love, the very day peace is signed, I'll come for you, free you from Warren and marry you.'

'No matter what happens?' she asked, her voice trembling badly.

'Yes, I'll come for you,' he said. 'No matter what happens.'

———◆———

'MY DEAR JAMES!' Koba held out her arms. 'Come in, *hartjie*, we miss you so much and I think about you every day.' She kissed him on both cheeks, hugging him long and hard. 'Are you well?'

'Yes, Tante Koba, I'm well. And you?' He was sober and rested and some colour had returned to his face. His hands trembled a little, but not for the want of drink.

'Spared through mercy! Come, come inside. We were just going to have our coffee and I've baked a milk tart.'

Victoria was sitting on the sofa arranging the cups. 'Coffee?' she asked.

He nodded and took a seat opposite her. Koba cut the tart and handed him a plate. She asked about the food in their mess, about the weather on campaign and then provided the latest news from Wintersrust.

'We were fortunate to receive a letter from Mary at last,' she said, sipping her coffee. 'It took such a long time to find its way here. God has been looking the other way, *hartjie*, Wintersrust hasn't been burned. Dear Lettie, her heart gave in, and, just as she was to leave her bed again, a stroke. It often happens; first the heart, and then a stroke. Anita is a good nurse—' she broke off, her eyes wide with delight. 'James! Dear Charles and his Anita were married three months ago! In the middle of the night.

Martin married them.' Leaning closer, she whispered, 'Now there's a little one on the way.'

'Charles, a father?' James smiled. 'Imagine! Have you told my parents, Victoria? It's not possible for him to write, being on the other side, so to speak.'

'Yes, I had no news about you, however.'

Koba caught the glance they exchanged and put down her cup. 'I must see to the hives. Spring is here and the bees are busy. I'll save you some honey, *hartjie*.' She ruffled James's hair on her way to the kitchen.

They sat in silence, drinking the coffee. 'Where's Stefanie?' he asked.

'Resting. She didn't sleep a wink last night, she told us.'

Neither has Radford, only stole into our room at five this morning. He brought a small parcel from his pocket and handed it to her. 'It's not much, but it was all I could find in Johannesburg.'

She fiddled with the ribbons before she opened it. Inside was a ring with a cluster of pearls around a small emerald.

'To match your eyes. Victoria, I want to apologise. I have acted childishly and been extremely rude to you.' He went to stand by the window, not knowing how to deal with her silence. 'I want to make amends, if you will allow me.' Still she said nothing. He turned and looked at her.

She put her hand to her throat. 'When one wants something, and it is forbidden, out of reach, one would do all to obtain it. And once one has it … James, I want you to know that what passed between Martin and I … it was all just an illusion, a daydream.'

Relief washed through him, but before he could respond, she took a deep breath and said, 'I've come to believe that I love you. I really do … love you.'

'You love me, despite everything?'

She nodded. 'Martin feels the same now. His country, his people, the war. They rule his life, are his life.'

'He told you all that? When?'

'I spent a night with him three months ago.'

'But how could you possibly …' he asked, bewildered, 'did you go to Wintersrust?'

'No. Johannesburg, he came to me.'

He grabbed the windowsill, steadying himself against the profound shock. An image of her, naked in Martin's arms, formed in his mind and he could not prevent himself from asking, 'Did … did you sleep with him?' The answer was in her eyes. He turned his face away from her to hide the hurt and jealousy that tore at him. The insult from his cousin was more than he could bear.

'James please, let's not argue about this. I know what I've done is unforgivable, and I'm not asking you to forgive me—'

He felt contempt contorting his face. 'The most wanted man, a Boer general, my cousin, consorting with my wife right here in our midst? Do you realise what you have done? I'm sick of playing by the rules! I'm sick of this war! And I'm sick of you! I'm through with you!' He grabbed his helmet and stick and made for the door.

The Crossing

September 1901

THE WIND CARRIED the rumble of the Orange River, thundering through a narrow gorge, into the night for miles around. To the exhausted commando, waiting in a range of hills half a mile from the gorge, it was a welcome yet ominous sound; they heard the fury of the water, smelled the musty vegetation, but no one except the scouts had set eyes on the river.

And now, Martin thought, *with our destination across the river, we find ourselves trapped*. Fighting a way out was impossible as their ammunition was almost gone, the horses exhausted. Barely three miles behind them was a large body of British troops, as blown as they were from the chase of the previous days. To the west, the scouts had spotted another force guarding the only possible crossing. To the east was the brooding, shifting darkness. The only place to ford the river was here; if the way were barred, they would be trapped against the river bank.

Martin stared fixedly into the darkness, waiting for his brothers to return. They had left at sunset to investigate the possibility of another crossing and should return before the half-moon set before midnight. His heart went out to them. They were worn out. Many a day they limped back to the commando, grim-faced, their clothes bloodied and bandoliers empty. Karel had set out with fourteen men and now there were only nine.

The horses snorted, tossed their manes, stomped the ground. A whisper came down the line; the scouts were coming in. The men waited in a strained, hopeful silence as the twins made their way to Martin, leading their horses.

'Come with us,' Karel said grimly.

They stepped out of earshot. Martin smelled their muddied clothes, heard water dripping off their horses. Karel put his arm around Legend's neck. Rudolf stood mute.

'Not two miles from here, east,' Karel said, exhaustion coming through in his voice, 'are close on five hundred guarding the only crossing point above the gorge. They've settled for the night, but are patrolling the bank further up.'

'Straight ahead?' Martin asked with little hope in his heart.

'The cliffs... no horse, not even Legend, can do that, but there's a way. Downstream ... a cut in the mountain wall ... steep, but we might get through. We can't cross there, the water is deep, but half a mile down, we might ... we might. The river widens out, the current might not be so strong. It's the only way, Martin.'

'We'll be less than a mile from the enemy to our right,' Rudolf said.

Martin was not given time to brood on this. 'We must start now if we want to get the men across before morning,' Karel urged.

'Then we go in small groups. Rudi, get Uncle Joep and Jan Viljoen.'

Joep came limping up, a hand clutched to his injured thigh. Jan supported him with an arm around his waist. Martin explained what was to be done. Joep pointed out that most of the men could not swim, but Jan came up with a solution. 'Karel, take me with the first lot. Show me the way. Rudolf can take another group. Three groups behind each other will see us through in no time—'

'Two groups. Rudi stays with me all the time!'

'All right!' Martin snapped, but immediately softened. 'Sorry Karel, Jan shouldn't have asked that of you.' He turned to Joep. 'Pa, prepare the men, but for God's sake don't tell them that we know nothing about the water. Go with the first group; stay there. If we get separated, we'll meet up in the mountains to the east.'

Joep called for twenty men to come forward and he, Jan and the twins led them away. Martin brought up the next group and waited at the descending point. Less than an hour later, Jan and the twins reappeared wet and exhausted, but smiling broadly, bringing the welcome news that the water was only waist deep for most of the way. With Jan guiding a group a little behind the twins, the crossing was completed before sunrise.

Martin crossed last and joined the commando in a ravine a mile further on. He found Jan holding on to Legend's reins. She stood quietly, blowing softly.

'Where's Karel?'

'Scouting. He says they could not clearly make out if the force on the left occupy both sides of the river.' Jan stroked Legend's nose hesitantly, wary of her dislike of strangers. 'After two crossings she's spent. If only we all had horses like her.'

'How's the wound, Pa?' Martin stretched out next to Joep on the hard ground.

Joep patted his thigh. 'Wet, but luckily it's only water, not blood.'

'Not even a little fire, Martin?' Jan asked. '*Magtig!* I'm freezing in places that should be kept warm.'

'No fires. The sun will be here soon,' Martin said. 'The Cape is wet and cold in winter, but it's spring. Things can only get better from now on.'

'Yes, spring will be kind to us and our horses, and we've left the bulk of the British army behind,' Joep said. 'Now let's find Jan Smuts, see him on his way and then head home.'

As the sun touched the sleeping earth and the exhausted commando, Karel and Rudolf came rushing back. 'Legend! Legend!' Karel wheezed, grabbing hold of her reins. 'How bloody stupid of me to leave you alone.'

'Martin, quickly!' Rudolf hung forward, his hands on his knees. 'There, before our eyes, at the foot of the height … shouting distance … a British camp. Maybe two thousand. Many horses and Armstrong guns.'

FOR DAYS, they moved east, west, south, often doubling back, desperately trying to stay out of range of the enemy. They did not always succeed; twelve men and thirty-three horses were lost. Death and sorrow became their constant companions, and, with survival uppermost in their minds, they looked into their souls, not knowing what the next day, the next hour, would bring.

Then the weather turned. First came a continuous drizzle, relenting a little in the afternoons, enabling them to dry their clothes and cook a hasty meal and allowing their horses to pluck a few mouthfuls of grass. Then, late one afternoon, while they were atop a high plateau, thick black clouds descended, and heavy rain set in. Soaked to the bone, their canvas hoods, blankets and clothes became a muddy burden.

Martin had thought that, if one of the twins were to break down under the strain of scouting and danger, it would be Rudolf. But for the love of a horse, Karel was crazed. He refused to scout because Legend was worn out. He would not be separated from Legend; he wouldn't die without her dying with him. Now Rudolf refused to scout without his twin by his side. They rode at the rear of the commando, keeping their distance.

'Martin, my friend, Karel is half-delirious with fever,' Jan Viljoen, his weather-beaten face wild with anxiety, reported to Martin, 'but will the scarecrow take any help! No, he swore at me.'

'Keep them going. Many are coming down with the cold.'

Jan leaned closer to Martin. 'We all stink, but Uncle Joep's wound is not healing. It stinks. It's rotten.'

'Oh God, Jan,' Martin said, his will crumbling. 'I have to find somewhere safe, some place where he can be taken care of.'

Still the rain swept down, turning the already saturated earth into a quagmire. The wind howled, bending trees towards the earth, flinging broken branches and uprooted bushes into the air. Darkness descended prematurely, the clouds hiding the night sky. They stumbled on, dragging their emaciated horses. Martin was desperate for a way to escape. A way to the north. But there was nowhere to go, nowhere to hide. He bit down on his shirt collar to stop his teeth from chattering. Every muscle in his body ached and screamed for rest and warmth. Buks's words taunted him. *You are dragging my father to his death.*

'Move! Move!' he ordered hoarsely, pushing an unwilling man on. 'Keep moving in circles. Don't let the horses stand. They'll never move again if you do! Move! Move!'

Strong arms gripped him from behind. 'Martin! Get a hold of yourself, *magtig*!' Martin saw Jan's beard tremble, his teeth chattering. 'Now listen! Listen to me, Martin!'

'I hear you, Jan!'

'There's a hut … not far. A shepherd is there, he knows a way down … a way not guarded by the English. Come, Martin!'

The commando followed the feeble light of the shepherd's storm lantern into the darkness. He led them to the northern side of the plateau. '*Meneer*, if you can get your horses down here … at the bottom swing northwest. No khakis there,' the old man said. 'It's a wide vlei in which you'll find yourselves.'

'Thank you, old father.' Martin shook the man's hand. 'God sent us to you.'

'Thank God for the darkness, *meneer*, no one would do it in the daylight.' The man disappeared into the rain.

Without further thought, Martin took his horse's bridle and disappeared into the ravine. The men followed, cursing, stumbling, their horses following blindly. Down in the foothills they found knee-deep muddy water. They struggled on, hour after weary hour, slipping and sliding. Many a horse was left where it collapsed, too feeble to carry on.

Martin first became aware of firmer ground when his horse could go no more. The wind had spent its fury, and the rain had slowed to a light drizzle. He decided to wait for daybreak. As the men caught up with him, he told them to tie the horses together in small groups, hoping that the closeness would give them warmth and a better chance of survival.

'Sit under your horses. Hold on to the man next to you as if he's your wife. Two bodies warming one another are better than one cold one.'

He helped Frans Viljoen with Joep. They wrapped Joep in their canvas hoods, placing him under the horses. Martin squatted next to him, with the Viljoens on his other side. He saw the twins close by. Karel rubbed Legend's flanks with his sodden blanket but kept slipping to the ground. He dragged himself up, rubbed her, all the while croaking to her. She whinnied and stood shivering fitfully.

Rudolf bent over Karel, who had sunk to his knees again. 'Karel, don't fall asleep now … please, Karel, stay awake, please! You'll die if you sleep … the sun will come, just another hour, please, Karel!' He pulled him into his arms. 'Legend will make it, you'll see, she'll make it … she understands, Karel.'

'You will fry in hell! But we're dying, Legend is dying from cold!' Karel shouted into the rain. 'Is this your hell, God? Is this your hell?' He slumped against Rudolf.

Rudolf struggled to keep him upright. 'Come … come, we'll dance! Remember the first dance with Annecke? Do you remember Karel? Come!' He croaked the tune of the 'Green Mountain Waltz' and Karel started swaying. 'Yes, yes, let's dance, Karel!' He sang, his voice forlorn and desperate.

Martin looked at his brothers locked in an embrace. He stumbled to his feet. 'Rudi, he's crazed with fever, let me help—'

'Leave us alone.'

'He's my brother too.'

'You're not my brother!' Karel rasped. 'You sent Pa to the British. You took James's wife. Annecke … you took Annecke from Rudi. You take *everything*!'

Annecke? Was it Annecke all along? Martin wondered. He stood for a while. Then he wrung the water from the blanket and rubbed Legend's flanks.

DAWN BROKE GREY AND MISERABLE, the sun a smudge on the horizon, but the rain had ceased. Twenty horses lay dead. Six men failed to respond to calls and shakes, their bodies numb, their hearts barely fluttering. Joep Maree was no longer conscious. His cheekbones stood out sharply, his grey beard matted with grime, his teeth clenched.

Martin gathered him in his arms, placing his cheek against Joep's forehead. 'Pa, please forgive me, Pa …' Joep's eyes fluttered open. They were wild. He mumbled incoherently, his breath sickly sweet.

'Frans, we must get these men to shelter,' Martin said quietly. 'Any shelter.'

Frans Viljoen nodded to Gert Vermaas and they set off. They were back within an hour, having found a farmstead only two miles away. 'The farmer is willing to help. There's a huge barn where we can hide for the day, as long as it's safe,' Frans said. 'He farms with horses, but the English have confiscated all of them. Now our horses will have stables and oats, and the women are already baking bread and making coffee.'

'Enemy around?'

'They passed through late yesterday,' Gert Vermaas said. 'This side of the mountain is inaccessible and therefore they don't expect us here. There's more news. A Boer force spent a few hours on this farm some days ago. General Smuts is looking for you.'

Tears of gratitude and relief pricked Martin's eyes, and his shoulders slumped for a moment. He looked at his weary men, knowing how dispirited they were, but he had to get them on the move again. He helped to place the sick men on the strongest horses, and the worn-out commando struggled on.

They found a warm welcome at the farmstead. The horses were stabled and given fodder. Soon the men settled in the barn and had fires going on the clay floor. Pots of coffee and steaming bread arrived. Martin bought four sheep from the farmer and told the men to slaughter them. The farmer's wife offered to take the sick men into her house. Martin and the Viljoens carried Joep inside.

Rudolf refused to let Karel go. They still had Legend with them, the only horse brought into the barn. They sat with the few scouts who had survived the trip. Martin walked over and squatted in front of them. Rudolf was forcing coffee through Karel's parched lips.

'Is Uncle Joep bad?' Rudolf did not meet Martin's eyes. 'Is Uncle Joep dying?'

Martin pressed his fingers to his eyes, trying to prevent this dreadful truth from overwhelming him. In the farmhouse, Joep, the man dearest to his heart, lay dying. But fifty more lives were in his hands, depending on his ability to think clearly. He had to get them home, back to their own soil.

'Yes, Uncle Joep is dying. His wound is rotten, the poison has spread through his body.'

Rudolf's face crumpled and he held on tighter to his twin. 'Will we ever get out of this, Ouboet? Will you get us home?'

'I'll try my best, Rudi.' Martin placed a comforting hand on Rudolf's shoulder. The scouts around them were snoring and he found it safe to speak. 'Rudi, those were harsh words Karel spoke last night.'

'What he said about Pa ... he says terrible things when he's desperate. And James's wife ... you saw her before we left, didn't you?'

Martin averted his eyes. He'd suspected that Rudolf knew about his trip to see Victoria, and thus Karel knew too. He wanted to tell them that seeing her had given him back his life, his soul. But he could not. It had left an emptiness that even the hard days of fighting and fleeing had not been able to fill. He had to get home, to his son, to the place where fighting the war, not just surviving, was important.

He rose, but there was one more question that needed to be answered. 'What he said about Annecke, is it true?' Rudolf did not respond. He looked at him closely and saw tears, but whether they were tears of fatigue he could not tell. 'Rudi, please tell me.'

After a while, Rudolf said, 'Outside, in this strange country, death is waiting for one of us or both. I don't want to deceive you any longer. She married you because she thought I was dead.'

Martin sank back on his haunches. 'What did you say, Rudi?'

'You heard me, Ouboet.' Rudolf closed his eyes. 'I'm sorry.'

Martin puzzled over Rudolf's words, but could not take them in; the exhaustion he'd suffered in the last months had taken its toll. He joined Jan and Frans at the fire. He would sleep and then find Jan Smuts.

The owner of the farm approached, his hat in his hand. 'General, your commandant … the gangrene has eaten into his mind. Come with me, he's going fast.'

Hunter's Revenge

November 1901

THE BRITISH CAMP at Rustenburg was on the large area the Boers used for weapon shows and *nagmaal* gatherings. Peter and James stood a little way from the sea of tents, their eyes travelling over the countryside. The mountains were resplendent in early summer; delicate fresh leaves, the acacias and the milkwood coming into bloom. Starlings, bee-eaters and shrikes tumbled through the air, catching insects on the wing. High above the mountains, black eagles soared in the air currents.

'Have you had your wound seen to?'

'Just a scratch.' James lifted his hand and allowed Peter to inspect the bandage. It was clean, with no blood seeping through.

Charles's hospital had been taken over and was overflowing with wounded and sick, requiring extra tents to be pitched around it. Peter knew James found it hard to go there. Some of Charles's things were still there – his books on the shelves and family photographs on the wall. And James was in a foul temper and drinking heavily again. Peter again wondered what had happened during James's last visit to Victoria. This time James had not confided in him.

Peter searched his mind for something positive to say, but the only piece of news he could come up with was that Colonel Butcher was due back soon, thus freeing the regiment from George Hunter's harsh authority.

The bugler's call for breakfast sounded. Peter picked up his helmet.

'Shall we have a bite before orders? Might be a trip in it for us.'

After breakfast they reported at the tented headquarters and found the other officers already gathered there. George Hunter picked up his swagger stick, pointing to a map of the area.

'We've reason to believe that many farmsteads are still being used as supply points. Four roads leading out of Rustenburg have been selected for today. Captain Radford, Lieutenant Miles, ride due east, follow this road.

Captain Shaw, Lieutenant Moore, take the road leading north. The farm of a certain Malan family, who have harboured wounded Boers, lies there.'

'We are cavalry, Major,' Murray Shaw grumbled. 'It's not our duty to burn farms—'

'Those are our orders. We are mounted infantry until cavalry is needed again.'

Shaw studied the map. 'And should we come across General de Winter's farm …?'

'It was spared, for obvious reasons.' Hunter kept his eyes on the map, his face flushing noticeably. 'We'd hoped to capture him on a visit to his family but he has eluded us so far. By destroying his farm, we hope to force him to acknowledge that the war is over. It will bring a speedy end to the resistance in this area and therefore the war.'

'Martin de Winter is not exactly a stranger to any of us,' Shaw said pointedly. 'Evicting his family—'

'Captain Shaw, need I remind you that the war has made him an enemy?'

'Sir, you know the man,' Peter said. 'He will not stray from his course.'

'These are orders from Pretoria, sir. I'm merely passing them on.' Hunter brought his stick down on the map. 'Captain Henderson,' the stick indicated a red-circled point. 'Take the road to the west, following the foothills of the mountain. I don't want a single house on that road spared. Is that clear?'

James stood with his eyes fixed on the red circle. The faces of the others registered disbelief when they realised what the order entailed: Hunter was ordering James to burn Wintersrust and evict his family.

Peter was the first to speak out. 'That's cruel!'

Hunter silenced him with a glare. 'All persons captured will be brought to a collecting point a mile south of town. I don't want them riding through here. I want you back by last light. Gentlemen, dismissed!'

The officers filed out. James made straight for the horse lines. The others conferred hastily, and then Peter rushed after him.

'I'll demand to swap assignments!' He fell into step with James.

'Don't you see, Radford? He's deliberately sending you in the opposite direction to prevent that!'

'The depraved bastard!' Peter headed back to the tent. He stormed inside. 'Permission to take on Captain Henderson's duty, sir! His brother's pregnant wife and his aunt live in the house you want him to burn.'

Hunter clasped his hands behind his back and rocked on his heels. 'I've reason to believe that Captain Henderson's loyalty is questionable. I'm allowing him the opportunity to restore his reputation.'

'No, you're not, Hunter! You're using this to settle old scores. James's loyalty questioned? It's absurd! I'm with him, constantly. My God, I should know.'

'Enough, sir! Don't you dare question my command.'

Peter turned to leave, but Hunter called him back. 'While on the interesting subject of loyalty; an officer, a captain, was seen leaving Mrs Warren's house in the early hours of the morning before we left Pretoria. Not Captain Henderson. He was in his room, but your bed was empty. Where were you that night?'

'My private life is none of your concern, sir.'

Hunter leant against the table, facing Peter squarely. 'Two reports have been made concerning Mrs Warren. Captain Bartlett is convinced that she gathers information on train movements and passes it on to the Boers, and Major Fernfield concurs. Paul Warren won't allow his wife's loyalty to the Crown to be questioned, and insists she couldn't possibly accomplish what their reports suggest. Do you agree with him, Radford? You were on rather intimate terms in Cape Town, weren't you?'

Peter was overwhelmed. James implicated in God knows what and Stefanie already under suspicion! He almost wanted to laugh at the absurdity of the situation: as long as her husband sought to safeguard his own position, Stefanie was safe from the firing squad. But not from Warren himself.

'I see, you refuse to venture an opinion. Quite frankly, I question his judgement.' Hunter dismissed Peter with a meaningful glance.

Peter's first thought was for James. 'We can't help him,' he said to the other officers when they gathered around him. He walked over to the horse lines, finding James mounted, ready to set off. He took hold of his horse's bridle. He saw Sergeant Adams watching them, and motioned James away from the men. 'The cards are on the table. Hunter is onto something.'

James nodded, his face set. 'I'm aware of that.' He gave his men the order to move out.

Peter held on to the bridle. 'Whatever it means, let *me* burn the farm. I'll suffer the consequences.'

'That will be the end for us both.' James gave spurs to his horse.

———

ANNECKE PLACED THE LAST of the bottled fruit on the shelves and stepped back to admire her handiwork. It was a nice little home, the cave; they could live quite happily here until the war was over. All that was needed was a gate to block the entrance so that the children could not take to wandering the mountain alone.

She took her music box from her apron pocket, placing it by the fire-side. She would not play the song today. The spring was worn, making the melody so much harder to bear. Charles had told her of a newspaper he had seen while visiting Oom Koos de la Rey's commando, detailing the havoc that Martin was causing in the Cape Colony. So he was alive, but what about Rudi?

She picked up her *kappie* and went outside. It was time to get home, for there was still much to be done. Besides, little Martin would need her by now.

'Good afternoon, Mrs de Winter.'

She swung around.

'No need to be alarmed. I'm a friend. And you're our general's wife.'

'Yes, my name is Annecke. Who … who are you?'

'The name is Patrick McFee. I'm with Karel's scouts. He asked me to keep an eye on the cave and the farms until you move up here. I saw that you bring things up here every day.'

'I've heard about you. Yes, we'll come up soon. Charles will help us with my mother. She's a little stronger now. We couldn't move her earlier. Do you know Charles?'

'Yes, our doctor, I know him. It's time you move here. Your farms have been undisturbed for too long and the English are in a vengeful mood. General de la Rey cut them up badly the day before yesterday …' he snatched his field glasses from his chest and brought them to his eyes. 'Thirty plus the officer … circling your father's house. They have come to burn the farms. The bastards!'

Annecke let out an anguished cry. 'My boy! I have to get my little boy!' She started scrambling down the rock.

He caught her by the arm. 'Annecke, the first law of survival is to think before you act, even if you have just a split second. We have time to work out a plan. When you get to the house, do exactly as the English say …'

'But we can't go to the camps! We have to flee!'

'Your mother can't run, they'll see you and catch you. I can save you by forcing you to stay with me, but then you'll be separated from your child. Listen to me carefully.' He spun her around, pulling her towards him. 'Calm down and listen, lass!' She wiped the tears from her face and nodded. 'You will get to a camp in a few days. No, no, don't worry. I'll get you out. That I promise. Here's what you must do; when you arrive at the camp, you write a letter to Stefanie—'

'Stefanie? But she's free with the English! She won't help us!'

McFee gave a short laugh, grabbed her hand and they set off down the mountain. 'Can you keep a secret, Annecke?'

'Yes, I'm good at keeping secrets.'

'She will help. Write to Stefanie, tell her where you are, which camp. I'll get the news from her. It might take a while, but I'll make a plan and get you out.'

She tripped over a rock. McFee set her on her feet again. They ran on. When they reached the drift, McFee pointed to the smoke rising in the sky. 'Soetvlei! They're still at your father's house. Now, be brave, be brave!' She nodded. 'That's a good lass! I'll come for you, I promise. Do you believe me?'

She nodded again. 'Thank you for helping me.'

'Now run! I'll watch from this tree. I have my rifle. If anyone touches you, or the others, I'll shoot him from here. I'm a good sniper, the best there is.'

———

JAMES LED HIS TROOP far around Wintersrust so that they reached Soetvlei first. Koba had told him that all the women and children were at Wintersrust. He had a plan, a desperate plan to warn them to get away from the house.

Soetvlei was deserted, the garden neglected. He signalled his troop to surround the farmstead. He dismounted, walked up the steps, knocked on the door. He allowed a minute or two and then faced the men. 'This is a Boer officer's farm. Before you set fire to it, search every possible place where documents could be. Lift the floorboards, search behind the rafters. Sergeant Adams, take charge!'

He handed his horse to a trooper. 'An edgy fellow, see that he's far from the fire.'

'Yes, sir, I'll keep him away.'

'Do you remember Lieutenant Sinclair?'

'Yes, sir, he bought it last year.'

'He was buried on this farm. I'm taking a walk to the graveyard.'

In the orchard, James paused. He heard the men's shouts and laughter as they ripped Soetvlei apart. *Forgive me, Aunt Lettie, Uncle Joep, forgive me*, he repeatedly mumbled as he raced on. Old Klaas's kraal was four hundred yards upstream. He doubled his pace and arrived at the huts, but found them deserted.

'Master James, have you come to burn your own blood's house?' Old Klaas said from behind him. 'I've told them to flee, but they can't leave *mies* Lettie behind, she's too sick. *Mies* Mary is not afraid of the English.'

James ripped a page from his notebook, scribbled a few words. 'Give them this. I'll give them enough time to get away. Please, hurry!'

Old Klaas took the note. 'I'll try, Master James.'

James raced back to Soetvlei. Time, he needed time. His chest was heaving when he arrived. He called Sergeant Adams. 'Found anything, Sergeant?' He was aware that Adams was looking closely at him.

'Only this, sir.' Adams handed him a few envelopes. 'Shall we get on with it, sir?'

James watched as the fire took hold of the house. Feigning interest in the papers, he saw Adams disappear in the direction of the drift, where he had just come from. Minutes later, a shot reverberated through the air. The men took what cover they could find. Nothing happened for a few minutes and then Corporal Johnson stood up.

'It were only the Sergeant!'

The men relaxed when Adams appeared.

'What were you shooting at, Sergeant?' James asked.

Adams appeared uncomfortable, not meeting James's eyes. 'A dog, sir. Came for me, sir!'

James stared at him; there were no dogs around. Before he could react, the rafters of the house snapped and, with an ear-splitting crack, the roof collapsed. He knew he could not delay going to Wintersrust much longer, and hoped fervently that Old Klaas had reached the farmstead and seen the women to safety. He gave the order to move out.

When they reached the drift, Sergeant Adams called out, 'Someone running over there, sir! A woman, sir!'

James reined in sharply. The little hope that he had clung to vanished and despair overwhelmed him. Annecke was running towards Wintersrust, her dark hair flying out behind her. From the stoep, Lena was anxiously calling for her. He wanted to go to them, take them to safety himself, but he dared not show himself; they would be devastated. *Dear God! How did I end up in this agonising absurdity?*

He composed his face and turned to his troop. 'This is Wintersrust, the residence of my cousin, General de Winter,' he said. Most men avoided his eyes but those who looked at him showed sympathy. 'They won't put up resistance, should we allow them time to prepare. Corporal Black, go to the house; tell Mrs de Winter that we'll give them an hour or two. Brew some tea, Johnson!'

He walked some way off, shaking with the effort to stay calm. The need for a drink crazed his mind. Johnson brought him tea. He forced himself to take a sip, but his shoulders shook as he retched.

'Sir? Are you all right, sir?'

James's eyes went to his horse at the drift. 'In my saddlebag is a bottle of brandy.'

Johnson nodded. He was back with the bottle tucked into his tunic a few minutes later. 'Anything else, sir?'

'Escort the women and children to the collecting point. I'm charging you with their safety. Thank you, Corporal.'

He waited until Johnson was away before taking a long pull from the bottle. He shuddered as the brandy burned into his stomach, but could not resist taking another mouthful. He willed himself not to look at the house, but his eyes were drawn to it. Lena brought the mule-cart to the stoep. Annecke piled blankets onto it. A mattress was placed on the cart. Mary and Lena led Lettie from the house. She was hanging between them for support. They reached the cart, but failed to get her onto it.

'Smith! Harper!' he heard Johnson's order. 'Go help with the sick woman.'

He averted his eyes, swallowing more brandy. When he looked towards the house again, Lettie was on the cart; Harper was helping Lena, who had a baby in her arms, onto it. Harper handed up the other children and held out his hand to Mary. She took it with dignity and took a seat on the cart. Annecke lifted a blond toddler onto her lap. *Martin's son?* He waited for Charles's wife to emerge from the house, but there was no sign of Anita.

Dusk fell when the mule-cart, looking small and forlorn, took the road to Rustenburg. James waited until it had disappeared from sight before he detailed two men to set fire to the house. The rest he ordered to stay at the drift.

A glow filled the house as if the lamps had been lit for the night, as he remembered it as a boy. It was the time that Uncle Marthinus would take the Dutch Bible and read the strange words that had brought serenity after a long day's play. He saw the devout expression on Martin's face; Charles concentrating on his uncle's words, lamplight reflecting off his glasses; his aunt's eyes caressing her husband's strong brown hands; Karel and Rudolf battling to keep their blue eyes open. He felt weary and his head drooped onto Stefanie's shoulder.

Flames billowed through the windows and doors and annihilated his memories. His feet carried him towards the house. The flames, yellow and scarlet, leapt into the thatched roof. The roar was deafening, the heat overpowering. He stood a few yards from the stoep, perspiration pouring off his face, smoke enveloping him, his eyes on the wicker chair that Oubaas de Winter had occupied for so long. The roof collapsed onto the stoep, the flames engulfing the chair in a second.

———

TWO WEEKS LATER, Martin and his battered commando neared their mountain hideout. The long ride from the south had been free of incident. They had travelled far to the west of the railway line in the sparsely populated country, moving only between sunset and sunrise. Snatching what rest they could during the day, they had made better time than expected, though it had been a gruelling ordeal for everyone, not least for the horses.

The twins, sent ahead to find General de la Rey, reported that Wintersrust and Soetvlei had been destroyed and that those responsible were still at Rustenburg, waiting for supplies from Potchefstroom. General de la Rey proposed to raid that convoy. Jan Viljoen, now commandant after Joep Maree's death, reminded Martin that supplies needed to be replenished, and Martin made plans to meet up with the rest of the commando and rendezvous with De la Rey.

'We wait until the convoy is close to Rustenburg before we attack. It might draw the force that burnt the farms out of town to assist them,' Martin said to Jan. 'I knew Wintersrust was going to be torched. Reprisal is a useless course, but, *wragtig*, I won't let an opportunity like this slip through my hands.'

They reached their old camp a few days later. There was backslapping, hugging and joking, and once again Jan Viljoen's roistering laugh filled the air. There were also tears when they remembered the dead left behind in the Cape. Martin found Charles surrounded by men wanting news of their families. Charles looked older, saddened, his eyes filled with weariness.

'You don't look overjoyed to see us,' Martin said, greeting him with a hug.

'I'm overwhelmed, grateful for your safe return.' Charles smiled, a tired smile. 'Get the twins. The news I have is … upsetting.'

Martin sent a man to fetch them. Karel had recovered, as Legend's condition had improved, and had taken control of the scouting again, but now Rudolf was sullen and refused to discuss Annecke with him.

Karel rushed up and hoisted Charles off his feet. 'Cousin! I've never seen so much rain in my life! Day after day—'

Martin interrupted. 'Charles has important news. Come!'

They walked out of earshot of the men. Charles fiddled with his glasses and the buttons on his collarless shirt. Martin waited, giving him time to arrange his words.

'Well, the farms aren't the worst of it, I'm afraid,' he said at last. 'Aunt Lettie had a heart attack after you left for the Cape. Anita pulled her through but then came a stroke. They were still at Wintersrust when … they were taken to the camps, except Anita. She wasn't there at the time.'

The three brothers overwhelmed him with anxious questions.

'Where's Buks?' Martin asked, shaking Charles's arm in his need to know.

Charles sighed deeply. 'When Buks and I reached the farms, they were still smouldering. Buks smashed his rifle and chucked his bandolier into the ruins. He rode away. I haven't seen or heard of him since. I found McFee there. He spoke to Annecke before it happened. He promised to get her out once Stefanie sends word where they are.'

'That would be easy,' Karel said.

'No, too dangerous,' Martin said. 'Oom Koos wrote that conditions in the camps have improved. The sickness is not so bad any more. They get better food and medicines now.'

'But the chance is that they might die!' Rudolf cried. 'If you don't care, I will get her out!'

'Come Rudi,' Karel said, taking him by the arm. 'We'll speak to McFee and get her out.'

'No, Karel!' Martin said. 'Can't you see that you will endanger them even more? You can't get all of them out, neither can you separate them. And there's my son. I will not allow you to endanger his life.'

'*Your* son?' Karel taunted.

'No! Don't … Karel!' Martin saw tears rolling down Rudolf's cheeks, his face distorted with anguish.

Then the truth spilled out: the note that Karel had only read when he had found his twin again; Rudolf defending his silence. Martin turned his back to them, his mind refusing to take in what had been revealed. It could not be. The boy was his, his son, the reason he was fighting for liberty. All he stood for had been taken from him – his farm, his very existence – but he would not allow his brothers to claim his son.

'You are mistaken. The boy is mine,' he said. 'Annecke knows that too. I spent the night with her before I left—', he broke off, not wanting to admit under pressure what had happened. 'I don't have to explain myself to you; she is my wife!'

'You forced her, didn't you?' Karel shouted and made a move towards Martin. Rudolf seized his arms, struggling to hold him back.

'Oh for God's sake, Karel!' Charles intervened, placing his body between the brothers. 'Only Annecke can tell us the paternity of her child. Leave it until the war is done.'

Karel shook free of Rudolf's hold, glaring at Martin. 'You want James's wife; we all know that. You met her in Johannesburg.'

To Martin's dismay, Charles joined in the row. 'You met Victoria?

Martin swung around and faced them. 'I will not be judged by any of you. *I had to go!* And that's all you need to understand. It is none of your concern!'

His anger silenced them. Karel pulled his twin to him. Rudolf's eyes were still brimming, but in them Martin read a plea for understanding.

'There's something else I have to tell you.' Charles made a hopeless gesture with his hands. 'James was the officer in charge when Wintersrust was burned.'

'James!' the three brothers exclaimed.

'Yes, James.' Charles told them how he had gone into Rustenburg under a white flag to find James, as he knew that the Hussars were stationed there. He had, however, only found Frank Crofton-Smith at his hospital. 'Frank told me that George Hunter ordered James to destroy the farms. McFee saw the burning; he'll tell you.'

'Hunter!' Karel let loose a string of profanities. 'Irishman!' he shouted.

McFee told about James sending Old Klaas to warn the women; about a trooper who shot Old Klaas before he could deliver the message. He told how the family had been treated and how, upon seeing the blaze, James had broken down.

'Your cousin was drunk,' McFee said. 'Crazed. It took his troopers to get him away from the house and onto his horse.'

Silence ensued, broken only by the crackling of a nearby fire, voices carried on the evening air and the melancholy notes of Gert Vermaas's harmonica. Rudolf stumbled into the twilight and sank to his haunches, his head in his hands. Rudolf's world was shattered, Martin realised through the anger and hurt surging through his mind. Rudolf needed hope; they all did. He too felt beaten, tired of struggling. But he was a general; he could not show weakness, even in the emotional chaos they found themselves in, or else they would fall apart, all of them. He pulled himself together with great effort.

'McFee, go to Stefanie; find out where my family is.'

McFee nodded and left.

'Karel, the garrison in Rustenburg and the convoy from Potchefstroom. Report daily.'

Karel muttered and followed McFee.

'Charles, please see to Rudi.'

Charles stood a moment longer, wanting to speak.

'See to Rudolf!'

A Bloodhound for the English

December 1901

ANNECKE AND LENA stood in the long line of women at the corrugated-iron shed, waiting for their weekly rations. The sun beat down, the children dragged at their skirts, and Lena's baby was crying.

Annecke shielded her boy's head with her *kappie* and moved a few paces on. It was their third Friday in the camp at Potchefstroom. There was seldom enough food and she had to collect sufficient for Mary too, as she refused to stand in the line.

Her mind was numb with all that had happened.

On arrival in the camp, they had received a tent and had to make do with what they brought from the farm. Lettie died soon after they arrived. The guards came for her body before they could wash and lay her out. It was one week into their incarceration before Annecke had the chance to follow the Irishman's orders. She wrote a long letter to Stefanie, but there was no sign of the Irishman. Every day she searched the river and the veld when they were allowed out to collect firewood and wash at the river, but there were so many places where he could hide.

'Lena, is the baby still feverish?'

'I think she's a little better, Annecke.' Lena moved on a few paces. 'I dare not take her to the doctor. He doesn't allow mothers to sit with—', she broke off, her eyes widening. 'Buks!'

Annecke saw her brother searching the line for them. Buks came running and gathered Lena and the baby into his arms. 'I've come to look after you,' he said. 'I've heard that those who have men in the field don't get their fair share of food.'

'Have you not heard that these men end up working for the British?' Lena pulled away from him.

'But Lena, I can't have you and our children here ...' Buks faltered, stunned by Lena's anger. He tried to reason with her, but the women in the line hissed at him and moved protectively around Lena. After a bit, he turned to Annecke. 'Where's your tent?'

Annecke gave him directions, imploring Lena to follow, but she refused to give up her place, crying silently, her face pressed into her baby's blanket.

An hour later, they received their food and arrived back at the tent to see Buks sitting with his children.

'Annecke, please don't leave me,' Lena whispered, handed the rations to Mary and asked her to take the children and start the meal. The children clung to their father, unwilling to release him so soon after his return. Lena spoke to them sharply and they burst into tears.

'So stuffy in here.' Mary looked pointedly at Buks, gathered the little ones and left.

Annecke stood uncomfortably, looking at her brother and his wife. Lena's dress was faded, the sleeves frayed at the edges. Her dull hair was scraped into a bun and her normally cheerful features now showed fear. Buks appeared dejected, his eyes dispirited. Thongs held his boots together, and his jacket was patched at the elbows and collar. Lena rocked her baby, but the child would not be consoled.

'Ma died when we got here, Buks,' Annecke said.

He nodded. 'Aunt Mary told me. Pa died in the Cape, just because Martin wants to keep the war going.'

Grief tore at Annecke's heart and she wept in silent sobs. Buks held her to him until her weeping subsided. Then he gently took Lena and Annecke by their shoulders and turned them to the entrance of the tent.

'What do you see?'

Annecke looked at the life they had lived for the past three weeks. The women, their suffering visible in the bitter set of their faces, were sharing scraps of food with their servants. Feuds erupted daily between those whose menfolk had given up, and those who still had theirs in the war. Grandfathers sat in the shade of tents, their hands hanging between their knees, their pipes cold in their mouths. The children played in the dust. They were thin and ragged, covered in sores.

'Do you see the white crosses behind the barbed wire?' Buks said. 'Do you know how many women and children have died? Thousands. Where will it end?' He turned Lena back to look at him. 'The war is over, my heart, it has been over for a year. Look what's happening to our land. There's hardly a farm left standing. I am going to force Martin to give up so that this can all end.'

'Martin is fighting for freedom,' Annecke said, her lips trembling.

'Don't blame him for the way the war is going, Buks. And don't blame him for Pa's death.'

'Annecke, the time for fighting is over,' Buks said, his voice pleading. 'If Martin gives up, a thousand men will lay down their weapons and so will those in Oom Koos de la Rey's commandos.'

'Will you lead the English to Martin?' she asked fearfully. 'He's my husband, your brother-in-law. How can you betray him?'

'There's no other way to prevent more suffering.'

'So, you have come to be a bloodhound for the English. I'm not going to turn my back on our people, not for your sake, but for our children's sake.' Lena's eyes brimmed with tears as she pressed her baby to her chest. 'I'm going to help Aunt Mary. When I get back, I don't want to see you here.'

They watched her walking through the tents to where Mary was cooking over an open fire. Buks stood a while longer before he took the path to the camp commandant's office. His shoulders were hunched, his hat pulled low over his face. Annecke had felt his tears when he had kissed her goodbye, but whether they were tears of anger or hopelessness, she could not tell.

They ate their meal of boiled beef and gruel. The children were fractious, squabbling and wailing. Lena tried to revive her baby, whose temperature had risen, her breathing rapid and uneven. She undressed her to sponge her down and saw red spots on her little belly.

'Measles!' The word hung in the tent like a death cry.

'The children have all had measles. They won't get it again.' Mary took the baby from Lena. 'Let me see.' She examined the baby's eyes and inspected the body. 'Lena, this is not measles, it's scarlet fever. It's not fatal, but highly contagious. The children will probably contract it, and even we may. It will spread through the camp. We have to report it.'

'What will they do, Ma?' Annecke pressed little Martin to her chest.

'They might isolate us for the duration of the fever.'

'All of us? Not just my baby?'

'Yes, all of us.' Mary placed her arms about Lena's shoulders. 'Come, let's make her comfortable. I shall go to Sister in the morning.'

———

STEFANIE'S COURAGE, already stretched to breaking point, was threatening to desert her. Three Boers from General Botha's force, spies like her, had been executed the previous month and she felt herself one step away from the firing squad. She had taken to crawling into Koba's bed at night, her head on Koba's comforting bosom. '*Hartjie, hartjie,*' Koba always said.

'The time has come for the Irishman to get you out of here.'

It was indeed time to disappear. Twice in the past month she had sneaked into Paul's room at the Pretoria Club. She knew his passion for keeping records, and, hidden in a hatbox, soon she found what she was looking for. Lists of names of the commandos of generals Botha, Beyers and Meyer, but not a word about Martin. *These papers were meant to be found,* she realised. On her way back to Church Square, she'd bumped into two men she'd seen before. She fled home without keeping her appointment with McFee, and sent Koba to warn him of her predicament. Koba came back with the dreadful news that Wintersrust was destroyed, her family taken to a camp, and that Martin, having returned from the Cape, was anxious to find them.

And now, with Christmas two weeks away, McFee was waiting in Church Square again to arrange her escape and get news from her of her family's whereabouts. But the confusion of thousands of families being herded to widely dispersed camps made it difficult to trace them.

Stefanie went into the garden, but the heat was overpowering and the stares of the soldiers under the willows irritated her. She returned to the sitting room and sank down on the sofa. The clock on the mantelpiece showed ten – two hours before Paul would collect her for luncheon at Burgers Park. She was so tired, so very tired.

I'm not getting enough sleep, but then, I'm two months late. Please God, don't let it be! I cannot involve a child in this nightmare! If Peter were to find out, he would confront Paul and they would both be doomed.

There came the sound of scraping boots at the front door. A sharp spasm went through Stefanie when she heard Victoria greeting the intelligence officer. 'Good morning, Major Bartlett!'

'Lady Victoria.' His voice filled the room. 'I don't want to impose on your morning, but I felt like a stroll. Getting out of the office for a bit.'

His khaki-clad figure came into view. Stefanie swallowed hard. 'How are you, Mrs Warren?'

'Well, thank you, Major.' She cleared her throat. 'Would you like some tea? We were just about to have some.'

'Yes, I would rather.' He sat opposite her, placing his helmet on the floor. 'Sir Alfred Milner is expected in the first week of January. Has your husband informed you of General Kitchener's request to perform for them?'

'Yes, he has. I'm honoured.' She tried to put some enthusiasm into her voice.

Bartlett took the tea, complimenting her on her music and the pleasure it brought to so many. He assured Victoria that Captain Henderson was in good health when he had last heard from the regiment.

Stefanie waited anxiously for the real reason for his visit. 'Unfortunately

I've also brought some distressing news,' Bartlett said, eventually coming to it. 'Your brother's farm was destroyed. Regulations, as you know. We have to force him to give up the war. You understand, don't you, Mrs Warren?'

'The news is all over Pretoria, Captain Bartlett,' Victoria said icily.

Stefanie avoided Bartlett's eyes. 'Where is my mother?'

'In a shelter at Potchefstroom.' Bartlett held his cup out for more tea. 'Scarlet fever laid your family low. Unfortunately two children succumbed; one of them was General de Winter's son. Please accept my condolences.'

Bartlett drained his tea while the women took in the news. Then he brought an envelope from his pocket. 'A letter for you. It has been opened; all letters have to be censored.' He picked up his helmet. 'I thank you for the tea; it was most refreshing. And, once again, my condolences. Good day, ladies.'

Victoria saw him to the door. Stefanie sat with the letter unopened on her lap.

'I think you should read it,' Victoria said. 'Going for a stroll, getting out of the office? Did you fall for that? The Translation Section must be working around the clock. Not all letters are inspected, but yours certainly are. Whatever is in there has caught his interest. By giving you that letter he wants you to know that he knows.'

'Knows what?' Stefanie's heart beat against her ribs.

'That you're under suspicion. That's the way they do things, I believe.' Victoria sat down beside her. 'They can't catch you at it, so they put the fear of God into you, hoping that you will be driven to make a mistake. They gave me the impression that you carry messages to your people, but I thought it wise to keep my silence. I felt it was a trap.'

'How ... who gave you this idea?'

'I was questioned by Major Bartlett over the months. A week after Martin turned up so unexpectedly, General Kitchener sent for me, but it was not for a pleasant chat over a cup of tea. They're suspicious, but without proof they dare not arrest you. I'll get Tante Koba. Read your letter, I won't intrude.'

With dread in her heart, she opened the letter. There was news about the camp and Lettie Maree's death, but also a plea: *the Irishman will come to you; tell him where we are so that he can rescue us.* She was still staring at the words when Koba arrived.

'Annecke's little one is gone, says Vicky. My Annecke, my little lamb, God has not been kind to her for her little sin.' Koba dug into her apron pocket for her handkerchief and blew her nose loudly.

'Annecke ... sweet Annecke, in her innocence, has betrayed me.' Stefanie handed her the letter. 'Tante Koba, please, please,' she placed her arm around Koba's shoulders. 'Don't cry now. I need you now. I must write to Martin;

Patrick is waiting, but I dare not go there. I'm being followed. Everywhere I look, everywhere I go … Will you find Patrick for me?'

Koba stowed her handkerchief. 'Yes, *hartjie*, I'll go. Should I find the bloodhounds on my trail, I'll give them a piece of my mind, and there are plenty of pieces to be had.'

Warren's hansom arrived after Koba had left to deliver the letter. Stefanie could not control herself when she saw his face. 'I refuse to accompany you. Martin's son died in the camp. I refuse to go out. I refuse!'

Warren took a few steps closer to her. 'You really do look unwell, my dear. You have an important engagement coming up after the New Year. Come, let me take you to Dr Bernstein.'

With a tremendous effort, Stefanie pulled herself together. 'No, I'm fine … the news upset me … the deaths …' She went up to her room to wash her face and do up her hair.

Warren seemed in high spirits as they drove through the tree-lined streets. 'I've splendid news, my dear!'

She tensed. The old regard flickered in his eyes.

'We'll be going home to Cape Town soon. Sir Alfred's visit coincides with the last phase of my project. Now it's up to Kitchener to see that it's carried out.'

'Home? My home is here.'

'The war is over, my dear.' He took her hand in his. She snatched it back. He shook his head, but there was no anger in his eyes. 'We've had our differences; the war is solely to blame for that. But we shall have children now.' He smiled. 'You see, my dear, I've decided to forgive you for your little adventure. I'm human, after all.'

When she found her voice, its firmness surprised even her. 'I shall not go to Cape Town with you. Ever again.'

'You are my wife and will leave with me, or I shall personally see that General Kitchener is given proof that you've fooled all of us, including him.'

'Paul Warren, his wife a traitor?' She was amazed at her sudden lack of fear, but it returned in waves at his next threat.

'Captain Radford won't be spared. He escorted you to Johannesburg while you were carrying information stolen from my study. He'll go down with you. Collaborating with the enemy is punishable by death.'

Reprisal is a Useless Course

December 1901

THE DE WINTER brothers stood on a rise watching Patrick McFee making his way through the commando. Karel and Rudolf had just brought news that the convoy had left Potchefstroom and was well on the way to Rustenburg. The cavalry was still in the town, Karel said, but would probably be sent to escort the convoy. He left it at that and Martin was grateful; like the paternity of his son, the fact that they might face James in battle was not discussed.

Karel's eyes narrowed. 'Something is chasing the Irishman.'

'Patrick! You're in time to loot some whisky,' Martin said when McFee dismounted. 'We attack in a few days.'

'Yes, whisky is what I need now, General.' McFee, breathing hard, handed him a letter.

'How is Stefanie?' Martin felt for his pocketknife to cut the string binding the letter, but his hands froze at McFee's reply.

'I didn't see Stefanie, General. Your dear aunt came to the square. Stefanie, she said, is in trouble. It's all in there.' McFee indicated the letter and added urgently, 'Apart from that, General, four miles from here – English, under a white flag, with a message for you. They refused to give it to a lone rider, an Irish traitor, they said.'

Martin called Jan and Frans Viljoen to get fifty men to ride with him. McFee led the way, and after ten minutes they came across a group of British soldiers.

'Cavalrymen.' Karel studied them through his glasses.

Martin took the glasses, scanning the group. 'Good heavens! That large man is Captain Shaw, from James's regiment.'

They rode at a canter to within a hundred yards of them.

'Wait here! A general shouldn't be at the beck and call of a captain!' Karel dug his heels into Legend's flanks. Rudolf and McFee followed at a more sedate pace.

Martin saw how Karel pulled Legend into a rear, her hooves cleaving the air close to Shaw's face. He could not hear what was said but, by Karel's wild gestures and McFee's aggressive stance, he surmised that it was not pleasant. He raised his hat in greeting when Karel pointed back at him; Shaw saluted. Karel and the other two galloped back, leaving Shaw and his group in a cloud of dust.

'Open it!' Karel handed Martin the missive.

Martin ripped the envelope and took out the single page. He closed his eyes, the note crumpled in his hands, his knuckles white. 'Jan, get the commando on the way,' he said. 'We'll follow soon.'

'Is it Stefanie?' Karel demanded when Jan and the men rode off. Martin dismounted and stuffed the note in his pocket. 'It's my son ... it's little Martin. He died in the camp.'

Rudolf went ashen, reached for Martin's hand and clung to it. 'I'm sorry, Ouboet. I only saw him once ...'

Martin pressed his hand when he recognised the old panic rising in his brother's voice. 'He was a fine boy,' he said hoarsely, 'a true De Winter.'

'Stefanie is in trouble,' Karel broke in roughly. 'Open her letter! Read it aloud, Martin.'

Martin unfolded the letter and cleared his throat.

> *My dearest brother, General Kitchener is on my trail. But I cannot leave just yet. I am not scared, please trust me. I am being very brave. Pa will be so proud of me. I am not a runaway horse after all. Yes, I also know the story of the wild horses. I think about it every day. My only regret is that I will not be able to help you again.*
>
> *There is a concert after the New Year that I dare not miss. Tell Patrick to come after the concert and to be especially careful. If I am still at liberty, I want him to take me out of Pretoria. If not, ask him to remember me as a devoted friend.*

'She sounds desperate,' Karel said. 'She's in bad trouble.'

Martin nodded and read on. 'Uncle Joep and now Aunt Lettie ... dear God ... Buks's child ... scarlet fever.'

'Go on!' Karel urged.

> *I don't know which little one it was. They're in a camp at Potchefstroom, and all of them are in quarantine for a few weeks.*
>
> *Please remember me to all. Tell Karel and Rudi and dear Charles that I love them so very much. Also tell Karel that there*

*is a God after all. In this terrible world we live in now, I have
found love so deep, so complete, only God could have created it.
Your loving sister.*

The veld was strangely quiet. The midday sun beat down. In the distance, the commando was making its way westwards, raising a pillar of dust. Martin folded the pages with care and placed them in his pocket. The sweat on his brow ran into the tears on his bearded cheeks. Rudolf wept silently.

Only Karel's eyes were dry, burning with vengeance. 'Get up!' He pointed wildly at the departing commando. 'For Stefanie's sake, come! We have to keep on running!'

———

'WOULD YOU GENTLEMEN be familiar with the name of General de Winter's horse? Major Hunter? Perhaps you know the name, sir?' Murray Shaw took his place in the mess tent long after the others had started their dinner.

His fellow officers gave him bemused glances. Since Hunter had sent James to burn Wintersrust, resentment had built up against him, and showed all too clearly in their manner. 'Not even a guess?' Shaw motioned to the mess steward to fill his wine glass. 'I shall have to enlighten you then. The horse's name is Pegasus.'

Hunter flushed and put down his knife and fork.

'Not so long ago,' Shaw continued, patting his moustache with the napkin. 'General de Winter was leading us a merry dance in the Cape. And now he appears on the ridges outside town. Ten days, gentlemen! It took him ten days to make a journey of five hundred miles.' He nodded his head sagely. 'I would rather leave the fellow in peace. Had me walking to Pretoria on my bare feet last time we met. Not exactly a pleasant trip. Major Hunter can testify to that.'

Hunter's chair scraped as he rose and stormed out. The others waited until their plates were cleared and the orderlies were out of earshot before turning their attention to Shaw.

'You saw Martin?' Peter said. 'Is that where you've been for the past three days?'

'Yes, I was ordered by Colonel Butcher to deliver a cable. Martin de Winter was spotted over a week ago. Hunter was informed, naturally, but is clearly of the opinion that it's no concern of ours.'

'What happened?' John Miles asked. 'Did you speak to him, sir?'

'Unfortunately not. A fierce black horse came thundering down. Nearly trampled me to death. Wild-looking individual, as fierce as his horse, demanded the note. Spoke perfect English, mind you. His friends caught up with him and, take my word, his exact image stood next to him.' He gave James a meaningful glance.

'My twin cousins. Martin's brothers.' James pushed his dessert away and called for another bottle of wine. 'Legend, the black mare I've so often told you about. She must be … eight, nine years now.'

'Ah, that explains it; they know our names,' Shaw said. 'Well, then an Irishman warned me to stay under the safety of the white flag …'

'Irish?' Peter interrupted sharply. 'What did he look like?'

'Yes, an Irishman, Radford,' Shaw said. 'He's rather upset at us for having burned his general's house.'

'We'll tangle with them soon enough. Colonel Butcher has ordered the regiment to prepare to leave at first light tomorrow,' John Miles said.

'Henderson, a word in private?' Shaw beckoned to James and they walked off.

Peter left the table and walked to their tent. He shrugged off his tunic and searched for brandy in James's trunk. He thought of James's soot-stained face when he had arrived back late the night after having burned Wintersrust. He shuddered.

He sank down on the camp bed, contemplating the bottle in his hand. *I'm going to end up as James did that night. I have to tell them. I have no choice, Stefanie. And it will be worse, much worse.*

He closed his eyes and felt her against him, her hair brushing his face, his chest. And her contrasting moods. Her mouth set in a line, then soft under his. Blue eyes flashing fire, filling up with tears, only to shine so beautifully with love the next moment. *My love, my bride. Just another Irishman? This must be pure coincidence. Again?* Fear for the future rose from deep inside him, and for the first time in his life he felt unable to face up to it.

James appeared in the tent entrance, hands in his pockets. 'The burning of Wintersrust … it's only now, tonight I realise why … the bastard! He could've reported me a year ago, but he wanted to repay me in person for stealing Victoria.' He swore heatedly. 'Scores settled, don't you think Radford?'

'Let's hope so, whatever it is.'

'Yes, all settled … I say, are you all right? Don't want battle against the Rustenburg lot? Kill one of her brothers, is that it? The time will come, *Engelsman*, and we'll face each other across the barrel of a rifle, Jan Viljoen said years ago. We were hunting, I lost my temper—'

478

'You always do.'

'Yes, don't I just?' James chuckled. 'Don't worry, Radford, old boy.' His voice rose sarcastically. 'The De Winters are forgiving me! That's the message I got from Shaw. Rudolf asked him to tell me that.'

'You're tight, James.'

'Yes, I'm drunk, Peter, have been since this bloody war started.' He sat down next to Peter and pointed to the bottle in his hand. 'Looking for the answer in that? Well, don't bother, Radford, because it's not there, believe me.'

Peter longed to confide in James about his fears for Stefanie and the unbearable choice he faced, but it would be catastrophic – for Stefanie, for James, for himself. 'Henderson, will you help me onto my horse in the morning?' He opened the bottle. 'If the answer isn't in here, it suits me; I don't want to know the answer.'

———————

THE ATTACK CAME at dawn two days later. Four hundred soldiers were guarding thirty wagons encamped on the banks of the Renoster River, which cut steeply into the earth twenty miles southwest of Rustenburg. The first warning came when the pickets were shot at close range. The men scrambled out of the tents into rifle fire directed from the surrounding thickets. Officers and sergeants shouted furiously, attempting to bring order to the ranks, while horses and oxen stampeded, trampling the dead and wounded. A group of Boers broke from across the river, charging into the camp, yelling wildly, shooting from the saddle. They vaulted off their horses and threw themselves at the soldiers.

James searched the faces desperately. For a second he saw Peter, locked in the embrace of a Boer. Peter slammed his pistol into the Boer and pulled the trigger. The Boer collapsed on top of him, blood spilling onto Peter. A horse reared, its hooves beating repeatedly down on a bloodied, beardless young Boer. A few yards from James a roan mare was on her side, her head thrashing the ground, her back broken. He saw John Miles toppled over, blood spurting from his head.

A tent caught fire and collapsed on the entangled figures inside. A sickly stench filled the air. A wagon loaded with ammunition exploded, setting the surrounding wagons alight. The pale morning sky lit up. Men were running frantically, their clothes blazing torches. Then the Armstrong field guns opened up, forcing the Boers back.

'To your right!' Colonel Butcher's command rang out.

The Hussars grabbed fresh clips of ammunition, stuffed them into their pockets, and staggered up the steep bank. Not fifty yards ahead, the Boers were scrambling for their horses. James threw himself to the ground and fired into their fleeing backs. Then all movement around them ceased, and there was only the sound of the Armstrong guns firing.

'Quite a destructive fellow.' Shaw tapped James on his shoulder and pointed to a lone Boer, torch in hand, setting fire to wagons as he passed them.

James raised his pistol and pulled the trigger. The lone rider fell forward across his horse, disappearing into the thicket.

'Not a bad shot, Henderson.' Shaw rose.

'Where are you going?'

'To get dressed, my dear fellow. We'll have to give chase, I should think. After all, we are the cavalry.'

Only then did James notice Shaw was still in his underclothes. He looked at the destruction and confusion around him, wanting to search every face, every black horse. He restrained himself, and then ran to where his troops were encamped and found Corporal Johnson saddling his horse. His own mount, tied to a tree, was saddled, pulling at the reins.

Minutes later, he led his troop away from the carnage, stopping briefly for orders from Colonel Butcher. Two miles from the battlefield he saw a group of Boers watching them from a koppie. A few shots whizzed through the air before they disappeared. James spotted them again as they rounded a clump of thorn bushes at the base of the koppie. Suddenly the Boers swung their horses around and charged at them.

A bullet caught him high in the chest. Turning his horse around, he fell from the saddle, crashing headlong into the ground. He lay stunned, vaguely aware of wild yelling, shots and horses thundering around and past him. He felt his chest; his hands came away sticky with blood. He tried to raise himself, but was powerless against the blackness descending over him.

A MILE from where James lay, Jan Viljoen urged his men back to where Charles had pitched a few tents to treat the wounded. News had reached him that Martin had been hit in the first wave of attack of the morning.

'Who's that?' Rudolf pointed to a horse that came galloping to catch up with them.

'Karel! Karel!' Gert Swart brought his horse to a sharp halt. 'Come! We shot your cousin! They were coming at us … the officer … went down … I want a pair of boots … I found him. I swear it's him! *Magtig*! Come, he's bleeding!'

Jan ordered his men back to the main commando while he and the twins, followed by McFee, rushed off with Gert. They found James lying on his side, his tunic covered in blood.

Karel flew from the saddle, flung himself down next to him. 'James! Oh no! James! Rudi! We killed James!'

Jan aimed a few slaps at Karel's head. 'Shut your mouth! He's not dead.' Jan removed James's helmet, which was hanging around his neck by the strap. '*Engelsman!* Open your eyes, *Engelsman!*' He rolled James onto his back and loosened his high collar while Karel emptied his water bottle over his face.

McFee squatted next to them. 'Chest wound. Sit him up.'

Karel lifted him a little. McFee opened his tunic, inspecting the wound. 'Aha, just above his old scar. It doesn't look serious.' He lifted James's eyelids. 'He's just stunned, knocked his head is what I think. He'll come round. More water, Rudolf.'

Rudolf poured water into his mouth. James groaned feebly.

'*Engelsman!*' Jan roared. 'You're coming around!'

'Jan Viljoen?' James mumbled.

'Yes, it's me, your old friend. And now you are my prisoner. I need someone who can drink and fight with me, and who can do it better than you?'

James retched, blood trickled onto his lips. '*Got!* The lung is bleeding inside,' Jan said. 'We're wasting time.'

'No … no … bit my tongue …'

'What shall we do? We no longer take prisoners,' McFee said. 'We could take him to his brother, but what then?'

'Not Charles, not Martin … not yet …' James struggled up, but the effort was too much and he fainted.

'Jan, only Karel knows about this, but now's the time to tell you.' Rudolf told them how James had helped him escape from the British hospital in Cape Town. 'Can't we do the same for him? Get him back to his friends?'

'My good *Engelsman*,' Jan said hoarsely. He sniffed and wiped his hands over his eyes. 'He is still out and will be for some time. We can't just leave him here.'

'We take him closer to the British camp, put him in their path,' McFee suggested. 'They'll find him. They always come for their wounded and dead.'

'No! We will take him in! *Into* their camp! There's someone there I need to see.' Karel jumped to his feet. 'A flag and bandages.' He mounted and sped off.

A few wounded were lying on canvas sheets at Charles's dressing station when Karel arrived. The smell of chloroform told Karel that Charles was operating. He stormed into the tent. Charles was bent over Gert Vermaas, whose belly was a bloody mess.

'Where's Rudi?' Charles asked without looking up.

'Fine, not wounded. I need some things, Charles.'

'Help yourself. I can't leave now,' he said.

'Do I put lint into a chest wound, a high one, just below the shoulder?'

'Only as a temporary measure. Needs drains. Stop the bleeding. Bring him in. Who is it?'

Karel grabbed a handful of bandages and lint, rushed out, snatched the Red Cross flag, makeshift pole and all, and was gone before the orderlies could protest.

———

OVER FIFTY SOLDIERS lay dead or wounded in the devastated British camp. Many horses and oxen had been killed; the rest had taken to the veld. The remaining wagons were being used to carry the dead and wounded to Rustenburg. Tents were hastily erected in which the doctors went about their task of patching up the wounded. A large hollow was dug in the river bank, the last resting place for thirty-two Boers. The only sounds disturbing the men at their tasks were sporadic shots as the bellowing and moaning of suffering animals were silenced.

Colonel Butcher watched as his cavalry rode in after the pursuit. No prisoners, only more wounded. The officers made their reports before going to see to their men. A trooper hurried over with a kettle of tea and cups.

'What a mess!' said George Hunter, helping himself to a cup of tea.

'Yes, quite,' Butcher said. 'The Boers took only eight wagons. Why only eight?'

'This is De Winter's work, Colonel.'

'Oh yes … Ah, here's Moore and Shaw.' Butcher raised his field glasses. 'And there's Radford limping in. Only Henderson still out.'

Peter saw his wounded to the hospital tent and came to report. 'Lost two men this morning; five wounded, sir. The Boers have made themselves scarce.'

Butcher nodded. 'You're wounded, Captain?'

'No, sir, came through without a scratch.' Peter looked at his tunic; the blood of the Boer he had killed had formed brown patches, caked with dust. 'Where's Henderson? We lost Miles, I hear.'

'Yes, and Smithers wounded.' Butcher raised his glasses again. 'I see a movement in the distance. There!' He handed Peter the glasses.

Peter looked at the approaching horsemen, not taking his eyes off them until they were close. He lowered the glasses and waited with dread in his heart.

Sergeant Adams came to report. 'One dead, three wounded, Colonel.

Captain Henderson … missing, I think, sir.'

Butcher raised his eyebrows. 'Missing? You think?'

'Captured, sir. Captain Henderson was hit, sir. We went back for him, but the Boers took him away, sir.'

AN HOUR LATER a corporal arrived and saluted. 'Red Cross flag coming in, sir.'

Peter snatched the field glasses from the table, training them on the flag. When the group drew closer, he recognised Jan Viljoen in the lead. Another man held the flag. A few paces behind them came two more riders with James on the black horse, leaning against the rider. He recognised Legend and knew that the rider was the wild twin, Karel.

The procession came to a halt. Colonel Butcher ordered a stretcher to be fetched, but they did not appear to be in a hurry to hand James over. The officers watched as the huge black-bearded Boer dismounted and scanned the destruction around them.

'*Got!*' Jan Viljoen said. 'How the poor animals have suffered.' His eyes searched the officers. 'Who is in charge here?'

'Colonel Butcher.' He stepped forward.

'Commandant Jan Viljoen, of Rustenburg commando. Where's my good friend Doctor Frank from Magersfontein and Nooitgedacht? He always rides with the Horse Officers. I've brought my *Engelsman* to him.'

'Your friend, Commandant Viljoen, is at the hospital tent,' Butcher said evenly. 'You may see him there if you wish. Could we see to Captain Henderson first?'

'Jan, hurry up! James has fainted again,' Rudolf called in Afrikaans.

Jan rushed over to Legend. The fourth man, his slouch hat pulled low over his face, dropped the flag and went to assist Karel in lowering James into Jan's arms.

'I can manage,' James croaked. 'Put me down.'

'Ah, now you can walk, can you, James?' Jan released him abruptly. His knees buckled and he fell against Legend, clutching at Karel's leg. Jan picked him up. He convulsed in a coughing fit, blood trickling from his mouth. 'I told you to shut your mouth or else you'll bleed to death and I would've ridden into the enemy's territory for nothing!' Jan smiled at Butcher. 'My *Engelsman* is in a pretty fighting mood as usual.'

Jan lowered James onto the stretcher. 'Guard my back,' he said to the fourth man. They followed the orderlies carrying the stretcher to the hospital tent.

Peter caught Jan's aside and frowned, but like the others, he could not take his eyes off the twins. They wore no jackets; their shirts, crossed with bandoliers, hung over riding breeches obviously taken from their enemy. Their hair was down to their shoulders, hats hanging down their backs. They were still mounted but had moved closer to each other, their eyes searching the officers' faces as if looking for someone in particular. Peter's heart lurched when Karel's eyes met his; Stefanie, angry and proud, was looking at him.

'Will someone please explain that it is perfectly safe to dismount,' Butcher said.

'We understand you *perfectly* well!' Karel mimicked, flew off Legend, placed his hands on his hips and walked into the circle of officers. Karel turned to Butcher and spoke in a level tone. 'My name is Karel de Winter. This is my brother Rudolf. The man we brought in is my cousin. We almost killed him today.'

'Ah, but young man,' Butcher said. 'Captain Henderson is also your enemy for the time being.'

Ignoring Butcher's comment, Karel continued, 'James has another cousin, as you know. My older brother, General Martin de Winter. He's a brave man, but there's no one braver than James is. Shall I tell you why? He was ordered … *forced* to burn our farm. And he did! It takes a very brave man to destroy what is dear to him. Do you agree?'

'Mr De Winter, you're sadly mistaken,' Butcher said. 'I'd never order a man to destroy his own kin's home. There's a chivalry between—'

Karel interrupted with a harsh laugh. '*You* didn't order him!' He walked in measured steps to Hunter until there were only a few inches separating their faces. 'You, George Hunter, forced James to burn Wintersrust and to send his family to the camps. My brother's son died in the camp. You killed him, George Hunter. If there is a God in this world, he might forgive you. But I'm not God, neither are my brothers. I had you in my sights today, but then I thought, no, you won't die in battle; that's for brave men only. From now on, you won't know a moment's peace. We will watch your every move, every convoy, every trail you ride, and then, when you least expect it …'

Hunter returned Karel's stare with disdain. 'How will you come by this information, *Captain Patterson*? Will you be informed by your sister?'

'We have no sister! Mrs Warren is a British whore! Even you could've used her for all we care!'

'No, Karel!' Peter stepped forward. 'I cannot allow you to question her honour.'

'Enough, gentlemen!' Colonel Butcher stepped in. 'Captain Radford, you're obviously acquainted with the brothers. See that they have some refreshment while they wait.'

Peter glared at Karel, when from behind them came an Irish voice.

'Time to get moving, Karel, your cousin will be fine. Commandant Viljoen is on his way.'

At the voice, Peter turned. And there he stood, the Irish corporal, the man he'd seen with Stefanie in Pretoria. He stared at McFee, numbed, believing but not wanting to believe, his heart breaking and crying out; *there was, after all, only one Irishman.*

'I'm happy to say that my *Engelsman* has no broken bones,' Jan Viljoen said expansively as he arrived. 'The bullet passed straight through! He'll be drinking, fighting and chasing women again tomorrow.'

'Would you like some tea, Commandant Viljoen?' Butcher offered.

'I thank you for your kindness.' Jan put out his hand to Butcher. 'We have to go. May God be with you till the end of this war.'

'When will that be, Commandant Viljoen?' Shaw asked as Jan started a round of hand-shaking. 'It's for your people to decide.'

'Yes, so it is! You burned our farms, depleted the herds, invaded our capital and chased our President across the sea. Now we've nothing more to lose. Except,' Jan held up his hand, 'our independence. So we fight!'

'You might lose your life.' Moore shook Jan's hand.

'Only God can decide on that, *Engelsman.*' Jan came to Peter. 'Have you been wounded again, Peter, my friend?' He touched Peter's bloodied tunic.

Peter shook his head numbly and took Jan's hand. 'Thank you for returning James,' was all he could manage.

'Go well, my friend. We'll hunt together after the war.' Jan came to Hunter.

'No, Jan!' Karel said. 'It was him!'

Jan towered over Hunter, his black eyes flashing hatred. He spat on the ground at Hunter's feet, turned and mounted. Karel took a flying leap onto Legend.

Rudolf was still looking at Peter. He took the few steps to him and held out his hand. Peter took it. Their eyes met and held. Then Rudolf whispered two words, barely audible, but Peter caught them.

'Save her!'

Despair, Despair

LATE THAT AFTERNOON, Martin became aware of his surroundings. His body felt light, as if floating, but when he raised his head, a pain seared through his chest. He cursed aloud.

'You're coming round,' he heard Charles's voice through the haze in his head.

He recalled the attack, and being brought to Charles, and he remembered the overpowering smell of chloroform. 'Not a lucky shot this time?'

'No, cousin, I dug a bullet from your shoulder. Your collarbone is fractured; you'll be on your back for a few weeks.' Charles smiled, but Martin saw the lines around his mouth, the weary eyes behind the glasses.

He licked his parched lips. 'How did we fare?'

Charles held a mug of water to his mouth. 'Ten men to be buried; over twenty wounded in my tents, but ... Oom Koos de la Rey ... he was here earlier, said that a part of your commando was wiped out, all dead or captured. They charged into the British camp when they saw you wounded.' Charles wiped Martin's face and beard with a damp cloth. 'That's not all, I'm afraid. Gert Swart has it that an officer came charging at them. In this wide, huge expanse of veld ... so many men ...' his voice tailed off and he whispered, 'It was James. They took him to the British camp.'

Martin tried to sit up, but pain overwhelmed him. Charles eased him back onto the mattress. Martin groaned. 'James ...'

'A chest wound. Frank Crofton-Smith says he'll be fine, Jan tells me.' Charles opened the tent flaps. 'Cousin, I kept you from the others. You were talking ... saying some rather rough things.'

Martin turned his face away from Charles. His thoughts had been dark lately and he didn't want to know what he'd given away.

The twins stepped in. Their eyes went to his heavily bandaged chest. 'Has he come round?' Karel asked.

'Yes, but he's in pain.' Charles sat down next to Martin's stretcher. Karel and Rudolf sank to the ground. A despairing silence reigned in the tent.

'He'll save her, he loves her,' Rudolf said, and added after a long pause, 'I saw it in his eyes.'

'Won't be murder, not in war,' Karel said.

Martin looked at his brothers. He did not want to know what they were talking about. He was weary of war, of death, of emotional crises. His heart wept for his country, for Stefanie, for Joep Maree, for Buks's heavy loss. He needed a place to hide. He needed the solitude, the peace of the cave.

Outside the sun was setting. Through the opening of the tent, they saw the sky change from orange to red and then to a gentle rose. The plaintive voices of the commando drifted into the tent from where they sang at the graves of those who had died in the day's battle.

'We need to get to the cave,' Martin said, knowing that that was what they all felt in their hearts.

———

JAMES FLEXED HIS FINGERS. There was a dull pain in his shoulder. He looked at the container at his side; a tube connected it to his chest a few inches from the wound, a pinkish froth half-filled it. He scanned the room; he must be in Charles's hospital. There was another bed close to his: Neil Smithers, his throat and chest white with bandages.

Frank Crofton-Smith bent over his bed. 'How are you feeling, James?'

'Just a splitting headache.'

Frank nodded. 'Concussion. You must've hit the ground pretty hard. Shall I give you something?'

'No, I'll be fine. What time is it?'

'After three. We arrived in Rustenburg in the morning hours, but you wouldn't know about that. I drugged you heavily. Peter has looked in a few times, but will be back later.' He moved to Smithers's bed and checked the tube protruding from his throat. 'Still unconscious. Must be off, have my hands full.'

James looked out of the window. The air was heavy, clouds obscuring the mountains. The anger, jealousy and humiliation he had felt on hearing about Vicky and Martin's betrayal had eased since he'd burnt Wintersrust. It was as if vengeance had been taken, yet that day, that dreadful day, he had not thought about it as revenge. The love that bound him to the De Winters, including to Martin, had shielded him from such an emotion. But to forgive Victoria, to offer his love again?

'Taking a nap?' Peter walked in and smiled but his eyes were troubled.

'Quite a time you had yesterday.'

'The indignity, being carried in by Jan Viljoen.'

'Yes, touching, actually. Any news from your family while you were out there?'

'Martin wounded, Charles working himself to a standstill. When is it going to dawn on them that they've lost the war?'

'Did your cousins ask after Stefanie?'

'Now that you mention it, no, not a word.'

Peter moved to the window. 'There's a storm brewing. When your cousins brought you in, Hunter called Karel "Captain Patterson". Colonel Butcher found it odd. He called Hunter to his office after we arrived back here. Then he questioned us all in detail about your sortie to Wintersrust. Sergeant Adams was also called in.' Raindrops splattered against the pane. 'It will be all right, won't it?'

'No, it won't, Peter.'

There was a pause before Peter spoke again. 'Another awful blunder when they brought you in. I declared myself openly, defending Stefanie's honour. Hunter provoked Karel, who then made a blatant attack on his sister … Oh God, what a mess, James!'

'Yes, what a mess,' James said as Peter contemplated the rain through the window. 'I helped Rudolf escape from the hospital. I know where Martin goes to rest. And burning Wintersrust … I was hopeless. I broke down. And Hunter knows it all. And now Colonel Butcher too, it seems.'

'Do you also know about Stefanie?'

'Stefanie? What about Stefanie?'

Peter told him about her alleged involvement in spying, and about the Irishman he had seen with her in Pretoria and when James was brought back to the camp. When he finished, he could barely look at James.

'Oh God, Radford! Are you going to report this?'

'For God's sake! Tell me what to do!'

'I love her too!' James coughed as pain shot through his chest. 'Do you expect me to tell you to send her to the firing squad? Is that what you want to hear, Peter? I won't say it. Sorry, Peter, I can't help, I cannot. Do what you must.'

THROUGH THE WINDOW Peter saw the regimental band form up and the troops with arms reversed.

'They're burying Miles,' he said. He thought back to Rudolf's plea. *Save her.* The sorrowful notes of the bugle filled the wet, heavy air. He closed his eyes. Stefanie and he had played their dangerous game of honour and duty.

Now it had brought them to the brink. They had run wildly, headlong; that was how their love was born, and what made it so overpowering. *I will not be a runaway horse, but neither will she.*

Six troopers raised their rifles to the sky. He saw Stefanie against a wall, her blue eyes challenging death. The volley tore through his heart.

He waited until the troops had dispersed. Then he walked to Colonel Butcher's office.

———————

ANNECKE WATCHED THE COLOURS of the setting sun through the barbed wire. *Tomorrow is Christmas and he still has not come for me.* In the afternoons when they went to gather wood, she searched every tree, behind every boulder, scanned the horizon, but was always disappointed. *The war will never end and the Irishman has forgotten about me.*

She could have become as hopeless as Mary was now, but Lena had not allowed it. 'At night on your mattress is the time to weep; we have to be brave like the others,' Lena had said. But now Lena and her children were gone. The camp commandant had sent for them one morning. They had not returned; Buks had traded their safety for Martin's life.

She looked at Mary on the mattress in the corner of the tent that they now shared with another family. She was painfully thin, her skin waxen, her eyes vacant. Her hands were on her chest, folded around a scrap of paper. She had not yet recovered from the scarlet fever when the note arrived informing them that Marthinus de Winter had died. Since then, she would take no water, no food.

Annecke's eyes travelled to the white crosses on the other side of the barbed wire. She wondered if she would ever find her son's grave. There were so many white crosses. Were there names on them? A white coffin had been sent in which to bury her son. He was a general's son, the camp commandant had said, and she did not tell him the truth. The coffin was so beautiful.

It was almost dark. She fetched water and gently washed Mary's face and hands, talking all the while about the cakes that Koba would be baking for Christmas, the fruit that had to be bottled, about Stefanie's beautiful dresses and about Anita and Charles's baby that would be born soon.

The voices of women talking, of children crying and laughing, floated on the evening air. She closed her eyes and tried to find solace in voices from the past. Warm nights on the stoep, watching the stars and the moon over the mountains. She wondered if the moon would also throw its beams through the roof of the cave. Moonbeams dancing in the cave at night and fireflies in the day. *We will always be safe here.* The light on Charles's glasses. *I've been to the place where nothing but our love matters.* Rudi's eyes soft and loving.

Christmas day dawned. Mary's eyes were open, but her chest was still. The guards would come for the dead on their morning rounds. Annecke spread a shawl on the ground and gathered her few things – her blue dress, underclothes and her Bible. She looked at her baby's clothes. There were children in the camp who were in desperate need of them.

She tied the corners of the shawl and went outside to wait for the Irishman.

PART EIGHT

THE RUNAWAY HORSES

A warmth within the breast would melt
The freezing reason's colder part,
And like a man in wrath the heart
Stood up and answer'd 'I have felt.'

Alfred, Lord Tennyson,
'In Memoriam. A.H.H'

The Last Recital

Pretoria, January 1902

IT HAD RAINED every afternoon in Pretoria for a week, but now it was as if the impending storm brought a forewarning of doom. The clouds were too low, the air too still, the people nervously glancing up, hurrying on, the horses skittish, snorting.

Stefanie sat slumped at the kitchen table. The news of her parents' deaths had left her numbed with grief, but for herself she felt no fear, just a strange sense of fatalism.

'The bees are angry today!' Koba walked into the kitchen, fanning her face with her black *kappie*. She poured coffee and sank down next to Stefanie. 'The bees know everything, like the ants, and today they tell me that it will be a terrible storm, like so many devils let loose upon us!' She tut-tutted. 'And you have to travel to Johannesburg in this weather.'

'We are leaving at five. The storm will be over by then.'

Koba bit into a rusk, sipping her coffee. '*Hartjie*, what will you wear tonight? I wanted to sew you a black satin frock, but there's no more black left in any shop. So many in mourning. And with the Commissioner and General Kitchener attending, you must look your best.'

'Paul wouldn't want me to wear black, not tonight.'

'Yes, *hartjie*, not tonight, of all nights.'

It was now the second week into the New Year. Every afternoon for the past week, Stuart Darnel, a violinist from Cape Town, had practised with her. She was to accompany him, but she could hardly manage. Her hands were faltering badly. And Paul dropped in at odd hours of the day, fearing that she might not be well enough to play and embarrass him at this most conspicuous occasion.

'I shall wear my waterfall dress and think of Peter dancing with me. It was such a happy night, Tante Koba.'

'It's too tight about the bosom now. Wear that beautiful rose silk.

Men like rose.'

The rose dress, Kitchener's New Year party, Peter declaring his love. That night she had looked her best.

'*Hartjie*, shall I pack the rose dress? I have to take Vicky to the hospital before the storm breaks. So many boys need to be fed, they can hardly hold a spoon to their mouths.'

'Thank you, Tante Koba, I'll pack myself. Isn't it too tiring for Vicky to go the hospital every day?'

'She thinks that she gives the men hope, the poor lamb.'

'Hope, Tante Koba? Hope in what?'

'In life, *hartjie*, life as we women know it.' She gathered Stefanie in her arms. 'Oh my little dove, Tante Koba will miss you so, but knowing that dear Charles will see to your baby is more than I could ask for.'

She buried her face in Koba's bosom, trying hard to hold back her tears. 'Is everything arranged, Tante Koba, my papers?'

'It will take the bees a day or so to settle again, but I got them. Under your mattress in a pillowcase, that's where I've hidden them,' Koba whispered. 'There's also an old black cotton dress and you will take my black *kappie*. Our Irishman says to have you at the station at three o'clock. He has the papers of Widow de Jager, who is going to Johannesburg and on to Potchefstroom. There, *hartjie*,' she rocked her gently when she started sobbing. 'Try not to be scared, *hartjie*, our Irishman will get you through safely.'

———

THE WIND WAS A MERE WHISPER before it gathered and gusted in a wild frenzy. Lightning ripped the air, followed by deafening cracks. The dark billowing clouds opened up and the storm broke over Colonel Butcher's force limping towards Pretoria.

At the head of the convoy, Peter struggled to bring his bucking horse under control. He had slept only in snatches since leaving Rustenburg. He thought about George Hunter, whose body lay in one of the wagons. Karel de Winter had carried out his threat. For three days he had sniped at George Hunter, harassing him, playing with him. First his shaving mirror, then a kettle on the open fire just as Hunter was reaching for it. A few well-placed shots to startle his horse. Then, at last light the previous evening, came a single shot between the eyes.

As they reached the edge of the city, the wagons carrying the wounded headed for Church Square, where the Palace of Justice now served as a hospital. The streets ran with rivulets and the iron wheels of the wagons turned them into mud, which slowed them down but there was little traffic due to the storm. Church Square reminded Peter of the danger Stefanie now faced. There was Beckett's store, where he had first seen her with the Irishman; the Transvaal Hotel, where she had performed so many times; and the Pretoria Club, where they had had their last carefree lovers' talk just before Martin had surprised them.

Peter handed his horse to a trooper and splashed his way to James's wagon.

'Lean on me, Henderson. Let's get you out of the bloody rain and mud.'

They limped into the entrance hall, where doctors were seeing to the new arrivals. The air reeked of ether, damp clothing and boiled food. The matron directed Peter to the officers' section. As they passed the open doors of one of the wards, Peter saw Victoria bending over a patient. He stole a glance at James, but he had not seen her. He helped James to the bed and removed his sodden tunic. He was about to pull off his boots when James grabbed hold of his arm.

'For God's sake, I implore you; don't go to Stefanie. You'll only implicate yourself. She may still get through this somehow.'

Peter nodded faintly. 'I'll be back; if not, I'll send Shaw. Take care, James.' With a wave of his hand he hurried to where he'd seen Victoria. She was walking down the passage when he caught up with her.

'Peter! What are you doing here? Are you ill?'

'No, we've just arrived back from Rustenburg.' He took her elbow and steered her on. 'Is there somewhere we can talk?'

She led him to the communal rest room and found an unoccupied corner at one of the windows. 'I brought James in. He's recovering from a slight wound and will most probably only spend the night.'

'Is he well otherwise?'

'I'm afraid not. Hunter ordered him to burn Wintersrust. And by God, Vicky, he did.' Looking through the window at the last of the wounded being offloaded and the rain still pouring down, he told her of the battle and of James being brought back by his cousins and of Karel killing Hunter.

'Things went from bad to worse. I can't explain now.' He passed a hand over his face and wet hair. 'Is Stefanie home?'

'Peter, don't even think of visiting her. You must not be seen near her.'

He pressed his fingers to his eyes. 'I have to see her! Please, Vicky, let me escort you home—'

'She's not there. Oh Peter, you can't go where she is.'

'Where is she? Please, tell me!'

'Nothing ever goes right in this world any more, does it?' Victoria sighed, pressing her knuckles to her cheek. 'Sir Alfred Milner is on a visit. Warren took Stefanie to Johannesburg to play for them. General Kitchener and his staff will be there. They've booked the Heights Hotel for the evening. She's suspected of spying, Peter.'

'I know. How is she?'

'Not well, I'm afraid. She's under terrible strain. She has to cope with her husband on the one hand and Major Bartlett on the other. Oh, Peter, should this be true, I won't condemn her. She's so courageous, so brave. Both her parents died last month ...'

'Yes, the news reached Rustenburg. James is distraught. Will you tell her ...' He rose; Kitchener would not be back in Pretoria until the following day. He needed to get to Johannesburg.

THE RAIN HAD CEASED, leaving the night air cool and fragrant. He had managed to catch the last train from Pretoria. Peter walked swiftly through the throngs of off-duty soldiers intent on a night's entertainment. A hot bath and a clean uniform had done little to restore him but he was driven by a desperate need to end the anxiety that ruled his reason.

When he rounded the corner of Commissioner Street, he saw a line of soldiers posted outside the Heights Hotel. It would be impossible to enter without an invitation. The windows were ablaze, the guests congregated in the reception room, glasses in their hands. He glimpsed a few women's dresses – pastel islands in a sea of black evening suits, scarlet and blue uniforms, gold braid and epaulettes.

He found himself on the opposite street corner, where Cape carts were parked. There was only one place to go, only one person who could help him now. He boarded the nearest cart and gave Rose Carter's address, refusing to think beyond the moment.

There were a few girls in the reception room when he arrived. It was too early for business and they looked at him with irritation. When they recognised him, however, they rushed over. 'I must see Madam Carter on an urgent matter,' he said, shaking his arms free.

'She doesn't come down till ten. You know that. Would you like a drink in the meantime?' James's French girl offered.

'Thank you, but no. Would you inform her of my request?'

She disappeared upstairs and was back in a minute, beckoning to him. He found Rose Carter in her suite on her chaise longue, reading a book.

She studied him over her half-glasses. 'Captain Radford? The war is not going well for you? Has something happened to Captain Henderson?'

'He's wounded – not seriously I'm happy to say.' He placed his helmet

on the low table and sat down beside her. 'I'd like your help in a matter …
somewhat unusual.'

She closed her book and lit a cigarette. 'A drink, Peter? Cognac?' She
indicated the decanter on the table. 'You're in a predicament of sorts?'

He poured them each a glass. 'Yes, and I'm willing to pay whatever it
takes.' He swallowed a mouthful and grimaced. 'I must get into the Heights
Hotel tonight.'

'Why don't you just walk in?' She puffed on her cigarette. 'It belongs
to the British brass tonight. I won't have enough girls to satisfy everyone
after eleven.' She chuckled and winked at Peter. 'I might even come out of
retirement for the evening.'

He smiled wanly and pressed on with his appeal. 'I've no authority to
go there and I mustn't be seen in Johannesburg tonight. But … *I have to see
her!*' His voice had a desperate ring to it and he closed his eyes, struggling for
control. 'I have to be with her. You do understand, don't you, Rose?'

She took a sip from her glass. 'Yes, it's clear.' She was thoughtful for a
while and then asked, in a businesslike way, 'The lady?'

'Mrs Warren.'

'The pianist? You're playing with dynamite, Peter. Warren tolerates no
opposition *whatsoever!*' She gestured to the decanter. Peter shook his head.
'Very well, I'll help you. Warren always takes a room at the Rand Club, never
at the hotel. There's a maid at the hotel who's been of use to me. She is trust-
worthy, but expensive. Ten pounds? Five now and the rest when it's done.'

He brought some notes from his pocket and placed them on the table.
'Ten pounds, plus another ten for her silence.'

'It's that important?' She patted his knee. 'Have a rest. Heaven knows,
it looks as if you could do with it!' She stubbed out her cigarette, and, as
she walked past him, she warned again. 'General de Winter's sister? You're
playing with fire, Lord Radford.'

AN HOUR LATER found him waiting in a maid's room at the back of the
hotel. 'It has to be when Mrs Warren is at the piano while everyone is in the
reception room,' the girl said. 'There's the dinner afterwards, so you'll have a
long wait. She knows that you'll be waiting in her room.'

'What did you say?'

She touched his chin. 'The man with the scar just there. Madame Carter
told me to say that. Nothing more.'

'Does Mr Warren visit her room?'

'No. Sometimes he escorts her as far as the door, but she never allows him in, or anyone else, not even a maid to help her undress.'

Piano music drifted through the open window. They slipped in by a back door, up the side stairs and down the long passage on the first floor. At the last door she turned the knob and pushed him inside. 'I'll come for you not later than four.' She blew him a kiss and closed the door behind her.

He looked about the room. A lamp on the dresser. Two easy chairs and a table, a washstand and a wardrobe. A blue hat sat on the table next to an arrangement of yellow roses, their smell sweet and delicate. An ice bucket with a bottle of champagne, two glasses beside it. He placed his helmet on the table next to her hat. His eyes went to the bed. The covers were turned down, a white nightdress laid out. He picked it up and held it to his face. Music floated up through the open window – a violin accompanied by piano.

The notes died away. There was silence, then applause, followed by complete silence. Music again. A Chopin Nocturne. He lay back on the pillows. Images swam through his mind. Dancing to the music box, her hair flowing out behind her, the white silk dress. *My bride.* The enormity of what he had done struck him. *Dear God, I've betrayed her.* He became aware of tears on his cheeks. *She must not see me weep; she is brave, so brave.*

He saw the full moon gliding ghost-like over the mountains. The call of a jackal. The smell of pipe tobacco. Raw homebrew burning his tongue.

And then he saw them: wild horses running in pale moonlight. Manes flying, nostrils flaring, hooves thundering. *A magnificent sight*, her father's voice, deep and restful, *so wild, so free, so magnificent, a mad flight from an unknown fear. It comes to them in their weariness, the futility of the madness, they break away.* He saw horses paring off from the herd, their shadows following them, dark blotches in the ghostly light. They faltered, slower and slower, until they stood mute, their heads bowed, mist rising from their bodies. The ones with the wounded souls. The runaway horses.

DOWNSTAIRS, STEFANIE'S HEART ached with bittersweet anguish. It flowed through her fingers, finding its way into the music. Peter was close by, and the world did not exist but for the song of farewell she was sending him.

The applause was insistent, appreciative, but the faces, the clapping hands, were a blur. Now there was only the eternity of the dinner to get through. Wine, fish, wine, lamb, mint sauce, peaches, champagne. Candlelight, polite conversation, gentle voices, strong voices.

'You've outdone yourself, my dear,' said Warren.

'Simply brilliant, Mrs Warren,' Sir Alfred Milner murmured.

'I truly admire your talent.' There was a touch of warmth in Kitchener's voice, sincere admiration in his eyes.

'We are immensely pleased to hear that soon you will be entertaining us again in Cape Town.' Milner's voice again. Kitchener and Paul looking at her, both waiting for a reaction, for different reasons.

'Yes, we leave for Cape Town soon,' she said. A quizzical glance from Kitchener, relief in Paul's eyes.

The dinner dragged to an end. 'We still have some work to get through over port and cigars,' Paul told her, taking her elbow. 'Shall I escort you to your room, my dear? You really do look unwell.'

'I'm tired and need to go to bed,' she tried to smile. 'You get on with your work.'

'Tomorrow then, my dear,' he said warmly and made a slight bow over her hand.

She walked up the wide staircase, down the long passage and reached her door. She pushed it open, her eyes searching the room. Her music sheets and reticule flew to the floor as she rushed to the bed. She knelt, put out her hands to touch his face but pulled them away again.

He was lying on his back, his tunic buttons gleaming in the lamplight, the crimson ribbon of the Victoria Cross and campaign ribbons on his left breast. The high collar of his tunic pressed into his cheek, the blond hair soft, curly in his neck and over his forehead. She saw dark smudges under his eyes, lines of fatigue between his eyebrows. She looked at his mouth; his lips were slightly parted as he breathed lightly in his sleep.

She laid her hand gently against his cheek. His eyes opened wearily and focused on her; they were red-rimmed, as if he had been crying. She believed she was seeing into his very soul. The fire was gone; she had not seen him so defenceless before. He put out his hand and touched her face, his fingers tracing her lips, her chin, her eyebrows. His lips moved, she read the words. *My love, my love.*

'I have reported you,' he whispered.

Deep inside her, the courage that had driven her, held her together, died. 'Oh no! Oh Peter,' her voice broke into a sob. 'Peter ... I knew you would. Oh, what have I done to you?'

THERE WAS NO REPROACH or surprise in her voice, only despair. Her eyes filled with tears. They hung on her lashes for a moment and then spilled down her cheeks. He lifted her onto the bed, crushing her against him. 'I no longer want to be brave,' he heard through her weeping. 'Don't want to ... be brave ... never wanted to be brave.' He was thankful that she could not see his face. He waited until her sobbing had subsided before releasing her. He removed his tunic, hung it over the bedpost and went to the washstand.

'I don't want to die,' she said in a small voice.

He splashed water over his face and pressed a towel to it. 'Neither do I.' Her tear-stained face questioned him. 'I have to testify against you, send you to the firing squad.'

A shudder raced through her. 'Will they come for me tonight?'

'Not tonight. In a day or so, but … this is as far as I can take it,' he said, silently entreating her to understand.

'Paul knows … Oh, Peter, he wants to drag you into this.'

'Warren has nothing to go on. Only if they find me here tonight will I be guilty of collaboration.'

She leaned her head against his chest. He felt that she was trembling despite the warm night. 'Are you ill, my love?'

'I'm so tired, so very tired. Peter, I want to sleep … just sleep …'

Fear rushed through him when he realised that, like him, she was past caring about her fate.

Downstairs, the function was ending. Male voices, rising and falling, the thudding of boots as the soldiers snapped to attention. He closed the window. 'Do you know of somewhere safe to go?'

She pulled her nightdress over her underclothes and climbed in between the sheets. He sat on the side, leaning over her. 'I will tell you a secret, my love,' she whispered. 'There's a place of peace. A mysterious place. Kitchener won't find me; he'll never find me.'

He placed his pistol on the night table, removed his boots and lay down next to her. 'Where will I find you after the war, my love?'

She placed her lips to his ear. 'Home of the Fireflies. After the war, only then, ask James where it is.'

He repeated the name, his mouth moving against her throat. *Be brave, my love*, he beseeched silently as sleep threatened to overwhelm him. *Be brave just a little while longer, for both of us; I have no courage left.*

THE DOOR OPENED noiselessly. Paul Warren had escorted his guests back to the hotel and noticed the light under her door. His eyes took in the helmet on the table, her dress over the back of the chair, the uniform tunic over the bedpost. Peter Radford was asleep in her arms, his hand against her cheek. There was a pistol on the night table. Stefanie's blue eyes met his. There was no fear, no alarm in them. He looked at her for a terrible moment and left.

500

The Bees Are Angry Today

STEFANIE'S MIND WAS AS CALM and clear as the morning sky she saw through the window of the train taking her back to Pretoria. There was not a trace of cloud, no storm in the making, the tempest of the past weeks spent.

Peter had kissed her goodbye and left quietly, without knowing that Warren had seen him. *Only if they find me here tonight, my love, will I be guilty of collaboration.* Paul Warren would not report them directly. He would first want to avenge his humiliation, and only then put them before the firing squad.

But she was one step ahead of him. One frightening, desperate step. The eternal fires of hell would be waiting. *Or is there no God, no life hereafter, Karel, my angry, fierce little brother?*

The Fountains came into view. Her eyes went to Paul; his face was bright, smug. The train steamed into the station. She felt his hand under her elbow – firm, almost brutal. His carriage was waiting as ordered. They rode down Prinsloo Street, the houses, gardens and pedestrians a blur. When they reached Koba's house, Paul spoke for the first time that morning. 'I'll send for you. Don't attempt to run away; you won't get far.'

Koba was in the kitchen preparing fruit for bottling. She greeted Stefanie fondly and made her sit at the table. 'It's going to be a long, long day,' she said, pouring tea. 'We have to keep busy to help it along, *hartjie*. Tell me about your evening, the nice things.'

Over tea she told Koba about the menu, the music and the women's dresses. Koba told her about James recovering from his wound. 'And Vicky is poorly today. She is having a rest. James will not see her. She says it's for the best …'

Koba prattled on while spooning hot syrup into bottles. Stefanie's eyes strayed through the window to the beehives at the far end of the garden. She took a bottle and dripped a little syrup into it. She wandered through the rose garden looking to see where the most bees were congregated. She saw Paul's face as he'd lain in hospital in Cape Town, struggling to breathe. Before her courage could fail her, she placed the bottle under a bush and unscrewed the top. She picked some roses and a few sprigs of honeysuckle and went back into the kitchen.

She took Koba's hands in hers and made her sit at the table. 'I want you to swear on the Bible that what I ask of you now, you'll promise to do. Please, Tante Koba.'

'*Hartjie!*' Koba looked offended. 'It's not necessary to swear on the Bible.'

'Swear not to tell anyone, *no living soul*, about my baby. I saw Peter last night. He has no will left to stand up for his honour as a soldier, only for his honour as a man. Should he know, he'll come to me and then he will be executed. Do you understand?'

'No, no, I don't understand, *hartjie,*' she said tearfully. 'You'll be far away—'

'I have one more thing to do before I leave, Tante Koba. I'm going to Paul's room at the Club. I want you to fetch me back. Park the cart just off Schoeman Street. I'll find you, and if I'm not there before three, find Patrick and give him my papers.'

'But you must not go to the Club! Patrick will get to the station minutes before three—'

Stefanie stood up. 'Paul is going to send for me, Tante Koba. Wait at Schoeman Street with the cart.'

When Koba went to Victoria's room carrying her lunch on a tray, Stefanie stole back into the garden. A dozen bees buzzed in the bottle. She screwed the lid shut, punched a few holes in it and carried it up to her room. She chose her largest handbag, placing the bottle inside. There was a faint humming as the bees settled down. She would shake the bottle to get them angry again.

She dressed in a linen skirt, a long-sleeved blouse with a high neck, and a hat with a net covering her face. She pulled on her gloves and sat at the window, forcing herself to think of familiar things. The sky is blue; red roses have a stronger smell than pink ones; there are gold and brown streaks in Martin's beard; Charles always walks with his hands behind his back; Karel's eyes are fierce, sceptical, Rudi's dreamy and soft; James, so beautiful when he smiles. Peter's face against her breast, the love in his eyes. Eternal love. Eternal fires of hell.

Warren's carriage drew up at Koba's front gate shortly after two. When Stefanie reached the stairs, Koba was waiting there. 'I know where to find our Irishman. I'll send him to the Club to keep an eye out,' Koba whispered.

Stefanie passed her, her eyes fixed on the door.

'CAPTAIN RADFORD'S REPORT supplied us with substantial information. How does he fit in, I wonder?' General Kitchener's voice was irritable. Enough time was wasted by reports on Mrs Warren's suspicious behaviour; it was time to act. The woman was too damned shrewd and not as innocent as her husband professed.

'I'm convinced that Captain Radford is innocent in this matter,' Colonel Butcher said. 'He's waiting outside. Shall I ask him to come in?'

'No, I shall deal with him in due course. Captain Maxwell!' Kitchener barked and the officer appeared at the door. 'Dismiss Radford. Send Bartlett in!'

Captain Bartlett appeared a minute later and saluted.

'Take a detail to Mrs Warren's house, but be sure that she is at home before you show yourselves. Arrest her and bring her in. Ask Lady Victoria to leave the premises. I don't want her involved in this.'

'What about the aunt, Mrs van Wyk?'

'Leave her there. This is sure to stir the town and we might want to keep a close eye on everyone who visits her. Search the premises.'

Captain Bartlett saluted and left.

Kitchener flicked through the report on Captain James Stuart Henderson. *Disobeyed orders concerning the burning of a farm.* He read the crumpled note attached. *Fireflies. You have an hour. James.* He turned the page. *Allowed an enemy to go undiscovered and assisted him to escape from Wynberg Hospital.* He read the third accusation. *Aware of the whereabouts of General de Winter's hideout without coming forward.*

'What damnable nonsense! Fireflies! Aware of this! Aware of that! Suspicions of this! Where's the rest of the report? I need a detailed report, the evidence. Where is Major Hunter?'

'He died yesterday, sir. Shot through the head.'

'Is there anyone else who can shed some light on these allegations?'

'Sergeant Adams, who brought the note to Hunter and was present when Captain Henderson burned the farmhouse.'

'Why, sir, *why* was James Henderson detailed to burn General de Winter's farm?' Kitchener slammed his hand on the desk. 'His family's farm? God knows I tried to avoid the burning of that farm for as long as decently possible.'

'Major Hunter gave the order in my absence. It's a long and detailed story.'

Kitchener paced the floor before he came to a decision. 'Hunter's death allows me time to write to Stuart Henderson at the War Office. Cables are too public. This is all in the past and poses no threat, surely.' He pointed at the report. 'It should be dealt with carefully. I owe it to Stuart Henderson as a friend. Could we keep this to ourselves for the time being?'

———◆———

PAUL WARREN WAS IN A VICTORIOUS MOOD. He'd achieved what he'd set out to do. The Boer nation was crushed, its spirit extinguished. The National Scouts, the *Hensoppers*, his brainchild, were bringing the war to an end. Brother against brother, father against son, friend against friend. Buks Maree against his brother-in-law, General Martin de Winter.

He poured some cognac and reread the document he'd brought from his office. Maree would bring De Winter to the convoy on the twentieth, a week from now; the route and the names of Maree's contact men were listed. In the last paragraph he stressed the need to capture De Winter alive. He would be indispensable to peace negotiations – one of the few Boers with whom one could reason.

He sipped from his glass. He was homesick for the Cape: the wet winters, the breeze from the sea, his comfortable home and his wife where she belonged. He thought of Peter in Stefanie's arms. But Radford would leave the country soon. It would not do to alienate the British nobility, not when a man had his sights set on a knighthood. Nor would divorce be an option. The humiliation of a failed marriage could put an end to his career and that he could not – would not – allow.

The door opened and Stefanie walked in. He closed the curtains, locked the door and slipped the key into his pocket. Her eyes were on his face, a strange look in them. He saw her hands clutching her handbag, noticed the bulk of something inside it. A weapon, it flashed through his mind.

'Did you have an amusing evening? Radford appeared to be quite spent for a man of his calibre.' He kept his voice neutral, his eyes not leaving her face. 'I had a most satisfactory meeting. Your brother will be brought in soon. Alive!' He pointed to the document on the table. 'What you failed to find in my hatbox; Buks Maree is on his way to meet up with him. He said that without your brother they won't fight, and with him here in Pretoria peace will soon be signed. I've endorsed it all, my dear.'

THE VOID in Stefanie's mind filled. Martin would not allow the British to take him alive. Buks had admired him, had always supported him and she feared to think what terrible thing could have driven him to turn against Martin.

She looked at the man she had married, her husband only in name. Once, in the past, she'd admired him. Paul was just another man, successful in all he did. Like Martin. They were only on opposite sides. She looked at the clock; it was getting close to three. McFee was waiting. But it was not too late to save Peter's life, Martin's life. *Is it the war, driving us all insane in order to save those we love?* Yes, a passing madness. But it had to be done. So Fate decreed.

She sank down on the chair behind her, her fingers on the clasp of her handbag. She had unscrewed the lid before entering the room. She swallowed hard, willing her fingers to open the bag. Conflicting values, what was right, what was wrong, competed madly in her head, leaving her paralysed. A firing squad, Peter standing proud, but helpless; Martin's bullet-ridden body. *Nagmaal* at Rustenburg; *Thou shall not kill*, the fifth commandment.

'What do you want from me?' she asked, defeated, when the fury in her head had subsided.

'To come home with me, to be my wife.' Warren moved closer, his legs touching her dress.

'What will happen to Peter Radford?' she asked.

'If you choose to resist me, he'll pay for his indiscretion with his life.' He grabbed the bag from her lap, opened it and put his hand into it. 'Want to shoot me?'

The bees swarmed out, buzzing furiously. A few settled on his hands, face and neck. He uttered a strangled cry, slapping at his face. She grabbed the bottle, opened a window and threw it out. There was a sharp sting on her cheek, another on her neck. She stared at Paul, horrified. He was clawing at his tie, his face already swollen, his breathing laboured.

'Get ... doctor ...' He stumbled to the door.

'The key! Where's the key?' She lunged for his jacket, searching wildly through the pockets. With trembling hands she unlocked the door. 'Help! Please help!' she screamed into the courtyard.

Paul collapsed, gasping. She fumbled with his tie and the collar studs. A few men came rushing in. 'Please get him to the hospital! Oh, please hurry! Bee stings! Tell the doctor!' she sobbed uncontrollably.

Four men lifted Warren and carried him out. As she sank down on the floor, her eyes fell on the document next to the cognac. Martin's death sentence! She grabbed her hat and bag, clasped the document to her breast and rushed outside. When she reached the cart in Schoeman Street, she found Koba in an anxious state. On the seat beside Koba was the canning bottle, a few bees still trapped by the syrup. She clutched her stomach and retched.

'Patrick was here. He found it outside the window.' Koba flicked the reins. 'What have you done, *hartjie*? What have you done?'

'Hurry, Tante Koba! Hurry!'

'The guilty make haste. We should not be seen as such.' Koba kept the horse at a dignified pace. 'I told Patrick to get to the station. There are too many eyes about. We will still make it!'

When they arrived home, Koba drove the cart into the stable and helped Stefanie into the kitchen. Victoria was packing rusks and cold meats into Koba's large basket.

'I thought that you could take these to James—' Her eyes widened. 'Stefanie!'

'He's dead ... killed him!'

'No, no, Stefanie! Pull yourself together.' Koba shook her roughly. 'Stay here with Vicky; I'll get your things.'

'Who's dead?' Victoria asked as Koba steamed into the sitting room. Koba burst back into the kitchen, her face filled with consternation.

'In the street! Many soldiers are coming to the house!'

Stefanie looked at the document in her hand. 'Tante Koba, I *must* get to Patrick! Buks is going to have Martin shot.'

Koba stared horrified. 'Our Buks?'

The sound of marching feet reached the front door and circled the house.

'Is Martin to be betrayed by his own—?' Victoria snatched the document, pushed it down her dress between her breasts and rushed to her bedroom.

'The station, Vicky ... go to the station,' Koba called after her in an urgent whisper.

There was a hammering on the door. Captain Bartlett marched in, followed by two troopers, who stood on either side of Stefanie. 'Mrs Warren, you are under arrest.' He turned to Koba. '*Mevrou*, I have orders to search your house. General Kitchener has reason to believe that it's being used for espionage.'

'You won't find anything here.' Victoria walked back into the room, carrying her hat and gloves. 'I've lived here for a year now, I would know.'

'Lady Victoria, I shall have to ask you to leave the premises,' Bartlett said. 'Is there anywhere that my sergeant can take you?'

She donned her hat, went to kitchen and came back with Koba's basket. 'I was about to leave and will use Mrs van Wyk's cart.' She pulled on her gloves. 'I've packed this for my husband, who is in hospital. Do you want to search it too?'

Bartlett sent her an agitated glare. 'I shall send for you at the hospital when you are free to return.' He turned to the sergeant at the door. 'Allow Lady Victoria to leave the premises.'

VICTORIA SAW HOW Bontes was hauled from his room at the stables, and she heard the troops moving into Koba's cellar. She drove the cart to the station, her heart pounding, but she stared ahead, holding the reins tightly in her hands. *And now I am a traitor.* She felt no shame. Stefanie's face would stay with her forever, the gratitude in her eyes for taking the letter to the station in order to save Martin.

She parked at the station and handed the cart into the care of a boy who was always there, hoping for a small reward. She joined the crowd waiting on the platform. The train puffed to a halt, billowing steam. A man in well-worn clothes came to stand beside her.

'Lady Victoria, where's Stefanie?'

She hastily explained to McFee what was happening at the house. Shielding her neck with her hat, she pulled the document from her dress. He took it and disappeared back into the crowd. In a daze she made her way to the hospital. She left the cart on the square and picked up the basket. The stairs were almost too much for her and she had to muster all her courage to will her tears away.

In the hall, she sank down in the nearest chair.

A nurse recognised her and came over. 'Lady Victoria, have you come for your husband? The doctor has not seen Captain Henderson yet. There was an emergency. The poor man died. Quite dreadful ...' she sighed. 'Shall I take you to your husband's room?'

Victoria shook her head. 'I need to sit a while. What happened to him ... the man?'

'Mr Warren was attacked by a swarm of bees. It happens in summer. It's the heat, apparently. We have sent for his wife.'

The nurse left. Victoria was stunned by the news that the nurse had so carelessly revealed. Paul Warren dead. Stefanie's incoherent words, about having killed someone, hit her forcefully. Her anguished thoughts raced to Koba. She needed to be with her, to help her to deal with this tragedy now unfolding, but knew that her presence was not wanted while the house was being searched. She prepared to wait for Major Bartlett.

Soon it was visiting hour. She saw Peter heading through the hall, walking swiftly. She wanted to call out to him, wanting to give him the dreadful news of Stefanie, but her voice failed her. Following him with her eyes, she noted the room he entered. She picked up the basket, lugged it down the passage. At the door she paused to catch her breath before pushing it open. James was sitting up in bed, Peter leaning against the wall. He had been so exhausted when she'd seen him the previous afternoon, but looked even worse now; the smudges under his eyes were purple shadows. She cleared her throat, but no words would come.

'Victoria? What's the matter?' James said, surprise obvious in his voice at seeing her. Her mouth opened and closed, still she struggled for words. 'For heaven's sake, pull yourself together!'

She took a deep breath and related the news of the house being searched, the bee attack and Warren's death.

'Good God!' James said. 'Stefanie? Where is she?'

Victoria's eyes went to Peter. He looked at her with agonising hope in his eyes. 'She was arrested.'

There was a shocked silence. Victoria crossed the room to Peter, but was uncertain of how to comfort him. She had not seen him so devastated and helpless. 'She always gets through everything ... somehow,' she said.

Peter gave a barely discernible nod, but whether it was to thank her or in agreement she could not tell as he sank against the wall, shielding his face with his hands. 'No more ... can't stand it ... no more,' he said, despair all too obvious in his voice.

James lay back on the pillows and closed his eyes. 'Why on earth did she get involved in this? War! Espionage! A woman's place is—'

'In bed? Is that it?' Victoria flared angrily before she could stop herself. His inability to deal with emotional crisis moved her deeply, but her concern for Peter and Stefanie overruled her reason. 'Is everything so damn simple to you? Your cousin might face a firing squad and you take refuge in anger. It is, to say the least, pathetic ...'

'You forget yourself, Victoria!' James snapped.

She lowered her eyes. 'Please forgive me, I shouldn't have said that,' she said miserably, looking at Peter. 'Please forgive me.'

———

WHILE THE SOLDIERS had searched the house, Koba had treated the stings on Stefanie's face, plaited her hair and hung a shawl over her shoulders as she had trembled uncontrollably when a trooper had walked past her, carrying the pillowcase containing all her correspondence.

Now, at Pretoria gaol, a cell was being prepared for her. She registered the sharp smell of disinfectant, a mattress, a washbowl and pitcher, a bucket, blankets and a pillow. *A pillow.* Major Bartlett was still speaking to her. 'Case ... days to prepare ... nothing more expected of you ...'

Nothing more expected. Nothing more ... nothing more. She kept her eyes fixed on the pillow, walked into the cell and lay down. Her head touched the pillow; she sank into oblivion.

Be It On Your Head

WHILE MARTIN WAS recovering from his wound in the safety of the cave, the scouts kept a constant vigil on the surroundings and stayed in contact with Jan Viljoen, who was in command of the scattered Rustenburg commando.

Here is truly peace and tranquillity, the agony of the world an outsider, Martin thought. He lay on his back, following the play of sunlight through the fissures in the rock. The New Year had been marred by the deaths of his parents, but death was no stranger and acceptance gradually replaced the grief in his heart, leaving a dull ache.

He tried to think about continuing the war, but found only a void. What he'd witnessed on the trek to the Cape Colony tortured him. The wide plains of the Free State, once teeming with game, dotted with farmsteads, were now a scorched wasteland. Families had been brutally torn apart, the men fleeing helplessly, their clothes in rags, their bodies emaciated, their eyes haunted, their once-proud horses reduced to hollow-eyed, pitiful beasts. The thousands of white crosses at the camps were mute testimony to the deprivation their women and children had suffered. *That is our destiny too,* his judgement confirmed.

When he ventured out onto the rock slab, he tried to look beyond the desolation of his home and life to where the veld stretched into the distance, hazy in the summer sun. *My land given into my care by my God, by the trust my people have in me. But God has been so far removed from me in the past two years; I can no longer find Him. Am I being tested now, weighed? Here I stand; judge me, I have given all.*

In the evenings he observed the others. Charles and Anita talked about the coming of their child. Rudolf stared into the fire, lost in a world only Karel could enter. Koba had said many years ago that a woman's love would come between them, but, so strong was their bond, it was as if Rudolf's love for Annecke had strengthened it. But Rudolf was emotionally exhausted and if he were to fall apart Karel would go wild again.

A woman's love. He had found Annecke's music box on a shelf. He wanted to hear the song again, but the spring was broken and no sound came from it. In the small hours of the night, he thought about Victoria, the only woman he had truly loved. He felt her body under his, firelight flickering over them, the gold in her hair, fire mounting in his body, lost in an uncontrollable need, fighting the final surrender, yet wanting it, needing it like a drowning man needs air, and then the ecstasy devastating all that had driven him on.

He thought of Annecke. She was Rudolf's love. He'd come to accept it and now wondered if she could make Rudolf whole again. Yet he dared not allow a rescue attempt; the risk was too great.

He thought of another risk that had also been too overwhelming, yet he had taken it and lost the man he had secretly clung to. The man who had given him courage and guidance when he desperately needed support. Joep Maree's tortured face haunted him. The wracking sobs as he struggled for breath had merged with his own raw sorrow when Joep died in his arms.

And Buks Maree. The scouts brought news that he had rejoined the commando a week after Christmas. McFee did not trust this return after an absence of months, growling that it smacked of intent, of betrayal. Martin wanted to trust Buks, but his reason cautioned against it. Buks had nowhere else to go, but his threat before the Cape expedition was a black reminder. *Be it on your head if my farm is destroyed, my family sent to the camps.*

THEN CAME THE NIGHT McFee rushed into the cave. Alone. Everyone sat in despairing silence listening to his account of Stefanie's arrest. Charles was the first to speak. 'What will happen to her, Martin?'

'Depends on the evidence found, if any,' Martin said after he had thought it over. 'She might have been taken in for questioning only. Who's going to testify? Warren? George Hunter?'

'Hunter is dead,' Karel said. 'I sniped him. I said I would and I did.'

'So is Warren,' McFee smiled. 'It seems a good number of bees flew into his room.'

The others looked at one another, alarmed.

'Bees, Patrick?' Charles asked.

'It's summer, Doctor, bees are everywhere.' He handed Martin a document. 'Lady Victoria brought this to the station. Stefanie found it minutes before the soldiers came. General, I warned you about Buks Maree.'

Martin looked at the paper, unwilling to open it. Karel swore, grabbed it from him. He read the first lines by the firelight. 'Traitor! Buks is to lead you into an ambush this coming Friday. You have to shoot him!' He pushed the document back into Martin's hands. 'You have the proof right there! In your hands!'

'No! Don't execute Buks,' Rudolf cried. 'He's your friend, your brother-in-law. You have known him all your life.'

'Rudi, Martin is a general first and his brother-in-law second,' Charles said hopelessly.

Karel stood up, cursing wildly. 'Martin, he knows where you are. He won't get you to the ambush; he'll bring them here – to the cave!'

'Surely he won't betray the cave,' Charles frowned. 'We agreed that it's neutral ground.'

Martin read Warren's report, hoping to find something that might be used in Buks's favour. But he'd sent many to the firing squad with no written evidence against them and here, in his hands was a guilty verdict. 'Oom Koos and General Viljoen must deal with it. I cannot judge where my brother-in-law is involved. Karel, get Buks arrested now and taken to Cypherfontein. I don't want you to be there. McFee, you keep my brothers away from there.'

Karel shouldered the Mausers and led Rudolf outside. Charles put his arm around Anita's waist and guided her to their curtained-off section. McFee waited until they were out of earshot and leaned close to Martin. His voice was so low that Martin had to strain to catch the words.

'General, we were going to bring her papers out. They might have been confiscated. It was chaos at the house. I had a look from afar, mingled with the onlookers. What now, General, what now?'

An icy hand gripped Martin's heart. 'I don't ... don't know. With all those papers ... she has no chance,' he said, tears of despair blinding him. 'Thank you, Patrick, thank you for keeping it from the others.'

'I shall leave now, General. Send for me if you need me.'

Martin went to his mattress, pulled the blanket over his head, and turned his face into the pillow.

MARTIN LEFT FOR CYPHERFONTEIN before daybreak, accompanied by the Viljoen brothers and fifty men. Rudolf and Karel watched them making their way down the mountain on the south side. McFee arrived, bringing two mugs of coffee.

'Have you done what I've asked of you, Irishman?' Karel asked.

'Yes, I didn't spend all my time in Pretoria. I took the train to

Potchefstroom. Not a lively place, not at all, hardly a drop to drink.'

'Can it be done?'

'Easy. The river is thickly wooded; there are enough hiding places close to the camp. The women go out to do washing and gather firewood. But getting to Potchefstroom won't be easy. Riding as khakis ... no, no. The bloody blockhouses!'

'Martin has forbidden us to go,' Rudolf said.

'*The General* will be gone for some time, Rudi. At Cypherfontein!' Karel laughed.

'I sent Annecke a note with a kindly *predikant* to say that I'll come for her soon,' McFee said. 'And that I will do.'

FOUR DAYS LATER, Buks Maree faced the three generals and two commandants at the table in the dining room at Cypherfontein. The tick of the clock on the wall was the only sound in the room. He kept his eyes on the clock; it was twenty minutes to ten. Acknowledging betrayal was the extreme penalty on the soul. He was not a *hensopper*, but a betrayer, a traitor. Even if he could atone, Lena, his children, the district, the *Volk*, would not forgive him. It would be a living death. There was nothing left but to stand strong, be a man, in his last hour.

Martin had come to him the previous day. The pain and bitterness in his voice was raw, but his words were sincere. They talked about the deaths of their parents and their children. Martin said that he understood fully what had driven him to do what he'd done, but wanted to know if he would have brought the ambush to the cave. With tears in his eyes, Buks swore he would not have betrayed the cave.

Now General Viljoen read out the document and passed it on to De la Rey.

'Jacobus Maree,' De la Rey said. 'Were you planning to do what this letter says? Lead Martin into an ambush?'

'Yes, Oom Koos.'

'Why, Buks?' De la Rey asked despondently.

'To bring an end to the war, the destruction of our country, the death of our people.'

'By having General de Winter killed?' General Slabbert asked, his moustache bristling.

'I was promised that he would be captured alive.'

'Do you really think that Martin would *hensop*? Give his rifle to the traitors?'

'You're blinded by his courage and name, Oom Koos. Last year we were exhausted, on our knees. Martin saw it, you saw it, yet you refused to acknowledge that the end had come. The war is over. It's in the hearts of the ten thousand Boers now fighting for the British. The time for fighting for freedom is long past. We can't win the war, so we must end it.'

'You took it on yourself to do that? Hoist the Union Jack over our nation!' General de la Rey called the guards. 'Take him away and shoot him.'

Buks looked at the clock; it was not yet ten.

OUTSIDE, MARTIN SAT under the orange trees, a few yards away from Jan Viljoen and his brother Frans. His eyes would not leave the wooden crosses in the near distance; the same fate now awaited Buks. The Viljoens discussed things in which they found comfort – the homestead at Vrede that needed to be rebuilt, their cattle – masking their anger and despair at Buks's betrayal. They broke off as General de la Rey emerged from the house and walked to them.

'The grave is being dug,' De la Rey said. He removed his hat and placed his hand on Martin's shoulder. 'I'm sorry, son, he admitted what was in the letter.'

There was such anguish in Martin's heart that he could not speak.

'Then Buks behaved like a man, Oom Koos,' Jan Viljoen said.

'Yes, he behaved like a man, Jan. The *predikant* is with him now.'

Half an hour later, six burghers, rifles in their hands, walked with Buks between them.

They averted their eyes when the shots echoed through the morning air.

God, have mercy on his soul for he has seen the truth, Martin found himself praying.

The Blockhouse

THE AREA AROUND POTCHEFSTROOM swarmed with patrols and convoys supplying the blockhouse line all the way to Krugersdorp. The half-moon guided the three riders for the first hours of the night, but travelling by day was careful and slow. On the second morning they reached the Mooi River and followed it down to within two miles of the concentration camp. There they found a rock overhang close to the river bank, a safe hideout for the day.

McFee handed his rifle to Karel, tucking a knife into his belt. He crossed himself and disappeared into the thick vegetation, following the river to the pools where the camp inmates came in the afternoons. He scaled the trunk of a large wild fig and prepared to wait. When the gates opened, the women and their coloured servants staggered through, carrying washing. The children rushed for the water. A few old men wandered about. He scanned the women through his field glasses and happened on a lone one, carrying a bundle, walking up and down the river bank. She didn't gather wood or wash clothes, but made her way to a rock and sat watching the veld.

He had found Annecke.

He sauntered over. A few paces from her, he bent over to tie the laces of his boots. 'Please stay calm,' he whispered. 'It's the Irishman. I've come for you.'

She did not reply. He looked up and his heart froze. She was thin, her dress filthy, her long hair unkempt, her eyes haunted.

'The Irishman?' she asked at last, hope fragile in her voice.

'Yes, the Irishman, I'm here now,' he said gently. 'Follow me. Don't run or talk to anyone, just follow me at a distance.'

He straightened up and ambled past a group of children searching for wood. When he reached the tree, he glanced over his shoulder. With her eyes fixed on him, she walked slowly, and it took some time before she caught up with him. He lifted her into the lower branches, scrambled up and hauled her into the thick crown.

'My baby died,' she whispered.

'Yes, we've heard, my brave lass.' He took the bundle and put his arms around her. 'Come rest a while, I'll hold you. We must be quiet.'

She closed her eyes and leant against his chest like an obedient child.

THE TWINS TOOK TURNS keeping watch on the columns of dust in the distance. The day was unbearably long. At nightfall they led the horses to the river for a drink, shared a piece of biltong and some water. They stretched out on a flat rock above the overhang and watched the half-moon travelling its course in the western sky.

'How much longer, do you think?'

'An hour or so. McFee will leave well after dark. Why don't you sleep a bit, Rudi?'

'I'm not sleepy. I'll check the horses.' He disappeared under the rock overhang, where they had secured the horses. Legend gave a soft whinny and nuzzled his neck. 'No Legend, I'm not Karel. I'm the clean one. Has your nose failed you?' She nibbled on his fingers. 'Are you trying to tell me something Legend? Is there danger ahead?' She snorted.

He crawled back up the rock and found Karel scanning the night sky through his field glasses. 'What are you doing?'

'Looking for God,' Karel said, but this time there was no scorn in his voice. 'When I was alone, after Magersfontein, I looked at the heavens for hours. Once I thought I saw Pa's wild horses running across the full moon. It looked so real, Rudi.' He gave a low chuckle. 'It was only clouds, of course.'

There was a rustle in the bush a little way off. Moments later a pheasant cried piercingly. 'Wild cat out hunting,' Karel grunted. He waited a moment and then said quietly, 'Rudi, I've killed enough; I want to farm again.'

Rudolf turned on his side and looked at his twin in the moonlight. 'Karel, do you remember what Pa said that night before the war started? He said that everything must have a beginning and an end ...'

Karel frowned into the darkness. 'Yes, Rudi, that's what I feel. The night, at Paardeberg, when I crawled out of Cronjé's laager and killed that man with my knife ...' he hissed through his teeth. 'The first man I killed. I'll never forget him, Rudi. All the others, yes, but he was so scared, so young, like us. I thought then that there must be a place where he goes to, a place we are before the beginning and after the end.'

'Does he go somewhere where he can grow old? Is that what you want to know?'

'He arrived in the British heaven a young man,' Karel laughed but turned pensive again. 'For the first time, I wonder about things, Rudi. The other day Anita allowed me to put my hand on her belly when Charles's son was restless. The little one kicked so hard and he's not even in this world yet. It was different to when you put your hand on a cow's belly. And I think about Legend. An exceptional horse, everyone says. It's not just my training that has made her so unique. She was created differently from other horses.

James, his hands, shoulders, the way he sits a horse – a rare thing, Tante Koba said, that everything about him is so perfectly created. God was in a very generous mood that day, she said. And things that one can only feel: Martin's courage – a strange, awesome thing. He never wavers. Never! And now he's going to execute Buks.'

'He wavered once. He met James's wife.'

'Yes, but it was dark. No one saw him,' Karel said. 'And that's another thing; love between a man and a woman. Ma and Pa dying so soon after each other. She died because Pa died, not because she was ill, Rudi, that's what I believe. She loved Pa above all else, above us. I miss Pa. Ma … yes, I think about her too … but for us it's always Tante Koba. Tante Koba says this, Tante Koba says that. Even Charles is like that now.'

Rudolf closed his eyes and sighed despondently. 'But the war has destroyed us all … all of us.'

'No, Rudi, Annecke could be yours again.'

'No, she is Martin's wife; she was always going to be his wife. I see that now. And I don't want to be separated from you again.'

'Rudi, I'm not scared any more.' Karel raised the glasses to the moon as it emerged from the clouds. 'If I'm going to lose you again, I'll know where to find you – in that secret place where everything comes full circle. You'll be there waiting for me and I'll come and find you. Don't be scared.' He hooked his little finger around Rudolf's. 'I'll come for you …'

Legend gave an urgent snort. A nightjar called. They slid down the rock, searching the darkness around them. The call was repeated, very close. And then McFee was there with Annecke slung across his back.

'Hurry! She's done in. Get the horses!'

Rudolf rushed the horses from the hiding place and watched as Karel held his water bottle to Annecke's mouth. McFee mounted and Karel lifted her onto the saddle in front of him. They led the horses away from the river. Karel took the lead, McFee with Annecke in the middle and Rudolf bringing up the rear.

Once they cleared the last observation post, Karel led the way parallel with the blockhouse line, sometimes walking the horses, then at a faster pace. When the sun was well up, he spied a burnt-out farmstead not far from a thicket on a rise. He observed the ruins through his field glasses and announcing it safe, led them there.

'There's a dam. I'll water the horses. Irishman, keep watch.'

Rudolf squatted next to Annecke. He choked back the lump in his throat. She was wasted, her eyes liquid pools in her small face, her fingers fretting with her *kappie* strings. He wanted to gather her to him, promise her that they would be together again, that they would have another son. But promises would be futile. His eyes filled with hot tears and his shoulders heaved. He turned his face from her, taking deep breaths.

'You're as pretty as ever, but thin as a bird. We have to feed you up.' He took her hands in his. 'I'm so sorry about our little one. I know that he was my child, but the note … it came too late.'

She nodded her head miserably. 'He was buried in a white coffin. I told them that he was not the General's son … but they didn't believe me …'

'It's all over now,' Rudolf whispered, stroking her hands. 'It's all over. Soon we will be in the cave. It's always better there … in the cave. Sleep now; we have a long night ahead.' He took his blanket from his saddle, spread it on the ground and made a pillow for Annecke with his jacket. 'Sleep, you are safe now.' He kissed her on the forehead, picked up his rifle and joined McFee.

IN THE LATE AFTERNOON they watered the horses again. Then, carefully scouting ahead, Karel guided them on. They travelled steadily, alternating Annecke between the three horses. With the moon still above the western horizon, they swung north and came to within a hundred yards of the blockhouse near where they would have to cross the railway. Karel dismounted and told them to wait. Crawling into the scrub, he cut the barbed wire and the telegraph line.

'Rudi and I go first,' he whispered when he got back to the others. 'McFee, give us ten minutes. We'll guard you until you're through and away.'

Leading their horses, the twins slipped through and reached the low scrub on the other side. They trained their rifles on the blockhouse two hundred yards to their right. But the fusillade came from their left, splitting the night into orange streaks. They emptied their magazines in that direction, and saw McFee vaulting onto his horse, covering Annecke with his body. The horse shot through the gap in the wire and thundered past, followed by shots from the blockhouse. Standing back to back, they kept up constant fire in both directions. When McFee's horse faded from earshot, they scrambled into the saddles. Another fusillade whined overhead but soon all they could hear was the beat of their horses' hooves.

Karel pulled Legend into an easy pace. His hands searched over her, checking that she was unharmed. 'Bloody Scotsmen! They sleep with one eye open. We'll give the horses a breather …'

Legend whinnied urgently. They heard the danger clearly – horses coming after them. 'The bastards! They're following! Damn moonlight!'

Karel put a fresh clip into his Mauser. 'Reload but don't shoot, Rudi; they will spot us. The Irishman will grow wings, don't worry!'

They raced away, twenty yards apart. Karel saw Rudolf a little ahead of him, half-turned in the saddle, the night alive with bullets cracking around them.

Karel slammed forward in the saddle. Warm blood spread down his back. He shuddered as another shot caught him sideways. Gasping, his mouth filled with blood. The Mauser slipped from his hands, and he grabbed hold of Legend's mane, urging her on. She veered into a thicket and went for a hundred yards before she collapsed.

He fell clear of the saddle and lay face down. Through his heaving and choking, he heard Legend's feeble whinny. With a tremendous effort, he dragged himself to her and searched her body with his hand. There was a gash in her side, blood pumping out freely. 'No ... no ...' he wept. Inch by inch, he reached her head and buried his face in her mane.

Death Comes at an Early Age

KOBA AND VICTORIA sat in the garden, poring over the newspapers. Victoria read out an article claiming that General Louis Botha, the Boer commander, had sent a cable asking General Kitchener to allow Mrs Warren civilian representation in court. Kitchener had refused, insisting that Stefanie's trial was a military matter and that, with the evidence found in her possession, legal help would be pointless. Nevertheless he consented to have the case heard in the law courts and to admit newspaper reporters only.

'See here, Tante Koba.' Victoria placed her finger on another bold headline. *General de Winter executes brother-in-law. Civil war threatens.*

'Yes, *hartjie*. The news leaked from Rustenburg a few days ago,' Koba said squinting at the paper. 'I saw it coming, felt it in my heart. Our Buks, such a fine young man, and now a traitor.'

'I saved Martin's life by taking that letter.' Victoria waved a bee from the tea long gone cold. 'But condemned Buks Maree to a death without honour. In a way, I betrayed my own people. It's all so confusing ...'

Koba looked about her garden. The morning was hot, the roses in full bloom, the bees busily going about their task. She folded the newspaper and swatted at some bees that were worrying the sugar bowl. A shudder raced through her big body. Stefanie, her husband, and bees. What had driven her to such extremes? Her love for Peter. Not his unborn child, but Peter. Like Buks's love for his land. 'Like Martin, Buks loved his country, but in a different way,' she said. 'Not in the way a man should in times of war, but still, the love he had for the land, the earth. Yes, he cared for every calf born, every acre he ploughed.'

'Tante Koba, have you considered that Stefanie might go the same way as Buks?'

'You're only a traitor if you betray your own, *hartjie*. Buks was caught, judged and shot by his own people, because he betrayed them. Stefanie will be judged by the British because she spied on the British. And Stefanie is a Boer; that's the difference. General Kitchener knows all about spying. Let the court have its day.'

Koba leaned back in her chair, looking into the middle distance. Over the weeks, Victoria's love for both James and Martin, the guilt-ridden confusion of it all, had been revealed. Passion was so often confused with love. But James, dear proud James. Betrayal could ruin love, but love would break through in the end; it had that power. Time was all James needed.

———————

JAMES INHALED DEEPLY on his cheroot. It was late afternoon. He sat in the garden of the regiment's house in the shade of a wild fig, contemplating the brandy on the table beside him. He was convalescing, and so was not allowed to smoke or drink. But like Peter, he was living in a world suspended between hope and despair.

He crushed out the cheroot, reaching for the glass. Statements had been taken from all officers, but only Peter would testify in court. He'd been questioned extensively about Peter, but, when it came to Peter's involvement with Stefanie, his mind had conveniently gone blank. He was certain that Koba and Victoria – who surely knew a lot more than they let on – would be discreet if questioned.

There was a deep silence about Peter that James could not penetrate. He was scared to sleep, he confessed; nightmares of firing squads haunted him. It was only a matter of time, James felt, before Peter's self-imposed barricade would crumble, the weight of what he was carrying too much to bear. It needed to happen before Stefanie's trial. But it would take a bottle of brandy to ease Peter through the agony, and he, James, was waiting and ready.

He looked about the garden. The shade of the trees was leaning to the east, throwing patterns on the lawn. The flowers wilted in the late January heat and there were only a few birds hopping about the shrubs. A shrike came to rest on a branch above his head, his beak gaping as he too felt the pressing heat.

He longed to see Koba. Although the guards had been removed, no visitors were allowed, as she was under house arrest. Thoughts about Koba inevitably turned to Victoria. When she had stumbled into his hospital room, he had dearly wanted to comfort her, but he still did not know how to deal with her betrayal. He sighed and drank from his glass. He and Peter had been invincible before love had snared them, but love was like a sabre, cutting deep and bleeding dry.

It was nearing dusk. He finished what was left in his glass and was about to get to his feet when he caught sight of the moon above the trees to the east. A day-moon, not far from full. A few more days and Stefanie would be shot when the full moon set. At dawn. Was there enough evidence to condemn him to the same fate? Colonel Butcher had informed him that, before he was killed, Hunter had made certain allegations against him, but it would take time to establish the facts. He could not rule out a court martial, Butcher had warned.

Not yet thirty, Stefanie and I, and with death sentences hanging over our heads. He thought about what Koba had said so many years ago: death comes at an early age in this country of ours.

———————

THAT AFTERNOON, Karel de Winter was buried at Wintersrust. The trees and the tall summer grass glistened, washed by the gentle rain that had fallen in the morning. The sun broke through the clouds, casting a rainbow over the small gathering of mourners.

Martin stood at the head of the grave, next to General Jansen, who was leading the prayers. His face was a mask of control but he was bleeding inside. Here, at his brother's open grave, the truth of his nation's plight was bared in his soul.

Buks's betrayal had shaken his faith in his leadership. Had Buks been right? Was he leading his weary commandos to death? They followed him blindly, but what was going on in their hearts? Most possessed only the clothes they wore and the horses they rode; farming and a home life were a distant memory. They had nowhere else to go. Was that why they remained with him? Did the answer lie in the hearts of those Boers who were now with the enemy? Where to now? Surrender?

Tears of despair rolled into his beard. He looked at Karel's crude coffin and all at once he longed for death.

He heard a stifled sob from Charles. Anita held his glasses, her arm about him, her lips moving in prayer. Annecke stood in Charles's arms, her face pale, her eyes bewildered.

Martin's eyes shifted to the Viljoen brothers on the other side of the grave. Jan cried noisily, his big hands wringing his hat. Behind them were McFee and the scouts, stunned and angry. Rudolf stood alone, his eyes not leaving the coffin. Martin thought about the time, two years previously, when Rudolf had disappeared. Karel had not shed a tear. And now it was the same. But this time there could be no wondering whether Karel was

521

still alive, there would be no searching of the countryside, there could be no hoping for a miracle: Karel had died in Rudolf's arms.

That dreadful day. McFee and Annecke, clutching a pathetic bundle, had rushed into the camp at Cypherfontein, the horse lathered and trembling, McFee calling desperately for Charles. 'Karel is down, Rudolf is searching for him. I need the doctor! I need the doctor!'

They found them later that day lying against the stiffening carcass of Legend, Rudolf asleep with his twin's bloodied body cradled in his arms, Karel's eyes unseeingly on Rudolf's face, a hand still entangled in Legend's mane. The men stared in silence until Jan Viljoen's loud wail rung out. 'God! Oh Almighty God! Look what You have done,' he cried to the heavens.

Rudolf had opened his eyes and, laying Karel down gently, stumbled to his feet. 'Karel and Legend died together. As he wanted.'

Just those words. Too tragic. Too overwhelming. A terrible anguish and unjust anger caught at Martin's throat. 'You are responsible for our brother's death! You, Annecke and McFee! I told you not to go!'

General Jansen touched Martin's arm, dragging him away from his anguished memories. He scattered a handful of earth into his brother's coffin and walked a little way off. Charles joined him and they watched as McFee placed Legend's worn-out saddle on the coffin and the scouts began filling the grave.

'Martin, I know how hard this is for you,' Charles said, clearing his throat several times. 'Please, I implore you, take pity on Rudi and Annecke. She has lost her child; she suffered in the camp. And with Karel's death … she's in deep shock. I fear for her reason. And Rudi, he's where Karel was … only love can help now, Martin.'

Martin kept his eyes on those gathered at the grave. Anita was laying a wreath of summer flowers and Gert Swart was hammering a cross into the earth. 'Was the boy mine, Charles? Do you know?'

Charles paused, his eyes closed behind his lenses. 'I will always remember him as your son, Martin.'

Martin waited for the scouts to complete their task, and for General Jansen and the men to move to their horses, before he joined Annecke and Rudolf at the grave. They stood forlorn and apart. Annecke could not speak for misery. Rudolf seemed unmoved by her plight, his dry eyes steady on Martin's face.

Annecke started weeping. Martin pulled her into his arms, pressing her face into his shoulder. 'I loved the boy, our son. Will it help a little to know that?' He stroked her back. 'You are my wife, my little wife, and you have been a good wife to me, but now I have to set you free.'

'I didn't mean to hurt you, Martin,' she sobbed.

'I know,' he said into her hair. 'You would never hurt anyone intentionally. Go with Charles to the cave. Go, rest, and get well.'

Charles put his arms around Annecke and Anita and led them away from the cemetery. Martin walked the few paces to Rudolf. 'Rudi, when we found Karel and you, I spoke in anger. I'm sorry. Our brother, our parents are dead. Annecke's parents and brother are dead. But we are still here. She needs help, Rudi, and only you can help her.'

Rudolf did not reply. 'I know that I've not been a brother to you in the way I should've been or wanted to be. I apologise for my neglect. Can you find it in your heart to give me another chance?'

'I'm not angry with you. I've always admired you, Ouboet.'

Martin pulled him into an embrace and held him for a while. 'Go to Annecke. Look after her for both of us. I'll be waiting for you to come back to the commando.'

'I've killed enough.' Rudolf's voice was strange, detached. 'I'm staying here with Karel.'

—————

STEFANIE WAS HAUNTED by images of bees, trains and firing squads. In the weeks before her arrest, she'd thought she would be terrified if caught, but now she was past fear. Only guilt filled her mind and heart. *I killed my husband! I deserve to die.*

Early one morning, the baby made its presence felt by barely discernible movements. She had not considered her child before; there had been too many desperate measures to stay ahead of the fate that now awaited her. In the small hours of the morning, as she listened to the night wind and the guards' boots crunching on the gravel outside, she wept for the child that would die with her. She tried to reach Peter to set him free of their love, but only Paul's face, struggling for breath, his eyes condemning her to hell, came to her.

The day before her hearing, a British officer arrived with a parcel of fresh clothes from Koba. Colonel Spencer was a kindly man, with soft features and a sympathetic voice. He sat next to her on the narrow cot for an hour and outlined the procedures that would be followed in court. Although she was guilty beyond all doubt, he said, witnesses would testify to establish her guilt and the involvement, if any, of British personnel. As she had been refused legal assistance, it would be best to acknowledge all she had done. The trial would be over in a few hours.

When he left, she stared out of the high window into the square of blue sky. Her thoughts went to Peter. Should the prosecutor probe too deeply, their last night in Johannesburg might be revealed. *The truth does not always come out in court*, Martin had told her many times. And there were some truths that had to be kept out of court to save Peter from a fate that might be worse than hers, if not the same. When he left, Colonel Spencer had said: you are a woman, not a soldier; there is the slightest possibility of a lengthy jail sentence or deportation, not execution.

She had nevertheless asked him; 'How do they say it in court? The death sentence? I want to know. Please write it down, the exact wording.' She was not going to be caught unawares.

After some hesitation, he had scribbled on a piece of paper and held it out to her.

———

'WOULD YOU CONSIDER IT? If offered?' James pointed at Peter's pistol lying on his discarded tunic. They had sneaked into Koba's garden long after dark and were now well into their second bottle of brandy, leaning with their backs against the willow.

'There's nothing honourable about taking one's own life.' Peter squinted through the cheroot smoke at James. 'And you?'

James laughed. 'I want to retire with a bang, yes, but not with that sort of bang. Father would've ordered it. And I refuse to give him the satisfaction. Once … the day he forced me to marry, actually, yes, *that day*, I promised him the biggest, the most talked-about scandal ever and I intend doing just that.'

'Where would you like to be buried?'

'Under Tante Koba's peach tree—', he broke off, frowning. 'No, no, where the fireflies live.'

'Home of the Fireflies. Is that it?'

James grabbed his arm. 'What do you know about that?'

'Only the name. She didn't tell me where … or what it is.'

'I won't tell you either, Radford. Don't look at me like that. Rather look at the moon. Over there, shining so brightly.'

'If you say so.' Peter looked at the moon. 'What a mess we've got ourselves into, James. Except Vicky … she has kept her head.'

James inhaled deeply on his cheroot. 'She has betrayed, in her way.' He had wanted to confide in Peter for some time, but now he blurted it out. 'She met Martin right here under our noses. Spent a night with him in Johannesburg. The strangest thing is that Vicky says she loves me, yet she met him.'

'God, James!' Peter slumped back on the grass. They looked at the moon and listened to the frogs croaking in the river. Peter raised himself on his elbow. His face was alive with excitement, his eyes ablaze with the old reckless fire. 'My God, must've been something! Think about it, Henderson. Meeting an enemy general, an old lover and the war raging all around. The temptation, the danger! Wouldn't you have done it, given the chance?'

James looked at him puzzled. 'Now that you put it that way, never thought about it ... yes, I would've, I suppose. But she's my wife.'

'Love was not the issue when you married her. Survival was. Victoria's thirst for adventure ensured your survival. You drove her to meeting Martin when you cut her out, spending your time at Rose Carter's.'

'And wasn't it fun while it lasted.' James squinted at the moon through his glass. 'Now it's all gone.'

'Yes, all gone. Splendid innings you had, though.'

'You're slurring, Radford!'

'Am I? Yes, slurring. Where was I? Oh, yes! Hear me.' Peter placed his hand on James's arm. 'Stefanie is like you, like me, addicted to danger. I know because I love Stefanie. That's why I love her. Vicky has a taste for adventure. That's why you love her; you wouldn't have otherwise, not you. And that's why she did it, meeting Martin. The thrill of danger—'

'The thrill of danger, Radford, doesn't thrill any more.' James gulped more brandy. 'You also did it, Radford, didn't you? Bluffed your way in and spent the night with an enemy spy.'

Peter's face filled with sadness. 'I knew she was involved and she knew I was aware of it, knowing that I might have to report her. We kept on raising the stakes. I asked her to marry me; she said yes.'

'*Marry you?* Well done, Radford. You've rewritten the Ten Commandments. Let's drink to that!'

The reality of the situation came home to him. He looked at Peter, who was stretched out on the grass. 'Where did we go wrong? Were the stakes too high, Peter? We know how to play, burned our fingers before. What went wrong this time? Love? Is that what brought us down?'

'No, not love ... loyalty ... the stakes we've put on the table. And now I'd pay double to reverse it all. Somehow, I think, it was bound to end this way. She will be sentenced to death. And I, well ... what I've done ... I deserve to be shot. And I welcome it.'

James looked at the empty bottles. He was still reasonably sober but Peter was not. In a few hours it would be morning. Peter had turned on his side and his shoulders were heaving. He recalled the night he had raped Victoria and drunk himself into oblivion. He had cried that night, alone, and would have welcomed Peter's comfort. *But I don't know how to comfort, I'm not sober enough to deal with this. Lately I'm never sober enough to deal with anything.*

He flung his glass away and put an unsteady hand on Peter's shoulder.

'Tomorrow will be worse, but I'll be there ... with you, I mean.'

'Now you're slurring, Henderson.'

'Yes I am, Radford. But tomorrow I'll be sober.'

He covered Peter with his tunic and waited for the morning.

Nothing But the Truth

CHURCH SQUARE WAS A SEA of restless people. The colours of the Vierkleur were sported around the brims of hats and decorated the *kappies* of the black-clad women. Dutch hymns were sung, overpowering all other sound and making the troops, out in large numbers, clutch their rifles nervously.

Peter arrived shortly before ten o'clock, escorted by his fellow officers. They dismounted, tossing their horses' reins into the hands of a private. Murray Shaw strode ahead, followed by Peter between James and William Moore. The eyes of the crowd followed them with unconcealed hate as they walked up the steps of the court building. Inside, a clerk showed them to an anteroom, where Colonel Butcher waited.

Butcher took in Peter's ashen face and bloodshot eyes. 'Captain Radford? You look spent. Will you cope with this?'

'I'll cope, sir.'

'Well, good luck. We'll be here when it's over.' He turned to the others. 'At ease.'

They removed their helmets and gloves and sank down in the chairs.

The court clerk put his head around the door. 'The prisoner is on her way, Colonel. Those who are to testify are requested to take their seats.'

James touched Peter's shoulder when he left for the witness' waiting room.

Major Fernfield and Captain Bartlett were apparently engrossed in their newspapers when Peter entered the room. He went to a window overlooking the Square. Minutes later, a commotion broke out where Schoeman Street led into the Square. A large body of troops, obscuring the closed carriage in their midst, made slow progress through the crowd, and came to a halt at the steps. The troops formed up in double rows, their backs to the carriage, rifles unslung. An officer opened the door. Stefanie stepped out, ignoring his offered hand. Dressed in a long-sleeved navy dress with a high neck and white buttons down the front, her hair done up in a plait and twisted around her head, she looked very much a Boer girl, very different from the former society lady.

A roar erupted from the crowd. She raised her hand in acknowledgement. The women's voices rose in song again. It was an eerie sound. The national anthem, the *Volkslied*. Peter had heard it before, the day President Kruger had seen his heroes off to war. And there, standing so bravely was one of those heroes. His throat and eyes hurt, but his gaze did not waver from her until she had ascended the stairs, disappearing from view.

SIX TROOPERS escorted Stefanie into the courtroom, to a large desk set at right angles to a raised dais and facing the witness stand. The court officials entered, and a panel of five judges took their places on the dais. A handful of newspaper reporters sat on the front benches.

She sat with her hands on her lap, her chin lifted, her eyes taking in the wood-panelled room, the high ceiling. Here in this room, Martin had conducted many successful cases. She felt her brother's powerful presence and tried to reach him in her mind.

Her eyes travelled to the officers on the dais. These judges would oblige her by revealing all the great deeds that Martin and she had achieved together. Her last ounce of courage she would save to protect Peter.

Colonel Hancock, the prosecutor, stood up and read out the charges. His voice was curt. 'Stefanie Warren, you are hereby accused of treason against His Majesty's Government in the annexed state of the Transvaal, your infiltration into, and spying upon, His Majesty's Forces, as well as collaboration with the enemy forces. How do you plead?'

'I proudly acknowledge my attempt to help my brother, General de Winter, and my *Volk*. However, I didn't need your soldiers' help to accomplish what I did.'

'Mrs Warren, that will do!' the officer seated in the middle of the panel, a thin-faced, distinguished-looking man with a straight moustache said. 'I am General Duncan. You will address me during the proceedings.' He nodded to the prosecutor. 'Carry on, Colonel.'

Colonel Hancock adjusted his spectacles. 'I present to the court letters written by General Martin de Winter – the brother of the accused – to generals Botha, De la Rey and Smuts, and one from De Wet. The charge is of sending information out of the country. A stamp, used to confirm that correspondence has been censored, disappeared from Major Fernfield's mail office on a day Mrs Warren took tea with him there. General Smuts mentions in this letter, and I quote, "Johannesburg is a safe place from which to reach Den Haag" unquote. I call Major Edwin Fernfield as witness.'

Fernfield, looking pained, was sworn in.

Before Colonel Hancock resumed, General Duncan asked, 'Mrs Warren, did you take the stamp? Acknowledgement will save us time.'

'Yes, it enabled me to mail letters to Den Haag. I informed the world of the situation in the concentration camps – the real situation. I passed on letters from Boer leaders to President Kruger in Holland. He needs the comfort of knowing the truth, that his people have not given up the struggle.'

Colonel Hancock turned to Fernfield, asking him questions about Stefanie's behaviour at social functions. 'Has Mrs Warren at any time attempted to enlist your help in this matter?'

'No, never, sir.'

'Describe your relationship to the accused.'

'We are both pianists, sir, we mixed socially only.'

'Thank you, Major. You may step down.'

Hancock turned to the second charge, that of supplying the commandos with information regarding the movements of troops. 'In a case last month against a Boer infiltrator, it was revealed that General Botha had been warned well in advance, in January last year and again in May, of the drive against him, and had been given the strengths and routes of the units involved. This information was known to only a few staff officers.'

Captain Bartlett was called to the witness stand. He testified that, ever since her visits to Melrose House began, the commandos had been aware of the movements of the approaching forces.

'On the nineteenth of January 1901, Mrs Warren was at Melrose House entertaining the staff. General Kitchener ordered me to watch her closely. I could not find any indication of suspicious behaviour then or during her visits thereafter, but, over the months, vital information repeatedly leaked out. In many of General de Winter's letters, he refers to the tapping of telephone lines.'

General Duncan raised his eyebrows at her, demanding an answer.

She nodded. 'Two specific telephone lines leading from Melrose House were tapped frequently by my younger brothers.'

There was a buzz at this acknowledgement and it took some time before order was restored. Hancock questioned Bartlett about her supposed attempts at infiltration, but he had no information on the matter.

The next charge dealt with the removal from Government House of secret information pertaining to train destinations and cargoes. A clerk testified that a Boer colleague, Dolf Meyer, who had signed the oath of allegiance to the King, had disappeared on the day of Stefanie's arrest. Two more witnesses were brought in to establish her involvement.

She sat quietly, wondering when Peter would be called to the witness stand. It came about with a charge that she did not connect with Peter at all.

'A number of letters clearly indicate that Mrs Warren was involved in the blowing up of ammunition dumps and the destruction of telephone communications.' Hancock read out a long list of such incidents. 'In this letter, written by General de la Rey, he says, and I quote, "We prevented them getting there on time, allowing De Wet to move his laager further south," unquote. The railway was blown up, thus preventing Colonel Powell's force from attacking General de Wet when he was encircled at Dewetsdorp.' He picked up another letter from the desk. 'I quote from a letter by General de Winter: "Spot on! Fireworks, and it was not even Guy Fawkes."'

'Blowing up trains needs dynamite. Cutting telegraph wire is dangerous business,' General Duncan frowned. 'The next witness, Colonel Hancock.'

'Captain Peter Christopher Radford.'

Stefanie felt a tiny movement under the corsets she had pulled in tightly to hide her pregnancy. She swallowed hard. From deep in her heart, courage returned in strong waves.

IN A STRAINED VOICE, Peter answered the questions put to him. They commenced with her meeting with McFee at Church Square.

'Captain Radford,' Hancock said. 'In your statement, you say that the day you saw Mrs Warren and a corporal in conversation on Church Square coincided with the destruction of an ammunition depot, and of a troop train that was set alight in Pretoria station. You saw the same man on a later date. Could you tell the court where this was?'

'At the Renoster River, twenty-five miles west of Rustenburg.'

'Under what circumstances, Captain?' Hancock asked.

'Captain Henderson was wounded. The Boers brought him into our camp. This man was with them.'

Hancock nodded. 'Did Mrs Warren at any stage attempt to pry information from you?'

'No, sir.'

'Captain Radford, are you quite sure about that? You were frequently seen with her at social occasions.'

'Yes, sir, she did not.'

Hancock consulted his files and frowned. 'On the same afternoon that you saw Mrs Warren with this Irish corporal on Church Square, a note was delivered to you at your quarters. In his statement, the trooper on duty that day testified that an Irishman, a corporal, delivered it. Was it the same corporal?'

'Whether it was the same man, I do not know, sir,' Peter said curtly.

'You specifically wanted a description of the man. The trooper testified to this. Why was that, Captain Radford?'

Peter desperately tried to formulate an answer. 'When I saw them, the corporal and Mrs Warren, she gave him a note.'

'And the note delivered to you? Was it the note from Mrs Warren?' Duncan prodded. 'Need I remind you that you are under oath, sir?'

'Yes, the note was from Mrs Warren.'

'What was the note about?'

A murmur went through the court. For the first time Stefanie looked at Peter. The enormity of what he had to reveal struck him forcefully. Not only was he sending her to her death but he was also destroying her reputation. His hands shook, and sweat broke out over his body. *No, I shall not do that. If she has to die, the least I can do is to ensure that her honour is intact.* He held her gaze, trying to convey a plea for forgiveness, remorse and, above all, his love, infallible and unchanged.

'Captain Radford, answer the question, sir,' General Duncan ordered.

Peter tore his eyes from Stefanie, clasping his hands behind his back. 'It was of a personal nature, sir, and not relevant to these proceedings.'

'It is most relevant, Captain Radford; Mrs Warren stands accused of espionage,' Duncan said, but no reply came from Peter. 'You are under oath, sir! I shall have you arrested for contempt of court and for suspicion of collaboration. Answer the question! What was the note about?'

Then Stefanie spoke up in the silence that reigned in the court. 'I requested him to meet me in Meyers Park that evening.'

'A meeting?' General Duncan's eyebrows rose. 'To what purpose, Mrs Warren?'

'As Captain Radford said, a personal matter. But it is irrelevant; he didn't comply with my request. He did not meet me *at Meyers Park* that night.'

Peter heard the veiled warning in her words. He needed to concentrate on her words, find where she was leading. *I went to your room and asked you to marry me, but yes, not Meyers Park. I did not go to Meyers Park.* He turned his attention back to Hancock, but the next question needed a truth that he did not want to convey.

'What exactly was your relationship with Mrs Warren, Captain Radford? A request to meet in the middle of night? Lovers?'

Peter caught Stefanie's barely discernible nod, but still he hesitated, trying to formulate an answer that would not dishonour her.

'Captain Radford? What is your answer?' General Duncan persisted.

'There's nothing dishonourable about our relationship,' Peter said.

'The late Paul Warren was not her natural husband. She has consented to become my wife once the war is over.'

Peter saw how the newspapermen scribbled furiously. The news would reach England by the morning and he was thankful. His father would be proud of him; he had stuck to the truth, testified in public his love for the woman he had condemned.

'In time of war, Captain Radford?' General Duncan asked, his expression disbelieving. 'You asked the sister of an enemy general to marry you, sir?'

'I met her under different circumstances, sir, eight years ago in Pretoria and again two years ago in Cape Town. The war intervened.'

A chuckle rippled through the rows of newspapermen.

'Sir, you did not meet Mrs Warren at Meyers Park that specific night. Why was that, Captain? Were you suspicious, perhaps?' Hancock demanded. 'Knowing Mrs Warren for so many years, and knowing her so well, did it not cross your mind that her sympathies were with her own people?'

'Yes, sir, naturally, it did. Exactly why I did not comply with her request to meet in Meyers Park. I thought it wise to wait for the war to end before continuing our meetings.'

'Colonel Hancock, sir,' Stefanie spoke up, 'could you ask Captain Radford, *prior* to receiving the note,' she looked fixedly at Peter, 'when last he met with me?'

'Could we have an answer, sir?' Colonel Hancock said when Peter did not reply.

Peter searched his mind, desperate to give the right answer. He thought about Stefanie's question and the reason behind it. 'Not since early March, sir,' he said, when he had thought it over.

'Almost a year ago.' General Duncan consulted his notes. 'And barely two months since arriving in Pretoria.' He looked at Stefanie long and hard. 'Mrs Warren, you agreed to marry Captain Radford, yet you betrayed his trust by spying. Is that what you had in mind?'

'I did my duty to my country, as he did his by reporting me when he discovered the truth,' she said in an unsteady voice. 'That's why we are all here today.'

Sighs of sympathy and excited conversations came from the reporters. *That will also reach England*, Peter thought; his family would get the full story.

RELIEF FLOODED through Stefanie as she watched Peter leave the court. She had succeeded; he was free. Her chin slumped to her chest, concealing the tears from Hancock and the judges. Weariness engulfed her and she prayed for the proceedings to be done.

'Are we through, Colonel Hancock?' She heard General Duncan ask.

'A last incident, sir. Boers converted to our cause have been executed in their efforts to bring their leaders to us. Information concerning the orders of these National Scouts were stolen and passed on. General de Winter indicated in this letter, and I quote, "Don't mess with that devil, Stef, even you are no match for him," unquote. He was referring to the late Mr Warren.'

'Mrs Warren,' Hancock said, 'I have here an affidavit from Mr Warren's secretary stating that a document concerning General de Winter disappeared from Mr Warren's rooms on the day of his demise. I believe you were with him when the bees attacked him. Most unfortunate. The Boer who was to lead us to General de Winter was executed last week. Did you take this document?'

The guilt of her role in Buks's death mixed with relief at Martin's escape. She met Hancock's gaze. 'Yes, the bees …' she took a deep breath, willingly the terrifying memory of that day away. 'I gave it to my Irish friend minutes before my arrest. I saved my brother's life, I now hear, and caused a dear friend's death.'

Hancock brought a photograph to Stefanie. 'This was found with your letters. Would you identify the persons for the court's benefit?' She refused to look at it, keeping her eyes on her hands folded on her lap. 'Very well, this man in the centre is General de Winter.' He held out the photograph to the officers on the dais. 'The inscription on the back reads "June 1901. Home of the Fireflies. We miss you dearly." Mrs Warren, would you please tell the court where that is?'

'Is there any point to this, Colonel Hancock?' General Duncan asked.

'Yes, it might lead us to General de Winter, sir.'

'Answer the question, Mrs Warren,' General Duncan demanded. 'Where is this place?'

Stefanie stood up, blood rising to her face. 'Do you *honestly* expect me to betray my brother?' Her voice was hoarse, filled with disgust. 'Not under any oath, not on pain of death!'

A minute ticked by, during which the reporters scribbled and the panel conferred in muted voices. General Duncan nodded to Hancock. He delivered his final address, pointing out that she had admitted all the charges against her.

'Do you have anything else to say, Mrs Warren?' Duncan asked.

'Yes, I want it to be known that I pressured my brother, General de Winter, into accepting my help. He would never have done so otherwise.'

The case was declared closed and a recess announced. The panel left the room. The restless noise of the crowd outside pushed its way in through the windows. Only five minutes later the panel reappeared and motioned Stefanie to rise.

'This court finds you guilty on the charge of espionage. The court sentences you to death by firing squad. The sentence will be carried out on Friday ... tomorrow, it seems.'

The soldiers came to escort her away. She walked with her head high, looking straight ahead. Outside a deafening roar hailed her. Her name was shouted. A few shots cracked and echoed on. There was a moment's silence before the women's voices rose in song once more.

———◆———

THE SUN WAS ALREADY LOW when James arrived at Pretoria gaol. He gave the written permission, hastily obtained from General Duncan, to the prison officer and handed over his pistol as requested.

Fear and anger twisted inside him – fear that he was going to fail Peter and Stefanie, and anger at his helplessness in emotional crisis. Peter was confined to his quarters, awaiting a disciplinary hearing. He had asked him to go to Stefanie without delay and kiss her goodbye in his stead. *But I can't do it, knowing she's going to die!* His head pounded furiously, the need for a drink overpowering.

She sat on the iron cot, her arms supported on her knees, her fingertips pressed together, staring into the flame of the candle on the little table in front of her. He stood in the door, uncertain of what to do or say. He leaned against the wall, pushing his hands into his pockets.

'Jamie, are you brave enough for this?' she asked. 'I'm not, I hate being brave.'

He forced himself to meet her eyes. They shone with tears in the candle-light. 'Of course I'm brave, Stef.' His voice faltered, but he tried to smile.

She pulled the shawl close around her, looking at him steadily. 'Oh Jamie, what a perfect mess I've landed myself in. But I'm not scared, not really. Tante Koba always says "an eye for an eye". And how true it is. I deserve to die. I killed my husband. I killed Paul Warren. I had to. He left me no choice.'

The bees killed him, he wanted to say, but the truth showed clearly in her eyes.

'Peter came to me at the Heights Hotel. He was asleep when Paul walked in. The next day ... I put the bees in a jar and took them to Paul's room. I knew one sting could kill him. But then, I ... I couldn't ... but he opened my bag ... and the bees ...'

'Dear God,' James said, sympathy raw in his voice as the terrible event presented itself in his mind. 'It was a most dreadful tragedy. You can't kill. Not you, Stefanie.'

She searched his face, a desperate trust in her eyes. 'Do you really think so?'

'Yes, yes! I know that beyond doubt.'

'Thank you, Jamie.' She looked into the flame of the candle. 'Please tell Peter why I had to go to Paul's room.'

'No! He has suffered enough. It'll destroy him.'

'Reporting me destroyed him, James. Knowing what really happened might give him a little comfort. That's why I told you. I wouldn't have burdened you with something so horrible otherwise, Jamie.'

The guard reminded James that his time was up. He nodded and straightened up. 'Is there anything that you want me to do for you?' he asked to delay the final moment.

'I want to see Tante Koba. Will she come?'

'I will fetch her.' He held his arms out to her. 'Peter asked me to say goodbye. He will always love you, he says.'

She sat for a while longer, pressing her fingers to her mouth. Then she rose, her hands nervously clutching at her shawl. 'We are not runaways, are we, Jamie?' she said, her smile betraying the desolation in her eyes.

He pulled her into his arms.

ALL WAS IN DARKNESS at Koba's house. James tied his horse to the gate and made his way onto the stoep. The front door stood ajar, as if Koba was waiting for him. A candle flickered feebly in the sitting room. Koba was in her rocking chair, Victoria by her side, holding her hand. In her other hand, Koba had a letter. When she saw him, she placed it in her apron pocket.

'Thank God you've come.' Victoria stood up. 'I cannot help here, it's too tragic. I think it's best if I leave you with her.'

James nodded. Victoria touched Koba's cheek and felt her way down the dark passage. He placed his helmet on the floor, and took the chair Victoria had vacated. 'Have you been to the square, Tante Koba?'

'Yes, *hartjie*. I saw them taking Stefanie away. They sang for her so beautifully.'

He reached across and took her hand. 'I want to take you to Stefanie.' The rocking chair moved faster, Koba's eyes remained fixed on her hands, a concentrated frown on her face. The candle flickered out. James struck a match and went to the kitchen to find a lamp. When he returned, Koba was fiddling in her pocket again.

'Has General Kitchener been told?' she asked.

He placed the lamp on the table. 'He must sign the sentence, Tante Koba.'

The rocking chair stopped abruptly. She squinted at the clock on the mantelpiece. 'What time is it?'

'Past eight, Tante Koba.'

'James, go hitch Bles.' She came to her feet and went to her bedroom.

He went to the stables, hitched the horse to the cart and brought it round to the front. While waiting for her, he stood by the piano, looking at the framed pictures on the wall, but the faces stared blankly back at him. All except Stefanie's. He put his fingers to his lips; their kiss was still alive. He would always feel it, remember it with the deepest sorrow and love.

When Koba reappeared, she had on her black Sunday dress and a black hat. He picked up his helmet. 'You can't come where I'm going, *hartjie*,' she said as if talking to a child. 'Stay here and wait for me. They won't shoot Stefanie. Tante Koba will fix this.'

'Tante Koba, this is something not even you can fix. Come, I promised Stefanie—' She brushed past him to the door. 'Where are you going, Tante Koba?'

'To that nice colonel of yours. I'll be careful with my words. He'll speak to Kitchener on my behalf.' She was on the cart and away before he could protest.

He sank down onto the sofa, burying his face in his hands. *We are not runaways, Jamie.* Stefanie's words came back to him forcefully. There was something he needed to do. It could not wait much longer.

Feeling his way down the dark passage, he went to the bedroom, knocked softly and pushed the door open. Victoria was in bed and looked at him questioningly. 'James? Shall I get you some coffee? Something to eat?'

'No, I'm fine ... fine.' He looked at her copper hair tumbling down her shoulders, her green eyes filled with anguish. He leaned his shoulder against the doorframe and stood quietly, ordering his thoughts. 'I can't promise you a future. There's a court martial hanging over my head. It's best you stay ignorant of it. But should I get through this somehow, will you come to India with me?' He saw joy welling up in her eyes, giving him the courage to push on. 'I cannot deal with this now. I'm too vulnerable, too fragile. I'll be back, but not, *please*, not before the war ends and all else is done. I promise.'

'You have forgiven me.'

'Yes. I did not want to love you ... but I do. And should a future be granted, I want to forget that our marriage is just an arrangement. I want you to be my wife, Vicky.'

'I am your wife, James,' she smiled at him.

He returned her smile, left and closed the door behind him.

———————

KOBA PARKED HER CART at the regiment's headquarters, collected herself and strode purposefully to the house. On the veranda she found Murray Shaw and William Moore, with Peter between them, sitting in their shirtsleeves, a decanter on the floor beside them.

'I want to see your colonel.' She took Shaw by his arm. 'Take me to him. And you, young man, keep Peter here,' she said to Moore. 'The storm is almost spent.'

They looked at the clear moonlit night and back at her, but she paid them no heed. Shaw took her to an outbuilding, once the dairy and now Butcher's office.

Butcher ushered her inside. 'Shall we have a small sherry?'

'A large one, my dear man. It's needed.' She fanned herself with her hat before placing it on his desk. While he was getting the sherry, she checked the windows and pulled the curtains before she motioned him to take a seat next to her. 'Now, my dear Colonel, what's the name of Peter's father?'

'Mrs Van Wyk,' he said kindly and handed her a glass. 'I'm aware of Peter's relationship with your niece, but, please believe me, there's nothing that his father—'

'Is he a lord?' She gulped from her glass.

'Well, he's an Earl—'

'And is the Earl a friend of your new King?'

'I suppose they are acquainted …'

She patted his knee, bringing a startled look to his face. 'I want your word that what I'm going to say will not be mentioned other than to save Stefanie.'

'You have my word, Mrs van Wyk.' He nodded, sipping his sherry.

'If they shoot her on Friday, they will also kill the grandchild of the Earl, Peter's father.' She wagged her finger at him. 'Your King will not like it.'

Butcher spluttered. 'I beg your pardon?'

'My dear man, Stefanie couldn't tell Peter. He's a fearless young man. Remember how he charged straight into the bullets to save the guns? If he'd known about his child, he would've thrown all caution to the moon and gone to be with Stefanie. You see, when she found herself with child, she gave up spying, but that horrible man Warren …'

Butcher drained his glass, Koba followed suit. 'Mrs van Wyk, are you telling me that your niece is with child?'

'Six months ago, the night before you and your boys left for Rustenburg, Peter was in my house. It's the only night he has been there. The next morning, I made him coffee—'

'Mrs van Wyk, this has to be reported, at once. To execute a pregnant woman—', he rose, but Koba pulled him back.

'Wait, my dear man! I swore on the Bible that I would not tell a soul. God will forgive me, but dear Stefanie will not. What will happen to Peter should this get out? He'll be put before the wall and shot. She would rather die and take the little one with her. And the child is innocent; it did not ask for this calamity. And poor Peter, his crime is that he loves her, a Boer woman.'

'Yes, what utter confusion, I dare say—'

Koba carried on breathlessly. 'Mr Warren passed away only two weeks ago. But we cannot put it at his door.' She leaned closer, whispering confidentially, 'Peter was her first and only man. Mr Warren didn't bed women, preferred men! People know; they talk about it in Cape Town, in Johannesburg. James, Peter and even General Kitchener.'

'Well, I'd better see General Kitchener and explain this to him. After all that was said in court today ... it might take some time. Allow me to escort you home. I'll bring you news in due course.'

'No, dear man, I'll wait here. Take my cart. It's there under the tree.' She reached for her handkerchief. 'The horse is called Bles. Say her name and she will move. And please pour me a little more of that sweet wine of yours.'

An hour later, Colonel Butcher returned. His footsteps were hurried and she heard him calling an order to the officers on the stoep. The door burst open. By the look on his face, she knew that she'd succeeded in saving Stefanie's life. He put his arm around her shoulders. 'Her sentence has been commuted, Mrs van Wyk. She'll be moved to another destination tomorrow and her condition kept secret. The newspapers will say that General Kitchener has reduced the sentence to imprisonment in the interest of ending the war.'

She nodded, wiping her tears with the handkerchief she had clutched in her hand while Butcher had been away. 'I knew that General Kitchener has a heart somewhere behind those cold eyes and wild moustaches. Now, my dear man, what about Peter? Will he be told about his child?' She hoisted herself up, stiff from the long wait.

'It's my duty to inform him.' He helped her to her feet, picking up her hat. 'Mrs van Wyk, it's out of our hands now.'

'I must tell James about dear Karel's death, but not tonight. It was a bloody day, Colonel.'

'Karel? The young De Winter?' he asked and she caught the dismay in his voice.

'Yes, Karel and his beloved horse, both taken one fateful night.' She told him about the letter Anita had sent with a *predikant*. 'It's in my apron pocket. It arrived this day, of all days, and so soon after the court condemned Stefanie.'

'A bloody day indeed, Mrs van Wyk.'

'My hat, dear Colonel.' She held out her hand for the hat. 'Be a father to Peter; tell him to honour Stefanie's example of sacrifice. He should not be thoughtless now. The war is almost done.'

When she drove off, she heard him call to the men on the veranda. She spurred Bles on in her urgency to get to James, to set him free of the burden that had forced him to his knees over the past year. Although he had tried to hide his eyes earlier, she had seen them aching for forgiveness and comfort. Yes, comfort.

SHEER EXHAUSTION had overtaken James. He drifted in and out of sleep on the sofa. When Koba came bursting into the sitting room, he roused himself. He had never seen her so drained and dishevelled. Her hat was askew, her chest heaving, her white handkerchief protruding from the front of her dress.

'*Hartjie* …' She tossed the hat onto a chair, motioned to him to move up a little. She sank down beside him and leaned back into the sofa. 'Tante Koba is in need of a little comfort, *hartjie*. Can you give me some? Come, come closer, put your head here on my shoulder … just here.' She patted the hollow of her shoulder just above her generous breast. 'Just here.'

He brought his face to her shoulder and felt her strong arm going around his back, her cheek coming to rest against his hair. He breathed in the smell of the summer of 1886 – freshly baked bread, spices, home remedies and rosewater. Through the warmth of her breast he felt her heart beating. The solace he longed for overwhelmed him.

'Tante Koba has fixed it, *hartjie*,' she whispered.

Adrift

A FEW LEAVES on the weeping willow at the vlei had already turned yellow, forming a colourful pattern as the branches swept in the gentle movement of the wind. The golden weavers hung from their woven nests, protesting shrilly at the presence of the man under the tree. Brown ducks glided on the water and a heron stood a distance away, catching frogs in quick movements of its long neck.

Rudolf lived in a wilderness of his own, far beyond the war. Peace would not come to him again. Beauty had died with Legend. Love was an emotion buried with Karel.

Here, under the willow, he had experienced precious times with Annecke. He had listened to Karel, who wanted him to be happy, to love. He and Karel had suffered to the depths of their souls when they were separated for four months. But Annecke had been waiting for him. *What God has joined together let no man put asunder, Koba had said so many years ago.* Their little boy, his son, had paid the highest price. Then Legend died. And Karel too.

He had stumbled upon Karel and Legend in the dark. But only when the morning light found its way through the leaves of the thorn trees had he died. Not with a shudder, but with a gentle sigh. He had looked into Karel's eyes and saw the moment.

But Karel did not leave him. Their bond had transported him into a place where he would find him again, where Karel would be waiting so that they should grow old together. He had closed his eyes and felt how he was lifted away from this life, from the war, from Annecke, from all else that could separate them again. There was no death. They were still together.

And now he was waiting for mercy. Everything comes full circle, to that circle where God is, where Karel was waiting for him. God would grant him death. He would ride with Karel again over the vast plains to the north. Karel had just ridden ahead of him.

A nightjar's call broke into his faraway world. Nightjars did not call during the day. McFee was coming for him. He took the sliver of mirror he'd found in the ruins of Wintersrust from his pocket and, looking into his twin's eyes, told him that he would soon be with him.

———————

JAMES BROUGHT HIS HORSE to a halt when yet another ruined farmstead came into view. Looking at the pathetic remains, his stomach churned with the memories of the day he had burned Wintersrust and Soetvlei. But the feeling lasted only for a moment. He had come to accept that the war was to blame. And the war was practically over. The drive moving steadily from the south against De la Rey and De Winter would bring the commandos to their knees.

No, not to their knees, he thought, *they are there already.* General Louis Botha's commandos in the east had been scattered by a similar drive. Now, unable to regroup, they were ineffective as a fighting force. He'd spoken to a few Boer prisoners before leaving Pretoria, who'd admitted openly that the war was a hopeless cause. In the Free State, the exhausted commandos of General de Wet could attack only when in desperate need of ammunition. But here in the northwest, the war was not done yet.

The 2nd Hussars were accompanying a convoy to Rustenburg, dropping supplies at the blockhouses – corrugated-iron structures standing forlornly in the semi-desert countryside, the telegraph line their only connection with the outside world. It was a tedious job. They had not sighted a commando yet, only lone riders in the distance – scouts, they reckoned.

James watched as the lumbering convoy passed. Although it was well into April, the days were still hot. Sweat gathered on his forehead and his helmet felt too tight, as did his high collar. He screwed up his eyes against the glare reflecting off the corrugated-iron sheets piled on some wagons.

Sergeant Adams rode up and saluted. 'Colonel Butcher says we are to halt for the night, sir. There's water in the well behind the house ... the place, sir.'

'The ruins, Sergeant. Find a spot away from these beasts. Get fires going and bring the furniture,' he ordered as he had done every night for the past weeks.

They had found a decent table and chairs at a deserted farmhouse. Every night, the officers watched the sunset and, later, the brilliant expanse of stars, while they dined informally at the table. They talked about the battles they had fought and, with the end of the war in sight, speculated about future postings. Colonel Butcher remarked how similar the countryside was to India – the stunted trees, dusty scrubland, scarcity of water and the wide spaces.

James lived in a curious half-world, not knowing what fate had in store for him, but he persuaded himself that he could face the day, when it came, with dignity, as Stefanie had done. Her courage, Peter's ability to face up to and deal with emotional crisis, and Koba's love had taught him to accept his plight. But he dared not hope. It had taken him a long time to forgive Victoria, but there was the possibility that he could face a court martial. The allegations George Hunter had made against him had not been forgotten, though finding proof was taking time.

Peter, cantering up, forced his thoughts back to the present. His tunic was unbuttoned, his Sam Browne hanging loosely. He had informed Colonel Butcher of his intention to resign his commission when the war ended, and now went about his duties mechanically, praying for that day to come. He had written to his family about Stefanie's plight and the child she was expecting, but his father could do very little until the war ended.

'Tonight we shall have one last shindig in the colonel's peaceful India.' Peter dismounted and called for a trooper to take their horses to be watered.

James cast him a weary glance and removed his gloves. 'Why our last, Radford?'

'Come, Henderson! Stretch the old legs a bit and you'll see. There's a view to behold.' He pointed to where the other officers were standing on a rise a few hundred feet from them. 'We're done with riding convoy, and over there is the reason why.'

They joined the other officers. In the far distance a dust cloud, stretching for miles, turned the westering sun into a ball of flame.

'General Hamilton's forces moving in,' Butcher said. 'Fifteen thousand strong. Short of cavalry, his latest grumble. We will oblige him soon, gentlemen.'

———

STRANGE HOW THE FLOWERS were more abundant now that they were not being tended, Annecke mused as she stood in the graveyard at Wintersrust. She'd gathered them that morning from the neglected garden and had placed them on two graves.

So many people from her little world had died, but they were at peace now. Her brother, her mother and father, her baby, Aunt Mary and Uncle Marthinus, all buried far away. But Karel was here. And the kind Englishman, Martin's friend who had touched her boy's hair. He was in the nearest corner of the graveyard. She looked at the metal cross that had been sent from Pretoria. It was so rusted, she could not read his name. She decided on the red carnations for his grave. The English liked red, Charles had said. And for Karel, wildflowers. He would not like fancy flowers.

Rudi was so hard, like Karel had been, and was constantly searching her Bible, muttering, learning verses off by heart. He did not tease her any more, whisper love words in her ear or kiss her. At night he cried like a baby, whispering Karel's name as if he was searching for him. Charles said that it would take a long time before he would accept Karel's death; they had to be patient.

She sighed, picking up her basket. It was a long way back to the cave and there were still the eggs and vegetables to gather, if there were any left. The English might have taken the eggs but they would not easily have found the vegetables. Anita had planted the seeds in the rich soil behind the empty cattle kraal. The English often rode through, bent on destroying Martin's and Oom Koos's commandos. Soon the whole British Army would be upon them. A large force, Charles had said, was moving up from the south, sweeping the earth like a giant broom. *All the King's horses and all the King's men*, Charles had sung to his baby.

She wondered if Charles had left the cave by now to rejoin the commando. It was hard for him to leave now that Anita had had the baby. Mary, a beautiful girl. Watching Anita suckling her brought back memories of her little boy. The aching emptiness his death had left made her think of Stefanie's baby, which would be born in jail. A fragile hope settled in her heart that she might have the baby to care for.

Stefanie was not well, the Irishman had said. He had been to the prison to see if it was possible to get her out. He had seen her, obviously with child, exercising in the courtyard. She had appeared so desolate, like a lost soul. Charles had promised that he would write to the authorities about the baby. Martin could not help. Since Karel's death he had not visited the cave. He was a general, and winning the war was all that mattered to him.

———◆———

NOT WINNING THE WAR, but keeping it going, giving the fighting generals and commander-in-chief time to make favourable terms with the British, a settlement that would not humiliate the *Volk* after almost three years of fighting. These were uppermost in Martin's mind as he made his way to where he had ordered his scattered commandos to gather. For the past week he had sat at the telegraph office at Cypherfontein, keeping contact with General de la Rey, who was at Vereeniging.

The commandos were unbeaten in battle, but the overwhelming numbers of their opponents and the desperate need for food were wearing them down. And now, embittered by the humiliations they had suffered, the British were intent on bringing a swift but bloody end to the war. They moved in large numbers, their convoys well guarded. The commandos attacked at many points simultaneously, like a pack of wild dogs, playing with their prey, tearing chunks out of it as they ran.

For months now, Martin had driven his men hard, splitting them up, bringing them together again, doing what circumstances demanded of him. But deep inside, he had lost all sense of time and order, of command. He only wanted to go on, to keep going until it was finished. He knew he was just riding the tide of events. He had many sleepless nights, sitting alone by a small fire a little way from his men, adrift in black despair.

He had spoken to General de la Rey before he had left for the preliminary peace talks. Oom Koos was weather-beaten now, his beard more salt than pepper, his face lined, but his deep-set eyes were filled with determination to serve the *Volk* to the end, to secure an honourable peace.

'Martin, there's a time for war and a time for peace,' De la Rey had said in parting. 'And that time, son, is upon us now – a time to heal, to make peace.'

And a time to weep, Martin thought now. The last cable from De la Rey had told him that peace would be secured but it was taking time; he had to prepare his men for the inevitable – surrender and the downfall of their republic. It was a heartbreaking task, shattering the little hope they clung to. Until then, they had to survive, to endure. They were in acute need of food, medical supplies and ammunition. But to attack, to risk the lives of his men, the survivors, when peace was in sight?

Another harsh reality forced its way into his thoughts. There was also a time to leave hate behind. To make peace with the darkness in his soul. A time to forgive. When the war was over, he would see James again. James, his cousin, not the enemy officer who had been ordered to destroy his home, his country. It would be hard, the hardest time. Deep in a forgotten corner of his heart, he would search for forgiveness and offer it to his cousin. And to his cousin's wife. He tried to imagine Victoria, but only a long-forgotten ache passed through his heart. The colour of her hair was all that came to him in faded fragments of another life.

THE FIRES WERE LIT, the pickets at their posts, when Martin rode into camp. As he walked to where Charles and the Viljoen brothers were sitting around a fire, he looked at his men. They doffed their hats and carried on with their tasks, stirring the porridge, carving biltong into it, brewing roots for coffee.

'The winter is almost with us again and we're dangerously low on ammunition,' Jan threw a stick onto the fire. 'The forces chasing us don't give us the opportunity to loot their wagons.'

'We need vegetables and salt,' Charles said, 'but where to find them? Some men have scurvy, their gums are bleeding. I'm at my wits' end.'

'Yes, yes, there are bitter times ahead,' Frans Viljoen said. 'This winter will be longer, colder, and we'll be hungrier than during the previous ones. And lonelier. When last did we get dispatches through to the Free State and to Botha? Yes, hard times.'

'Has General Jansen reached us?' Martin asked.

'Yes, he rode in earlier,' Jan said. 'Commandant Kemp and his commando are also with us, as you ordered. How did the *krygsraad* go?'

Martin ignored Jan's question. 'Are the scouts in?'

The Viljoens exchanged glances and reached for their pipes. 'The Irishman was here earlier.' Jan gave a shrill whistle. A young boy came over and was sent to find McFee.

Martin took a bottle of water and washed his face and hands. 'News, Patrick?' he asked when McFee walked up. 'Are we safe for the night?'

'Yes, General, for the night. North, past Rustenburg, is a force of seven thousand chasing General de la Rey's main force. To the south is an escape route, a narrow corridor, if we slip through, go around—'

'And the west?'

'Won't be easy, General. They've doubled their forces there. They don't want to be lured into the wastelands again. Nine thousand stretched over sixty miles, ready to move out as soon as they spot us. Kitchener's brother himself is the commander. There is a small force in the south on the farm Rooiwal. We can slip past them.'

'How many, Patrick?'

'Eight hundred infantry at the most, a few mounted and three field guns, but they might be hiding more somewhere. General, they are encamped for the night. Should we move early, skirt them before the first bugle—'

Martin nodded. 'We'll go south to Rooiwal. Come for orders later.' McFee was about to take his leave, but Martin called him back. 'How's Rudolf? I haven't seen him for weeks now.'

McFee frowned. 'He's ... not well, not well at all. He does not carry a rifle. Not to worry, General, I keep a close watch on him.'

'Patrick, you scout ahead tomorrow. Bring my brother here. The doctor can keep an eye on him.' Martin dismissed McFee, poured a mug of coffee, and took a place opposite Jan Viljoen. 'There was no *krygsraad*. I sat at Cypherfontein, keeping telegraph contact with Oom Koos. He is at Vereeniging. Louis Botha is also there.'

'Kitchener invited them to talk again?' Jan asked warily.

'Not this time, Jan. General Botha did the inviting. General de Wet is also there on behalf of President Steyn and the Free State government. And that makes all the difference: De Wet's presence. He refused to talk to the English for three years.'

'He's there because he has no choice, I suppose,' Charles said.

'All generals have been ordered to speak to our commandos. They have to say how they feel about negotiations, about ending the war.'

'And if we don't oblige?' Jan asked.

'The war will go on,' Charles said glumly.

They sat in silence. Men came to the fire, most wanting to see Martin or Jan, but Frans waved them away.

'Cousin, if we carry on, there will be nothing and no one left to fight for,' Charles said. 'I think we owe it to the *Volk* to call an end to the war. The prisoners on the islands must come home. This country was built up from nothing. We can do it again.'

'Thank you, Charles,' Martin nodded, staring into the fire. 'What do you say, Jan?'

He scratched his beard, chewed on the stem of his pipe, poked in the fire with a stick. 'If I, Jan Viljoen … if you say we fight on, we fight on. If you ask me to lay down my Mauser, I'll go back to my farm, build up my herds, teach my sons to ride and shoot and carry on with the fight some other year.'

A burgher approached and announced that the officers were assembled for the meeting, as ordered. The Viljoen brothers knocked their pipes against their boots and rose, but Martin remained, still staring into the fire. Jan placed his hand on his shoulder. 'Take your time, my good friend, find those wise words of yours. We'll wait.'

'Martin, it's over,' Charles said, deep sympathy in his voice. 'Accept defeat with the grace and dignity your opponents expect of you.'

'Charles, I'm not defeated. I thought about what Oom Koos said, about a time to make peace. That I can do, but surrender does not necessarily mean defeat. As Jan said, we will carry on with the fight some other year. I have to think about a new direction. I have to give hope for the future. I have to give them that, at least. Somewhere there have to be words meaningful enough to convey this to them.' He straightened his jacket, raked his fingers through his hair and stood up. He walked a few paces, and then half-turned back, staring into the darkness above the fires. 'Yes, the hardest time is now.'

THE EVENING BREEZE carried Martin's words, strong and persuasive as always. Charles found himself drawn to the wagon on which Martin stood surrounded by his commandos. Standing on the fringe, his eyes travelled over the weather-beaten faces reflected in the firelight. All they had fought for so bitterly for the past three years had been in vain, yet faith still shone in their eyes.

'Yes, we are a divided nation,' Martin was saying now, 'and a divided nation cannot govern itself. There's hate among us. Brother against brother, father against son. There are traitors in the *Volk, hensoppers*. They'll not be accepted back into our hearts. But we, the *bittereinders*, have stayed until the very end. We are the core of the new nation. We have been tested, weighed, and not been found wanting …'

Charles walked back to his ambulance. He'd seen enough despair and sorrow to last him a lifetime. He was weary of trekking day after day, and ridden with guilt for leaving so many wounded in the path of the enemy for want of supplies. Peace seemed so inviting, but the decision lay with the commandos.

Carefully folding his glasses into a handkerchief, he put them into his jacket pocket. They were the only pair he had left. He pulled his blanket over him. In the distance he heard the men cheering Martin. Once again they put their lives into his hands. He drifted off to sleep, thinking about his baby girl and wife living in a cave.

A touch on his shoulder roused him. Rudolf's face was close to his. Charles moved his blanket aside, threw more wood onto the fire. 'Coffee, Rudi? I still have a handful.'

'McFee said I ride with you tomorrow.' Rudolf sat down by the fire. 'McFee is the leader and I must do as he says.'

'Yes, Rudi, I don't think it's wise, you riding with the scouts any longer.' He busied himself with the coffee. 'Stay with me, Rudi. Wait with me for the end.'

'Thank you, Charles.' He sat for a while, staring blankly into the small flames of the fire. 'Is there a life hereafter?' he asked unexpectedly.

'A life hereafter?' Charles frowned and handed him a mug of coffee.

Rudolf raised his eyes to the starlit heavens. 'There has to be, but I don't know if it's a life like here on earth.'

'Heaven is a concept of something mysterious, Rudi.' He searched his mind for some words that would give comfort. 'It's like the cave, I suppose, a place of peace. Why, Rudi? You and Karel have always scorned these things.'

'I see Karel and Legend … I see them … riding across the veld with Lady beside them. The grass is green and tall, up to Legend's belly and the sky ... so clear ... and I see many horses following them. Could they be all those that died in the war?'

Around them the fires were dying out, the men curled up in their blanket rolls, a few talking restlessly.

'Rudi, how's Annecke? Have you been to the cave?'

'She's Martin's wife, Charles. She promised that in the presence of God. I told her so last week ...' his voice wavered. He swallowed hard. 'She was so sad when I told her, she cried, Charles.'

Charles looked at Rudolf; his face held a poignant sadness, his hands folded as if in prayer. He was so young, too young to die, and yet so utterly beaten.

He draped a blanket around Rudolf's shoulders and put a comforting arm around him. 'Rudi, yes, there's a place where Karel is waiting for you. But there time is of no importance. The waiting, whether it's for a year or a day or a lifetime ... it's all the same. Here we feel the separation, but we'll get through it somehow.' He pressed Rudolf's head to his shoulder.

Dawn into Darkness

THE SUN HESITANTLY PROBED the autumn mist blanketing the cave. Even the birdsong was restrained this morning, Annecke thought, where she sat outside on the rock slab. There was a chill in the air that had not been there the previous day. That's why the birds and the sun were unsure of themselves and that's why Anita's baby was crying, crying. It was cold in the cave.

A long winter lay waiting, the sun barely providing warmth before going to its home behind the sea in the far west. A weary, lonely journey, Koba had said, to make day after day after day. The moon at least had the stars for company and the souls of those who had been called away from earth. Yes, they only showed themselves at night; you could see them if you search long enough. But not during the day. The sun was God's fiery eye; the departed souls were free of His scrutiny; they had found rest and peace.

Peace? Was there really peace up there? The night sky, Koba also said, was the true heaven. The moon was God in a forgiving mood. That was why He only showed himself a few nights a month. The moon had not cast its beams through the roof of the cave. God's forgiveness had not reached her. Rudi was right; they had sinned and were now punished. He had shown her in the Bible. *Then when lust has conceived, it brings forth sin; and sin, when it is finished, brings forth death.*

'We lusted, Annecke. We sinned. Our child died for it, Karel and Legend died for it,' he had said. 'I don't want to sin again. You are Martin's wife, not mine.'

To love before marriage was a sin, but only a little sin if the wedding was planned, Koba said. To trespass one of God's commandments was an unforgivable sin. Adultery was the fancy word for it, and the punishment was severe. In biblical times she would have been stoned to death.

She looked at the sun; it had travelled a few inches. A long and weary journey ahead to the sea. She remembered the sea. When they had been in Cape Town for Stefanie's wedding, she and Koba watched the waves breaking on the clear white sand. It had frightened her then, the endless power and movement of the waves. The vlei was like the sea, only smaller and less powerful. On a windy day one could see small waves running into the reeds.

Her eyes shifted to the vlei. It was deep; the water was cold and muddy. She had not been near the vlei since her baby had almost drowned in it ... no ... not the baby ... he had not been born then; it was the rag doll.

She heard a baby cry, stood up, and made her way down the rock and past the waterfall. *Her baby is drowning, he is lying between the reeds, she must save him ... he is crying ... crying ...*

———

THE LAND WAS STILL CLOAKED in half-darkness when they crested a rise on the farm Rooiwal, thirty miles south of Rustenburg. Martin raised a restraining hand and the commandos came to a halt. A mile off was the British encampment, probably part of the main force that had hunted them ceaselessly for the past months. But there was much more. Martin raised his field glasses to his eyes. A hundred yards behind the encampment was a large convoy, strung out carelessly.

'They were not here at sunset,' McFee whispered. 'They arrived during the night. Some of the oxen are still at the yoke.'

Martin felt his men's eyes on him, imploring him to attack. The sight of the rows of wagons was tempting, the urge to plunder, to take revenge, instinctive. It was in their blood; they were battle-hardened survivors. He scanned the encampment carefully. A depression into the dry riverbed did not allow him to observe the infantry, but, further on, he saw a few dozen tents, men sleeping under canvas stretched over low scrub. No cooking fires yet, no movement, no sign of life. He spotted the cavalry horses, tethered, unsaddled. Only eight hundred men and three guns. His commandos numbered six hundred.

He lowered his glasses, beckoning to Jan Viljoen, Commandant Kemp and Wessels. 'Spread out, ride at full gallop,' he said. 'Jan and I will attack head-on. At six hundred yards, you outflank them on both sides. Get a Red Cross wagon and a few with supplies away as fast as you can. I'll keep them occupied, *hensop* them.'

Martin waited until the officers had moved their men into position. He unslung his Mauser from his back, raising it high above his head. Instantly the battle cry rose, and the air filled with the thundering of hooves.

Martin looked to his left. For a mile his commandos stretched across the veld at full charge. It was a magnificent sight – horses' manes flying, men low in the saddle, firing madly, murderously. *A decisive battle to end it all, the dream is shattered! One last charge for my scorched land, for Pa, for Buks, for Karel and for my men. For Uncle Joep! Uncle Joep!* He looked to his right and then over his shoulder. He saw Jan Viljoen's face split into a grimace, heard his wild roar. He saw Frans, his eyes fixed to the front as he fired. Far to the left, Commandant Kemp bent low in the saddle, his men unwavering behind him.

The British pickets began firing, tearing holes in the Boer line, but no man faltered. Eight hundred yards. Seven hundred yards. The ground slid past at a furious speed. The rushing horsemen obscured his view ahead. Through a gap, he saw British riflemen scrambling into position. Four hundred yards. This was madness.

'Retreat! Retreat!'

JAN VILJOEN tried to catch up with Martin, but he could not spot him. Through the clamour, he heard Martin's order to retreat. Jan was about to turn when he saw horses coming to a chaotic halt, men flying from their saddles.

'Retreat! Back!' he yelled, but still the men bundled forward.

And then he knew. He flew from the saddle, ran to where Martin had fallen, shoving men aside. 'Back! Back! Save yourselves!' He stumbled to the prone figure, falling to his knees. A shell exploded close by, bringing a shower of earth and rubble and flying splinters. With an anxious look, men swung their horses around and fled back over the rise. 'Ai, ai!' wailed Jan, turning Martin onto his back. Blood ran down his temple into his beard, and a crimson stain spread rapidly over his jacket.

'*My Got!*' Frans cried hoarsely as he fell down next to them.

'Frans! Brother,' Jan shouted above the crash of artillery and the thunder of the horses. 'We take him to Charles! Where's your horse?'

'Shot! Killed back there!' Frans pointed wildly.

They looked at each other, rivulets of sweat running down their faces, their breath coming in huge sobs. Their eyes flew back to Martin. Jan ripped Martin's shirt, revealing a gaping wound in his left breast. 'Martin? Can you hear me?' He placed his lips to Martin's ear. 'I'm here, your old friend, Jan Viljoen, I'm here.'

'Shot in the heart, Jan, shot in the heart,' Frans said hopelessly.

'Shot in the heart.' Jan took Martin's hand in both of his when his breath faded. Another shell ripped the earth not far from them. They looked back at the British lines, where infantrymen were rounding up a large number of

Boers. Dead and wounded littered the veld. Riderless horses, and a few with men clinging to the saddles, galloped past.

McFee appeared. 'Is our general down? For God's sake, come, the doctor is only two miles behind! Come!'

'He is dead, my friend,' Jan said.

McFee jumped from the saddle and bent over Martin. 'Our doctor brought many back who were breathing their last!'

They heaved Martin across McFee's mount. Frans lunged at the reins of a panic-stricken horse, and they left the battlefield in haste, McFee leading them to where Charles had taken shelter in a ruined farmstead.

They rode up to the outbuildings, where the Red Cross flag hung limp. Some of the commando, having heard of Martin going down, had already sought shelter there. Many wounded were stretched out on blankets, and in their midst stood Charles with his arm about Rudolf's shoulders. An open blanket lay prepared on the ground at their feet. Wordlessly, Jan and Frans lowered Martin onto the blanket.

Charles sank to his haunches and placed his fingers on Martin's neck. 'He's dead. Martin is dead,' he said strangely, formally, his bloodstained hands shaking when he drew his fingers over Martin's eyes.

Rudolf fell to his knees, attempting to wipe the blood from Martin's face and beard. Jan Viljoen hauled him to his feet, pulling him into his arms. 'Weep with me, my little friend, weep. God gave us tears, so we weep!'

Jan's noisy sobs filled the solemn air. Through his blurred vision, he saw men, hats in their hands, moving closer to stare at Martin in death. His eyes took in the rest of the commando, standing at their blown horses, their rifles hanging loosely, some barrels trailing in the sand. Barely an hour ago they were a fighting unit – resolute, desperately fanatical. Now he saw only worn-out men stunned by defeat and weariness. For them the war was done, the fight irretrievably lost.

Jan released Rudolf and shoved him over to Charles. He pulled himself upright, squaring his shoulders. 'Rest yourselves and your horses,' he shouted so that all could hear him, yet his voice carried understanding of their plight which was his too now. 'We leave in the hour. We shall ride through the night. To Wintersrust.'

JAMES AND HIS TROOP rode back to camp, bringing three wounded Boers with them. The large force that had attacked them at dawn had disappeared into the bush. It had been a magnificent sight: a horde of slouch-hatted figures sweeping down on the main camp, riding knee to knee, yelling their battle cry, shooting wildly from the saddle. Five hundred yards from the guns, the greater part of the force had broken away towards the flanks. The rest galloped on wildly, most mowed down by intense rifle fire, some reaching as close as thirty yards from the British lines. The order for the cavalry to follow up came only an hour after the charge and was called off after a fruitless hunt. The remaining Boers had got away, leaving only their dead and seriously wounded behind.

James and his fellow officers reasoned that the Boers had underestimated their strength and had not considered the infantry concealed in the riverbed. Now James heard from the wounded Boers that Martin had led the charge. They also told him that the charge had failed because men had seen Martin going down. Some said he was dead, others were adamant that he was only wounded, while some had it that his horse had taken the shot and that he had got clear away.

When they had ridden through the battlefield that morning, it had been in chaos – wounded, dead, medical personnel, orderlies shouting for stretchers. There were isolated shots as suffering horses were put out of their misery, and the remaining horses stood, heads bowed, exhausted from the charge, some with wounded still in the saddles. But now the wounded had been taken to the tents and the dead left outside awaiting identification before burial.

James stood undecided for a while. Where to start looking: the wounded or the dead?

Peter found him searching the faces of the dead Boers. 'You won't find him here, old boy,' Peter said quietly, taking James by the arm and steering him away. 'Yes, I've heard. He is wounded and the Boers took their general with them.'

'What got into him?' James said. 'What a senseless thing to do! And so close to the end. The war is over. It's no secret that the republics are negotiating for peace.'

They made their way away from the carnage. When they reached their tent, James flung his helmet down and stood in deep thought for a while.

'I have forgiven him. You know that, don't you?'

'I know that,' Peter said and handed James a glass of brandy.

———

THE NEWS of General Martin de Winter's death spread rapidly. It reached the 2nd Hussars late that night. Peter Radford obtained permission for him and James to attend the funeral, which was to take place at Wintersrust under a white flag.

Escorted by twenty troopers, they rode through the day into the gathering night. At Rustenburg they stayed at the officer's mess, and in the morning took the road to Wintersrust. The Red Cross flag and a white one hung from a pole tied to the ruins of Wintersrust. The Boer horses, still saddled, were feeding on the oats that had sprouted wild on the unploughed fields after the rains. A little way from the drift, the commandos were gathered at the graveyard.

James ordered their escort to wait at a distance. When they were halfway to the drift, a lone Boer came to meet them. The man doffed his hat.

'Mr Henderson, Mr Radford.'

'The Irishman,' Peter said.

'Yes, the Irishman. McFee is the name.' He turned to James. 'You have come to attend your cousin's funeral. Admirable, but when it's done you will take your victory and leave us with our sorrow.' He drew his finger down the sleeve of James's khaki tunic. 'The colour they have fought against for three years. There's no telling what some of them might do in their grief.'

'I was hoping to have a few words with my brother.'

'After the war, Mr Henderson, not now. Our doctor has his hands full. We have many, many wounded at our camp and he's saddened. Our General's wife, we found her wandering by the vlei. She's looking for her baby, although the child's been dead for months.'

'Annecke?'

'Poor lass …' McFee paused. 'Come, I'll take you in and bring you back. Leave your weapons here. It's best.'

They removed their pistols and sabres, placing them on the ground. McFee led at a fast pace. The Boers silently made way. 'The doctor's brother,' someone whispered. 'The General's cousin.' He stole a glance at the man; it was Gert Swart.

At the open grave, McFee led them to the side facing the family and took his place behind them. The Boers held their slouch hats in their hands. James and Peter removed their helmets. The *predikant* opened the Bible and the solemn High Dutch words filled the morning air. James stared fixedly into the grave, but his eyes were drawn upwards and he saw Rudolf next to the *predikant*. His eyes were shadowed and haunted.

James lowered his eyes and a pair of scuffed boots came into view. He found himself looking at Jan Viljoen, tears rolling into his wild black beard. Next to him was his brother Frans, a bloodied bandage around his head. Charles was weather-beaten, greying at the temples and was crying as openly as the Boers. James longed to put out his hands, touch him, comfort him. Then Charles's gaze met his and James found his longing reflected there.

Charles mouthed a few words, but he could not read them.

James tried to think of Martin and a vivid picture came to his mind. *One day I am going to be the president,* Martin had declared with such conviction. A great man must be humbled first before he's truly great, Jan Viljoen had said. *A nation, a man, it's the same with all God's creatures.* He thought how wrong his answer had been at the time. A nation, a man, a lion: yes, the British lion had been deeply humbled in the war.

The *predikant* closed the Bible and the voices of the Boers gathered in song, hoarse and plaintive. *Nearer my God to thee.* A boy's voice, not yet broken, rose clear above the singing, echoing the despair of his people. James stood with his head bowed until the hymn dragged to its sorrowful end.

Frans Viljoen held out a spade filled with soil to Rudolf. He trickled a handful into the grave and the spade was passed to Charles and Jan. James stared fixedly as the soil rained onto the coffin, trying to close his mind to his grief. Peter nudged him; the spade was held out to him. He stepped forward, threw a handful into the grave. Peter followed suit, but McFee was already urging them to leave.

The Boers silently made way, allowing them through. They had gone but halfway to where they had left their weapons when a shout came from the graveyard.

'*Engelsman!*'

They turned; there stood Jan Viljoen, holding his Mauser with both hands high above his head. As they watched, he brought it down forcefully on his knee, breaking it in half. He tossed it aside, doffed his hat and, not looking back, walked to the horses. His brother followed suit. One by one, and then in groups, the Boers smashed their rifles, some only opening the breeches and dumping the cartridges, others casting theirs, like fetters finally unchained, onto a growing pile. Then they mounted their horses and rode away.

'Dear God,' Peter said as he and James watched in awe. 'They are giving up the fight. Just turning their backs on it?'

James's eyes filled with hot tears of compassion. 'It's their way, Peter,' he said, his voice low and hoarse. 'Unlike us, they are free men.'

NO SOONER had they returned to camp than Corporal Johnson informed James that Colonel Butcher wanted to see him immediately.

'At ease, Captain, take a seat,' Butcher said when James closed the tent flap behind him. 'The order for your arrest came through in your absence.'

James undid his sabre and pistol, handing them to Butcher before taking a seat opposite him. 'Permission to smoke, sir?'

'Yes, and do have some port.'

James lit his cheroot and looked at the smoke spiralling upwards.

Butcher indicated the port. James poured a glass and passed it to him. 'How did it come about, James, this damnable mess you're in?'

'Colonel, my Tante Koba would have an answer, but I can only give you the bare facts. Stefanie saved Peter, and might still die for it. Karel rescued Annecke from the camp and died for it. I saved Captain Patterson – my cousin Rudolf, that is – from the hospital and now I will die for it. What an awful confusion we brought about, trying to save one another.'

'The futility of it,' Butcher said, his voice strained. 'But *you* need not die. It goes without saying that you have my support and that of your fellow officers. Apart from that, the War Office has recommended a hearing, not a court martial.'

James looked up sharply. 'I refuse to accept any assistance from my father. Especially in this matter.'

'Captain, put that aside for the time being. The charges are grave, but the circumstances, your Boer family, your excellent record, will be taken into account. General Henderson insists that you give your cooperation—'

'Father insists? No, sir!'

'Good heavens, man! Your honour and that of your father is at stake.'

'My honour, sir, was buried on an island in the Atlantic with my Uncle Marthinus. The day I was forced to burn his farm, that was the day when honour ceased to exist!'

Butcher took a cheroot from James's tin, nodded his thanks when James held a flame to it. They smoked in silence, sipping port, listening to the noises in the camp: soldiers walking past the tent, laughter, orders being shouted. Someone tripped over a guy-rope and cursed.

'James, I know that the war has been hard on you, but all is not lost,' Butcher said, his voice near pleading. 'At least give your father a chance. If not for his sake, then for that of your wife.'

James stabbed out his cheroot and pressed his fingers to his throbbing temples. He was desperately tired and forced himself to think about Victoria, but rational thought was disturbed by another picture: the tiger's head in his father's study, the cold glass eyes winking at him; his father hard and unforgiving. And he heard his own enraged voice damning his father, banishing him from his future.

'I appreciate your concern, sir,' he said at last. 'But what you ask of me is quite impossible. Should I accept my father's help, I would damn myself forever in his eyes. He knows why. I apologise for having brought this on you and the regiment. I'll take my chances with a court martial.'

The Bitter End

30 May 1902

A N ANXIOUS SILENCE hung over the war-ravaged land. The war dragged on, but it was dying. A few attacks here, a raid on a convoy there, all while the British continued their relentless sweeping of the earth, scattering the commandos over the veld laid waste by fire and death.

At Vereeniging, where the railway crossed the Vaal River into the Transvaal, the Boer generals gathered to decide the future of the republics. Vereeniging was a forsaken town – plundered shops and deserted houses, forlorn in the stark winter landscape. The grass blackened by frost, the river low and muddy, the trees bare. And in the distance were the ruins of farmhouses, and animal skeletons picked clean by vultures, bleached by the sun.

In a marquee provided by their enemy, the representatives of the commandos reported on their districts. The blockhouse system had been successful in hindering communication but now the picture became clear: devastation was complete; the land could no longer support them. In the Free State were only seven thousand men under arms, kept to the task by a never-wavering President Steyn. But like his land, he had suffered. His eyes were badly inflamed, and roaming the countryside in a buck-wagon had taken its toll. Yet he refused to admit defeat.

General de Wet summarised President Steyn's message, confirming the plea of many. 'We shall carry on despite the state our country is in. We have to fight to the bitter end!'

'Fight to the bitter end? Is what you are saying? But has the bitter end not come?' General Koos de la Rey asked.

Silence ensued, broken by the crackling of the open fires and the winter wind echoing the cries in their hearts. Peace had to be secured. The alternative was the destruction of their country and extinction of their nation. The

Volk was divided, a full-scale civil war, a result of the introduction of the National Scouts, the *hensoppers*, had become a reality. The land was on the brink of death, of ruin, total and complete.

The bitter end was indeed upon them.

Promises Fulfilled

Pretoria, June 1902

T HE WAR HAD been over for a week, but Pretoria was still in upheaval. Boer and Brit were caught up in the court martial of the British officer who had helped his Boer family during the war. The public was not allowed at a court martial, yet, when James was marched from the barracks to the court on the morning of his trial, a crowd gathered to catch a glimpse of him. Koba pushed her way to the front, waving her *kappie* energetically.

James had pleaded guilty on two of the three charges against him – disobeying an order and allowing an enemy to escape. Colonel Butcher and Peter Radford had found an army lawyer, Colonel Pears, who was willing to take on James's defence. Pears was impressed that James had refused his father's assistance, and believed that little was impossible should one handle it with patience and diligence.

The bleak courtroom must have once been a storeroom, James decided, judging by the high windows and concrete floor. There was hardly a sound audible from outside. And there at a long table sat the same five officers who had judged Stefanie, General Duncan in the centre.

James and Colonel Pears took their places at a table facing the panel. Colonel Hancock, the prosecutor, the witness box next to him, sat facing Pears. James looked at the files on Hancock's table – the evidence with which to condemn him.

It took the entire day to get through the testimonies of those who affirmed James's loyalty to his country during his short, but eventful career. Officers, troopers, non-commissioned officers were all given their turn, on Pears's insistence. He then elaborated on James's decorations – the DSO at the age of twenty-four, the VC two years later – reminding the court that these were not given lightly.

The trial began in earnest the following day with the charge of refusing to comply with an order when charged with the burning of Wintersrust. Sergeant Joe Adams testified that he had acted on orders from the late Major Hunter in reporting Captain Henderson's actions, but there had been nothing untoward except the note he had intercepted. He told the court how James had always followed orders, even when ordered to torch General de Winter's farm.

'The troopers stated that Captain Henderson cursed and made a spectacle of himself when the house was in flames,' Colonel Hancock, the prosecutor reminded him. 'Not the behaviour of an officer in the presence of his men.'

'The captain, for the first time, the only time, lost control for a few minutes, sir. Who would not if you had set fire to the—'

'The court is not interested in your speculations, Sergeant. What the court is interested in hearing is Captain Henderson's behaviour on that specific occasion. Would you care to elaborate?'

'I don't recall the details, sir.'

'Neither does a single member of the troop, it appears.' Hancock said in exasperation and turned to James. 'Can you perhaps recall, Captain Henderson?'

'I was not myself, sir.'

Colonel Pears turned to the panel. 'Major Hunter ordered the accused to burn his family's house – a most irregular order. Yet, even so, he carried out the order. Yes, he did try to warn his family to flee, but in that house, among others, were his mother's sister, his brother's pregnant wife—'

'General Kitchener's orders were that all inhabitants should go into camps,' Hancock objected. 'The accused disobeyed that order.'

'Women and children are dying in the camps, sir,' Pears said. 'The official figure is already at twenty thousand. Twenty thousand women and children! Captain Henderson was aware of that. How could he send his own blood to certain death? Surely there is just one grain of compassion left in this war-ravaged world of ours to understand that?'

'What happened to the family?' General Duncan interjected.

'Captain Henderson had them taken off to the camps, as was his duty, sir. Sadly, four of them did not survive, General de Winter's son and mother included.'

'In your opinion, Captain Henderson, would they have survived if they had gone to the place you call Fireflies?' General Duncan asked.

'Yes, sir,' James said. 'There's fresh water and food and they would not have come into contact with the disease that caused their deaths.'

'Thank you, Captain. Let's move on to the second charge, that of being aware of the location of General de Winter's hideout. A vague charge, most vague. Have you any proof at all of this, Colonel Hancock?'

'If Captain Henderson will oblige and tell us about this mysterious place of Fireflies, I might be able to prove that he was, at times, aware of General de Winter's whereabouts.'

James cast an obstinate glance at Hancock. He was not about to break the oath that he had taken as a boy.

'Captain Henderson?' General Duncan prodded.

James took a moment longer to order his words. 'The Fireflies place is close to the homestead. The late Major Hunter kept a watch on Wintersrust in order to catch General de Winter. My cousin would not have put our family in danger by visiting them while aware that the house was being watched. And if he did manage to make his way through the observers, how was I to know about it in time?'

There was a thoughtful silence and then Hancock asked half-heartedly, 'Captain, do you know of any occasion that General de Winter was on his farm?'

'I'm aware of one: last year, in July. He officiated at my brother's wedding, apparently.' James couldn't keep the ridicule from his voice. 'I was only told about this three months later by my aunt, Mrs van Wyk.'

'One more question concerning this charge,' General Duncan said. 'If the observers had known the location, they might have captured General de Winter. How far exactly is this place from the farmstead? Ten miles, fifteen perhaps? A distance like that would not have endangered his family.'

'As the crow flies, sir, not two miles from the house. It's visible from the house if one knows where to look,' James said. 'My cousin would not have chanced that.'

'Very well, we shall adjourn and deal with the final charge tomorrow,' General Duncan ruled and closed the second day's proceedings.

COLONEL PEARS responded to the charge concerning Rudolf's stay in hospital with a deliberate emotional approach. The court heard from the doctor, who had been sent for from Cape Town, that Captain John Patterson, alias Rudolf de Winter, was a scared individual. He elaborated on Rudolf's unstable condition and his plight while under his care.

'As is largely the case with identical twins,' he explained, 'Rudolf de Winter was in severe emotional shock while separated from his twin. His head wound most probably contributed to his unstable mental state.'

Colonel Hancock insisted that the court should see Rudolf as an enemy, not as James's sick relative, and implied clearly that this should also have been James's view. 'We've completely lost the point of this charge! The charge, gentlemen, is that Captain Henderson deliberately omitted to report the presence of an enemy combatant, not a family member, and allowed him to escape. Men have been executed for less.'

General Duncan conferred with the panel before asking Colonel Pears to deliver his concluding speech.

'I'm not asking you to clear Captain Henderson of guilt,' Pears said. 'He is guilty. He did try to warn his family before he burned their house. He admitted to letting his cousin walk unreported out of the hospital. One wounded Boer, a mentally unstable man, a beloved cousin, one of inseparable twins! Was it really a crime to let him go? A family torn apart by war and conflicting loyalties. You have to look beyond the war, look into the heart of this family, before you allow yourselves to judge one of its remaining members. Few of us have been called upon to bear the suffering they went through. Who are we to bring more suffering on them?'

The panel of judges took a recess and returned after ten minutes. James stood to attention. As he looked about the dismal room, the stern faces of the officers on the dais, a longing for the tranquillity of the cave rushed through him. He needed to feel it again, be there with those who had survived; he wanted to survive.

'Captain James Stuart Henderson, this court finds you guilty on two of the three charges. That of allowing one of the enemy to go free, and that of attempting to avoid having to carry out an order by trying to warn your family beforehand. Sentencing will take place tomorrow at ten.'

———

JAMES STOOD AT THE WINDOW overlooking the parade ground, waiting for the sentence to be carried out. Soon the sun would appear and he would dress for the last time in the uniform of the 2nd Hussars. He looked at the buttons and braid gleaming softly. A pang of regret went through his heart, but was quickly replaced by relief at the prospect of freedom – from the deep anxiety the war had brought, from the harsh reality of fighting a war against family. The scandal he'd promised his father was about to happen.

'The court finds that, by your actions, you are no longer fit to be an officer of His Majesty's Army, and therefore not fit to be a member of the 2nd Hussars. The charges of which you have been found guilty carry the sentence of execution by firing squad, but the tragic circumstances under which they were committed have been taken into account. The court therefore orders you to be cashiered.'

As he watched the sun spread over the parade ground, James tried to picture his father's reaction, but found that victory over the General had a hollow ring to it, like the victory in the war against the Boers. There was no satisfaction, no honour in it.

A guard brought a breakfast tray and reminded him that he had half an hour before the escort would come. When James reached for his breeches and was buttoning them, the door burst open. 'Radford! How did you get in?'

'Ha! Poisoned the guards.' Peter closed the door behind him. 'They're writhing on the ground. Terrible sight!'

'And what do you want? You're supposed to be on parade to witness my disgrace.'

'Quite spectacular it promises to be. But, seeing as I'm no longer permitted on the parade ground, I'll watch from this window, cheer them on.'

James looked at him closely. He was hugging his coat about him, but by the shoes and trousers it was obvious that he was not dressed in uniform. 'Why are you not allowed on the parade ground?'

'I beat you to it, Henderson. Was unceremoniously chucked out of the regiment yesterday. No flags, no drums!'

'What is it this time, sir?' James mimicked his father's voice.

'Love, lust and such doings, sir,' Peter returned. He handed James his shirt. 'I've come to ask you to be my best man. In prison! To a very pregnant bride. Can you beat that, Henderson?' Peter brought out a bottle and two glasses from under his coat. 'Couldn't make an important announcement like this without the old bubbly.'

James took the glasses from him. 'Surely not in prison. I don't believe you, Radford.'

'No, not in prison. Stefanie is to be moved into Tante Koba's care for the birth of the child.'

He twisted the cork from the bottle and filled the glasses James was holding out. 'Well, here's to matrimony and parenthood in the same breath.'

James clinked his glass against Peter's. 'And this is the reason why you were chucked out of the regiment?'

'General Kitchener gave me a minute of his precious time.' He clicked his heels together and twirled an imaginary moustache. 'Captain Radford, your father desires that his grandchild should not be born out of wedlock. I, however, won't allow an officer to marry a convicted spy. Your father is also aware of that, but, as is always the case, leaves the choice up to you. Gladly I'll leave, I wanted to shout, but fortunately kept my presence of mind and said that I would honour Father's wish. As is always the case.'

'Excellent! You always get through everything with a smile.' James sat on the bed and reached for his boots.

Peter came to sit beside him. 'I have permission to fetch Stefanie in the week. I've dreamed about this day constantly, longed for it … but Stefanie … I owe her so much. She's been through a dreadful time. I might be so overwhelmed. Make a total fool of myself.'

'You've done *that* before.' James pulled on his boots. 'I face the same sort of trouble. What awaits me out there,' he said, pointing to the window, 'feels like going to a picnic compared to what awaits at Tante Koba's house – my wife.'

Peter refilled their glasses and went to stand at the open window. 'The parade is forming up.'

James joined him. They watched as the Regimental Sergeant-Major marched through the lines and took his place under the hoisted Union Jack. Peter held out James's tunic. 'It won't be easy, old boy, but try not to lose your temper and don't spit in his face. He might shoot you on the spot. Where are your trinkets?'

James pointed to where his medals were on the table.

'They're actually mine.' Peter stuffed them into his pocket. 'Got wounded in order for you to get them. Twice!' He buttoned James's tunic. 'There are new challenges ahead for us. Think of them, it might help.'

'New challenges?' James ran a brush through his hair.

'Yes, I've been thinking. Three years ago we arrived here for cavalry charges and to deplete the champagne stock of the country. Look at us now – both of us husbands and me a father. I've never been either of those. Mustn't make a mess of it. I promised Father that I'd stay out of trouble for a few years—'

'A few years?' James pulled on his gloves. 'That's going to be pretty boring!'

'I'm planning to buy a farm in the Cape, breed horses, good Boer horses. Heaven knows, this country is in need of them now. Will you join me?'

'Sounds excellent, Radford. Where shall we—'

The guard opened the door. 'Captain Henderson, sir.'

James handed Peter his glass and straightened his shoulders. 'Where shall we buy these farms?' he asked on his way to the door.

'Near Cape Town?'

'Yes, at least they do play cricket around there.'

PETER SIGHED with relief. James would make it through. Putting his hand into his pocket, he clutched James's medals. Through the window he saw Colonel Butcher taking his place at the head of the parade. The drum started rolling. James marched onto the parade ground and saluted Colonel Butcher. He stood to attention as the Regimental Sergeant-Major cut the rank insignia and the regiment's emblem from James's tunic and cast them

564

on the ground. His buttons were forcefully ripped off. Only the medal ribbons remained on the stripped tunic, a forceful reminder of the brave cavalry officer he once was.

Peter caught James's eye as he briskly marched off the parade ground while the drum kept up a constant roll. He raised his glass and smiled, but James was too far away to see the tears of sympathy in his eyes.

———

STEFANIE LOOKED ABOUT THE ROOM that had been her shelter for four months. There was a bed with a good mattress and blankets, a comfortable chair, a small kist where she kept the clothes Koba had sent. There was no carpet, but at least there was an old sheet covering the barred window overlooking the courtyard.

There was also her table on which she had chalked a piano keyboard. It kept reality at bay for hours. Her fingers found their way to their favourite pieces, her voice singing the notes. The guards said she sang rather loudly, shrilly even. But not since they had showed her the British newspaper. *A Glorious Death. Young Boer General Slain Leading Troops into Battle,* the headline read.

When the news came, she had almost overcome her struggle against apathy and despair, weeks in which she'd eaten only for the baby's sake. She remembered little about the endless hours of weeping, not just for Martin but also for the desolation suffered by those who had followed him so reverently: she had feared for her sanity. Only Rudi was left, only Rudi, all alone, but for little Annecke, sole survivor of the Marees.

Stuffing her few belongings into a pillowcase, she sank down in the chair, rubbing her feet a little. Soon she would have to force them into her shoes. An escort would arrive at four to take her to Pretoria. Peace had been signed two weeks previously and amnesty for all prisoners of war had been declared.

She wondered when she would see Peter. She could not hold him to his promise of marriage. What they had endured, forced upon each other, might be too heavy to bear, too recent. A sharp pain caught at her back. The baby was active, restless, had been for the past few days. She could not sleep at night; lying on her back was impossible, nor could she lie on her sides for long. Endless nights spent in the chair, sleeping in fitful snatches, had exhausted her. Soon, she thought, alarmed, but Tante Koba would be there.

Tante Koba rescued you, rescued both of us, she whispered to her baby.

Tante Koba always fixes everything. She closed her eyes, summoning Koba's comforting presence, as she had every day since her internment. And, in Koba's strong arms, she drifted into her all-embracing love.

PETER PUSHED the cell door open. He stood quietly, too overcome to approach her. There were dark rings under her eyes and her beautiful hair had lost its lustre. He took in the shapeless dress stretching over her belly, her feet covered in thick stockings against the cold. All at once, remorse and guilt took hold, but he steeled himself against the past. *So much suffering endured, so much endured.* He vividly recalled James's face when he had walked off the parade ground. The hurt and degradation had touched James to the core, although he had made a brave attempt to hide it. When Peter had delivered him to Koba's door, anguish had showed through the determination in his eyes to honour his promise to Victoria.

You always get through everything with a smile, Radford. He swallowed hard and tried a smile. 'Stefanie …'

She started and struggled to sit up. As he moved forward to help, she held up her hands, warding him off. 'Please, don't come any closer, please, I don't want to cry …' she whispered, uttering the words that kept him at the door.

He nodded, smiling, but the smile hurt so much, he found it hard to breathe. He looked about the room, giving her time to compose herself. His eyes caught the piano keys drawn on the table.

'I played something for you … once … but the guards …' her voice faltered. She clasped her hands around her belly. 'How was it on the outside for you? Was it bad?'

'No, it wasn't bad. Quite peaceful actually, not having you interfering with the war. At least I knew you were safe in here.'

She nodded. 'Yes, I felt safe here.'

'May I come closer now? One kiss, just a little one, for my bride?'

'Your bride? Do you still want me? I cannot possibly hold you to your vows.'

Fear caught at his heart. 'I want you above all else in life,' he said with all the hope and love that he could muster.

She pressed her fingers to her mouth and he saw how she was willing her tears away. 'Do you know what happened the day Paul died? Did James … has he told you what happened that day? Did he tell you what I took there, wanting to kill him?'

'Yes, he told me.' He squatted next to her chair and took her hand. It was thin and cold, and he knew that he had to smile to get them both through this. 'You were driven beyond reason, yet you had the presence of mind to stop yourself from what you had planned in desperation. But you are such an old coward, my love. You didn't kill him.'

'But I wanted to. Aren't you a little bit scared of me … knowing that?'

He shook his head, smiling brightly. 'No, I'm not allergic to bee stings.'

'Oh, Peter, how can you make fun of this?' she placed her other hand on his.

'We have to, my love,' he whispered, touching her cheek. 'We have to erase it from our minds, and the only way I know is to make light of it some-how.' He placed his arms about her waist and gently lifted her to her feet. 'Come, the sun is shining and there's peace out there.'

Epilogue

SPRING ONCE AGAIN brought beauty to Wintersrust. The fruit trees were in blossom, the jasmine trailing its way around the ruins. Down by the vlei, the branches of the willow, bursting fresh green buds, were gently stirring and under them, the white lilies opened their faces to the morning breeze. The brown ducks had returned from the north, the herons stood watchfully, and the golden weavers were noisily fashioning their nests.

Koba's spring-wagon, flanked by two riders sitting their horses with the ease of cavalrymen, was also on its way. From where he sat on the bench, the reins in his hands, Charles listened absentmindedly to the chatter of the three young women under the hood who were now lauding Koba's remedy for colic.

When peace was signed, Koba had arrived in Rustenburg and had taken over his hospital to give him time *to gather himself* while she *gathered* those who drifted in from the veld and camps, restoring their health, soothing the bitterness in their hearts with her wittering. When the winter was over, James and Peter with wives had arrived from Pretoria. And now they were to meet Rudolf and Annecke, who refused to leave the shelter of the cave. But Wintersrust had to be rebuilt and James was determined to see to it.

The ruined farmstead came into view. The women's voices tailed off. The riders slowed down. Charles adjusted his new glasses and hurried the wagon through the drift to the graveyard, where Rudolf stood with his arm around Annecke's waist. He watched the others crowding around the two. It was a poignant reunion, tearful, yet so resolutely gay. They stood at Karel's grave for a while and, when they gathered around that of Martin, Charles joined them.

James squatted next to the grave, his fingers travelling over the rough wooden cross, his eyes roaming over the mountain, over the farm and into the distance, where a black eagle tested the spring currents. 'Like that eagle, this cross in all its simplicity symbolises what he lived for, what he stood for – his land, the freedom of his nation,' James said. 'A pure and noble ideal. It would be a pity to replace something so fitting with a granite stone.'

MUCH LATER, in the cave, Charles thought about James's words. Martin had been an exceptional man, too passionate perhaps; he could not submit to the changes the war had so forcefully wrought in their lives and souls. He gave the *Volk* a brief and memorable moment in history, but the death of the republic was the death of Martin's dream. An unfulfilled dream. Never to be fulfilled now.

His eyes went to the others around the rock table. James did not carry the look of a dishonoured man, but that of a man at peace with himself and obviously in love with his wife. Peter Radford was full of wonder at the world; it shone from his face when he held Jamie, his boy, in his arms, or when his eyes caressed Stefanie. Annecke's attention was divided between the two babies on the mattress. Rudolf was quiet, often looking at Annecke. Only time would soften the wound in his heart and erase the guilt over Karel's death, guilt with which he so needlessly burdened himself.

Charles pressed Anita's hand and stole a kiss on her cheek. He helped her unpack the large basket and light more candles.

Annecke walked over and stood by the table. She laid her hand against Rudolf's cheek. 'Look, Rudi, look,' she whispered, pointing to the roof. 'The moon. It does shine through the roof after all.'

A hush came over the table. Everyone looked up at the moonlight slanting through the fissures, here and there touching the walls, the floor. Like fireflies dancing.

Acknowledgements

IT TOOK MANY YEARS to write, research and live this story. My grateful thanks to Sharon Montgomery, who worked with me through the first drafts of the book, when it was double the length. Thank you to Jannie van der Merwe, Mara Timon, Anne Fischer and Johann Human for their support, constructive criticism and passion for the story – they kept me writing. Welcome aboard to my enthusiastic agent, Lynne Wood, of Lynne Wood and Associates. Thanks also to John Harris, Boer War battlefield guide, for his invaluable input on battles and tactics.

A big thank-you to Harry Bingham and the Writers' Workshop for their interest in my work. I am especially indebted to Linda Proud-Smith, historical novelist, who believed in my story. She showed me how to write it and kept me to it. Special thanks to Ingeborg Pelser at Jonathan Ball Publishers for her faith in the book, and to Alfred LeMaitre for his meticulous but gentle editing.